The Killing Ground

The shout of "airlock drill" woke Bran from sleep. He thought of making speed by omitting socks and underwear, but decided that Butcher Korbeith might take the omission as an excuse for having him killed. On the Butcher's ship, a cadet's first space trip was an all-or-nothing final exam; if you screwed up, they spaced you out the airlock.

Downship as fast as he dared go, he was eighth to reach the airlock dock. Quickly they all lined up. The guard checked off his list, and Korbeith began to stalk along the rank.

As he neared, Bran felt sweat gather at crotch and armpits, and begin to slither down his skin. *I never thought I could wish to be back at the Slaughterhouse!* In his mind a resolve formed. If Korbeith jabbed that great, knobby thumb at him, he would immediately, without thought, take his best shot at killing the man. No matter what happened then, if he could take the Butcher with him, that would have to do. *Sometimes to survive you have to become a monster.*

THE REBEL DYNASTY
Volume 1

STAR REBEL

•

REBEL'S QUEST

F. M. Busby

BANTAM BOOKS
TORONTO • NEW YORK • LONDON • SYDNEY • AUCKLAND

THE REBEL DYNASTY
Volume 1

A Bantam Spectra Book / December 1987

PRINTING HISTORY

ISBN 0-553-26954-2

Published simultaneously in the United States and Canada

Bantam Books are published by Bantam Books, Inc. Its trademark, consisting of the words "Bantam Books" and the portrayal of a rooster, is Registered in U.S. Patent and Trademark Office and in other countries. Marca Registrada. Bantam Books, Inc., 666 Fifth Avenue, New York, New York 10103.

PRINTED IN THE UNITED STATES OF AMERICA

KR 0 9 8 7 6 5 4 3 2 1

STAR REBEL

To Robert and Ginny,
with much gratitude

1. The Boy

Near to his thirteenth birthday, Bran Tregare lost his home, his family and his surname, which had been Moray.

Some of the reasons he didn't know or understand, but a few he did. His family, headed by his mother Liesel Hulzein, lived at an Australian outpost, in exile from the Hulzein Establishment's North American headquarters. An exile part disgrace and part sanctuary, caused by the fact that Bran and his sister Sparline had a father, the tall young man Hawkman Moray. Whereas their mother Liesel and her implacable older sister Erika, not to mention Bran's grandmother Renalle Hulzein, had none.

They were not illegitimate, those women, but parthenogenetic. Heidele Hulzein had conceived and birthed her daughter Renalle using micro-genetic techniques and no male whatsoever. "Not cloning," Bran's mother once explained, "but the melding of two gametes from the same person." And Renalle's daughters, Erika and Liesel, also carried the continuation of Heidele's original genes, and no others.

And there, or so Bran's father said, lay the problem. The tall, dark man, so obviously junior in age to his wife, told his children, "Renalle and Erika have faith only in their own genes. They won't admit that without an inmixture from time to time, the pattern can deteriorate." Sparline asked why it would, and Hawkman talked about cellular entropy, how a few genes or chromosomes always went wrong. With simpler organisms it wasn't too serious. His white grin transformed his dark face. "But humans are too complex to survive much of a defect rate. So that's why sexual reproduction, with the most vigorous gametes producing new mixes, works best for us. Your aunt and grandmother don't see it that way."

Bran nodded. At twelve he knew a little about sex. He'd know more, he thought, except that Sparline had caught him trying to learn some things with Sheylah, the cook's daughter, and ran and told. He knew she'd do that, so he ran too. Sheylah yelled after him in anger, but he kept going anyway.

Even so, his parents called him in, with Sparline as witness, for inquiry. He wasn't sure whether he was "before the mast" or only "on the carpet," but neither was much fun. Sparline grinned with triumph, getting back at Bran for the bird nest thing the week before, but all that happened was Bran being asked some questions about his own body. The answers were simple. Yes, lately sometimes that part stood up and felt very good. And no, he hadn't actually done anything about it, with Sheylah or with anyone else. His parents nodded at each other. Liesel said, "Before you do, come talk with one of us."

Hawkman added, "And especially, don't mess with the help."

That was all there was to it. Sparline looked disappointed. Though usually they got along well, on some levels there was a kind of running contest. This time, Bran thought, she hadn't won as big as she'd expected to.

Later, with Hawkman telling family problems, she and Bran listened quietly. Aunt Erika, it seemed, hadn't had great luck with gene-replicating herself. "Two miscarriages and a stillborn monster, before she managed your cousin Frieda. And that one's flawed." Which, he said, was why the children's own mother Liesel, after two self-fertilization misfires of her own, had defied Hulzein custom. "Came out here to run this boondocks operation, and—"

"And you and Mama fell in love and got married!" Sparline, Bran noted, had to get in *her* two cents' worth.

Hawkman laughed. "Not exactly. For genetic reasons, Liesel chose me; it's no secret. *Later* she paid me the high compliment of keeping me around for my own sake." But ancient history or not, their parents' genuine affection was apparent to both children. Suddenly, counting back, Bran realized that when he'd been born his mother had been thirty-two, and his father only sixteen.

Hawkman was still talking. "To the Hulzein Establishment—Renalle and Erika—you kids are a slap in the face. Their dynasty doesn't include two-parent children." He ruffled Bran's hair. "Let alone a male child. That's why we live here quietly, using my name, rather than flaunting ourselves at local Hulzein HQ." His eyes slitted. "The fact is, you're safer here. And yet—"

"And yet we mustn't disturb the balance." Bran turned to see that his mother had entered the room. "Against UET's tyranny in North America there's only three forces still effective. And with the New Mafia driven into hiding nearly as bad as the Underground itself, the Hulzein Establishment is the *only* opposition that dares show its head."

Hawkman grinned. "So that's why we, here, keep ours down."

Bran knew his share of recent history. Both the official version ("*that* pile of crap," Liesel called it), and some dissenting material from the family library and two parents who would answer questions. The official stuff mostly began with New Year One, right after the United Energy and Transport conglomerate won the governing bid from the Synthetic Foods Combine and took control of North America. And immediately began building Total Welfare centers and filling them with "clients." A more accurate term, said Liesel, would be government-owned slaves.

It was also in NY One that star travel had begun. "But UET didn't invent it," said Hawkman, "no matter what they claim now. Do you know about the Shrakken?"

Bran did. "Sure. There's some old fax sheets in the library. Telling how they traveled more than a hundred light years to get here. Pictures too, but faded." He remembered the tall, hairless aliens with their triangular eyes and inverted-V mouths. "And they walk on their toes, like a dog on its hind legs."

"But what *about* them?" Sparline asked.

Liesel snorted. "According to UET, the poor things fell prey to some Earthly disease or other. What really happened was, as soon as UET's Committee Police were sure the Shrakken didn't have faster-than-light communications, they pumped that ship full of cynanide gas one night—no more Shrakken. So UET had the ship, and their labs could analyze and copy it."

"So now," said Hawkman, "UET has interstellar travel, and their Space Academy has a bigger job than training pilots for asteroid mining."

Then he changed the subject, telling something of how things used to be. Years before UET achieved power and proclaimed New Year One there had been a time when elections involved voting by the citizenry rather than corporate bidding, and when North America hadn't been all one political unit. But the continent's largest segment, the United States of America, facing economic collapse, moved to the corporate system. "Otherwise," Hawkman said, "we might have gone under. I've never been sure the country chose right." He shrugged. "But of course 'perhaps' applies only to the future, never to the past."

He continued his story. The first two corporate elections, each closely fought, were won by Communications, Inc., and some measure of stability was restored. Then the Synthetic Foods combine made a landslide win, and capitalized on it by annexing Canada, Mexico, and most of Central America. In a new semblance of stability, SynFood held power for four elective terms. But United Energy and Transport had other ideas. "In the sixth corporate election," Hawkman concluded, "the deciding factor was UET's assassination section. We now know them as the Committee Police. And more and more nowadays, their power seems to be permanent."

UET didn't have it all gravy, though. True, with starships as weapons, North America need no longer accept forced immigration from freely breeding Third World countries. But at home, the Underground, loosely descended from the previous century's Counterculture, sometimes made dire examples of those who misused power too flagrantly. And the New Mafia, driven back from almost respectability (in one corporate election the group had even entered a bid) to shadow-legal status, now concentrated on blackmail and extortion from the powerful. "Oh, it's a right mess," Liesel said.

The third thorn in UET's side was quite different: the Hulzein Establishment's legal superstructure carried a long tradition of spotless escutcheon and pristine standing. "The underside of it, though," said Hawkman, "is trickier, and always has been. For every asset that shows on paper, your grandmother Renalle keeps ten that *don't* show, working for her."

"If we're to confuse the children," Liesel put in, "add that Hulzeins seldom make a move that serves only one purpose." As near as Bran could tell, his mother spoke in total sincerity.

What it boiled down to, the boy decided, was that his aunt and grandmother never gave an inch to *anybody,* whether it was UET or a Hulzein defecting from the parthenogenetic ideal. No one knew if the marauders who had tried to kill Bran and Sparline, and who did burn the house, came from either Erika or UET. The new house was better fortified, and fireproof. Hulzein money paid for it, and no argument on the matter reached the children's ears.

Once only, Bran saw his aunt Erika in person. She invited Liesel to a conference in North America, and Bran went along. That was Liesel's idea, but the deciding wasn't so simple. Renalle, the matriarch, wouldn't be present. "She's in

Israel," Liesel reported, "trying to wangle an Establishment branch there. Not much chance, I'd think. I expect the Hulzeins have some Jewish ancestry, but no political or religious ties to offer. And strict neutrality is the only safe way to keep UET's hands off a country."

Lying on a sofa, stretched out at his great length, Hawkman asked, "Will you attend Erika's conference alone?"

Liesel smiled. "I can't take *you;* you'd be a red flag to Erika's bull. And Sparline's too young to risk. Bran though—" Her eyes narrowed. "I think our son's cornered the family's devious streak." She turned to the boy. "How'd you like to go see Hulzeins on their own home ground?" Puzzled but interested, he nodded. "Then assuming we disguise you well, can you forget we're mother and son, and be only my serving-boy? Every minute, day and night, for the next two weeks?"

For only a moment, he thought. "Yes, I can."

"Yes, *what*?"

"Yes, Madame Hulzein!" He suppressed the grin that would have come, because it didn't fit the part he had to play.

His mother smiled. Hawkman nodded. Sparline still seemed dubious. And next day she looked at him—with his curly black hair bleached and dyed red, plastered flat, and cut straight across in front—and couldn't hold her laughter. "Old sad *horseface*!" Well, the mirror told him she was right, and the serving-boy's voluminous gold-trimmed costume, hardly cut for anyone of active ways, didn't help much either. But Bran did want to go on this journey, so he put up with everything and made no complaint.

Neither did he protest the crash course, administered by his mother's chief-of-maids. Bran had seen Alexa Duggan's stern ways with the lesser help, of course, but without really noticing. All his ten years he had been one of Alexa's employers, not a menial. The change jolted him. At first he couldn't take it seriously when she threatened him with a caning if his work did not improve (calling him "Jerrin," the name assumed for this role). His weak smile drew a harsher frown; he decided not to test the matter. The third day, after he'd slept two nights in the cubby off Alexa's room, she said, "If you mind your ways, Jerrin, and pay heed, perhaps you won't disgrace us after all."

Only Alexa on the journey would know who Bran really was. Except for his mother, of course. The other servants and the four guards came from Liesel's official headquarters.

Even if they had seen Bran as himself, they'd hardly recognize him as Jerrin.

The hard part was his parents ignoring everything about him except "Jerrin"—but he knew they had to. He didn't see Sparline at all, and decided that she couldn't be expected to keep his role straight.

Early one morning the party left. Loading a small mountain of gear, the dozen or so boarded four pogiecopters and flew for several hours across bare, reddish land to the nearest commercial port. Then a suborbital SST across the Pacific to North America. Nobody said exactly where, and Bran knew better than to ask. They were met by squat groundcars, two armed guards to each car, the cars and guards all wearing Erika Hulzein's monogram crest. Bran had seen it on letterheads in his mother's study.

He didn't know how long they rode. He slept most of the way. When Alexa shook him awake their car was stopped. Getting out, he met chill air. A dark, overcast night was lit by floodlights that showed the front of a large timber-beamed lodge. Shivering as he walked, he was glad to reach the warmth inside.

Sheer luxury overwhelmed him. Later he recalled few details, only that this place made his own well-appointed home look like an Outback trail cabin.

He did notice that the lodge was a weaponed fortress. A platoon of tanks might have cracked it, but nothing less. Of course UET's bombs could breach even the underground sanctuaries he saw next day. But as Hawkman explained later, back home, Erika's installation sat at the outskirts of a fair-sized city. "They'd have to be pretty desperate," he said, "to blow half the town."

Four days, the conference lasted. Mostly, young Bran was stuck with servants' quarters and company; he cared not greatly for either. Jimmy Kazich, an older youth in Erika's retinue, liked to mimic Bran's slight accent. "Sye soomthin' fer us in Orstr*eye*lian, won'tcher?"

Somehow shamed, and no longer willing to be, Bran faced the other. "Orl right. Oop yours!" Exaggerating Jimmy's own parody, and waiting. Not for long. Kazich slapped him. Shock brought tears, but no sound. Hand cupped to his slapped cheek, Bran shuffled forward, and as the larger boy leaned to grin at closer range, slammed the heel of his hand to Jimmy's nose. As hard as he could, bringing blood and yells, and suddenly the room full of adults. *"What's happened?"*

If an older girl, sixteen maybe, hadn't kept insisting that Jimmy struck first, Bran would have had the caning Alexa once threatened. Not from her, but from her counterpart on Erika's staff. As it went, though, he escaped with a scolding.

One thing about it: Jimmy Kazich didn't bother him again.

The conference dealt with strengthening the Hulzein branch of Argentina: whether, how much, and *how.* "Erika wants an ace in the hole," Liesel told Bran when the two were alone briefly, "a backup hideout. Our mother resists the idea, so while she's away, Erika wants to push it through." Pleased to be confided in, Bran nodded as though he understood.

He kept hoping to get a look at Erika Hulzein's gene-replicated daughter, his cousin Frieda, who was a year his senior, but no opportunity occured. With no chance to question his mother, finally Bran asked Alexa Duggan where Frieda was.

The woman shook her head. "She's sickly, poor child. Had a horrible fever a few weeks ago, and the treatments, what I've heard, even worse. She's out of intensive care now, but still bedridden." Then Duggan realized that Bran had broken his Jerrin role, and scowled at him. "Get on with you, young Jerrin. Haven't you chores to do, besides pestering me about your betters?"

So Bran scuttled off with an armful of clothes for the launderers. Duggan wasn't so bad, after all!

The visit ended with a banquet, and on this occasion Liesel's servants were themselves served, at a smaller table to one side. Before that, in the vacant end of the large room a series of unarmed combat bouts occurred. Erika Hulzein stood to announce them and Bran got his first good look at her. She looked like his mother and yet she didn't; Liesel's features were rounded, Erika's cut more sharply. Liesel's gray-flecked brown braids formed a crown; Erika's iron-grey hair hung straight, to chin-length. Erika stood half a decimeter the taller—but blade-thin, she probably weighed a few kilos less. And the edge to Erika's voice was one that Liesel used only rarely. All in all, Bran's aunt impressed him more than was comfortable.

Now, paired in combat, her trained athletes showed their

skills. Graceful, and at first harmless-looking, but in the third match a young woman came up pale, cradling a broken arm. And after that, more injuries occurred. Neither Erika nor the contestants seemed to be surprised.

Eight bouts, then a pause for appetizers and wine—which Erika did not sample. Then in four contests the eight winners reduced their number by half; all losers not in need of medical aid went to a table at the far side and got a belated start on the banquet. Another rest period, another elimination series, leaving only two persons undefeated. And one of the losers had to be carried off.

Momentarily distracted by his salad—those crinkly chartreuse tendrils *had* to be from off Earth—Bran looked up to see the two finalists ready for combat. Both were male: one brawny and built thick like a bear, the other slim and moving catlike. Their styles differed. The bear lunged and smote, while the cat evaded and flicked punishing blows that seemed effortless. At the end the bear lay prone, panting, bleeding slightly but not dangerously, and the cat stalked out in no hurry at all.

Liesel cleared her throat. "Very impressive, Erika. You train your people well." She gestured, and a servitor refilled her wine glass. "And is that all of it?"

With a quick headshake, Erika said, "One more stint. Soon now." And when the last victor returned, Erika stood and threw off her ornate gown. Under it she wore only brief, skintight fighting togs. "Now," she said, "we'll see." And she rounded the table to meet the man who moved like a cat.

He bowed at her. "Madame." Her answer was too quiet for others' hearing. Then, as in some strange dance, their movements joined. Fascinated, young Bran watched.

Some of the earlier bouts had been highly skilled, but this was like magic! Strikes and evasions, swift grace of attack and reprisal—sharp crack of a savage blow finding its mark, thump when defensive move sapped most of the force.

Suddenly, at the arena's marked-off edge, the cat had Erika trapped—and made his ultimate assault. Bran's eyes almost shut, but not quite, because he *couldn't* miss an instant of this, no matter what. The man's foot like a dagger, his arm slashing—but then, her leap perfectly timed, Erika seemed to *float* over the thrusts. Missing, he sprawled. She came down astraddle, fingers at his throat. He gasped, "Madame! I yield."

Erika Hulzein laughed, and patted her opponent gently. "You came close, Felipe, to making *me* yield." She stood, and gave him a hand up. "Well, it will come; I'm fifty-one and getting no younger." He tried to speak but she overrode him. "But when it does, my prize pupil, rest assured it won't be easy!" Bowing once more, the catlike man went to sit at the athletes' table. Calmly, Erika resumed her gown and her own seat. "And now, colleagues, let us dine." As near as Bran could see, she hadn't even worked up a sweat.

Not until the homeward suborbital flight did Bran find a chance to talk with his mother. "The way Aunt Erika fought... can I learn it?"

"Sure. You're a little young for combat work, though. What's your rush?"

He thought. "If anyone else can do it, maybe I need to."

Liesel nodded. "All right. We don't have the grade of instructors Erika has, let alone anyone like *her*. But what we do have, you're welcome to."

So once home he began training. He was small and skinny, and his coordination had a way to go yet, but he'd always had fast reflexes, and more strength than his slight build indicated. The Hulzein combat methods borrowed from several schools: The misdirection of the "gentle way" blended well with karate's emphasis on putting all one's *mind* into a blow or kick. And there was more, not the least being an overall conditioning program. He ran until he couldn't run any more, and then he kept going anyway. He climbed, he jumped, he swam—staying under water longer than he'd have believed possible at the start.

After a time, the boy began to run up against some of his natural limitations. He realized that although he could become very good at these skills he would never achieve the absolute top rankings. But by then he was more than capable of dealing with the likes of Jimmy Kazich.

Since the type is not rare, especially in that age group's schoolyards, he sometimes proved it.

At twelve Bran was small for his age. Sparline, a year younger, had two centimeters on him and probably three kilos, none of it excess bulk. Maybe girls did get their growth earlier, but Bran didn't have to like it. And if she picked on him he had to let her win. She hadn't done any combat training so if he used his with her, he'd hurt her for sure. It got pretty tiresome.

So one day he up and told her. Wide-eyed, she said, "You *let* me win?" He nodded. She reached, but only to hug him. "All right, Bran. I won't pick fights any more." And she didn't.

What she did was start lessons herself. Bran's instructor supervised several sessions before putting the siblings on their own. "And stay with practice rules, nothing all-out," the woman said. Bran knew what she meant. Against an adult instructor he could go full force because he simply wasn't strong enough to injure anyone both grown and trained. But with anyone near his own size and age, "practice rules" meant doing a move hard enough to prove it, but not to injure.

All right, Bran knew how to follow instructions. The worst Sparline suffered was a few bruises; at her age they healed quickly.

Nearing thirteen, Bran felt on the verge of something. He was still short—less than sixteen decimeters, to his father's twenty. But Hawkman said, "We Morays bloom late." So Bran waited. It wasn't as though he had any choice.

Besides being larger, the other boys in combat training showed signs of body hair where Bran had only fuzz. He supposed the difference shouldn't bother him, but it did anyway. Maybe that was why, when he threw a competitor in practice, he put extra effort into the throw. It didn't help his feelings much.

Still, he told himself, his mother stood honcho over this part of the Hulzein Establishment—and whether aunt Erika or grandma Renalle liked it or not, he was Liesel's co-heir.

But in a few brief moves, even that comfort vanished.

There was a morning of early sudden wakings and much confusion. Liesel was in the comm room, beating fist into palm: "They did it; UET's killed my mother!" Bran found the group—his parents, a few top aides, and Sparline—by following the sounds of commotion. Liesel paced, raging, while Hawkman talked at the overseas console. Pausing, he turned to say, "Long-term sabotage, Liesel. Ringers infiltrated. If Renalle could have laid hands on one of those experimental truth-field installations, UET couldn't have wormed in." Low-voiced, he talked again with the console, then reported, "They slagged the citadel's power plant, put all the central-powered weapons out of action. Only portables left, in the way of energy guns, to fight the sappers blasting in." Taut-faced, he shrugged. "You once said, Liesel, it'd take a regiment of tanks to invade that place. Well, that's what they used."

Hours later (and still no breakfast), the comm console went dead. Hawkman's far-end informant had escaped UET's holocaust in an aircar and reached a hidden ground-to-satellite terminal. Apparently UET had caught up to that person.

Gripping each of her children by a shoulder, Liesel sighed. "Well, you heard. UET's Committee Police jackals didn't take your grandmother easily. She was eighty-six, and nowhere near to wearing out." Incredibly, Liesel smiled. "Their own self-glorifying newscasters say she died firing a Mark-XVII two-hander, with a full squad of dead Police to mark the spot. And they only got her by coming down through stone shielding with a laser!"

In his mother's grasp, Bran stood taller. "I can't even aim a Mark-XVII yet, without resting it on something. But someday. . ."

Suddenly, she hugged him.

Three uneasy days later, Liesel called family council. "I needed to know what's left of the Establishment and what's gone. Now I do know." She spread her hands. "In North America we're wiped out. But Renalle didn't keep all her nest eggs in the one citadel, and UET didn't catch Erika. She's managed to shift a great proportion of the assets, and many key personnel, to her Argentine branch. Totally outside UET's grasp."

Liesel didn't look as relieved as her words might indicate. Hawkman said, "So, then—the recent terrible reverses aside, Liesel—what's bothering you?"

She shook her head. "Erika isn't answering or returning my calls. And the message her aide relays to me is a very old one." She shrugged. "Don't call us; we'll call you."

Bran knew how time zones affect calling schedules, and the Argentine problem worried him so he tried to monitor it. Still, one day he reached the comm room to find his mother and her sister already involved in a long-distance yelling match. Viewscreen circuit this time, and except for gaunter face and whiter hair, Aunt Erika hadn't changed much. The yelling, though: "—your mongrel brats, Liesel, will *never* come to power among Hulzeins. Oh, I'll see to that! And—"

"Erika!" If Liesel wanted to talk, Bran knew no one could

stop her. "I'm not *asking* for power. Surely we can discuss these matters and settle them to our mutual satisfaction. I don't—"

Erika Hulzein's voice was high and harsh. "You don't tell me what to do, Liesel. You never did and you never will! What you'll do is come here in . . . oh, three days from now. . . and I'll offer you a settlement and you'll take it!" The screen blanked.

In the sudden quiet Hawkman spoke softly. "You'll go?" Fuming, breathing fast and deeply, Liesel nodded.

Obviously trying to relax, she began pacing. "How did it get this bad between us? When we were little children . . . so close and loving, Erika and me . . . and mother too! Erika always looked after me, protected me. And later we stayed close. How—"

Still quiet, Hawkman's voice. "You heard what she said."

"Sure. Of course. It's the children. Like mother, Erika's still totally devoted to the parthenogenetic principle; she still thinks it's workable indefinitely. Well, I decided it wasn't, and I have two healthy kids. And Erika has poor, sickly Frieda."

She paused in her motion and stood still. "Peace take us, that's it! After Erika the partho dynasty depends all on Frieda. Who likely isn't up to it. Leaving me, and then Bran and Sparline." She snorted. "No wonder Erika's birthing porcupines. I—"

"And you still intend to go there?"

"Yes, Hawkman. Erika won't hurt me."

"She's not entirely sane just now, you realize. Keep that in mind and try not to provoke her."

"And you keep in mind that you're talking to a Hulzein!" But her tone and expression showed no ill humor. "Which is the devil of it. I'm up against another one." She frowned. "I *think* Erika could share power with me if I had a one-parent daughter. I'm not certain but I think so. In this case, though, sharing would be an attack on her dynastic principles . . . which come all the way from our grandmother Heidele who started the whole thing."

Liesel shrugged. "Well, I'll just have to convince her that I'm no threat to either one. And believe me, Hawkman, I won't lose track of that need. Or of my temper, either."

"You'll go with only a nominal retinue then?" When she nodded, Hawkman said, "All right. But one other thing needs to be done. Until we have assurance that Erika isn't going to strike out at us—on behalf of her dynastic principles, I mean—we must put Bran into hiding, out of her reach, because he's the one she sees as a threat.

"And I think I know how to do it."

"It's simple enough," Hawkman explained, "with a little computer-tap fiddling. We give him a slightly different identity and slip him into the entrance quota for the Space Academy."

Liesel frowned. "Safe from Erika's hands, but in UET's?"

"As a trainee, a cadet. And—"

"Do I have to use a phony name *again*?"

Hawkman shook his head. "Not entirely. You'll be simply Bran Tregare, not Moray, and that's the beauty of it, because your middle name comes from an old friend of mine, Sean Tregare. His wife was Alexa Duggan's sister Lisbeth. Sean and Lis both died in the Artificial Plague, when you were a baby." For a moment, old pain tightened his mouth. "But now—"

"Sure," said Liesel. "Feed into the computer net that Bran's their son; run that datum through all his records—schools, all of it. Perfectly natural that he'd be taken in by his aunt. And—" Now she smiled. "If I remember right, Sean Tregare held North American citizenship, so Bran can claim the same thing."

At first puzzled, even frightened by his father's proposal, now the boy began to feel excitement. "What you're saying—I could train to captain a *starship*?"

Liesel gave a laugh. "By contagion, Hawkman, you're assimilating Hulzein ways! Every move to serve more than one purpose." She turned to Bran. "We don't know it'll come to that. For now, the point is hiding you from Erika's inflamed temper, and it might be you won't find the Academy all that pleasant. If it's a bad situation, then when it's safe to do so, we'll pull you out." She paused. "Alexa, of course, should be our communications link. But if all goes well with you there, Bran, it would not be a bad idea at all for the Hulzein Establishment to have a hook into UET's space fleet."

Hawkman's grin crinkled his face. "For one thing, it would show Erika that mongrel brats might be damned useful allies."

Sometimes, Bran thought, being a Hulzein was a lot of *work*.

Liesel and a moderate entourage left one morning to visit Erika's Argentine base. Before boarding the copter she found brief time to hug and kiss her children. To Bran she said, "I know this is a drastic change for you to handle so fast. But we've established credentials for Alexa... to exchange messages with you at the Academy. Just be careful what you put in yours."

"Keep my cover, yes. And with aunt Erika, *you* be careful."

"I always do." Then she climbed aboard and the craft lifted.

Later that day, Bran left his home. Waiting to enter the same kind of air vehicle his mother had used, he traded handshakes and then a surprisingly fierce hug with his father, and an embrace and kiss with Sparline. His sister was crying—and suddenly so was he. Well, nothing wrong with that, except that somehow he thought such things wouldn't be approved at the Academy.

The trip wasn't much different from the one he'd had to Erika's headquarters. Pogiecopter, suborbital SST over the ocean, then from the port a groundcar—this time driven by a uniformed cadet, a large, older youth with a livid scar down his right cheek. Still sleepy from his dozing on the SST, Bran hardly noticed the winding road the car took, through dark stretches punctuated by occasional bursts of glaring light. Then the sky at one side began to lighten. Unable to determine the time difference from his point of departure, Bran realized he was seeing dawn begin.

The car pulled before a gate, the only break in heavy wire fencing that reached three meters above ground. The gate opened; the car went in. Now Bran saw the great grey slab of concrete. A building with no windows, like pictures he'd seen of Total Welfare Centers except those had a bit of blue to their coloring. The car stopped beside a door to the slab. The driver jumped out and motioned Bran out also. The door opened. Bran walked inside and he heard the door close.

Another young man met him. "You're who?" Bran told him. "Oh, a snotty, huh? New, *and* late. By an hour, *Mister* Tregare."

"I—the suborbital plane—hey, I just *rode* it, is all."

"*Smart* snotty, too! You first-timers are all alike." The bigger youth stepped forward. "You have to *learn*, don't you?"

Bran avoided the first blow, shucking his gear to give him mobility, but the second numbed his face and sent him sprawling.

"Welcome to the Slaughterhouse, snotty!"

2. The Slaughterhouse

Scrambling up into a crouch, one hand braced against the floor, Bran paused. The big stubble-headed bully was shuffling forward, and Bran recognized the move. "Don't kick me!" But the words came out a barked order, not a plea. This one was too big for him to fight, and somehow he knew that even if he won, he'd lose here. But still . . .

The other stopped moving, then laughed. "All right . . . You're new, so I'll tell you. In here, don't fight unless you're told to. But you take a punch pretty well." He held out a hand. "Come on, get up. I'll show you to your cadre section. You'll have time for breakfast and a haircut, after you draw your issue . . . before the commandant interviews you." As Bran picked up his things and turned to follow, the large youth said, "I'm curious. Just what did you think you'd do if I *did* kick you?"

Put your foot on backwards! "Oh, I dunno," Bran said. He was Hulzein enough to realize that it's foolish to tell *everything* you know.

And already he knew something about UET's Space Academy.

The older boy took him to a ten-bed squad room, where seven cadets of about Bran's own age were dressing and using the room's adjacent sanitary facilities. "Three bunks vacant," his guide said, "so take your pick," then left. Bran did so, and chose a vacant locker also, to stow his gear. Then he stood, waiting, expecting some sign of acknowledgment from the room's incumbent residents. But no such thing happened, and soon the seven, ignoring Bran entirely, moved to leave the room. Bewildered, he lunged to the doorway and stood barring it. "What *is* this? My name is Bran Tregare and I'm assigned here. Don't you give your new people decent help or greeting?"

The skinny, freckle-splotched boy at the front of the group made a placating gesture. "Sure we do. But you have to speak up first. Come on. Breakfast may not be good, but it's hot."

In the large, crowded mess hall. Bran found the prediction correct.

* * *

Now he knew that to learn anything he had to ask. After breakfast he learned that he also had to know *who* to ask, for when he put a question to a uniformed adult, the woman whipped a backhand slap across his mouth and told him "Don't try to jump levels, snotty!"

So it took him longer than he expected to find where to draw his grey-green jumpsuit and uniform, and where to get the haircut that left only stubble on his knobby skull. So naturally he was late for his interview with the commandant.

As he waited in the outer office, Bran tried to run through the altered "facts" he needed to remember. Parentage, sure. Age, upped one year because otherwise he'd be about three months too young. Surname, he'd practiced and wouldn't fluff it. Anything else?

Too late to think more; he was summoned. And walked in to face fat, scarred, cigar-chewing Colonel Harold Arbogast. He expected the man to look up from the papers on his desk. When it didn't happen, Bran cleared his throat and said, "Cadet Bran Tregare reporting, sir."

Now Arbogast looked at him, pouched bloodshot eyes under bushy, straggling eyebrows. Around the wet cigar the heavy mouth twisted. "Reporting late, you mean."

"Yes, sir." *Excuses don't work here.*

"You know how to salute, don't you?"

"Not yet, sir."

Right answer, for now the cigar came out. With it, the colonel pointed at Bran, and the mouth formed something that was probably meant to be a smile. "Let's check your credentials," and rapid-fire he asked questions. Just as fast, Bran gave the answers. Finally Arbogast nodded. "I see you're in Cadre D, Squad 8. Too late for you to make morning drills, even if you'd been here on time. Well, that'll give you time to get your shots this morning, and read the Regs. Ask for a copy on your way out."

"Yes, sir." Arbogast was looking down again, so Bran turned to leave.

"Just a minute, cadet." Bran swung back. "With the Academy Regulations, I can save you a little time. The main thing is that everything your superiors tell you to do, you do. And nothing else. Got that?"

Sure, whatever is not compulsory, is forbidden. Bran had read about that, somewhere. He didn't say it out loud, though.

And now it seemed he was truly free to go. In the outer office he asked for and was given a copy of the Academy Regs, and directions to the infirmary, where he received various inoculations. Some hurt more than others, and by the time he got back to his empty squad room he was feeling a little lightheaded. He figured he'd better read the Regs through, anyway.

It was pretty much the way Arbogast had said. There were separate buildings for each of the four cadres that made up the Southwest Quadrangle, and off-duty you stayed with your own. There was a definite hierarchy of seniority among cadets. One's superior was automatically right, and there was no appeal. Insubordination was a dire offense, and severity of punishment was pretty much up to the discretion of the higher-ranking offendee.

After reading carefully about halfway through, Bran skimmed the rest of the pamphlet. Already he thought he had the idea. *For a while, I can stand this place. But I hope they get me out soon.*

If one of his squadmates, looking harassed as well as bushed, hadn't stopped by the room on his way to lunch, Bran would have missed that meal, the shots had made him doze a little. Lunch was better than breakfast but not by much. Then Bran went with his squad out to the large central drill area, where each cadre trained in its own quadrant. The afternoon's subject was a series of marching maneuvers in formation, an art form as old as armies, and at first Bran thought it a harmless enough pastime. But then an instructor shouted someone's name and ran to intercept that person, giving the young man a slashing blow across the ribs with what appeared to be some kind of riding crop. More incidents of the same kind began to happen. Bewildered, Bran lost step on a Squads Right, heard his name called, and felt the quirt's burn across his right shoulder. Instinct made him crouch and start to turn—to see last night's bully hefting the short whip, grinning, ready to strike again.

So he turned back, sprang to regain place and step in the group. Counting cadence under his breath, he left the whip behind.

If the marching drill was bad, the calisthenics were worse. Bran was wiry and strong for his size, but never before had he been worked to exhaustion and then kicked or struck to force him to continue. Through a haze of fatigue he realized they weren't picking on *him*. Everyone got the same treatment. He saw one boy collapse and fail to rise no matter what was done to him. An instructor grabbed a foot and dragged the cadet off, out of the way. Gasping for breath, pausing a moment while no one seemed to notice him, Bran gathered strength for the next ordeal. And eventually the session came to an end. The squads marched back into the cadre building—with ten minutes to shower and change before dinner.

In the mess line, some were stopped and sent to another serving station at the room's far side. Facing Bran, the arbiter looked at a list and said, "Out there today, you stunk! But it's your first day, so I'll give you a break and not send you over to the bread-and-water line, this time. You get a real meal; enjoy it."

Maybe dinner was better than lunch, maybe not. Bran was too tired to know, and feverish, semi-nauseous. He concentrated on getting the food down and keeping it there, because he knew he was going to need it.

The following days didn't get any better, but somehow Bran managed to cope. He didn't exactly get used to the Academy's deliberate cruelty, but increasingly he learned to take the unremitting parts for granted; it was the new stuff that got to him, and always there *were* new outrages.

One evening after dinner he was unexpectedly penalized for some infraction he hadn't noticed at the time. "Tregare! Five laps around the drill field. Right now." On a full stomach, naturally, but no point in arguing; Bran went outside in the evening chill and did the five laps. He didn't hurry them a lot, though, and returned to his squad room at a leisurely pace. Only when he opened the room's door did he realize something was wrong there. "What the *hell*?"

The newest boy, who had come in only two days earlier, was spreadeagled face down and naked, with a larger cadet holding him there, raping him. Screwing him. Boogering him. As he yelled, and the others in the room stood back, white-faced watching.

Bran shook his head. "What you think you're *doing*? You can't—" Two boys held him back. Then the rapist was done, and that one, an upperclassman from two floors up, came over to Bran.

Bran's arms were held and he couldn't stop that bigger youth from cupping a palm around his jaw. "I can't *what*, snotty? Tell me, huh? Can't come back here tomorrow maybe, and do *you*?"

Nothing in Bran's whole life had scared him this badly. He knew that in the room or in the entire Academy he would find no help. *All right, damn it!* He jerked his head back from the hand's grip, then lunged to bite its reaching edge. He drew blood, and took a backhand across the face for his trouble. But now he was pretty sure his voice wouldn't tremble. So he said, keeping it slow, "You could, yes. But unless you killed me, you'd never be safe again." Sheer bluff and he knew it, so he held the other's gaze until that gaze turned away. Good thing, too—Bran's eyes were starting to water with the strain.

The big one shrugged. "Oh, turn him loose. You know better'n to jump me, don't you? I was kidding, anyway. You're not the type." And pulling his clothes together, he walked out.

The others tried to talk to Bran then but he wouldn't answer. Nor would he look at the naked one crying on the floor. He took his shoes off and climbed into bed without undressing further. He lay a long time, tensed, until the rest of the squad also went to bed and turned the light out. Much later, hearing their sleeping breaths, he found himself crying. He kept it quiet.

Every day he checked the comm room for messages from Alexa. For eleven days the visits were fruitless, but on the twelfth the orderly said, "Tregare, Bran, you say?" Bran nodded. "You know anybody in Australia?"

"Sure. I lived there." The sour-faced man seemed to want something more, so Bran added, "I was expecting word from my aunt. Ms. Alexa Duggan." And he gave the address.

The way the man looked at the flimsy he held, he might have been trying to memorize it. Finally he handed it over. "I guess it's for you, all right."

The orderly's grade of courtesy rated no thanks, but Bran gave him some, anyway. After all, he'd be dealing with the slob again. He took the message and walked the long corridor to the building's "inside" exit. Late afternoon sun warmed him as he sat on a bench facing the now vacant drill field.

Then he read the message. What it said on the face of it was idle chatter, nothing important. Just in case, though, he read it that way first. Then he counted the letters in the first three words, which gave him the three digits of the code sequence Alexa had used. And then he read the real message.

It didn't say much either. Liesel was still in Argentina, and her own reports, telefaxed or direct on viewscreen circuits, were largely noncommital.

Well, sometimes things did take a while. . . .

The next few days, not much new happened. In a tentative way, Bran became friends with the skinny, freckled boy who had first spoken to him. Jargy Hoad, his name was, and Jargy carried an air of irreverent independence that appealed to Bran. The other six in the room—the raped boy had simply vanished, transferred to another cadre without notice to his squad mates—the other six didn't impress Bran Tregare much, though four of them were second-year, not snotties. He could keep them straight in his mind because Ellsworth was fat, Donegan had buck teeth, Ahmad was black and said he was Muslim, Dale talked a lot and never said much, Pringle was just the opposite, and Hastings could do one-arm pushups. Jargy, though, was fun to be around, to talk to. To conspire with.

At first, all the two did was sneak extras out of mess at dinner, deciding who should swipe what in order to put together a late-night snack. They hid the stuff in shrubbery near their closest building exit, and went outside for the snacking: first, because they couldn't steal enough to feed the whole room; second, if they didn't share, someone would probably snitch; and third, share or not, Jargy said Dale would snitch anyway. "Reason he talks so much," said young Hoad, "is to cover what he's thinking."

Maybe so, maybe not, thought Bran—but Jargy's advice made sense.

There weren't any more rapes in Squad room 8. Between them, Jargy and Bran figured out how to stop those; Jargy told the rest of the squad. "What we do is, we get in the way a lot, and somebody opens the door so the whole floor can hear. Right, Bran?"

"Right." Staring at Dale, "Anybody goes to shut that door, or doesn't help stop one of those prongers, gets beat on a lot." It wasn't Bran's usual way of talking, but you had to learn things.

And one night the same upperclassman as before—his name was Channery—either drunk or on drugs, came barging in and hollered, "You're for me!" reaching for Ellsworth.

Jargy yelled for everybody to move in, and pretty soon the older cadet found he couldn't scare the interference away. He cursed a certain amount, and left. A little later, when Bran and Jargy went out for their stolen snack, they brought some back, waking Ellsworth to share it.

And from then on, Ellsworth joined the mess-raiding crew.

The Academy setup wasn't all that complicated, but since nobody told you much unless you asked, Bran found it took him quite a while to put even the most basic facts together. For instance, normal cadre strength was about a thousand, so this four-cadre campus (one of six such, he was told) should have held roughly four thousand cadets. But for some reason the whole place, not just Squad 8's room, was nearly twenty percent under quota. Somehow that datum gave Bran a vague unease. But alongside the real hell of the place, not enough to keep him worried.

The three classes of cadets were (unofficially) snotties, middies, and uppers; the official designations were for the records and nobody except officers used them much. Between cadets and Academy officers were a few graduates who hadn't been assigned space duty yet; the Regs called them graduate instructors but the cadets, speaking among themselves, called them "mules." Those young men commanded sub-cadres, groups of squads, something on the order of a hundred cadets. The mule overseeing the contingent that included Bran was a thin, intense youth who was having moderate luck at growing a mustache. His name was Jimar Peralta, and he had no mercy on cadets who made his contingent look bad. Never cross that one, Bran decided, unless you really need to!

Peralta wasn't all bad, though. Some of the upperclassmen—such as Channery—liked to pull really dirty, degrading tricks on snotties and middies, in the way of punishment. Channery's fat buddy, Guelph, once punished the last cadet to finish in a five-lap race by tying him to a post and leaving him there for two days. He could eat or drink, but he couldn't leave. Then, stinking and wet, the boy was chased around the drill field three times while Guelph's squad cut at him with their little whips.

Maybe Jimar Peralta didn't hear about that incident. The one he came in on—that Bran saw—was a run-the-gauntlet bit. Channery liked putting snotties through the gauntlet. The way it worked, you stripped to the waist while all the squads in your area lined up to whale hell out of you with their belts. Bran had it happen once and didn't want it again. Luckily he was a fast runner and fell only once. So he wound up hurting, but not really *hurt*.

One time, though, late in the afternoon Jargy Hoad tripped and fell during a race with everybody carrying full packs, and came in a woeful last. It was Channery who assigned the gauntlet, and stationed himself about halfway along the double line. Jargy was pale, looking desperate as he ran. Bran swung his belt in a deliberate miss. Jargy wasn't doing too bad; he ducked some swings and took the hits pretty well. Then Channery stepped out, blocking Jargy's run, and smashed Jargy across the face with the *buckle* end of his belt. You weren't, Bran knew, supposed to do that—but Channery did it, and grinned as Jargy got up to his knees and held both hands to his bleeding mouth.

The hell with the rules! And Bran was going for Channery, blind rage driving him, when a hand grabbed his shoulder and threw him to one side. Levering himself up, he saw that Jimar Peralta had Channery by the throat. "*Muerto*, you should be!"

Gasping, Channery tried to speak. "I don't understand."

"You stupid cockroach... sadist idiot! You put bad marks on the record of *my* unit, I'll have your balls on toast—and you'll serve them up!" The angry man shook his head. "More seriously, if you do such a thing again, *you and I* will duel with these belts. And I will have your face off your skull in two minutes!" Glaring, Peralta looked around. "Unit dismissed!" Channery slunk away. With a little extra time before dinner, Bran accompanied Jargy to the infirmary, where his lip was stitched.

The next day Channery was missing. Transferred or discharged, Bran didn't know. Or care much, either.

What he couldn't understand was where the Slaughterhouse drew the line between routine brutalities and unacceptable ones. Lisping a little with his swollen lip, Jargy tried to explain. "It's the way the colonel says to everybody, on our first day. Anything you're *told* to do is all right, but nothing else is."

"Oh? Then how about Channery's little rape games?"

Hoad looked uncomfortable. "Rotten, yeah. But he always waited until he was senior cadet on duty in the unit. And you try to snitch on a guy that ranks you—his word against ours, it would've been. No contest."

So Bran learned a little more about the way the system worked.

Jargy also had some thoughts about what made Peralta tick. "He's ambitious like nobody else I ever saw; he wants rank, and power. I came in at half-term last year so I saw him operate as an upper before he graduated. You know he wound up as cadet colonel, in charge of all four of our cadres?"

Bran whistled. For the moment, he'd forgotten how badly he wanted *out* of this place. "You mean, by the time *we* graduate, he'll be an admiral or something?"

Headshake. "Not that fast. But if he isn't close to commanding his own ship by then, my guess is he'll Escape."

Bran had heard the term, always stressed a little. Now he asked what it meant, and Jargy told him. "UET's losing ships. One of my dad's cousins went into the Underground, and we used to see him once in a while." Hoad laughed. "Late at night, usually, and disguised never twice the same.

"Anyway, he said UET first thought there was something dangerous in space—black holes or aliens or something—but then some of those lost ships turned up raiding UET colonies. For supplies and people, both. Cousin Larry claimed these Escaped Ships were setting up their own colonies, on planets UET never heard of. The Hidden Worlds, he called 'em."

"You think he's right, Jargy?"

Shrug. "How would I know?" But it was something to think about.

Every time Bran thought he'd adjusted to whatever the Slaughterhouse could throw at him, it came up with something worse. He'd been there nearly two months, stretching hope between weekly messages from Alexa Duggan—messages that only said she had no real news for him—when one afternoon Peralta summoned his unit to join a full cadre formation. For a moment the taut mask slipped and he looked human as he said, "They're starting the free-for-all season early this time. I hope none of you are chosen." And aside, Bran barely heard him mutter, "Goddamn waste of good talent!"

With all four cadres in tight formation surrounding the drill field's center, Colonel Arbogast himself waddled to climb a small stand that held public-address equipment. The colonel began,

"All right, men! We have a challenge from cadre C, for the honor and rations-differentials of your respective groups. Two men per cadre into the arena—and this one's to the death, so no snotties allowed. Losing cadre goes on bread and water, as usual, for a month or until next challenge, whichever comes first." He turned to his adjutant. "Draw the names, captain."

Standing next to Jargy Hoad, Bran nudged and whispered. "What *is* this?"

"What the man says . . . eight-man free-for-all, until somebody gets killed." He gave a half-sob. "Jeez! I hope I'm still a snotty, on the record!"

This is insane! But Bran kept asking. "What kind of fighting? What weapons? What rules?"

Jargy stifled a hysterical laugh. "No weapons. They go out there naked and try to kill each other. Only two rules: you lay off the eyes and balls, because blind guys and eunuchs aren't much good to the space fleet."

"How about dead ones?"

"I guess they don't care about that."

The fight was more horrible than Bran could have imagined. At first the boys were hesitant, but then their respective officers shouted some things Bran could not hear clearly, and he saw how their feelings changed to desperation and their actions to reckless abandon. Bran especially watched Ellsworth, the middie from his own squad room, and bit his knuckles when he saw Ellsworth caught and cruelly thrown, to rise with one arm hanging limp and twisted, then fall again. But the boy's next attacker, leaping in to grab the throat, caught a hard-driven heel at his own larynx and dropped, rolling over to hands and knees but unable to rise again as his face purpled and he collapsed. And shortly died.

Bran wanted to look away but he couldn't. He'd never seen anybody die before. Then Jargy's elbow nudged his ribs. "Wake up, Tregare! We're supposed to sing the goddamn 'Victory Song' now. If you don't remember the words, fake it."

Next day at parade, Peralta told the unit it was time to get into free-for-all practice. "Snotties rules, though, for everybody—bouts go to first disablement, only." The idea still didn't strike Bran as much fun. In fact he found himself shivering with fear as he waited for his first bout. The fact that Peralta didn't seem to approve of the whole matter was no help at all.

To avoid friends ganging up on strangers, the combats were set up among cadets from different squads. So that beginners would not inadvertently break the "eyes and balls" rules, the young combatants wore skimpy protective gear in those areas.

Nonetheless, the time came that Bran found himself in an arena with seven enemies. And until one of the eight was ruled disabled, the other seven could do damn near *anything* to him! Except deliberately kill him, of course, but accidental death didn't sound like such a great idea either. Nor did "disablement." Even sedated and with the dislocated shoulder strapped back into place, Ellsworth had with his moaning kept the whole squad room awake most of one night. And whether the injured boy had slept at all then, Bran couldn't be sure.

Now, moving and shifting with the other seven, trying for positions of advantage, Bran missed the sleep *he* hadn't got. The edge was off his timing. His first feint missed its purpose and he didn't dodge the counterblow cleanly; it stung him.

Suddenly Bran was scared. He knew he couldn't afford to be; it could freeze him, make him helpless. But he was anyway. The sweat of action went cold on his skin. His breathing came shallow. A kick rammed at his face, and missed only because the kicker was clumsy. Moving as if through water or mud, Bran backed away.

All right now, dammit! He drew a deep, shuddering breath and shouted, "Hai!" The boy coming toward him, startled, veered to one side, and Bran caught him with a neck chop. Not hard enough to drop him but the fellow did stagger for a moment.

Not the next one, though. A blow caught Bran's shoulder and spun him. He dropped and rolled, coming up to face that boy. He suddenly realized that he, Bran, was near to being the smallest of the eight combatants.

So the hell with it; he attacked. Right at the biggest kid, because this move had to be feint and bluff, and then off to the side where he put a good solid throw on someone he caught standing flatfooted. The boy got up, though, and Bran danced back away.

Now his moves were working. He struck and twisted and tripped and kicked and threw, and nobody was stopping him much, except that there were just too damned many of them and he wasn't *winning*.

Panting, his throat felt raw; much more of this he couldn't take. What was wrong? Then he realized—all his training had been to *stop* the opponent, to register a defeat the other would have to accept. But that wasn't what *this* was all about! His training hadn't been to injure people deliberately. But now—

The big kid was back. Two others, smaller, flanked him. So Bran had succeeded—if that was the word for it—in uniting three against him. Vision glazing, he felt his eyes narrow to slits as he chose his move. Shouting again, he leaped to kick both feet at the big one's chest, because he wanted someone he could get a good solid bounce off—sidewise almost, in a diving tackle at the shins of one of the flankers. And as he and that one landed in a heap, Bran heard the other's knee pop like a dry stick.

He got up; his opponent could only lie there and shriek pain. First disablement—the bout was over.

In the mess hall when the afternoon finally ended, Bran forced his dinner down. Not much later, back at the squad room, he threw it up again. Jargy tried to help him but no one could. "You did what you had to, Bran. That's how it is, here."

Coughing, wiping away the tears of nausea, Bran said, "Sure. Stupid is how. Rotten is how. Pure total shit." He shook his head. "You know what time it is?" Jargy told him, and he stood up and wiped his face on a towel. "I have to go check something."

He got to the comm room just before the message desk closed. Tonight the orderly was a woman, neither young nor old, who was the friendliest of the lot who worked there. When he came trotting in, breathing a little fast from the run, she smiled at him. "Well, now. Just in time, young Tregare. And I have one for you." She handed him the slim packet, and he paused to thank her—not only for reasons of policy but because he had truly come to like her.

He went outside to the bench where now, by ritual, he read all of Alexa's messages. Slowly, not expecting much news, he opened the envelope and read the surface text. Nothing there, so he studied the code group and reread from that standpoint. And then he sat frozen.

Because, give or take a phrasing or two, it said: "Erika gave an ultimatum. All of your mother's group have to get off Earth immediately. There's a money settlement which is not too unfair, but Liesel stays off Earth forever. We have to get everything together and board a ship on the 15th of the month which is less than a week from now. Liesel and Hawkman are making every effort to get you free of the Academy so that you can join us, so be ready. We all hope to see you soon. Earth isn't the *only* place to live."

Bran blinked, and wondered why he had no tears. Because the message made perfect sense, but there was one thing wrong with it.

It was dated two weeks ago.

3. "Only One Latrine..."

STUCK here! It couldn't be that way—but it was. His parents wouldn't have left him here—but they had. He tried to get his mind to function, to come up with some kind of answer, but it wouldn't. Maybe crying would have let out some of the hurt, but he couldn't even do that.

He tried to think, but no thought came to him—only the dull ache at his solar plexus, as though he'd been kicked there. Maybe if he could talk to somebody. But he couldn't—not even to Jargy, for Jargy didn't know who Bran's parents were, or that he'd had any hope of escape from the Slaughterhouse where Jargy didn't. No, he'd better not tell anyone about that stuff; it would only bring scorn onto him.

Blank-minded again, he sat while memory pictures tormented him: good things at home, people he loved. He shook his head: all that was gone. Then recall gave him Jargy's face being cut by Channery's belt buckle, the purple-faced death of the boy Ellsworth had kicked, and finally twisted-face screaming after Bran himself had scored "first disablement" on a stranger's knee.

It was intolerable, all of it. Bran stood. He didn't know how he could help his own condition but there was one thing he had to do.

* * *

Quiet-voiced and blank-faced, Bran asked his questions. The clerk in Active Files, two offices away from Colonel Arbogast, seemed glad of someone to talk to. "You have a message for Cadet-captain Channery? All I know is, he's over in Cadre H now, in the next quadrangle but one." He pointed, and Bran said, yes, he knew where it was. He didn't, for sure, but it shouldn't be hard to find. The clerk smiled a little. "Your best bet is, write the message down and I'll see it's forwarded."

Bran shook his head. "I'm to deliver it in person." And after a little waffling the clerk wrote him a temporary pass, to get him into the proper quadrangle.

A half hour or so later, in lingering dusk, Bran knocked on the door of Channery's quarters. Outlined against light from indoors, Channery held the door open and said, "Yeah?"

Standing in dimness, Bran said, "I have a message for you."

"Well, come the hell in, then!"

"I'm not authorized. Just to hand it to you." He stood there, and slowly Channery emerged. When he was within reach, Bran swung the belt, and again, and twice more after Channery fell to his knees, yelling, trying to shield face with hands, while between his fingers blood spurted.

Bran heard running footsteps, people coming to see what the yells were about. He took one more satisfying look at the blood and turned and ran.

He made one wrong turn, though; just short of his own cadre-group area, he was caught. With blood on the buckle of the belt he still carried.

The hearing held by Colonel Arbogast wasn't like any court trial Bran had ever heard of; what it consisted of was denunciation and sentencing. Channery, his face swathed in bandages, sat on the witness stand and, with a Major Forsythe (or something like that) feeding him leading questions, did most of the talking. According to Channery, Bran Tregare had been nothing but trouble from the day he arrived at the Academy. In spite of himself, Bran was fascinated by some of the incidents Channery made up out of whole cloth: his arrival didn't find Channery raping some kid; instead Bran was beating the kid up for no reason and Channery stopped him. And of course Channery hadn't barged in drunk, later, to try another rape. Oh, no—he had intervened to stop Bran Tregare from molesting one of his squad mates. Rape wasn't specified in that instance, but it was sure as hell hinted pretty strong.

Sitting in the dock, Bran's feelings flared through rage to amusement to despair: what chance *was* there for him? After a time he simply quit hearing what was said. Until Arbogast's hoarse voice told him to stand for sentencing.

He stood; the colonel said, "I don't understand boys like you. You came here well-recommended. *Why* did you do these things?" He gestured toward Channery, and even now, Bran couldn't help but be glad that he'd carved *that* bastard up a little, with his belt. At least he'd paid back for Jargy. . . .

But to Colonel Arbogast's question he had no answer. Why had he sought out Channery and ambushed him? Because this place left him no sanity, and when he found he had no escape from it, *he had to hit back*. And Channery was the only person he knew who really deserved it.

But he couldn't say any of that; to anyone else it would make no sense. Nor, probably, would what he did find himself shouting: "Because Cadet captain Channery is a cruel bully, and a boogering rapist, and a goddamned liar!"

Even before two cadet guards flung him back into his seat and held him there, Arbogast's face told him he had lost. The colonel, himself standing now, spoke in a voice that shook with rage. "You'd like me to throw you out of here, wouldn't you, you little sneak? Even if it's into Total Welfare, and that's where I'd put you! But it won't be so easy, Tregare. I've made men out of worse worms than you are—and I will this time, too." Regaining some semblance of calm, the man said, "I was going to let you off with ten days' ordinary detention. But your outburst, your attempt to traduce your superior officer the cadet-captain—I think, Tregare, you rate the special cell." He turned to the guards. "Take him there, strip him, throw him in, and set the controls. Ten days ought to do it, I should think."

The cell looked no different from the others. Each was a cube, roughly a meter in each dimension, made of heavy wire mesh and sitting over a drainage sink. The guards took Bran's clothes and shoved him inside and slammed the door. There was no room to lie down, except curled around on one side; neither was there a comfortable way to sit. In either case, his weight lay on the wire mesh. Suddenly he knew what other cadets had meant when they referred to punishment as "waffle ass."

Well, there wasn't much he could do about it, only try to shift his position a lot. That part wasn't too difficult because the place was so cold that he couldn't sleep, anyway. Maybe fatter guys could doze naked in what Bran estimated at sixteen-Celsius, but Bran couldn't. So for long hours he lay and shifted and shivered, and leaked and crapped, and had no way to clean himself, and more and more felt thirst and hunger with no relief, until finally his fatigue was too much and he dozed.

SHOCK! He came awake, arms and legs flailing, bruising himself against the cage's roughness. For moments he couldn't figure what had happened. Then he knew. Electrical shock, they'd used; the wire mesh must be in two insulated parts. *GodDAMN!*

Then he saw a kind of shallow bowl in the cage beside him. It was only about half-full; his awakening convulsions had spilled the rest of its contents. But—they would *have* to feed him, wouldn't they? So he smelled, then tasted what was left in the bowl. It wasn't good exactly, but he could eat it. So he did.

The unpredictable pattern never changed. As long as Bran could stay awake, he was neither electrically shocked nor fed. When he slept, they jolted him the hell awake and fed him the pig slop.

They had one more trick in reserve. Once when he dozed, he was jarred awake not by voltage but by a slanting blast of icy water. After his first yell, and his attempt to curl up away from the deluge, he decided he'd better take advantage of it. He turned this way and that to scrub himself as clean as he could. When, abruptly, the flow ended, he crouched with teeth chattering and wished for some way to dry himself. The evaporative process chilled him horribly, but eventually he was, for the most part, dry. His hair, short though it was, took a while longer.

But at least the torrent had washed both himself and the cell's floor mesh free of the stink of feces.

At this waking, though, he hadn't been fed. His hunger kept him from sleep, so did the extra chill. But finally he did lose consciousness, was jolted back to it, and ate again.

The only new trouble was that the blast of cold water had

been one blow too many against his body's powers of resistance. Whatever combinations of cold or flu virus he'd been harboring, now they struck. Chills and fever shook him, along with diarrhea and a grade of nausea that had him vomiting before he could finish a bowl of slops.

A point came when he simply lay, partly conscious, and tried to ignore the shocks. And then he passed out totally, and no longer had to try.

When he next woke, he was in a hospital bed, with an IV tube in his arm. Whether he'd lasted the colonel's ten days, he didn't know and didn't care. At any rate, he'd survived the special cell. This time, anyway.

The infirmary wasn't in the business of coddling patients. The first nurse to find Bran awake pulled the IV and slapped a band-aid on the puncture. There was a glass of water beside the bed; it was up to Bran to sit up and reach it, and a little later, at midday, he found that the same rules applied to lunch. A tray was set on the side table; he could either cope with it or go hungry. Shakily in both cases, he managed. Spilling a little, but not much. Lying back again, afterward, he slept more comfortably.

What woke him was the need to urinate. He looked around for the button that would summon a nurse; Bran had never been sick in a hospital before, but had visited them. No such button here, though; well, in the Slaughterhouse, that figured. So he clambered up out of bed and leaned over to the wall, and carefully edged his way, bracing his weight as best he could, out of the room and along the corridor. For once his luck was in; he turned to the right and the john was only a few meters away. Once relieved, for a moment he paused: why make two trips if one would do? But his bowels seemed totally quiescent. All right; he made his painful hobble back to the room and his own bed. And quickly slept again.

Next day, Bran was visited by Jargy Hoad. "Hey, Bran—I'm glad you're all right!"

"Who says I am?" Bran's voice came out sulky, but he had to grin.

"Brought you something." Jargy held out a honeycone. "Better eat it right away; it's starting to melt." Dubiously, wondering if he *could* eat, Bran took it. But the first bite was delicious; his difficulty was trying to eat slowly enough to enjoy the taste of all of it. Meanwhile Jargy kept talking. "You're a hero, kind of... you know that? Eight days in that hellhole... not quite the record, but you're close. Peralta came in the squad room and told us that." Jargy paused, then said, "But the big thing—by three or four days in the special cell, most cadets break down and start yelling, begging to be let out. Peralta says you never did, at all. Not even once."

Embarrassed, Bran shrugged. "Never thought to." He considered the idea, and added, "No point in it. They wouldn't let you out anyway." He frowned. "Nobody ever makes it the full ten days?"

"Not so far. Maybe next time you will."

Bran could see Jargy was kidding, but still he shivered. "I'd just as soon let somebody else set that record."

The honeycone was gone now; Bran wished there'd been two of them. Belatedly he thanked Jargy, then asked, "You hear anything? How long before I go back to regular duty?"

"You don't, exactly. One thing, classes started again, this week. Here." He lifted a book bag to the bedside stand. "I brought these, so you can read and catch up. The first two weeks you're out of here—or until the medics okay you for general duty—you're on classwork only."

Surprised, Bran said, "Somebody in this place has a heart?"

"It makes the colonel mad as hell probably, but once a cadet hits this infirmary, the medics have the say-so."

Something to remember, Bran thought. One for our side.

Restless after Hoad's short visited ended Bran looked at some of the books. Parts of the math he knew already, but by no means all. The introductory course on spaceships, starting simply with construction layout and later—he flipped to the back of the book, to see how advanced it got—winding up with elementary drive room procedures and control functions, fascinated him. When a nurse brought his dinner he was still reading, and continued until another told him to cut the lights and get some sleep. Then he lay thinking of what he'd read. *A ship. I want a ship!*

Sooner than he expected, Bran was released from the infirmary. As Jargy had said, for two weeks he faced only classroom work, and because Bran's prior education was a little spotty, that two weeks with some free study time was a godsend to him. When once again he was also scheduled for physical drills, for some days he had a hard time of it. Eventually his stamina rebuilt itself, and he began to learn to live with chronic fatigue as the normal order of things. Along with fear and resentment, of course.

He'd never given much thought to the abstract concepts of bravery and cowardice. Some things scared him and some didn't, and he knew that with other people the things could be different, both ways. And mainly, the point was that if something scared you, don't let the bastards *know* it. But the Slaughterhouse stretched that point a lot.

What really got to him were the free-for-alls. A week after he was back to drill status, one was called; for middies and uppers, and so to the death. No one from Bran's squad room was tapped this time, but still the watching was bad. The kill came when a squat, bandy-legged middie from Cadre C had the head of an opponent locked, the victim standing behind, and made what started to be an ordinary wrestling throw. But the Cadre C ape, instead of letting go, clenched arms more tightly around the other's neck and twisted to one side. Both fell in a heap, but no spectator missed the sound of cracking vertebrae.

Only a few days later came a similar tourney for snotties, and again, no one Bran knew personally got the call. He stood, hands clenched, hoping to see some minor injury that would qualify as first-disablement. But the deciding blow was a kick to the abdomen—the attacker's foot sinking totally out of sight—and the loser died of a ruptured spleen before the medics arrived. They took good care of the kicker's sprained toe, though.

That night, Bran's nightmares began.

He was going to lunch but he couldn't find the mess hall. Pretty soon he knew he'd be late for drill, so he forgot about eating and headed for the quadrangle. It started getting dark and he knew he was late, so he began running. But his legs would hardly move at all; he could barely totter along. He looked for the way to the drill field, but there was some construction in his path. He had to go around, and then to climb over a lot of half-built structures and scaffolding. When he got to the top of it, he could see the drill field, but nearly a hundred meters below—a sheer drop. So he'd have to go back down and find a new way to get there, but when he began his return he couldn't locate any way out of the maze.

He was underground now and couldn't find any familiar landmarks at all. The narrow passage was knee-deep in mud and something was behind him. He tried to run, and again his legs seemed almost paralyzed. Finally he saw light ahead, and *pushed* with one leg and then the other, and came to—

The special cell! With no choice, he entered it. . . .

And woke to hear himself making a soft, shrill whine. Sweat bathed him. He sat up, looked around in dim light until he was oriented, then lay back, feeling his pulse and breathing slowly return to normal.

Jeez! It had been three or four years since a dream fooled him that way; he'd learned to spot them, and break loose from the bad ones, when he was nine or ten. And he knew that the business of never being able to run in dreams was because he would *really* be trying to move his legs and the bedclothes wouldn't let him. Hawkman had explained that part, and Bran had tested it and proved it by sleeping coverless in warm weather.

But *this* one—! The rest of that night, he only half-dozed. The next was no better: He was in the mess hall and there was one egg too many on his tray so he had to run a gauntlet to his table. Channery and Jargy Hoad and Ellsworth and Colonel Arbogast were all swinging the buckle ends of belts at him and if he spilled his tray. . . He woke, not quite screaming because he was biting down hard on a mouthful of his righthand knuckles.

Whatever had started didn't seem to want to stop. He dreamed of free-for-alls; sometimes he was injured horribly and sometimes the horror was a ghastly thing he'd done to someone else. He tore someone's head apart and then found his opponent had been Jargy Hoad. Once he won some kind of drill contest, and his prize was to be raped by Channery, who opened his trousers to reveal a jagged belt buckle. As Colonel Arbogast chuckled . . .

It was the tension and fatigue, he decided, that gave the nightmares such power over him, so that he couldn't see they weren't real and wake up by normal effort of will.

The knowledge didn't help much. The damned things continued, and only eased off over a period of weeks.

* * *

At first he could keep them into nighttime, but after a while they invaded his days; of a sudden he would find himself wet with sweating from fear—from something that was said, or purely from memory of some deadly bout. He hated himself for what he considered to be his weakness. Some nights he woke up crying and only hoped no one had heard. He felt all too close to breaking, and knew that in this place he could not *afford* to break.

So the next time a snotties' bash was announced, Bran did the unthinkable: he volunteered for it. He lay awake the night before, dreading, and went through the next day and out into the arena feeling not alive but wooden, now and then wondering if he were simply and terminally stupid.

Four cadres, eight combatants: Bran's team mate was a new kid and looked as scared as Bran felt. No help there! But Bran had already chosen his tactic: two hands are stronger than one. So while the others were weaving and shifting cautiously, he made a great war whoop and charged. He made feints, kicks, and hand chops as he went—but these were only to clear path to his chosen target, who stood frozen. Bran grabbed a handshake hold with both hands, swung to turn under the other's arm for a standard wrestling throw—and then simply didn't let go. Between the dislocated shoulder and the ruined elbow, first disablement was clear enough.

With only a few twinges of conscience, that night he slept well.

What Bran liked about the math courses was applying the methods to spaceship operations, such as communication and navigation. Yeah, probably the latter should be called "astrogation," but it wasn't. And the way the ships chewed time, up near light speed: the relativity stuff fascinated him. On his desk calculator, if he entered a velocity as a decimal fraction of c, he could get the time-ratio (one-over-the-square-root-of-one-minus-vee-squared) by punching seven keys. Or, going the other way, from ratio to vee, the same.

Then one day the class was doing some trig, and suddenly it came to Bran that with trig functions he could do it even faster. Enter vee and then hit: Arc. Sin. cos. 1/x. *Four* moves, and again, the same in reverse. He didn't tell anybody, and later when the instructor had the class do a chart of t_0/t from zero to c in 0.1c steps, he finished in two-thirds the time of the next fastest student. The instructor was impressed.

It paid to do well in classwork, because the lowest scorers on any exam got to run the gauntlet. Nobody liked to beat his own classmates, so the system was for classes to trade victims for the ordeals. Across cadres, sometimes.

Bran was no genius, but being half Hulzein he had to be bright, and Hawkman was no slouch, either. The boy knew his IQ figures qualified him for nearly any kind of training a university could offer. In the Space Academy program, only once throughout his first term did he have to run the gauntlet. That time he was fogged from lack of sleep and misread the crucial high points question.

Jargy Hoad had it rougher. It wasn't that he was dumb, but that here *nobody* was dumb, so someone had to drag bottom. Jargy endured four gauntlets that term—about average.

The trouble was, you never knew when they were going to call one of those damned free-for-alls. There was no regular schedule to them. Bran wasn't sure whether a predictable pattern would be easier to live with or not. He decided it would, because then you wouldn't have to be scared *all* the time, and could start psyching up when the time approached.

And there was no knowing how they picked the poor bastards who had to fight. Scholarship had nothing to do with it, nor skill on the drill field. But somehow Bran knew the "draw" was a farce. Once he muttered as much, and Peralta heard him and told him he'd do well not to talk that way. So he shut up.

But it seemed that Bran's unheard-of volunteering for a bout had gained him considerable respite from further ones. Time after time the "draw" missed him. Not his squad mates, though.

Ellsworth caught it, bragged that he'd repeat his earlier triumph, but was whipsawed by two Cadre B men and limped on crutches for a month or so. At least he wasn't the one killed. Neither was Donegan, whose front teeth were no longer buck, but artificial. Jargy had an easy one. On a muddy day he tripped and slid past the entire confrontation. By the time he got up, the action had moved away from him. All he had to do was watch.

Hastings, the strong man, managed by dint of vicious defense, black Ahmad by grace and quickness. The quiet Pringle went berserk and chased all seven opponents—including his supposed ally—out of the ring. When the one he'd rabbit punched couldn't get up for awhile, the umpires counted it as disablement. Mouthy Dale tried a spectacular leap-kick, missed, and cracked two of his own vertebrae when he landed. He was invalided out of the Slaughterhouse. Jargy Hoad said, "Some guys just get lucky."

Near the last day of his snotty year, Bran got tagged again. That night and next morning he couldn't keep his food down. Taking Ellsworth's example to heart ("Never try to repeat," the fat youth had said later. "They'll be watching for it."), Bran tried a different tactic. When the fight began, he yelled and charged, made chops and kicks far short of any goal, jumped back, yelled some more, and charged again. What he was being was a threat and a distraction. At no time did he engage in actual combat. He made one leap-kick, a deliberate miss, sprawled and rolled, thinking to entice the opponent to come after him. But while they circled, feinted, and taunted each other, someone else wrapped the match up with a neck chop.

Well, at least no *real* disablement, in that bout.

With the end of that term's classes, ship training began. Not in space, of course, but in two old, long-grounded hulks—the *Il Duce* and the *Caesar*—that stood like towers behind the Cadre H barracks. But just being *in* a ship gave Bran a strange, thrilled feeling.

The *Caesar* had been an armed ship. Bran was glad to be assigned to it rather than to the unarmed *Duce*. Of course the six turrets were now empty of projectors, just as the drive room no longer held a Nielson cube. But the controls—at the pilots' chairs, turrets, or drive room—connected to computer simulations and gave proper indications on the instruments. Peralta said, the first day his groups were allowed on the *Caesar*, "Don't consider these simulations as toys. Treat it all as real. If you do, you'll learn how to handle a ship." Bran believed him.

Ships, except for being armed or not, were pretty well standardized, from Control at top to the drive room and landing legs at bottom. In between, as you climbed, came space for cargo and supplies, crew's quarters, the galley complex, and officers' quarters. Well, it wasn't quite that simple. For instance, the drive room didn't occupy its full vertical section of the ship, but was itself surrounded by cargo holds. And quarters were stratified, with ratings living topside of unrated crew, and control officers occupying the deck above engineering officers.

Total ship's complement was usually about one hundred, give or take a few. So Peralta's subgroup made a good simulation.

Even if the ship hadn't fascinated Bran, the change from sadistic drills and calisthenic ordeals would have been welcome. Onship the cadets were first shown through the various sections, given study assignments on each aspect, and then put to practical test. Faced with the different types of control simulations, Bran found that his skills varied. When the first ten-day results were posted, he rated: Navigation, Very Good. Communications Control, Excellent. Weaponry, Fair. Drive Room Operation, Fair to Good. Overall Capability, Good to Very Good.

Those results were a little misleading. Bran found drive room work so easy as to be totally boring. Deliberately he had made a poor showing there. Because if ever he did get onto a ship, he wanted to be riding up front, not down with the Nielson cube.

His weaponry rating bothered him. To be a control officer he needed to be fairly expert at a turret. And right now, he wasn't.

It shouldn't, he felt, be all that difficult for him. A projector consisted of two lasers that operated above the UV band and converged to give a heterodyne frequency in the peak infrared. "Tune it right, and you could boil tungsten in less than a second," one instructor said. The trouble was, the things weren't tunable. What you did was, take about four shots for ranging-in. These wouldn't be in peak heat range—but your next five or six shots, before the heating of circuit components drifted your heterodyne-freq *past* top performance—were deadly.

A gunner's controls were really quite simple. The ship's computer picked a target for you—then you had only two choices to make. One was to get your beam-convergence on target, which meant moving a lever toward either of your two range lights, to extinguish it if it lit up. Any time both lights were out and your heterodyne was near to peak heat, your projector fired.

The other control was an override foot pedal, which doubled your combined range-heterodyne tolerance for allowing fire. "And that," said one instructor, adjusting the eye patch that interrupted her face-splitting scar, "is the main reason for having human gunners at all. Of course you use override to get off your warm-up shots. When you're testing on sims, shots on override give only half credit."

Bran knew what she meant. On test runs, any time your shot was a damaging hit, a central viewscreen lit up with a dot. At a run's end, the computer spit out a tab indicating what percentage of time you'd had effective energy on target—that you *could* have had—according to what the simulation had your target doing. Like changing course or pulling a quick accel or decel to evade. But hits made by using override counted only half.

But the point of having override at all, Bran learned, was that in a really tight spot, people can try to guess right and computers can't.

Bran's problem with gunnery didn't take him too long to figure out. Only thing was, he didn't know how to fix it. The ratings were simple: Fair was a 30-40% average on the sims; Good was 40-50 and Very Good 50-60. In Weapons he hadn't heard of any Excellent ratings. Which didn't mean there weren't any. . .

But he needed at least a Good, to get branched into Control Officers' training, and so far he was averaging a lousy 38. The thing was, his coordination was too ragged, and that was because he was running on the thin edge of fatigue. The damned nightmares cut into his sleep too much, and they wouldn't stop.

It had been over a month since the most recent free-for-all, but he couldn't keep from dreading and expecting the next one, any day. And he'd had to run a gauntlet, for coming last in a gunnery competition, and somebody's belt-end had caught him across the right eye and left him seeing blurry for a couple of days. No buckle, but the leather was bad enough. Even after his vision cleared, he had to squint through the swelling, to see much.

By now, though, at night he did not cry. He merely hated.

But Bran was, after all, an heir of the Hulzein Establishment. So eventually he began to think back, if only in desperation, to sayings he'd heard from his mother Liesel

Hulzein and his father Hawkman Moray. And remembered something Liesel had said: "About so-called insoluble problems. First you find the logic. Then you find the handle on it. And then you twist it."

So once again Bran volunteered for a snotties' free-for-all, and made a great lot of attention-drawing commotion while doing his best to avoid any real action. As soon as he saw a disablement happen, he took a wild dive at a rather passive opponent and wound up with the both of them bruised enough to be excused from the rougher stuff for a time. Bran didn't know about the other guy, but he made sure to land with one arm on a sharp rock in the ring, gashing himself enough to bleed a reasonable amount.

Blood didn't scare Bran. He'd seen plenty of his own, having had the usual quota of silly childish accidents—which tend to happen to kids whose confidence exceeds their knowledge. His aim now was to get loose from the physical harassment by way of injury, and from the nightmares by way of temporary freedom from all the goddamned physical *hazing*. ("Whatever works," said Liesel Hulzein.)

So now he was free of mandatory combats and from calisthenic risks. He had time available for studies and his mind was clear—for the moment—of the usual dread. He'd learned the hard way to avoid thinking too far ahead, in this place. So he settled down and brought his gunnery average from a lousy 38 to a quite respectable 54. Which put him into the Control Officers curriculum.

For now—things being the way they were—that was good enough.

The term was ending. Pretty soon there'd be the summer session, and then Bran would be a middie, not a snotty. The graduation ceremonies for the uppers came on a sweltering day. Putting on his dress uniform for the first time since an all-cadres parade, he began sweating before he had his jacket buttoned.

All the way across their own quadrangle and the next, going to the main parade ground, the cadres marched at attention, loudspeakers blaring music at them. From the first time he'd heard it, Bran had hated the Academy's official march, "UET Forever," and now the sound of it made him grit his teeth.

Eventually all the cadres formed up. Now, thought Bran,

maybe the show would get on the road! No such luck. Two cadres abreast, the entire Academy complement raised dust marching the full field perimeter, to pass in review before Colonel Arbogast.

Bran was in Cadre D's right-hand file, third in line behind Ellsworth, his squad leader, so that not too much dust was kicked up where he had to breathe it. He winced for Jargy Hoad, bringing up the rear as lance-corporal. But soon, heat and all, dust and hated marching song, the rhythm of the march got to Bran. In a sort of hypnosis without conscious effort, he went through his paces.

To his right, just ahead, a motion caught his eye—a motion that didn't fit the rhythmic pattern. He almost lost step himself, but caught the beat and recovered. Now he watched, to see what had distracted him, and for the first time noticed the cadre beside him was H, and that leading it was Channery. And Channery wasn't doing too well.

He was limping, for one thing—his paces hesitant, not firm, and sometimes off rhythm. His balance didn't look too good either. And now as the columns turned, the final wheeling before the march past Arbogast's reviewing stand, Bran saw Channery's face. That it was red and sweating was no surprise, but as Bran watched, the face twitched and twisted into agonized grimace, fought its way toward standard parade blankness, then writhed again. One thing for certain: Channery had troubles. *Well, it couldn't happen to a nicer guy!*

Weaving noticeably but staying on his feet, Channery made it through the interminable graduation ceremonies. A couple of times Colonel Arbogast paused and stared at the cadet-captain, making the colonel's rambling tirade all that much longer. But it had to end sometime and finally it did. With shirt and undershorts sticking solidly to him, and sweat running down his arms and legs, Bran set his mind to lasting out the grim march back to barracks.

Channery, staggering and hardly keeping step at all, made less than fifty yards of the departure. One foot tripped on the other and he fell. The first ranks of his cadre stepped over him and then Bran was past and could see no more—whether anyone stepped on Channery, or who dragged him away.

Back at quarters, Bran, Jargy Hoad and Ellsworth were first into the showers. They ran the water fully cold and allowed no one to change that setting. Coming out of the shower, hearing others squabble over the water temperature and not caring, Bran didn't bother with a towel; evaporation in the hot room dried him soon enough. Then he lay on his bunk, trying to relax, and was half-dozing when Jargy poked at him and said, "Chow time, Bran." Once in the mess hall, he had a better appetite then he'd expected, and afterward he and Jargy walked around the shady borders of the quadrangle, taking it easy and not saying much.

When they returned to the squad room, they found a party going.

Jimar Peralta wasn't exactly drunk, but sober wasn't the word, either. Still in dress uniform—or again, more likely, for his garb showed no sweat stains or other signs of the day's ordeal—the graduate instructor sat on a vacant bunk and waved greetings to Bran and Jargy. "Got my posting today, cadets!" He tipped up the beer he was working on, and pointed to two cases that sat alongside the bunk. "So I'm standing drinks for all my squads." He scowled and grinned at the same time. "Just remember—give your juniors a treat when *you* ship out."

Caught by Peralta's gaze, Bran said, "Sure; I've heard about that," and nodded. "First time I've seen it, though."

Wave of hand. "Then drink up, snotty! Oops—you're not one now, are you, Tregare? *Middie*, I meant. All right?"

Bran grinned, and took a beer. He looked around; he and Jargy were running late at this party; everyone else already had a start. Well, that was all right; he had no intention of getting tanked. But a small friendly load couldn't hurt anything at all. . . .

He raised the plastic can. "Thanks, Mr. Peralta. Here's to you and space."

"I accept . . . with pleasure." For a moment Peralta looked around vaguely, then again he put his attention to Tregare. "Hey! Something I heard, might tickle you a little bit. Since you did special-cell time for assaulting cadet-captain Channery."

Suddenly Bran felt chilled—was he to be punished *again*? But Peralta's expression, a little slack, was still pleasant. He said, "Y'know why Channery looked so bad today, and finally couldn't make it?" Bran shook his head; he didn't look to see how anyone else responded. And Peralta laughed, then hiccupped once before he said, "Somebody in his cadre filled his boots with water and put 'em in the freezer! He didn't find out until about five minutes to making formation—too late to fix anything. He had to borrow! Somebody else's *old* boots."

Bran couldn't see why the idea was so funny that Peralta couldn't talk for laughing. He waited, then asked. "Well," said Peralta, "the whole lot must have been in on it. Because the only boots Channery could lay hands on—or feet into . . ." More laughter. Bran waited, and Peralta said, "Anybody here ever try to march five miles, in boots three sizes too small?"

All that came to Bran's mind was that he hoped the Slaughterhouse didn't hear about this and use it as a new way of punishment.

Bran had never drunk much alcohol at any one time. At home he'd been accustomed to a little wine at dinner or a cold beer to ease the heat of summer outdoor hiking. The few times during his first term here that beer had been smuggled into the squad room, it had been a matter of one or two cans per cadet, barely enough to feel the effects at all. Now, though, when Peralta's two cases were gone, somehow another two were delivered. Bran himself was on his fourth can, and his head felt strange—partly dizzy, partly godlike, and all mixed together.

One thing came clear to him, though: he had to take a leak. So he stood, feeling a slight imbalance, and went for the john. But the door was locked. He stood and he stood, and finally it opened. Ahmad came out. Bran went inside, wondering why Ahmad had closed off the group facility but not caring much. He relieved himself of a great lot of secondhand beer. As the flow splashed in the receptable he heard singing from the squad room, and when he rejoined the group, Peralta said, "Once more now!" And the group sang:

"When I was a boy at UET.
Twice a day they maybe let you pee.
Sometime later, when we were men,
They told us we could hold it twice as long again.
So *that* is the reason, you can plainly see,
Why there's only one latrine in all of UET.
Yes, *that* is the reason, you can plainly see,
Why there's only one latrine in all of UET!

"Yay!" shouted Jimar Peralta, and lay back on the bunk where he sat, kicking both feet into the air—but not spilling a drop of his beer. Then he sat up, blinked, and said, "That's something you don't sing when there's any brass around. It's a verse of the Underground fight song, mind you. I learned it in a tavern, over the wall one time in my middie year—and don't ask me how to do that, because if you can't work it for yourselves you don't deserve to know." Again he blinked. "That's all of that."

To Bran's left, Hastings said, "I know that tune. It's from Gilbert and Solomon."

"That's *Sullivan*." Bran's tone sounded disgusted. But Hastings nodded assent—no argument.

Bran opened another beer. He was past his limit, but he was tracking and felt good. And this was term's end, Peralta was buying, and the hell with it! He started a song he'd heard Hawkman sing: "Cocaine Bill and Morphine Sue, walkin' down the avenue, two by two . . ." But nobody else knew enough of it to keep it going. Peralta had the first two verses, and Pringle knew the fourth, but Donegan had a different version, and pretty soon Bran lost his way in his own song, and gave up.

The singing ran down. Bran took another leak, no locked doors this time, and came back to open his fifth or sixth beer. Somebody was looking over to him. Jimar Peralta, who said, "Tregare? You make it through this hellhole. I want to see you in space." Bran accepted the offered handshake. Peralta stood. "Sorry. . . must go, gentlemen and snotties, if any. I will see you—" Suddenly he leaped, landed on his toes and stood arched, taut, like a matador evading the bull's rush and turning to attack. "—in space. *If* any of you make it that far!"

Head buzzing with mild disorientation, Bran sat while the others talked and sang, joked, argued—once Ellsworth and Ahmad almost but not quite came to fighting. He would just as soon have gone to sleep but he wasn't sleepy. So he sat, sipping beer that became more and more warm and stale, while one by one the roommates put themselves to bed. Some undressed, some not, but finally there was Bran, sitting in dim light, needing to work up the energy to shuck his clothes and sack out.

He was unlacing the first shoe when the intercom chimed; quickly he went to answer. "Yes? Bran Tregare, Squad 8, Cadre D."

A chuckle. Then, "Peralta here. Did I leave the personnel folder in your room? Please look for it."

One look; on the vacant bunk where the man had sat was the folder. "Yes, it's here."

"Good. Could you bring it to me? I'll phone down to pass you through the guardpoints."

"Sure. Of course. Right away." Bran retied his shoe, picked up Peralta's folder and set out on the trek through two quadrangles to deliver it. The journey was uneventful. He was back to quarters within the half hour, and again began to undress.

But when he lay in bed he could not immediately relax into sleep. Because he hadn't been able to resist the temptation to look into the personnel folder, before he took it to Peralta.

Most of the contents were routine, and Bran looked mostly at the entries for his own squad. But after each official summary of a cadet's standing, Peralta had added his own notes. He rated Ellsworth: "Adequate, but not much more." Jargy Hoad: "Good officer material perhaps, but too easy-going as yet." Hastings: "Sturdy chap, but this one is a rating, not an officer." Donegan: "Successful graduation not predicted." Ahmad: "A good one, I think."

And then, following some other remarks, Tregare: "If this boy survives, put him on an armed ship. Gunnery scores aren't everything; he may be the deadliest of the lot."

4. The Killings

With most of the graduating uppers posted out, either to space or to other groundside facilities, the Slaughterhouse seemed half-empty. Not for long, though. During the next weekend, Cadre B was dispersed among the other cadre buildings, while its own was occupied by an all-female cadre. "Oh, sure," Ellsworth said. "Every summer they shut down the women's section, move them in here. Saves money, I guess."

Seeing them on the drill field, Bran didn't find stubble-headed girls all that attractive. Still he was glad that no free-for-alls were demanded—combat drills, sure, but with practice rules in force, so nobody had to hurt anybody.

One day he put a throw on a freckle-faced redhead, shorter than himself but chunky, letting her down as easily as he could. When he helped her up she came upright slowly, and said, "Do you ever walk around the drill field, evenings? I do, sometimes."

Wondering if she meant what he thought she meant, he looked at her. "Tonight, I could."

She nodded. "Two hours after mess. Northwest corner." So, Bran decided, he had himself a date.

In the squad room after dinner, Bran felt uncomfortable. With their two new roommates from Cadre B, there was plenty to talk about, but tonight Bran couldn't seem to join in. More than a half hour before his scheduled rendezvous, he left the room and went outdoors. Then he didn't know what to do with himself. He'd feel funny showing up this early, to sit and wait a long time.

So he walked the field's perimeter, the long way around, taking it slow and easy. As he neared the tree-darkened corner the girl had specified, he saw her approaching from the other direction. As they met, she took his hand and steered them deeper into the shadows. Then she kissed him—and Sheylah the head cook's daughter had never kissed like *that*.

"Don't wait!" she said, and without quite knowing how it all happened, Bran found himself wriggling on the grass with her, their clothes off and discarded, him trying to find where it was supposed to *go*. For a moment he thought he heard a whish of shrubbery; then a whipstroke lashed his shoulder.

"All right, cadets! Up!" *He knew that voice*, and now as they obeyed, it said, "I don't know who you are, missy, and I don't want to. Pick up your clothes and get going. No—out *that* way, where it's darker. When you're out of sight from here, you can get dressed."

Bran watched, as in the dimness the redhead collected her clothes and scuttled away. Then he turned to the interloper, who had stepped back so that faint light lit her face. It was the gunnery instructor with the scarred face and the eyepatch. She was smiling.

"Why—?" He realized he didn't know what to ask. "Who—?"

She stepped forward. "You know me. Murphy. Maybe you never got the name." Low-voiced, she chuckled. "I see you picked your weapon scores up, some."

"Yes." Naked, he felt vulnerable, but the dark helped. He said, "Why are you here? I mean, what business—?" Crazy, to challenge an instructor, he knew—but dammit, what business of *hers*?

Murphy cleared her throat. "I don't know your chubby little friend but I do know *you*, Tregare, so watch your manners."

"Yes. Sure. You let her go. What happens to me?"

"You'll see." Incredibly, Murphy was taking off her clothes.

At thirteen he had never come before. It was close to tearing him in half and it lasted most of forever. When he knew himself again he was lying with his neck and head across Murphy's bosom, his face cuddled against her scarred cheek and her arms around him. "Your first time, it would be? Are you all right now?"

"Yes." And yes. But still he needed to know. "Why?"

Her laugh carried a brittle edge. "If you plowed that little ginch, likely as not you'd knock her up. You know what happens then? She gets Welfared—Total Welfare and no way out." She paused. "Me, now: I get off-base privileges, so my right thigh itches with a contraceptive implant. No problem."

"But—"

"Not charity for you, young Tregare. Believe it or never, kid, I used to be a good-looking female. But combat's a tough game. And it's funny, how losing an eye and picking up a red gully down the face takes a girl off the market."

Abruptly she pushed him off and away, and stood. As she dressed hurriedly, she said, "We don't owe each other anything; you don't have to know me. I—"

Half-dressed, he moved to her and held her. "Hey, Murphy. . . don't! You've been *good* to me. I—"

Hugging, her hand stroked down his back and side. "Sure, kid. You'd try. But if I was staying around here, I wouldn't have done this. Tuesday I transfer out . . . never mind where. So you can feel fine about good ol' Murphy, without ever having to see me again in daylight." She kissed him hard, then walked away fast.

He couldn't decide, the next day or two, how he felt about it all, with Murphy. Because he had no way to know how he was *supposed* to feel, and now he realized that he'd always depended, to some extent, on other people's ideas to guide him.

And one morning, waking up thinking and having no good ideas at all, he said to himself the hell with it. From now on, Bran Tregare would take his best shot at steering his own head. As to Murphy—well, what was wrong with just plain gratitude?

That day was one of ordinary ship drills, and that night, well before dawn, a great *whump* woke him. With no way to know what had happened, gradually he dozed off again. Not until after normal rising and breakfast did he learn what the *whump* was all about. In the mess were three persons in Space Service uniforms, and the mess attendant who slopped food onto Bran's tray said, "See those three? They brought the scoutship."

So then Bran knew what was happening, a little. Scoutships were small spacecraft that berthed twelve and approxed a trillion mile range, root to root. From light to zerch, maybe four times the distance in close to the same time. Real starships, or armed ones anyway, carried two scouts each. They could be combat auxiliaries or emergency lifecraft—supplied to feed six people six months. What happened after that, the manuals didn't say.

But Bran felt excitement. For the scoutship's presence meant that finally the Slaughterhouse would take some cadets into *space*.

Not all, though, and even after more scouts came, so that there were a dozen assembled, Bran despaired of his chances. Especially when the first two lifted carrying picked squads, chosen for performance. But then the system changed; personnel were tagged individually, by no method Bran could figure out, and his name came up for the tenth scout.

He packed his kit, going by the list on the handout sheet, the night before lift-off. And, considering, slept surprisingly well.

The scoutship, which carried no name but only a number, was a much-simplified miniature of the *Caesar*. Drive occupied all volume below the airlock. In ascending order, then, came the supplies hold, sleeping quarters with twelve acceleration couches, and the forward area which combined a mini-galley and control facilities with what passed for "social space."

And while it might not have been strictly true that there was only one latrine in all of U.E.T., there was only one on the good ship SX-2517. Everyone had better stay healthy!

Control was cramped by the addition of seats so that the entire complement could watch the viewscreens and monitors, and hear the lecture comments of scout commander Pell Quinlan and his aide, Janith Reggs. Quinlan was a tall, slim young man with tawny hair and a complexion that nearly matched it; he spoke in what might have been called an urgent drawl. Reggs was older, maybe close to thirty, a quiet woman with a round face, carrying a noticeable few pounds more than her best weight. But while Quinlan outranked her, Bran observed that when Reggs said anything, the man listened.

Everyone strapped in, watching the front screen: Quinlan said, "Now!" and his hands played across the control panel. From below came the building roar of Drive; the scout pushed up against them, and lifted off. Accel force made Bran heavy; in the screen the sky went black much sooner than he'd expected. "Out of atmosphere," Quinlan reported, needlessly.

And then, conferring with Reggs, he set course, and eased the difference between accel and the counter-gee field down to Earth-normal. "Okay, Janith," he said, "Give 'em the spiel."

Janith Reggs was good with numbers, getting across what they meant. Accel, distance, time, Big Vee and how it *changed* time if you got it up there much, toward c. *(Vee. Arc. Sine. Cosine. 1/x. Correct as hell, ma'am!)* "We don't have the acceleration," she said, "of a full-sized ship. Even though this scout's power has been augmented by a considerable fraction." She paused, with her characteristic gesture of running a hand back through her dark brown hair. Always, Bran noticed, it fell back into the same pattern of short, crisp waves. Beat the hell out of stubble. . . . But she was saying "—will be in space for six weeks by Earth time, and upon our return you will all have two ages." She cleared her throat. "Let's assume that your chronological and biological ages then differ by exactly two days. And that we go out in a straight line, accelerating to a given velocity and then slowing to rest, and come back the same way." She smiled, and in that smile Bran saw something besides amiability. "Now who can tell me, from those data, what our top velocity will be?"

Getting out his calculator, Bran thought about it, and knew that his steady-vee assumptions lacked the answer. He'd have to work up an equation and integrate it, and *he had nothing to write on*. Well, neither did anybody else, so figure what he could first. Okay, five percent time-differential *(1/x. Arc. Cosine. Sine: BINGO—roughly 0.3c.)* But that was average, not peak Vee. He felt confused—was this aspect of the function linear, or should he skew his guess a little? Sure; enough to be in range either way.

He waved his hand and caught her attention. She nodded, and he said, "About half-c, maybe a little more."

Her brows raised. She said, "Let's see what our other students estimate, perhaps giving the question more severe analysis." But the others' results, coming slowly and stated haltingly, varied nearly from 0.1c to 0.9, and the explanations varied as much. Finally Reggs said, "Tregare? Explain *your* method. Because you're the closest to correct, and with the tools at hand, I'd like to know how you did it. If it wasn't a plain lucky guess." Scowl. "Well, speak up!"

So he told her, figuring that her question was honest, not a trick. At the end she nodded. "I see. You knew which facts you had and which you didn't, and then made an educated guess. Not bad, not bad at all—because someday in space, in a *real* emergency, any of you may have to make vital decisions on insufficient data. Well, one of you knows how, and I hope the rest paid attention."

Heading out from Earth, Bran had expected to get a tourist's view of the moon and maybe even a planet or two. Instead, the scoutship bent course north out of the ecliptic—not directly toward Polaris but only a few degrees off. So when increasing velocity began to Doppler-shift the colors of stars in the forward viewscreen and move their apparent positions nearer to center-front, there weren't all that many to color-shift or move, which made it easier to check the computer corrections that put real positions and colors on the aux screen. Probably, Bran guessed, this was the reason for heading on a star-scarce course.

* * *

Navigation turned out to be Bran's best skill—aside from dealing with communications gear, which he knew from childhood. Gunnery wasn't emphasized in scoutship training, because scouts carried only one turret that pointed straight ahead and had no traverse capability, so the pilot could either try to shoot or not, and the computer would either let the shot go or it wouldn't, depending on range conditions. Well, Bran wasn't planning on being a scoutship pilot, anyway.

One thing he couldn't help noticing was that Pell Quinlan was in command over Janith Reggs, who obviously knew more that Quinlan did. It wasn't that Quinlan was dumb, but that Reggs was smarter. The discrepancy puzzled Bran but he didn't know how to ask about it. Then one "day" it was his turn to be given his first space-walk training, and it was Janith Reggs who helped adjust the too-large suit to him as they waited in the air lock. She was making sure that their mutual life line was properly secured, both to them and to the stanchion by the entrance, when suddenly Bran realized that the air lock's bulkheads totally shielded their suit radios from any outside listener.

So he asked. "Ms. Reggs, you have seniority on Mr. Quinlan and you know more. Nothing against him, but how come he's in charge and not you?"

She had her gloved hand on the hatch control, but didn't operate it. Through his faceplate and her own, Bran couldn't be sure of the bitterness he thought he saw in her brief smile. She said, "How long have you been at the Academy? Not long, I imagine—or you'd know that UET *never* gives command to women. Not of anything at all... even a scoutship. We can be anything else, including second-in-command, but never first."

"But... that can't be true. Why, there are women on UET's Presiding Committee, that runs the whole *show*."

"I know," she said. "But that's *ownership*—the Committee is the majority shareholders, with some kind of arbitrary cutoff as to amount of holdings, that they don't tell us about. So not even Minos Pangreen, the Chairman, can keep women off his precious Committee." Bran heard her laugh but her face didn't show it. "The funny part is that Pangreen has no sons. His daughter will inherit." She shook her head. "Enough talk. We're taking too much time" The hatch opened, and Bran had his first experience of space itself.

For the first few steps he took walking the scout's hull, Bran thought he'd never get the hang of it—how to activate his bootsole magnets for solid footing, then release a foot to move, with any kind of continuity, let alone grace. But after an error that left him dangling at the end of his life line, so that Reggs had to pull him back in, the burst of panic-adrenalin seemed to give an edge to his coordination. And soon he was stepping along the hull, almost automatically handling the suit and its magnets, while he scanned the visible star field, distorted by the scout's fraction of light speed. He found himself forgetting to breathe.

Not thinking that others might hear, he said, "Oh, Ms. Reggs! *This*—it's worth all of it! The Slaughterhouse, all the crap. I—"

In a sharp tone she interrupted. "*All of us* know that the Academy can be rather grim sometimes." He caught the message—their talk here was not private. "But as you say, the goal is worth it." He looked at her, and nodded his thanks for her help, saying something trite and bland to cover his lapse.

All too soon it was time to go inside again. In the air lock they unsuited, and Bran learned that spacesuits make you sweat in a particularly stinking fashion. Reggs said, "Quinlan says we're crowding our water-recycling schedule. So I hope you don't mind sharing a shower."

He wasn't sure if he did or not, because he wasn't sure what the offer included. While he was trying to think what to answer, she said, "I like you, Tregare, I like your work and I like your thinking, though you'd be well-advised to keep some of it close to your vest." When he only nodded, she went on, now beginning to undress, "Six weeks is a long time, and there won't be all that many chances. Would you like to?"

"I—"

"Or do you only do it with the other boys? Or ever?"

He shook his head. "No boys. And just once, so far." Her clothes were off now, and without them, somehow the extra weight didn't show so much. She reached for him, and he nodded.

While she helped him strip, she said, "To the others, we'll have to pretend this didn't happen."

"Yes, I know, Ms. Reggs."

"Janith. Here, I mean. Ms. Reggs outside of here." She kissed him. The two of them crowded into the tiny booth, and had to move cautiously to get the spray everywhere that both needed it. Then, having sex standing up was fun but not easy—and a good thing, at climax, that there was no *room* for him to fall down. When his legs felt solid again, they washed a little more before indulging in a final hug. This time, in the kissing, he did a better share of it.

"Thank you, Janith."

"And you, Bran Tregare." They got dried and dressed. Just in time for dinner.

Later, Quinlan and Reggs did a wrap-up report on the cadets' spacewalk performances. Bran was pleased to place high in the evaluations, but he wasn't tops of the group. Where he truly excelled was in piloting maneuvers, nudging the scout through simulated combat situations. By instinct, before anyone had the chance to instruct him, in evasive action he was "cheating" on turns by throwing the scout semi-broadside and hitting max drive blast, firing his single turret on override all the way. After one practice session Pell Quinlan said, "If I ever rate command of a combat ship, Tregare, I'd like you to pilot for me."

Janith Reggs spoke in mild protest. "But can't everyone learn that?"

"Learn, sure," Quinlan answered. "But this kid did it *without* learning anything."

So maybe, Bran decided, Quinlan did know some things that Reggs didn't. He still liked her a lot, though.

After reaching a respectable but minor fraction of light speed, instead of going into straight line decel, the scout turned. One day in classroom mode Reggs asked, "At any velocity, how much energy does a right-angle turn require?" Bran fussed at the question, trying to rig equations and getting nowhere. Then the answer hit him: a right-angle means killing *all* your velocity and building a new vector from scratch.

So he had the answer: "Ms. Reggs? Same energy as to slow to zerch and then accel to the same vee."

"May we see your validating equations, Tregare?"

"I haven't worked them out. That's just how it is."

Reluctantly, she nodded. "True. But now try a thirty-degree turn." And it took him nearly an hour to realize that all he needed for *any* degree of turn was to plug in the sines and cosines.

* * *

The scout made its circuit and returned to Earth. Now Bran had, as the saying went, "two ages." His personal chronometer registered nearly forty-eight hours less than did its counterparts that had remained on Earth. Well, thought Bran, it's a start. . . . He exchanged leavetakings with his shipmates, paying special heed to Reggs and Quinlan. Was the slight twitch of the woman's eyelid meant as a wink? No matter. He kept his own face as straight as possible but tried to put extra warmth into their final handshake, and was rewarded with a barely noticeable nod.

Off the scout, then Bran toted his kit across the quadrangles to Cadre D. He found his squad room empty, but heard water running in its adjoining facilities. After he'd set his kit on his bunk and begun unpacking, the water noise stopped and he turned to see a new cadet, still drying himself, come out to the main area. A tall, skinny kid, sandy-haired and strong-jawed, with greenish eyes and a lopsided smile. Who said, "You'll be one who lives here, I'd think? As it happens, so am I, now. I'm Bernardez."

"Bran Tregare." They shook hands, after Bernardez took a moment to be sure that his was dry. "I'm just back from my first scoutship tour, as a new middie. Have you been here long?"

"As of yesterday, so such things go, I hadn't set eyes on the place. Nor am I entirely certain that I'd cared to . . . meaning no offense, you understand. But my father died, and my stepmama couldn't see me out the door soon enough, so here I am and now it's to make the best of it." The smile flickered. "I am, so it's told me, a snotty. Not a title I'd choose, but with the customs of the country we must all make do, and so shall I." With a grace of movement that belied his gawky appearance, Bernardez slipped into his jumpsuit and zipped it. "Tell me, Tregare, are you fond of Irish whiskies? For I've brought a trifle and I hear that this place has such things as inspections and confiscations. So . . . should we foil such malfeasance by drinking the lovely stuff?"

Bran felt a grin stretch his face. This Bernardez was *fun*—never mind how he'd last the course when the worst stuff hit, but maybe Bran and Jargy could give him some helpful advice.

For now, though: "I can't think of a better idea, and thanks." His try at imitating the Bernardez style, Bran thought, hadn't come off too well. But the friendly part worked all right.

Bran wasn't used to straight spirits, no water or even ice, but sipping slowly, he loved the taste of it. He sat back and listened while Bernardez talked a mix of personal history, opinions, and total sheer speculation. "While my father claimed the family to be vanguard of Spain into Ireland, I find this hard to reconcile with his claim of collateral relationship to the Pope." Bernardez paused. "What do *you* think, Tregare?"

Bran shook his head. "Damned if I know."

By the time Jargy Hoad and some other roommates came in, Bran was more drunk than not and had missed dinner. Jargy seemed to have a lot of news to relate, but said, "No, not tonight, Bran. Get some sleep and we'll talk tomorrow." Sleepy enough, Bran agreed.

The extra slumber eased the change from ship's to Earth time, and cleared his head. Although he'd hoped for more work on the *Caesar*, the morning began with calisthenics and the following gauntlet runs for losers, and then a free-for-all. Before his guts could knot into their worst agony, the announcement came that this one was for snotties, to disablement only.

The second name called for it was Cecil Bernardez.

Oh, damn! The newcomer had no chance to know any of the angles—how to protect himself or help his odds. And Bran *liked* the oddly talking, mouthy kid.

But all he could do was watch and hope. The eight victims were equipped with protection for eyes and balls, and herded into the central ring. *"Go to it!"*

The bout was quick. Bernardez charged in and decked an opponent with his first blow, and the other stayed down. The only trouble was that Bernardez dropped his man with a clenched fist to the head, and even before the decision was signaled, it was obvious that Bernardez was nursing a broken hand in the other. *Fist* fighting, of all things!

But events can't be argued with. Bran saw Bernardez taken off to the infirmary; he'd be back to the squad room tomorrow. Meanwhile Jargy was still bursting with news, but it wasn't until after dinner, he and Bran walking the twilit perimeter, that Bran got to hear any of it. Some, he wasn't awfully pleased about.

"Channery got himself Welfared!"

Well, that part didn't hurt Bran's feelings. "What happened?"

"After the graduation party he hauled a snotty into his quarters—guess for what!—and got caught in the act." Then Jargy shrugged. "They Welfared the kid, too—and the way I hear, anybody could see that Channery'd beaten him into doing it."

Bran felt the rage come, but didn't give over to it. He took a deep breath, and tried to keep his voice steady. "Nothing new, is there? When was there ever any fairness in this place?"

Jargy's speech, then, held an odd edge. "Could be worse. The old commandant, before Arbogast—the guys were saying . . . about five years ago, two kids got caught like that. And on the way to Welfare, stopped by the local Committee Police HQ and had what they call a minor operation." He paused. "The commandant circulated pictures."

Bran didn't have to ask. Not only that, but he couldn't. Unexpected shock had him close to fainting. He forced himself to smile, and finally said, "I guess it's lucky I like women."

Horror offstage, though—atrocities he hadn't really seen—couldn't drag Bran's spirits down for long. Next day Bernardez returned from medical custody. The new kid seemed to be popular with all the group, for he got a whooping great welcome. Jargy yelled, "You get a good heavy cast on that hand, did you? Fine for clubbing, next time you're picked."

Bernardez shook his head. "No. Soft cast. Which, I admit, does in truth restrict my options."

Bran asked, "If you get picked for it, what'll you do?"

Bernardez shrugged. "Combat, I must own, is not my specialty. But in some other sports I was never the most rule-bound of players." He grinned, and said nothing more.

Bran wasn't sure who'd sneaked the beer in, but there was a fair amount of it, which led to friendly wrestling and lots of off-key singing. Such as the Underground fight song's second verse:

"In the Slaughterhouse, just to get along,
Even if you're right, you admit you're wrong.
How it works is, if you get off free,
They change the rulings retroactively."

And everyone yelled: "So *that* is the reason, you can plainly see, why there's only one latrine in all of UET!

And next morning when Bran woke up, feeling not too bad but not exactly tops, either, the refrain still rang in his head.

Whether out of spite or sheer chance, Cecil Bernardez did get chosen for the next snotties' free-for-all. Jargy said, "You could beg off for hurt, you know," but Bernardez shook his head. "Should they have such a want of me, I could hardly avoid the issue for long."

Bran watched as Bernardez with his crippled hand went out to the fighting area. The thing began. Bernardez dodged, feinted with his casted hand and avoided breaking the other by striking only light blows with it, still clench-fisted. Someone his height but heavier came charging. Bernardez slipped to one side and brought a foot sharply to his attacker's knee. The other went sprawling, and rolled over clutching the knee with both hands.

First disablement. End of bout. In barracks after dinner, Bernardez said, "I've lived a time in the eastern Canadian sector, and soccer was one of the sports in which I was sometimes less than totally sportsmanlike." He sighed. "But—I much misdoubt that any such trick will avail more than once. Twice, at the most."

Whoever controlled the draw seemed to have it in for Bernardez. Time and again, still with the cast on his broken hand, he was chosen for snotty fights and caught a number of bruising injuries. But his footwork kept him free of serious damage, and after a few bouts, even the instructors began rooting for him. "Kick'em, Bernardez!" And after one fight when the boy dropped an opponent with a high, spinning kick but fell exhausted, Bran and his squad mates ran out onto the field and carried Bernardez off in triumph. "Come on, Kickem!" Bran shouted. "Let's go get chow!"

From then on, the young man was known as Kickem Bernardez.

If a minor triumph could elate cadets so much, it was because there were few bright spots in the Academy's grim brutality. Bran was so accustomed to living with fear that he hardly remembered what *not* being afraid was like. But still, as he said to Kickem once, "I don't think you *ever* get used to it, really." He said nothing, though, about his recurrent nightmares.

And recently, in fact, his dreams had begun taking new directions. He found himself dreaming of being with his family—either back with them, before coming to the Slaughterhouse, or else somehow miraculously reunited with them after escaping the Academy by some means he could never quite remember. Very pleasant dreams, these were. Bran hated them.

The first time he dreamed that way, he felt so wonderful! And then woke, and had to give it all up and accept his grim reality *again*. And again, and again—his dreaming mind couldn't seem to learn that it was being deceived, so every waking was a devastating shock. The result was that instead of merely missing his parents and sister, and feeling vaguely betrayed, he came to hate them. Because they had *promised* to get him out of here.

Until the new dreams, he'd almost forgotten any goals other than surviving the Slaughterhouse and getting into space. And in a way the loss of alternatives had made things easier for him. Now, though, the continual dream-reminders of a better life set his mind against itself, and the conflict was too much for him. His only way was to *reject* Hawkman and Liesel and Sparline.

Sometimes, without wishing to do it, he found himself arguing both sides of a dialogue: They didn't *mean* to leave me here. Then why *did* they? Couldn't help it; something went wrong. Sure; people who break promises *always* have an excuse. They tried, though; I bet they tried. Not hard enough; I'm still here.

What it finally boiled down to, was that when he got to space and eventually Escaped, he would *never* have anything to do with his family again. That was the first time he realized that Escape was his second goal. Survival, of course, was his first.

The family dreams ceased. By contrast, the nightmares were welcome. Even when he *knew* he was going to be killed.

The Slaughterhouse never gave any reasons for what it did; one day early in Tregare's middie year, Kickem Bernardez was transferred to Cadre G, in the same quadrangle where Bran had once belt-whipped Channery. For the brief farewell party, Ellsworth sneaked some beer in. "Gonna miss you, Kickem," said Jargy Hoad.

"And be it known," said Kickem, "that Bernardez is of no mood to leave valued comrades." In spite of the boy's flair for big talk, Bran saw that he meant it. "Though I'm told that my new leadership can't be faulted: cadet-captain Ragir Parnell is, I understand, well-liked by his cadre."

Bran felt sadness; he reached to shake the other's hand. "Maybe we can visit back and forth, some."

"And highly welcome that would be, Bran Tregare."

For a time, Bran and Jargy and Kickem did arrange to meet. But the formalities of getting quadrangle-passes, the time-consuming delays, made the intervals longer and then indefinite. A few times Bran met and spoke with Kickem's cadre leader. Ragir Parnell had a quiet way about him, a bit somber but not unpleasant. The tall young man's long face, topped by sandy stubble, wasn't given much to smiling. But he seemed more amiable than not, and Kickem said he dealt a fair-minded grade of leadership. Since Tregare's own cadre had had three cadet-captains transferred in and then out again, in as many months—and not one of them could pour sand from a boot without cutting a hole in the toe, to hear Jargy tell it—the two friends felt that maybe Kickem had the best of it.

Not much later, the killing free-for-alls began, and with them a recurrence of Bran's occasional nightmares. He'd seen enough death by now that at spectator's distance he could almost blank his mind and force himself not to react. Almost, but not quite. Then, for the third death-fight, his own name was drawn.

That night he went over the wall and came back drunk, hoping to sleep without dreams. Mostly it worked, and he woke feeling less debilitated than he deserved. Feeling a little woozy but not much, he put away most of a fair-sized breakfast and it stayed down. As soon as the meal "settled" he took advantage of a free hour to run a few laps and do some stretching exercises.

When time came for the combat formation, he felt as ready as he could ever be for that sort of ordeal. He marched out with his squad, heard Colonel Arbogast's insane announcements, and walked to join the other seven cadets while they all stripped and made the circle to face each other.

Then it began. The circle shrank into a knot of violence.

His legs weren't working right. They twitched and jerked, instead of moving smoothly. Then a big youth lunged at him and suddenly he could move the way he always had. Bran made a leap, caught his attacker over the ear with one foot, landed with a smooth roll, and came up to find nobody in immediate threat to him.

He looked around. A lot of inconclusive grappling and flailing was going on—as usual in the early stages. Well, he had to look good for the records, so Bran decked one slow learner with a chop block, bounced up to leap and do a chest kick on the biggest guy in the crowd, and found his target staggering from someone else's hit—wide open for a flying head scissors. So he did that, and there was a hit from the side, and a lot of rolling across the ground while he still held his scissors clamp.

When everybody untangled, the big guy's neck was broken, and he caught Bran's breakfast all over his head, neck and shoulders.

There was no point at all in eating lunch.

For the next two killing bouts he didn't get called, so he began to sleep better. But on a deeper level he knew his luck couldn't last, and sure enough, on a windy drizzly morning the drills were interrupted by Arbogast yelling on the loudhailer. An impromptu combat, a killing one. Of the eight names announced, Bran's was the sixth. His gut froze in him. To the center of the field, meeting the others, he walked like a half-paralyzed cripple.

Peace take it, they WON'T kill me! Forcing himself to deepen his fast, shallow breathing, to swing his arms and put snap into his steps, Bran thought of how to make his mind put its own force into every blow. Australia was behind him now, but there he had learned what he now needed to use.

But when the melee began, Bran's foot slipped on the wet grass; his thrust fingers scooped an attacker's eye loose to roll free. While everyone stood frozen, watching as the half-blinded youth pawed at his face and at the ground, Bran swallowed the bitter acid that erupted into his throat. He made one step back, one forward, and kicked to the throat.

The maimed boy fell, with no will left, even to clutch at the injury that killed him.

Looking through a haze that shifted, listening through sounds that made no sense, Bran Tregare saw Colonel Arbogast and heard words that complimented him on his victory.

But for violating the no-eyes-no-balls rule, he still had to run the gauntlet. Just belt-ends, though. No buckles.

Later he realized that for minutes he was in range to put Arbogast's head on backward. He thought about it, and shrugged, because he'd have been killed for it.

The thing was, Bran Tregare had more to pay back, to UET and its Slaughterhouse, than *any* one death could satisfy.

His work in the melees had earned Tregare a vicious kind of respect—seldom now did opponents attack him singly. Still thin, though he had added some height, his wiry strength and Hulzein training made him more dangerous than he probably looked. Well, after this year, only one more to go!

Except that no one had boots full of ice, the graduation ceremonies were much the same as before. Cadre D's relatively new cadet-commander hosted a niggardly going-away party; in less than an hour the beer was finished. Bran and Jargy managed a call to Cadre G and reached Bernardez. "Of a certainty," said Kickem, "you must join me here. I shall request of cadet-captain—outgoing—Parnell that he furnish you the necessary bona fides to bring you hither." Since the guards had also been treated to beer, there wasn't any great problem about it.

Kickem's squad room was nearly empty. One cadet was passed out on his bunk. The rest, said Bernardez, were over the wall. So for the three of them there was beer in plenty.

They sat, drinking slowly and talking in quiet tones. On their minds were their respective futures. One more year of Slaughterhouse for Bran Tregare, a bit less for Jargy Hoad who had entered at near mid-term. "And two more of these eternities," said Kickem, "for my not entirely wretched self." For in Cadre G, Bernardez had found better treatment, and better luck in the "draw."

Tregare began to answer, but the door opened and Ragir Parnell entered. The tall youth was weaving a little, but his eyes still tracked as he said, "Ah, Kickem's friends from his old squad. Am I right?" He waved a hand, spilling beer from the flask it held. "Be welcome, of course." He sat, a little heavily. "Well, lads, you may congratulate me. I'm posted to space. I'm not certain as to which ship yet, but one thing I do know. I was slated for the *MacArthur*, commanded by Arger Korbeith. But that ship isn't back yet; the murdering bastard is late."

Bran cleared his throat. "I don't understand."

Parnell shook his head. "Pray to peace that you never do."

Again the summer period was scoutship training time. Bran and Jargy drew assignment to the same vessel, QR-1610, somewhat older than the one Bran had ridden a year before. Jargy described its commander, Malloy, as wearing the map of Ireland on his face. Malloy had red hair and freckles, with an expression partly tough and partly pleasant. For the most part he talked seldom, but sometimes the dam broke—Not right away, though—not on the trip's outgoing leg.

As had been the case on SX-2517, the scout's *segundo* was female. Unlike Janith Reggs, Dien Talmuth had a sour way to her. Youngish, slim, not bad looking when now and then she forgot to wear her usual sneer, Talmuth rebuffed all attempts at friendly conversation. Bran thought he knew why. Reggs had told him that UET totally denied command to women. Janith could live with the restriction. Talmuth apparently could not.

So Bran tried to stay pretty much out of her way.

From a training standpoint, the scout's trip went well. In most aspects, Bran and Jargy ranked high in tested skills. Not first place usually, for either, but seldom worse than second or third. The competition, out in space with no brutal penalties in store, was fun for both. And, as during the previous summer, Bran found he could outdo anyone on board when it came to *maneuvering* the scout. After one contest, Malloy put a hand on Bran's shoulder. "You've got the reflexes for it, same as I have. If they don't put you to an armed ship 'twould be an awful waste."

And hadn't Peralta written much the same? Bran felt good.

The trip ended, and Bran was sorry it had to. It was back to the Slaughterhouse, to the forced fighting, to the fear again. But when Malloy landed QR-1610 on the Academy grounds he held his crew aboard that night, ordered beer and booze brought in, and staged a party. "I'm entitled," he said, "and I damned well shall."

Good party, Bran thought. He was more used to drinking, now; he could pace his intake and avoid losing control. He made one pass at the young woman who had topped his and Jargy's efforts in several phases of training, and knew enough not to be disappointed when her answer was no. It was time for singing, anyway.

The third verse of the Underground fight song wasn't all that encouraging:

> "When you post to space, your odds are dim;
> Your life's at the mercy of the captain's whim.
> Ride with the Butcher and you'll get a shock;
> Just one error and you're out the lock!
> And *that* is the reason, you can plainly see,
> Why there's only one latrine in all of UET!"

Bemused, Bran sang through the repetition of the chorus.

Later, a bit more taken with drink, having been turned down by Dien Talmuth and not much surprised by that outcome, Bran found himself sitting alongside Malloy, who was talking.

". . . one of the first ships ever to vanish, and now it turns up on Terranova," Malloy said. "Called *Ridgerunner* now—went in and raided, and got away clean. That's how—" Malloy fell silent.

"How what?" Bran asked. Malloy turned and looked at him, owl-eyed, but said nothing. "*What?*" Bran repeated.

Squinting, one eye almost closed, Malloy nodded. "How *I'll* do it someday, you hot pilot, you!" The man looked around, saw nobody paying heed to him, and said, "*Pig In The Parlor.*"

Puzzled, Bran said, "I beg your pardon?"

"*Pig In The Parlor!* When I take my ship, that's its name."

Bran thought, then said, "You mean Escape?"

Then Malloy's hand was to Bran's throat, and the man said, "You and I know what I said. Anyone else does, you're a dead cadet."

Bran shook his head. He knew Malloy was too drunk for thinking and he wasn't sure how to handle the mess. He said, "I didn't hear you say anything." Then, seeing the light of reason in Malloy's eyes, added, "But I won't forget the advice either."

Malloy laughed. "Good for you, Tregare." And the crisis was over. After a time everyone bunked down, and next day debarked.

Beginning his third year, as an upper, Bran found himself moved to a different squad room, becoming its leader. Jargy also had a squad of his own—still in Cadre D though, so visiting back and forth was no problem. But seldom could the two of them get all the red tape coordinated to make a joint visit to Kickem in Cadre G. Separately sometimes, but not often together.

All seven of Bran's squad mates—four snotties, three middies—were unfamiliar to him. And the way he was feeling nowadays, he was content to leave it at that. He learned their names and paid heed to their failings, and conscientiously tried to help and advise them toward survival as best he could, but all attempts at more personal acquaintance he discouraged. Because he didn't need more friends who would likely be hurt or even killed; he had enough grief of his own.

So all of them—Spencer, Delegans, Marshal, Tarenz, Bills, Gannister, Kloche, and fat little Schweik—formed a tight loyal clique of themselves, in which he had no part. Which suited Bran Tregare just fine; he felt a relief from pressure.

But he sometimes thought, *is this place turning me into some kind of monster? Or just a machine?*

Riding on nerve's edge, Bran drove himself to excellence—or as close as he could manage—in all aspects of upper-year training; classwork, physical drills, even the dreaded death-fights. Plus, as an upper he now had access to training on ship-control computer simulations for as many hours as he chose, and after a time his reports began to carry an Outstanding rating.

The way he knew about the reports was that he courted the young woman who was Colonel Arbogast's most junior secretary. At first he didn't care that he was using her for his own purposes. Then he came to like her and felt guilty about his duplicity. And finally he liked her enough to confess, and by that time *she* didn't care, so he didn't have to either. Lindya Haines was a small person, thin and dark and intense, and with her Bran found that he had known as much about sex as a mole knows about agriculture. The learning was quite an experience.

Bran's proficiency ratings had him well into the running for cadet-officer honors. When the listings were posted, Jargy Hoad came over to Bran's squad room and they had a couple of beers. Jargy said, "We're neither of us likely to be up for cadet-colonel, like Peralta—but captain's a good bet, and *you* might make major."

Bran looked over his tipped-up beer, tipped it back down, and swallowed. "Don't bet any money on it. Not me, anyway. You, maybe."

Jargy protested, but when the promotions were announced, Bran's pessimism was justified. Jargy made cadet-captain; Bran remained a squad leader. *Colonels and elephants never forget;* Arbogast wouldn't have forgotten sentencing Bran to the special cell.

Bran had no right to be disappointed about the promotions and he knew as much. But when, a day later, he was picked for a free-for-all, inside him something froze. *Be DAMNED if I will!* But he knew he had to; there wasn't any way out of it. He'd heard of the group that sat down and refused to fight—some years back, that was. On a third refusal of the commandant's orders, they'd simply been gunned down where they sat. And then there was the group that had somehow communicated and agreed to gang up on one of their number and kill him fast. They were congratulated, then told to go ahead and fight to *another* death. Not that that case had any bearing on Bran's current problem; well, he hoped not.

No way out. But then—suddenly, Bran Tregare knew exactly what he was going to do, next day. Or try to do, anyway . . .

Standing naked, one of eight in the drill field arena, even with the heat Bran found himself shivering. Could he do it? Arbogast's hoarse voice brayed "Start." Without hesitation, Bran moved. No choosing of targets. Whoever was nearest, came first. Moving at top speed while others vacillated, he kicked an opponent's knee sidewise, gave a near-lethal neck chop, and broke an elbow.

Three down—four to go. He had to pause a moment to see where everyone else was. Then: jump, kick, drop the man. Stiff fingers to a throat; trip the next man for later. And then the remaining contender put out a defending hand. Bran took it, twisted, had the man in front of him and ran him full speed, head to head, into the one trying to get to his feet. *Seven down!*

Panting, he stood and faced Arbogast. Growling past the mouthed cigar, the colonel said, "Well, go ahead. Finish one of them."

Bran shook his head. "I don't have to. They're all disabled, out of action."

Arbogast stood. "You haven't *finished*."

"I'm not under attack, colonel, sir. No need."

"Finish it. That's an order."

Too much. "Take your order and—"

Which is how Bran Tregare became the first cadet to survive a full ten days in the special cell, with the cold, the electric shocks, and the ice-water showers. He was tougher now, and the experience didn't even put him into the infirmary. Though for a few days after his release, he was glad that his reputation saved him from challenges he couldn't possibly have handled.

"Are you crazy?" said Jargy Hoad, visiting Bran's squad room.

"Probably. This whole place is; you know that."

"But to try such a trick . . ."

"I thought it might work. You disable all the rest, that should be enough. Only thing was, I wasn't all that sure of doing it."

"Well, you did it, all right. And got ten days in Special."

Bran shuddered. "I'll never get the chance to kill Arbogast. A cadet wouldn't have a prayer—and the way ships chew time up toward light speed, he'll be long buried by the time I'm back from my first real space cruise. If I—if they let me—if I ever get out there at all. . . . But—" Bran leaned forward. "He's just one of a *lot* of bastards. And Jargy—someday I'm going to get rid of some of those."

Before next visiting Lindya Haines, Bran waited a while. For one thing he wasn't sure how she felt about UET and Arbogast and the Slaughterhouse in general. And he wasn't certain that he could smooth out his own feelings and, if need be, use tact. Well, tact had never been one of his greater talents! But one evening, sending a bottle of wine in advance as a peace offering, he went to see Lindya.

His fears were needless; her first words were, "Oh, Bran! *How* could that bastritch treat you so?" Arbogast she meant; sure. So they cuddled and kissed and drank some of the wine, before they got laid, and the rest after, with the dinner she'd prepared. And later talked with the Tri-V running unnoticed, and hit the bed again. Twice, before Bran decided he'd better not risk staying the night and maybe being caught absent from his squad duties.

But before he dressed, they kissed goodnight while her tiny warm breasts nudged his chest and made him wish he could stay longer.

At the age of fifteen, Bran Tregare recognized few limitations. Except, of course, for the official and enforced ones.

Next evening, Bernardez came over for a visit. Not often could he manage it, for Cadre G was tight with passes.

They were talking—no drinks tonight, for the illicit pipeline was temporarily crimped—when Bran's squad came in. Looking embarrassed, they sat here and there, not saying much. Bran's conversation with Kickem also died. How could they talk in front of these strangers?

Then, clearing his throat, little Schweik spoke up. "Tregare . . . in these forced combats, how many kills do you have?"

Bewildered, Bran shook his head. "How should I know?"

Delegans drew a shocked breath. "You mean, so many you've lost count? Or just don't care?"

Rage came, but Bran sat on it. "It's not that. It's—I hate it, I hate to think of it, I try to put it out of my mind." He found himself close to going for Delegans, and held himself back. "Can you understand that?"

Looking pale, Delegans nodded. "Yes. I think so."

Kickem stood. "Gotta go, Bran. Long day tomorrow."

"Sure. See ya." After, the squad was quieter than usual.

Still no more than a squad leader, Bran graduated. The next day, the board showed him posted for space. Standing beside him, Jargy said, "Oh, Jesus, Bran!"

"What's the matter?"

"You see the ship you're on? It's the *MacArthur.* Bran, you're shipping under Butcher Korbeith."

5. The Butcher

The *MacArthur* was an older ship but very well maintained. Toting his gear upship from the main airlock, Bran noticed that the bulkheads were spotless and the "ladders"—stairs, really—had new nonskid plastic on the treads. As an officer-cadet he was quartered on the top level of the crew's space, one deck below the galley. The cubicle held two bunks, two chairs, and two small desks. It shared sanitary facilities with three other such rooms arranged in a cluster. Someone else's possessions lay on one of the bunks; Bran dumped his on the other and, as directed by the boarding officer, went up to the galley. Like the one on the *Caesar*, it seated about forty—a little more than one-third of the ship's complement. At the moment only a few off-duty crew members were having coffee and snacks, but off to one side sat about a dozen young people who were obviously cadets.

With them sat a uniformed woman with a tattoo on her cheek. She motioned to Bran. "Over here." Then, "Soon as your whole group's here, the captain will be down to give you a talk."

"Sure. Thanks for letting me know." He was staring at the tattoo. In a pattern of red, green, and blue, it was the lower quadrant—right-angled point upward—of a circle, its radius about a centimeter and a half.

The woman cleared her throat. "Never saw an officer before?"

"I—of course. At the Slau—the Academy. Colonel Arbogast, and—" Other cadets were entering. He paused.

"A spacing officer, I meant. Arbogast only spaced as a rating. He got commissioned after he went groundside." She gave a quick laugh. "He used to be younger than me, if that tells you anything. Anyway, I noticed you gawking the tattoo—that shows I rank as Third Officer. Second adds the left quadrant." She pointed. "And First adds the right. Captain has the full circle. Admirals and such—" But looking past Bran, she sprang to her feet. "Ten-*hut*!"

Standing quickly, Bran turned to face Captain Arger Korbeith. The man was a hulking giant, with huge, knobby hands and the outsized, distorted features that told of a hyperactive pituitary gland. Acromegaly, Bran recalled. Korbeith's shaggy hair was a dirty blond color above his sallow face. His expression was that of someone confronting the latest error of an unhousebroken pet. "At ease." The term, "gravel-voiced" might have been invented just for him. "Sit down before you fall down." Except for one who almost did fall down in the process, the cadets obeyed.

Korbeith looked them over. "Another snot-nosed batch. Take forever to make spacers out of the likes of you! A quicker way for some, though. Keep your tails clean or you'll find out." Slightly stooped, like an animal about to spring, he stood a moment. "Any questions? And state your name first."

Sooner than ask that man a question, Bran would have banged his head against a brick wall. He held his breath, hoping for silence, but a young woman said, "Megan Delange, sir. What did you mean?"

Korbeith's heavy brows rose, unhooding deepset yellowish eyes. "One more word, *slut*, and you'll be the first to learn." He paused, waiting. His questioner shook her head. Korbeith's laugh had the sound of gravel. "Hope for you yet, maybe. Not much, but some." Turning with speed and grace that belied his awkward stance, the captain left the galley.

Silence extended, then across the large room some crew members began talking together, one giving a high-pitched laugh. Bran turned to the third officer. "Is it all right to ask *you* questions? If it isn't, I withdraw the request." He looked, gauging her. Her broad-cheekboned face looked pleasant enough, with its wide mouth and firm chin below grey eyes and a totally inadequate childlike nose. She looked trustworthy.

As she said, "Ask away. But first, who's asking?" Bran gave his name. She nodded. "And I'm Eunice Parsons. To you cadet types, Officer Parsons. So now ask."

The answers were much as he'd expected. As her hand worried the short, sand-colored curls below her uniform cap, Bran began to get the picture. At the Slaughterhouse, rumor repeated enough to gain fact-status had said that a graduated cadet's first space trip was an all-or-nothing final exam. If you screwed up, they spaced you out the air lock.

"On most ships," Parsons went on, "that doesn't happen much. Which is to say, maybe every second or third trip on the average there's a real muckup in the group and an example *has* to be made. But—" She paused, obviously hating what came next. "Four training runs this ship's made, with this captain. He never spaces less than three." Shuddering, "seven, once."

For a moment, Bran fugued back to the party on Malloy's scout.

"Ride with the Butcher and you'll get a shock;
Just one error and you're out the lock!"

Somehow he managed to take a deep breath without making noise about it. Others around him, who had also listened, weren't quite as successful. Bran said, "I thank you for the warning, Officer Parsons."

"I hope it helps you, Cadet Tregare."

Going down to his room, Tregare calculated. Two dozen cadets was max quota. The actual number might be two or three less, depending. The odds weren't all that bad, but they weren't too good either. In the Slaughterhouse at least you had a chance to *fight* for your life. Not here, though.

It took him a moment to remember his room's right number. Then he opened the door and got a surprise. Sitting on the bunk that wasn't his, a slim person looked up at him. His roommate was female.

The realization didn't come immediately, because the blouse showed no evidence of breasts, and the sidewise view concealed any spread of hips. The person had been an early graduate, because the black hair ran to nearly two centimeters, rather than Bran's five millimeter stubble. But, first subliminally and then consciously, Bran noticed the slimness of ankles, and of wrists that had no bony knobs to the outside. No Adam's apple. No sign of facial hair (and the sideburns ended in a curve, not a shaved straight line). Earrings, small, not immediately noticed. Then she turned to face him, and he was sure.

"Well!" he said. "We're roommates, are we?"

Her voice was husky, mid-pitched. "It seems so. Don't get any ideas, roomie. My contraceptive implant runs out this week or maybe last, and getting spaced for preggy isn't my idea of a great career."

Already she was ahead of him. He said, "You've heard about the Butcher? I didn't see you upside, in the galley."

"I wasn't there. Besides, I'd heard it all before. One of our instructors shipped with Korbeith once—and lived." She laughed. "Well, *obviously* . . . right?" She stood and reached out a hand. "Just because I have to be off limits, I don't mean to be unfriendly. I'm Salome Harkness. Sally for short."

Her handclasp was warm, firm. "Bran Tregare. From Australia originally, but that's a time ago."

"San Francisco. Well, a hundred miles east, nearly, but these days it's all the same." So then they talked for a while.

To start with, duty on the *MacArthur* wasn't too bad. Hard work, long hours, strict discipline. On watch duty (he caught the 1600-2400 stint, not— thank peace!—the 0800-1600 stretch when Korbeith usually sat in.), the cadets took turns on the comm board, weapons positions, first or second navigators' chairs, or one of the pilots' seats. They did not, ever, *do* anything unless given specific orders; their jobs were to make observations, calculations, estimates of what they would do if the task were truly theirs to perform. Their notes were handed over to the watch officer and, presumably, evaluated by someone. Stressful chores, but Bran enjoyed them more than not.

Then, following the after-watch meal, cadets put in six hours of scutwork. Mostly scrubbing—floors, doors, bulkheads, or anything else that held still for it. Then maybe a couple of hours at Drive-monitoring. Then sleep, which came easily.

But it beat hell out of worrying about free-for-all fights.

Ten days off Earth—exhausted, Bran had slept through liftoff and hadn't even noticed—the first scare came. Captain Arger Korbeith called a meeting of his twenty-two cadets. In the galley again, but this time he sat and they stood. In his rasping voice, the captain called each cadet by name and proceeded to read short excerpts from that person's Performance Report. As: "Megan Delange. Failed to note a rock on collision course." Headshake. "May not be with us much longer, Delange." His target was the young woman who had made the mistake of asking him a question; Tregare saw her go pale.

A few more, and then, "Bran Tregare" A nod. "Performance none so bad. Too bad your earlier record doesn't match up." The brows raised; the yellow eyes glinted. "Twice in Arbogast's special cell, I see. Too bad we don't have time for that onship."

Tregare felt his gut heave; "Too bad," he'd heard, was a term to fear. But he didn't throw up; he didn't dare.

* * *

He was lying on his bunk, trying to get his breath to come evenly, when he heard the door open. "Hey! Are you all right?" And Sally Harkness came to sit and hug him. He turned to look up at her, and knew his attempted smile wasn't making it. But she said, "He scared me, too. Come on, let's just hold each other."

But after awhile his natural impulse came to him, so he wiggled loose from her. "It's no good. You *can't*."

She grinned at him. "You've always done only the one thing? Let me show you." Her blouse came off, and Bran was surprised to find that breasts could at the same time be so small and so tempting.

Then she showed him some things he hadn't known, and after that they didn't bother to hide nudity from each other.

Bran was "on watch" when his comm instruments indicated an object approaching, on a converging course with slight skew. Parsons had the watch. Bran said, "A ship there, I think."

The woman's face went taut. "Get off the board, Tregare." Wondering, he stood and moved to another seat. Then after quickly talking into a hushphone, she said, "Only the captain speaks a ship met in space. Or his named speaker."

Bran nodded, and everyone waited until Korbeith entered, bringing with him a thin, slouching man who looked tired and perhaps defeated. Korbeith shoved him toward the comm chair. "Say it all just right, Meardon. No mistakes. You hear me?"

The man nodded, and his hands moved to open the offship circuits. "Open screens," said Korbeith, as he moved to be off to one side, out of the screen's view. "Now *talk*."

Meardon's voice sounded the way he looked: a whine. "Hello the ship," he said. "Can't make out your insigne from this distance. We're still keeping the *MacArthur* name on here for a while. Heading toward—" He spoke gibberish and at the same time overloaded his voice amplifiers to peak distortion, then eased the control back and said, "—but we'll be a time getting there. And what's your own course, and who have you seen lately?"

The offship viewscreen lit, but the picture wobbled. If Bran had ever seen the man shown there, he couldn't have recognized him. The voice came flat. "The *MacArthur*, eh? Or was. Tell me, how did Butcher Korbeith die?"

Meardon paused. "Now why should you ask that? And who asks?"

"Cade Moaker asks, and I don't mind telling you, since you're not armed and can't cut course to ram, that you're speaking *Cut Loose Charlie* now. Not the *Dictator*, these days. You got that?" Now, at the other end a pause, then: "Meardon, isn't it? You never could fool me and you can't now, either. The Butcher's still alive, isn't he? And you're still gobbling his leavings!"

"You're wrong, Moaker. I—"

"Eat crap, Meardon! And don't bother trying to peg my destination, because ahead in my course there's still a dogleg."

The circuit went dead. Meardon tried twice more, until Korbeith said, "Drop it, you fool!" and left the control room.

Then Bran dared to look up, and saw that nearly everyone else had been having the same problem. Lagging behind the captain by several paces, Meardon slunk out. Bran caught the gaze of Eunice Parsons; his raised brows and his gesture asked a question.

Parsons beckoned him closer, and he sat. She said, "Once Meardon—First Officer then—thought to mutiny and Escape. As you might guess, he lost. But Korbeith found it useful to have it leaked to the grapevine, on this and that world, that Meardon succeeded. So now he keeps the skinny rat as a slave decoy, to try to trap out passing ships and get leads to Hidden Worlds."

Bran shivered. "Why doesn't Meardon kill himself?"

"Same reason his mutiny failed. No guts."

Two "days" later the intercom alarm woke Bran in midsleep. A quick look told him he'd had less than four hours' rest. Then a voice rasped, "All cadets! Assemble for airlock drill! On the run!" The room lights came on; Sally had reached the switch first. "Thanks," Bran said. "What uniform, you suppose?"

"Regular duty, I expect. He said, a drill." So they dressed quickly and descended the stairs considerably faster than safety regs permitted, making themselves the fifth and sixth cadets to arrive at the airlock deck area.

It wasn't merely a quartet of their peers waiting, though. There Arger Korbeith stood, flanked by two armed guards to either side. Bran didn't dare speak, but he and Sally exchanged a quick glance, and he was pretty sure her thought was the same as his own: *Now the Butcher strikes!*

It seemed forever, but probably less than two minutes passed before the last cadet arrived, perhaps thirty seconds after the next-to-last. Korbeith looked at the laggard and cleared his throat. "Your name, *sir*?"

The young man's face reddened. "Pendleton, sir. Keith Pendleton. I—"

"If you were intending to make an excuse, I advise against it." He nodded to the guard who looked to be the oldest of them.

That man made a kindly-seeming smile. "Form one rank. Take normal interval. Dress it up, there; straighten that line!" When he was satisfied, he nodded. "Now strip. Clothes off, *now*. Fold them neatly and place them one pace behind your position, then form rank again." He broke hesitation with, "Move it!"

Shucking his uniform as fast as he could, Bran tried to think. Then he had the answer: not merely simple humiliation, but economy. If you're going to space somebody out the air lock, why waste perfectly good garments? Neither first nor last to do so, he rejoined the lineup. And waited, as Korbeith glared.

The captain strode to face the boy at the right end of the group, stared at him, said nothing, and moved to the next, paused, moved again. Tension built; Pendleton the late arrival was now under Korbeith's scrutiny. The big man started to turn away, swung back, jerked his thumb toward his target; the guards started forward, but then Korbeith shook his head. "No, not this time. Next drill, let's see if he can be *first* here."

Standing to Bran's right, Salome Harkness was seventh to endure Korbeith's inspection. It ended quickly, and then it was Bran's turn. Resolutely he avoided the yellow-eyed gaze, staring straight ahead at the enlarged Adam's apple. Korbeith mumbled something, and only when he moved on did Bran realize the words had included, ". . . no good. Should space him. But later . . ."

The man stopped only briefly before the next few cadets, then paused a time at Megan Delange. Bran's sidewise glance showed him beads of sweat at the forehead edge of her blond stubble, and barely noticeable, she was swaying on her feet. Korbeith's smile had rocks in it. "You'll keep."

He went past the last two people without looking at them. The guards followed him, and they left the area. No one bothered to dismiss the cadets, or direct them to clothe themselves; for close to a minute the all stood there, unable to decide what to do. There were a number of relieved exhalations but no talk, until Bran said, "In two hours I'm due on watch." He put on his shirt, pants, and shoes, bundled the rest of his clothes into one hand, and walked away. Whether the others followed his lead, he didn't know or care. But Sally Harkness entered their room while he was still putting the clothes away.

As she herself undressed, she said, "Peace take me, I've *never* been so afraid. But he didn't kill anybody, after all. Do you suppose, Tregare, that it's all a big hoax? A scare?"

Only one true answer. "No, I don't. This way the bastard can build up suspense more. That's all."

If Korbeith indeed enjoyed playing cat and mouse, he had little patience for it. On Tregare's second next duty stint, about halfway through, came the "Airlock drill!" call. Rising from the comm board, Bran turned to the watch officer: "Relief, sir?" The man nodded, and Bran took off in sprint gear: Control was the topmost inhabited upship level, so of all the cadet group he had the farthest to go. He took stairs in three and four-step jumps, and when he came to a vacant flight, no one in his way, took a flying leap, a quick grab at the handrail, and swung to take a free bound to the next deck.

And still, by about two seconds, he was last to assemble. Well, *bluff, dammit*! Catching a deep breath he took a good cadet brace and threw Korbeith his best salute. "Cadet Tregare, sir, reporting directly from watch duty!" Explanation, not excuse—and grudgingly, the Butcher nodded.

"So fall in, cadet." And then the smiling guard gave the orders to strip, and again they all stood side by side while Korbeith stalked down the line. Bran strugged to get his pulse and breathing down to normal. There was nothing he could do about his fear, except try to conceal it. While they all waited...

So quiet. From well along the line, Bran could hear Korbeith's gravel-mumbled threats. "If you shape up, you might be *worth* spacing out the lock." "Can't imagine why Arbogast passed you." Long pause, and the chronic scowl intensified. "I'm saving you for later." To Bran's right stood

Megan Delange. In his peripheral vision he could see that her knees were shaking as Korbeith moved to tower above her. "Any question this time?" She shook her head. The captain took a step to face Bran, then jerked his thumb back to Delange. "That one."

Then it was horror. Korbeith stood back, and two guards, the older one still with his falsely-kind smile, came to grab the young woman by her arms. Her knees buckled and her head sagged back; she made a keening sound, a mewling whimper that hurt Bran's ears. All instinct said to *help* her, but he knew he couldn't. He could only watch—and that, he couldn't avoid.

While a third guard opened the main air lock's inner door, the other two dragged the woman toward it. Suddenly she stiffened, shaking almost loose from one captor—but the man grabbed her again, one hand on her arm and the other giving her left breast a vicious twist. Her eyes rolled up until only white was showing; her scream shrilled echoes in the place, but still the two guards pulled her along. Then all at once her body rejected whatever it could manage—urine, feces, and vomit splattered everything and everyone within range of her. Down along the line, Bran saw two other cadets throw up, and fought to hold his own gorge.

Ignoring their soiled uniforms, the guards heaved Megan Delange into the air lock chamber. The portal slammed shut.

Bran couldn't remember whether the thick plastic window fogged up with entrance of air or evacuation. In this case it didn't matter. The outer door opened, and Megan Delange went spinning, her balance not yet caught from the rough throw into the chamber, out into the vacuum.

Until that moment the captain's gravelly laugh had never paused. Now it did, and with the silence that came while no one else seemed to draw breath, Bran heard a harsh mumble. Maybe it was the chamber's acoustics that brought the words. But the voice was Arger Korbeith's. And as Megan Delange plunged dead into space, Bran heard, "*You* go out there, not *me*. *You* pay, not *me*. *Nobody* can pay enough, but you'll never stop paying. And *you* go out. . . ."

Then other people began breathing and talking, and Bran lost track of the Butcher's litany. If it were real. If *any* of this was.

At least it's done, Bran thought; but he was wrong; Arger Korbeith had more for them. Above the airlock door a viewscreen lit, and the harsh voice said, "You will now observe the results." A camera with a zoom lensing and a brilliant floodlight had followed Delange into her experience of explosive decompression, so now the surviving cadets were treated to a replay of young Megan's dying convulsions. The camera operator was no expert; the lighting showed only her decompressed body against blackness of sky, and the body grew and shrank as camera adjustments failed to match the dying woman's rate of receding from the ship.

The colors were off, but purple was probably about right for the face. Compared to what else happened to it, and especially the eyes, the rest didn't matter.

Shocked to calmness of a sort, Bran stood through several repeated showings, trying not to hear Korbeith's chuckles. All around Bran, people were tossing their cookies, but he held his down. Until Korbeith graveled out a particularly lewd comment that in other context Bran could have ignored; suddenly he spewed.

It wouldn't have made any difference; the entire cadet contingent spent the next hour swabbing up the whole mess.

When Bran and Sally finally got back to quarters and showered up, they held each other and that was all either wanted. Bran was shaking and couldn't stop for a while. When he did steady, he said, "Harkness, I'm swearing an oath."

Her hug tightened. "Yes, Tregare?"

Against her warm arms, his head thrashed. "I don't know how or when or where or how long—but one day I will kill Arger Korbeith.

"If he doesn't kill me first."

Again she hugged harder. "Or if I don't." She said, "Him, I mean." Then Bran wanted her, but even for surrogate sex, he was too pooped.

Tensed, unable to relax, Bran waited to see what Korbeith would do next. But for days there were nothing but normal duty assignments. Cat and mouse, yes. Mouse wasn't Bran's favorite role. But he didn't exactly have a choice.

He tried to learn more, about what the Butcher's *pattern* might be, but it was hard to figure who to ask. Ratings (and unrated) in the crew simply clammed up to cadets, and it was about the same with First Officer Orrin Peale and Second

Officer Wendel Rheinhardt. The Engineering officers kept pretty much to themselves—not much chance there.

So it came down to Eunice Parsons, the Third. She'd talked with Bran before, but for a time the watch skeds kept him from meeting her in galley. But then he caught her having a mid-watch snack, and sat beside her. After casual greetings he got his nerve up to ask.

She looked at him. "Well, why not? I've never seen that scared people work better, so—" The pattern was fairly simple. After the first cadet was spaced, Korbeith tended to call random drills, but usually staged an execution only at the end of a training program. The programs generally ran about two or three weeks. "Be careful who you tell this to," she added. "If it gets back to the captain that the cadets know anything, he'll change his system. It's happened." Bran thanked her, and told no one except Sally Harkness.

Training progressed, and in spite of himself Bran enjoyed it. At the Slaughterhouse there had been practically no drill with sidearms. On the *MacArthur*, the group regularly had target practice on a range set up in the ship's machine shop, just above the Drive room. The energy weapons, both the light ones and the big, heavy two-handers, had their outputs locked down to a level that would barely melt butter but which gave clear indications on the targets, both stationary and moving. The vicious little needle guns that fired a stream of tiny slugs at ear-wrenching velocity as air was riven were, for practice, loaded with fragile plastic pellets propelled at a much slower rate of speed. It wouldn't do to catch one in the eye, of course, but a cadet's jumpsuit would protect against anything more than an angry bruise. Since Korbeith himself frequently observed the practicing, Bran could see the point. Given real ammo, what cadet could resist using it on the Butcher?

As on the scoutships, navigation was stressed, and again Bran starred at it. The *MacArthur*'s mission, aside from the training aspect, was to rendezvous with a series of patrol ships, stationed at intervals along a line between Earth's solar system and a planet known as Stronghold. The odd thing about Stronghold, as Bran had noticed before on star charts, was that it lay in the opposite direction from all of UET's other explorations. Remembering his father's story of UET killing the alien Shrakken and stealing their ship, Bran thought he knew what Stronghold was all about. And the patrol ships too. Again he told his guesses only to Salome Harkness.

But the *MacArthur* was going nowhere near Stronghold, only a few percent of the distance to that world. Orrin Peale, the First, handed the cadets the problem of figuring their max distance. "It takes roughly a month for us to get up as near to c as makes no calculable difference for scheduling purposes. Using nearly twelve gees—and don't ask me how the Drive field neutralizes all but one of those in the ship and its immediate vicinity. My job's Control, not Engineering. Now then, cadets . . . with that information, tell me roughly how far we'll be from Earth after one month accel and the next one in decel. For that's exactly what we'll be doing. Going to the farthest ship first and catching the others on the way home." He coughed. "And the ratio of subjective time to objective, also."

Zerch to light? Bran already knew that one: t/t_0 (elapsed) was pi-over-four. He stood, said so, and got an approving nod.

The other part took him a minute, in his head, to set up. Then with his hand-calc, it was easy. "Slightly under eight hundred billion kilometers, sir. Between a seventh and an eighth of a light-year." Which wasn't much of a bite toward *any* extrasolar planet, but still one hell of a way from Earth.

Along with a nod, this time Officer Peale almost smiled.

Again the shout of "Airlock drill" woke Bran from sleep. He thought of making speed by omitting socks and underwear, but decided that Korbeith might take the omission as excuse for having him killed, and spent the few extra seconds. Downship as fast as he dared go, he was eighth to reach the air lock deck and pleased to see Sally just ahead of him.

Quickly they all lined up. The guard with the plastic implant for a smile (or so it now seemed, to Bran) checked off his list, and Korbeith began his stalk along rank.

Despite the assurances from Parsons, Bran felt sweat gather at crotch and armpits, and begin to slither down his skin. *I never thought I could wish to be back at the Slaughterhouse!* In his mind a resolve formed. If Korbeith jabbed that great, knobby thumb at *him*, he would immediately, without thought, take his best shot at killing the man. No matter, then, what happened—if he could take the Butcher with him, that would have to do. *You HAVE to become a monster!*

To Bran's right stood Keith Pendleton, the boy who had arrived last at the initial drill but who had indeed been first there for the second, when Megan Delange died. Squinting to that side, Bran saw Korbeith make a dismissing motion toward the guards—with the hand Pendleton couldn't see. then the captain stared Keith up and down, mumbled a threat Bran couldn't quite make out, moved along to Bran and then jerked his thumb back at Pendleton. "That one." Then Korbeith stood still.

The condemned youth turned pale as death. But he didn't sway or fall; his knees locked and he stood rigid. For about ten seconds that seemed a hundred times longer, the tableau held. Then came Korbeith's jarring laugh. "Not yet, Pendleton . . . not yet. Have to keep you snotnoses alert . . . that's all."

He moved to give Bran his glowering stare, but Tregare hardly noticed; he stood, his mind in a confused whirl, as the captain gave a snort and a few foul words, and moved to the next person. *If he'd pulled that on me, I'd have jumped him; I'd be dead now.*

So he changed his plan. Only when the guards came at him, would he make his try to kill Butcher Korbeith.

But true to the Third Officer's estimate, that time no one went out the air lock.

New training segments on the *MacArthur* tended to begin abruptly and without notice. When Tregare next checked in for watch duty he was told to report to the deck level just above the improvised target range. Arriving there earlier than most of the cadet group, he found Second Officer Rheinhardt inspecting a mechanism, hanging from an overhead track, that looked like a metal skeleton festooned with straps and servomotor units. Bran found himself looking at something that leaned in a corner of the room—an oversized spacesuit that obviously carried a lot of mechanical paraphernalia. Rheinhardt caught his gaze, and said, "That's a power suit. This is the trainer for it." When all the cadets were present, Rheinhardt had two of them help him into the heavy suit. When he had himself fastened up properly, but leaving the helmet off, he said, "This thing gives you more than ten times normal strength, via the servo assists. It takes practice, because you have to learn not to overload the circuits or else you could wreck it. But I'll show you." He beckoned to Bran, and with one hand lifted him high and bounced him gently. Setting him down, Rheinhardt then picked up, again one-handed, a machine tool that had to mass at least three hundred kilos. He moved slowly, carefully, and put it back to rest. "I won't show you how this thing can jump, because I don't want to dent the deck. Here, help me out of this." Pendleton and another cadet obliged.

Salome Harkness asked, "Sir? What do we *use* it for?"

"Good question. Well, mostly for outside work, handling heavy components that would be hell to work with, no matter how many people you had, without the power assists."

Bran said, "Sir? Are we going to work in that suit?"

He wasn't surprised when Rheinhardt made a headshake. "No. You'll work with the trainer. Only officers use the suit."

Sure. Let me in that thing and I'd own this ship!

But the trainer, as Rheinhardt explained, simulated all the inertial aspects, the vast weight and the power-multiplication. Over the next three duty periods, taking turns, Bran got the feel of the surrogate mechanism—how to judge his timing and coordinate his moves. At the end, he felt he could operate the suit all right—if the trainer's parameters made an accurate facsimile. And Rheinhardt assured the group that in fact it did.

But when the cadets did their first practice at outside work, they wore ordinary, non-powered spacesuits. Orrin Peale took first position on the life line. Everyone seemed both nervous and eager, but then came a complaining voice: Keith Pendleton's. "This suit's marked redlined. Not safe."

"That's for extended use, son." In his own suit, waiting for his helmet to unfog, Bran couldn't see who spoke, but the voice sounded like that of the plastic-smiled guard. "Don't worry. I'll be right next to you, and keep an eye peeled to see you're all right. Which you will be. This time we're due out only half an hour. But I'll put us at the end, if it makes you feel better. So we could get back in fast."

It sounded like a lot more explanation than the question needed, but Bran was too excited to pay much heed. After a wait that probably wasn't as long as it seemed, the first half of the group entered the airlock. It cycled, evacuating its air back into the ship, and the outside hatch opened. Last in line, of his contingent, Bran crept out onto the ship's hull.

And gasped. Space seen directly from the scoutships had

been spectacular, but *this*—the *MacArthur* was well past half of c, out where even at such speed the interstellar gas made no threat to a suited person—and the view was like nothing he'd ever imagined. Behind, except for the Drive's spreading aura, nothing but blackness—ahead, stars crowded into an unrealistically tight vista, and colors shifted out of all recognition.

The lock had closed, recycled, and opened out. Now the other half of the group emerged. Bran saw the two life lines being connected; then came Officer Peale's order to move off. "Just follow me. We're going all the way around the ship, a bit the long way with a lengthwise slant to our path. What you do is concentrate and get used to handling the suit outside."

So they began to walk, to clomp along with their magnetic boots on the ship's rind. Progress was jerky, as one or another cadet lost footgrip or held it too long. Life line segments tended to go too taut or too loose, disturbing someone's balance. But all in all it didn't go badly. Bran found that his earlier scoutship practice came back to him easily enough, and now and then he risked a look at that fantastic sky.

They were nearly all the way around, and he saw the airlock hatch ahead, when behind him he heard a commotion. Well, it had to be behind because the voices were Pendleton's and Plastic Smile's. "Help me!" "Watch it, boy. What—?"

Looking back, Bran saw the last suit in the line drifting away. Faster and faster, until it vanished in distance.

When they got inside, both groups, Plastic Smile hurried the unsuiting and quickly sent the cadets to quarters. Bran wanted to look at something but didn't get any chance to do so.

When Salome joined him in their room, she grabbed to hug him. "Oh, Bran! I saw the life line. It was *cut*."

He nodded. "And on orders; sure. Well, if you're going to waste a suit, make sure it's worn out already."

Her eyes widened. "You think that?" She gave half a sob. "How much air do you think he had?"

Without meaning to, he snarled at her. "How should I know? And what difference does it make? It all depends on how long the Butcher likes his victims to suffer first."

But now he knew. Air lock drills were only part of it. The Butcher had other ways.

6. Reunion

While the *MacArthur* still built toward c, the Butcher called two more drills. All the remaining cadets lived through the first one, but next time Plastic Smile and his sidekick took a young man to the air lock and he went naked into space. The victim seemed frozen by Korbeith's verdict; he said nothing, and his body held its contents until the vacuum hit. Two cadets vomited, but not Bran Tregare. Not before he was back to quarters, anyway.

The ship, Bran knew from briefings, was on sked to hit a Vee of 0.995c—a t_0/t ratio, briefly at peak, of about ten. Or maybe one-tenth; Bran could never keep straight which was t and which was t_0, and who cared? Ships chewed time, was all.

Turnover date was no secret, though, and Bran looked forward to watching the maneuver. No such luck: Korbeith ordered all cadets to quarters, "—and strap in. Anyone injured during zero-gee time, I needn't tell you what happens."

Sure as hell you don't, you murdering bastard.

Bran would have settled for strapping in, but Salome came up with a more imaginative idea. So they rigged tie lines, and during the turnover, floating free, they made love. One of their ways, that was safe for them, simply wouldn't work without gravity—so they made do with the other. And so much for the Butcher!

Now the *MacArthur* went into its month of decel. Training continued, and in three more airlock drills, only once was a cadet spaced. Always, every time, Tregare thought *he* would be the one to go. *But, peace willing, not alone!* The strain was costing him sleep, wrecking his appetite, winding him up to a tighter pitch all the time. If it hadn't been for Sally Harkness, he knew he'd have cracked, long since.

His closest call was the airlock drill two days before scheduled rendezvous with the patrol ship *Barbarossa*. Two places to Bran's left stood Sally, and at her turn Korbeith paused to mumble longer than usual. Then he jerked his thumb—"That one!"—and if Tregare hadn't seen the behind-hand signal, warding off the guards' move, he'd have charged and hoped to kill. As it was, he barely restrained himself. And back in their room fell shaking onto his bunk, needing love's comfort but physically incapable of taking it.

"That's all right," she said, holding him. "We're still alive and there's always tomorrow."

How Officer Rheinhardt came to his death, Tregare never knew. The ship was told only that Eunice Parsons had been promoted from Third to Second, that a rating was breveted to Third, temporarily, and (hardly made clear, but implied) that a new, permanent Third Officer was being transferred from the *Barbarossa*. This last news came after the two ships had met and docked, and the various Control and Engineering officers had exchanged guesting between vessels.

Rheinhardt had been a good, likable officer, clear in his instructions and fair in the ways he treated his cadet students. With some foreboding, Bran awaited meeting with the man's replacement. During ships' rendezvous the event didn't occur. After pullout, heading back for Earth by way of stoppage at other patrol-ship stations, he still hadn't met the new Third. So when he entered the galley, fresh off watch, the sight of a familiar face started him. *Peralta!*

The man hadn't changed much: still slim, but more muscular. His face held firmer lines, and now the mustache was considerably more successful, though still trimmed to leanness. Bran saw that Peralta had recognized him, but showed no overt sign of the recognition. So maybe there were rules Bran didn't know yet. For damn sure he wasn't going to run up yelling buddy-buddy; for all Bran knew, that could mean a quick route to the air lock.

So, setting his tray aside because for one thing he really wasn't all that hungry, Bran got himself a cup of coffee and strolled over to the table where Jimar Peralta sat. If he got the invitation to sit down, fine. If not, he'd go eat.

Peralta *had* to see Tregare coming but he didn't look up. Well, maybe this was how it was. Bran walked to the table, refrained from setting his cup down, and said, "Mr. Peralta?"

Now Peralta's gaze acknowledged Bran's existence. "Yes?"

"You'd be our new Third Officer, sir?"

A nod. "I would, yes."

"Congratulations, sir. From Cadet Bran Tregare."

He knew he'd said the right thing when Peralta grinned and offered a handshake. "Sit down, Tregare. Join me. It's irregular, but permitted." Bran sat. "Now what's been happening with you?"

Others were in earshot. Still he had to say what he felt. "I've been on this ship two months and I'm still alive, Sir."

With a slight frown, a twitch of head that wasn't quite a shake, Peralta answered, more loudly than seemed to be called for. "Very commendable, Cadet Tregare. Your attitude does you credit." Abruptly his voice dropped. "You talk too much. In public, don't." Voice raised again. "What news from our colleagues at the Academy?"

Chatter? All right; Bran gave some. "Jargy Hoad—you'll remember him—made cadet-captain our upper year. Kickem Bernardez—no, he was after your time—well, anyway . . ." Bran talked for the audience, assuming anyone was listening, and Peralta responded in kind. Then said, "You'd better go now, good as it is to see you." And, "Visiting must be at *my* instigation."

Bran nodded. "I understand."

"I hope so, Tregare." That was all of it, so Bran left.

In training work, Peralta treated Bran as if they hadn't known each other before—which, of course, was as it should be. The man was not unfair; if Bran or anyone else did especially well on any assignment, Peralta gave a compliment. On the other hand, any cadet who goofed caught the Third Officer's best grade of sarcasm. Bran didn't goof often, or badly.

Once he was able to answer a question without bothering to calculate—because, from curiosity, he'd already worked it out. "On your outward leg," Peralta said, "you hit very close to c before turnover. What did that run add to the difference between your two ages?"

"Not quite seventeen days," Bran answered, while others were just beginning to set up the problem on their hand-calcs. Peralta waited for an explanation, so Bran added, "It's the pi-over-four factor, for t/t_0 at steady accel from zerch to light, and back down. So sixty ship days roughly, equal nearly seventy-seven back on Earth."

"Did you do that in your head?"

"No, sir. I got to wondering last week, and figured it then."

Peralta made a faint smile. "Very good. Now we'll put a

more complicated question. Our return to Earth is in two segments. Consider—" Bran's hand was up. "Yes, Tregare?"

"I thought we were to meet three more ships."

"And so did the captain. But the orders have been changed. Shall we continue?" Bran shut up, listened to the problem as given, and came in with the second-closest approximate answer.

Only the top performer got commended, though.

Back in quarters, Bran did some battery-assisted thinking. Before, he simply hadn't considered the matter. Now he realized that a four-segment return to Earth, each with accel and then with decel to rest (approximate), would have taken more than four times as long as the outward run. By ship's time, that was; on Korbeith's ship, Earth chronology meant doodly zilch.

So the change of orders was a break, and the nineteen surviving cadets could certainly use one. Still, they had four [illegible] months, anyway, under the Butcher's sway. *Scheist!*

So when Salome came in he was in no mood to talk. She tried to rally him but he wouldn't respond, until finally she jumped and grabbed him, laughing, knowing he was ticklish and would either snap out of it or get angry. Balanced on the edge of that choice, suddenly he laughed. "Watch it, lady! Tregare never forgives a tickle!" They had most of their clothes off when the intercom sounded.

"Third Officer Peralta here. Inspection tour in five minutes." Pouting, but grinning along with it, Sally Harkness got dressed. Except for mussed hair—now it was long enough to be mussed—she looked relatively sedate as she opened the door to Peralta.

Bran stood at attention. "Ready for inspection, sir."

Closing the door, Peralta waved a hand. "Inspection completed, cadets. Let's sit down. I have a few things to say."

Bran sat, with Sally beside him, Peralta taking the other bunk. Bran said, "Sorry, no beer to offer, sir. This ship doesn't seem to have much of a pipeline." Immediately, from Peralta's expression, he knew he was on the wrong track. "Sorry, sir. I'll shut up."

"You'd better." The Third Officer looked at Salome Harkness. "I see that in assignment of roommates, Bran Tregare has had better luck than he deserves." Her brows raised, and Peralta quickly added, "That's a compliment, cadet, not a proposition." Bran didn't know what to say, so he kept silent.

And so, for a time, did Peralta. Until he sighed and said, "This is a bad ship; we all know that. I'm relatively safe. Entirely so, I'd have said, until the circumstances of my posting here as Third Officer. If anyone knows what happened to Rheinhardt, no one's saying." He shrugged. "But I'll manage, I think; the captain seems to like my style and I shan't disabuse him of his opinion. You, though—" He shook his head. "I told you once, Tregare, I'd like to have you spacing with me. On my own ship, I meant, when I have one. *And I will*, peace allowing it. But how any of you cadets can guarantee to survive, I have no idea."

Harkness leaned forward. "You've heard something, sir?"

"Just grapevine. The captain seems to be working himself up to something."

"Is there anything—" As soon as he said it, Bran knew the answer.

"Anything *I* can do?" Peralta shook his head. "That's what I wanted you to know. I'm against this killing, the same as back at the Slaughterhouse, but there is not one damned thing I can do about it. I wouldn't even try." He leaned forward. "Because I want command and I intend to have it. And nothing in this universe is going to get in my way. Nothing: not even friends."

And seeing the tautness of face and eyes, Bran knew that argument wouldn't help. Jargy had pegged Peralta right enough.

But on the next space walk around the *MacArthur*'s outside, when two cadets waffled at being placed at either end of the lifeline (well, look what had happened to Pendleton! But no one mentioned that), Peralta took one end himself and Orrin Peale took the other. Plastic Smile wasn't present, so Bran thought the fears might be unwarranted. But still he gave both officers a good mark in his mental book.

At the next airlock drill, two days short of rendezvous with the armed ship *T'chaka*, the cadets stood shivering, naked in a temperature hardly exceeding 12-Celsius, and saw Third Officer Jimar Peralta standing at the captain's flank. After a silent wait, Korbeith said, "Third Officer, you do the honors. Inspect, and choose which of them to space."

Peralta nodded. "Yes, sir." He moved to confront the cadet

at the right of the line, looked her up and down, moved on. Unlike Korbeith he said no word, taking shorter or longer times to inspect each possible victim. As he faced Bran, one eyelid dipped so slightly that Tregare thought he might have imagined it. Then at the end, Peralta turned to face Arger Korbeith.

"Sir?"

"Yes, Third. Have you chosen?"

Headshake. "No, sir."

"Why not?"

"Sir, I've had nearly eight weeks, working with these cadets. And I must say, you've done an admirable job of culling. I—"

"You can't find *anyone*?"

"No one person. Captain, sir, in my opinion their performances are pretty much on a par. So in my judgment, if any are to be spaced, all should be." Peralta didn't quite shrug, but gave a faint suggestion of that move. "That would be up to you, sir."

For a heart-stopping moment, seeing blood suffuse Korbeith's sallow complexion, Bran thought they were all dead. *But not alone!* For he would take his last chance at Korbeith, live or die.

Then the Butcher relaxed his stance; the gravel laugh came. "If I dumped the lot, Peralta, you'd go with them." Then he stalked away, and again Bran found himself able to breathe.

Later, alone with Sally and still winding down from tension, he said, "He's a fox, Peralta is! If he's on your side, that's wonderful."

"But if he isn't?"

"Yeah. That's the problem. How do you know?"

Rendezvous with the *T'chaka* came and was done with; Bran didn't get onto that ship and saw no one from it. The *MacArthur* went into accel mode: two months, roughly, short of Earth return. Training stayed heavy but not intolerable; scutwork details shrank to token chores. Despite what the late Officer Rheinhardt had said, cadets did get actual training in one of the ship's two power suits. But with the suit-powered energy projector, much more massive and destructive than a regular two-hander, disconnected and removed. While a guard or officer, in the other suit, had the potent weapon ready for use. And the whole thing, the suit training, took place in a locked hold. No, Arger Korbeith was taking no chances of a cadet getting loose with a suit—not in *his* ship.

Never mind; Bran Tregare enjoyed the learning. At first the time-lags, the discrepancies between his body's moves and the servo responses, felt awkward. But then he caught the hang of it—a little, though not entirely, like swimming in Great Salt Lake (which he had done one summer, but had almost forgotten by now). In his third session he had the coordination down pat: the move, the pause, the suit's *action*. So when he thought he'd achieved mastery, what else but to *try* it?

Risky, it would be, for now Peralta inhabited the weaponed suit, and the man was cat-quick. But in a power suit, not quite so fast. All right, give it a go! So moving toward the other suited man, Bran said, "Let's see if I can do something, here," and heard his amplified voice boom echoes from the confining bulkheads. Peralta nodded; good enough. Bran feinted to the right, held the feint long enough for Peralta to reach, then took advantage of the suits' delay-factor to come back the other way while Peralta had only begun to move.

The next instant, he had the other man's energy projector in his armored hands. But before Peralta, recovering his balance, could launch any attack, Bran was handing the weapon back to him. "No offense meant, sir. I just wanted to see if I could *do* it."

Halting his move, the Third Officer reached and took back the big gun. Inside the helmet, Tregare saw his nod. "Good action, cadet. You know, I trust, that if you'd failed to take the gun, you'd be dead now? Not by my will, but by my trained reflexes."

"Not quite that definite, no, sir. I did know I had to cut it pretty fine."

"Indeed." Peralta had punched the door control; it opened, and for the first time helpers came to get both men out of the suits. So Tregare knew something else now, or thought he did: a trainee's suit must have outside controls on it, so that someone else could turn it off. For otherwise the unprotected helpers could be made hostage, or simply slaughtered, by a really desperate cadet.

One more item to keep in mind...

* * *

When he told Sally about it all, she shook her head and then laughed. "You take such chances!"

He thought about it. "In this mess, is there any other way?"

"I guess not. But—" He was caressing her. "Careful, there. Mmm—that's safer. And now why don't you—?"

He did. Sometimes it bothered him, what they had to settle for. But as long as Sally agreed, it would have to do him.

Parsons had said the Butcher never spaced less than three cadets per trip; that much, he had done (if Keith Pendleton, cast adrift in a defective suit, also counted. And how many more deaths would Korbeith's urge need?). Patience wasn't Bran's best skill, and constant fear would never come to be a comfortable companion. He lost sleep, dreamed badly, and ran on raw adrenalin.

One day I'll kill him. If he doesn't kill me first. The saying helped Bran at first waking, and also in getting to sleep. No one, ever, had given him such fear; while Korbeith lived, Bran felt he could never be a whole person. Alive and functional, maybe, but incomplete. *So I have to. Someday, some way, I have to.*

He knew the goal was unrealistic, but still he was stuck with it. All his life, maybe, however long that might turn out to be. The main thing was outliving the Butcher; he thought on it.

When Peralta next paid Bran and Sally an "inspection" visit, he'd been wining. In fact he brought along a bottle, still nearly full. "Be my guests," he said. "I've had plenty. Not in the usual sense, but on this ship, more than enough." So, with thanks, the two sipped the tart, ruby red stuff.

"Very good," Bran said, and Salome nodded. Bran changed the subject. "What have you been doing since you left the—the Academy?" Thinking back, he frowned. "Someone said—I forget who—that you were trying for the next fleet to Stronghold."

"I was." Peralta's chuckle held no amusement. "But got bumped last minute into patrol duty on the *Barbarossa*. Been there ever since, 'til now. Not much action, and *no* promotions."

"But you're Third now. . . ."

"Your Mr. Rheinhardt's bad luck was my good. Oops. . . drink to his memory for me, will you? That's right. Anyway, I was senior to all cadet-status personnel on the *Barbarossa* and also here on the *MacArthur*, so I got the nod. Not my idea of a prize assignment, as you might guess, but Third Officer is Third Officer. And once back on Earth . . ."

"You have plans, sir?" Soft-voiced, Sally spoke.

Peralta laughed. "Always. But I never reveal them ahead of time." More soberly, he said, "This much I'll say. Some think promotions come faster at HQ, but percentagewise, they don't. You have to go out, to go places." Again he laughed. "Peace take it, I've made a joke!" He leaned forward. "Out in space, except for the piddle of patrol duty, your ship can—" He waved his arms wide. "—can find a new colony planet, nail an Escaped ship or its destination, maybe even locate a Hidden World. The bonuses for *that*, if it ever happens . . ."

"Nail an Escaped ship?" Bran thought. "Then you'd be trying for a berth on an armed one."

"If I could manage it. Of course." Maybe Peralta didn't think he was carrying much of a load, but Bran did. "And then there's the wild card situation. Which we need not discuss here."

But when the wine was gone, and Peralta also, Bran and Sally discussed it. "It stands to reason," he said, "that most ships make their Escapes by way of mutiny. Captains have the least incentive to bolt. Which, afterward, means promotions among the survivors, and one of these is to *command*. And that's what Peralta wants most. He can taste it."

On the *MacArthur* there was no question of mutiny or Escape. Off the grapevine, once crew members began talking to cadets, Bran had picked up several stories, and he passed them along to Salome Harkness. "It was tried once, on Korbeith's previous ship. I forget its name now. He got the ship back to Earth with only six other people alive."

"That's not possible. In these ships, for Control alone—and the Drive—"

"Korbeith proved different. He ran with two on duty in Control, rather than four, and two filling in for the usual three on Drive. Everybody standing double watches, sixteen hours out of twenty-four. And one in the galley, and no maintenance. He needed luck on that last, but he got it."

"Only seven alive?" She shook her head. "The others?" Then she said, "No, I guess I don't have to ask about that."

"Hardly." Inside him Bran grinned; he was starting to sound like Peralta. "Anyway, the word is that Korbeith has this ship loaded with special weapons systems, and carries the only keys to them. He can gas whole levels, if he wants to. And his guards—" (especially, Bran had heard, Plastic Smile) "—he has them addicted to some drug, and of course he has the only supply on board."

Sally frowned. "Are you *sure* about all this?"

"Course not. But it fits his patterns, and sure's hell I don't intend to find out."

At the next air lock drill, just short of turnover, the Butcher stood before Bran a long time. Mumbling, "No damn good. Past time—skinny, useless—waste of rations . . ." trailing off so that Bran, against his will, strained to hear. Then, with that quick way he turned, Korbeith twitched his thumb at Bran.

"That one." Only the fact that momentarily he froze, before noticing that the guards hadn't moved, saved Bran then. Because he was primed to go, and his target was that jutting larynx. The hell with eyes and balls, their loss didn't kill.

But the tiny, involuntary pause, giving him time to realize the guards' immobility meant Korbeith had waved them off, saved Tregare. He felt himself redden as the great rasp of the Butcher's laughter came. "Almost had you there, didn't I? Well, you're not home yet." But that time he killed no one.

Back in quarters Bran expected to be incapable with Sally. Instead he found himself ready, and again, and again—until finally she said, "I'm sorry, but it's starting to *hurt*."

So he apologized, and she said he needn't, that it was all right and she understood, and—somewhere in there, he fell asleep.

But that was why, at turnover next day, they played no games at all.

In some ways the last month was the worst. The closer they got to Earth, the more Bran felt they had to lose, should Korbeith choose one of them for spacing. Wound up tighter than ever, he had to forgo coffee entirely; combined with a constant adrenalin overload, it literally made him ill. Food was a chore. He needed the fuel value but had to force it down and fight to hold it there—not always successfully.

The next one Korbeith spaced was a quiet young woman whose work, Bran knew from the reports he'd seen, was exemplary. When the Butcher chose her, she simply fainted—or pretended the faint perhaps, since Plastic Smile was unable to force her to show wakefulness before he dumped her into the air lock.

As the lock's outer hatch opened, Bran saw the Butcher's lips move. Stationed at the far end of the line, this time he couldn't hear the words. But seeing the heavy mouth move, he knew what Korbeith was saying. "*You* go out there, not *me*. *You* pay . . ." And pay for what? Tregare had no idea. Except that it might have to do with the ship Korbeith had brought home with only six other living persons aboard. At any rate, the Butcher left, and air lock drill was over.

After that one, Bran was not sane, knew he wasn't, and didn't really want to be.

In the galley, after watch-observation duty, Bran went to dump his tray and put it in the rack. As he set the tray down, alongside the stack he saw a thin, sharp-pointed tool, something like an old-fashioned ice pick. He had no idea of its use, but somehow he liked the looks of it. Under cover of pretending to adjust the stack of trays, he grasped the tool and put it up his sleeve. Then he left the galley.

Restless, he stalked through the ship—up a deck, prowl the corridors, up another, down three—he wasn't sure where he was going. But when he saw Plastic Smile ahead, turning a corner and going out of sight, he knew who he was looking for.

He followed the man, and the pursuit didn't take long, because Plastic Smile came to a door and rummaged to bring out a set of keys. As he put one to the door's lock, Tregare was close behind him and tapped his shoulder. The man turned.

"What—" He got no farther. Between larynx and chin, the point entered slanting upward, rasped between vertebrae and hit the spinal cord. When the guard didn't drop immediately, Bran wiggled the haft to enlarge the wound. Then as Plastic Smile began to crumple, the cadet wiped his palm over the tool's handgrip. *No fingerprints*. And only then realized he hadn't even looked to see that the corridor was clear of witnesses.

It was, though.

Heading back toward quarters, feeling the cold sweat of reaction running down his body, briefly Tregare wondered if he should have kept the impromptu weapon. *There's always Korbeith*. But he decided if he had it, he could be caught with it. And if the galley stocked one of them, no doubt there were more. Now that he knew about them.

The sweat of fear stank on him; he showered clean before Sally got back. Then things weren't so good; sexually he was totally unresponsive. No matter what they tried, nothing worked.

Why? His total rage, his frustration when the Butcher baited him and laughed—he'd expected *that* to unman him, but the effect had been just the opposite. Now he'd taken revenge, and somehow the secret triumph left him drained.

There was no way to talk about it. He couldn't tell anyone, not even Salome Harkness, that he had killed Plastic Smile. So he hugged Sally and said, "Delayed reaction, I guess. Sorry."

"Don't worry about it, Tregare. I can wait for next time."

Bran dreaded what could happen when Korbeith got into retaliatory gear. For two days nothing. Then the Butcher called a selective assembly in the galley. Lower-rated and unrated crew members weren't invited, and the watch contingent was present by intercom-viewscreen only. Still the place was packed.

There weren't enough seats; some ratings doubled up and some sat on the deck, as Arger Korbeith stalked and glowered. "Won't put up with murder!" *Except by your own doing, you piece of dung*. "No shelter for killers, no mercy." *I'll drink to that*. "So—" Korbeith pointed to one of his other guards. "—get up here, and talk!" And to Bran Tregare's amazement, the guard who had been Plastic Smile's colleague in the spacing of cadets was dragged to a chair and tied to it. Whereat Arger Korbeith raged and swore and hit the bound man, and had other things done to him that Bran didn't like to see, until the man confessed to killing Plastic Smile—whose true name Bran never did register.

Korbeith turned to his two remaining guards. "Take him down to the airlock. Officers and cadets, follow. The rest of you, dismissed."

Bewildered, Tregare moved downship with the rest. Why had the guard confessed to what he hadn't done? The torture? Or a mind-softening effect of the drugs used by Korbeith's guard force? It made no difference; Bran was off the hook for Plastic Smile. And now he remembered: this guard, headed for the airlock, was the one who had given the vicious wrench to the naked breast of the woman Bran had first seen spaced, and then had helped to space her. *Go to hell, then!*

Airlock drill didn't seem the same with clothes on. Only the condemned guard was stripped. But this time the procedure was different; Korbeith ordered the man equipped with a breathing mask, oxygen tube, and life line. Then his two ex-cohorts horsed him into the air lock and secured the life line to a bulkhead bitt. When they were out and the inner door closed, Korbeith himself punched the opening of the hatch to space, to cold, to vacuum.

So that the man could breathe while his body's internal pressures bloated and ruptured him, while the chill of space froze him from the outside in. As the Butcher's lips moved. *You* go out there, not *me*. . . .

Bran didn't throw up. Korbeith had worn that reflex out. Among other things . . .

Slow, Bran was, going back upship. When he entered the bunkroom Sally was toweling and still part dripping from her shower. She looked at him, a question in her face. He shook his head, went to stand in hot spray longer than customs said he should, then came out to face her.

Frustration burst. "It's no damn *good*!"

She came to him. "I know. But it's not much longer. Back to Earth; then we get reassigned. They told us that."

He pushed her off; he had to. "You *don't* know." She waited. He said, "That bastard didn't kill the other one. I did." Then he told her all of it. "I didn't want to tell you."

"Oh, Bran! I'm so glad you did." And then, between them, everything was suddenly all right.

Why was it, he thought, that so many of the bright spots of his life had to do with women? Well, why argue?

In bed then, it was for him close to the best time ever. Afterward he told her so, then frowned. "Sally—is this ship turning me into a killing freak? I don't want it to. I don't want love tied into death. I *don't*."

She held him. "No, Bran, that's not it. After you'd killed that smiling hyena, you *couldn't*—remember? But now that we have it straight between us, you can. If you're a freak for something, Bran Tregare, it just might be honesty."

Suddenly his tears flowed. He couldn't stop them, and after a few moments he didn't try. When he was done, still in Sally's tight hug, he felt a lot better.

And he slept without nightmares.

Approaching Earth, the *MacArthur* simulated invasion maneuvers. Korbeith might be a sadistic murdering son of a sow, but Bran had to admit that the Butcher knew his tactics. Sitting up in Control on his watch-observer stints, he saw how the *MacArthur* utilized its approach angle, coming from above the ecliptic, then some deceptive changes in rate of deceleration, and finally a twitch of course that hid the ship behind Jupiter's radiation belts, to first appear on Earth's screens in what would have been a highly effective attack stance. But of course no such thing was intended; it was all for training purposes, and the captain had given safe-conduct signals to all outlying patrols. Still, it *was* damned good training.

Inside the moon's orbit, the ship neared Earth. Not long now, Tregare thought, until they'd all be groundside. And *out* of this insane mess. But that wasn't how it happened. A bit lower than synchronous height, the *MacArthur* stopped descent and went to circling the planet below. Cadets, having strapped in according to orders, were then commanded to go downship. Nude this time, leaving all clothes in quarters.

Airlock drill. What else?

With little earlier chance to learn weightless maneuvering, Bran and Sally made awkward going of it. And so, it seemed, did every cadet they met along the way. Nobody, though, after three turnovers and two dockings, suffered from null-gee nausea.

At the air lock deck, with his two remaining guards, Butcher Korbeith *stood*. Sure; those three had boots with controlled magnets. The cadets, of course, didn't.

There was a cable, though, strung across the area, and the cadets were told to line up by grabbing onto it. When the captain was satisfied with their spacing along the thing, he said, with the laugh Bran had learned to despise, "Back to Earth, we're all going. But maybe a head start for some of you; beat the ship down there." And he stalked to scan the cable-holding line-up.

There was no way to stand at attention so Bran didn't try; instead he twisted to watch the Butcher's progress and actions. Korbeith mumbled something to the first cadet, pushed the young man free of the cable and bellowed, "You have thirty seconds to get back into place." But then, as the cadet floundered, moved along and paid no heed.

Next in line was Sally Harkness. Gasping, as the Butcher put his great hands on her and *kneaded,* she turned pale. "And you'll reach Earth ahead of us, won't you? And make a fine bright light to guide us in, as you hit air. *Won't* you, slut?"

Sanity was lost. Tregare pulled on the cable, gathered his legs up to make thrust, and launched for Korbeith's throat. All without making a sound. His breath hissed through gaping jaws. But as the Butcher jerked Harkness free of her hold, the cable moved with his pull; Bran was sent spinning off the wrong way.

He met a bulkhead with one hand and one foot, tried to angle his carom back toward Korbeith, but missed again. The guards had the woman now, but somehow again she grasped the cable.

Then from the air lock—from outside it—came a muffled clang, and the other noises that happened when a small craft docked there. And the intercom sounded: "Attention! The vice-admiral's inspection lighter, approaching on the port bow, will be docking at the main air lock. The captain is requested to attend the vice-admiral there, as soon as possible." The voice was Peralta's.

Bran caught grip on the cable again, and turned to see Arger Korbeith's face twist into fury. "Two hours early, that bastard's here!" His knobby hand swept air. "All right, you cadets! Back to quarters and get dressed. Prepare for the vice-admiral's inspection." He glared. "Move it!"

But as Bran and the rest turned to shove off, to make their ways upship, the airlock warning sounded. Bran paused, and saw that the lock was opened to the other spacecraft, and five uniformed figures had entered. Then the outside hatch closed, the inner one opened, and the five boarded the *MacArthur.*

Since neither Korbeith nor either guard had worked the local operating levers, the lock had been handled from Control.

Of the five, the leader was slim, and neither tall nor young. His greeting wave to Korbeith was not quite a salute, but thoroughly proper. "Captain! We've met, but not for some years, even bio. I'm Vice-admiral Kaner. Was up to Luna, and thought I'd stop by and—" Suddenly, Kaner seemed to notice the covey of floating, naked cadets. He laughed. "Ah! Initiations, at the end of their first trip? Not kosher by the regs, strictly—but back on the old *Zhukov*, when I commanded there, a little of such sport did add zest to the end of a long trip. And no one was hurt—or hardly ever. I trust it's the same here."

Korbeith's grey-sallow face held an ochre tinge. Before he could answer, Kaner said, "Shoo these youngsters back to their digs, will you, captain? Give 'em time to prep for my inspection. And—" He tapped the folder he carried under one arm. "For some of them, depending on proficiency ratings, I have immediate space assignments. Ships waiting for personnel, so I may ferry a few down with me ahead of you." Bran hoped he'd be one of those. Anything, to get off *this* deathtrap!

Neither he nor Sally were quite fully dressed when the knock came. "Not the inspection *already*?" But, being closest, she opened the door. Graceful, experienced in zero-gee, Peralta glided in, caught a stanchion, and halted.

He motioned for Salome to close the door, then said, "I'm passing the word. During inspection, or if you have the luck to ride groundside with the vice-ad, make *no* accusations against Korbeith." As both Bran and Sally tried to speak, the Third Officer waved them silent. "His superiors know all about him . . . have for years. He is, in a word, despised among them. Don't ask how I know; I have my pipelines. But the point is, the brass is an Old Boys' league. They cover for each other, no matter what." One eyebrow raised. "Do you understand?"

Reluctantly, Tregare nodded. "Yeah. I guess so." But then he had to grin. "We sure lucked out back there. When the Butcher couldn't kill Sally, because the admiral showed up."

Peralta shook his head. "Not all luck, cadet. The second officer and I heard rumors. So, somehow—and nobody can prove it on us—Korbeith's invitation for Kaner to come inspecting got updated by a couple of hours. Close timing, but it worked."

Bran tried to thank him, but Peralta would have none of

that. "I hate waste. Here, as at the Slaughterhouse." Then the man moved to the door, was out it, and pulled it closed behind him.

Inspection wasn't soon, but it was fast. Intercom orders were to leave room doors ajar, so Bran complied. Hearing the vice-admiral's group approach, Bran and Sally braced against bunks and held stanchions, to give a semblance of standing at attention. Kaner walked in magnetic boots as if moving in normal gravity. Entering, he looked around the cubicle, nodded, and gave a faint smile. "Quite satisfactory. Now then . . . Tregare and Harkness, isn't it?" Both affirmed. Kaner leafed through a notebook. "Yes, you're both posted for the hurry-up transfer. So get your gear together, and be at the air lock in thirty minutes. Or less."

He turned, and as though walking on Earth itself, strolled out. Just past the door, Bran saw Arger Korbeith standing, and before he also turned to follow the vice-admiral, the Butcher gave Tregare and Sally the most murderous gaze Bran had ever seen.

But now the Butcher was out of it. Or so Bran hoped.

Packing was no problem. Sally and Tregare were among the first to assemble near the air lock, beating Kaner's deadline by almost ten minutes. Then they waited, while Bran began to wonder if it might be all a cruel trick. Sally wanted to talk, but now he couldn't. Eventually, Kaner and his cortege arrived. The vice-admiral bade Korbeith goodbye—after what Peralta had said, Bran could hear the sarcasm in the compliments—and the group boarded the tiny dispatch craft. Twelve, in all.

The vice-admiral himself took the pilot's console—and once the preliminaries were done and the lighter undocked, proved himself a pilot after Bran's own heart. As Bran and Sally, sitting side-by-side, gripped hands together, he laughed. "The man's taking her down like a real bat. Oh, peace! He knows how to *fly*!"

Sally released held breath. "I'm glad you think so."

Then they were groundside. Exactly where, on Earth, they weren't told, but it was a big spaceport and there weren't all that many of such size, so Bran had his guesses.

He and Sally were immediately hauled off to transient quarters and assigned a room. And, after dining at the mess hall, mostly empty because they were between regular mealtimes, they made the most of it. Because it was their last chance for love or talk, either one.

Lying quietly for a time, drinking wine provided by a friendly, bribable mess attendant, Bran felt both sad and happy. "We lived through it, Sally. We got past the Butcher."

"Yes. I don't suppose we'll go to the same ship. Will we ever see each other again?"

His free hand grasped hers. "I'd hope so. But with the Long View, ships chewing time and all, might be our ages wouldn't match."

Like a cat, she dipped to bite his knuckles. "I won't care. If one of us is older, we'll simply not pay attention." She sat straight now. "Bran? What are your plans? What do you want to *do*?"

He knew he could trust her, and logic said that transient barracks weren't worth bugging, so he spoke freely. "Escape. What else?"

Salome Harkness frowned. "I thought it was Peralta, not you, who wants command so bad he can taste it."

Bran shook his head. "Not just command—though I wouldn't spurn it if it showed up under my pillow someday." He leaned forward. "Bloody *freedom*, is what. Getting out from under UET's heel. And then twisting UET's goddamn tail 'til it comes right off!"

Until he saw her shrinking back from him, he had no idea how tightly his face was making some kind of predatory grimace. Trying to relax, at least he softened his voice. "You've been through most of it, same as I have. Don't you want to hit back? Don't you burn to see those bastards *dead*?"

Eyes wide, she leaned to hug him, and hid her face against his shoulder. "Oh, Bran! You mustn't let them *make* you like this!"

Well, she was a fighter too; he'd put everything too strong, was all. He soothed her until it came time for love again, and afterward mentioned UET not once.

Next morning Bran was rousted out early and told to report, gear and all, to his new ship. "You're Third Officer. Your papers are aboard." So with little time to spare he got Salome Harkness wide enough awake to know who she was kissing goodbye, collected his belongings to go sit for his Third Officer's cheek tattoo, and rode a shuttle-route groundcar out to the hardened area where the big ships sat. As the car approached one of those great towers, he stared at it. The insigne read *Tamurlaine*.

And even from some distance, he could see that it was an armed ship.

7. The *Tamurlaine*

Climbing the ship's ramp, Tregare realized he was still in cadet uniform. So before the air lock guard challenged him, he thought out what to say. "Bran Tregare: just completed my cadet trip with Captain Korbeith on the *MacArthur*." On the face of the guard, a thirtyish First rating, initial supercilious expression changed to something like respect. "My assignment here as Third Officer came as a hurry-up. In fact Vice-admiral Kaner brought several of us groundside in his inspection lighter, ahead of our ship's landing." What else? "My papers are aboard, they tell me. You can call up to Control and make sure. And I suppose I can draw proper uniform when there's time for that."

When the guard's tough-looking face made a half-smile, he didn't look like a bad sort at all. "No need to call; you're on my list, sir. Your instructions are to go to Third's quarters and wait for the captain's summons. My advice, though, is to stop by Supply on your way and draw the uniform first thing. You're reporting early, and the captain's a bit of a stickler for the formalities."

"I see. Thanks."

"Nothing like your recent captain, though; if I've heard right about *him*, my sincere congratulations for being here at all. At least three out the lock, it's said, every trip."

This could be a plant. "It is? That's interesting."

"As you say, sir. Well, welcome aboard."

Although the *Tamurlaine*'s internal arrangements differed slightly from the *MacArthur*'s, Bran found Supply easily enough. The man and woman on duty there found garments that fit him without need of alteration. He changed cap, jacket and trousers on the spot; the rest of the gear was interchangeable. Then he went up to Third Officer's quarters, on the deck between the galley and Control.

The room was slightly larger than the one he'd shared with Salome Harkness but it held more amenities, and had its own bathing and sanitary facilities adjoining. Before leaving his groundside billet he'd had no chance to shower. Banking on the guard's guess about the timing, he did so now, and shaved. He wasn't yet growing much in the way of whiskers, so it seemed as well to keep his face bare of the immature fuzz. Just in the interests of his Third Officer image, that was.

Then he waited until the intercom made its announcing sound, and a voice said, "Third Officer Tregare?"

"Tregare here." Was this the captain? "Sir." Just in case.

"Captain Rigueres speaking. Is it convenient for you to join me in my digs now, and meet your fellow officers?" From the assured tone of voice, Bran decided it had damn well *better* be convenient.

"Right away, sir. Tregare out."

Bran had never seen inside Korbeith's "digs" but Peralta had dropped hints that they were furnished in rather sybaritic style. Captain Rigueres, it turned out, didn't indulge himself in such ways. The ample space was more bare than not, with only a few very good pieces of space-adapted furniture, and on the bulkheads three differing but harmonious pieces of art work; he had a seascape, a half-lit Earth as viewed from low orbit, and a forest scene on a planet that obviously was not Earth. Rigueres apparently liked what he liked, and the hell with quantity.

Shorter than Bran but blocky-wide, not fat, the man gave a handshake that stopped short of crunching. Under crinkly iron-grey hair and heavy straggling brows, his squarish face seemed set in a scowl. "Tregare, eh? Welcome aboard." Without the intercom's distortion, his voice was a rumbling growl, deeper even than Korbeith's, but with no rasp to it. "And wouldn't surprise me that you're glad to be here." Eyes don't really twinkle, but now Bran saw how the expression had come about. "Well, this isn't the *Mac*, but nonetheless I run a tight ship."

He stepped back, turned slightly sidewise, and gestured to the other two men in the room. "Your other two superior officers. Mr. Monteffial, my First—" An average-sized man, olive-skinned and dark-haired, made a wary, quiet grin as he moved to shake hands: firmly, no-nonsense, but no excess pressure.

"Leon Monteffial. My pleasure."

"Bran Tregare. And mine."

As they stepped back again, the captain said, "—and Mr. Farnsworth, my Second."

Tall Farnsworth's face went from blank indifference to almost enthusiastic welcome. As his left hand pushed his bushy fair hair back from a slightly sunburned forehead, his right hand shook Bran's in a clasp neither limp nor aggressive. "Welcome, I'm sure," he said. "Cleet Farnsworth."

Monteffial chuckled. "And that's two e's, Tregare," he said, "not cleat as in track shoes."

"Thanks; I'll remember," and then Bran noticed that Farnsworth didn't especially seem to care for the clarification. "And I appreciate your welcome, Mr. Farnsworth."

The man nodded. "Well, we're all on the same team, aren't we? Which reminds me—" He turned. "Captain, there's a First rating holding down the watch for me. I realize it's only groundside duty, but still—"

Rigueres nodded. "Of course, Mr. Farnsworth. Excused." And as the tall man, his skin pale where the sun hadn't pinkened him, left, the captain said, "Sorry to cut the socializing so short, but Farnsworth's right. I have some cargo manifests to check over. Mr. Monteffial, would you take over the courtesies by showing Mr. Tregare around the ship? Whatever he wishes to see?"

"Of course, sir." Monteffial gave a formal salute, so Bran did also. Then they departed the captain's digs. "Where to?" said Monteffial. "If you'd like, we could start with a drink, on me."

Tregare nodded. "Sounds good. Sorry I can't make the same offer, but the *MacArthur* kept cadets in dry mode, and groundside I had no time to stock up."

Monteffial paused at a door, opened it and ushered Bran inside. His place was less than that of Rigueres but more than Third's quarters. Which made sense. "Here we are. And not to worry. As Third you can draw on ship's stores, within reason, against pay. And you'll have your cadet pay on account, to start with." Bran realized no one had told him about his cadet pay, and he'd been too preoccupied to think about it. Mainly being scared. He said something amiable and noncommittal, as Monteffial asked him what he'd like to drink.

"Anything simple and not sweet. Beer, dry wine, bourbon..."

Nodding, the First said, "The latter, then. I had some old-fashioned sour mash once. This stuff imitates it almost perfectly." Whether or not, Bran found the flavor impressive.

"Cheers, definitely," he said. "And do I get the lecture now?"

"Lecture?" Monteffial smiled. "Orientation, yes. I knew you'd realize why we're here—one-on-one, as they say. All right. You want to know what this ship's like, and that's what the captain means me to tell you. You made it through and safely off the *Mac;* this one's nothing like that, praise peace!"

He stared under lowered brows. "As far as I know the skipper's spaced only one person in his whole career. Off this ship, but before I joined it. What happened was, a senior rating talked on a monitored comm line and Rigueres heard the recording."

"*That's* all?"

"The rating, identified because he initiated the call from his duty station, was trying to recruit cohorts for an attempt at mutiny and Escape. And on that subject, Captain Rigueres is death. Literally."

Tregare blinked. "Well, I can see—"

"Can you? Think of this. The Academy—and six years out of it I can say Academy without thinking Slaughterhouse first—it's an exercise in the harshest of conditioning, toward blind loyalty and obedience. But like all conditioning, the effects depend on what the conditionee brings to the process. On the captain it worked perfectly. On others, the opposite—they go into a trapped-rat syndrome and will chew their own leg off to try to get away." He shrugged. "Most of us—most fall short of complete acceptance but settle in, anyway. Do you understand?"

Bran wasn't at all sure he did, but he nodded. "Monteffial—"

"In private, make it Leon."

"Bran here. And how about Mr. Farnsworth?"

"Precisely. *Mister* Farnsworth. Until he tells you otherwise. Cleet's picky. He's only been out once, and new at Second. So—"

Bran waved a hand, just slightly. "Reminds me. What happened to your previous Third?"

"Our previous Second. That's what moved Cleet up. Well, nothing *happened* to her, except that she was overdue for a First, and when we landed there was a ship here with that berth open, so she moved to it." He shook his head. "You missed a good farewell party."

Now Leon frowned. "Back to orientation. Tregare—you've been out on only a short haul. You must not have had time to see your family on this quick stopover, and your next visit might be twenty years from now, Earth time. How do you feel about it?"

Bran felt his face go wooden; he thought fast. The truth should do—or, rather, part of it. "I didn't have much family living. What was left went off Earth. The message that was supposed to tell me where, somebody lost. So—"

Monteffial grimaced. "No way for you to find them, then?"

"Just keep going out, I guess. And maybe get lucky." *But if I do find them, they'll never know it.*

"Maybe you're lucky already. Let me tell you something...." And the way it went was that Leon Monteffial, fresh out of the Slaughterhouse except for his relatively brief cadet trip, had shipped out as Third on a ship that returned twenty Earth-years later, with him aging less than two. Family ties couldn't take the discrepancy; he was effectively orphaned and disowned. "Not because they wanted to, mind you. It's just—not everyone can deal with the Long View."

Bran signed agreement, to whatever the First meant. On the man's lean face a wry grin built.

"So I thought I'd take out some insurance, you see, against my next return. How, you ask?" But Bran didn't ask, so the other went on. "I looked for a very young nubile maiden to love and court, and I leveled with her that I'd be gone for years and come back younger than she, but meanwhile she'd have her allotment from my pay and I wasn't asking from her any such foolish thing as decades of chastity—but merely that she *be here* for me when I returned."

He sighed. "She thought it was all very romantic. We even married Oldstyle. I was in special training—my first trip out, I'd been only a rating at the start but moved up fast—so we had ourselves a great half a year before I went out again. But when I got back—"

Bran had to break the pause. "Yes?"

"I never found her. I didn't try. It was all clear in the records. I don't know how long it took her to decide to find somebody else, and I don't care. Or how long it took both of them to see their best course. But what they finally did was—there's still a law that seven years' absence equals a spouse's desertion."

"So after seven years—"

"You're not thinking, Tregare. Seven years, hell! Not until my ship was announced coming in soon. *Then* she divorced me, and gave up her monthly share of my pay." His laugh grated. "At least I didn't pick me a stupid one." Draining his glass, the man stood. "Time, I guess, to give you the grand tour of the ship. Whatever you'd like to familiarize yourself with."

Bran's glass was dry long since. "Yes, sir. Ready when you are."

Ships were all pretty much the same. Where the *Tamurlaine* differed from the *Mac*—and now Bran could think of Korbeith's command by that nickname—it closely resembled the now-gutted but once-armed *Caesar*, where Tregare had trained as a snotty.

The *Tam*'s (well, he wouldn't say that out loud) turrets were fully armed. As the First showed him the equipment in Turret Two, Bran saw that the projector was heavily insulated for as far forward as a gunner was likely to reach, even by accident. Farther ahead, the cooling fins were bare. But, as Monteffial said, "You'd have to reach hard to burn yourself. Unless you were a gorilla."

Dutifully, Bran chuckled. Then asked, "Are all the turrets set up with computer simulations? Practice runs . . . the way they did it back at the—oh hell!—the *Academy*?"

Monteffial's laugh burst out. "Takes a while, doesn't it? Well, not all; just Two and Six. That's not policy; it's only that when we got the conversion, the shops were short on circuitry."

"I see. But anybody can schedule sim practice, on free time?"

Monteffial looked at him. "Not *anybody*. You can. I can. Anybody authorized. But not just anybody."

"Oh, sure," Bran said. "That's what I meant." But he hadn't.

When the First Officer told him it was coming on time for chow, Bran took the word gratefully. Trudging upship and down in Monteffial's wake, he'd seen enough of the *Tamurlaine* to last him a time. The Drive area was no different than any other he'd seen. Control was, for the operating consoles differed from those of unarmed ships and were of a newer design than the *Caesar*'s. But two or three watches at those controls, Bran thought, and he'd have it straight, where everything was.

So it was with relief that he followed the First into the galley. Ratings and crew stood in line with trays, but Monteffial nudged Bran away toward the table where Captain Rigueres sat. Now he thought about it, Tregare recalled that Korbeith and his officers were served in place. It had been a long day. . . . So he followed, and sat between his leader and a woman he hadn't met.

Well, he should say hello. He turned to her and she turned to him. "Bran Tregare, new Third. Pleased to—"

"Airda Kroll. Call me Airedale." The round-faced woman, sandy curls tumbling down to her eyebrows and around her face, came close to fitting her nickname and had a wrestler's grip to her handshake. "First Engineer." Meaning she was counterpart, among the Engineering officers, to Monteffial in Control.

Enduring the hand clench with only defensive resistance, Bran said, "Pleasure to meet colleagues. I—"

Headshake. Until her head tipped back a little, her eyes were hidden; then they showed grey. "You follow illusion. There is no pleasure, only duty. But enjoy illusion while you can."

Bran's dinner was served. Confused and silent, he ate it.

Afterward, leaving the galley with the First Officer, Bran asked, "What shakes with *her*?"

"I have no idea. It's some religious sect."

"New? I never heard of anything like it."

"No." Monteffial paused, looked to Tregare. "It's something that happened a long time ago. She's been out a lot, and I think her special religion came and went, died on the vine while she was away. Maybe sixty years back. You see?"

"Yeah, I think I do. The Long View, you mean."

"Right. Anyway, she causes no trouble, and does her job."

"Sure." But *the Long View*. At Bran's nape, a chill came.

Before Tregare's first watch duty he got some sleep and had only hazy, residual nightmares. He was off-duty when the ship lifted, but like any conscientious junior officer he sat in at Control—to observe and learn. The *Tamurlaine* went up not quite like a real bat, but not exactly coasting either; Tregare watched his monitors and decided that Captain Rigueres knew how to fly a ship. Especially when he skimmed past Luna and set his course by making a sling turn that Bran himself would not have dared try, without computer verification. And how could Rigueres have had *time* to get that? Lifting off at a slant, and—

Well, sooner or later, Bran decided, he'd figure it all out.

The ship's routine came easily to him. The feel of it took longer. Rather soon it became clear that the captain's apparent joviality was a surface thing. His reports entered in the log were merciless on even the most minor errors. And although not a killer like Korbeith, Rigueres had a mind for unusual turns of punishment. As, the time a rating reported five minutes late for watch duty. His next turn, the man stood watch in full spacesuit, except for helmet and gloves. Besides the discomfort of it, the order meant that to report on time, the rating had to go to the equipment deck nearly an hour before his watch began—to be fitted into the suit, and then to plod upship wearing the heavy thing.

"And nearly as long afterward," Monteffial confided, "to get back downship and check the damned thing in."

They were having a drink together—Bran's treat and in his quarters. He answered, "So, two hours extra duty, and the whole of it miserable. Seems a little strong."

Leon shrugged. "It's authorized in Regs. Well, hell—so are the Butcher's killings. Not some of the finer touches he does, though, if I've heard right."

Bran liked the First, but still he wasn't going to put anything on record, just in case. "There's lots of rumors. I suppose some may have a little truth to them."

Monteffial gave his quick smile. "Cagey, aren't you? Well, that's good, Bran. I wouldn't feel safe drinking with someone who spilled everything he knew. The dogs, you see."

"Dogs? There aren't any dogs on a ship."

The other man laughed. "You *are* new. Which is why I can be sure *you're* not a Police dog. They don't come quite so young."

Frowning. Bran asked, "Committee Police, you mean? But—"

The First leaned forward. "Relax a minute. It's not a traitorous act to hate the guts of the Committee Police, unless they hear you do it. Because everybody does. My point is that on every ship there's probably a dog or two, pretending to be an ordinary rating and bugging everything he can manage. Or a she; there's Police bitches, too. And one problem we have here is that they scare hell out of the captain. He overreacts."

Bran was a point or two behind. "They bug the ship?"

"And Captain Rigueres keeps his comm-crew, which I expect you'll be heading before long, busy debugging it." Quick wave of hand. "Oh, it's all quite sublegal. The dogs aren't supposed to bug us. The captain isn't supposed to know they're doing it. But it's always legitimate to remove unauthorized electronics. Y'see?"

Tregare was catching up now. "He overreacts, you say?"

Nod. "He's tougher than need be because he's scared the dogs will catch him being not tough *enough*."

"Oh, shit." Bran looked at his wrist chrono. "Time for one more, Leon, before chow. Right?"

"Right."

In the galley, Bran found he'd drawn his turn at sitting honcho over at the cadets' table. Once before he'd had this duty, but then he knew none of the two dozen and simply ate first and asked questions over coffee. By this time he could put names to five or six of the two dozen faces, so he knew he'd have to talk more, want to or not. Under Korbeith on the *MacArthur*, certainly there'd been none of this fraternizing.

Being served at that table, waiting for it, would take longer than he wished, so Tregare simply formed up at the end of the cadets' line, picking up a tray, same as they did. He saw the captain, at the officers' table, give him a stare that was less than approving and jerk a thumb toward the head of the line. In return, Bran made what he hoped was a placating wave of hand, and patted his stomach. Still grim of face, Rigueres nodded.

Finally seated, his tray loaded with food not so good as the other officers were getting, Bran ate. He sat at the table's head, saying brief greetings to the cadets at either side of him, since it happened he did know both by name. To his left was Waxy (Waxwell) Marston, a skinny blond beanpole who seemed to ask good questions—so far, at least. And at his right sat a stocky little woman with dark brown stubbled hair: Laina Polder. Whether from fear or shyness, she had trouble speaking up. Now, feeling tense from what Monteffial had said, Bran hoped none of them would ask too much.

He got through the meal without having to say a great deal, but over coffee the questions flowed. Most of them had no good answers: "Sir, if you were going to settle on a colony planet, which would you choose?" He'd never been to one and hadn't seen the brochures, so he had no idea. He said so.

"What's it like, sir, to return to Earth out of your time?" So he explained that as yet he had not had that experience.

"What about the Escaped Ships and the Hidden Worlds?"

He turned and looked at that questioner. Looked hard. A chubby, teddy-bear type, either all innocence or working at it. What was his name? Oh, yes—Cameron. Henry Lane (Hank) Cameron. According to Leon Monteffial, much too young to be a Police dog. But maybe not. So Tregare said, "You mean, what do I think about those rumors? I don't. I have no knowledge whatsoever."

The teddy-bear shut up.

"Are you glad you came to space, sir? If you had it to do over, would you?" The soft voice, with husky undertones, came from Laina Polder, to Bran's right. The very harmlessness of the question somehow set him scowling at her; he saw her lower lip begin to tremble, shook his head, and saw that the gesture only made things worse for her. Keeping his voice low, then, best he could, he said, "I think I made my best choice, and I stand by it." She nodded, and the next questions came.

But through those exchanges, Polder's question stuck to him. For he'd been given no choice at all. Had he?

Tregare's guess had been right; after only a couple of weeks at watch duties, he had the somewhat unfamiliar controls down almost pat. On the comm-board, which included viewscreen and other monitor controls, his work was excellent enough to draw a logged compliment from Rigueres himself. That came after the captain, sitting in to observe Tregare's watch, asked for a four-way split picture on the main viewscreen: outside view of an approaching ship that would pass at rather near range, Control-to-Control voice-and-picture circuit for conversation while the proximity lasted, outside view of a group of cadets taking their first spacesuited hike around the *Tamurlaine*'s hull, and of course the normal "ahead" picture.

A lot of tricky coordination there, but Tregare brought it off nicely. At the time, Rigueres gave him not even a nod. But scanning the log, routine fashion, when he began his next watch, Bran found the commendation entered. Phrased in stuffy, understated language, to be sure—but better than a swift kick!

Not so good was that returning to his quarters after that watch, he found that someone had searched the place—and hadn't even bothered to try to hide the disarrangement of his things. The Police dogs? Probably. He had no idea what they could be looking for; certainly he had nothing to hide: no contraband, no incriminating letters or personal notes, no unauthorized weapons, nothing.

The incident's only result was in his own thinking: *UET is a shit trap and always will be. Whatever happens, don't forget that.*

Little, stocky Polder, Bran soon decided, had a crush on him. How he felt about it, he wasn't quite certain. She was a nice enough kid, and in the log her training reports weren't bad—she wasn't officer material but would probably wind up with a respectable rating. And Sally Harkness was a world ago, and Bran cared for celibacy hardly at all. But on this ship he wasn't too certain how these things were considered.

So, next chance he had, he invited Leon Monteffial to his quarters for a couple of pre-dinner drinks. Well, dinner for the First; on Bran's watch-sked it was a late night snack.

After the pouring and the ritual "Cheers," Tregare tried to think of a way to ask his question, and said, "There's this young woman, seems to like me. And I wondered—"

Monteffial's smile went wide. "Advice to the lovelorn? I thought better of you."

"No, not that." Bran shook his head. "That part I'll handle all right, win or lose. It's—it's the ship's customs, that I don't know. What's allowed and what isn't. I mean, how would *you* conduct yourself in this kind of situation?"

The First laughed. "If you don't know, my own discretion is working better than I'd thought." His expression sobered. "Well, the captain's not quite prudish, but very traditional. Without some kind of contract—Freestyle marriage at the least—I'd advise you not to move a roomie in. I haven't; my own young woman and I maintain our official separate quarters and make do with visiting. What with the changing watch skeds that ratings have to put up with, the arrangement's probably easier on both of us." He paused. "Does that answer your question?"

"I think so. Thanks. Next time I have a chance to talk with that cadet, I'll try to find out how serious she is about—"

Monteffial's hand gestured a stop. "Hold on there. Cadet? No, Tregare." He shook his head. "If you were a rating, yes. Or if she were. But officer and cadet? It's a—a sort of social barrier, you could say."

"But that's silly. A cadet's only one step away from *being* an officer." But then he realized that Polder wasn't.

As Leon answered, "You were. Some aren't."

And Bran nodded. "Yeah. I know. Well . . ."

"I'm not saying you couldn't play a little. Just keep it damned quiet, is all."

"No, I don't think so. And thanks for telling me." But for some reason he was depressed as *all* hell.

Monteffial was still talking. ". . . reasons aren't all bad. He took that with any great difference in rank, there's too much likelihood of coercion entering in. Such as—"

"You mean clout, Leon?"

"Yes, I guess that's it."

"I can't argue with that," said Bran Tregare. *Channery.*

From then on, the way Polder tagged him at each chance, big-eyed and hanging on his every word, seemed embarrassingly obvious. To Bran, Monteffial's good-natured grin seemed like a taunt. And chilly Farnsworth, one day at mess after Bran had—more or less gently—shooed Polder away, said, "Tregare, if you don't want trouble, you'd best chase that puppy bitch back to her kennel."

Because Bran had, after all, halfway encouraged Laina's earlier attentions, he found it hard to answer the Second's sneering comment. Finally he said, "Don't worry. There's no involvement. She's new, and a little starstruck, and I guess I'm the only officer who'd talk to her."

Giving a snort, Farnsworth said, "I should hope so! You won't find *me* slumming with cadets." He stood, and left. Looking after him, Bran wondered which would be doing the slumming.

But still, Tregare had a problem. He didn't want to hurt

the kid's feelings. But he did want her off his back. So he waited his chance for a private chat with Laina Polder.

That opportunity came when he drew spacewalk detail, bringing up the end of the life line while once again the cadet group donned suits and marched a long slanting oval around the *Tamurlaine*'s hull. This time he knew there'd be pauses for inspection of hullside gear; outside camera modules, antenna arrays, and so forth. So, with any luck, time for talking.

He didn't have to arrange anything; Polder herself made sure she was next ahead of him in line. Leaning to help check her suit closures, he spoke quietly. "First substantial inspection stop, we turn off our suit radios and touch helmets. Private talk; okay?"

"Oh, yes!" Her eyes widened, and he knew she'd taken his meaning wrong. *Damn all!*

The lead group entered the lock; it cycled and they went out. Bran's group, he trailing, followed. The lines were connected. Just like on the *Mac*, Bran thought, except that he wasn't Plastic Smile, out to kill a cadet. The slow, clomping walk began.

Polder was probably goggling at the velocity-distorted view of space. By now, Bran was used to it; he waited for a stop that would last long enough for him to speak his piece. The first—to view a cluster of viewscreen inputs—was too brief, and so was a pause to inspect turret-ranging antennas. But then the group reached the smaller, topside air lock.

Too bad Polder would have to miss the lecture, but there'd be other exposures to that. Bran made a switchoff sign to her. As he turned his own communicator off, he saw her make a nod.

Gently, not to give noisy impact, he touched his helmet to hers. "Polder? I have to tell you something."

"Yes. I know." Very faint, her voice. "And I will. Any time you want me. Just ask."

"*No*, dammit! I mean, that's what I need to say. Cadets and officers can't fraternize that way; the captain won't stand for it. So forget the idea." He heard her gulp breath, and said, "Cadet, on this ship you're walking a tightrope. So am I. Don't let's get them crossed and raise our risks. You understand?"

"I—I guess so. May I still—?" But the life line jerked at her, and then as she moved with it, at Tregare. He turned his radio on and motioned for her to do the same. The tour went on.

Back inside, everyone unsuiting, he saw her looking at him. Where her look fell—between reproach and resentment—he couldn't know. But when she spoke to him after that, the circumstances were always public and her address almost stiffly formal.

He hated it—and at the same time, felt somewhat relieved.

Next time Tregare walked the ship hullside, it was in a power suit. Monteffial was in the other one, the two linked by a lifeline and further safeguarded by remote-control magnetic anchors at the line's ends. Purpose of the excursion was visual inspection of Drive nodes (through nine-nines-dark filters) at the ship's stern, and projector turret muzzles at the bow—with a perfunctory check, between, of antenna systems.

The drill was a bit cumbersome, but not hard to get used to. Carry your front anchor, slide it out ahead along the hull at bare minimum magnetic attraction, then sock it solid. Back anchor line being taut, ease that anchor almost loose and slide it in. A monotonous routine, but not difficult.

Neither Bran nor Leon were carrying the heavy energy guns that plugged into the suits' power sources. For one thing, no need on this chore. And for another—"Well," Leon had said, "there's no point in allowing capability for damage to the ship." That remark took Bran a time to digest, but he did manage it.

Back inside later, he didn't bother to ask Monteffial about the correctness of his guess.

Pale Farnsworth, the Second, was a real pain in all the wrong places. He was snide, upstage, and maddeningly likely to be correct in his gripes. Bran tried to be friendly, and was snubbed. He tried total formality, and as long as he could stick to it, the ploy worked fairly well—but formality wasn't really Tregare's long suit. At one drink break in the First's digs, he asked about the problem.

Slumped, relaxed as usual, Monteffial shrugged. "Cleet's a perfectionist, that's all. By now he's accepted that I'm not perfect and never will be. Unfortunately, he still has hopes for you."

To the downfall of such hopes, Bran raised his glass.

* * *

Rigueres hadn't disclosed the *Tamurlaine*'s destination, but he did condescend to announce, twenty-four hours ahead, the time of Turnover—when the ship would cut Drive, go zero-gee, turn end-for-end, and begin decel for target. Bran was on watch at the time. The captain didn't come to Control, but made his statement over the intercom, all-ship broadcast. Better than nothing . . .

Bran could see no particular reason why Turnover should be preceded by a quick eyeball inspection of the entire ship, but that's what the captain wanted, so that's what he got. Since Bran was at the bottom of the officers' totem pole, he figured to be stuck with inspecting the cargo areas. But Rigueres broke the job into more than three parts, delegating two Chief Ratings to assist. The cargo duty fell to a thin, blond man named Gonnelson, whose outstanding characteristic was that except to answer a question, he seldom spoke.

Bran drew the bow section, everything upship from Control—which meant the projector turret rooms and the staging deck below them (with its small aux air lock). He decided to start at the top and work down.

As he expected, the turrets were in top shape, except that someone had left Number Two switched to the Test Simulations position. Not serious, unless a gunner needed to *use* the weapon in a hurry and forgot to check. Undecided, Bran finally shrugged and logged the minor violation. He hated to get anyone in trouble, but maybe the minor black mark would cause the negligent party to pull his or her socks up. It couldn't hurt.

He still didn't like being a snitch, but sometimes you had to.

The staging deck looked good too. He noticed a couple of pieces of reserve gear secured rather sloppily, logged the matter, and corrected it. All right; nothing left but to check the air lock, to see that nothing had been left to rattle around loose in there.

The local operating panel—like the main lock, this could also be managed from a console in Control—showed outer door closed, chamber pressure normal. As it all should be. So he thumbed the switch to open the inner hatch—and nothing happened.

Either he had a malfunction, or the Close switch down in Control had been thrown. Or else the inside switch was holding the hatch secured. He looked through the heavy plastic window. No light inside, but in the dim shadows, did he see movement? Again he tried for Open, this time punching the Override button. And the door opened, and the inside lights came on.

What the hell? One man lay on top of another, just like Channery and his victim. *"Get up!"* The first man came to his feet and began to arrange his clothes. He was small and compact, snub-nosed and dark-haired, a Second rating, a technician named Deverel.

The second man, tall and lanky, with thinning pale red hair above a high forehead, took longer about it. Quite calmly, he said, "So we're dead, Hain. Sooner or later, we knew it had to happen."

Not in negation but confusion, Tregare shook his head. "I thought—I couldn't see how such a small man could rape you. But—"

The bigger one made a one-sided smile. "No. It wasn't rape. We've been lovers for years. No point in hiding that now."

Before Tregare could think of what to say next, Deverel cut in. "Hadn't you better call up some troops, sir? After all, we're two to one here, and you're not armed." Tregare braced for combat, but the man said, "No. We won't try to space you. Want to know why?" Bewildered now, Bran nodded. "At the cost of an innocent man's life, ours wouldn't really be worth it." Deverel frowned. "You still don't see how it works, do you? Well, Anse and I knew our risk and chose to take it. You didn't. It's not your fault that you caught us—or that UET proscribed our natures as a capital offense. Besides, word is, you're a decent officer."

Tregare had to regain the initiative. "How about first things first? Names? Ratings? Assignments?"

"As opposed to assignations? Sorry, sir," Deverel said. "A little gallows humor, there. Yes—Hain Deverel, rating Second, electronics and servo gear."

"Anse Kenekke, rating Third. Drive technician. Dead man."

"Dammit!" Tregare said. "I can't—" He was going to say "—condone such behavior." But this wasn't like Channery's brutality. Was condoning or condemning any of his business? "I can't understand any of this, is all. To me it makes no sense. Another thing I can't see is why you two didn't go for officer training. You both score high on the proficiency lists."

"We were in it," said Kenekke. "We dropped out, so we'd have a chance to ship together. And for five years, we've done so."

"And even now, with UET about to kill us, it's *worth* it." With that, Deverel's defiant air evaporated. He stood slumped.

Looking at the two men, Tregare wavered. The business of their not threatening him hardly applied. Considering their respective grades of training, Bran was fairly sure he could have taken the both of them. But *they* didn't know that, and still . . .

Abruptly, he decided. But how to say it? He began, "I hope you're right that I'm a good officer on here. I intend to be. But what UET says and what I think, aren't always the same thing." Deverel tried to speak, but Tregare overrode him. "I may not understand you, but I don't see where you're harming the ship, or anyone in it. So I'm neither taking you in nor turning you in. I didn't see you. Got that straight? I didn't *see* you. So next time you get in a jam, if you do, don't make me out a liar." He paused. "And try to keep a little better track of what goes *on* in this ship. The captain announced this inspection hours ago."

He turned to leave, but Deverel said, "Sir? You say you don't always agree with UET. Do you mean—Escape, perhaps?"

Oh, no! A trap? "I mean no such thing. What I do mean—well, in your shoes I'd think seriously about jumping ship. The colonies, I hear, are more easygoing."

Then he did turn away and leave. What the two men said as he left might have been thanks, or maybe something else. He didn't care much.

Nor did he care what they did after he was gone.

8. Strains and Actions

Turnover came during Tregare's watch. Taking the seat he used when supervising, Captain Rigueres sat in to observe. When Bran, going by protocol, offered the job of turnover to the captain, Rigueres declined. *So the old devil trusts my skills.*

When the countdown clock was close to chiming, Tregare called down to Drive, to Chief Engineer Mallory. "Cut

Drive, Chief. Ready to turn ship—*now*!" He didn't know Mallory at all well, had been in conversation with him maybe twenty minutes of the entire trip, so far. The man was older than most officers on active duty, and his record was very good indeed. Now Mallory acknowledged; the Drive hummed down to near-silence, and weight diminished to nothing.

Bran set to swinging ship. One-eighty degrees, no more, no less. The way he did this was to energize, carefully varying the thrusts, two of the three smaller aux-Drive nodes that at the ship's rear end formed a hexagon with the three mighty nodes of the main Drive. The way Rigueres had programmed turnover, the *Tamurlaine* wasn't going to pivot directly over one of the aux nodes, either singly active or silent with the other two sharing equal loads. It was going to be two nodes loading differently, and Bran's job to figure the balance and avoid skew in the turning. And then make the complementary thrusts, to stop the rotation.

Well, same as back at the . . . Academy. He plugged in the sines and cosines, and it worked.

Somehow, the decel end of the trip seemed to go more quickly than the accel leg. In truth it *was* slightly shorter, because of the resistance of the interstellar gas, which impeded accel but helped decel. But some of the difference, Bran realized, was subjective to him. For one thing, he'd done his learning, most of it; now he knew more of how he stood, on here. And for another, shortly after turnover—just off-watch, in the galley, in fact—he'd arranged himself a liaison.

Well, the officers' table was vacant so he'd sat with the ratings. Not quite according to Regs, maybe, but not prohibited. And as he ate, Chief Rating Nadine Ling sat down beside him. He'd seen her around a lot but they'd seldom shared the watch duty. Now he gave her a good look.

She was small, slight, and cute as all hell. Unusually for a woman of Asian descent, she had her hair in short tight curls, almost an Afro. The overall result, he liked.

If you don't ask, you'll never know. So he said to her, "You have a little free time now? Like for a drink, maybe?"

For a moment, eyes narrowed, she gave him a stare. And then nodded. "I think I can find the time."

So, once done eating, they went to his quarters. The drinks had to wait a while, because he didn't even have to ask; she came to him and that was that. First, because it had been so long for him, he blew it too fast. Then he got the drinks poured, but things started happening again, so the ice melted. That time worked better, a lot better. And there was plenty more ice.

Sitting up then, while she tickled his chest with her cold, condensation-moistened glass, he said, "Why, Nadine?"

She knew what he meant, because she said, "I watch the people I work with. I like the way you handle things."

"And here? We'll be back here?"

Grinning, she got him with an ice cube. When the writhing was done, and then the laughing, she gave him a sober-faced look. "Damned right we will."

On Tweedle, one of the Twin Worlds that present the same faces always to each other and make their own quicker dance together, along with their more leisurely path around the primary—on Tweedle, then, the *Tamurlaine* hit groundside.

In a way, Tregare hated to see the trip end. He knew there'd be personnel transfers; either he'd be one of them or he wouldn't, and the same for Nadine Ling. The way it went, she left the ship and he didn't. At least they had a mutual off-watch shift for the farewell, and made the most of it.

About half the cadets were offshipped, too. Among them was Laina Polder. Tregare would have liked to say something nice to her in the line of good-bye, but didn't get the chance to do so.

Two days passed before Bran got any time groundside. He'd hoped to be able to share leave with Leon Monteffial. No soap, though. Rigueres allowed only one officer offship at a time. He himself, Bran noted, took only his fair share of leave time, if that. "He's not all bad," said Tregare to Monteffial, at watch-change.

Leon grinned. "Probably afraid that if he gets too far from the ship, we'd take off without him!"

At any rate, one day at about noon, local time, Bran stepped groundside for the first time. Groundside was hot under a sky somewhat darker than he expected. Atmosphere was lighter, something like Earth at about twenty-five hundred meters. On this day no breeze blew, and the planet's sun shone whiter than Earth's but spanned a smaller apparent radius.

A group of ratings was climbing aboard a shuttle groundcar. The port was several kilometers from Capitol City, which mostly filled a river-mouth valley. Bran brought up the tail of the group, not pushing rank, and took the first vacant seat he came to, beside a red-haired First rating he didn't recognize. Not bad looking, he thought, even with the bright hair skinned back to a tight coil at her nape.

She wouldn't look at him, though; her face went blank and she sat as far from him as possible. What in the worlds—? He turned to her. "Seems strange, all this time on the ship, but I don't seem to know you."

First she blushed, then went pale. "Sir? I—I was just transferred onto the *Tamurlaine*. Off the *Bonaparte*, with nearly two months' wait groundside in between."

She went silent, so Bran said, "I'm Bran Tregare, Third Officer. It's my first trip as brass. Came aboard at Earth, straight from my cadet trip. On the *MacArthur*, that was." He waited, and finally had to ask, "And you are—?"

"Uh—Phyls Dolan, rating First, navigation. But, sir . . ."

"Yes, Dolan?"

"Officers and ratings don't socialize."

He had to laugh, regardless that the sound turned others to look. "Well, sure, we have to pay *some* heed to rank. For instance, the galley has an officers' table. But if I come in and find it empty, I can join the ratings, for company." She looked shocked. "I guess the *Tamurlaine* isn't as stiffbacked as the *Bonaparte* must be." She seemed to relax a little, so he expanded on the theme. "Mind you, we couldn't move your gear into my quarters. The captain wouldn't like that. But I can invite you up for a drink, any time you like, and—"

Really pale, she went then. And biting her knuckles as she said, "Oh, sir! Please don't. *Please!* I mean, if you say so, but—"

"Hey, wait a minute!" He wanted to ease her anxiety, but knew he mustn't touch her, not at all. "You're reading me wrong, Dolan. I don't know how your text reads, but mine says not a damn thing about command performances. When I said a drink, that's what I meant." He paused. "Tell you what . . . once into town, I'll buy you a drink in the first good bar we sight. Give you a look at my drinking manner, firsthand."

"Yes, sir." The rest of the way, she sat looking down at her clasped hands, while Bran wondered why he was bothering.

* * *

The bar was mostly red plastic and dim lights. It could have been any one of like thousands, on Earth. Bran found them an alcove out of the main line of blast. The drinks list carried bourbon. Dolan surprised Bran by seconding his order. She also consented to clink glasses with him—"Cheers"—and seemed a little less tense now.

Too bad to spoil it, but Bran had questions. "Dolan? I want some straight answers. On your last ship, you didn't have the right to say no?"

Her headshake was frantic. "I mustn't say anything. I—"

"Cool down. You're not talking to UET now. You're talking to Bran Tregare, who sometimes knows when to keep his mouth shut. And I don't care about names—probably wouldn't recognize them anyway, and what're the odds on our meeting that ship again?" She still wasn't saying anything. Bran leaned forward. "All I want to know is, are you scared here because you think rank can take you any time, like it or not?" A faint nod. "Well then, Dolan, drink up and cheer up. Because that's just plain not the case. With other personnel, it might be—but our sonsabitches don't happen to be *that* kind of sonofabitch."

With the second round of drinks, Bran ordered a tray of snacks. The cheeses were pleasant, the meat tidbits were unfamiliar but tasty. Except for a purple jellied mass that smelled like pickled overshoe, the treat was a success. And Dolan seemed more relaxed than not.

So Tregare said, "Now we'll try something. I am going to proposition you. 'You want to?' You've just been propositioned." He saw her stiffening, and said quickly. "If you say yes, you have to buy me a drink. If you say no—well, I'm afraid you still have to buy me a drink. Because it's just about your *turn*."

It took maybe thirty seconds, but she laughed. So it was all right. Even though she never did answer the question.

Dolan's alcoholic capacity wasn't all that much. When Bran saw she probably shouldn't finish the drink she'd bought, he walked her outside and along the street to a shuttlecar stop. The walk helped. He decided it was safe to send her back to the ship by herself, and when the car came along, he did so. "You'll be okay?" he said, as she prepared to get in.

"Sure thing," she said. "Sir. And thanks."

"My pleasure." She got to her seat all right; as he watched, the car pulled away. Even if she went to sleep along the way, he thought, somebody would get her safely aboard the ship.

Restless now, he turned back along the street. He wanted no more drink just yet, but he was hungry. So he looked for a good medium-grade eating house. Nothing too specialized: he passed up a place that advertised "Highland Cuisine for the real Highlander." On the other hand, "The You Never Left Earth Restaurant And Boozerium" didn't take his fancy much, either; after all, what he'd tried of local stuff wasn't half bad.

The building he stopped to look at was a rambling shanty, much added-to. Its sign read "Ask For What You Want," and that seemed fair enough, so he went in. The high-beamed roof, with no ceiling below, made the interior cooler than outdoors had been. The decor was out of chaos by improvisation; Bran liked it.

Only about a third of the tables were occupied. Human instincts being what they are, those were the ones around the area's perimeter; the middle section sat empty. For no reason he could think of, Bran went to sit at the room's center.

Service was faster than he expected; a young woman, got up in an exotic fashion quite new to him, brought water and a menu. He was too busy looking at her to think of ordering a drink; as she walked away, he decided maybe that was just as well.

On the Tri-V, back on Earth, he'd seen some weird get-ups, but nothing like this woman's. Her breasts seemed to be compressed flat to her chest, but through two transparent plastic bubbles, oversized nipples showed. Her hair stood straight out in all directions, in spikes about four centimeters long, each sprayed or coated with more transparent plastic. Between her thighs, just below her short skirt swung a metal bell, that chimed softly as she walked—in short, precise steps, because two ankle bracelets were joined by a slim, gold-colored chain not more than forty centimeters in length. Bran shook his head: *strange*.

The menu made little sense to him. When the woman returned he asked "What's your own favorite meal here?" and ordered according to her answer, including a small bottle of native wine. And when the food came, he found it surprisingly good. No pickled overshoes, not even one.

He was having coffee, and one glass short of emptying the wine bottle, when nearby movement caught his attention. He looked up and saw Deverel and Kenekke about to pass his table. For a moment he paused, then stood and said, "Join me? Though I'm nearly done here, now." The place had filled up quite a bit, so his offer made sense any way you looked at it.

Kenekke looked at Deverel. The latter hesitated, then said, "Yes. Thanks, sir. I guess we're hitting the crowded time."

They sat. The two new arrivals took Bran's recommendation on the wine. Each studied a menu, then ordered items Bran had never heard of. "You're more adventurous than I am," he said. Their expressions tightened. "The food here, I mean." Both men nodded, and the conversation went from sparse to nonexistent.

Hell with it. Gently, Bran swirled the remaining wine in his glass. "I'm curious. Would you be taking my advice?"

Kenekke said, "Which part, sir?" Before Bran could answer, the strangely got-up woman brought the two dinners. Looking and scenting, Bran was rather glad he had not ordered either of them. But the two ratings, digging in, seemed to enjoy them well enough.

"I meant, are you being sensible enough to jump ship?" His only question, really, so he drained his glass and stood, waiting. But Deverel's hand caught his wrist, and the glass was full again.

"I don't think so, sir," the small man said. "If it's all the same with you. We've dodged risk, Anse and I, since second year at the Slaughterhouse. I don't think we're done yet, and this world doesn't tempt us much." Deverel's eyes narrowed. "Unless, of course, sir, you're *telling* us to get off."

Again Tregare sat. He shook his head. "No such thing. Advice, was all; I think you might be best off the *Tamurlaine*, for your own sakes."

"And if we don't agree?" Kenekke said it.

"Then I wish you luck." Bran stood, drank his glass dry, and set it firmly on the table, upside down.

And said, before walking away. "Remember one thing. I *still* didn't see you."

He went to three different bars for one drink at each, found nothing much to interest him in any way, and caught the shuttle car back to port. Upship in the galley, two ratings were drunk.

So was Second Officer Farnsworth, Bran was told, but he'd been put to bed.

So who cared?

The next time Monteffial relieved Bran at watch-change, the First said, "Would you fill in for the ramp guard a few minutes? He asked me, but I didn't want to be logged in late." Tregare knew what the man meant: put a perfectly good *reason* into the log, and captains and promotion boards read an *excuse*. ". . . on leave yesterday, ate the wrong thing, I guess. He's been running a lot. So if—"

"Sure. And if there's much of his watch left, maybe I can find someone to handle the rest of it." Then, not forgetting the formal stuff—because any rating on watch might be a Police dog—he saluted. "Relief acknowledged, First Officer." Monteffial said his part of it, and Bran left Control.

Down at the main air lock, the ramp guard certainly looked miserable enough. "Here, give me your order sheet," Bran said. "I'll hold your post down for awhile. No hurry." The man started to leave. "Whoops, there—I'll need that gunbelt," so the man unbuckled it, handed it over, and hobbled away. Bran hoped the fellow would reach a latrine without mishap.

The guard station was quiet enough, with no one approaching either to leave the ship or from below, to climb ramp and enter. Tregare took time to scan the order sheet. Not much to keep track of. The leave roster wasn't included, so all he had to do about personnel leaving or entering was check their passes and log their passage.

He'd buckled on the gunbelt without paying much heed to it. He noticed that it was too loose, so that the gun rode uncomfortably low on his hip. He adjusted the thing, then realized he hadn't checked the weapon itself, because it had been Monteffial who'd asked him to take this chore and he trusted the First. But what if the *illness* was faked, and the captain inspected him and he hadn't checked a faulty weapon? UET did love traps! So Tregare drew the gun—it was one of the smaller energy projectors, not a needler—and was relieved to find it fully charged. Still, being careful never hurt . . .

He looked back to the order sheet. Another group of cadets would be boarding today, but no exact time was given. Four this time, which would probably fill the ship's quota.

The ailing guard had been away for nearly a half hour, and

Bran was beginning to wish he'd asked the man how much longer his trick would last, when he saw the group approaching the ramp below. He waited as they were led upramp to the lock, noting only that two cadets were male and two female.

It wasn't until he scanned the assignment sheet that he realized one of the cadets was Kickem Bernardez.

Remembering Peralta on the *MacArthur,* Tregare restrained his first impulse. He saw Kickem about to blurt a greeting, and gave a slight, headshaking frown. He decided to improvise a new formality: greeting each cadet by name and with a handshake. "Cadet Higgins. I'm Bran Tregare, Third Officer. Welcome aboard." And so on. Kickem was third in line. To him, Bran added, "Bernardez? I'd like you to report to my quarters at eighteen hundred hours, your other duties permitting."

Kickem's "Yes, sir" came in a voice as cold as his stare.

A few minutes later the guard returned. "Sorry, sir. I ran up to the medic station and got a pill. I think I'll be all right now—and I'll never eat *that* stuff again." He took the gunbelt, loosened it to fit him, and buckled it. "And thanks a whole great lot, sir. You saved my life!"

"Glad to help . . . Pritchard, isn't it? Well, maybe someday you can do *me* a favor. Or pass it along to somebody else." They exchanged salutes, and Bran went upship. A quick thought came to him. He detoured by way of the ship's Stores and drew a bottle of a liquor he didn't have on hand in quarters.

After a shower and his "evening" meal, he returned to his digs and waited. Almost on the dot of eighteen hundred, the knock came. He opened the door to admit Kickem Bernardez.

Ramrod straight, the cadet snapped a salute. "Cadet Bernardez reporting as ordered, sir. Since this is the way it seems to be, now that some of us have advanced above others."

For a moment, Tregare couldn't talk for spluttering. "Admirable, cadet. That's exactly the way it is in public. But right now, Kickem, we're not in public. For instance, I remember a business with some Irish whisky a long time ago."

"You'd be saying—"

"Well, I got a bottle of the stuff from Stores today. How'd

you like to get down off your high horse, Kickem, and have some?"

And then they were whooping and pounding each other on the back.

"It was Peralta who showed me. He came on as Third, on the *Mac*. Anybody around except trusted friends, keep it formal. But—"

Kickem sampled his second drink. "Well, I *thought* that to be the case, Tregare, but was not wholly certain. and then to needle you a bit, in the bargain, was more than I could find it in me to resist."

So they traded stories. Hearing of Korbeith, Bernardez went sober-faced and shook his head. His first ship had been a strict one, sure enough, "—but nothing like the Butcher, was Captain Pemberton. A mercy you survived, Bran."

"Don't I know it! Now then . . . this is only your second run . . . Am I right?" True enough; at the end of this one, Kickem hoped to be posted somewhere as Third Officer.

"Except now it is that I'll be loath to move along, Bran. For wouldn't it be a marvel, were we to be shipping together when—" He paused. "But it may be I shouldn't ask of that."

Bran knew what he meant. *Escape!* He spoke carefully. "So far, I wouldn't have an answer for you. Nobody's said."

In no hurry, they finished the bottle. Flushed and cheerful but still in good control, Kickem left in time to get some sleep before his first watch period. Alone, Bran considered the question his friend had posed. Were Escape plans afoot on the *Tamurlaine*? Well, sure. The real question was who was in on them, and how many, and how far along? Which meant . . . what would the chances be?

Monteffial had *almost* dropped solid hints—that is, he'd dropped some but they weren't very solid. Farnsworth wouldn't tell you the time of day off your own chronometer. The ratings always gossiped, but how much of substance their talk held, Bran had no way or judging. He was still too new on this ship.

But for now, the hell with it. He could use some sleep, too.

Two days later, as scheduled, the *Tamurlaine* lifted off. Monteffial did the honors. When Farnsworth took the watch an hour later, the First caught up with Tregare in the galley, "Hey, there, Third!" He clapped a hand to Bran's shoulder.

Bran, seated, looked up. "Yes, sir?"

"Would you like to help celebrate my lift-off? A small party, but invite a guest or two if you like—people who can spare an hour or two, maybe three, starting at fifteen hundred. Compatible persons, you understand. Plus your own date, if you have one."

Leon had already had a couple of drinks, maybe more. No doubt of that. Bran thought, then said, "I don't know about a date. Since Nadine was transferred off, I haven't—" He cleared his throat. "Well, if I run into someone to ask. But one thing, sir. There's a fella came aboard not long ago, we were friends at the Slaughterhouse. He was a year my junior there. And—"

Monteffial frowned. "So what's the problem? Invite him."

"It's only that for this trip, he's still in cadet status."

Wave of hand. "Bring him along. What's his name, by the way?"

"Bernardez, Kick—I mean, Cecil Bernardez."

Monteffial laughed. "Oh, that one. I've noticed him. Glib tongue hiding a good brain is my guess. Yes, bring him."

So when Tregare went to quarters he got on the intercom to Kickem. The cadet's roommate answered, and Tregare said, "Is Bernardez here, and awake or due to be awake soon?" He was, and came onto the circuit. Bran gave it the formal treatment: cadet Bernardez, and please report suitably dressed, and so forth.

So at the proper hour, after a couple of drinks in private, Tregare and Bernardez arrived at Monteffial's party. Knowing how these things went, Bran took along a couple of bottles to contribute. Kickem, being a cadet, couldn't obtain any.

The two new arrivals made it seven men and four women attending. Nobody was drunk, nor totally sober either. Leon Monteffial was dancing with a tall brunette First rating. The others, sitting or standing, drank and ate and talked. After looking embarrassed for a few minutes, Kickem got into an amiable argument with the Second Engineer. With an arm around her, he looked well enough at ease.

Bran, though, felt edgy. He joined in conversations but didn't stay with them long. Finally he decided he didn't like being there solo, so he left and went down to the galley. Inside he saw no one he really wanted to escort to Monteffial's celebration, so he turned to leave. And met, coming in, rating-First Phyls Dolan. The redhead still had her hair skinned back tightly to a coil. She always seemed to do that.

As she moved to pass him, Bran took her arm. "Dolan? How'd you like to be my guest at a high-class party? It's the First Officer's, to celebrate his lift-off."

She began to shake her head. "Oh, no, sir, I—"

Softly but with emphasis, Tregare said, "Don't misunderstand, Dolan. This is a *nice* party. It may get a little loud, I wouldn't be surprised, but perfectly respectable, all the way."

"But I haven't eaten yet."

"The First has laid on a fine spread. Come on." For a moment she still pulled away; then she looked at him eye-to-eye and finally nodded.

In a group, Dolan was more fun. When other ratings whooped greetings to her, she smiled and waved back. She ate with enthusiasm, drank moderately, and danced with a lot more skill that Bran Tregare could muster. He tried, though.

As he had predicted to Dolan, the group did get steadily louder. Nothing raucous, no ill-feeling, just louder talk and the occasional burst of song. Yes, it was "getting a little drunk, out." Not Bran, though. Back at the Slaughterhouse he'd learned to pace his drinks, to get level and stay there, and now he did just that. Here and there he heard talk that sounded decidedly indiscreet; he hoped no dogs were present, or for that matter, bugs.

As he and Phyls Dolan finished a dance, her coiled hair beginning to sag loose and she trying to push it back into place, their host called to him. "Tregare? Over here."

Patting Dolan's hand, Bran said, "I'll be right back," and went to Monteffial. The First had a load, all right; he stood with one hand braced on a chair back. "Tregare? Gotta close down. Question first, though. In here." He moved, and Bran followed, to the side-cubby that held the bed. It wasn't closed off, exactly, but the alcove gave privacy for talk.

As Monteffial plunked down, heavily, to sit on the bed, Tregare asked, "Questions? At this time of the party?"

A nod. "Just one. Escape. How you feel about it?"

"That's not a good question to ask, out loud. Is it?"

"So don't answer now. Think about it, though. Because when it gets asked big, no *time* to think. Unnerstan'?"

"Maybe. And maybe thanks, too." Monteffial was leaning back, close to falling asleep. Bran said, "You need any help?"

Eyes half closed, the First murmured, "Send her in here. Lady with me, you know. Close the party down first. Her, I mean. She'll do it. Just tell her, all right?"

"Sure. Right away. And thanks for the party, Leon."

He went back to the main group. Already it had thinned out some. The tall, dark-haired First rating—the one Bran figured to be with Monteffial—sat alone. He went over to her. "Leon asked you to close the party down. Then he'd like to see you."

She chuckled. "I hope he's still awake to do that."

"If you hurry it up, he will be." He gave her a wink for her smile and turned to find Phyls Dolan. The task wasn't hard; he heard a squeal and there she was, brushing liquid off her blouse. He went to her. "Everything all right?"

Someone else was brushing at her also, trying to apologize. Dolan said, "Never mind, Jennings. I bumped into you as much as you bumped into me." The other moved away, and Tregare guessed he knew what happened.

He said to her, "The First wants the party cleared now. I expect we ought to set a good example. All right?"

She shrugged; her hair sagged farther. "I suppose so. I did want one more drink, but Jennings and I collided, so—well, if the party's closing, I can do without."

"Maybe, maybe not." One hand gentle at her arm, he moved them through the latestayers toward the door. Out in the corridor, he said, "I offered you a drink once. The offer's still good."

For a moment she froze in place, then moved again, the two of them out of step now. "*Just* a drink, you said, though." He nodded, and she caught step with him. "All right."

Down the hall; then at the door he reached in to put the lights on and let her enter ahead of him. "Small place, isn't it?" he said, and started over toward his minimal bar setup to mix her the drink. Her hand grasped his shoulder; he turned to face her. She was shaking her hair lose; the tumbled reddish mass fell to hang nearly at her waistline. Her face held no expression at all, as she moved, facing him but not quite touching.

Throat tight, he said, "Look, I told you. You can have the drink, Dolan. You don't have to do *anything*."

"I know." Now she smiled. "Maybe that's why I want to."

* * *

It was, for Tregare, a great trip, the short haul from Tweedle over to its twin Twaddle, to pick up cargo. And then another relatively brief jump to Penfoyle Gate. As Tregare had told Phyls Dolan at their first meeting, they couldn't move in together on a ship commanded by Rigueres, but sure as hell they could enjoy time together, whenever neither was on watch duty.

It wasn't that Bran let the joys of friendly love get in the way of his shipside training—nor did Phyls Dolan. Merely, they made the most of what spare time the ship's schedules allowed them. And on the *Tamurlaine*, if you kept your official nose clean, you had some unofficial leeway. And certainly no Butcher Korbeith to give you nightmares.

As the grapevine linked her with Tregare, Dolan seemed to change a lot in a hurry. She dropped her anxious, defensive stance, obviously more at ease. She styled her hair in varied, less severe ways. When Bran complimented her, she said, "Maybe you're good for me, Tregare."

He knew what it was. He was Third Officer, and now Dolan was under his protection. No matter—he liked the result.

Among the cadets, Kickem Bernardez rated well, ranking usually in the top three. The exceptions came when Farnsworth did the scoring. As Kickem said to Bran once, "The Second—somehow I've got me on the wrong side of that cold man. Ah, well—not even the genius of Bernardez can charm everyone."

Bran was tempted to up his own scoring of his friend's skills in compensation, but decided against it. Once you start making allowances, where do you stop? So he kept his reports totally factual to the best of his judgment.

Any time he couldn't meet Dolan after a watch trick, Tregare spent some time training on sims. The second backup pilot position was hooked up to simulate various maneuvers, including takeoffs and landings. After one watch, Bran ran landings for nearly an hour. The computer threw him different situations; what he had to do was *adapt* to them. Such as gusting typhoon winds that shifted suddenly: that one, Tregare knew, was a real case, recorded at Hardnose. He hadn't run it before, and now he fought the simulated tiltings and drifts, and brought the imaged ship to ground—safe, but just barely so.

A voice behind him, not quite recognizable through his muffling headset, said, "Did that landing satisfy you?"

As he peeled the set off, Bran said, "Hell, no. Theoretically I made it, but I'm glad that was a sim, not real. Because I'm not sure I know enough, yet, to handle it."

"You think you're up to handling Penfoyle Gate?"

Before he answered, Tregare turned to see who was asking. It was Captain Rigueres, and the word for his grin, then, was mean.

Bran thought, then said, "Unless there's something tricky about it, sir, that isn't in the scoopsheets, I think I am."

"You are so assigned, Third Officer. Any necessary change of watch schedules, I'll arrange immediately." Tregare felt questions in him that he couldn't get into words; Rigueres answered them anyway. "Either you can or you can't; we have to find out. I'll be on the aux board, and if you're blowing it I'll cut you out and take over. And find me a new Third." Still shark-grinning, the captain turned and left.

For a while, Bran sat. Well, now it was on the line; for sure. Should he practice some more. No, dammit! He'd done that; now either he knew it or he didn't. Thoughts swirling, he went to his quarters. He could have used some company—Dolan, Kickem, maybe Leon—but one of those had the watch and the other two would be asleep now. Too tired to hit the galley, he had a snack from his goodies stash and lay much too long before he finally achieved sleep himself.

Three ship's days until the landing, and upshifting his watch trick by eight hours didn't help. Mainly, Bran stewed. Only once could he and Dolan get together to any purpose, and he was too jittery; he could perform but not complete it. He had no appetite. He forced himself to eat, but not much, after one full meal that didn't stay down. He wondered: would it have been easier if he hadn't known ahead of time, if Rigueres had simply called him to the job at the last minute? It didn't matter; he was stuck with what *was*.

So when the time came he went to Control with all his guts knotted into a lump just below his throat—or so it felt.

And the damned landing went off like clockwork. Not a glitch, not one. "Quite adequate, Third Officer," said Rigueres.

* * *

Penfoyle Gate. Discovered, naturally, by a Captain Penfoyle. The Gate part came from the planet's location, which made it a good refueling station on several runs between colony worlds.

The planet itself was only marginally habitable; located anywhere else, it would have been ignored. The temperature was chilly, sunlight red and dim. Air barely tolerable: thin and dry and impure. Take three steps and pant, take another and cough. Once Bran and Phyls Dolan reached the first group of buildings, covered by an airdome, they learned they could rent respirators. But new visitors to the Gate had to run the atmospheric gauntlet once, first. In a way, Tregare could see the point of it.

He and Dolan found a bar that served snacks, and were sipping drinks in wait of food when Bran said, "Sure, Phyls. They have to live with it all the time, here. So they want to make damn sure we know how bad it is, so's we respect them for it."

One copper-colored eyebrow she raised. "And do you?"

"I think so, yes." Pausing, he said, "Except, if I lived here I imagine I'd be working on a way to get the hell out."

"Tregare," said Dolan, "somehow I'm not all that surprised."

Two days later, after the one brief visit groundside, Tregare's watch trick saw the windup of cargo offload and onload. Tired after a lot of cross-checking and correction of mistakes, Bran went to quarters and took a relaxing hot-water soak. As he came out, drying himself, at the door he heard a knock. He wrapped the towel around his waist and opened the door.

Kickem was there, bottle in one hand and sobriety a bit aft. "Tregare! News of Bernardez, and brought by none other than himself!"

What the—? "Get *in* here."

Laughing Bernardez entered. "Oh, 'tis all right, Tregare. You speak no longer to cadet Bernardez, but to the newly designated Third Officer of that illustrious name. I'm posted to the *J. E. Hoover*, Mister Tregare, sir and friend. Due to shove out in a few days, the exact number of which eludes me just now."

Tipping up his bottle, Kickem took a swallow, then handed it over. "Join me?" So although Bran didn't much care for tequila, he took a swig anyway. Bernardez said, "My shared room wouldn't hold so much as a bridge game. Tregare, would you host, here, my farewells?"

Bran hugged his friend. "Hell, yes, Kickem. Say who you want, and I'll get on the holler box for you."

The party was just the right size—almost too big but not quite. Leon Monteffial brought his tall brunette lady—by now, Tregare knew her name: Erdis Blaine. Kickem came with four other cadets: one male, three female. Bran got Phyls Dolan on the intercom and she managed to swap watch shifts with one of her counterparts; jumping shifts did beat the hell out of you, but that was no excuse for missing a good party. Farnsworth brought a woman from groundside; neither of them said much to anyone else, but at least he wasn't finding fault all the time. There were some other people that Bran knew fairly well, or somewhat, and some he knew hardly at all. Well, with over a hundred people on three shifts, that's the way it went. And the party, he thought, went better than not.

Even though it had to break up at a time when he and Dolan couldn't possibly enjoy each other before her next watch sked.

At main air lock next day, Bran saw Kickem Bernardez off the ship. "Best luck. And we'll be seeing each other."

Bernardez nodded. "I purely hope so. Good landings, Tregare." Seeing Kickem walk away, Bran knew how much he would miss him.

On Tregare's next watch trick in Control, toward the end of it he heard raised voices from one of the auxiliary positions, but couldn't make out any of the words of it. None of his business, likely, so when Farnsworth relieved him, Bran went down to the galley and had some soup and coffee. He was nearly done with all of it when Monteffial, carrying a cup of coffee, came and sat beside him. Scowling, and saying, "Oh, total rotten *shit*!"

Tregare looked at him. "Something *bad*, wrong now?"

The First looked back to Bran, then shook his head. "Max worst, I think." The coffee was good, but a sip didn't seem to help.

Bran hesitated; what *was* this? Then he said, "You want to tell it? Or not?" Because, don't push too hard. . . .

Leon Monteffial wrenched his shoulders through a tension-popping shrug that had to be painful. "Trouble just boarded, Bran. We have us a Major Bluten and two goons with him. Committee Police, the whole shit-eating lot!"

"But what can they do on a *ship*?"

Then Monteffial told Tregare what they could probably do. "They spy, they snoop; they get all the reports from their undercover Police dogs and bitches. They note down everything anyone says, that they could possibly consider incriminating. And at our next stop, which you can bet your ass will have a sizable Police garrison, their troops board us and arrest people."

Bran shook his head. "I hadn't heard of this before."

"I have. It happened on the *Leamington* a time ago. Two of my best friends were hauled off in cuffs and Welfared." Monteffial swallowed coffee and made a face.

To distract his friend—because Leon looked close to blowing wide open—Tregare said, "Bluten's an odd name. What origin, d'you suppose?"

Monteffial snorted. "It won't be his real one. 'Blut' means blood, in German. And that tells me something."

"Yeah? What?"

"The sonofabitch probably thinks he has a sense of humor."

It wasn't until his next meal that Tregare saw the Police group. Major Bluten was a slim, ruddy man of medium height. From the thighs up he didn't look all that slim, for he and both his followers, one male and one female, wore protective garb—bulky tunics that were armored against needle guns and insulated to withstand a certain amount of energy fire. The red-and-blue helmets, which looked like ordinary plastic but weren't, they carried slung at their belts, along with their weapons—Bluten wore the medium-heavy one-handed energy projector while the other two made do with needlers.

Just inside the galley entrance, the major stopped to speak with his troops. The man was short and bulky, the woman taller but equally large of frame. Both had heavy features under stubble haircuts. They might have been siblings, or cousins.

Nodding at Bluten's words, the two went to fill trays and then moved to sit at the senior-ratings' table, where no one greeted them or looked directly at them. The major himself came to the officers' table. It wasn't at all filled; Bran sat across from Chief Engineer Mallory and beside Second Officer Farnsworth. The Second Engineer was there, too—and as usual, not saying much.

Having seen how the ratings reacted to Police, Bran waited to see how his own colleagues would respond. As Bluten sat, Mallory gave him one quick look, said, "Major," nodded, and looked down to his food again. So Bran did the same, and the other two followed suit. A mess attendant brought Bluten's dinner, did not make the usual queries about beverages or dessert, and left. Everyone kept eating. Nobody spoke.

After a time, Major Bluten set his fork down loudly enough that it had to be on purpose. Side-glances showed Bran that no one was admitting having noticed, so he didn't either.

Bluten cleared his throat. "I want your attention and I will have it. Look at me." All right. Bran did so, keeping his face as expressionless as he could manage. "That's better. Now let's understand each other, right from the start. I am on a routine surveillance mission, not a witch hunt. If our HQ thought this ship had any special problems I'd have brought at least a full squad aboard with me, not a mere two aides. We allow for a certain bias by your branch of the service, against mine, but I sincerely advise you not to push it too hard."

He's been leaning forward, tensed. Now he eased back. "Any questions?" Silence. "All right. You had your chance."

Appetite somehow gone, Bran finished his meal anyway. He'd be damned if he'd let the bastard know he'd scored, any!

When Tregare got to his quarters, having taken an hour of sim training in Control, he found all his gear out in the corridor. *Now* what? *Damn!* He keyed the door open and swung it wide, to see a naked Cleet Farnsworth in the act of disengaging from an equally nude woman—the one Farnsworth had brought in earlier from groundside.

"I'm sorry," Bran said. "Didn't know you were in here." But—"Come to that, Second Officer, why the hell *are* you?"

Showing no embarrassment, Farnsworth headed for the bathroom cubicle. "Tell you in a minute." The woman followed him and shut that door; Bran was left standing, looking at his room filled with Farnsworth's belongings. *What the hell?*

After a time Farnsworth emerged, took the woman's clothes into the other room, came back out, and dressed without hurry. "The major's equivalent rank is just behind the captain," he said. "So he bumped the First. Who bumped me. And I've bumped *you*."

Sure. RHIP. "Yeah. I see it. But who do *I* bump?"

Farnsworth, shirt half on, shrugged. "You don't have to. Down on the next deck there's at least two Chief rating rooms empty. Pick the one you like." He sniggered. "Just be glad, you and your redhead, you won't be stuck with a roommate."

Why did Farnsworth make himself so impossible to like? Never mind; Bran made a lukewarm reprise of his apology for intruding, and went out to haul his stuff one deck downship. Of the two vacant Chiefs' rooms he picked the smaller, because it had been cleaned more recently.

When Tregare went to Control to observe lift-off, he looked for a seat near enough to follow the pilot's moves on monitor instruments. Before he found one, Captain Rigueres called to him. "Sit over here, Third. Beside me. Let's see if you can take the ship up."

All Bran's nerves flashed fire. He stood frozen. Well, he'd wondered if no notice would be better than prolonged anxiety. Now he decided there wasn't all that much difference. Numbly he moved and sat beside Rigueres. "Thank you, sir." Without thought he began his pre-lift checkoff list, feeling nothing more than if the occasion had been merely another sim.

When the count hit sixty, he turned and asked, "Sir? How fast a lift would you prefer? Gentle, or more vigorous?"

Squinting, Rigueres gave his shark grin. "I had in mind to leave you the choice. Now that you ask, though—let's make a real exercise out of it. Consider that our survival depends on getting us upstairs at max—except, Tregare, stay one notch below *real* redline, for your max. And—" A moment's pause. "I want some evasive action, soon as you have a bit of speed up; two dodging moves, and then back on course. Understand?" Not waiting for answer, the captain shouted, "Get *on* it, man! Your count is three."

Two, one—*lift*. Evasive action, the man wanted? Bran tilted the ship at first movement, let it skitter sidewise across the empty side of the port as the *Tamurlaine* built thrust, blowing gouts of dust and melt as the Drive nodes beat at soil and paving. Then the Drive took full hold; the gees hit, and the ship accelerated faster than Bran would have imagined.

His funny stuff at lift wouldn't count. Tregare threw a side-vector, angled off course and took two separate corrections to bring the *Tamurlaine* back to its programmed route. He checked his figures against the computer's expectations for an average lift, and said, "Lift-off complete, sir. On course, forty seconds uptime from sked. Continue as ordered?"

Until Tregare looked over to him, Rigueres said nothing. Then he said, "Not bad, Third. But I don't recall asking you to sweep the field on your way out."

"Sorry, sir. Just wanted to see if I could do it."

The captain nodded. "I see. Well, you did. You get a commendation—and two days' house arrest, for not asking first."

Well, you can't win 'em all. . . .

Rigueres hadn't specified solitary confinement, so during Bran's two days of restriction, Phyls Dolan took the chance of bringing him his meals and staying to visit. Tregare enjoyed the visiting, but not the news Dolan brought. "That Bluten, the Policebastard—he and his two enforcers are scheduling everyone for interviews. It scares me."

"You haven't been called in yet? Who has?"

She told him, and there didn't seem to be much pattern to it. Monteffial hadn't been tagged, but Farnsworth had. Mallory had been in, but none of his junior Engineering officers. Of the ratings, and unrated crew, Bluten's selections appeared random.

"Any leakback?" Bran asked. "Anybody have an idea what they're after?"

She shook her head. "Not a peep, Bran."

He pulled her to him. "Then the hell with it, for now. Tomorrow I'm back on duty. Time enough to worry, then."

But after Dolan had left, and six hours before Bran's house arrest was supposed to end, Bluten called him by intercom. "Tregare? We have an appointment. In First's quarters, as I assume you know. In one hour."

Watch this vulture! "I'm afraid there's a mistake, major. Any appointment I keep at that time will have to be here. I'm still under house arrest—as I assume *you* know."

"Don't hand me that space cadet stuff. This is a direct order, not an invitation to tea. Are you going to be here?"

"Not without the captain's permission, I'm not. Or rather—"

overriding Bluten's angry voice, "I'll report to you when the captain okays it to me directly, or in six hours. Whichever comes first. Will that be satisfactory?"

Without answering, Bluten cut the circuit. Bran thought fast. If the major griped to Rigueres, the odds against a straight story ran to a lot of zeroes. He checked the time; the captain would likely be in Control now. He punched for the comm officer and asked to speak with Rigueres. For a moment he heard the captain saying, "Just a moment, major. I'll get right back to you." Then, to Tregare, "Yes?"

Bran told it fast and kept it factual, putting in no personal opinion until the end: ". . . seemed to irritate the major. So I thought I'd ask your permission, sir, to meet his schedule. I would add the out-of-quarters time to my period of house arrest, of course."

He was almost sure he heard Rigueres suppress a chuckle. "You needn't do that, Third. Permission granted. I'll tell Major Bluten to expect you, right on time."

"Thank you, sir." *So now I can stick my neck in the noose.*

The Policebitch opened the door to him. Of the two goons, Tregare decided, she looked to be the meaner. Not that there was much choice between them. Bluten sat behind a desk. Looking up only briefly, he pawed for a folder and opened it, then again looked at Bran. "A right smart ass, aren't we, Third? Got to the Old Man first, with a slanted story, eh? Well, well . . ."

"I told the captain our problem and asked his permission to keep this appointment. He granted it. That's all." Bluten hadn't offered him a seat, but he sat anyway in the chair facing across the desk. *Take charge a little. Not too much . . .* The man glared, but made no comment.

Leafing through the paper, Bluten stopped at one. "Bran Tregare." He read off the biographical data as fabricated by Hawkman for the Academy, and the gist of the records from then on. "Substantially correct?"

"No errors, major, that I can detect."

"Punishment twice . . . in the special cell. That's odd. Once does it, for most. Explain?"

"No excuses, major. I made mistakes. That's the size of it."

"Error-prone cadets seldom finish a trip with Arger Korbeith."

"Maybe by that time, major, the lesson stuck."

"Maybe." Bluten shoved the folder aside. Elbows on the

desk, hands clasped, he leaned forward. "All right—who else is in on the Escape plot? If you give me a full list, I can save you."

If anything saved Tregare then, it was the total idiocy of the whole thing. Without intent or control he burst into helpless laughter. He saw Major Bluten's face turn red, but it only made him howl the louder. He tried to stop, but couldn't. Bluten shouted; it didn't help. Finally the major sat back, scowling up a storm, and waited for the paroxysm to run down. Then, still fighting the occasional fit of giggles—and inwardly appalled at himself, for peace knew *what* this maniac would do now—Bran said, "I—major, I'm sorry. It's just that—" Giggle fit. "—that I'm on my third hop with this ship, and I've yet to hear a *hint* of conspiracy." He wiped his eyes; his laughter had them streaming tears. "Peace be witness, major; that's truth."

And it very nearly was, too. At least, the vague bits he *had* heard were so far from the major's ideas that—well, that the pompous accusation had kicked him offbase. Giggle.

Stern-faced, the major tried a new tack. "What drugs do you happen to be on, just now? Oh, I can tell; you spacers can't fool me. Don't be afraid to admit it; we have treatment programs, and—"

Tregare suppressed a resurgence of the laughing. This part wasn't as dumb as it might sound; there *were* some exotic offworld drugs making the rounds of UET's ships, and Bran had heard of several though he hadn't yet been offered any. But what to say, now?

He shook his head. "No. Nothing, unless you count a drink now and then." Bluten looked skeptical; Bran said, "A blood test would verify what I say. If you like, I'll volunteer for one."

The major stared, glowered, and finally shook his head. "No. You're not smart enough to try a bluff, so you're clean." *Just keep thinking that! It might come in handy.*

There were a few more trick questions, but they were all so far off any personal mark of Tregare's that they gave him no trouble. Apparently Bluten had a fixed routine that he pulled on everybody whether it fit or not. This time it hadn't, much.

At the end of it, Bluten stood when Tregare did, and came around the desk with his hand outstretched. "I'm glad we got our earlier problems straightened out, Third. The grade of cooperation on this ship is hardly outstanding, but a few people like yourself help the average a lot." *Me, he's talking about?* And the bastard wanted to shake hands! Deliberately, Bran thought of the time he'd cleared away some chicken manure with his bare hands; that way, when he shook Bluten's hand he could smile about it.

The female goon showed him to the door and a bit outside it, holding his arm as she edged the door back to block the view from inside. Then she turned Bran to face her, her sullen face in a frown, and dug a vicious finger into the nerve at the back of his elbow. The arm screamed pain as its lower part went numb. Bran's feet shifted in reflex moves: *one hand now and she has twenty kilos on me! But—* But she let go of him, made a sour smile as she stepped back, and said, "Just to show you, buster, you're not all *that* smart. You didn't fool the major none. So watch it."

The cheap trick wasn't worth retaliation just now, and any threat would be stupid, so he let her back away and close the door to him. Rubbing his elbow, as sensation painfully returned, Tregare went downship, to soak under a hot shower.

He got some sleep then, until time for his first watch at the end of house arrest. He didn't know which Chief Rating had filled in for him, and frankly didn't care. The watch shift ran smoothly. From the log he learned that the *Tamurlaine*'s destination was Terranova's spaceport at Summit Bay. So Monteffial was probably right; at that well-established colony, UET would have a sizable Police garrison. The idea worried him, but he didn't know what he could possibly do about it.

His next two days, things seemed to be easing off; in the galley or up in Control, people weren't so tense. During one break he and Dolan managed a visit in his room. After his next watch, Leon Monteffial invited Bran up for drinks.

And then, while they were talking, relaxed and amiable, it all hit.

Farnsworth on the intercom from Control: "First! Up here right away!"

"Sure, Cleet. But what is it?"

"Not for open lines. Get here, will you?"

"Right." Monteffial shut the squawkbox down. Turning to Bran he said, "If I need you, Tregare, I could best reach you in your temporary quarters." He paused. "Where all your equipment is." And Monteffial tucked an energy weapon inside his belt, under his jacket. Bran felt his eyes widen, as he nodded.

"On my way," he said, and then was.

Down in quarters, Bran wasn't sure what he wanted to carry. Because what *was* this hassle? Monteffial seemed to think it could need weapons—well, Tregare had a lightweight energy projector and a needle gun. He didn't like the charge indication on the blaster, and the needler was smaller and easier to hide, so he tucked that one in his waistband. At the back, the way Hawkman Moray had shown him long ago. "They don't expect that. . . ."

He was armed, but nothing was happening. Nervous, Bran thought to add a concealed knife to his armament. *If nothing's blowing, I'll look silly as hell.* He waited.

Then the intercom blared, and it sounded as if all hell was breaking loose.

9. The Mechanics of Mutiny

Monteffial's voice. "—Police major raped her and maybe worse, so Dolan killed him. I don't know how, yet. The other two Police are running loose and shooting on sight. Captain took Dolan downship; he intends to space her, to clear the ship's record with the Police."

Farnsworth: "Monteffial, we *have* to go along with that!"

Bran opened intercom to Control: "Like hell we do! Leon—this is Escape! Are you with me?"

"But you can't—" That was Farnsworth.

Monteffial then: "I think we have to, Cleet. Tregare's right."

"Hell, he's not even briefed, Leon. And there's no schedule."

"Are you with us, Cleet, or are you dead?" A pause. "That's better. Now then—" Monteffial's voice changed, as he loaded the intercom with more circuit outlets. "All hands—"

Not waiting to hear more, Bran left quarters, plunging downship as if the Butcher himself had summoned.

Still he wasn't first to the air lock. Captain Rigueres, disheveled and wild-eyed, held the half-clothed Phyls Dolan by a choke collar. Her head flailed; she didn't seem to know where she was, as Rigueres shoved her into the lock and closed the inner hatch. He put his hand on the lever that would space the woman. "Everybody hold it . . . right there!"

Everybody? From one side Monteffial entered. From the other came the Police goons, their handguns out. And Bran found he'd pulled his needle gun and was aiming it.

Following Monteffial, Farnsworth waved his arms, shouting, "Be calm! Don't dispute the captain's authority. . . . but sir, maybe you should delay your decision and—"

Everybody was in the way; stepping from side to side, Bran still couldn't get a clear shot. He moved closer, as Monteffial said, "Don't do it, captain! You won't have to—this is Escape, now."

Rigueres made a snarl. "Oh, no! You'll never make *me* a traitor." Tregare saw the man's arm start to move. The Police male was in the way, so Bran fired through him. As the man fell, Tregare took better aim, but then Monteffial's charge took *him* into the line of fire. Cursing, Bran moved to try for a better shot, and the Police female blindsided him and knocked him flat.

He rolled and came up, in time to see Rigueres pull the air lock handle as Monteffial reached him, and to see Phyls Dolan blown out into vacuum. In less than a second she disappeared from view.

Slowly, it seemed to Tregare, he got up. His gun was gone. But then, until slugged down from behind, he killed some people.

He woke up strapped to a cot, with a head he wished he could give away to someone else. For a time he didn't make sense and knew it, but couldn't help it. Then, a few hours later, he had to face Leon. The man had a bruised face and a bandaged hand.

He said, "A right mess *you* made. Are you all right?"

"No more than you, maybe less. What happened?" Before Monteffial could answer, Bran said, "He spaced her. The bastard spaced her. That's the last I remember." He tried to sit up, and Monteffial loosened the straps, so he could. "If he's still alive, he's mine!"

"He's not. I cut his throat. A second too late, dammit." The man shook his head. "I hadn't wanted Rigueres dead; hadn't planned things that way. But the way it went—too much killing, but that one I can't truly regret."

"Killing. And you say *I* made a mess. Tell me?"

Leon's hand on Bran's shoulder found unexpected soreness. "Rigueres had the intercom open; that's why the pack of loyalists came in and rushed us." The First squinted. "You really don't remember? Well, you cut the Police goon nearly in half with your needler, trying for the skipper, and hit *him*, too—but penetration slowed the needles down: no stopping power left."

Tregare nodded; the other went on. "I'm told it was the other goon who decked you from a little behind your view. Anyway, when—when Dolan was blown out, you made a yell I never want to hear again. And you took a jump at the Police one, and spun in midair, and she went down with her head on backwards. Then you had you knife out, and spread four sets of guts on the deck, and—well, I think you lost track of who was who. When Deverel rabbit-punched you down, it was *me* you were headed for."

"Deverel?" *Peace take me—six, I killed?*

"He saved your life, Tregare. The way you were, then, I'd've had to shoot you to save myself."

"Berserk, eh? Never happened to me before. Not too unusual in the family stories, though." But that was Hawkman Moray's family, and here Bran's Moray ancestry was unknown. He said, "I'll thank Deverel, then. Assuming I'm allowed. Leon, you haven't said, yet, whether I'm under charges for any of this."

Monteffial laughed. "Charges? Hell, Tregare, you're Second Hat now, behind me as captain and Cleet as First. And by the Agowa formula—you've heard of it?—that Escaped ships use to allot shares, you *own* ten percent of the ship. We had to hold the divvy meeting without you; that kind of thing mustn't wait."

The rumor-mill info came back to him now. Agowa, sure: Control officers split a fifty percent share, 20-15-10-5; the Engineering officers did the same with twenty percent, 8-6-4-2. The other thirty percent went to the crew, with ratings getting double shares. And now he also remembered that on Escaped ships you'd be "Second Hat," not Second Officer. Any buildup of tradition, he supposed, was good for morale.

Now he said, "That's good to know. You have any idea when I can get up and go to work?" Because he didn't want to lie here, trying not to remember Phyls Dolan.

"Soon as the medics check you clear." The new captain looked at his chrono. "You get your next look in about an hour, I think." He stood. "I have to go now. We're shorthanded, you understand. Sixteen dead in the fighting, and something like twenty diehard loyalists locked in Hold, Starboard Lower for safekeeping."

"You're not—" He couldn't say it.

"Spacing them? Not unless we have to. If we make it to a Hidden World, maybe the place can use some cheap labor."

Alone again, Bran tried to wall himself away from grief for the dead woman who, frozen now and far behind the ship, swept through the interstellar gas. Slowing gradually, from the friction of that tenuous medium, to coast forever—or maybe to make a small spark someday, against a star's glare.

But when someone standing by the bed coughed to get his attention, tears blurred his vision.

Quickly, he wiped his eyes. "Who—?"

"Hain Deverel, sir. I wanted to say—hitting you and all—"

"Deverel!" Bran reached out a hand, and the man took it. "The First—I mean, the new captain—told me. Said if you hadn't put me down, he'd've had to shoot me. I owe you, man."

"No you don't, sir. But maybe now we're even."

It took Tregare moments to think what the rating meant. Then he said, "All right. That's fine. And now you're safe, aren't you? You and—" The other name escaped him.

"Anse. Anse Kenekke. Yes, we're safe now. And that I *do* owe you, because they tell me it was you who pulled the trigger to force Escape."

Headshake. "Not me. A dead woman did that—or maybe the Police bastard who drove her to killing him. All I did was—" Well, hell, he *had* forced the issue at that. Change the subject. "Kenekke's all right too, I take it?"

Deverel grinned. "Anse? He's the one that secured the Drive for us." Now he talked fast. "When the new skipper made his all-ship call, announcing Escape, the Drive room had its problems."

"Mallory?" Sure, the older man could be a strong loyalist.

"Not him. But it was watch-change; the First and Second were both there. Chief Mallory just stood back and said he was out of it; whoever won, he'd tune the Drive for. The Second had a gun; he said we'd stand by UET or he'd blow the Nielson cube and all of it. The First, the one they call Airedale, she yelled something about duty and pleasure and illusion—Anse says she never did make much sense, except doing her work right—and tackled the Second. He killed her, and Anse killed him, by hand, before the man could get his gun free to use again. Stronger than he might look, Anse is. And then he had Drive secured, and no more problems. The Third, when he got there, he's solid with us—and up to First now, come to think of it." He paused. "There's several Drive techs in line for the Second and Third openings. If you could put in a good word for Anse?"

"I'd like to. Two problems, though. I don't know anything about his training scores, and I don't have all that much clout, anyway. But if Captain Monteffial asks for my opinion, I'll try."

"That's fair. Thank you, sir." And Deverel left.

A little later, the Chief Medic came in. Not a full-fledged doctor, but trained well enough. Bran knew her only slightly, from a physical exam during which she jabbed like hell at all the tenderer spots she was supposed to check. Must have trained at the Slaughterhouse, where cadets got used to cringing during physicals. Eda Ghormley was thin, middle-aged, with iron grey hair and a slight stoop. Aside from the jabbing fingers she was easygoing enough, and spoke pleasantly despite her chronic frown.

Right away she took the conversational lead. "Tregare . . . haven't seen you much, in the line of business. Can't hurt an officer by hitting him on the head, but let's check a few things anyway." So—some questions, while she measured pulse, temperature, peered at his pupils, tested reflexes and coordination. And then said, "About an hour from now, after you eat, you get a sleepy pill and one shift's snooze right here. Then, unless you find something bothering you besides bruises and such, you're cleared for duty. All right?"

"Right. Thanks, Chief."

"Yes. Well, thanks for *your* part, in getting us free of those shitbags. I've waited a long time, for Escape."

Getting up after sleeping and dressing, Bran found stiffness and soreness he hadn't noticed. Nothing serious, though; he went up to Control to check the watch sked, and found he had several hours free yet before relieving Farnsworth. He also found that there'd been some fighting here. Needle projectiles and energy bolts had clobbered some instruments.

Well, that was his line of work—but first he needed something to eat. He went down to the galley.

Alone at the officers' table, Monteffial was finishing his meal. Tregare filled a tray and joined him. The new captain said, "Feeling better?"

"I'll live." He explained about the repair he planned to start, then asked, "Have you picked a new Third yet? And the new Engineering officers?"

"Leaving that part up to Mallory. He knows his people better than I do. But for Third Hat—Tregare, I have a problem."

"Nobody's qualified? Or too many?"

"Neither. I could pick any one of three Chief ratings and justify the choice. Or rather, *we* could, because you and Cleet get a vote each, too. But the best qualified person isn't a Chief yet, just a First."

"So promote him, Leon. I'll vote your selection."

One sided, Monteffial grinned. "Afraid not. The trouble is, you see, the First I mentioned is Erdis Blaine. Now wouldn't the new captain make everybody happy by naming his woman Third Hat, over the heads of three who have seniority on her?"

Bran nodded. "Yeah, I see it. Well, make her a Chief anyway, for future reference."

"I plan to. There's more than one vacancy at that rank now."

Impatient with the subject, Tregare said, "Okay . . . but who *do* you peg for Third?"

The captain paused. "It's a tossup, mostly, but I lean toward Gonnelson."

"The man who never uses one word if he can get by with none. At least he won't be nagging the watch to death. Well, if you think he can handle the job, I'm for it."

"He looks to be turning into a fine pilot—good marks, fast reflexes, solid judgment. Gets along well with the Drive room—just tells them the bare bones of what he wants and lets them do it, without fussing over details."

"Yeah." Bran knew what he meant. Farnsworth, for instance practically told Mallory which knob to turn, and how far.

Monteffial stood. "Gotta go. Oh, yes . . . one more thing. Not right away, but when you find time for it, I'd like you to replace the antenna cluster just aft of the topside air lock.

Groden, down in Stores, will have the parts assembly ready for you, and the tools."

"Sure. It'll have to be after my upcoming watch, though." Then he thought. "Just a minute. Who do you want me to take along on the job? I mean, that stuff's more than a one-man load."

"Gotcha!" Leon grinned. "Not in the power suit, it isn't. Use the two-anchor system, though; no showboating."

"Right. I'm not much for hitchhiking."

Before his watch began, Tregare had more than half of the damaged instruments replaced. He sent the removed items down to the Shops level by one of the cadet observers. Then after relieving Farnsworth he let his Comm board technician take the pilot's chair, telling her to notify him of *any* change on the monitors. So, during the first half of his watch, he restored the consoles to full function—except for one aux board, where he put a cable splicer to work on a burned-through trunk line.

At the half-watch break he patched the main forward screen, and the intercom, down to the galley. And was starting to leave for that oasis when the intercom came on. "Captain here. Tregare, would you mind taking your break in my quarters? Little meeting going on. Shouldn't take long."

So he changed the patching to put view and squawkbox to the captain's digs. Bran hadn't had time yet to move into Second's quarters, but Monteffial and Farnsworth, he knew, had made their own moves already. Gonnelson, whether he'd relocated into Tregare's previous room, Bran didn't know about.

Entering the skipper's suite, Bran found the lanky, blond Gonnelson there as well as the two senior officers. Walking over to the stand that held the coffee urn, Bran made a head move at Gonnelson and said, "You tell him yet, Leon?" Monteffial nodded, so shifting his coffee cup to his left hand, Tregare went over and offered a handshake; Gonnelson took it. "Congratulations, Third Hat. I expect we'll all work together just fine."

"Yes. Thanks." Two low-voiced words, then nothing more.

Well, there were worse habits than not being gabby. Bran turned back to the other two. "A meeting, you said?"

"Yes," the captain said. "Let's sit down." That done, he went on. "Question of where we go next. Cleet thinks we should go on in to Terranova, per sked, bluff it out and get refueled on the strength of our original mission documents. Fake the log from about two jumps back, to leave Rigueres off and promote everybody. What do you think?"

It took no thinking. "We don't have a chance in hell, getting away with that. And the Uties we have, locked up—we'd need to space the lot. I—"

"No such thing," Farnsworth put it. "Stick 'em in freeze, listed as high-priority passengers for our next stop."

Freeze. Tregare knew, when he stopped to think, that the ship had freeze chambers. The *MacArthur* had none, because Korbeith in his independent way had had them removed. But Bran had seen the *Tamurlaine*'s during his first hurried tour of the ship; he'd forgotten about them, was all. But how many were there? He frowned. "Twelve of those, we have; right? And twenty prisoners."

"Which is too many," Farnsworth said. "I keep telling you—" He spoke now to Monteffial. "—nearly half of those, now they've had time to think, are safe to let loose and put to work. Then we wouldn't be so bloody shorthanded, and—"

"And on Terranova," Bran cut in, "they'll all go on groundside leave and keep their little mouths shut. *Sure* they would." He shook his head. "I can't go with any of that. Captain, what's *your* idea?"

Monteffial cleared his throat. "Well, it also has its risks. But different ones. I haven't told anyone before, but I have what purports to be a coded set of coordinates for five Hidden Worlds. To reach one of these would require only a thirty-degree course change, which I believe is within the limits of our fuel reserves. So—"

Thirty degrees. Let's see: pi-over-six radians. Plug in the sines and cosines; yes. A right-angle change took as much energy as slowing to zerch and coming back up to speed, like a planetary stopover. But a lesser turn—decel would be one-minus-the-cosine of the angle, and accel factor would be the sine. Pi-over-six; okay: decel, dot-one-three-four. Accel a flat point-five. A little over five-eighths then, total, of stopover fuel need. Discounting gravity, because the Drive field fed it back, mostly. Tregare blanked his hand-calc.

He said the numbers. "Leon—do we *have* that much extra?"

"And enough more to let us sleep easy."

"Then do we vote on this, or what?"

Monteffial said, "I suppose so. I vote for the Hidden World."

"Terranova," said Cleet Farnsworth.

Bran laughed. "I'll take thirty degrees and out!"

Gonnelson, as they all looked at him, kept them waiting. Having been granted a vote, he could lock it all up now, if he chose, in stalemale. Finally the serious face tilted to face the others. "Not Terranova," he said.

Monteffial whooped, then said, "A drink on that. Bran, you have time for a short one, not enough to muddle you for watch!" He poured neat spirits; the four clinked glasses and drank.

Farnsworth, though, looked as though his drink was sour.

What with one thing and another, including Monteffial's change of course to the Hidden World, it was two more ship's days before Tregare found himself with enough free time to do the outside work, replacing the antenna array. First, of course, he tried fiddling with the gear from Control, hoping that the glitch was merely an adjustment problem. *Always try the easy answers first*. No luck, though; the problem was definitely outside. So he called down to rating-First Groden and made sure the parts and tools were ready to go. Then he gave a little thought to the logistics of outside work, and went looking for Hain Deverel.

He found him just leaving the galley. "Deverel? You got a minute?"

"Yes, sir. Can I help you?"

At Tregare's gesture, the shorter man accompanied him along the corridor. ". . . outside, see, in the power suit. And I need somebody dependable to cover for me at the main air lock. Maybe an hour, not more, is my guess. Would it be convenient for you, now?"

"No problems at all, sir. And I'm glad it's me you asked."

Gently, Bran tapped the man's shoulder. "So am I."

With less whinging and creebing than Tregare expected, "Gripin' Groden" issued the necessary equipment. Carrying the stuff out of Stores and along a passage to the stairway landing, Tregare and Deverel found it a full load. They left it, to go up a deck, where Bran was able to instruct the other man how to help with the power suit. He checked the thing out; all systems seemed to be working well, except for one gyro that was a little slow at engaging and disengaging. Well, he didn't plan to have to bend over or straighten up in any big hurry.

They went back for the parts and tools. In the suit, Bran carried the lot like an armful of kindling. They went to the air lock staging area. There wasn't any reason for personnel to be there, and no one was.

The lock's inner hatch was open. As Bran prepared to close and seal the suit's helmet, he said, "Okay, Hain. All you need to do is stay here and see that the lock's kept open for me to come back in, and that nothing interferes with coming in *all* the way."

"Yes, sir. But what would interfere?"

Tregare shook his head. "Maybe cross-up from Control. Somebody doing an inspection and putting the outhatch closed. *I* don't know what's antsing me. . . . just plain jitters, maybe. Anyway, I'll feel lots better with you standing in, here."

"Come to think of it, sir, so will I."

"Okay . . . here goes." Tregare sealed up, entered the air lock, and attached his lifeline with the two anchors. When the lock cycled to vacuum, the outer hatch opened. He climbed outside.

Working both magnetic anchors by himself was a nuisance, but Bran kept patience and used care all the way. When he reached the antenna clump he saw why it wasn't working; some chunk of cosmic debris had wiped half of it off and twisted the rest.

The wreckage wasn't worth taking inside; the shops wouldn't be able to salvage any of it. When Bran got it free of the connections, he heaved it off into space. He'd used four different tools; now they all floated on the short lines that fastened them to his suit belt. Carefully he untied the replacement bundle, fitted it to the heavy connector, and pulled in the wrench he needed to fasten the assembly in place. Once it was secured, he did the unfolding and attached the accessories, taking loose only one at a time and cinching it down firmly before reaching for the next part. In the back of his mind he thought that for a first outside job, he wasn't doing half bad!

Then he was done with it. He had no idea how long he'd taken, but hoped he was within the limit he'd told Deverel.

He started back, and restrained the impatience that made him want to shortcut the twin anchor routine. So it took him longer than he liked, to get back to the main air lock. At one point he thought he felt the ship jerk under him. But he got there without mishap, climbed in, and secured his life line and anchors in their usual places.

Through the heavy plastic window of the inner hatch he could see Deverel, and gave him the high sign. The outer hatch closed, pressure swirled in, and eventually the inner door opened. Bran went through it; it closed behind him.

Deverel was talking, but until the helmet got unsealed, Bran couldn't hear him. Then he did. "The ship, Tregare! Farnsworth's retaken it—him and the Utie loyalists. It's been announced—Captain Monteffial's dead, and we're back on course to Terranova!"

At first he couldn't make sense out of any of it, so he kept asking. Coming inside from outside was always disorienting—but *this*? "Say again, Deverel—*how* did they do it?"

Farnsworth. A sleeper. Well, he'd always dragged his feet on Escape. Now with only officers and a few selected people carrying arms, Farnsworth and one or two of his flunkeys had opened the arms room and put weapons in the hands of all the UET loyalist prisoners—and turned them loose to conquer.

Deverel shook his head. "I don't know who killed Captain Monteffial. It wasn't Farnsworth, because he was up in Control, announcing himself captain, when somebody reported having killed Monteffial in his quarters." Deverel's face tightened. "Tregare, sir, what can we *do*?"

Sometimes things took no thinking at all. "Seal the helmet on my suit, Deverel. I'm going upship. You stay here; you should be safe enough."

"I want to help!"

"You already have. But from now, you hardly can't."

There wasn't time to sidetrack and get the suit's energy projector—even if he could have hooked it up by himself, from inside the suit. No—best to go straight upship and take what came. So Bran Tregare headed for the nearest landing and began climbing.

At first he didn't see anyone else. Then he came up to a group of unarmed people who seemed to be screaming as they ran away. They were probably on his side, but there wasn't a way he could spare the time to tell them that.

A few decks before the level of his own quarters, he was intercepted by four gunholders. A quick glance told him they were among the Utie ex-prisoners—now, according to Deverel, part of Farnsworth's troops. No time to quibble about it—both needle pellets and energy beams raked his suit's armor. Well, *hell*! One man was within reach, so Tregare reached. He swung the man against the other three; it took two swipes but he decked them. Then he found he wasn't holding the man any longer—just the man's arm. He used it to club down one Utie who was still trying to get up, then threw it away. That move was a mistake; the faulty gyro, when he went to straighten up too fast, began to precess and almost turned him sideways.

All right—easy now! He paused to look. One man wasn't quite dead, but close to it, so Bran stomped on his head. No point in leaving loose ends. Weapons might be a good idea; he looked around and picked up one medium energy weapon and one light one. There was a needler lying handy, but he had only two hands and no place to tuck anything away. So—upship again.

Somebody must have ducked away and made an intercom call, because three decks up he ran into an ambush—maybe a dozen armed people blasting at him when he came up into view at the landing. *Peace on it!* Spraying energy bolts with the heavier gun in his left hand, he ran at the two closest attackers. They were standing against a bulkhead. The suit's impact made mush of them.

Well, nobody said it was going to be neat and tidy. Three were still alive. They ran, and he didn't bother to shoot.

Farther upship. He was shot at, and he shot back. He left several dead and let some flee unscathed. The suit's right knee mechanism was heating up; the gyros for bending down and straightening chattered and paused at the wrong times. He had to keep his moves simple now, or the damn suit could collapse on him.

Coming to the galley level he heard a lot of shouting. Whose, he had no idea, and by now he couldn't afford to care. He thought of something Hawkman had told his once. When he climbed far enough to look across at floor level, he flipped on the suit's outside speakers and *yelled*, then dropped out of sight for a few seconds. And then raised his heavier gun up and sprayed the level without even looking. When the noise stopped he raised himself up and scanned the area. There were three corpses and no one alive. Whether the three kills were his or someone else's, he'd probably never know.

Not far now, to Control. And to Farnsworth, who'd had Monteffial killed, who had tried to give this ship back to UET. Farnsworth, that pigass—oh, forget about cussing, *get* him. So Bran started up the last climb.

He expected a grenade, but maybe Farnsworth had forgotten to stock up on those. He expected a flood of armed troops, but maybe good ol' Cleet had run a little short. He didn't know *what* the hell he expected. So he just climbed on up.

Farnsworth didn't have much ready for him, special. A few troops, and one of the projectors that would have fit onto the power suit. Not much, but enough. "Hold it right there," said Farnsworth. "I don't know who you are, in there, but I'm captain now and I offer you amnesty if you'll surrender. Is it a deal?"

"Tell me a little more, captain," said Tregare. He was inching the suit forward, trying to look as if he weren't. "I'm not sure I understand all what's happened."

"Well, it's simple enough," Farnsworth said. "There was a traitorous mutiny, and now that's rectified. Except that you and I have to reach an understanding."

"That's no problem. I understand fine. A deal, then?" He strode toward Farnsworth. Everything would have worked if the heavy-projector man hadn't caught on; the blast caught the suit's control pack and jammed the lower limbs. Bran grabbed for Farnsworth; the thrown missile that smashed into the gunner's face and knocked him unconscious, was Farnsworth's head. Then, the explosion came.

"I'm getting tired," said Bran Tregare, "of waking up in hospital."

"Then try taking better care of yourself." Eda Ghormley's voice still belied her sour expression. "Captains shouldn't take so many chances. Can you tolerate visitors? There's one here."

Bran took a quick self-check. Head thudding, ears ringing, stomach vacillating between hunger and nausea, but—"Visitors.

Yes." Because if he was captain, he had to know more about it, and fast.

The visitor was Erdis Blaine; she looked a little red-eyed puffy but mostly in control. Bran asked first. "Who's got the watch? What's the drill? Tell me fast." Then, realizing she had her own problems, "I wish to hell they hadn't got Leon."

She sniffed once and almost managed a smile. "Me, too. Nicest guy I—well, Gonnelson's standing in for you, Tregare, and just temporarily, Al Druffel and I are filling in on the other watches. The other Chief rating in line, he was on the wrong side. Somebody killed him. Probably you."

What a mess. Tregare said, "Tell Gonnelson I confirm his choices. You and Druffel, which of you is senior?"

"He is; he's a Chief."

"Then I guess he's Second Hat and you're Third. All right?"

Now she did smile. "Anything that works." She paused. "Tregare—did anybody ever tell you you're a real pisser?"

He looked at her. "I wouldn't know what that means."

"You don't have to; you just [illegible]

Not feeling up to it, Tregare after one sleep cut loose from medical custody and called council in Control, since he also wasn't up to moving into captain's quarters. On hand he had Gonnelson, Druffel, Baine, and old Mallory representing the Drive room. To avoid distracting the ratings who were holding down the watch positions, Tregare's group took seats well away from them.

"I missed the other meeting," he began, "so if I pass up anything we should do, somebody clue me in. First, who's got a roster of surviving personnel?" Gonnelson handed him a flimsy. He made a quick count. "Sixty-seven of us. Jeez, we *are* shorthanded."

"Five of those," said Al Druffel, "were Farnsworth's."

"How come they're still alive?" Tregare raised one eyebrow.

"Because you haven't ordered them killed," said Erdis Blaine. "And three of them are cadets. . . ."

He thought. Hell, he wasn't Korbeith! "Then let's leave it at that. Any holding ratings are unrated as of now, though. And no two of those five are to work together or live together. So I don't think they'll give us any trouble." Blaine pointed out the names, and Bran checkmarked them. "If they keep their noses clean, they can earn promotion like anybody else."

Again he looked down the list. "We need to make some promotions. Well, for starters, let's make it official that I'm captain, Gonnelson First Hat, Druffel Second, Blaine Third. Any questions?" Most of them nodded. "How about your people, Mallory? Your Third Engineer—what's his name? —he'll be First now, I imagine."

"That's right. Junior Lee Beauregard. Georgia boy." Mallory cleared his throat. "My Chief Tech moves up to Second Engineer: Ingrid Nakamura. Now for Third I've jumped a fella several grades, just because he's a damn good Tech. Man named Anse Kenekke."

"I've met him." At the corner of vision Tregare saw movement. The man in the pilot's seat had looked around; it was Deverel. "Good choice."

"And I've made other promotions, to fill in the supervisory spots, which I'll log in after this meeting. If you approve."

"I said it before, Mallory. You're the one, knows your Drive people. You call 'em, I'll okay your choices." He paused. "Upship here we need some promoting, too. I have some ideas for about half the top rating slots and can use suggestions for the rest. Here's who I favor for the vacancies at Chief level." He named the people; one of them was Hain Deverel.

The only question came from Druffel, about upgrading Groden, down in Stores. "That man would bitch at his own funeral."

"Does his job," said Gonnelson, surprising Bran.

Tregare thought of something. "How long's he been a First?"

"Five years, maybe," Druffel said. "Rubs people the wrong way."

Chuckling, Bran said, "Let's see if a raise might help his disposition some." Druffel nodded, and Groden got his Chief's rating. Then suggestions were offered for the lesser promotions; without any real arguments, most of them were passed.

That much done, Tregare said, "Gonnelson, I noticed by the log that you corrected Farnsworth's change of course almost as soon as somebody got me out of that suit, cold as a clam, and cleared you some space to work. So—" The man looked alarmed, about to apologize; Bran waved a hand. "I checked it; you're solidly on the route Monteffial punched in.

All I want to do, here, is give you a public commendation for initiative. *And* accurate work. By not waiting, you saved us some fuel, too."

What else? Oh, sure; the new divvy. The figures were no news to anyone, but his reciting them made it all official. "We'll need to refigure crew's shares, rated and unrated, but that won't take long."

"How about Farnsworth's Uties?" Blaine asked it. "Are you giving them shares?"

"As unrateds, sure," Tregare answered. "Way I see it, since we're not killing them they have jobs. Jobs determine shares. Anything else wouldn't be fair, all around."

After a couple of minor questions, Bran called the meeting closed and went to log the results into the ship's computer. He grinned at the young woman in the seat beside the terminal he used. "Better be careful when I feed this stuff in. Wouldn't want to give Tinhead a headache."

As he started to leave, Erdis Blaine intercepted him. "Captain, you'll be moving into your new quarters, I imagine, as soon as possible."

He hadn't thought that far ahead, but... he nodded. "Yeah. I suppose so. Why?"

"It's just—well, I've tried to get Leon's things packed for storage, figuring what should be sent to his family if he still had one, and if there's any way to do so. What to simply throw out—" He saw tears forming but she blinked them away. "But I just haven't had *time* to get it all done. And my own stuff. I'd moved in with him, you know. Or maybe you didn't. So there's all *that* to move, too. And—"

He touched her shoulder. "Hold it, Blaine. There's no rush, except that I do need to do my sleeping where the remote command facilities are. But my own personal junk—there's not enough of it to crowd anything. Just clear a corner maybe, and part of a closet. I'll wedge in okay. And you don't have to move right away either, if it's inconvenient."

She backed away from his touch. He hadn't meant more than comfort, so he felt foolish. She said, "Look, Captain. I like you, and I think we all owe you a lot. But I *loved* Leon, and I can't switch men that fast."

Angered for no real reason, Bran Tregare kept his tone calm. "All right, I see why you'd take the offer that way. But believe it or not, all I meant was—" Grief came. He fought it, and couldn't quite hide his feelings. "Blaine, I'm still hurting over Phyls Dolan. You might think a fast tumble would help, but that's not how it feels. What I meant was, just that you could *stay* if you wanted, long as you wanted." Now he could smile a little. "Hell, wouldn't be the first time I had a lady roommate in a 'mustn't touch' setup. So *now* how about it?"

"Tregare . . . I mean, captain—"

"We're off duty. Tregare's okay. So's Bran."

"They'll all think we are."

"Do you care? I don't."

"I snore. Or so Leon claims."

"People snore, I nudge 'til they quit."

"Then it's a deal."

Bran hauled his gear—three loads, but he didn't bother asking anyone to help—up to captain's digs. Erdis Blaine had cleared him more than enough space; when she got everything out, the place was going to look rather bare. Oh, well, things always tended to accumulate faster than a person expected.

He moved some clothing—Leon's—that Blaine had piled on the chair facing the remote-command facilities module, and set to checking that equipment. Druffel had the watch; Bran coached him through some of the operating functions and found that skipper's quarters could monitor not only the main viewscreen, with whatever he ordered combined on that versatile instrument, but could also obtain miniature insets of the two aux screens that flanked the big one. And he could separate or combine various facets of the intercom net, and—well, when he'd checked out nearly all the console, he decided he could damn near fly the ship from here! Well, he didn't have access to direct control of gunnery or of the Drive, or the air locks. But to everything else, or nearly so.

Somehow, Bran had in mind that Leon Monteffial had taken all necessary action with regard to the *Tamurlaine*'s new course and destination. When he checked the log and it told him differently, he was too depressed to bother with cursing. Or to blame anyone else for not noticing. All he said was, "Druffel. Ask Mallory how soon he can be ready for Turnover."

"Turnover?"

"I believe you know the term." Then, ashamed of taking his irritation out on the man, Tregare added, "I should have checked earlier. Just found out, here. Turnover was due about the time I was flatbacked after Farnsworth's caper." So that, of course, was why Monteffial hadn't done it; the man was dead then.

Mallory needed only an hour or so to prepare; Bran spent the time in useless stewing. What the delay meant, was that to bring the ship to the Hidden World known as New Hope, he was going to have to run decel near to max, or else go past, too fast to land or even orbit, and loop back. Either way a waste of fuel, the same as pushing a groundcar or aircar at full throttle. Well, either the fuel reserves would be enough, or they wouldn't.

Turnover went smoothly; Bran tipped the *Tamurlaine* over, directly in line with the idle thruster and balancing with the other two, then used the third to dead-stop rotation at as near a solid one-eighty as the instruments would measure. The calcs were more complicated than that, actually, because the ship was still in change of course. But the vectors could be considered separately, and still add up right, so Tregare didn't worry about the overall equation.

When he told Mallory to set decel at point-nine-two max, the old Chief Engineer said, "Nine-two? Confirm, please?"

Tregare sighed. "Confirmed, I'm afraid. We turned late. Call it my fault. There's nobody else alive to blame."

Clearing his throat, Mallory said, "I see. Don't fret, lad . . . Captain, I mean. The Drive's tuned quite finely, as I always try to keep it—but I'll just see if from now on we can't tune it a little finer."

"Thanks, Chief. I'm sure you will." Well, if Mallory couldn't do it, Tregare knew no one who could.

Blaine had exaggerated about her snoring. Once in a while a soft burring vibration, but never loud nor for long at a time. The way the watch sked was running, they didn't usually share the big bed for the full sleeping period of either. Sometimes Tregare came to bed while she was sleeping and found her gone when he woke, sometimes the other way around.

When their skeds did synch, for once, he found himself embarrassed. He entered quarters, and there she was, undressing for bed just as he intended to do. The thing was, it was only about the second time they'd both been around for disrobing together, and the first had been when he was bedding down and she arising. Which was, somehow, different.

Bran nodded to her. "Hi, Blaine." And went into the bathroom for a while. When he was done there, he picked up his clothes and went out to the main room, and hung them over a chair. She'd left the light dim for him, so he supposed she was trying to go to sleep. But when he went to bed, he saw her lying there looking at him. He got in, staying on his own side as usual. "Good night, Blaine."

"Are you sure, Tregare? I've been wondering."

He came close to snapping out a curt reply; dammit, was he supposed to be able to respond to this kind of turnaround in thirty seconds or less? So he said, "Can we talk some?"

Her words came fast. What were they *doing*, living like monks and nuns when maybe the ship couldn't even hit groundside and they'd just drift and die? And—but tired as he was, he could see what drove her. And it wasn't sex, as such.

"Come here, Blaine. What you need is a good cuddle. And me too, maybe. But that's all, for right now."

So they did.

Mallory nursed the Drive; Tregare refined his navigation figures and finally saw his way clear, when the *Tamurlaine* hit half-c going downhill, to cut decel to point-eight-seven of max.

When they came in hailing distance of New Hope, they had close to three days' fuel in solid reserve.

10. New Hope

What Tregare expected of the Hidden World, he wasn't sure. But this one didn't make things easy. The voice from groundside came from a loop tape, and repeated, ". . . colony world New Hope, to the approaching ship. Identify yourself, please. Name, last port of call, roster of officers to check against our own records, and other ships of recent contact with you. We welcome all news and will reciprocate in kind." Pause. Silence with slurred undernoise. "This is the colony world New Hope—"

Bran cut the sound to a murmur. *Colony* world? That

meant UET, but Monteffial vouched for this one as Hidden. He looked over to Gonnelson, who nominally had the watch, and decided not to ask questions.

But he couldn't help muttering out loud a little. All right, he had an *armed* ship. But little use would those turrets do him, sitting groundside and pointing straight up. So if New Hope turned out phony, how would he handle it?

"Scoutship." The voice jarred him; then he realized it was Gonnelson answering his unheeding mumbles.

He turned to look at his First Hat. "Thanks, Gonnelson. You're right." For he'd forgotten the scouts. Rigueres had ignored them in training, and unarmed ships (like the *Mac*) didn't carry the little spacecraft. Tregare first began berating himself for losing track of things, then thought: *well, it got a little hectic on here*. So he shrugged, and thought some more.

"Gonnelson? Those scouts checked out for use?" The man nodded. "Who by? You do it yourself?" Another nod. "Good enough; I think you just now gave me some answers." He reached for his offship transmit switch. "So maybe it's time to talk to groundside."

Tregare didn't bother with the loop-tape approach; he spoke live on circuit. "The ship *Tamurlaine*, calling New Hope spaceport. Captain Bran Tregare speaking. We last lifted from Penfoyle Gate; before that, the Twin Worlds. Our officers' roster? Your news might list Rigueres, Monteffial, and Farnsworth; unfortunately, none of those gentlemen have survived to greet you. Tregare over."

He turned to Gonnelson. "If this is a UET plant—if they send up missiles—I'll walk this ship across their town and wipe it off!"

"Fuel," said Gonnelson, and Tregare sagged in his chair.

"Fuel, yeh. All right. You can land this thing?" The man nodded, and Bran knew that Gonnelson never overstated. So he said, "Then you do it. And just outside atmosphere, I'll take one of the scouts out and ride you shotgun, going down and until we know things are right, groundside."

Gonnelson shook his head. "Talking."

Bran knew what he meant. "Druffel and Blaine'll be with you, to handle that part. I'll brief 'em first. All right?"

Groundside, after a pause, was answering now. "*Tamurlaine*? That's an armed ship. None of those ever Escaped before. *If* you did. Which is to say, if you're Escaped, what's the ship's new name? And why aren't you using it? Answer immediately!"

Bran shook his head. No time to think up excuses. Level first and maybe regret it later. He said, "Peace take you, I came on this ship as Third Officer, after one cadet tour with Butcher Korbeith. Whom one day, if ever we meet again, I will kill. Escape happened on here before I had any chance to learn the rules of it, or the niceties and protocols. We are coming in to land, New Hope; we intend to give fair treatment and expect the same in return. Are my intentions satisfactory to you?"

The pause was too long; groundside was having fast confab. Finally the voice came. "Set your computer for fast feed and we'll give you a landing trajectory. New Hope out."

Tregare said to Gonnelson, "Put this input in storage first; before it goes into Tinhead, we inspect." But when they checked the data, it came out solid enough. So Tregare called Al Druffel and Erdis Blaine, explained what he wanted them to do during and after landing, and signed off. He told Gonnelson, "I'll grab my kit and go snooze in the portside scoutship. Call me about a half hour before you hit gas, and then keep a channel open between us." He grinned. "If you want, you can put Blaine on it."

The snooze part had been a touch of bravado on Tregare's part, but once aboard the scoutship and leaning back in its pilot's seat, he actually did doze off.

Druffel's voice woke him. "Skipper? Captain Tregare?" Bran acknowledged. "Roughly thirty minutes to hitting atmo, sir. Instructions? And do you want the landing site coordinates, and the trajectory, in your computer, sir?"

All that stuff? Hell, he had no map recorded, and—"No need, Druffel," he said. "In about twenty minutes we talk again and you spit this scout out. Once through the no-comm ionization layer, we talk again. But no point in bothering the computer with it."

"Yes, sir." Druffel paused, talking to someone, not loud enough for Bran to make it out. "One thing, Captain. Will you want to dock with us groundside, under gravity?"

Oh, hell. Bran thought fast. "No. I haven't done that. Don't know if I could. No . . . we get things settled, I hope, and I'll land alongside. Then either these people have a big hoist we can use, or we dock this scout after we get upstairs again."

Another pause. More talk Bran couldn't quite hear. Then, "Yes, sir. That will work. One way or the other."

"Good." Another thought. "Flash me the map once, though, so I can spot the port. I might just want to be there first." On the screen the image flickered, then steadied; Tregare put it into the records. "Okay, thanks. Call me in twenty minutes."

He cut the circuit, ate a quick snack, and hit the john. His nerves could have used a quick drink but maybe his reflexes couldn't, so perhaps just as well he had no booze aboard. He sat again, fingering the controls, and waited. When the voice came again—Blaine's, this time—he was more than ready for it.

"Docking chamber pumping to vacuum, sir. Count ninety, to opening. Further instructions, sir?"

He couldn't think of any, except—"Anybody takes offensive action against the ship, walk the Drive across them. And then sit down near as you can to the fuel dump, if you can spot it. I'll try to give you backup."

"And if our landing is peaceful, sir?"

Tregare laughed. "Hell, you don't need any orders for *that*."

The time came, the hatch opened, and the scout made its exit to clear space. The *Tamurlaine*'s inward path was crossing the terminator into a hemisphere of daylight on the world below; Tregare checked his map on the screen and—off toward the horizon—he spotted the port. Already the edge of atmo dragged and jerked at the scout, making it look as if the larger ship, to one side, bucked and pitched. But Tregare knew the *Tam* was holding course; it was his own scoutship being bounced around as it entered the top of atmosphere.

He watched his hull-temp readings; they looked fine. The ship, though, was lagging him, drifting off the back edge of his portside screen. Well, should he hang back and stay with it, or go groundside like a bat?

A moment, Tregare thought. Then he grinned. The *Tamurlaine* had to do a conservative, least-fuel grounding. The scout's fuel needs, by comparison, were hardly noticeable. Tregare pointed his small aux craft straight down. *Like a bat!*

Surprising, how long the scout took, getting down to aircraft altitudes—and then how little time he had to level off, and not churn dirt. He didn't actually plow a furrow, Tregare didn't, but he decided not to tell anybody what his altimeter read when he pulled out of his dive. For one thing they probably wouldn't believe him, and accuse him of bragging. Hell with it. Next time, if ever, he'd know to take it a little easier.

Slowing now to speed that wouldn't break windows groundside, if they *had* windows, Bran spotted the approach route to the mapped spaceport. He opened channel to the *Tamurlaine;* in a little while the ionization roar cleared. "Tregare here. Downside and close to the port. Going to make a pass there. Keep in touch."

Static partially obscured the answer, but Druffel was agreeing. Tregare saw the spaceport just ahead; he went across it at just below sonic speed, looped around and eased past the place again, slower. Nobody shot at him so he pulled up and circled, waiting for the *Tam* to descend. And finally he watched the ship land, on the one of four landing circles nearest a building. Port Control, probably. When the dust settled, he saw a group of people leave the building and approach the ship. If any were armed, it was with nothing more than handguns. So, keeping the *Tamurlaine* between the groundside people and his scout—to protect them from his own, lesser landing blast—Tregare set down.

He did the shutdown checkoff in a hurry, lowered his ramp, and went down it three steps at a time. By walking quickly, he intercepted the groundside people as they reached the place where the *Tamurlaine*'s ramp was descending and would soon touch.

Leading the party were a man in late middle age and a somewhat younger woman. Bran couldn't figure who was in charge, so "ladies first." Extending a hand, he said, "Bran Tregare, captain of the *Tamurlaine*, which we haven't got around to rename yet." He saw them looking past him, between the big ship's landing legs, at the scout. "I came down by the scenic route, you might say."

Squinting against bright sky, the woman pushed back short, tousled hair, more sandy-colored than anything else. At close range Bran saw that maybe she was younger than she looked. Her skin was weathered and darkened. Outdoors too much? She said, "I'm Corlys Haines, Port Commander, and I'd like you to meet"—Gesturing to the man beside her—"Council President Edd Crilly. With two d's." Crilly's gaunt, lined face creased into a smile as he in turn shook hands. He mumbled something that sounded polite, before Haines introduced Bran to a stocky, freckled man, roundfaced under greying, reddish hair. "Ezra Drake, our security chief. He's the one who'll want to know all your spacing histories, to put together a picture of who's been on which ships and where they've been."

Another handshake, and Bran nodded. "The Long View, eh? I hope the information flow goes both ways."

"Once we've checked you out," Drake said, "it does."

Down the ship's ramp, now, came Druffel and Blaine, followed by a squadsized group of senior ratings. So Gonnelson, to avoid a talking situation, had stayed in Control. Tregare introduced his two Hats to the three persons he'd met, mentioned that his First had stayed aboard to hold down the watch, and wondered how to get down to business. Well, just *start:* "Well have to go over our cargo manifest together, I expect, to see about trading for fuel and supplies. I suppose you do some long-term trading with other-Hidden Worlds, so maybe we can work up a dicker to handle some cargo for you. And—"

Palm out, Drake's hand came up. "Hold it. You're not cleared yet. You can get on with your preliminary negotiations if you like, but no fuel or data goes on that ship until I okay it. Understood?"

Bran scowled, then thought about it. Drake didn't sound unfriendly, nor like being arrogant for the fun of it; he was doing his job. "Understood," Tregare said. "But if the checking's holding us up, let's get on with it."

"Fine. Your group here first; all right?" Drake waved a hand toward the nearby building. "Over there."

"Sure," Bran said. Then, "Just a minute." He hadn't taken a talkset aboard the scout, so he borrowed Druffel's and called Gonnelson. "Post somebody to the scout, will you? Can't leave it vacant and open." Gonnelson acknowledged. "Right, then. Thanks, First." Tregare waited until a rating came down from the ship, entered the scout, and drew the ramp up. Then he turned back to Drake. "Sorry to hold things up. Let's go."

And during the short walk to the amber-colored concrete building, which looked like any box of offices on any world, Bran finally had time to notice and enjoy the clear air—plenty of oh-two here—and the springiness of step that came with a lighter-than-Earth gravity. Sky glare was a little more than he liked; next time he'd bring sunglasses. He had no close look at local vegetation; the port area was bare, and the brush around the edges too far distant to show any detail, except that it seemed to be mostly a pale grey-green, and wafted no scents across the landing area.

And then they all went inside.

* * *

Drake himself questioned Tregare. There was nothing tricky about the man's approach, no traps in the Major Bluten fashion. Drake simply wanted all the info Bran could remember about ships and rosters and destinations. Also anything he could recall from the Slaughterhouse. "If somebody graduated in the year Z," Drake put it, "then when he shows up in another report, at Z-plus-ten, we have that much more tie-in on him."

Bran had just about run out of data, which was why they were into chatter. "Do all Hidden Worlds have data banks like yours?"

"I hope so. I try to send the word along, and copies of our stuff, with any ship that cooperates." He paused. "Actually, I didn't originate the idea. I got it from Cade Moaker on *Cut Loose Charlie*. He brought a packet from Number One, a sort of starting kit."

Moaker. Bran had forgotten the *Mac*'s fly-by with that ship. Now he told it. Drake nodded. "He wouldn't have been from here, on that one. The coordinates and vectors don't fit."

Relaxed now, sitting back, Tregare said, "Any more you want?"

"From you, no. Unless you think of something else for me. And far as I'm concerned, your ship's cleared. You can go ahead with the dealings." Drake stood. "But I'll appreciate it if you'll send your people over in groups of twelve, to fill in anything else they may have for us. Will you set up a circuit to me from your Control room, so we can cut out the delays with the walking back and forth?"

"Sure." Ready to leave, Bran shook hands. "See you." He found his other people had finished too. They walked back to the ship.

Drake's systematic checking went fast. On his advice, Tregare dumped the five survivors of Farnsworth's team offship, bag and baggage. "We'll relocate them to a settlement a few hundred kilometers north," the man said. "They won't be the first of their kind, by any means. It's an ongoing problem, and our solution usually works out."

Another order of business was recruiting to fill the ship's vacancies. There were plenty of young people with an eye to space for the unskilled slots, but a shortage of trained spacers.

Bran wound up with a full roster plus a few supernumeraries, but realized he was going to have to set up an intensive training program. So, not to waste time, put his officers on it immediately.

On the financial end of things, Tregare lucked out. Quite a lot of his cargo was electronic components, stuff that carried high value in small bulk. His fuel and supplies put a smaller dent in his assets than he might have expected. And rather than commission to carry New Hope's cargo, he bought it outright and would sell it the same way. The Long View . . .

When the Council threw a banquet for the *Tam*'s officers and top ratings—about twenty in all—Tregare turned up with a couple of good ideas. He was seated between Corlys Haines and a Professor Landis. First, Haines asked him if he intended to visit only Hidden Worlds in future, or bluff it out at UET colonies also. "Raiding can be profitable, I'm told."

"Yeah, I've heard that. Matter of fact, I've been working on a faked log to use for bona fides if we hit UET territory."

She touched his left cheek. "Then you and your new officers had better do something about your symbols of rank."

Right. His cheek proclaimed him Third Officer, while Gonnelson and Druffel and Blaine had no markings at all. Now why hadn't he thought of *that* objection when Farnsworth wanted the ship to go on in to Terranova? He said, "You have anybody here who can do it for us?"

"Yes." It was agreed; Haines left to make a brief call, and returned to say that the needle artist would visit the ship the next day.

Meanwhile, Bran had been talking with the professor, and he found the talk interesting. Landis headed a technical group stranded here by Escape of the ship they'd been riding. "And I have a prize gang of lab jockeys, captain, and a rather good lab"—he spread his hands—"we could hire out to design all sorts of gear and arrange the building of it, but all this place wants is better farm machinery!" He laughed. "Well, not quite that bad, but nearly."

The man started to change subjects, but Tregare raised a finger. "Let me think a minute." Actually he didn't have to think about anything except how to say it.

The equation was this: he wanted to do UET in the eye, and peace take it, he would! But one ship wasn't enough; he needed allies. The trouble was, far as he knew, no other armed ship had Escaped, ever.

But that didn't mean that maybe an Escaped ship couldn't be armed later. So Tregare asked Landis about that. "Say I give you a spare turret projector out of ship's Stores, along with the specs for it, and for the circuitry. And the other stuff—missiles and counter-missiles, which I haven't studied all that much. Hull plate adapters, all that." He stared at the prof. "How'd you like to build me some weapons, and arm other Escaped ships I send here?" Because there *was* a Hidden Worlds grapevine, and ships left messages for each other; *it could work*.

Landis squinted. "It won't come cheap. You will pay how?"

"Plain old Weltmarks." The *Tam*, Bran had found, carried UET's money in good supply. Well, a ship would have to. And New Hope, at least, operated on that same currency. So?

"We can deal, captain. And I know a way to improve on UET's turrets. You'll come, yourself, for the weapons?"

"Or send somebody, with my personal password. Say, my name, plus my ship's new name."

"Which is what?"

"Unknown at present." Call it *Unknown*, maybe? No, but the French word for it. Yes. "*Inconnu*."

So with one word Tregare made a deal and renamed the *Tam*.

The tattoo artist wasn't all that expert. The Hats' emblems looked well enough, but when the scabs came off, Tregare found that on his own cheek the colors, new parts and old, didn't quite match. Which would have been okay if he'd realized ahead, and asked for each succeeding segment to differ a little. But this way it was obvious that he'd gone from Third to Captain in one jump. And the faked log was already getting too complex to tamper with, to try to make plausible three promotions all marked on him at the same place. Tregare shrugged. *Hell with it*.

The ship, its scout docked by Gonnelson following liftoff, was in space again. Or rather, *Inconnu* was there for the first time. Still wearing the *Tamurlaine's* insigne, though, because nobody had designed one for *Inconnu*, and the ship was headed for UET's colony on Hardnose, an icebound world.

The need for heavy training schedules made the trip seem to go faster. And while Hardnose was a small colony and not apt to hold much in the way of high brass or Committee

Police, still it seemed a good idea that officers and ratings get the faked log down pretty well. Thinking in terms of the Long View and of spatial geometry, Tregare decided there wasn't much chance of any vessel from Earth leaving data this soon, that would contradict his effort at computerized fiction. Or so he hoped.

At icy, high-albedo Hardnose, the approach and hailing and landing all went easily. Now the question was, could *Inconnu* get away with pretending to be UET's *Tamurlaine*?

How easy it was, Tregare could hardly believe. But all officialdom was in a dither, trying to hunt down a group of deserters from the only other ship in port, the *Attila*. That ship's First Officer had headed a leave party of nearly a dozen, including the officer's lady, and the group hadn't returned. Two were caught, but seemed to know nothing of the others' whereabouts. Since Committee Police had done the interrogating, Tregare tended to believe that the two, before they died, had been telling the truth. So even in this relatively small place there had to be a local Underground hiding the fugitives.

On Hardnose, ships' business went slowly. Before Tregare was done with his, the *Attila* lifted away, maybe with replacements and maybe not. Bran didn't care and didn't ask.

What he did care about was how to find the deserters. Still shorthanded when it came to skills, he could use some experienced people, and obviously the ones hiding out would like a way to escape UET.

But how to go about it? Tregare was too easily recognized to try scouting the local underworld on his own. His officers, each sporting the appropriate cheek tattoo, were no better qualified. So who in hell *could* he send on such a mission?

Then, walking along a corridor, he met Deverel and Kenekke. *These guys know how to keep cover. They have to*. So he said, "Talk with you two for a minute? My digs. And drinks go with the offer." After a quick look at each other, both nodded, and followed Tregare's brisk gait. In his quarters, Deverel accepted the drink. Kenekke settled for water.

Bran explained the problem. "I don't know how you can make contact but I'd appreciate your giving it a try. If you do locate these people, especially that First Officer, port security here is so lax that we can sneak people to the ship in the courtesy groundcar."

He waited, then Deverel nodded, and Kenekke said, "I guess we can give it a try, sir. But why us?"

Bran tried to think how to put it, "Because, to stay alive in UET, you *had* to be pretty good at keeping the bastards guessing." Both men laughed; then, with handshakes, the deal was on.

For three days, no luck; Tregare had to start thinking in terms of how long he could stall his scheduled lift-off. Then, late one night, Deverel brought two Tech ratings around to be hoisted in by the cargo hatch—no air lock, that point of entry, and only Tregare's own alerted guard watching. Bran interviewed the two, a young couple. The male did most of the talking but looked to the woman for corroboration and was sometimes corrected in his details. "True; the First didn't *tell* us to jump ship. He just talked slow, around a table in this big bar, and said if anyone was going back to the *Attila*, don't say anything about some of us maybe not going back." It sounded reasonable.

The next night, Tregare met the prodigal First and his freemate. The officer, now wearing crewman's fatigues, gave a bad first impression. Hulking and swarthy, a bit stooped, the man wore gargoyle's scars on his face. Blinking as he came from the dim corridor into Tregare's better-lighted quarters, he faced Bran and offered a handshake. As Bran took it, the man said, "I'm Derek Limmer, off the *Attila* and done with it, I hope. With me is Vanessa Largane." The scarred face grimaced. "I am not to blame for my looks, captain. At the Slaughterhouse when I was fourteen, it was a matter of too many belt buckles and not enough dodging."

As the low, resonant voice stopped, Tregare didn't know what to say. Finally, "Those bastards do have a lot to answer for."

Now the woman stepped forward. "And I'm Largane." As Tregare accepted her handshake, his breath caught—she was so damned beautiful! Tall, slim, with delicate features and tilted grey eyes, a mass of honey-tinted hair falling well past her shoulders. Strength to the slightly wide mouth, though, as she smiled. "Derek and I are a team. For some time now."

"Yes." Bran nodded. "Welcome aboard, both of you. Drinks, maybe?" They agreed and he accommodated them. "Now—two of your people are here already. Any more, that you know of, looking for a way off this icecube?"

"All the remaining five, I'd judge," said Limmer, "if they and your people can make connections."

"We'll try," Bran said. "Now let's exchange news."

Two more refugees from the *Attila* were aboard when Tregare lifted from Hardnose. Of the other three no trace could be found, and time was running out; sooner or later UET was going to get suspicious of the delays.

Bran felt lucky to have Limmer on the ship; the man was obviously capable, and from the start, after those first moments, Tregare felt full trust in him. And a good thing, too, because *Inconnu* was short one Control officer. Not in body but in function: Druffel, groundside, had tried a local competitive variation of downhill ski racing, and now had one leg in a cast from waist to ankle. Maybe a couple of drinks too many and maybe not; only the result mattered, so Bran didn't ask.

What he did was call a meeting of officers, in hospital which was really more of an infirmary, and invited Limmer also. Deverel was on watch along with Erdis Blaine and could hold the job down alone long enough for the necessary talk, Bran felt. Arriving while Eda Ghormley was still fussing over Druffel's complaints about the way the cast itched, Bran waited for the others to get there.

When everyone was on hand—and Druffel wasn't in such bad shape that people couldn't find seating on the edge of his bed—Tregare opened the proceedings. "While Second Hat Al Druffel is out of commission I want to appoint Derek Limmer, here, as Acting Second." He paused. "Any comments?"

Gonnelson said, "He held First." No more; he'd said it all.

Tregare nodded. "True. But I'm not demoting my own people."

Erdis Blaine frowned. "Why Acting? I mean, I know it's temporary, until Al's back fit for duty, but—"

Low-voiced as always, Limmer spoke. "Because permanent ranks carry shares with them; I know that much. And I brought nothing with me, from the *Attila*, that would enable me to buy in."

Waiting until he saw that no one else had anything to say, Tregare wrapped it up. "Then it's settled. And Derek—your time as Acting Second will earn you work-credit shares in *Inconnu* at that rank's rate. All right?" Some nods, no objections. "Adjourned."

* * *

The UET trip-sked handed to Tregare on Hardnose had the *Tamurlaine* going next to Johnson's Walk. But the hell with that; scanning Monteffial's list of Hidden Worlds' descriptions and coordinates, Bran changed course—out of detection range from Hardnose but still at such low-vee that the change cost little in terms of fuel—and headed for a planet called Freedom's Ring. According to the list it had a lot of Escaped traffic, and Tregare wanted all the information he could get.

So *Inconnu* built vee. And Bran looked at the circuit modification diagrams he'd got from Landis on New Hope. It was about time he did that, for Landis had a good thing here. The trouble with ships' projectors, as Bran already knew, was that the heterodyne was off-peak at the start, drifted through peak for five or six shots and then went off the other way, weakening again. Landis had circuitry that gave the gunner *control* over the heterodyne frequency—peace take it, that gunner could *stay* at peak energy. If the thing worked.

Tregare put Deverel on the modification job, handing him the specs, and letting him pick his own work crew. And a couple of days after turnover, listened while the small man explained the modified turret controls, and tried them out. They worked!

Took a little getting used to, though. Tregare sat in at Turret Six on some sims Deverel had improvised. You still had your range lights, for convergence, to keep unlit, and the hand lever for that function. And still the override pedal for desperation shots. But now, between the range lights, Tregare faced a small screen that lit up with a glowing ellipse. When heterodyne frequency was perfect, you had a circle. Off either way, the circle tilted, became an ellipse, and what you had to do was push your other handlever against that tilt, ease it back. Took a bit of doing, to learn the coordination, double observation and both hands, but after a while Bran thought he had the idea. At the end of the sim run he pushed up out of the gunner's seat, and turned to face Deverel.

"Hain," he said, "between you and Landis, I think we can shoot UET's ass off. If ever we get the chance."

Sooner than he expected, that chance came. Off-duty, coming out of the shower, he heard his intercom chime and went to answer it. "Captain?" Some rating talking; Tregare didn't recognize the voice. "Come up here? There's a ship overhauling us."

Half-wet, half-dry, he pulled on pants and shoes, and ran upship to Control. Gonnelson had the watch, but Erdis Blaine was there too, and it was she who explained, pointing to the main screen that pretty much told its own story. ". . . still on accel, captain, but the speeds are close; it'll be a relatively slow pass. Slight skew in our courses but not enough to shorten the contact period. And as you can see—"

"Yeah." Tregare nodded. "I see it's armed. So one gets you twenty, it's UET."

Blaine moved over to give him the aux pilot seat. Gonnelson had started to vacate the main one but Bran wasn't going to take over from his First Hat. Not that blatantly, anyway. He turned to the comm board. "Any calls coming yet?"

"Signals, yes, sir. But not strong enough to read yet."

"Stay on it." The woman nodded, fiddling with her tuning knobs. As voice tones grew toward intelligibility, Bran waited.

"... the *Tamurlaine*. For the *Hannibal*, Commodore Sherman calling the *Tamurlaine*. Come in, Rigueres, you old war horse! If you're still a captain, you owe me a bottle!"

A *commodore*? This one would know too much to be fooled by the ship's usual cover story. So fake it! But how much? Well, for starters: "First Officer Tregare speaking for Captain Farnsworth, who will be up to greet you if there's time. Sir, I'm sure Commodore Rigueres would congratulate you on equalling his rank, but you'll have to compare promotion dates to see who won your bet, and I'm afraid I have no exact data for you, sir."

"You don't, eh?" Now, inset on the screen along with the picture of the accelerating *Hannibal* facing *Inconnu* on decel, the commodore appeared; a lean-faced man with a mustache waxed into toothpick-length spears. The man scowled. "Answer me two questions, First Officer! Name your last two ports of call, and your next destination. And fast!"

Without even a star map, Bran couldn't begin to invent a plausible set of routes. He shook his head. "Begging your pardon, sir, but without the captain's authorization . . ." He let it trail off, hoping to stall a little. This pass couldn't last forever.

Not much luck. The commodore's voice raised to a shout. "To the *Tamurlaine*—I order you, a *direct order*, damn it!—to cut your Drive. *Now!* The *Hannibal* will match velocities and dock air lock extensions with you. Then we'll see what's going on."

Tregare panicked. "Sir . . . I can't . . . the captain's authority . . ." He knew he was dithering but couldn't think what to do.

"You will do it," the commodore yelled, "or I'll blow you out of space!"

Bran's thoughts came together. He looked to Gonnelson. "How long until they're into effective range?"

"A minute. Less."

Tregare was out of the seat and moving. "Swing us to *point* straight at them. No time to mess with traverse, but hook all six turrets to slave on Six. I'm going up there."

Protests came but he overrode them. "Gonnelson, you drive this ship! Blaine, feed me a running report up to Turret Six. And right now, everybody *shut up*!"

Then he ran.

In Turret Six he found the function switch on Simulation, thanked something or other for the time he'd had to correct that mistake once before, strapped into his seat, and activated his gunnery position. No bother with Tinhead-the-computer fiddling with traverses; Gonnelson had *Inconnu* headed dead on, and heterodyne was warming up as Tregare batted the other control back and forth, while he got the feel of his range lights.

He felt a jar; the *Hannibal* was firing. He got a circle on the middle screen, held it, and wiggled the controls until both range lights went dead. The odd part was that only a tiny indicator light told him he was firing. Then Blaine's voice came. "Oh my God, Tregare! You got them. You blew that ship apart!"

Stiff-legged with soreness incurred somehow when he wasn't noticing, Tregare went downship to Control. "All right," he said. "Tell me what happened. No screens up there, y'know."

"Better," said Gonnelson. "Show you. Tape." He switched the forward view to an aux screen; on the main one Tregare saw the *Hannibal* approach, swinging to the screen-center as Gonnelson had turned *Inconnu* for dead-on aim.

Incredibly fast, the *Hannibal*'s image grew. Then, between the two ships came flashing bursts, as UET's gunner strove for accurate beam convergence; Bran couldn't see the twin UV beams, and the lights vanished as heterodyne went into the peak-heat infro-red range. Suddenly the picture jerked and jiggled; almost, Tregare could feel again *Inconnu*'s shudder at the impact. Sheer radiation pressure, that was! "—much more time," Erdis Blaine was saying, "and they'd have got us."

Flashes going the other way now. "That's where *you* started shooting," The woman said, unnecessarily, as a little behind the *Hannibal*'s turreted nose, blinding bursts of plasma erupted. "Dead on into Control," she said. "The Drive didn't blow, but—"

He wasn't listening now; he saw the other ship go into a slow pinwheeling motion toward the screen's edge. Cargo holds, under his fire, exploded. Just before the *Hannibal* went off-screen, two specks, showing Drive radiation, left it and also vanished. "Scouts," said Gonnelson. "Got away."

"Which direction?" Tregare asked. As Blaine figured the defining angles, Bran shook his head. "That was in real time, wasn't it? Up in the turret, seemed to take a lot longer."

Blaine quoted her figures now. "A UET colony off that way, I think," said Derek Limmer. "I've seen the listing but don't remember the name or coordinates."

"Close enough, they might make it?" Tregare asked.

Limmer peered at him. "I wonder how you mean that."

Bran shrugged. "I mean, I hope they do. But sure as hell we can't go picking up after UETs mistakes."

"The *Hannibal*," said Gonnelson.

"You can't worry about that one, Tregare," Blaine protested. "It went spinning off our screens before you got back down here."

Well, sure, it *would*. Up at these speeds, a very little bit of Drive change could make a lot of distance in a big hurry. Bran shrugged. "Sherman was the one, wouldn't let it go."

Derek Limmer blinked. His scarred face made the sneering grimace that Bran knew he meant for a smile. "One thing's certain, captain. If any from the *Hannibal* get back to UET, you'll have a new nickname. . . . Tregare, the Pirate."

Limmer was there to relieve Blaine from watch; she'd stayed over, was all, but finally left. Tregare remained longer, talking and winding down, then stopped for a galley snack before he headed for quarters and sleep. He found the captain's digs lighted only enough so that a man wouldn't trip over the furniture. In the big bed, slight sounds of fuzzy breathing came from Erdis Blaine, who hadn't moved out yet.

Tregare hit the bathroom and then came out to go to bed. Maybe he should find out about Blaine—and about himself. He climbed in, turned and put a hand to Erdis Blaine's shoulder. "You awake?" In case the guess was wrong, he said it softly.

"Yes. And I sort of expected you tonight, Tregare."

"How's that?" The idea was going sour already.

"You're the kingbird now. Don't you need to celebrate?"

Celebrate making death? Not hardly. But he pulled her to him. "No, Blaine. It's like the time, a while back; I told you, you needed a cuddle. Now *I* do. So get you over here."

But one of these days . . . It's been too damn long.

11. "... Like Hogan's Goat"

When he and Blaine did become lovers, about three days short of Freedom's Ring, it happened almost by accident. He came half-awake to find himself somewhat entangled with the woman, and more than somewhat aroused. Her hands had something to do with it, and his own, moving more or less by instinct or habit, weren't quite idle either. Jolted into wakefulness, Tregare at first felt annoyance: was she trying to seduce him in his sleep? Then he saw that Erdis Blaine wasn't fully awake either. Smiling then, he saw to it that she was quite aware of what was going on.

When he finally decided he couldn't manage still another time, he sat up and said, "Sure worth the wait. For me, anyway." She gave him wordless agreement, and with that reassurance, suddenly his mind turned to the matter of hunger. "What you like for breakfast?" She told him; he nodded. "Same here," and he got on the intercom, to the effect that a few minutes later he accepted delivery of a breakfast tray from the galley. Since he had shoved all the papers to one side of his work table, they had a place to eat. "Enough eggs? How's the sausage?"

After swallowing, Blaine said, "Plenty. And fine."

Bran laughed. "We ought to eat this way more often. If your watch sked and my routines ever synch better." Then, when they'd finished the coffee, it was time to get dressed and go to work.

They kissed first, though, and she said, "Tregare? Now we have to talk a lot, really get to know each other."

"I think we do already—all this time living around the edges of us. But you're on, Blaine."

"Erdis."

"Oh, yeah . . . right. Erdis."

Except for a near absence of axial tilt, Freedom's Ring was quite like Earth—in size, gravity, and mean temperatures as determined by the characteristics and distance of its primary. "Main difference," said Tregare holding court in Control with all his Hats in attendance, "is lack of seasonal changes. You want summer, head toward the equator. Winter, head away from it. The seasonal climates sort of stay put. Lucky for people, the main island chain slants across the equator, with snow on one end but not quite so cold on the other."

The ship hit what should have been hailing distance, but this Hidden World had no beacon radiating any message. Or not right now, at least. So Tregare decided he should open communications.

Well within detection range if anybody happened to be watching—and with the screen on hi-mag, he could spot settlements but hadn't yet figured which ones might have spaceports—he got on the horn to groundside. "The ship *Inconnu*. Bran Tregare, captain, speaking for *Inconnu*. Calling groundside. Come in, please, Freedom's Ring." No answer yet. "I got your coordinates from Ezra Drake, the Security chief of New Hope. Part of the list he had from Cade Moaker on *Cut Loose Charlie*." Pause. "Freedom's Ring. *Inconnu* here. Come in, please."

After a time the aux screen flickered and lit, as a voice built volume until words came clear. ". . . about the delay, *Inconnu*. We've been reading you, though. We have no listing on the man Drake but Cade Moaker has been here and we do know of New Hope. So if you'll ready a tape input for fast-feed, I will transmit directions for your setdown. Please acknowledge."

Once Tregare's comm operator had complied, Bran said, "Ready." And watched as the digital data ran the screen full of eye-hurting blips—because the operator hadn't disengaged the two functions. Hmmm . . . ex-cadet Hank Cameron would wait a time for his next promotion.

* * *

Ideologies, Tregare thought, made nomenclature rather predictable. Located not quite far enough from the equator if you weren't too fond of hot weather, the main spaceport of Freedom's Ring was named Liberty Port. Tregare, handling the controls himself, landed without incident. Well, just for the hell of it he came down a little bit slaunchwise, off-target, and "walked" the ship a hundred meters or so to the designated landing circle. In response to the port's squawks, he apologized. When Blaine jumped him about it, and Gonnelson asked, "Why?" Tregare said, "I needed to know if I could do that. I found out."

Jonny Payce, in charge of Liberty Port, looked surprisingly young for the job. On closer inspection Tregare decided the looks were a little deceiving. The short, sandy-haired man was simply one of a type that holds age well.

In Payce's office, with Limmer and Erdis Blaine accompanying Tregare, they shared a snack and some drinks with the administrator and two of his aides. Compared to New Hope, this place conducted negotiations casually and quickly. In about half an hour, most of the buying and selling of cargo items was tentatively settled. "Subject to confirmation check," Payce said. He hitched his chair around, so he could stretch his legs. "Captain? Do you have your next destination picked yet?"

Tregare set down his empty wine glass, savoring the faintly spicy aftertaste. The younger aide refilled it. "Not for sure. Why?"

"You've heard of Number One?" Bran had, so he nodded. Maybe not the first Hidden World ever established, but one of the early ones—and now, because of an odd development, the most heavily populated by far. "You know the story?" Bran did, but this time he restrained the nod and raised his eyebrows. Maybe Payce knew more on the subject; it could pay to listen. The man flexed his knees, pulling his feet back so he could lean forward. "The damnedest thing. When the *Churchill* made its Escape, it was carrying among other things a load of frozen sperm and ova plus an experimental batch of pre-fertilized zygotes, also in freeze, intended to produce cheap labor for the mines on Iron Hat. And zoom-wombs to incubate them too, from zygote to infant in less than two months. You hadn't heard that?"

"Just rumors," said Derek Limmer. "It's true, then?"

"Right. And when the *Churchill* landed on Number One, the oligarchs there saw a chance to up population by a couple of decimal places in a hurry, and they went for it. Insisted on trading for the entire lot, or no refueling."

Tregare cleared his throat. "Two decimal places? Just how did they handle that many little kids, all at once?"

Payce laughed. "With difficulty, or so I've heard."

"Interesting," said Bran. "But what's the point? With regard to us, I mean?"

"Just that if you're not already set on going someplace else next, I have a standing contract to send certain types of cargo to Number One, any chance I get." He shrugged. "Some rare earth ores they're short on, some food-grain seed to vary their farm output—things like that. And they pay bonus rates, which you and we here would share." Tregare felt his skepticism showing, but Payce said, "Tregare, we never cheat a ship. Some places have tried it, and the word always gets around. And Escaped ships stick up for each other; we know that. Cheating bounces back."

Digesting the new knowledge, Bran said, "On Number One, who would I deal with? These oligarchs, you say. Any names?"

Jonny Payce cleared his throat. "I don't think there's any centralized governing body, as such. The whole thing sounds somewhat like feudalism in the Middle Ages on Earth. At any rate, my contracts are specifically with Hulzein Lodge, and that clan handles the dealings on Number One, from then on."

Hulzein? Bran's entire body went taut; he fought to relax, not to show his reaction. When he thought he could control his voice, he tried to think what to say.

Payce beat him to it: "I don't know how much you've heard about the Hulzein Establishment in Argentina, on Earth. You see—" Tregare halfway quit listening; for one thing, this Payce had his facts more than half wrong. But—". . . not a direct branch out of Argentina, I understand, but a semi-independent operation. A Hulzein 'connection,' I think it's called. Headed by a woman named Liesel Hulzein."

So that's where they went. "Yes, I've heard of that one." He thought about it. Number One, with its larger population, sounded like a place he needed to see. Already he'd found that New Hope and Freedom's Ring didn't have the facilities or the know-how for problems such as repairing the power suit he'd wrecked in retaking the ship from Farnsworth's gang. Though the areas of strength and weakness in expertise were spotty. Entering this Port Admin building, for instance, he'd heard some people discussing knowledgeably, the problems of stabilizing a Nielson cube, the heart of a starship's Drive. Confusing...

Payce still talked. At his next pause, Tregare said, "Number One sounds like a good bet, all right. Sure—let's work out the money angle, and I'll take your load there."

I'll deal with my family. I won't meet with them, is all. Because the hurt, from when they'd abandoned him to UET's Slaughterhouse, was still too great. The conscious rejection he'd had to make there, to free himself from tempting dreams of his home, heartbreaking when he woke, was solid in him. Dammit, they *could* have rescued him: surely Liesel had Underground and New Mafia contacts that could have worked for her even after she and Hawkman and Sparline left Earth. She *could* have done...

Reason tried to tell him that maybe Erika's surveillance had been too tight for any such action—but he was having none of reason. The old emotions, the old bitterness, still gripped him too hard.

By effort he shook himself free of it, and paid heed to Jonny Payce and Derek Limmer.

Leaving Admin, the three walked back toward *Inconnu*. There was another ship in port, standing off to one side. Jonny Payce hadn't mentioned it, so Tregare hadn't done any asking. He looked across the landing area, squinting past his own ship at the other one. Its insignia looked faded, but that had to be sheer pummeling from random encounters with interstellar dust; he could still make out the name and graphic emblem: *Spiral Nebula*.

On impulse, Bran stopped. "An idea. You want to look in on this ship, say hello?"

Erdis shook her head. "I'm overdue to relieve Gonnelson on watch. Actually, he took mine." Sure, the man who hated to talk had traded watches, so he wouldn't have to come visiting.

"Sure; okay." Tregare turned. "How about you, Limmer?"

The scarred man gestured assent. "Why not, Tregare?" So

Blaine walked off to *Inconnu*, and the men went to the other ship. At the foot of *Spiral Nebula*'s ramp they found no guard. Looking up they saw a woman, uniformed but hatless, her gun set leaning to one side, lounging at the air lock hatch. "Looks sloppy," Limmer said, "but let's not judge too soon."

"Right," Tregare said, but he'd already made judgment because he couldn't help doing it—and so, he suspected, had Derek Limmer.

They climbed the ramp. The surprising thing was how long it took the woman to notice them. On drugsticks? Probably. When they were only a few stairsteps below her she suddenly gasped, grabbed for her gun and nearly dropped it, then aimed it in a way that made Tregare uneasy. "Stop right there! What the hell do you think you're doing?"

There was no time to argue; the knuckle of her trigger finger was white. Tregare pitched his voice to carry. "Ten-HUT!" And the woman came to attention, holding her gun at a position that resembled Inspection Arms but didn't quite make it. "At ease," Tregare said, and then, "Would you please call your captain, and ask if he will accept a visit from Captain Tregare and Second Hat Limmer of *Inconnu*, just landed today?"

He saw the light disorientation, from the drugsticks, leave her. Her hands relaxed; she put the gun aside. "Oh—? Yes, sir. Sorry, sir. I—just a moment, please." She got on the horn then, keeping it in hush mode so that Tregare caught not a word of what was said, until she hung up. Then she said, "Welcome aboard, sirs. There'll be an escort down soon, to show you up to Captain Marrigan."

While they waited, Tregare looked around. The plastic underfoot was worn, through in places to the metal deck. The bulkheads, both the plastic-covered sections and the bare anodized metal, bore greasy smudges that looked as if they'd been there a long time. The deck part he could understand; this was an older ship and things do wear out. But the poor maintenance . . . mentally he shrugged. None of his business.

A heavy-set, thirtyish Chief rating clattered down the main stairs and came to greet them. He was ruddy of face and spoke loudly; Bran couldn't decide whether the fellow's manner was joviality or bluster, but gave benefit of the doubt. "My name's Corbett, gentlemen. The skipper's ready to see you now, if you'll follow me."

On the stairs the first handrail was loose; up the well came a faint scent of leaking gases. Refrigerant from the second stage of cryogenic environment for the Nielson cube, Bran recognized. The smell was only a faint trace; maybe someone had been changing a fitting or two.

Still it bothered Tregare: when, on *Spiral Nebula*, was he going to find something in *good* shape?

Captain's digs seemed cluttered, but comfortable enough. The man inside stood. "Brooks Marrigan, captain of *Spiral Nebula*. Used to be the *Wellington*, but of course that's a long time ago."

As they shook hands, Tregare gave his own name, "—captain of *Inconnu*, which until recently was the *Tamurlaine* and still bears that insignia. And my Second Hat here, Derek Limmer, who jumped ship off the *Attila*, back at Hardnose."

"Pleased, gentlemen. Something to drink, will you have?" They accepted, and at least the booze was good. Sitting, then, the three men traded news—always a preoccupation of spacers, Bran thought, living by the Long View as they did.

It wasn't that Marrigan sounded old, or looked it, but that he sounded like a defeated man. He perked up, though, when Tregare related the destruction of the *Hannibal*. "An armed ship, you have, Tregare? For our side, I think that's a first. Or do you know of others?"

As Limmer shook his head, Bran said "No." Before Marrigan could say more, Tregare got to the subject that was really bothering him. "Marrigan—is this ship in trouble?" He'd dealt with enough cadets to know when someone was trying to figure how to duck a question, so he cut in quickly. "Are you broke, or what?"

"Not—well, I—oh, hell!" Slumping back in his chair, Marrigan said, "Four trips ago. Up to then we'd been doing fine. But I put in at Dixie Belle and did an almost total swap of cargo there, and the bastards skinned us. They knew, and I didn't, that the bottom had dropped out of the market, for most of what they sold me. And since then, it's been like trying to play poker, table stakes and down to your bare ass."

Tregare's thinking moved fast. "Maybe we could make a deal."

But Marrigan wasn't done telling his grievance. "I should have stayed with safe goods, but they said we could make a killing." He leaned forward. "Do you know—Tregare, Limmer? —on that world they countenance slavery? Just like UET's

Total Welfare, except that Dixie Belle doesn't bother to put a fancy name to it. Somebody ought to—Tregare, your armed ship—you should—"

Limmer cut in. "Not necessary, not now. On Hardnose, hiding out, I heard what happened there on Dixie Belle." With a good sense of timing, or so Tregare guessed, the Second Hat waited until he had full attention, then said, "Dominguez, on *Buonatierra*, took offense at that aspect of Dixie Belle's system. He laid down an ultimatum: abolish slavery. He was laughed at, and told that *Bonnie* wouldn't be refueled." He made the smile that looked like a sneer. "Dominguez didn't have fuel for a real trip, but he was by no means dry in the tanks. He gave warning, of a sort—if they wanted to keep their town, they'd do things his way. 'Frig it off,' he was told. So the man lifted *Buonatierra* about fifty meters, held it there, squandering fuel like mad, then tilted and walked his Drive across the major government complex and the rich part of the city where the major slaveowners lived. And landed alongside the refueling facility. Nobody argued."

Marrigan looked pale. "But—didn't he kill a lot of innocent people? How can you condone that?"

"What choice did he have?" Tregare's voice came flat. "All the weapon he had was the Drive. It was use it or don't. Me, I agree with Dominguez."

"Well, actually," said Limmer, "the area he pulverized turned out to be highly underpopulated. The slaveowners thought he was bluffing and stood fast, but others had better sense, and vamoosed."

Tregare laughed. "Derek, you know how to wrap up a story with a ribbon around it!" Then, serious again, "Marrigan, what's your problem here? The bones of it." The man stayed silent. Irritated, Bran went on. "I said already, maybe we could help."

Marrigan sighed. "The Drive's bad—the Nielson cube and its support gear. Maybe it'll last the next trip, maybe not."

"So? I heard they have some here. And repair facilities."

The other man shook his head. "But I can't afford it. If we pay that, we can still buy fuel—just barely—but then at our next stop we'll have no assets left for trade. Or not enough."

Pausing first, Tregare said, "What if I buy you a new Drive?"

* * *

Walking back toward *Inconnu*, Bran said, "The trouble is, Limmer, the man's not realistic. I didn't ask much of a handle for our ship's money—just the promise of cooperation, later, on an operation I haven't even figured out yet, all the way. But he wouldn't budge."

"Maybe I wouldn't, either. How far *have* you figured it?"

Bran turned to face his Second Hat. "That one day I twist UET's tail like it's never been done. It'll take a bunch of ships to do it, so I have to start lining 'em up, one way or the other. . . . Use the grapevine, the mail drops, whatever. Buy in, take over, make agreements . . . *I* don't know what all, yet. I—"

"Tregare?" Bran stopped talking, and listened. "For what it's worth, I've changed my mind. In Marrigan's shoes I'd take your offer. But he's wearing them, not me."

Back on *Inconnu*, Tregare couldn't let the idea go. He paced his quarters, wishing Blaine weren't on watch, so he could bounce ideas at her and get feedback. But when he called her up in Control, all he said was, "Can you put me through to Jonny Payce, please?"

"Right, skipper." And in a few minutes Payce came on screen.

"Tregare here, Mr. Payce—or do you hold a rank I should use?"

The man chuckled. "Technically I guess I'm a commodore, though I've never served as a ship's officer. But 'mister' is all right. Call me anything—"

"—except late for dinner!" Both men laughed, then Tregare said, "You have Nielson cubes, and the means to install or repair them. Right?" Payce nodded. "What do the cost figures look like?"

Hearing the numbers, Bran whistled. Payce said, "Yes, I realize that's more than twice what costs would be on Earth. But we're not gouging. We have one new Nielson and one that's used but totally reconditioned here, and equal to new; I'd ride with it any time. And the figures—our markups, figuring parts and trouble-shooting and research, as well as normal labor—runs to slightly under twenty percent. We're heavily invested in these items, and they're scarce. Who knows when we'll get another?"

Tregare grinned. "Right away, maybe. What kind of trade-in can you offer on a cube that landed safe and is still chilled?"

"Forty percent of total job cost." No hesitation; this, then, wasn't an item up for dickering. "But where—? I mean, I didn't realize your Drive needed any major work."

"It doesn't. Thanks, commodore. I'll get back to you."

The money part would work. *Inconnu* could afford to fix *Spiral Nebula*'s Drive and to help a little with seed-money to put the cargo business on a paying basis. What was bothering Tregare, now, was the Marrigan part.

Over dinner in quarters, he and Erdis Blaine kicked the problem around. But not right after her watch. First they went to bed, and there she liked to take her time. Well, so did he.

She said, "The man won't give you any commitment, for his ship to join in helping you someday?"

Headshake. "It's his ship. Nobody else gets any say in it."

"Then what can you do? If he just lifts anyway, I mean?"

"Who says I have to let him?"

A couple of times Tregare tried to talk with Brooks Marrigan; finally he realized he wasn't getting anywhere. When the other ship's cargo was fully loaded, Bran knew he had to move. Hain Deverel, on the comm board up in Control, put the call through.

"Marrigan? Tregare here. We need to talk."

On screen the man looked haunted by devils. "Nothing to say, Captain. Except what we all say: good landings. Because *Spiral Nebula* lifts in about two hours."

Tregare beat his fist on the chair. "You *can't*. Marrigan, your Drive's not up to it. If you take that ship out, two to one you lose it, and you're all dead."

"That's my business, I think. And—"

"Have you taken a vote, polled your crew? Do *they* want to gamble on your insane pride?"

He'd gone too far there, Bran saw; Marrigan was ready to cut the circuit. Quickly Tregare said, "Don't cut! Because there's one more thing you need to know." Waiting, he said nothing else.

Until Marrigan answered, "I don't understand. *I* need to know?"

Tregare sank the hook. "Yeah, you do. And so does your

crew. You wouldn't have the guts, though, to pipe me on your all-ship broadcast circuit. I might say something you wouldn't like."

The intercom sounded; Deverel said, "Commodore Payce on the line, captain. Picked up one side of the argument, I think. He—"

Caught between tension and amusement, Tregare said, "Oh, what the hell, Deverel; patch him in. Conference circuit—the more the merrier." And when Payce appeared as an inset on the screen, Bran said, "Hi, commodore. You're coming in at the middle, so could you please just listen now, and I'll explain later?"

Payce started to speak, then nodded, as from *Spiral Nebula* Brooks Marrigan said, "My crew can hear anything I can. Speak your piece, Tregare."

All right! "Bran Tregare here, on the armed ship *Inconnu*, to all personnel of *Spiral Nebula*. Your Drive's no good; if you lift with it, as it is, you're all dead."

Screaming, Marrigan: "That's your opinion! I—"

"It's an opinion I can enforce."

"What do you mean?" Marrigan, sounding not quite so sure.

"I mean, you lift, you'll never reach vacuum. I'll blow you before you get there. Six turrets; you don't stand a chance."

Payce stuck an oar in. "You can't do that!"

"Try me," said Tregare. Intense now, wound up to busting, he yelled, "Damn you, Marrigan! We're so few, the Escaped Ships! We can't spare any; I can't let you waste yours."

"But you can essay to kill us all?"

Now almost sure of his ground, Tregare said, "Ask your crew, Marrigan. See if you can get your people to do a lift for you. I don't think you can."

"So that's it!" Well, Jonny Payce, at least, had caught on.

Marrigan's voice came as a growl. "This is piracy."

And now Tregare could relax. "Not a bit of it, Captain Marrigan. Consider yourself overruled, is all. I'm quite willing—determined, in fact—to buy you out, based on your own computer estimate of the ship's assets. And to buy out any who want to get off with you as well." Fast thinking, now. "Those who want to stay with the ship, and work with the command cadre I'll be installing, are welcome. And when you lift, it'll be with a solid Drive system. I guarantee that."

He was guessing, by this time, the costs and credits, and

where the deal would leave *Inconnu* in the assets column. But *he wanted this ship*. Imagining the chaos on it right now, he waited.

In Marrigan's voice when he finally answered, there was no mistaking the sadness. "If it were only me, Tregare, I'd blow the Drive and you with it, sitting so close, and the hell with you. But not my people. And . . . and not, I find, my ship, either. I can't work under you or anyone else, not these days, so I couldn't accept your offer of alliance. But"—well, maybe he hiccuped—"I'll get off. You can buy me out. *And damn you to bloody hell, Tregare!*"

No answer at all seemed the kindest thing.

A few more than twenty left *Spiral Nebula* with its captain. Tregare, along with Gonnelson and Limmer, interviewed personnel on *Inconnu* to work up the command cadre. At the same time they recruited replacements from groundside, most for *Inconnu* but a few for the other ship. It began to seem, Tregare thought, that any ship was better off running overmanned than the other way.

Nebula's Drive was almost ready. Old Mallory stood in to help that ship's Chief Engineer study the fine tuning after the new Nielson cube was in place. The groundside techs knew their stuff, sure—but it wasn't the same as making adjustments when you were running at a t/t_0 of maybe twenty. Or was it the other way around? Well, symbols or not, Tregare knew what he meant.

The "trade-in" of *Nebula*'s Nielson cube was the item that put Tregare's dealings in the black. Without it, he'd have run *Inconnu*'s assets down too thin. As it was, *Nebula* would have to deal close to the vest for a trip or two, but it was no longer in real trouble. And *Inconnu* had shed a little surplus, was all.

The main problem, though, Tregare hadn't tackled yet.

When he called Gonnelson down to captain's quarters for the talk, Erdis Blaine stayed away. Both she and Bran knew that the First Hat's trouble with talking was even worse with women present.

Gonnelson came in, nodded, muttered some kind of greeting, and accepted the one drink which was all he would take on any given occasion. He sat down, and looked at Bran Tregare.

Bran said, "*Spiral Nebula*. It's your command, if you want it. You're first in line and you're damned good with a ship. I know you have trouble talking, but your Hats can help with that stuff. I—"

"*No!*" First time Bran had ever seen the man throw a drink down in one gulp. Gonnelson shook his head. "Not command. No."

"Why? Tell me why. You have to." Headshake. Bran said, "This is one time you're taking a second drink, and that's an order." He poured it, and Gonnelson took one sip. "Now tell me."

It took a while and it didn't come easy. Haltingly, a few words at a time, between repeated questions from Tregare, the man told his story.

"Had it."

"Command? You had command?" Nod. "Where? Did you take it willingly?" Headshake. "*Where*, dammit?"

"Slaughterhouse."

"You were in officers' training? I didn't know that. When?"

"No. Combat cadre. Okay—Tregare knew about those. They were a slaughterhouse sideline, for ratings, not officers, and—suddenly Bran's indrawn breath hissed as he made a gasp. The training maneuvers!

He said, carefully, "They put you into command for a combat exercise?" Nod. "They use live ammo for those, don't they?" Gonnelson's face made any other answer needless. Tregare winced, as he said, "How big a command? A platoon, or what? And what happened? What the hell *happened*?"

"Ambush. Whole cadre." The man's shoulders had begun to shake and heave. "Lost nearly whole *cadre* . . . dead."

Wishing he'd never started this questioning, now Tregare had to follow through with it. "That can happen. But how? *Why?*"

"Orders. Right orders. Knew them. Couldn't *say* in time." Gonnelson didn't seem to notice the tears running down his face. Shaking his head, he looked ready to throw up. "Not command! Please?"

"All right." Tregare went to him, hugging the man's head to his shoulder. "If you can't, you can't. You're one hell of a good First Hat, though; you know that?" Gonnelson's body had been shaking; the movement eased. Tregare said, "I still think you earned your second drink." He sat back and raised his own. "Cheers, First?"

After a moment Gonnelson said, "Cheers," and drank.

* * *

So time to call conference, all the Hats. Captain's digs had the most ease, so that's where Tregare gathered his people. With everyone seated and comfortable, comestibles handy, he began.

"*Inconnu* now owns a chunk of *Spiral Nebula*. Well, you all know that. Thing is, we've set up a command cadre to run it for us, but nobody's in charge yet." He looked around the group. "Gonnelson was first in line but he declined, and his reasons are his own business. So I guess you're next, Limmer. Can we deal here?"

The scarred man blinked, and said, "If you mean, will I honor your call on that ship's services—something you mentioned after our first visit with Marrigan—yes, you have my word on that. There's one problem. Working in the Long View, how do you let me know what's wanted, and when?"

To Bran Tregare the question was nothing new. "The grapevine, Limmer. The mail drops. Passing computer info at every landing, and between ships that come into comm range." He shook himself loose from tension. "Look . . . I *know* the odds are bad, hitting enough contacts by way of the Long View to put anything together in one place at one time." Even to him it sounded hopeless. So he laughed. "So if I need to get six ships together, I'll try for sixty. Or more. There'll be ships Escaping, we haven't even heard of. So don't worry, Limmer. If you aren't with me when I pull off the coup I haven't even figured out yet . . . well, somebody will be."

When Derek Limmer laughed, the sneer left his smile. He raised his glass. "Tregare . . . I hope I'll be there."

"One more thing," Bran asked. "You renaming the ship?"

"I hadn't decided. Why? Aside from future IDs, of course."

Tregare held his laughter. "The shape that bucket was in, I thought of calling it '*. . . Like Hogan's Goat*.' But now—"

"No," said Limmer. "Now it's *not* fucked up." He chuckled. "Still, though . . . Tregare, what would you say to *Left-hand Thread*?"

Huh? Pause. "Hey . . . I *like* it!"

For the refurbished ship's lift-off, Tregare threw a good party in *Inconnu*'s galley. He missed the lift itself by sleeping through it. A time later, the intercom brought him awake. "Yeah?"

"Captain?" Some rating on the horn; the name escaped him now. "A ship coming in, close to comm range. You want to speak to it?"

He sat up. "Why? We got a problem?"

"Not that I know of, sir. But I thought I'd ask."

"Thanks. But if we don't know 'em. I expect we can wait 'til they get set down." Another thought came. "You get anything says maybe there *is* a problem, call me five minutes ago. Okay?"

"Yes, Captain." Tregare cut the circuit and started to lie back for a little more sleep. But Erdis Blaine had awakened and was sitting up. It turned out that she had a better idea.

The incoming ship was newly Escaped and now called itself *March Hair*. It came in on awkward trajectory and did not land well. Nothing serious, but Tregare wouldn't have allowed that pilot to set *his* ship down. Expecting the usual exchange of courtesies, he waited in quarters a while, but no message came, so Bran went down to the galley and ate more breakfast than he really needed, because his appetite felt like it. He was dawdling over an excess of coffee when the officer's-table intercom squawked at him. "Is there an officer available in the galley? There is none in Control just now. We have a request, an officer off *March Hair* who wants to talk with the captain. And says it's urgent. Is there—?"

Tregare hit the switch. "Captain here. Send—I mean, *escort* this other ship's officer to the galley. I'll be here." He didn't need any more coffee but he ordered another pot anyway. Then he waited.

The person the guards bought in wasn't wearing officer's uniform, exactly; it was sort of a mix. But that didn't matter. Bran stood; without thinking, he yelled welcome. Because the man coming in was Jargy Hoad.

"Bran! Tregare! What luck!" They were hugging, shouting, pounding each other around the edges with no intent to hurt.

Tregare it was who first came to caution. "Yeah, good to see you; glad you're here. But what *is* this?" He held them both still. "What's wrong, Jargy?"

Hoad didn't look much older, and seemed still good-humored. "I need off that ship, is all, Bran. The wrong man came up captain—nobody's fault, it just happened. But Grecht and I have hated each other's guts the whole time. I get off, or it'll be a killing."

"Which way?"

"I think I'm faster. But that's not the point, Bran. Escape leaves a lot of strain among the survivors. Well, you'd know about that, wouldn't you? *March Hair*'s people are solid, basically, but the situation won't take any more upheavals and still hold together. And—" He shrugged. "I think Grecht has more folks on his side than I have on mine."

"So?" Tregare wanted Jargy to do the saying of it.

"Tregare, do you have berth for me on here? Or would I have to ride as supercargo?"

"Is Grecht buying you out? What Hat are you wearing?"

"Third, before Escape. First now. But Grecht only wants to pay me off as Third."

Tregare knew his own grin, then, wasn't looking amiable. "Is that right? You mind if I speak with your Captain Grecht? I think I can change his mind for him."

If something works, use it. Tregare put a call through comm to *March Hair*, identified himself, and asked for Grecht. He expected to dislike the man on sight and was surprised to see a pleasant-looking young man with a blond crewcut and cheerful smile. The smile went away, though, when Bran said, "I intend to make sure you deal fairly with my friend Jargy Hoad." He then explained, much as he had to Brooks Marrigan, the alternative. "So it's fifteen percent, Captain Grecht, not five. I won't need to check your figures; Jargy knows the totals. So figure what you want to pay in cargo and how much in Weltmarks, and if I like it, we've got us a deal."

Grecht chewed his lip. "Let me think a minute."

"Sure. Take your time." Tregare cut his audio transmission and went to the intercom. "Watch officer. Tregare here. On the double, get an armed squad to cover the boarding ramp, from inside." His order acknowledged, he turned back to Jargy and Erdis Blaine, who had just joined them. "Pure precaution. In case Grecht got any ideas about direct action."

Blaine said, "He couldn't pull a lift on you, could he?"

Jargy Hoad chuckled. "Not hardly. He's refueling, and Bran already knew that." Then, "Ready to talk now, Grecht is."

". . . can work it out," the other captain was saying. "Not

more than a third in money. I'm afraid. As to cargo..." Grecht began citing items and quantities. Playing it off the top of his head, Tregare made his choices, checking his own computer extension terminal to validate pricings, and saying yes more often than no. Sooner than Bran expected, the dickering was done with.

Wrapping it up, he said, "Fine, Captain Grecht. Tomorrow we can sign papers and take delivery." The call ended, and Bran said, "I told you, Jargy, I could change his mind."

"Sure," said Hoad. "And thanks. But if I were you, I'd keep those armed guards at the boarding ramp."

"You're not me, lucky for you. But I will."

"That's good." Jargy nodded toward the woman. "I don't think we've met, exactly. Would you introduce us, Tregare?"

"Oh. Oh, sure. Erdis Blaine, my Third Hat. Jargy Hoad, Erdis—he and I were in the same squad room, our snotties year at the Slaughterhouse. He's going to be our new Second."

"Second?" Her face went slack, then made a frown. "But I—"

He reached for her hand, but she pulled it away. "Erdis, I know you expected Second. And if Jargy hadn't turned up, you'd have it. Or if I'd promoted you earlier—just like Gonnelson and Limmer, I wouldn't have set you back, no matter what. But, you see—Jargy's had the full Slaughterhouse, same as me. And while you're doing just fine, training and all, he's simply better qualified." Her face was tight, her expression withdrawn. "Can you accept that?"

Before she could answer, Hoad said, "A moment, here. Bran, what's *Inconnu*'s going rate for Second, and for Third?" When Tregare, taking a few seconds to calculate, gave him the figures, Jargy said, "No problem. This is a rich ship; my last one wasn't. Third's all I can afford to buy in for, and glad to do it."

Still angry, Blaine said, "I'm sure the captain is willing to lend the difference to his old roomie, against your future duty credits. Welcome aboard, Second Hat."

This time Bran did capture her hand. She tugged, but he wouldn't let go. "Wrong, Blaine. Welcome our new *Third* Hat. I was sticking to my own rules a minute ago, and I still am."

Narrow-eyed, she looked at him. "You're not just doing this to soothe the spoiled brat's temper tantrum? Bran—"

Jargy Hoad's laugh broke the tension. "I'd think, Blaine,

that you'd know Tregare better than that, shipping together. If you want to change his mind, pressure is absolutely the worst possible tactic."

Seeming puzzled, she said, "Then what's the best one?"

"As just now," said Hoad. "Provide new facts." He stood. "I brought a runaway's kit aboard, in case it wasn't feasible to rescue all my gear from *March Hair.* In it is something I think we might use just now. I won't be long."

As he walked away, leaving the galley, Bran leaned closer to the woman. "Don't ever think I undervalue my *new* roomie." Then she smiled, and squeezed the hand he still had on her own.

Taking longer at his errand than Tregare expected, Hoad came back carrying a bottle of wine. Passing the serving counter he picked up glasses, then came and sat. "While I was at it," he said, "I hauled my kit upship and set it in the corridor, just outside Third's quarters." Somehow he made a ceremony of pulling an ordinary cork, then poured for the three of them. "This comes from Far Corner, a colony noted for tart and tangy wines. Sort of appropriate, I thought"—he raised his glass and waited while the others followed suit—"to toast the promotion of Erdis Blaine to Second Hat on *Inconnu.*"

They drank, and Tregare was surprised to see Blaine brushing at her eyes. She said, "It should be yours, Jargy. I—"

"Don't give it a thought. If I know Bran Tregare, and I think I do, before we're done we'll each have our own ships."

And before the wine was done, with a couple of other people joining in, the occasion became almost a party. At the end of it, Blaine said to Hoad, "You can move your gear right into Third's quarters, if you like. I have a few things in the place, which I'll get out soon, but I don't live there."

Asking no questions, Jargy said, "Sure; thanks," and left. Soon after, Tregare and Blaine went to their own quarters. Once inside, she turned and embraced him.

"Bran? I like your friend. I'm glad he's here."

"Yeah. Jargy's one of the good ones, all right."

Cash and cargo both, Jargy Hoad's shares in *March Hair* were delivered on board *Inconnu;* checked, accepted, and signed for. Grecht himself brought the packet of Weltmark certificates. When the man's entrance was announced, Bran was hosting Jargy a drink. On the intercom he said, "Escort Captain Grecht to my quarters, please."

Hoad gulped his drink, and stood. "I'll leave, if you don't mind. I've seen all I want to of that sonofabitch." He paused. "Unless you might want a little backing, Bran. He's tricky."

Tregare suppressed his laugh. "On *my* ship? Thanks anyway."

So Jargy left, and soon a rating ushered Grecht in, then departed. The blond man had his smile back; after shaking hands he gave Tregare the heavy envelope. "You'll want to check this."

"That's right. Sit down. You'll have a drink?"

The amenities taken care of, the counting went fast, and Bran looked at this man his friend disliked so much. "The numbers check out. We're free and clear." But he was still curious. So *ask*. "Grecht . . . I've known Jargy Hoad a long time. Easygoing, I'd always thought. How come you two couldn't live on the same ship? Not that it's any of my business, come to that."

Grecht finished his drink, and stood. "Precisely. But I'll tell you, anyway. I own my ship, and that includes the people on it. Hoad couldn't accept the principle."

Incredulous, Tregare gazed at the man. "Neither could I."

"So you'd have sneaked off too, tail between your legs?"

No such thing had Jargy done. Two questions here. But only one answer. "No," said Tregare. "I'd have killed you."

Grecht didn't stay much longer.

12. A Job To Do

For lift-off from Freedom's Ring. Tregare gave Erdis Blaine the office. He'd have liked to have done it himself, and drift a little sidewise toward *March Hair* and maybe scare Grecht's guts out into his shorts, but that wouldn't be fair to a lot of other people, so he didn't. And Gonnelson had done a lift, and so had Jargy. It was Blaine's turn. And she did fine with it.

They headed for Number One now. Not a straight shot, because that would pass too close to a UET colony, and the course also needed a bulge to miss a dust cloud expanding from where a star had once erupted as a medium-sized nova.

Tregare looked through what records he had from Escaped ships, and hoped he wasn't missing anything essential.

One item caught his notice. His totally random choice of direction in which to bulge his course would take *Inconnu* well within range of a Hidden World listed in his new information. Tregare called a conference; his Control officers plus the Chief Engineer. Holding up a rough sketch, he said, "Shegler's Moon. It's not all that far off our planned course, and close enough that if we go there we'll have a time-ratio of five at Turnover. Question is, should we have a look at the place?"

Mallory didn't care. Jargy said, "Why not?" Erdis Blaine favored the idea. Gonnelson's hand made a sweeping palm-up gesture, sidewise toward Tregare.

"I guess you mean, Gonnelson, it's up to me?" The man nodded. "Okay; consensus says we go there. So—"

"I'm surprised, Bran," said Jargy Hoad. "I'd have expected you to do all your own deciding, not take votes."

Looking, Tregare saw that his old friend was sincere, not needling him. "Well—" He thought about it. "When it comes down to squat, there's no time for voting. And what this ship's going to *do*, someday—anybody doesn't agree, I buy them out. But on stuff like this, the major owning shares should have a say."

"And the minor ones?" Erdis Blaine asked that.

Impatient now, Bran shook his head. "Those are courtesy shares, a system of wages, and you know it. If we have to ask people who don't know what the problem is, we're in deep."

Enough of that; he began telling them about Shegler's Moon. The system's star massed about one-point-five of Sol and ran hotter and whiter. The satellite's primary combined a mass of about three Earths, an atmosphere like that of Venus, and an orbital distance that beat Mars somewhat. "The Moon itself, the Escaped outpost, is maybe eight thousand kilos across—light on gee and thin on air."

Hoad leaned forward. "It hardly sounds like a great place to settle on. All the frequent eclipses, for one thing."

"Not all that many," said Bran. "Good tilt on the orbit." He read them the rest of it straight off the data sheets: temperature range, availability of water, edible vegetation but no vertebrate animal life. "Until their frozen zygote supply grew up to be cows and such, most of the protein came from a meat tank. But this latest report—some years old by now—

says they have a stable colony going. And a good fuel-production plant, of course, for refueling ships."

"That part I'd figured," said Mallory. "Or else you wouldn't have suggested we go there at all."

So *Inconnu*, still wearing the *Tamurlaine*'s insignia, cut course for Shegler's. With the ship still coming up toward a vee that would halve ship's time compared to that of planets, Jargy Hoad on watch called down to Tregare's quarters. "Bran? Something up ahead. I think we're overhauling somebody. Not straight on. There's some skew between us. You want a look?"

"Be right up." He dressed and went to Control. "What have you spotted?"

In space the passage of a starship left—well, indications. Not a "wake" exactly, but etheric turmoil that jiggled outside viewscreen images and put a bit of hash into communication channels if those were open. If the disturbances were on the increase, it meant you were closing your distance.

"You want to swing over and check this, Bran? Intercept?"

"Couldn't hurt to have a look. Assuming it's not too much work." Meaning cost in fuel, and they both knew it. For maybe thirty seconds he watched a couple of instruments, then said, "I'd guess we're overhauling, but only by a little. Means he's still on accel, whoever, but running it well below max. Why don't you up ours a smidgen, not too much, and see what happens."

Less than two days later the other ship showed on the detectors, and then, at top mag, as a shimmering dot on viewscreen. Gonnelson had the watch as Tregare said, "I think we've converged enough, for now. Let's run parallel for a while, so that when we pull up with them, their Drive won't garble the comm."

Gonnelson nodded, and corrected course. Tregare went to get some sleep, and it wasn't until he rose and was finishing breakfast that Blaine called him by intercom. "Tregare? We don't have comm yet, but we do have a make on that ship's beacon. It's the *J. E. Hoover*, Captain Durer commanding."

Kickem's on that ship, or was! "I'll be right up."

And it was Kickem's voice, stretched and splattered by distance and wavering magnetic fields, that came from the viewscreen's speaker as Tregare entered Control. The screen itself, at high mag, showed a rear three-quarter view of the ship. ". . . repeat, the *Hoover* here, First Officer Bernardez speaking for Captain Durer who is, unfortunately, unable to give you proper greeting at the moment, though I do take the liberty of sending you his best wishes. And who might yourselves be, out here so far from no place but temporarily sharing course with us?"

Tregare waved the comm tech off and sat in his place. Kickem was up to First on the *Hoover*? This was going to take some thinking. "Third Officer Bran Tregare of the armed ship *Tamurlaine*, speaking for Captain Rigueres who is also indisposed at the moment." *Now what? Oh, yeah . . .* "*Hoover*, you are directed to name your most recent port of call and next destination." That's what the *Hannibal* had pulled, so maybe it was S.O.P. And if Kickem could maybe use a hand . . .

A pause, then, "Tregare, is it? A time it's been. Well now, only Captain Durer himself is authorized, you understand, to put our mission's details onto open circuits. However—"

Bran flipped his switch to Transmit. "Then I hope you're authorized to match course and vee, and stand by for boarding. Because otherwise, *Hoover*, we'll have to fire on you."

Fire on Kickem's ship? But sometimes a man has to bluff. Because here was Bran's chance to help his friend Escape.

From the other end he heard argument: Bernardez and at least two others. Somebody wanted to flip ship, a dangerous form of near-instant Turnover, and lose the *Tamurlaine* by taking max decel at a random angle and then flipping again, to run for it. Sounded as if Kickem disagreed, but Bran couldn't be sure of that.

Well, the hell with it. The way the argument stood, Bran had the wrong people on his side and the right ones against him. So into his mike he blasted a shrill whistle, and when relative quiet came from the *Hoover* he said, "Correction. My orders still stand: heave to! But those orders are from the escaped ship *Inconnu*, Bran Tregare commanding." He took a deep, shuddering breath. "I'm sorry, Kickem, but this is the best way I can see, to do it."

For a moment he wasn't sure what he was hearing. Then he knew it for Kickem's laughter. Finally, "Oh, Bran! Always so cautious, we have to be. And your ship with those great dangerous projector turrets, to blow us out of space. But no need, no need at all. For in fact I was not, myself, utterly truthful. Because although we've not changed the *Hoover*'s name as yet, to make it easier for us to trade advantageously at UET colonies, let me inform you that you now speak with the ship's new captain." Another laugh. "Yes, Tregare . . . it's my ship now!"

Wanting to believe, Bran said, "How many latrines you got on it?"

After a moment, Kickem said, "A great lot more than only one!" And then, totally and necessarily out of synch with each other, what with distance and delay, the two ships' Control crews sang about UET's lack of sanitary facilities.

A few hours of running parallel, the ships' computers indicated, wouldn't cost much in time or fuel, though a physical meeting would—and was tricky work, as well. So talk had to suffice. "Your Captain Durer's indisposition is permanent, then?" Tregare asked. "Same as happened to Rigueres?"

On screen, picture clear now at closer distance, Bernardez shook his head. "No such thing. We had us, you must understand, some great good luck. At Escape we managed to take Durer's woman, and two of his best friends, as hostages. The man announced surrender and enforced it. We had only two Utie loyalists dead, and one of ours. Durer and the other Uties we left safely on Fair Ball." Bran felt his face change, and Kickem must have seen, for he sighed. "Not so lucky in your own case? In usual, I gather, it seldom is." Then Bernardez took on a more cheerful look. "Almost forgetting, I was. We have a great lot of data for you, secret reports fom UET's most sequestered files. For this ship, mind you, was on its way as no less than a special courier to the fortress world Stronghold. So if any of our pilfered records should interest you . . ."

"Sure." The aux circuit was set up, and soon the comm panel lights showed digital info coming in on fast-feed. When he'd ever get a chance to scan through it all, Tregare had no idea. Someday, though, and maybe soon enough to make use of it. But right now, he had to ask something. "Kickem? What's your planning? I mean, you have a ship. So now what?"

When the other didn't answer immediately, Bran said, "I'm

going to do something about UET. Right yet, I'm not sure what. But whatever, it'll take more ships than one, so I'm trying to line some up. For whenever the idea whips into shape." He told of taking Marrigan's ship for Derek Limmer, and their agreement. "Bernardez, I'll take ships, buy into them, make free alliances, anything—to put a fleet together." Quickly he explained how he was trying to spread word—and later get answers—on the grapevine already begun on the Hidden Worlds by Cade Moaker. He mentioned his plans to arm Escaped ships from his arsenal on New Hope.

"From what I hear, I'll want my main base on Number One. It has the population to support a reasonable grade of production." Bernardez nodded, agreeing with the coordinates Bran gave then. "So what I want to know, Kickem—if I get something set up, and it looks like it might work . . ." He paused. "Are you with me?"

Bernardez smiled. "Had you gone and achieved this thing, Bran Tregare—and having the chance to invite me along, not done so—why, the insult would have been near to mortal."

[illegible] diverged.

Through this volume of space a number of world-to-world routes funneled. Shortly after *Inconnu* passed peak-vee and Turnover another ship entered detection range. Its beacon, though, was either faulty or deliberately turned off, and no amount of hailing via loop-tapes brought any response. Checking his coordinates against graphic viewscreen simulations, Tregare could make no good guess as to the ship's origin or destination, and the angle between courses was far too great for possible interception. "For all I know," he said to Erdis Blaine, "it could be a Shrakken." And then needed to explain to the woman who had heard nothing but the vaguest of rumors, how UET hadn't invented stardrive at all, but had murdered visiting aliens to steal their ship. He repeated Hawkman's story of Committee Police and cyanide gas.

At the end, she nodded. "Yes, Bran. That's the way they work."

Approaching time for Turnover, Bran called Mallory and discussed the argument he'd partially heard from the *Hoover*. "This quick-flip thing they mentioned. It's been done, I gather—but is it dangerous to the ship?"

After a pause, the Chief Engineer said, "Not if you do it right the first time. Should you end up pinwheeling, though, it could take considerable time and fuel to get straightened out again. But why—"

"Because it sounds like a useful tactic—and I want to be able to do anything that anybody else can."

They compromised. At Turnover, Tregare swung ship about four times as fast as normal, but still only half as quickly as the combat maneuver. At Mallory's suggestion he fed all his moves into Tinhead in real time, then worked to refine the parameters and get rid of minor errors. And finally he put the entire maneuver onto a program requiring only a single key punched to activate it.

Although he warned the crew and asked them to secure all gear, more damage than usual resulted. But he felt it was worth it.

Approaching Shegler's Moon, *Inconnu* detected no call-beacon, and for a time Tregare's own calls, put on a loop-tape when he got tired of repeating himself, brought no answer. Not until about an hour before the ship could have landed did groundside respond. "Shegler's to *Inconnu*. You can land if you want to, but we have nothing to trade just now, and very little spare manpower or facilities for servicing. Fuel is short here, and—" The whining voice continued explaining its inhospitality.

Inconnu wasn't short of fuel; Tregare figured he could make Number One, with a little to spare. But still he intended to top off, any place he landed. "*Inconnu*, Bran Tregare commanding, will land in fifty-four minutes, give or take a couple. We're not in need of servicing, and require only a moderate amount of fuel, for which we pay going rates. Who'm I talking to down there, by the way?"

It was like pulling stumps with a lame mule, but Tregare did get his answers. The voice was Mace Henry, and, yes, there was a *little* fuel, but because of unnamed difficulties, a surcharge was in order, and ships' personnel were quarantined to the landing area, no fraternizing in the settlement, and . . .

Disgusted, Tregare said, "We'll talk that small stuff when we're down. Bran Tregare out." And turned to Gonnelson and Jargy Hoad, saying, "I don't know what these folks' trouble is, but let's make sure it stays theirs and not ours." He knew both scoutships were checked out in top shape. Now he saw to it that an armed squad would protect ship's security groundside, at all times. And wound up by adding, "I don't think this outfit has missiles and I have no idea why they'd want to use them. But heading down, let's have the scouts manned, just in case."

"Aren't we getting a little paranoid?" said Jargy.

Tregare grinned. "Maybe. Just so we don't get a little dead."

Landing was no problem. Gonnelson took *Inconnu* down. As with any task that didn't need talking, he did it superbly. Once groundside, Tregare headed for what had to be the Port Admin building. With him he took along Erdis Blaine and three armed guards. Going toward and into Admin he thought the place seemed normal enough but the people didn't. For one thing, they weren't much given to saying hello to strangers.

Entering Mace Henry's office, he and Blaine left the guards outside; after all, one man wasn't much menace. As Tregare went to Henry's desk, giving his half of the introductions and offering a handshake, the other man stood to accept. "Yes. Captain Tregare. I trust your ship's not staying long?"

"That depends. Let's talk about fuel first." As Henry stalled and waffled, Bran tried to decide what was *wrong* about him. He stood and moved like a healthy person. His complexion was good. But there was something hangdog in his manner. Finally Tregare thought he saw what was haywire here; the man was scared. *Of what?* Still listening with half his attention, he caught a phrase and shook his head. "Forget your surcharge. Straight rates."

"Out of the question. Our problems here—"

Tregare nodded to Erdis Blaine. *Time for the whipsaw.* Blaine said, "We could believe your problems, possibly, if you'd show us some figures to back them up."

"Well, I—" The expression of Henry's face, then, Tregare couldn't figure out. The man stood. "One moment. In the other office . . . I'll have to . . ." he moved to a door, opened it, and went into another room.

Blaine said, "What do you think he's up to?"

"Why not find out?" Tregare walked over to that door, put his ear to it and listened.

Not much at first, then Mace Henry's voice. "Habbeger.

Captain Habbeger . . . from Port Captain Henry." Then, more like talking to himself, "I hope that damn satellite relay's working," and again speaking better, "Habbeger, this one's trouble. I think you'd better come around here and be ready to intercept."

Impatient, Tregare waited, back where Henry had last seen him, until the Port Captain brought out a folder of papers and tried to smother everything in figures and confusion. A few minutes, Bran put up with that garbage; then he said, "When can you start refueling?" Tomorrow afternoon, maybe later. "All right; I'll pay the surcharge. Call me at my ship." He motioned to Blaine and they left. Outside the office, the guards followed.

Halfway back to *Inconnu*, Blaine said, "You're paying his squeeze? Ships don't pay blackmail. Tregare—?"

The only squeeze was his hand on hers. "That's tomorrow afternoon. Erdis, we won't be here then."

"I don't understand."

"Neither do I, for sure. But that bastard made a call out to space. And he asked a fella name of Habbeger to come intercept us." He looked at her. "Guess whose uniform *that* one's wearing."

Nobody on *Inconnu* was ready for lift-off to be scheduled so soon; none of the necessary checkoff lists had been done. Tregare raised his voice some, then, and the jobs went faster. He and Deverel did the comm-system work themselves, and four hours after Bran and Erdis left Henry's office, Tregare called the Port's comm. "*Inconnu* lifting in five minutes. Clear the safety zone."

"You can't do that!" Not Henry this time; the voice was unfamiliar. Not that it made any difference who was yelling.

"I'm doing it. Clear the area. Any dead are *your* fault." He didn't shut down the voice input that kept blithering at him; he simply paid no more heed to it. From down below he heard ringing noises that sounded like projectile weapons hitting *Inconnu*'s hull. In that case they might be trying energy bolts, too—so the hell with trying to be nice; he reached over and cracked his Drive-node output. Not enough to raise ship, but plenty to fry the landing circle and a little more. *Fuck around long enough, Henry, you'll win a prize!*

The five-minute notice had been for Mallory, not for the

convenience of groundside. Bran used the rest of the time to make sure his assigned gunners had the turrets ready. Missiles he didn't know, but he asked who did and Gonnelson said "Me," so the silent man held down that seat, with the fate of four fusion heads under his splayed fingers. Erdis Blaine had the counter-missiles, though neither she nor Bran knew much about those. And Jargy Hoad was riding sidekick.

Good enough. On mark, Tregare took *Inconnu* up like a bat.

Just under redline max but not by much. Bran kept his indicators. Not straight up but heading around Shegler's toward its primary, he went. Because that was where any interceptor would have to come from, and he wanted the sonofabitch in front of him, not behind.

Coming in, he hadn't had time or occasion to take a good look at that oversized version of Venus; now he did. Awesome, the thing was; bright slanting light from the system's white star showed the heavy, roiling atmosphere, hundreds of kilos deep.

Not much time for looking, though, for at one side of the planet and straight at him came not one but three intercepting ships. And they had to be UET's, and if they were all unarmed, the Easter bunny came on Christmas.

Tregare hit his talk-switch. Forget viewscreen contact, just say it. What was the name? Oh, yeah—"Habbeger! Get your ass out of my way! Bran Tregare here, speaking for *Inconnu*."

". . . surrender, and amnesty will be considered. I repeat, Captain Habbeger offers amnesty if you surrender. If not—"

It was all bullshit so Tregare didn't bother talking. Three oncoming ships, and his hi-mag view showed that only one was armed, were coming in straight side-by-side triangle formation.

Well, that left the middle, didn't it?

Ahead of any viewscreen indication, Tinhead piped up the oncoming missiles and spotted the ship that threw them. And as programmed, the computer took control of all six turrets and blew those missiles before any human gunner had a chance to act. No time, in that situation, for any niceties about range or convergence—it was, Tregare knew, a case of blast *right now.*

There was time, though, for Bran to say, "Gonnelson! Hold

your missiles! You'll get another chance." Couldn't say any more because he was punching to gain control of turrets and now Tinhead let loose and Tregare got one good rake across a UET ship. Not the armed one, the missile thrower; it wasn't closest in line, so Tinhead didn't let him have it. But he holed the other one pretty good; its Drive didn't blow and it didn't tumble, but if that one got home at all, he figured it would limp a lot.

Then he had *Inconnu* through the middle of them, past and free and clear. Except, he couldn't be satisfied with that.

He called the Drive room. "Mallory! Prepare to flip."

"If we have to, captain." The voice had a sigh in it.

"Do we want to nail an armed Utie, or don't we?"

"Yes, *sir*!" Pause. "Wait for the count, though."

So Tregare did, and when it came he swung ship so fast that the centrifugal and then the stopping forces left him dazed. Only fixed purpose let him hit max accel to chase the retreating, separating triangle of UET ships and aim for the one he wanted.

They lost us; they don't know where we are! And the hell with sportsmanship; too much came back to him: the forced death fights, the gauntlet-running, the Special Cell, the panic fear of Butcher Korbeith. He said, "Gonnelson? Can you put me a missile into that armed ship up ahead?" With no word, the man nodded. Tregare said, "Then do it."

The missile was fast but Habbeger's ship was still spreading debris as *Inconnu* flashed past it; some hit and clanged against the hull. But not all of that ship was dead. Going away, Tregare felt *Inconnu* jerk and shudder; its thrust fell away to less than half of max. "Mallory? What's wrong?"

The older man's voice sounded tired. "Their turrets didn't quit soon enough. Got us across the Drive nodes. I think we can land once, if that damned tricky settlement will let us. But I wouldn't bet more than even odds on that landing."

It took some tricky juggling, trying to balance the burned nodes against the aux ones. Long gone now, the two surviving UET ships—one probably damaged a lot, and the other away free. Both unarmed, they were no danger to *Inconnu*—but now UET would know of Shegler's Moon, and someday claim it. So that, Bran now realized, was why Mace Henry and the whole place had been running scared; they'd been retaken, was all, and trying to cover their own ass.

Not good enough, that excuse, or so Tregare saw it. If they'd trusted him, helped him, things could have gone better.

Well. Relying on Mallory's advice, Bran eased *Inconnu* back toward Shegler's and called the Port. Mace Henry answered, and told *Inconnu*, "We can't allow you back here. The trouble—"

Blaine had been doing the talking; Tregare took over. "You haven't seen trouble yet. You try to stop me landing, you give me any problems on Drive repairs, *then* you'll see trouble." He was fuming, mad as hell and glad of it. He said, "Gonnelson? Mallory? Can you two land this thing if I clear it at groundside?"

He got qualified assents, and turned to Jargy Hoad. "What you say, once this bucket hits a good place to orbit, we take the scouts downside and show these closet Uties how the cow ate the cabbage?"

Jargy grinned. "Sounds good to me."

Shegler's had no missiles worth worrying about. The scoutships dodged th[illegible] enough, and Tregare saw them explode harmlessly, upstairs. "Jargy? Two launching sites, I spotted. You see any more?"

"Just the two. I'll take the one nearest me."

The scout's projectors weren't in the same league with the ones ships carried, but they did the job. Both missile sites went up, taking quite a lot of Shegler's soil with them. Circling, waiting for the dust to settle or drift downwind, Tregare spotted the ionization trails of projectors reaching up from groundside. Big ones, too—but not geared for traverse fast enough to nail a scout. Bran yelled to Jargy, and the two methodically wiped out the gun emplacements. Then Tregare made three fast passes over the settlement, at speeds intended to break every window in the place and maybe a few other things, and then two slow ones, to draw fire from anyone who still had some. Nothing happened. "Looks like Shegler's has shot its wad," said Jargy.

"Seems as if." He called up to *Inconnu*. "Gonnelson? I think it's safe to land now. Let's see if you and Mallory can set yourselves down like a crate of eggs." No answer, but after a while the ship's ID-beacon came in, signal strengthening, so he knew it was on the way down.

Anything more, now? He first rejected the idea that came to him, then reconsidered it. Item one: *that Henry could've warned us*. Item two: *maybe these people need a little more convincing*.

So before he landed his scoutship, Tregare made one more pass, and blew the Port Admin building purely all to hell.

The Port itself, it turned out, had been the government of Shegler's Moon. Now there wasn't any. So while *Inconnu* sat, undergoing repairs, the only government was Bran Tregare. The main item of business was refueling and repair of *Inconnu*, but he did take time to ask who among the survivors had held down what kind of semi-executive job previously, and made some appointments. To the woman he assigned to replace the late Mace Henry, he said, "After I leave, you're in charge for just as long as you can keep things under control. Can you?"

She pushed short, greying hair back from her thin face. "After the way you shot hell out of us, what do *you* care? And what's the point? Now UET knows about us. When they come back—"

"By groundside time, that'll be years from now. If they bother, even. Still—" He thought about it. "In your shoes, I'd think in terms of evacuating. A few at a time, whenever a ship comes in and has room to take some extra aboard." Pause. "Guarantee me no Utios in the lot. I could take on maybe a dozen. More, if they're real friendly and don't mind sleeping crowded." He shrugged. "Food, things like that . . . they're no problem."

She looked at him. "Suppose we did that. The last few left here . . . what do *they* do?"

He knew what she meant, but that wasn't what he answered. "They blow the fuel plant, so UET doesn't get the use of it."

She shook her head. "Tregare, you're a real monster. You know that?"

He couldn't let his hurt show. "Well, I had some help."

Before Mallory pronounced *Inconnu*'s Drive solid again, Tregare did a little trading, after all—remembering Number One's reputation for being interested in new food plants, he swapped some electronic components for a few bags of seed. He took aboard seventeen evacuees from Shegler's: mostly tech people, but also a mother with two children. He wasn't too crazy about having kids loose in a ship, but they behaved themselves all right. And finally, quite a bit later than he'd expected at the time of landing, Bran lifted *Inconnu* off

Shegler's Moon. Just out of atmo, Gonnelson docked one scout and Jargy the other.

He picked his time so as to use the Venus-like primary for a vee-enhancing sling turn that put him dead on for Number One—no need, on this leg, to take any detours. The first couple of days he worried about the Drive and hung around Control a lot. Then, deciding that Mallory knew his stuff, he went back to his normal routine.

He didn't know why things weren't so good between him and Erdis Blaine, but they were not. Down on Shegler's he'd been too busy and harassed to have much time with her—time that did either of them a lot of good, anyway. Now when he could relax with her, it wasn't working. She'd miss one rendezvous after another and make some kind of excuse. He never checked up on her, because if he had to do that, the whole thing wasn't worth it.

And then about once a week or a little less often, she'd meet with him in quarters and be totally passionate, sometimes so much so that it put him off his stride and he bungled.

The trouble was, he had so much on his mind that he couldn't really concentrate on his problems with Erdis. Maybe if he could have (and he realized as much), things might get straightened out. But he couldn't . . .

When she'd taken to leaving him a lot of spare time he didn't want, he started using some of it to scan through the mass of UET data that Kickem Bernardez had fast-fed to Tinhead. And found some things he knew were probably significant, but not *why*. Or how he might be able to use them.

There was the list of UET colonies, with their coordinates and descriptions. Some of them he could keep in mind—Terranova, the Twin Worlds (well, he'd *been* there, and at Penfoyle Gate and Hardnose), Iron Hat the mining world, Far Corner, Franklin's Jump—and some he couldn't remember. Well, he'd better think more solidly along those lines. Because one way to help give UET the trots was to raid their colonies. Even unarmed ships did that sometimes—and anything they could do, *Inconnu* could do better!

Then there was the rather cryptic description of UET's fortress world, Stronghold. Not a fortified *planet*, of course, but an armed outpost on a world to the far side of Earth from all other UET explorations. And Bran could find no other reason for the venture, except Hawkman Moray's theory: that Stronghold was UET's guardpoint against any approach by the alien Shrakken.

Appended to that block of data was a listing of ships and dates. Future dates, if Bran hadn't lost track of planets' time. For a time the codings, not cryptographic but mere abbreviations, had him puzzled; then he figured it out. Maybe. If he had it right, every two years UET on Earth sent to Stronghold a group of ships to add to that world's arsenal. Not all of those, he gathered, stayed at Stronghold. Some returned as messengers to Earth and others went out patrolling or on missions to other colonies, for reasons not at all clear in the text at hand.

But every two years, something like six or eight ships, one out of three armed (on the average), went to Stronghold.

Somewhere in this load of facts there had to be an angle. But right now Tregare couldn't see what it was.

Turnover came and went. The planet Number One was about three or four months in *Inconnu*'s future, and in Bran Tregare's. He thought about it. His family was there—or so he'd been given to believe. He'd have to deal with them; anywhere a Hulzein was, that person would be a major factor in the local setup. But he did not want to see them, and he wouldn't. Well, there were ways. . . .

Everything he'd seen, heard or read said that Number One was his best bet for a permanent base, to set up whatever offensive he would someday mount against UET. That might take some doing. *Inconnu*, though, carried leverage with it wherever it went.

All right. When he got to Number One he'd play it by ear, because, when had he ever had the chance to do it any other way?

Between Tregare and Erdis Blaine the tension grew. He was mostly too busy to pay attention, but sometimes it got to him. Then, only a few hours short of detection range from Number One, that planet spotted and identified by Tinhead, Bran went to quarters for a quick shower and change of clothes, and found Erdis drying herself from her own bath. He said, "You heading for watch, or chow, or what?" He didn't care much.

"If you're not busy just now, how about bed?"

"I—" I can't shift my head so fast, just like that, was what he had in mind to say. But it had been a time, and for a change his annoyance worked for him instead of against him when it came to arousal, so he peeled his clothes off. "Wait a bit. I need a shower first."

Neither of them clothed, she came and hugged him. "After." So they did everything they ever had done, and to his mind very well indeed, and then lay together, half-embracing. And she said, "Buy me out, Bran. At Number One. I'm leaving the ship."

How many ways can you say "I don't understand"? Bran tried several; none worked. Finally he said, "Just *tell* me." She nodded and tried to explain.

"I can't stay with you, and on this ship I can't live away from you." *It made no sense*. He asked more. "I know your past," she said. "For a long time, to me it justified your actions." She shook her head. "But not what you did on Shegler's. The woman there, that you told me about—she pegged you, Bran. You [illegible] becoming a monster. And I can't live with that."

Memory hit him. Fighting inside himself, determined *not* to strike this woman and stop the hurt she was giving him, he said, "You're the third to call me that. The one on Shegler's was the second."

"And the first?"

If you smile, they don't know they got to you. "Me. Back at the Slaughterhouse."

There was more to it, and long before Tregare could admit it out loud, he accepted her need to be off the ship, away from him. If that's how she felt—*how many hours 'til we land and she gets the hell off?* She was talking and talking, off into the kind of diatribe that never says what it's *about*. By the chin, not hard, he grabbed her. "Erdis? You got more on your mind, for peace's sake get to it!"

Not pulling away at all, she tilted her face up to the angle he'd always found the most lovely. "I'm not leaving you behind entirely, Bran. Part of you stays with me."

To cover his puzzlement, he said, "Nothing I'll really need, I hope?"

She shook her head. "Hardly. Just your child."

But how—? "But how—?"

"Coming out from Shegler's I didn't renew my contra implant. Because I've loved and valued you, Bran—for some qualities you may not even know you have, by now. But you've let yourself be warped; Shegler's showed me that."

Let? Butcher Korbeith? The Slaughterhouse? LET?

But he held silence as she said, "So I can't be with you any longer. But your child, Bran, won't carry your hate." Trying to smile, she almost made it. "You understand?"

Almost gently, he said, "No. No, I don't." Suddenly thirsty he poured bourbon and gulped half of it too fast, but kept himself from coughing. "But you don't understand, either."

How to say it? "It's nice you and my kid can live peaceful on a Hidden World and not hate. Nice. But I can't do that. I had it from Arbogast and Channery and Korbeith and—" He shook his head. "Never mind that. What it is, somebody has to *do* something about those bastards, and it's not going to be any nice bunny rabbit. It's going to be people like Derek Limmer and Jargy Hoad and Kickem Bernardez—and like *me*. From here it doesn't look like what you say, but I guess I have to live with that. If I'm a monster, as you call me, I had a lot of help getting there."

His gaze unfocused. Looking back in time he said, "I thought when I got away from Korbeith, and then from UET itself . . . but I expect you're right. The longer it goes, the meaner it gets."

He stood. "You better move into Second's quarters. I'll have your stuff brought over." He had another thought. "The ship can't pay your shares off all in cash, but I'll see you get good marketable cargo for the rest—and maybe I know a connection on the planet that can help you handle it the best way." Yes, his family owed him that much, even though they'd deal through intermediaries. If they didn't think so, he'd show them different.

Offering no kiss or handshake, she said, "Goodbye, Bran."

He nodded. "That's right. Except on business, we won't see each other again." He watched the door close behind her.

He felt he should want another drink, but lay down without one. After a while, Jargy called on intercom. Tregare answered, "I'm busy. I expect to be that way for some time. You and Gonnelson do the hails and landing; don't call me unless there's a problem. All right?" All right, so he lay back again.

I'll take Stronghold, that's what. Don't know how yet, but I will. Kickem's data, that's the key. . . .

What was it with him and women? Murphy, now—with the raw-scarred face and the eyepatch—catch *her* bleeding tears over any dead Uties? Not hardly. Or Janith Reggs on the scoutship? Well, maybe. Salome Harkness . . . and where was she, by now? Escaped, Bran hoped. Either way, they were probably years out of synch with each other. But she'd been a fighter, and likely still was.

Without volition his mind scanned ahead, and his gut clenched. Phyls Dolan, tumbling frozen between stars, forever. No matter what he did to Uties, he'd never pay them back for Phyls. But Erdis couldn't see it that way; she hadn't been there. On the ship itself, yes, but not where it happened.

Headshake. *After Stronghold*—there'd be more of a move he could make, some way.

My family. Well, they'd dumped him, so that was that.

With the lights softened, he squinted into dimness. The way things were, no point in worrying about people who couldn't see what the problem was. The way things were.

The hell with it. I've got a job to do.

REBEL'S QUEST

For all rebels who find themselves

1. Prologue: Bulletin on Tregare

"Testing—one, two—all right, the recorder's working. Alden Bartlett dictating. Shelly, do this one up and get it into Distribution right away. I'll just rough it; you fill in from the files and streamline the chat. This hot number came down from Committee Chairman Minos Pangreen his own brass-bound self.

"What it is, is an All-Worlds, All-Ships Bulletin on Tregare the Pirate, so use official headings: United Energy and Transport, Presiding Committee, old Pangreen the Chairman, UET crest, all that. Do it up pretty.

"All right; subject, Bran Tregare. Born Australia, New Year 9 or 10—look it up—to Sean Tregare, citizen of North America, and Lisbeth Duggan. No surviving family on Earth or at any legitimate colony, so we don't have that kind of handle on him.

"Entered the Slaughterhouse, oops, Space Academy, at age thirteen, graduated in normal sequence at sixteen. Good scores but no outstanding cadet promotions. Two turns in the Special Punishment cell, which should have told somebody something.

"On graduation, did his cadet cruise on the *MacArthur*, Arger Korbeith commanding. I hear the Butcher's still complaining he should have spaced that kid while he had the chance. Put four or five others out the airlock, that trip, but missed the kingsnake. Everybody guesses wrong now and then. . . .

"Back here at Earth, Tregare was transferred to the *Tamurlaine* as Third Officer. The ship went as directed to the Twin Worlds—Tweedle first—and then to Penfoyle Gate. Then lifted for Terranova but never arrived there, so it's assumed that's when the ship Escaped. At next contact it was renamed *Inconnu* and Tregare was captain. It's usual enough that the old captain doesn't survive a mutiny but this guy seems to have wiped out *all* his superiors. Boil this all down a lot, will you, Shelly?

"That next contact was with the *Hannibal* under Commodore Sherman. Tregare blew the ship apart, but its scouts got away and reached Johnson's Walk safely, which is why we know the story. And from then on . . .

"Some of these reports contradict each other. That is, unless someone invented a faster-than-light Drive and Tregare has it, he couldn't have been to all the places and done all the things listed in here. My guess is that when a ship or colony of ours gets creamed, they figure they'll look better if they blame it on the Bogey Man. But leave my guesses off, Shelly; this thing's going out over Pangreen's name.

"After the *Hannibal* incident, next contact was when he hit three ships off Shegler's Moon. He got the armed ship *Cortez* with a missile and his turrets crippled the *Goering*, so that it spiraled down onto Shegler's primary. That world is like Venus only a lot bigger, so there went the *Goering*. The *Charlemagne* got away to tell us about it.

"There's a lot more, but I have an appointment coming up, so could you crib the rest from the files? Don't bother trying to sort out what's relativistically possible and what's not; I can't figure the Long View of space-time myself and won't ask you to try it.

"But here's some speculations that haven't been filed yet. That Tregare's allied himself with some unknown species of aliens possessing FTL travel. That somewhere he's found or set up ship-building facilities, and is building a fleet of ships—twenty, fifty, maybe a hundred. Well, to say the least, these things are unlikely—but the guesses have official sanction, so put them in anyway. Labeled *as* guesses, of course.

"Another is that he's the one who hijacked the ship with all the frozen sperm and ova and conceived-zygotes, and the Zoomwombs to hatch them in, and is force-growing thousands of Instant Troops to attack us with. If you put that one in, Shelly, look up the dates and add those, too. I think that ship disappeared while Tregare was still on the *MacArthur*.

"But it's not our business to tell our bosses they work too hard at scaring themselves. If Tregare did even half the real items they say he did, he's the single biggest menace our government faces. So just set down the facts and let our beloved readers, All-Worlds and All-Ships, do their own editorializing. Right?

"Hmmm—I see here that somebody wants Tregare boosted to the top Wanted slot: Escaped Target Number One. Could be a reasonable priority, at that. I mean, how long has it been—twenty years, maybe?—that anybody's heard anything about Cade Moaker and *Cut Loose Charlie*? But Tregare, we hear a lot about—enough that Upstairs gets nervous and we catch it. Actually, the way this Tregare operates—well, never mind that. Pangreen will either up the Target rating or he won't.

"End Bulletin draft, subject Bran Tregare known as Tregare the Pirate. Alden Bartlett out.

"And Shelly—if you can get this out today, tomorrow I buy you a three-drink lunch and we take the afternoon off."

A long time later, so long that the readout paper had yellowed and gone brittle, Bran Tregare read that Bulletin. Smiling a little, he shook his head. They had a few things right, UET did, but not many. The fake ID had held up, he noticed—UET had no idea he was the son of Hawkman Moray and Liesel Hulzein, and nephew to Erika Hulzein whose Establishment in Argentina was a major thorn in UET's paw. Not that those connections did him any good: Erika had been after his hide, and his parents had run off and left him to the nonexistent mercies of the Slaughterhouse. And had gone to the world called Number One.

UET had some of the early stuff straight. Yeah, he'd blasted the *Hannibal*. He hadn't known before that his second armed-ship kill was the *Cortez*, or that he'd also nailed one of the other two; he'd been too busy trying to cope with a crippled Drive. He wondered how the Escaped colony on Shegler's had fared after discovery by UET, but the Bulletin didn't say.

They couldn't know of his stops, once he was captain of *Inconnu*, at the Hidden Worlds of New Hope and Freedom's Ring, and his visit in between, to UET's base on Hardnose, was considered to be a hoax by someone else. On the other hand it had been Raoul Vanois in *Carcharodon*, not Tregare, who raided the mining colony on Iron Hat.

UET's speculations about alien alliances and FTL Drives made him laugh out loud. Well, the wilder their beliefs, the less apt they were to be set for what he *was* planning!

He did wish they were right about the shipbuilding part, but to his knowledge only one Hidden World had built any kind of ship: Number One had a cargo shuttle that worked fine for in-system work but lacked interstellar range.

He read more: yes, this escapade was his; the next wasn't. And so on. He wished to hell he *had* been the one to wipe out the slavers on Dixie Belle, but that was the work of a man named Dominguez, whom Tregare had never met but would like to, someday.

And of course the Zoomwomb-and-zygotes caper was long

before his time. It had given the planet Number One its rather surprising population in a hurry, but by none of his own doing.

"Bran? I thought you said something about a drink. I am certainly ready for one." Still dripping from the shower, Tregare's wife wrung water from her long, dark hair and put a towel around it. To look at Rissa Kerguelen one would hardly guess that she and Bran had married in a dueling ring, after she had fought—naked and unarmed—with a man twice her weight, and killed him. It had been a long time since Stagon dal Nardo had any place in Tregare's thoughts; he didn't stay there long.

"Sure. A minute." A quick scan covered the rest of the Bulletin; he set it down. "You want some chuckles, look this over." He stood, and went to make the promised drinks.

Thinking: UET didn't know about his alliances, either—Limmer on *Lefthand Thread*, for instance. Hell, they didn't even know that Kickem Bernardez had taken the *Hoover*.

And reminiscing: *Number One, yeah. That's where it all really started.*

2. Number One

Tregare was dozing. Jargy Hoad, his oldtime Slaughterhouse roomie and now his Third Hat, had the watch as *Inconnu* neared the planet. Tregare had a lot of thinking to do, but right now he was too tired to do it.

Second Hat Erdis Blaine, his sometime lover, was leaving the ship at Number One. The trouble with Erdis was that she thought life should be played fair. She didn't realize, and couldn't accept, that fighting the monolithic tyranny of UET a man had to use whatever worked. In Tregare's view, treachery was rewarded by death. Back at Shegler's Moon, *Inconnu*'s most recent stopover, Port Administration had tried to cover its ass with UET by selling Tregare out. After he'd fought clear of the ambushing UET ships—all three of them—he went back and blew Port Admin purely to hell. The word would spread, and the lesson needed to be made clear. But Erdis couldn't see that, so she was getting off. Well, if he was a monster, as she said, he'd had plenty of help. . . .

Before the breakup, Erdis had for some reason decided to

get pregnant. That wasn't Tregare's worry, since she hadn't asked his consent. His problem was figuring how to buy out her officer's-shares in the ship itself. Might be best to pay largely in cargo bought, back at Freedom's Ring, especially for delivery here. But Freedom's Ring's contracts were with the Hulzein connection on Number One, and that meant Liesel Hulzein, Tregare's mother. And probably his father Hawkman Moray and his sister Sparline. Long ago, appalled and heartbroken when he knew they'd left him in UET's Slaughterhouse when they went off Earth, he'd vowed never to see or speak with any of them again. Thirteen he was, then; even now, maybe close to ten subjective bio-years later, that hurt was fierce.

But he'd figure something out, some way to handle things. . . . Bran dozed.

The intercom brought him awake. "Bran. Jargy here."

Getting his face out of the pillow and throwing covers back, Tregare sat up and flipped the talk-switch. "Yeah? Anything wrong?"

"Nothing at all. But come up to Control anyway. We're close to hitting air, and I don't think the view is anything you'll want to miss. I mean, on tape it couldn't be quite the same."

Tregare shook himself fully awake. "Sure. I'll be right up."

The view from Control was something, all right. With the downscreen on hi-mag, Tregare saw first an endless-seeming plain; just below the ship, now, was a huge water sink. He checked; as planned, *Inconnu* was coming down headed toward the Hidden World's arbitrary West—traveling with the terminator and expecting to land before crossing it from dawn into darkness.

Ahead lay several parallel ranges of hills. Jargy pointed. "Take a good look. I read about the Big Hills, on the data sheets, but now I believe them."

Still a bit sleepy, after all, Bran said, "They don't look so much." Then he checked the instruments. "We're still forty kilos up? I just changed my mind!" Because the slanting afternoon sunlight now showed him something of the sheer size of those rounded masses—foothills, they weren't.

"Aircars can't cross them," Jargy said. "Even with oxy for the passengers, the cars simply won't climb that high. And you notice how far they extend, north–south—not feasible to go around. So this perfectly good plain, less than a hundred kilos from the main port, is hardly explored at all."

Flipping through the info, noting the average height of the Big Hills, Tregare could see why. He said, "Gives me an idea. Remember, I'm thinking of a base here? Well, how about on this side of the Hills? With the ship and the two scouts we could move supplies over—and sure's hell the locals wouldn't bother us!"

The locals! Who was he kidding? His family, here on this world, was what still worried him. Too many nights he'd lain, shivering in fear of Slaughterhouse brutality, hating his parents for leaving him there while they escaped to a safe world. But so what? He didn't have to see them, did he? Maybe not—but why was his body giving him all the sensations of panic?

Grimly he shook his mind loose from the problem. Those people weren't his real enemy, UET was. And this wasn't Airlock Drill on the *MacArthur*, standing naked in the line of cadets and waiting for Butcher Korbeith to have one of them spaced. Bran had vowed to kill that man someday; if he ever did, maybe these flashbacks of fear would vanish. But to do it, first he had to get on with the job at hand: gather ships under his command, and *attack*. Not that the Butcher was his only target; he was after any part of UET's cruel reign that he could bite off. And here was where he planned to start it. . . .

The Long View—the fact that up near light-speed ships might experience one year while planets went through twenty—the Long View made things difficult. The trick, though, was to learn how to use it. By passing info to every Escaped Ship met in space and to the Port computer of every Hidden World he visited, Bran Tregare was building a longterm communications net. He wasn't the man who'd first begun it, but he knew a good thing when he saw one.

So someday, he hoped, there would be a rendezvous of ships to join him, here on Number One. And he'd need a base to service them and arm them—as many as he could round up, but six or eight at the very least, or it wouldn't work.

So for now, get his base set up. And when he'd prepared it the best he could, for the gathering he hoped to bring about eventually, take off again on a two-purpose mission: to make more contacts with Escaped Ships, and to bite UET's tail to the bone!

Jargy Hoad's voice broke Tregare's fugue; for a moment he couldn't remember what he'd been saying. Oh yes, about the locals not bothering them, east of the Hills. Jargy's grin indicated that he agreed, and he said, "You know, that's not a bad idea." So, approaching the Big Hills the two men scanned the terrain in search of a good site. At first Bran liked a ledge area to one side of a canyon, but a better look showed it slanting too much. Jargy picked a dry lake, but as Tregare pointed out, nothing said it was dry all the time. Then Bran spotted, on the long slope where the Big Hills themselves began, an ancient crater with a fairsized ringwall and a floor more flat than not.

"It's closer and it's better," he said. "I wouldn't risk landing the ship there yet, but a scout I would. Hang a bulldozer outside the scout, and in four, five days—a week, maybe—we'd have us a nice flat port."

He realized he'd said the plan in shorthand, but Hoad knew what he meant. "Sure. Except, do you know anyone who knows how to run a bulldozer?"

"Course not. That's what groundsiders are for. We hire some."

Radar confirmed eye judgment that the flatlands on the west side of the Big Hills were nearly a kilometer lower than the eastern plain. A little to the north of their path Bran spotted the major settlement: "The capital city, or whatever." One Point One, it was called, and it was bigger than any town he had yet seen on a Hidden World. Well, with the Zoomwombs and all, it would be. First Hat Gonnelson, doing pilot, swung course toward the place.

The port looked fairly large, too, and now held three ships, none of them armed. Earlier, at hailing distance, Tregare had talked with the port's spokesman-on-duty, and had been impressed by the way this place simply took incoming ships in stride. There was no hassle, no apparent anxiety. Finally he'd asked: "You people don't seem nervous about new ships, the way some places are. How come?"

A little bit, then, the voice flattened out. "Most places don't have our grade of missile defense."

A hard line to top, so Bran said, "Well, now I know." Certainly he appreciated the logic. Now as Gonnelson brought *Inconnu* down, drifting expertly toward One Point One's port, Tregare saw something odd, off to the north—across the Big Hills ran a zigzag mark. There wasn't time to do more than swing an aux screen's camera over that way, and put it on hi-mag and hi-speed, both, so he did that much. Later he'd have a look. . . .

On the landing circle the port had designated, Gonnelson brought *Inconnu* to rest without a jar. "Good job," said Tregare, and clapped a hand to the man's shoulder—briefly, because he knew that Gonnelson was no more comfortable with touching than with talking: a little went a long way. But a little couldn't hurt, either.

Bran watched Gonnelson run down through the grounding checklist; halfway through, realizing he didn't need to monitor, he turned to Jargy Hoad. "On the commercial stuff, you deal for the ship. The talking part, I mean. Anybody asks for me, I'm busy. And—"

"Wait a minute." Hoad waved a hand. "I don't know prices, any of that stuff. Bran, how can I—?"

"We have folks who do. Groden, down in Stores, for one."

"Ol' Gripin' Groden?"

"Not any more. Held back too long on promotion, was all. He's a lot different now. And anyway, you can pull most of the info out of Tinhead."

Jargy frowned. "Still, though—Third Hat, dealing for the ship?"

"Second. Didn't I tell you? Erdis, she's getting off. And rules or no rules—compared to you, Al Druffel just doesn't hack it." Before Hoad could ask anything, Tregare said, "The thing is, most of our cargo for here is consigned to Hulzein Lodge. I have my own reasons—tell you sometime, or maybe not—I'll deal with those people but I won't talk with them. So you handle that part."

After a pause, Jargy nodded. "If you say so."

To the port Tregare gave the correct protocol, both from upstairs and after landing. Such as "Bran Tregare, captain, speaking for the armed ship *Inconnu*." They wanted the ship's history and he gave it straight: nothing to hide, here. But when it came to commerce he said, "Our Second Hat, Jargy Hoad, is authorized to handle all that. Don't bother me with it." And mostly, nobody did.

He had one bad moment, going into Control while Jargy was on a direct circuit to Hulzein Lodge and dickering on delivery charges, to the Lodge rather than directly to the port. On the screen Bran Tregare saw his mother Liesel

Hulzein, and noticed that now her crown of braided hair carried a lot more grey in it. Behind her stood the tall man, Hawkman Moray—he hadn't changed much. For seconds Bran looked to see if maybe his sister Sparline might be in the group, then he shook his head and moved to make sure that he himself wouldn't be seen from the far end.

He was moving to leave Control entirely when Liesel's voice cut through, saying, "I've had enough of this! Liesel Hulzein speaking, and I know damned well that the captain of *Inconnu*, the armed Escaped ship, is Bran Tregare. I want to talk to him! I have the right—after all, he—"

Hawkman gripped her shoulder. "No, Liesel. He may not want it known." Tregare gave a thankful sigh.

Voice disguise is easy: with one hand Bran pinched his nostrils closed; with the other he grabbed a talkset. "Captain's orders are that *Inconnu* deals with Hulzein Lodge through the Second Hat. He says you'll know why."

He saw Hawkman frown before saying, "Yes. It's an old grudge. Something we did, or didn't do, a long time ago. We'd hoped—but apparently he still believes we had a choice."

Oh, hell! But he wouldn't open that can of worms again. Tregare cut the circuit. He left Control. In fact, he ran.

After a cup of coffee to calm down with, he went back up to take care of the business he'd had in mind. Immediately on landing he'd fed all the news he had to the port's computer and milked it of word from other ships. And had called the three currently in port, asking to meet with their captains and giving a guarded version of his own plans: ". . . and to our mutual advantage I'd like to make agreements with any ship that's willing. Call me back when you have time."

For none of the three captains had been available to talk with him on the comm. One was Cade Moaker on *Cut Loose Charlie;* to him Tregare added, "We had a close pass once, when I was a cadet on the *MacArthur;* I was in Control at the time and heard you tell Korbeith's hyena off. Loved it. And I was lucky enough to survive riding with the Butcher. Just barely, though."

The other two, Bran hadn't heard of: Rasmussen on *NonStop*, who was down with some exotic brand of the flu, or Krieg Elman who commanded a ship now known as *Stump Farm*. That one's spokeswoman didn't seem to want to give Tregare the time of day, much less any commitment for her captain to meet with him.

Now, though, Moaker was willing to talk. On the screen the man looked old but vigorous. He said, "What you say of your plans, I like. But can't join in." He shook his head. "Old *Charlie*'s past it, pretty much. Not just the Nielson Cube, which isn't all that close to crapping, but throughout. We're good for two more hops, I'd say—but I'll settle for one. I take the conservative approach. From here, where I'm loading up on what I expect to need, we head for a colony that can use our technical help, and set up in business there."

Bran scratched his head. "What's wrong with right here?"

Moaker grinned; he looked younger that way. "Too much competition. I'm thinking of Fair Ball; ever heard of it?" Tregare hadn't, and so indicated; Moaker fed him the coordinates. And then said, "Not all my people are ready to settle down with the old man. And for this jaunt I don't need a full crew. So if you can use any additional help? I won't send you anyone I can't recommend fully."

"Why—thanks, captain. Happens I can use several. And if you'll be in port a few days more, I'd be pleased to host you on here, you and your officers."

"Thank you; we'll see. Pleasure talking with you, Tregare." Moaker cut the circuit, leaving Bran with the thought: *I wish that man could stay around for the big fight.*

He checked the other ships. Rasmussen was slightly up and around but not very, and Krieg Elman was still unavailable.

So much for that. Tregare was hungry, and went downship to fix that problem.

Commerce ran more smoothly than not. The Hulzein contracts gave Jargy no problems; other cargo sold well, and exchange rates were favorable. Not buying for future trade just now, Tregare began loading up on materials for his base, across the Hills. Alsen Bleeker, a thin hollow-cheeked man crowding middle age, tried to push a little price-gouging, over and above agreed terms—on pain of holding up the ship's refueling. But Tregare had seen his tanks filled—ship's and scouts' both—first of all his dealings. So he told Bleeker to trundle his goods back to the warehouse. "You're not the only source, and maybe you can use the exercise. You come here again, figure to deal square." Not even a quick offer of extra discount changed his mind. To Jargy he muttered, "A little rough on him, maybe. But I want the word to get around." And thought, *If my own side wants to gouge me, isolating the base is a damn good idea*.

Done with trade, for now, Tregare went offship. It was late morning, warm and slightly breezy; from his first exposure to local air and sky he'd liked this planet. As he neared the edge of the landing area a woman stepped out of a groundcar rental office. "You need some wheels?"

She was skinny, with short, shaggy red hair and a freckled complexion that could have used more care. Thirtyish, maybe. "No. An aircar, later. This time I'm walking."

Her grin was missing some bicuspids. "Aircars, I can get. Where is it you have in mind to walk?"

None of her business, but maybe she could help. "I want a bulldozer, including the operator. Stuff for a job where we have to lift the gear there, to do it."

"Lift? No aircar's going to lift a bulldozer, mister."

"Once I find the dozer, I'll take care of that part."

She gave directions, then said, "You're off that ship there." Right. "How's your captain? A real [illegible], like most?"

So she didn't know about officers' cheek tattoos. "You could say that."

Her directions worked, though. Following them he found a ramshackle setup with miscellaneous equipment sitting all around; the sign read "J. MacDougall & Assoc, Gen'l Contractors." MacDougall was scowling Black Irish but talked amiably enough. Assoc was Pete Aguinaldo who smiled as if he hadn't been unstoned in recent memory, but his answers made sense. Tregare hired them, and a dozer, and a portable "walking" hoist the scoutship could power, and some things he took MacDougall's word were necessary. "Day after tomorrow, then," said Tregare. "Midmorning?" Agreed; everyone shook hands, and Tregare left.

Heading back to *Inconnu*, the smells from a streetside food booth attracted him; he bought and ate, with considerable relish, two spicy concoctions of ground meat wrapped in some kind of leaves and served on a stick. Not bad at all!

When he passed the rental office the redhead wasn't outside, so he went in. "I got the equipment lined up; thanks for your help. Now—you said you could get me an aircar?" She could. He explained that he wouldn't need a driver; she agreed to provide a map and come along as guide; Tregare nodded. "Fifteen, twenty minutes, you said? Fine, I should be back from the ship by then."

Aboard, he brought Gonnelson and Jargy up to date. Erdis Blaine wanted to talk but now wasn't the time. "Tonight. Okay?" He ran and then reran the brief flash of tape, the zigzag line on the Big Hills. Either it was important or it wasn't—now he intended to find out.

Groundside again, Bran saw the aircar waiting. He walked over, climbed inside, and said to the redhead, "We okay to go? You got the map, and all?" He activated the propulsors.

"Right here." Pause. "My name's Keri Freling. What's yours?"

"Tregare." He began to taxi. "Point me north, will you?"

Looking startled, finally accepting that he wanted business, not chatter, she answered, "Sure. Sure, Tregare."

Neither reckless nor cautious, he took the car up. Pointing north, as he'd asked, she explained that here they were outside the city's jurisdiction. ". . . but don't fly over One Point One, below six hundred meters, without learning the altitude lanes." She gave him a pamphlet covering those; he tucked it into a pocket.

Turning east toward the Hills, Bran topped the first range and headed north again. Freling asked, "Where are we going?"

On the massive upslope to his right Tregare saw a complex of buildings dominated by a large, timbered structure. "What's all that?"

"It's Hulzein Lodge. Don't go much closer; those people don't take to uninvited visitors."

"I wasn't planning to." *Not hardly!* He looked from his unfolded map to the view ahead. Yeah—not too much farther now . . .

"What are you looking for?"

"Show you in a minute." A west-reaching headland blocked his view. "Freling? You know how to use the oxy gear? I'd like to go up over this." He got his mask from under the seat.

"Why, yes. But—" Then she put hers on and shut up. And as Tregare lifted over the mass ahead, before him was one end of the Big Hills' zigzag scar that his screens had shown him from above. This end looked as if a giant axe had made it.

* * *

Freling grabbed his shoulder. "No! Don't go in there."

He eased his power back. "Why not?"

"It's a trap. Five aircars—six, maybe—have tried it. Not one came back."

"Maybe they didn't know enough."

Her grip jerked at him. "Those were *experts* here; you've just arrived. What makes you think—?" Her hand shuddered. "If you want to try it, take me back to the port first. And post a deposit to cover the cost of the aircar!"

"Fair enough." He turned back, and dropped altitude until they could stow the oxy masks. Her silence gave him time to think. *Was* the place a trap? A blind alley, the end of it too narrow for turning back? Or maybe those "experts" hadn't seen it from topside, didn't know how sharply it zagged, and which way.

Tregare did, though. *And with the scout, I'll check it.*

He took them back in a moderate hurry, not really fast. Over the city he circled, well above the traffic limit, until the pamphlet and rooftop lane markers gave him a good idea how the system worked. He landed in front of Freling's office and paid her off. "Thanks for the guided tour."

"If you'd like more of them, we're here. There's a lot to see: the Slab Jumbles, for instance. . . ."

"If I do want more, you're first in line." But if he needed an aircar, it was simpler to buy one. Or better, two.

Walking back to the Port, at its edge he detoured for a closer look at something he'd heard about. Having bought a deteriorated spare Nielson Cube from a visiting ship, a consortium of oligarchs had set out to build a ship of its own. Not for interstellar use, or anywhere near full-sized. But for a hull with only a few times the bulk of a scoutship, and the short hauls of in-system freight runs, a half-power Nielson Cube should give safe service indefinitely.

Tregare looked up at the partially-completed structure. The frame girders were all in place; hull plates covered them, starting from the bottom, about halfway.

It all looked workable; too bad Bran couldn't be here to see the packet's first lift.

One more look, while he wondered what kind of share Hulzein Lodge might have in this enterprise. Then he turned away and walked to his ship.

* * *

Aboard *Inconnu* he found things going smoothly. He stopped by the galley, intending to ask for a tray to be sent to his quarters, but was told, "It's already been ordered, captain. I'll send it along in about twenty minutes." He acknowledged with thanks, and when he got to quarters he knew what to expect. Erdis Blaine, dolled up fit to kill and smelling great.

Arms outstretched, face turned up for his kiss. The big farewell scene; right? So she wouldn't have to feel any guilt or remorse, but rather, could feel generous and righteous, both.

Tregare wasn't having any. Firmly, though without violence, he moved her away and to one side. "That horse is dead. You shot it."

"But, Bran—"

"Dinner, we can share. But not bed." And by the time the tray arrived, and the wine, she saw he wasn't really listening, and dropped the subject.

Later, as she stood to leave, she said, "Bran, if you hate me so much, why are you being so fair in buying me out?"

The woman, [illegible] take her, didn't understand *anything*. "I don't hate you." He suppressed the pang of bitterness. And wondered why good-hearted, decent people like Erdis here, couldn't get it through their heads that dealing with the monstrous *in*decency of UET, you had to take all the edge you could get. Inwardly, Bran sighed. As things were, it wasn't exactly that he was going to miss Erdis Blaine. What he missed already, and had for some time, was the real affection they'd had together.

His child that she was carrying did not—*could* not—concern him. All he had to do with it was a cell he'd given her with no such aim, without even his consent for its use in this fashion. And with Blaine's ship-shares as Second Hat, the kid sure wouldn't be hurting for child support money.

Shaking his head, Tregare got back to now. "Hate you? Hell, even if I did—Blaine, on an Escaped Ship a captain *is* fair, or he doesn't stay captain very long."

Maybe she got the point, maybe not. Next morning, after he'd arranged her transportation to the hotel Maison Renalle, he did give her a goodbye kiss. But his mind was more than halfway stuck in what he needed to do next, across the Big Hills.

As she left, another worry hit him. Al Druffel, ever since he broke his leg skiing, back on New Hope, had been out of business as Third Hat. Now it turned out the ligaments needed extensive surgery, so Druffel was selling off, going groundside. And where was Bran going to find himself a new Third?

When MacDougall called, ahead of midmorning on the scheduled day, Tregare was well-breakfasted and ready to move. "An hour? Fine. See you." In finding Mac, Bran decided he'd been lucky. The man didn't dawdle.

Arrangements set with Gonnelson, Tregare went up to the starboard scoutship. The hatch opened; he took the small craft up and out. He had time for a short jaunt north; running higher than any aircar could, he headed for the zigzag gash through the Big Hills. And got his first good look at it.

He had no idea what forces produced the original cut, but later there had been lateral slippage along a fault line, to make the Z-turn near the top of the western slope. Going from the port it would be first a quick left and then almost as abrupt a right turn. To try this, without knowing the layout ahead of time—no wonder nobody came back!

But why *hadn't* anyone known the terrain? After a moment, Tregare had the answer: only ships' people could have seen the thing from upstairs, and they weren't the ones who would be interested, or mention it.

How about altitude? Checking his radar altimeter against the one calibrated with the Port as zero, he overflew the pass. And nodded: in this atmosphere, an aircar could take a medium load through, with a hundred meters to spare.

Unless there was something else he didn't know yet. . . .

Back to the Port. From upstairs Tregare saw a tractor nearing *Inconnu*, towing two cargo flats. Among the gear he recognized only the bulldozer and a hoist. MacDougall was prompt—good enough. Bran landed, and went aboard ship, where he rounded up some people to help with the heavy lifting. Hain Deverel was senior, so Tregare put him in charge. "We're going across the Hills. Pick two more to stay with you, working with the contractor. About two weeks, I'd guess; then I come get all of you, and the gear. Okay?"

"Two weeks?" Deverel didn't sound happy, and—*oh, hell*. Now Bran realized: the man didn't want to be away, that long, from his longtime lover Anse Kenekke. Tregare had never understood that kind of thing, but these two men he liked and trusted.

He said, "I'm sorry, Hain, but you *are* the best for this job. And for quarters, now, there'll be only a couple of pre-fabs."

Deverel shrugged. "Two weeks. All right."

Deploying the "walking hoist," by degrees Mac and Pete walked it up the scout's flank. In the open cargo hatch they planted it for best leverage to raise the dozer. That mass would have to ride sidesaddle, outside—but besides the hoist's own cables, lashings were made around the scout's hull. Bran nodded. "You've got it solid, Mac. It's not going any place except where we do."

Inside the scoutship, all stowage checked, Tregare said, "With the dozer hanging out there, this bucket's going to ride weird. I don't want anybody hurt. So—Deverel, you ride sidebar for me, and everybody else go down one deck and strap into the accel couches. Okay?"

With the others gone, the two men strapped in. Deverel said, "What am I here for? I've done no piloting."

"Time you learned, maybe." The Drive's hum built to stability; from below came word the passengers were secured. "You look like officer material to me, when the chance comes."

He hit the power switch; the scout lifted.

Lift took a bad slant; Tregare pulled a hard bias to get straightened up. That done, he looked over to Deverel. "This off-balance thing, with the dozer, pay it no mind. The rest of it, running this crate, watch me and ask questions." But the man seemed to find no questions to ask.

Up crowding black sky with stars in it, Tregare drifted his unbalanced load across the Hills, then southeast toward his crater. Short of it by maybe twenty kilos he spotted an east-slope plateau that gave him an idea. An aux base, a home-office retreat apart from the jangle of activity when other ships arrived. Base One, with the crater as Base Two. It could work. . . .

To the north, a glimpse of the zigzag pass reminded him of something. "Hain, why I wanted you up here and nobody else, is I don't want the rest seeing some things from upstairs."

Slowly, the man said, "But you don't mind if I see."

"Why should I? You trusted *me*, didn't you?"

* * *

The crater floor wasn't all that level, but at the southeast part Bran found a flattish spot and set down. When the tilt subsided, he could exhale without making noise.

With everybody up, then, they moved the dozer and other gear groundside. Once the talus slope was dozed down and leveled, the prefab huts were erected near the crater's west wall. Shouting over the dozer's roar, Tregare told Mac, "Give the site as much clear space as you can manage, level, and stomped down hard with the treads. Get the middle really firm; the edges aren't so critical." Because ships, landing, needed more solidity than buildings did. And to move things faster, he had to cut every corner he could find.

Near the scout was a gap in the crater wall; the floor sloped off into a gully. Ideal place for fuel tanks; next time he'd bring explosives to blast the shape of hole he needed, and cross-filament synthetics for his tank liners.

So far, so good. On a portable talkset he twiddled frequencies until he hit the right skip to bounce above the Big Hills and connect him with *Inconnu*, where Gonnelson reported all was well. To Mac, Bran said, "This HF stuff may take some fiddling. Up freqs daytimes, down 'em at night is the rule." he shrugged. "Pretty soon I'll bring in stuff that uses scatter, and can ignore skip. But this week, here's what we've got."

Then, making sure his instructions were clear, Tregare left his three ratings and two employees, and took the two extras back aboard the scout, heading for *Inconnu*.

Without the dozer's lopside weight, lift-off went better.

Back aboard ship, after scrubbing up, Bran checked tapes of incoming calls. He found an invitation from Rasmussen, captain of *NonStop*, to bring a colleague or two ". . . and join me for dinner here. I don't quite understand your proposal but we can discuss it. Answer at your convenience."

On screen the man was wedge-faced, dark-haired, pleasant of voice, and sounded reasonable. So, checking his chrono, Tregare called in an acceptance and rounded up Jargy Hoad to go with him. They arrived in good time.

Rasmussen was a good host and *NonStop*'s galley had at least one superb chef, but no deal was closed. ". . . like your plan, Tregare. Getting a fleet together, looking to take the fight to UET. But just now I have other commitments."

Bran shook his head. "*Later*, I'm talking about." And explained the loose data network operating on the Long View, to set the rendezvous of allies here on Number One. Hoping his arsenal setup on New Hope was in gear by now, he said, "For your help on the mission, I arm your ship for free." He leaned forward. "On that mission, though, I don't share command. So what do you say?"

Rasmussen liked it but couldn't promise anything. "If I *can* make your rendezvous, I'm with you." So as Bran and Jargy left *NonStop*, everybody shook hands, and Tregare had to settle for that. Better than nothing, he supposed. . . .

Up in Control on *Inconnu*, Bran found messages waiting. The first of any importance was from Cade Moaker on *Cut Loose Charlie*. "You said you could use some people. If you have a Hat berth open, my Second's looking for one. Decided she's not ready, just yet, to settle down groundside on Fair Ball."

Since he needed a replacement for Druffel, Tregare called back, and soon Moaker was onscreen. Beside him stood a young woman. "Ola Stannert," Moaker said. "Captain Tregare."

Nodding greetings, Bran looked at her: medium height, slim, bio-age in the twenties. Good cheekbones, generous mouth, eye-color probably distorted by the circuit. Straight blond hair that fell behind her shoulders, so he couldn't tell the length of it. She said, in a low-pitched voice that still carried well, "I think I'd like being on an armed ship."

Within five minutes the deal was made: given Moaker's recommendation, Tregare felt no need to ask a lot of questions. Her shares in *Charlie* bought her in as Third Hat and left her a surplus; she didn't seem to mind having to drop one grade. Her cheek bore no tattoo, so she wasn't a Slaughterhouse graduate—not in officer grade, anyway. These things ascertained, Tregare said, "Move in when you're cleared with *Charlie*. And in advance, welcome aboard."

"Thank you, captain. A day or two, I expect." He cut the circuit.

"I'm glad you filled that Third slot. I'd been wondering."

Tregare looked around. "Hi, Jargy. Didn't hear you come in. Hang on a sec, while I check the rest of the input backlog, and I'll buy you a drink."

When the screen lit again, the pictured woman looked familiar but he couldn't place her. Fairly tall, he thought, if she'd been standing. Strong features, highlighted by dark eyes under challenging brows. Midnight hair, bulked out with the waviness that indicated frequent braiding. Age? Not too far off his own, likely.

The voice resonated. "This is Sparline Moray and I want to talk with Captain Bran Tregare. I have good reason; there are things to be said, and we are, after all—um, somewhat related. I'll accept a return call, any hour, at Hulzein Lodge."

Tregare's face went hot. To his comm-tech he said, "Tell Hulzein Lodge there'll be no return call." *So they'd sicced his sister on him, had they?* He stood; the rest of the incomings could wait. "Come on, Jargy. The drink. My digs." Damn, though—with the puppy fat gone, Sparline was one striking woman.

Down in quarters, drinks poured, Jargy said, "Tregare, you never mentioned being Hulzein-related. I know a little about those people, and—"

Tregare used sipping-time to think how to put it. "You heard what she said: somewhat related. But not closely." *Not now, anyway.* "And that's how I intend to keep it." Satisfied or not, Hoad pushed the matter no more.

Al Druffel, his ship-shares paid off fairly, left the ship on crutches; Tregare noted that the young ex-officer made sure to tip the unrated crew members who carried his gear. Maybe Number One's medics could fix the leg; Bran hoped so.

Back in quarters he found the intercom chiming. "Somebody here to see you, captain, from *Stump Farm*. It's not their skipper."

"Yeah?" He yawned. "Show'm up here, in five minutes. Whoever does that, bring me a snack, too. The galley knows what I want. If our visitor's hungry, double it."

The crewman escorting *Stump Farm*'s envoy brought a single-sized snack but double coffee, so Bran poured for two but ate for one. "Talk in a few minutes. Okay?" As he ate, he looked at the woman.

Average height, a little sturdy, with a pleasant face under short curly dark hair. Age youngish, but grown-up, not a kid. Done eating, he poured them both more coffee. "Krieg Elman send you? About time our two ships talked some."

She shook her head. "He doesn't know I'm here. He's crazy. I want off that ship! I can't get my First Hat shares out of Elman, but if I have to, I'll ride unrated. Because I don't want to be on *Stump Farm* when that maniac blows the Drive."

Changing his mind about four times in five seconds, Tregare said, "You know who I am. Now what's *your* name?"

Leanne Prestor. First Hat since Escape, which no officers

had survived; Elman had held Chief's rating. "Oh, he can handle the ship all right, but he thinks everybody's out to get him." A shaky laugh. "Not just UET, which *is*, of course. Any other Escaped ship, anyone groundside—even here, on a Hidden World. Everybody wants his ship; that's his obsession. He doesn't trust any of us, his own people. And his standard reaction, seeing threats that aren't there, is to start yelling that he's going to blow the Drive." She shuddered. "And one of these days he'll forget he's bluffing, and really do it."

Tregare thought. No Brooks Marrigan here, so wedded to *Spiral Nebula* that he'd take it out in obviously unsafe condition, yet unable to defy Tregare's threat to blow *Nebula* apart rather than let Marrigan lose it in space for lack of repairs. Bitter as hell about his own helplessness in the face of Tregare's ultimatum, Marrigan had sold off, so now Derek Limmer had a refurbished ship, *Lefthand Thread*, and Tregare had an ally. Back on Freedom's Ring, that hassle had been.

This mess, though, was different. *Damn!* All four ships were grounded close together. If Elman did go apecrap he'd take out the whole lot.

Several ideas came and went, then one stuck. Tregare said, "Prestor? You leave anything you really need, on *Stump Farm*?"

"No. If I went back, I probably couldn't get off again. Captain—do I have a ride on here?"

"Sure. No Hat berths open, though. Will a Chief's rating do you?"

Her relief was evident, but Tregare had no time to listen to thanks. "Then let me figure this." He had separate scramble codes set up with each ship so he didn't need to warn Rasmussen or Moaker. Calling Control he got a call put through to *Stump Farm*.

"Bran Tregare for *Inconnu*, to Captain Krieg Elman. Listen quick; no need for answer, and maybe no time, either." He gave Prestor a wink. "Elman, hear me! We all have to lift off fast. I can't for a few minutes so I may get caught; I hope you can go right away. Because there's UET ships coming in. And you know what that means.

"Get your ass upstairs fast, Elman! And good luck."

Less than fifteen minutes later, *Stump Farm* lifted. Then everything went to hell. Because Port Admin announced that a ship *was* coming in. No names, no ident, just the fact.

Tregare hauled Prestor up to Control with him and aimed an aux screen topside, waiting. The action didn't take long.

Shaking his head, wondering just how bad a person's luck could get, for a while he hardly noticed Leanne Prestor's queries. When he did notice, he told her, "I don't know who the hell that was, coming in, but now it doesn't matter much. Because whoever it might have been, your Krieg Elman took care of it. He rammed.

"And blew *both* Drives."

3. Bases Loaded

Being depressed, Tregare decided, really got him down. He alternated between guilt and anger, and was comfortable with neither. Dammit, was it *his* fault for taking Prestor's warnings seriously and spooking Elman to lift scared? He couldn't have known that there'd be an incoming ship to trigger the man's paranoia.

And yet, if he hadn't been so quick to make his smart move, maybe two shipsful of people wouldn't be plasma, now.

So when Deverel called to say the crater site was leveled and ready for more equipment, Tregare welcomed the distraction; he went out and bought two aircars. He left one for Gonnelson to test-drive; the other, he'd wring out himself to find out if that zigzag pass would really work. Because if it did, the project could move a lot faster.

And if the pass turned out to be a trap he couldn't handle, maybe he deserved it. But that was no conscious part of Bran's thinking as he headed north, then across the first Hills range well clear of Hulzein Lodge, and north again.

In the way his blood pulsed, he felt the challenge ahead.

The giant axe-cut looked no less awesome than before. Flying past it for a quick preparatory scan, he caught whipsaw from turbulent air. He circled away, then cut in, pointing directly at the gap. Climbing, he gunned the car hard.

At first he thought he had the handle, but once between the towering walls his car was caught by gusts that lifted and dropped him, threw him to the side and nearly into one jagged scarp. He swung the car's nose down and away, hit full power and pointed for the most room he had, up ahead. Pulling for height, hoping the car would take the stress.

It shuddered like coming apart, but then he was past the turbulence. Now he needed altitude; he pushed for it and got it.

But ahead—when suddenly he saw only a wall there, he gave it what time he could afford and then swung hard left; at both sides he missed death by not very much. The abrupt swing right he was ready for, and made with no real difficulty. Then he concentrated on keeping proper distance from the rising ground below and cleared the summit easily. After that, down the Big Hills' eastern slope, he could coast and enjoy it.

But two things were for sure. One, for saving a lot of time and fuel, this pass was the edge he needed. And second, anybody who got through it the first time needed some luck.

At the crater, progress was good. The floor was reasonably level, the prefabs set up around the edges, and all loose gear stowed away, out of the weather. Tregare congratulated everyone, and set them to gathering their duffel for a ride back to town. Mainly he didn't want to try the pass in less than full daylight, but no point in worrying people, so he didn't say so—he just rushed them some.

Westbound was easier because the wind was on his side. He had more altitude, up where the zigzag notch was wider. It still made a hairy passage, but nothing like the first time. When he could, Bran sneaked glances at his passengers. Deverel, narrow-eyed, tried to watch terrain, instruments, and controls, all at once. The two lesser ratings looked to be trying to decide whether to be scared or not. White-knuckled, Mac likely didn't know his face held a fighting grin. Aguinaldo's smile showed only bliss. "Nice," he said, as the car shot past turbulence and turned, high over flattish lowland, toward the Port.

Visibly, MacDougall forced himself to relax. "You did that well. I'm good with aircars, but I'm not sure my coordination's still fast enough for that run."

"Mine is," said Pete.

Mac turned on him. "Maybe if *I'd* just smoked three drugsticks, I'd think the same of myself."

The lazy smile didn't change. "Sure, I like the sticks. But not when it counts. I didn't say I'd want to try it *now*."

Avoiding the western ridge, Tregare skirted its northern

end for a straight course to the Port, and dropped Mac and Pete off at their business. "When the next load's ready, in a day or two, I'll call you." Then he made the short hop to his ship.

Boarding *Inconnu*, Tregare and Deverel hit the galley for coffee, and Bran got filled in on the fine points of how the work had gone. Then Deverel said, "Something puzzles me. Going over there, you didn't want the others to see anything. Coming back, though—"

"Why'd I change my mind? Didn't realize I had. Didn't think about it at all." But why? Then he knew. "I ran into a true paranoid. Fella used to be named Krieg Elman. And I must have decided I don't want to be one."

Then they discussed further details of the new base.

Ola Stannert was aboard and in Third's quarters. Tregare put her on a split watch, half with Jargy to teach her the ship, and half with Gonnelson so she'd learn how to communicate with Gonnelson. She learned fast; Bran was gratified.

The blond hair, he noticed, reached in full mass to well below her shoulders. Tregare found her attractive, but he was a little late; Jargy Hoad already had the inside track.

Cordially, but without naming his destination, Rasmussen made his farewells and lifted *NonStop*. Forty minutes later he made an urgent call to *Inconnu*. Bran ran upship, hotfoot, and took the comm. "Tregare here."

Screen showed Rasmussen standing by his own screen, which gave an outside view: the dark of space dotted not only with stars but with moving objects, dimly seen. ". . . debris, Tregare, from *Stump Farm* and the ship Elman rammed. I can't afford to slow down, collect any of this stuff and land it. But maybe one of your scoutships—" He gave the figures: coordinates and approximate drift factor. "In case you want to check it out, and see who it was that Elman wiped off the books."

And it's my fault. "Yeah, I'll do that. Thanks, Rasmussen. And again, good landings to you."

Signing off, Tregare turned to Jargy, who had the watch. The first half, it was now, before Stannert was to join him. Well, change of sked: "Tell the Third she's taking Gonnelson's watch. All of it, by herself. No problem, I think. Okay?"

"Sure, Bran. Care to say why, though?"

"What you heard. I'm taking the aboard-ship scout upstairs. And try to pick up enough scraps to figure out who I killed, when I sent Krieg Elman off with his head up his tail."

Only Tregare would be walking space, but Gonnelson needed a suit, too. Because if they salvaged something too big for the scout's airlock, they might have to hang it half-outside. Tregare wasn't planning to ride an open lock when they plowed air, so to get him inside they'd have to dump the scout's own air. He didn't say all that: just "We'll both need suits," and the First nodded.

Suited, then, both men clambered through the airlock, past hastily-loaded clutter of cables and fasteners; in case they needed to salvage something really big, Tregare could hang it on the outside. Figuring to waste fuel coming down slow, and preserve any outside cargo unburned.

When Gonnelson got them upstairs, Tregare navigating, the main drift of debris was easy to find, and to match vee with. Outside the lock Bran anchored the longest lifeline he had, took his best jump, and corrected with energy-gun bursts. He found plenty to salvage, and hooked each item to the cable with wraparounds. Some of the things surprised him, but now was no time to think about them. When he came to something too big to handle but too good to leave, he used the gun to cut it down to manageable size for outside transport. Then he hauled himself, and his collection, back to the scout.

Stowage and tying took him nearly an hour; going back inside, he was pooped. In the lock he signaled Gonnelson to dump the scout's air, and held on through the decompressive blast, then went on in and closed the lock behind him. Sitting, then, and strapped down, he said, "I wish I could have got more, but this is about all we can get through air, safe. So let's do it. But slow."

Groundside, because they couldn't possibly dock with *Inconnu*, they let air into the scout, climbed past the gathered litter, and boarded the ship. With his helmet off, Tregare gave orders. "A work crew to get all that salvage off the scout and spread out for looksee." Then he called Cade Moaker. "Got some things to show you. A turret projector, for starts. That ship Elman rammed was UET, and armed."

"I'll be over. Mind if I bring the Port Commissioner? I think he should be in on this."

"Sure." Tregare hadn't had occasion to meet Layne Ingalls, "the Commish," but had heard well of the man. Now, though, Bran needed to get out of his suit and wash away the stink a suit built so fast. Soon, no longer poisoning the air downwind, he went groundside again.

A little on the elderly side, Ingalls moved well. Shaking hands: "Glad to meet you, Tregare. Now what's all this stuff you've brought down, eh? I know about the two ships that smashed, upstairs, but—"

Cade Moaker interrupted. "The idea, Commissioner, is to determine the identity of the incoming ship."

Tregare's turn. "Right. And we have it." He showed the remains of the heterodyne projector, then a mostly-legible insigne on a scrap of hull plate. "The *Pizarro*, sir. An armed ship, as you can see. More important, though—" He held up readout sheets from his prize exhibit, the *Pizarro*'s core files, the item he'd burned loose from its surrounding framework. "The *Pizarro* took, in space, an Escaped Ship I'd never heard of before: *Swing Low*."

Ingalls cleared his throat. "I know the ship; it's been here."

Tregare frowned. "That's the problem." At Ingalls's startled look, he said, "*Swing Low* didn't quit easy; at capture, it was hopelessly crippled. The *Pizarro* spaced all survivors, then gutted the ship of information and supplies. And using that info, came here."

Ingalls went pale. "You mean—?"

"I mean you better hope the *Pizarro* had no chance to spill your coordinates to any other Utics, between killing that ship and coming here. And I mean, maybe your missile defenses can handle an armed ship's attack—but because Krieg Elman was insane enough to ram on suspicion, you don't have to find out. For a while, at least." *And my own guilt*—UET or no UET, he'd still triggered a lot of death. But this way, he could live with it.

His handtalker pinged; from shipside, Jargy Hoad told him that some of Number One's oligarchs were coming to join the session.

"Yeah? Like who?"

"Varied folks. A Harkeen, which I think is a clan title, not the individual name. And somebody from something called the No Name Cooperative, carrying two swords I don't see how anyone could swing, so let's hope they're ceremonial. And a tall gent named Hawkman Moray, from Hulzein Lodge, and—"

Forcing himself, Bran unfroze. "Jargy! Get down here right away, and take over. I'll come up and do your watch." He cut circuit, gave Moaker and Ingalls quick goodbyes without explanation, and headed for the ship. *That was close*.

Upship in Control, Bran put an aux screen viewer on the groundside confab. Jargy had it in hand okay. Dammit, why couldn't his family leave him alone? They'd done it before. . . .

As the new delegation, all five of them, joined the group below, Tregare listened to the signal from Jargy's talkset. The No Name fellow, with the absurd swords, was trying to run things. But Hawkman Moray's great height gave him a psychological edge; with a few quiet words he got the session on track, so Commissioner Ingalls could report the new information.

At the end, Hawkman said, "How long since *Swing Low* was here? Five years?"

"Six, maybe," said Ingalls. "I can look it up."

Running through the t/t_0 calculations, Tregare watched Jargy work his own hand-calc before Hoad said, "The *Pizarro* had to catch *Swing Low* not more than two point six lightyears out." He cut through attempted interruptions. "So unless, on the way here, the *Pizarro* passed another UET ship within talk range, UET has no word of you. The odds are good. And—" Jargy grinned. "Even if they did, it'd be twenty years before UET could get here in any real force."

"We have to think ahead!" A nasal voice, Alsen Bleeker's. "We need an armed ship, for defense. Why not this one, right here?"

"No," said Hawkman Moray. "I—I used to know its captain. You won't be hiring that man to sit guard on a mudball."

Too right, Hawkman! Tregare punched Jargy's beeper and told the man what to say, then listened. "While we're here, you can count on *Inconnu*'s help if you need it. But when we leave, that's up to the captain."

Bleeker and Big Swords tried to make a fuss. The Commish merely shrugged. Hawkman, looking up at the ship, nodded. *He still knows me. Too bad it can't help*.

Next day, wanting to expedite delivery of some supplies, Tregare rented one of Keri Freling's groundcars and drove across One Point One to the Harkeen warehouse complex. He parked near the office entrance, went inside, and found that business face-to-face went faster than over a phone. He dealt with a chubby man, Harkeen by name as well as by affiliation, and soon cleared the paperwork and saw the first consignments loaded and headed for the Port.

So he shook hands, thanked Neyford Harkeen, and went outside. Beside his groundcar stood a tall, bulky young man, scowling and dark-browed. Tregare veered to walk around and past him, but the youth grabbed Bran's arm. "Just a minute, you!"

Tregare restrained his first impulse and made no move. "Yes?"

"Your damned groundcar. That's where *I* park."

Three adjacent spaces were empty; Bran couldn't see what the problem was. "There wasn't any sign up. Sorry," and he waited for this lout to let go of him.

But the left hand came to clench on Tregare's jacket while the right, releasing his arm, made a ham-sized fist and drew back. The hell with it—Tregare took two fingers of the grabbing hand in each of his own, stepped back abruptly, and leaned down. A moment he stood, his would-be assailant kneeling and howling; then one more tug put the youth's face in the dirt.

When the other got up, Bran saw no intent of further attack. He said, "Maybe you did own a grievance. But you got too quick with your hands."

"I'll get you for this! I'll see you dead! My family—" The hulking boy spat, but the drops fell short. He turned, cradling the injured hand in the other, and limped away.

From behind Tregare, Neyford Harkeen said, "No idle threat, I'm afraid. Though with due precaution you should be relatively safe from the dal Nardos."

"Who?" Neyford repeated the name. "They're big around here?"

"On the way to being. Not nice people, I'm afraid. No one says so publicly, but the dal Nardos progress largely by extortion and assassination."

"And nobody does anything about it?"

Harkeen shrugged. "Some try; they turn up dead, and by coincidence their heirs are named dal Nardo. You see, there's no overall organization here. Oligarchs work independently, and—"

Tregare nodded. "Feudalism. But you *could* gang up."

"Or hire outside help. Captain Tregare—"

"No. People have to clean up their own mess."

"It might be yours, too. If young Stagon complains to his father—"

"He's the honcho?" Harkeen nodded. "Look—you said we got nothing to worry about. Make up your mind!"

Neyford Harkeen waffled. Yes, but. If. Maybe. But still. So they went back inside, and Harkeen put a call through to dal Nardo HQ. When Lestrad dal Nardo came on circuit, Tregare told him what happened outside; carefully, he made sure he had all the details right. Dal Nardo answered, "That's not the way my son reports it. You've made yourself fair game, captain—you and all your people. Guard yourself, if you can."

Allowing himself no laughter, Tregare said, "Looking at an armed ship and two armed scouts, you say a stupid thing like that? *Listen*, now—" And he detailed what could happen to any or all dal Nardo holdings if that clan bothered Bran Tregare enough to notice. Adding: "Stomping overgrown kids isn't my line, but that one of yours is bigger than I am, and needs some manners."

He cut the circuit and turned to Harkeen, who didn't seem to realize his mouth was open. "What you do with people like that," said Tregare, "you explain why they're not going to mess with you."

Then he left. Going back to the ship, his car was followed by two larger ones, the armored kind. He guessed he knew whose they were, but all they did was follow. And if Lestrad dal Nardo wanted to *look* tough, who cared?

The scout was loaded, with the makings of three prefabs lashed to the outside. Mac and Pete brought a crate of explosives and the gadgetry needed to use the stuff. This time Bran was ferrying a bigger work crew, with Deverel again in charge. And what with the extra huts, Anse Kenekke was also in the group.

At midafternoon Tregare set the scout down in the crater he thought of as Base Two, though his plateau above as yet bore no trace of the projected Base One. Unloading and planning took longer than he expected, especially laying out the fuel tank sites. So instead of flying and landing in dark, Tregare slept over. The scout's bunks were hardly luxurious, but comfortable enough.

Back at *Inconnu* next morning, Bran got bad news from the Commish: one of Mallory's Drive techs had died in a Port-area bar fight. Tregare's first thought was that it could be a dal Nardo move, but Ingalls said the other fighter was a loner, fresh in from hunting bushstompers south of the Slab

Jumbles. "Just an ordinary fight, over a woman who wanted no part of either of them."

So when Ingalls asked if Tregare wanted to add punitive charges to the Port's court docket, Bran shook his head. "My crewman and your hunter, they were both unlucky." Feeling old and tired, he added, "It's the Port's case; I'm out of it."

Lestrad dal Nardo might be backed off, but he hadn't quit. Everywhere Bran went in One Point One—arranging for supplies to be loaded in the ship and scouts—he was followed. Blatantly. After a time he got tired of it. He waited his best chance, though; in the area of small shops and food booths one day, he noticed he had only one bloodhound, a hulking bruiser behaving like the Menace on Tri-V. All right. Tregare picked his spot, turned a corner quickly, and stood waiting.

When the man, hurrying to catch up, came around the building's corner to see Bran facing him, he stopped short. "You following me, or going someplace?"

"I—going someplace. What'd you think?"

"Then go there. Me, I think I'll hang around a while."

No fast thinker, this one. "You can't tell me what to do."

"Wrong. I just did. Move it."

"Let's see you *make* me move." The man pulled out a knife, and pointed it—weaving in what he probably thought was a pro stance—at Bran. "I'm staying, smart guy."

Enough of this crap! As he spoke, Tregare took the knife away and heard elbow ligaments rip loose. Slapping the empty hand up against an exposed corner-beam, he drove the blade through flesh and deeply into wood.

"Yeah. Stay right here. Long as you want." He walked away, not heeding the man's suddenly-shrill cursing. Bystanders gawked, but no one interfered.

Apparently the lesson took; after that incident, Bran spotted no more followers.

One more time Tregare took the scout across the Hills, to check that his fuel tanks were ready for filling and to have landing circles marked on the crater's leveled floor. Those matters seen to, he lifted *Inconnu* and brought that ship to his developing Base Two. Gonnelson followed in one scout, Jargy Hoad in the other.

In a couple of days the camp shook down into an operative routine; Bran felt the base was coming along well. When the major projects were on track he went upslope in one of the aircars he'd brought along in the ship's starboard scout bay, to have a closer look at his cliffside plateau. Coming in over the lower dropoff he taxied through sparse, grasslike ground cover, almost to the westward-rising cliff. And got out, and walked around.

The place wouldn't need much bulldozing, just some minor leveling of the inevitable talus slope, for building foundations. He stood, maybe fifty meters out from that slope, and looked eastward. Ahead and to his right the ground hummocked a little, but mostly the shelf made a gentle slope. All right—storage buildings close under the cliff, and a headquarters cabin—where to put that? Some of the oligarchs' infighting included bombing from aircars, and the zigzag pass wouldn't be his personal monopoly forever. Turning, he looked up, estimating the angle to the cliff's edge. And laughed. Right where he stood, a car couldn't drop over and land a bomb on him, without slowing enough to be dead meat for ground fire. Some smallish missiles . . .

He piled loose rocks to mark the spot, and took the aircar back to Base Two.

With one storage tank complete and secured, Tregare pumped much of *Inconnu*'s fuel into it and took the ship across the Hills for a refill. "I'd like to stock up for half a dozen ships," he told Jargy when they were back again, "but even watching for price dips, I can't afford it."

"You shouldn't need to. Any ally who meets rendezvous in shape to join up can probably buy its own."

"I know," said Bran. "I just want to make sure."

Jargy cuffed Tregare's shoulder. "You worry too much."

With the walking hoist, MacDougall was pulling the dozer up the side of one scout, to ride outside. When everything was cinched down properly, Bran got the work crew aboard and lifted to the plateau. Gonnelson, with Ola Stannert to talk for him, could handle things for a while at Base Two.

The bulldozing went fast; so did erection of storage buildings, mostly prefab but some timber-framed. Number One's trees, taken from the plateau's south end where cliff eased into a gentler slope, gave good lumber. Using the energy gun from his disabled power suit, clamping it under an improvised chute, Tregare shaped square timbers by having the cut logs pushed through. "And everybody keep your hands on *this* side, so's you don't lose any."

He wanted the cabin to be a mini-fortress, so it took longer. Thick walls and roof of solid wood, metal-reinforced. Windows with no ground-level look-in from outside—the one facing uphill looked at blank cliff face. Under the building an escape hole dropped to a tunnel ending in a ravine to the south, and partway along that tunnel was an upward egress to a brushy hummock. "I'll make a pillbox there. Use it to cover the front entrance."

Jargy shook his head. "To defend against *what*?"

"I don't know. *Anything*, I guess." But after two more supply trips to the crater and one to the Port, Tregare figured his little Base One to be fairly well secured. Especially with the small defense missiles he'd bribed out of Alson Blecker's warehouse without that gentleman's knowledge; those were now installed at the plateau's outer edge, ready for hookup.

Some of the small detail was a bother. Time wouldn't allow bringing and burying enough pipe to get sewage wastes off the plateau completely. So, since the place would have to depend on a water table rather near the surface, Tregare settled for building a fancy outhouse and heat-fusing the pit to keep it sealed; three times, he had to recharge the energy gun.

Once the cabin's double-plastic windows were in, he took the work crew down to Base Two and began loading the scout with some appliances and fittings he needed, plus a fair amount of food and drink. He was bringing his final load offship—no point in bothering the help with this little stuff—when Leanne Prestor said, "Captain? I'd like to talk with you."

He turned around to her. "That'd be fine, except right now I have some work to do, upslope. Later, maybe?"

"Why couldn't I go along? And help with the work?"

I don't need any help. But this woman was the only person who had recognized the danger of *Stump Farm*'s paranoid captain *and* had the initiative to get away; it might not hurt to get to know her better. So Tregare said, "If you can arrange leave off your watch in the next ten minutes, come along."

"Right." Sturdy legs pumping, she ran up *Inconnu*'s ramp. Tregare put his gear aboard the scout, went back to collect a few last-minute odds and ends, and returned to find Prestor waiting in the co-pilot's seat. "I'm covered for tonight's watch. If necessary, I can arrange for tomorrow's, too."

Tregare didn't let his brows rise in inquiry. "That's fine. But I expect we'll be back then." He warmed the scout's Drive and lifted. Flying to the plateau they didn't talk. Bran had some questions, but he figured they could wait.

Once landed, he and Prestor carried supplies and equipment, mostly to the cabin but some to the storage sheds. Then they got to work on the plumbing, so he could start the pump and fill the attic water tank. Next he hooked up to the kitchen facilities, and the folding tub in the bathroom. Prestor made a good helper; she understood instructions, and talked only to the point at hand. She didn't need to know that the tub could pivot to expose the trapdoor leading to his tunnel, so Tregare didn't tell her.

Under the west-rising cliff, sunset came early. Wiping sweat from his forehead, Bran said, "The rest of it can wait; let's call it a day. You getting hungry? I am."

"Why, yes." She pushed at the hair over her forehead; her own perspiration made it curlier than usual. "I hope you can cook, though. Even if I knew where things are, here, I'm not very good at it."

"No problem—there's frozen stew." He saw she didn't know which way to take the remark, so he said, "You watch, while I figure how this combustion stove works, and learn from my mistakes." Then she smiled, and wandered around the cabin as though trying to memorize it. There wasn't that much; one entered through the only door, at the right of the front wall, into a room that took up half the building. Its left front corner held a wooden bedframe with two bunk-sized mattresses, and now a pair of rolled-up sleeping bags. The cabin's rear half was kitchen and dining nook on the right side, bathroom on the left. Not a lot to keep in mind, but Tregare let her look all she wanted until the stew came to boil; then he gave chow call.

The slab-topped table he'd built himself; the chairs were cheap flimsies from One Point One. The stew was good, and the small cooler he'd brought along worked fast, so they had cold beer, too. When he piled the used utensils into it, the compact dishcleaner also worked. He hoped the water heater wasn't too slow, because a hot bath felt like a good idea.

First, though, seeing through a front window that day had begun to turn to twilight, he said, "Come on outside and see something." He went out, and she followed.

The way the cliff shadowed the plateau, no sunset was visible now. But looking eastward the two saw sunlight leaving the Big Hills' lower slopes, and shadow chasing that light out across the plain below, before the bright reflection shimmered on the horizon a moment and disappeared. Then, suddenly it seemed a lot darker.

Cooler, too. So indoors Tregare lit up the front room's combustion heater. As the place warmed, he checked at the sink and found the water hot. "Prestor? I haven't found the shower gear yet, but if you want firsts on tub dunks, go ahead."

He liked the smile she gave him. "Why, thank you." She entered the bathroom. Looking for something constructive to do, Bran settled for unrolling the sleeping bags and arranging them, each on its own mattress. Then he sat, thinking for only a brief time until she came out, hair damp and face pink. "It's all yours, captain."

He took no great time at it, himself. And came out to find Leanne Prestor lying at the far side of the two sleeping bags she'd zipped together to make only one.

Until now, he'd had no sexual thought. Slowly, he said, "You don't have to—I didn't intend anything."

Again she smiled. "I did."

"Why?" Yes. Why me? And why so fast? And was he ready, so soon, to deal again with someone else's feelings? The physical part, sure. But still . . .

He waited, and she said, "Because you don't just dither, you *do* things and you know what you're doing." Now she frowned a little. "You're dangerous; I know that. But maybe that's part of it—like having a tiger that I know won't hurt me." Pause, then, "You wouldn't, would you?"

"No." But—*Erdis!* "Not on purpose, I wouldn't." He thought about it. "You got to realize, people don't always have the choice. But if you still—"

"I still. Come *on.*"

For Tregare it had been a time, so sleep had to wait until they'd had "seconds," and next morning saw more activity before they arose.

The only eggs were freeze-dried; Bran served them scrambled. Along with toast and juice and coffee, he figured it made a damn good breakfast. Down to coffee, Leanne said, "I should tell it straight. Onship I'd *like* to move in with you, but I don't have to."

This one talks up fast. "You're ahead of me. Spell it."

She pouted cute, but Tregare waited for the words. "We're good here. On the ship, though . . ."

"On the ship, *what*?"

"Sometimes officers and ratings can roomie and sometimes not. On *Inconnu*, which way is it?"

"Well—" He stalled, partly because he hadn't really thought about it and partly because his instinct went against being rushed. Was this too soon? And distracting him further, a kind of buzzing started inside his head. No—not *in* his head—he was really hearing it. And now it built to thunder, and he knew—a ship was lifting, crossing above him while still plowing air. Not *Inconnu;* the direction was wrong. This ship was coming from the Port at One Point One. He hadn't known any were there now, but if one had landed from westward, the sound might not have been noticed here, with the Big Hills between to deflect it.

He started to sit back, to put his mind to Leanne's question, but from above the sounds changed. Not just the ship, its thunder softening with distance and climb into thinner air, but something approaching, now.

An aircar. No, more than one, and not far off. *How the hell did they get over here?* And then came the *ssisss* of a falling object and a clanging explosion too close not to jar things. Why, the bastards were bombing him!

There wasn't time for anything, so he didn't take it. "Get under the bed!" and he saw her go in that direction. All he wore was pants and socks; they'd have to do, as he realized the damn missile-control panel wasn't hooked up yet so he'd have to try to get to the scout. He was out the door and running, feeling the sharp rocks cutting at his feet, while he tried to think how to jigger the scout's control fre-quencies to launch some missiles. Once they were up, they'd seek heat and metal, but what the *hell* were his launch codes?

Sound and shadow passed above him; something hit his leg and hurt a lot; he heard the rattle that meant a whole batch of needle projectiles had hit the ground behind him. He didn't look at the leg—it was still working, so it could wait. Then he was up the ramp and into the scoutship.

For seconds that seemed longer, he paused. *The launch codes!* He was too hassled to be able to remember anything about them. He put the viewscreen on and saw two aircars circling; one dropped a bomb and all too soon the scout rocked to the blast.

Hell with it—if he waited, he was dead. So he hit the Drive switch and took the scout up cold. Well, not quite; it hadn't wholly cooled from its last flight. But still a risky move.

The scout made it, though. Tregare got off the ground alive. And went up past the two aircars and made a sharper turn than he really should have, and came down in one elegant S-curve that put his projector fire across both cars, blowing them into nothing much.

Then he landed, right about where the scout had sat before, and went back into the cabin.

She probably hadn't gone under the bed at all, for what good that might have done her. Leanne Prestor sat on that bed, drinking what looked like a cup of coffee. She said, "You want some?"

Wrung out all to hell, Tregare didn't appreciate anybody trying to show how nothing bothered. He took the cup. "Yeah, gimme that."

First she was silent, then she said, "I'm sorry. You're so damned competent; I was only trying to keep up a little. Tregare—what *did* happen? All I know is, there was a lot of shooting, and I was scared out of my skivvies."

Put that way, he could understand. "Me too. Two aircars with bombs and needleguns, it was. I don't know how they got here. I took the scout up and wiped them." He felt the blood on his leg. "Hey—take a look here? I guess I got hit some. Not too bad?"

"It doesn't seem so. The needle went straight through, nowhere near the bone. Where's your first-aid kit?" And when the wound was patched to Bran's satisfaction, she said, "You never did answer my question."

He was going to ask "Which one?" but then he remembered. And said, "I'd purely enjoy you moving in with me. Don't let anyone accuse you of trading on my rank, though. Which means, don't give 'em any excuse to."

She nodded. "Yes, of course. I won't cause trouble."

* * *

Not that he figured on any more attacks right away, but Tregare wanted those missiles in working order. Leanne asked why he had no such things down at Base Two and he explained that not only did *Inconnu* have its own missiles ". . . makes these here look like kids' firecrackers . . ." but also its projector turrets had traverse capability, which the scout's lacked.

She couldn't help him on the hookup, except with fetch-and-carry work; circuitry wasn't her specialty. But he found himself enjoying her company anyway; she seemed to know when it was okay to talk and when to shut up and let him think.

Originally he'd planned for manual launch control, with radar and sonic alarms to alert the operator. Now he decided to jigger that setup a little, adding the option of letting the alarms do launching automatically. "Not all at once," he said, explaining to himself as much as to Prestor. "Send up two, first. When they blow, either on impact or burnout, if the target's still there, then another two fire. And so on."

This was one of the times for talking. She said, "So how do *you* come here and land me in one piece?"

That answer he already knew. "The system's either on manual or automatic; I can switch it here or by a coded signal when I'm leaving or coming in." He made half a grin. "Just so nobody forgets the drill, is all."

There were a few more things he wanted to do before leaving. Most of them got done but some would have to wait for another time. At midafternoon he said, "Time to pack it in," and they put tools and apparatus in some sort of order and boarded the scout. When they were strapped in he called *Inconnu* and got Jargy Hoad.

"It's going well here, Tregare. How's it with you?"

"A little flap, nothing serious. Tell you later. Just wanted to say, have somebody cover Prestor's watch again tonight."

Hoad acknowledged; Tregare cut the circuit. As he waited for the Drive to warm up, Leanne said, "I could stand my watch."

"Not from One Point One you can't. That's where we're going."

When he lifted, Bran first cruised the downslope below his plateau. He saw some fragments of aircar wreckage but, he decided, nothing big enough to identify—even if he could have landed, or taken time to investigate on foot. So forget it . . .

He took the scout high, crossing the Big Hills, and tilted to get a good look at their overall contours in this area. He landed in the open space nearest the Port Admin building and said, "I'm going to talk with the Commish. Want to come along, or stay here?"

"I'm coming with you. Tregare, this is why you brought us here, isn't it? I certainly don't intend to miss it."

Tregare called the Commissioner, whose secretary said that Layne Ingalls was in conference but should be free in half an hour; could he call back? "Yeah, sure," and Bran confirmed his call code and primary frequency for that purpose. Call closed, he turned to Leanne Prestor. "Dry work. We have some time to kill. Fix us drinks, maybe? Bourbon, ice, for me."

She said, "Half an hour? You know, we could—"

"Drinks. Please. Or I could fix 'em."

"Tregare—I'm not supposed to ask? Is that it?"

His hand slapped his seat's armrest. "Hell, no. Asking's okay; it's fine. Just, this time I have to say no. Two reasons. One is, I killed some people this morning and I'd kind of like to find out who they were, if I can. The other—well, in bed I don't like time restrictions. Now—"

But she was already moving. "Drinks coming up." When she handed him his, she said, "I like knowing the reasons for things."

Ingalls called back on schedule; a few minutes later Tregare introduced Chief Rating Prestor to the Commissioner and they all sat. "And what's on your mind?" Ingalls said.

All right. "What ship lifted off this morning, heading east?"

"Only one has departed all week. This morning, yes. That was Dominguez on *Buonatierra*."

"Damn! I wanted to meet that man." For a moment, Tregare forgot his present concerns. "Did he check the data grapevine, where we all leave word?"

"Yes, he took full computer readouts. But the man was in a hurry. Refueled, restocked, and left. Something about a rendezvous, though how you people can compute such things in the Long View—"

"Yeah. It's not easy." But right now was a shorter view.

"Dominguez, though. You know if his cargo included any aircars?"

Ingalls nodded. "Yes. Two. And that's odd. Because they weren't packaged for stowing. In fact, when I saw them, not long before *Buonatierra* lifted, those cars were simply sitting just inside the cargo hatch, and the local pilots who delivered them seemed to be doing routine maintenance."

Tregare leaned forward. "Those pilots. They belong to anybody in particular? Some clan, some oligarch?"

"Mmm, no. They hire out. Not particularly savory characters, I might add. They work for—"

"The dal Nardos, maybe?"

"Sometimes. And the No Names. And last summer one of them did a month of chasing poachers off the fishing grounds that young Fennerabilis is trying to develop. More legitimate than most of their enterprises, that one. I'm just as glad they're gone with Dominguez." *Not with Dominguez, but gone, yes*. "Why—"

Tregare stood. After a moment, so did Prestor. Bran said, "This morning a ship went over where I was and two aircars came down bombing and shooting. Anybody wants to investigate, I can tell 'em where the pieces landed. How the investigators get there, across the Big Hills, is their problem."

Briefly, Ingalls looked startled. Then he nodded. "Quite so. I assume that if I asked your cooperation—?"

"You'd get it. But hardly anyone else would."

"Yes," Ola Stannert answered. "The floodlights are working."

"Good," said Tregare. "Expect us pretty quick now." He lifted the scout, started toward the Big Hills and then swung back. On his comm-panel he punched a call into the local system for Layne Ingalls's office and got relayed to the Commissioner's home. "Tregare here. I think I know which is the dal Nardo estate"—he gave the coordinates he'd spotted on the map—"but I want to be sure. Confirm?"

"Why, yes; that's correct. But, Tregare, you can't just—"

"I know, Ingalls. I'm not certain they hired the bombing—just positive. And they didn't kill me, so I'll return the favor."

"What are you going to *do*?"

"Teach Lestrad dal Nardo something he can't learn any younger."

* * *

Prestor was gasping and protesting but Tregare didn't have time for it. He'd spotted the dal Nardo mansion, and drifted toward it, while he talked with the Commish. Now he dropped near to ground level; the scout tilted, its Drive raising hell with the immediate landscape. All around the great house, twice, he walked the small craft, turning the ornamental grounds to pure chaos. Then he lifted the scout high and took it across the Big Hills slowly. Because he figured he had some talking to do.

He looked to Leanne. "What's your problem? You said you liked me because I know what I'm doing, but when I do it you get all shook up. You having second thoughts, maybe?"

Her head moved, not decisively. "But you—you just took this scout and *smashed* somebody's property. I—"

"Not somebody's. Lestrad dal Nardo's. Case you didn't notice, it's his people tried to bomb us out, at the cabin; nobody else here had reason to." He overrode her attempt to interrupt. "He's leaned on me before; I *told* him what would happen if he kept it up. He did, and I did. Any more questions?"

She had none, but he gave answers anyway. "It's close to time for lifting *Inconnu* off Number One. What I need here is almost done, and it's years before I—" No, he didn't have to tell her about the fleet he wanted, or when rendezvous could occur. "—before I come back here. What I do is, I use those years on fast time, *ships'* time—making contacts I need, and plainly raising hell with UET any chance I get. I don't waste that time sitting here and getting old." His right fist clenched. "I want UET scared, up to its neck in puke. So I have to go *hit* the bastards. And I can't leave some scorpion behind who thinks he can go eat eggs out of my nest when I'm not looking. You understand that?"

"Yes."

"Good." But another thought came. "From now on, when I do something, why don't you just figure I have a reason for it? And do the asking later."

Her smile came a little shaky. "Yes, I think I can do that."

The remaining twilight let him land, with no need for instrument work, alongside *Inconnu*. In that ship's galley, because he and Prestor hadn't eaten since leaving the cabin, he talked while he ate. "What I want to know, Jargy, is how they knew where I was."

"MacDougall. Aguinaldo." Gonnelson said it. "Their—"

Needing to swallow before talking, Tregare shook his head. "No. Mac and Pete wouldn't cross us."

Jargy Hoad said, "Their crew, he means. Moved back and forth a lot, in the other scout, to have days-off in town. So somebody got to one of them. More, maybe. Right?" Gonnelson nodded.

Tregare could see it but he didn't like it. "How soon can we dump most of the outsiders and do our own work?"

Hoad grinned. "Yesterday. Mac and Pete stay, and three they vouch for. The rest are superfluous now, anyway."

"Yeah. Good, Jargy." Bran thought ahead. He needed talk with MacDougall and Aguinaldo, but tomorrow would do. Right now, he turned to Prestor. "How long you need to get your stuff together?"

"Twenty minutes, maybe thirty."

"All right. About then, I'll come help."

As she left, Jargy Hoad said quietly, "You have a new roommate, Bran? Funny thing; I'm not at all surprised."

"Funnier still," said Bran Tregare. "*I* am."

Next day in his quarters he hosted Mac and Pete to lunch. His point was that when he took *Inconnu* off Number One, fairly soon now, he needed reliable caretaker service for both his bases. "And some missiles here, too, of course, with a control booth, and control capabilities for both places, from either one."

No problem on any of that; the big question was: "All right; now can you two arrange a setup to keep these bases in shape for me while I'm gone? Even if it's twenty or thirty years?"

Mac shook his head. "I can't handle something like that. The administrative part, sure. But the on-the-spot stuff—I'll be in town with no ship or scout for transport, and I don't intend to risk my neck in an aircar, as often as I'd need to, crossing that pass of yours."

Even without drugs, Pete Aguinaldo's smile was lazy. "That part's mine. Okay, Mac?" And the other nodded. "Then we have a deal."

There was more to it: contracts to be filed with the Port Commissioner's office, legal arrangements for the long term (privately, Tregare had little faith in those, but as a matter of form he negotiated and finally signed).

Then there was a certain amount of commerce back and forth across the Big Hills, until Bases One and Two were as complete as Bran could manage, and *Inconnu* primed to lift. The ship would run crowded, because he wanted supernumeraries just in case, after having to scrounge for troops to man Derek Limmer's ship.

Tregare enjoyed the ride when Pete Aguinaldo first took an aircar through the pass from the coastal side. The man eased in toward the "chimney" at medium speed and altitude; when the turbulence hit he went with it, mostly, letting it bounce him to the sides of the cut but not quite into disaster, and steadily increasing push to gain height. Bran had to admit that Aguinaldo was doing this with less effort than he had used. And when the dogleg loomed, Pete swung the car at an angle well ahead of time, then hit max thrust to take an economical diagonal across that zigzag. Straightened out after the second turn, the car made its final climb easily. Tregare said, "I like how you did that. The dogleg. How'd you gauge it so well?"

"I noticed, before. On your right, just at the turn, there's a pile of white boulders. Maybe some aircar wreckage in it, too. Anyway, when I saw that coming up, I—well, it's like putting a groundcar into a sideways skid, and then pouring on the traction."

"I never got fancy with groundcars," Bran said. "Just ships and scouts. But the way you took that zigzag sure works fine."

"Going back should be easier."

When Pete left, after dining on *Inconnu*, Tregare considered his arrangements and found them good: the maintenance skeds for skeleton crews at both bases, the funding arrangements through the Port, with MacDougall working the investment side, on commission. As good as could be set up, he decided, when you have to go with absentee management. If only his plans didn't need so much *time* . . .

He was tired, needing sleep before morning lift-off from Number One, but he checked the comm for messages. Most, his watch officers had handled—but Stannert told him one was personal so he played the tape. It was Sparline, his sister, and his gut knotted so hard that for moments her words made no sense to him. Then, "*I* didn't leave you there, Bran! Peace take you, I was only twelve years old. I had no—"

He couldn't listen any more. Shaking his head, trying to dislodge its sudden ache, he said, "Stannert, tell them there'll be no answer." And more to himself than to her, "I *can't*.

When they left me at the Slaughterhouse, that door closed. It stays that way." And how could he do this to Sparline? He *had* to, was all.

He said, "We lift at oh-six-hundred. For Target Place." *And about* time *we got this show on the road!*

4. Deuces Wild

Ola Stannert had been Second Hat on Moaker's *Cut Loose Charlie*, so Bran figured to let her do the lift-off. But at nearly the last day, Chief Engineer Mallory came up and said, "Tregare, I'm getting too old for this deadly game you're into. I have some good years left and I'd like to spend them on this world; I've asked around, when we were over at One Point One, and I can do well here as a consultant. Will you buy me out?"

"Well, sure. Sorry to lose you, Mallory, but I see your point." It took some figuring but there were no real problems. For one thing, with Tregare leaving investment funds at the Port, Mallory didn't need his shares all paid off right now. So the two men shook hands, and Mallory and his belongings rode the scout's last trip to One Point One.

The trouble now, though, was that Ola Stannert couldn't always decipher Junior Lee Beauregard's accent, which he himself described as "mushmouth Southron." Redheaded, freckled Junior Lee was a competent Chief Engineer, but his speech patterns did take some getting used to. Tregare had learned to ignore the differences consciously, and listen to what Junior Lee *meant*. So Bran did the lift himself.

"Drive ready, Chief Engineer?"

"As ever will be, skipper."

"Then here we go." And whoever had tuned *Inconnu*'s Drive, Mallory or Beauregard, the ship lifted on a rock-steady thrust.

Target Place itself wasn't all that desirable as a destination, but starting from Number One it lay not too far off a route that hit several Hidden Worlds without much zigzag, and passed within reasonable detour distance of some UET colonies. "In case we get the itch to check one of those out," said

Tregare. "Just for instance, if we make a turn to bend around Franklin's Jump on the way to Target Place, we'd have our vee down enough to decel and raid if we wanted to."

"Would you want to?" Leanne asked. They were in quarters, and Tregare got the idea she wasn't paying much attention.

So he said, "Depends; we'll see." Then, looking at her, "Your mind's on something else. What is it?" It couldn't be sex, he thought, because they'd had that before dinner, and were still polishing off the coffee and wine, after.

She fooled him, though. "Bran? If I wanted to spend a night with somebody else, would that be all right?"

Jolted some, he said, "Somebody you have in mind?"

She shook her head. "Not really. But if I did, could I?"

He thought about it. "Sure you could. Right after you move out of here."

"But, Bran—!" She looked startled. "I didn't think you were possessive. Or monogamous, so to speak. And how many women have you roomed with, anyway?" He wasn't in a mood to count back; he waved the question away. "Well, at least you've never gone in for permanence. So why—?"

"Give me a minute." He had to think; he knew he had a reason but he didn't have it quite figured out. Then he nodded. "If I was Third Hat, Leanne, or Second, this wouldn't apply. You could do what you want and still be with me. But I'm captain, and that's different."

"I don't understand."

"So listen, and maybe you will. Captain's woman can change, leave to go with somebody else, that's okay—but she can't play around. It's—I guess it's a matter of dignity. Something silly like that." He looked closely at her. "You understand now?"

After a time, she nodded. "I think I do."

"And you'll go by my rules, on this?"

"Yes. Yes, I will, Tregare."

"That's good. Here, let me pour you some more coffee." But she couldn't let it go. She asked what he'd do if a woman—not her, especially, but any—broke those rules. He had no idea, but she wanted an answer. So finally, half seriously, he said, "I'd throw all her gear out the airlock, and let her new fella find her some clothes."

She smiled. "That's reasonable, I guess."

Inconnu built vee to the point where someone had to decide whether to bend course over past Franklin's Jump or head straight for Target Place. Tregare met with his Hats and took a vote: three wanted to scout the Jump and Gonnelson didn't care either way. So Bran sat shotgun, off to one side at a monitor position, while Ola Stannert fed vees and vectors into Tinhead and got back Drive coefficients she could call downship to Junior Lee. "And for each change, act on the count, Chief. Understood?"

"Purely shall, ma'am," and Stannert seemed to get his meaning.

Through the stages—swinging ship a little, easing accel, coasting, taking sights, swing some more, all of it—Tregare followed the action because he didn't know Ola Stannert's grade of skill yet and needed to check her work. So far, so good—his mind drifted to other concerns. . . .

Monogamous, Leanne had said. Well, was he, or not? In practice, he guessed he had been—in principle, he didn't know. But since he'd put that onto Leanne Prestor, then while they were together he'd do the same by her. Not that he'd had any other ideas.

"Complete, captain," Ola Stannert announced. "Course should put us past Franklin's Jump at the edge of detection range; vee roughly point-one c if no corrections are made. Confirmed?"

Startled back to now, he took a quick scan. "Seems like it. Any changes we need should be small. Good job, Stannert."

Running the ship crowded, Tregare found, seemed to cause a lot of small hassles. People got in each other's way, and tensions sometimes popped. Fights happened; accusations were made. Bran hadn't had to hold any kind of ship's court before; now it looked as if he needed to.

Well, *when in doubt, delegate!* Tregare didn't remember who'd told him that, or when, but it seemed like a good idea. So he said to Jargy Hoad, "Screening this crap, you're in charge. Set up a complaint desk—Ola Stannert running it, maybe. Prestor says she'll take it for a quarter-shift each day; see who else you can get."

Any time Jargy looked solemn, Bran Tregare got wary as to what the kicker was. Hoad said, "And what do *you* do?"

Bran sighed. "You know that, if you think a minute. The desk handles the easy ones, you interview the remaining bitchers and try to get them to settle out of court, or whatever. If they won't, *then* I hold Captain's Court and my verdict is peace-take-it *final.*"

Jargy Hoad grinned. "Not bad, Bran. It might even work."

When he finally had to sit court, after stalling as long as he could, Tregare showed up with a bad mood and a lousy headache. After an uncharacteristic bout of indigestion the night before, he hadn't slept very well. The galley seemed too informal, so he held the session in his own quarters. And sat, sipping coffee with Leanne, while the people involved took their own sweet time getting there.

Finally Jargy came in with two men who glowered at each other a lot, and a red-haired woman who ignored both of them. The place was fairly well filled so they had a little trouble finding seats. Bran said, "This the first case?"

"That's right," said Jargy, and named the complainants. Gaines, the short, dark man, had come aboard at Shegler's Moon. Lanky, sandy-haired Martin was new on the ship, from Number One. Item at issue was that when Martin's wife, the redhead whose name was Sheila, left Martin for Gaines, she took along some jewelry. "Family heirlooms, he says," Hoad added. "They won't give 'em back."

Tregare cleared his throat. "You folks know you have the right to counsel, if you can find anybody knows how to do that?"

No counsel; they'd all speak for themselves. And did, at length, until Tregare wished he'd never heard of any of them. Finally he shook his head. "*I* can't say how the gift was given or who has rights to it now. So I'll tell you how it's going to be." Everybody stayed quiet until Tregare said, "Spread the disputed goods out there in front of us. Then you have five minutes to decide who owns what." Leanne was whispering to him that he couldn't *do* that; he shushed her and could sense her outrage. "*Later,* dammit!"

Gaines spoke. "But that's just it; we haven't been able to agree. What if we still can't?"

"Don't worry about it," said Tregare. "Anything you can't agree who owns it, goes out the airlock."

Well, he'd read something like that when he was a kid, from a book of one of the old Christian sects. It worked for Suleiman. . . .

Now Martin was hollering. "I'm a citizen of Number One, and under that world's codes I claim the right of challenge!"

This was new to Bran; he leaned forward. "Challenge to what?"

"To a duel, of course," Martin said. "And to the death. Being the challenging party, it's my right to specify that."

Sheila whispered to Gaines, and that man spoke. "And as the challenged party I get to name the weapons!"

"Not on Number One you don't!" Martin again. "The referees decide which is the disadvantaged party, and that person—"

"Everybody shut up!" said Bran Tregare. "On this ship, I make the rules." He paused: don't be *too* bossy. "Let's hear your choices, for weapons."

Gaines wanted energy guns. Martin preferred the needle-throwers. Bran shook his head. "Neither of those. Not on shipboard. You want to cut through a bulkhead and wreck circuitry in there? Or bounce those needles around the audience?" Before they could answer, he had his solution. In early North American history there had been a frontiersman named Bowie. . . .

". . . so what we do, you see, is tie your left wrists together and then give you knives to use with your right hands. Unless one of you is left-handed, in which case that'll be your knife hand. Now whether you want this with clothes or without 'em—" Then Martin and Gaines and Sheila were all yelling quite a lot, and Jargy Hoad was trying not to laugh.

The settlement was, Martin got about two-thirds of his jewelry back, and everybody promised to leave everybody else alone.

"You really know how to pin people into a corner, don't you?" Bran and Prestor were alone in quarters now, and he could see she wanted to argue some more, hours after the "court" was done.

He shrugged. "You saw how it was. You got a better idea?"

Pausing, she said, "I—right *now,* I don't have an easy answer. But what you did was sheer barbarism. There has to be something better, and I—"

"Barbarism, yeah." He didn't want to get angry but he was, anyway. "Now look. Everything I have, Prestor, including my life, I got the hard way. At the Slaughterhouse, riding with the Butcher, and taking this ship. So now don't try to tell me how to handle it."

Her eyes teared and she turned away. Before bed there

was no more talk, and in bed, no contact. Tregare didn't like what was happening between them but he didn't know what to do about it. He got up and had a drink and smoked one of his infrequent cigars, none of it helped much but he did feel a little better. Maybe . . .

Next evening they made it up, more or less; at least he screwed his brains out, for what that was worth. And he did like Leanne Prestor, and in many ways respected her. But in some others he had to think her brain was half cornflakes. So what he did was try to keep their talk where she made sense. And mostly it worked.

Going in toward Franklin's Jump, Tregare watched Gonnelson bring *Inconnu*'s vee down to the point that gave all the options: slow and land, up the vee and leave, or anything in between. The ship's beacon was turned off and approach was at the far end of detection range from the planet; coasting, *Inconnu* wouldn't look like much of anything from groundside.

So they coasted, and time passed, and Tregare tried to find something to help him decide what to do here.

And then they saw a ship lifting from Franklin's Jump. Lifting like a real bat.

"What's its course?" Tregare asked, and the comm tech said it looked to be heading not far off their own. Figures for vee and accel first varied and then came clearer. Tregare said, "Gonnelson, let's go after that ship. I want it."

Surprisingly, the chase wasn't easy; initial course divergence cut the hell out of *Inconnu*'s velocity advantage. By the time Bran had his ship chasing on-line he'd lost overhaul capability. For now, anyway. The other ship was gaining distance, it had the edge in vee, and accel was about even. When Tregare asked Tinhead for the third derivative of distance with respect to time, it came out as near to zero as made no difference.

So the way things were, he wasn't going to catch up. "Damn all!" he said. "On accel, we should have the edge. That ship's not armed, and UET always arms the ships that turn up with the best Drive coefficients." Because, mass-production or not, some Drives simply wound up with more oof than others did.

"Loading," said Gonnelson, and suddenly Bran knew what

his First Hat meant. *Inconnu* was hauling close to max load; if the ship ahead was running light, even a considerably less powerful Drive could give it an advantage in boost.

"Yeah, right," and he called the Drive room. "Beauregard? We need some more push."

There was a pause, then Junior Lee said, "Cap'n, you got you all the Drive they is."

Tregare scanned his instruments and spotted something. "At this level of excitation, you're right. But we still have safety margin on the exciter. Junior Lee, run that thing up to redline!"

"Redline? For certain sure, you want that?"

Curbing an impulse to sarcasm, Bran said, "Yes, Chief. Do it."

The third-derivative indicator got off the zero pin. *Inconnu*'s accel grew; its vee approached and then surpassed that of its quarry, and that ship's lead in distance decreased. Instruments showed the Drive working near its limits—but not, Tregare hoped, too close to the edge. Accel leveled, third derivative hit zero again. But second derivative was on his side now; *Inconnu* was gaining. He queried Tinhead some more. Catching up would be futile if he simply flashed past the ship ahead; he had to match vees so that no matter how fast they were going, they'd be nearly at rest with respect to each other. Well, he knew how to extract those parameters, and after a while he got them. And put them on the auxiliary display board for Gonnelson and succeeding watch officers.

Tinhead set the forced rendezvous at ten hours minimum. "Gonnelson, I need a snack and some sleep. Carry on."

The man nodded, and Tregare left Control.

Back to quarters after eating, Bran found Leanne in bed but awake, reading. She said, "Will you catch that ship, do you think?"

"I'm working on it."

"And then what?"

Distracted, he shook his head. "Take it, if I can. Bring it over to the Escaped side. Install my own cadre, with an alliance agreement for when I get my fleet together. You know that."

"I know you think it can be done. And I hope you're right."

"Then why ask?"

"It's the details I was wondering about."

Without volition, he laughed. "Those, I haven't figured yet." Thinking about them, though, had him strung out too tight for anything more than a little cuddling then, before sleep.

He woke feeling better, knowing his plans in rough if not in fine. In the galley he said "Light and quick," ate that way, and went up to control.

Jargy Hoad, on watch, said, "We have their beacon. It's the *Peron*, and they're headed for Stronghold. I don't know who's commanding; we're not in talk range yet."

"How about our beacon?"

"By it we're still the *Tamurlaine*. Is that how you want it?"

Bran nodded. "For starters. Until we're up close, anyway."

And *Inconnu* was closing. Tregare watched as Jargy eased the accel back slowly, working toward a least-time rendezvous. When the two ships came first into talk range and then into firing distance, Bran opened his ship-to-ship circuits. Voice only, at first. "Hello, the *Peron*. The armed ship *Tamurlaine* here, Bran Tregare commanding. As authorized by the Presiding Committee I direct you to cut Drive for rendezvous and boarding. Will your captain acknowledge, please?"

No answer, so he repeated it, then added, "What's wrong with you people? You know the standing orders. Either you respond and comply or we are compelled to fire on you. So answer me!"

The voice that came, then, sounded breathless. "Sorry, sir. The captain's not available just now. We're having some trouble on here." Tregare saw the *Peron*'s Drive nodes flicker and their field die, and Jargy made moves to match the change. "If you'll give us a little time—"

Tregare quit listening; he cut his send switch and on another circuit gave orders. "Boarding party. Get suited up; no time to horse around with a connecting tube. Everybody armed." He heard answer and said, "As many as can get in the airlock, jammed up. Yeah, I know some suits are redlined for maintenance. All you need is about five minutes over and five back—pick the marginals on that basis."

When he had the operation underway he cut back to the *Peron*. What had the man been saying? Oh, yeah—"Well, time's what you don't have. Here's how it's going to be.

When we match up close, open your airlock. If you don't, I will. My boarding party's armed and doesn't want to see any guns at all on your people; you understand me? Have *all* your personnel in the galley; coasting, you don't need a watch officer. Anybody found anyplace else gets shot down."

"Our Drive crew—"

"Get 'em upship, fast." Here he was on thin ice and knew it, but couldn't think of a better idea. Then he did. "Either I take that ship over, for sorting out, or I blow it. That's up to you. But spread *this* word: no one who follows my orders will be killed or punished. Any resistance, though, can get folks dead. You got it?"

At the other end of the circuit he heard argument, but one voice overrode the rest. "Don't you understand? There's no damned *choice*!"

"Glad to hear somebody's smart. We're matching now, so get on with your part of it." And Tregare cut the circuit.

He looked around to see Jargy Hoad standing. The man said, "Request relief from watch, skipper."

"Sure. I'll cover. You better hurry, though."

"Right. Before all the suits are taken."

"When you have the galley over there, put that viewscreen through to here. Two-way. I'd kind of like to sit in."

As Jargy left, Leanne Prestor came over to Tregare's seat. "Bran, what's he doing? Do you know?"

"Course I do. He figured it out, without me telling him. We take this ship, it's his, and we're allied. So naturally it's his place to lead the boarding party."

When the aux screen lit, Tregare saw that the *Peron*'s galley was wall-to-wall with standing people. To one side stood most of Jargy's spacesuited contingent, the majority with helmets tipped back so they could hear better. The screen at that end must have come alive at the same time, because Hoad looked up at it and nodded. "Ship secured, Bran, except for a few diehards. Had to shoot a couple on the way upship, and two, three more are being hunted in the cargo area. We have Drive and Control solid, though." Bran released a sigh; it takes only one fanatic to blow a Drive. He gave Jargy a quick acknowledgment and commendation, then shut up and listened, as Hoad addressed the group.

"We've interrupted an Escape attempt, I gather. Well, I have my own ideas, how to handle these things—and they don't include murder." Tregare grinned—*nice going, Jargy!* "So I want the leading activists in the attempt to come over here." Silence, no moves. "You might as well; if you don't, someone else will point you out." Then, from various places in the room, three men and one woman began moving toward Jargy. When they reached him, he said to the overall group, "You people stay put here, for now. I'm taking these four upship for a private talk."

When Hoad and two guards escorted the four out of the galley, Tregare waited until the screen switched to a view of the *Peron*'s control room. Then he said, "Jargy? You hear me?"

"See and hear you both, Tregare."

"You want to tell 'em the real situation, or should I?"

"You give the overall; I'll handle the detail." So Tregare explained that the *Peron* had been taken not by UET but by an Escaped Ship, and that now the idea was to sort out the Utie loyalists and put them away safely in empty cargo area until they could be grounded in isolation on a Hidden World. "So we need your help, telling us who's safe to run loose and who needs locking up. And the trick is, none of 'em knows what's happening until we have all the nuts and bolts in the right bins."

"Thanks, Bran," said Jargy. "I can take it from here."

The *Peron*'s computer log had data Bran could use; he fired it into Tinhead, ran correlations with stuff he already had, and came up with some interesting ideas. Some of those, of course, would have to wait on the Long View and some long chances.

The *Peron*'s mutiny or Escape, depending on who was telling the story, had been less bloody than most. Partly, of course, because of Tregare's intervention while everything was still up for grabs. The captain, caught unarmed, had fled upship to take refuge in the topside airlock; then, desperate, he went outside in a suit. And when the Drive was cut, his lifeline came loose.

All three Hats were in on the Escape effort and had survived. In fact, there had been only a dozen fatal casualties, and four of those fell to Jargy Hoad's boarding party. Surviving Uties numbered slightly under forty, and Tregare refused to take any of those aboard *Inconnu*. "You might's well go on to Target Place, Jargy. You can dump 'em there."

"Why couldn't you?"

"Junior Lee isn't sure we can get there."

"What—?"

"Oh, we'll get *some*place. But to make that kind of bend in our course, and still land—he says maybe so, maybe not."

Between the two ships, now, came a certain amount of personnel transfer. Tregare had supernumeraries, Hoad was shorthanded and could use a cadre of people he knew. Ola Stannert was of course leaving *Inconnu* with Jargy. But on the *Peron*, Second Hat Frei Relliger wanted to leave, so the Hat berths evened out pretty well.

First, though, Bran had a talk with the tall, blond young man. Hosting the session in his quarters, Tregare saw Relliger seated and furnished with a drink, then said, "It's nice you want to join my ship. But I'm curious. Why is it you want to leave the one you're on?"

The man shrugged. "Woman trouble. Which is to say, about three months ago I lost mine to the First Engineer. I thought I'd get over it—but seeing them together on the ship so much, it just keeps getting worse for me. You understand?"

Tregare didn't, but he nodded anyway. "This kind of thing happen to you much? I mean, any part of life you care to name, we all win some and lose some. What I want to know: is it, you just can't stand losses?"

Chewing his lip, Relliger paused. Then his expression cleared. "No, sir. That's not it. Thinking back, I've had my share of lumps, and taken them. Including some in the romance department." He sighed. "This was different. I really thought—but then it all fell apart, and I'm not handling it well."

"How bad?"

"Killing bad. I never felt that way before, and I don't like it. It's not the way I *am*."

Tregare thought about it. "Maybe it's the way you're turning."

"No, sir. Or I'd have done it. Just being off that ship, now, the pressure's gone."

"All right. Welcome aboard."

Relliger's *Peron* shares bought him a Third Hat on *Inconnu*, near enough to work out, so Tregare staked Leanne Prestor to the Second's berth. He didn't ask where Jargy was going to fit Stannert into the *Peron*'s hierarchy of officers, and Hoad didn't volunteer the information.

Now connected by a transfer tube, the two ships drifted for several days while all these matters were settled and a certain amount of stores were shifted both ways, to forestall shortages on either vessel. And when these chores were done, Bran and Jargy met to share a farewell drink in Tregare's quarters.

"You have all the computer stuff," said Bran, "on our rendezvous some day, when I get the big job figured out."

"That I have. Cheers." Each man sipped a little. "And I'll keep in touch, best we can over the Long View, and leave word myself, of course, whenever I can."

Tregare leaned forward. "Who do I leave word *for*?"

Looking puzzled, after a moment Hoad laughed. "Oh, yes. Not the *Peron*, you mean. Well, it took a lot of thinking, but I finally have it. The gamble, Bran, when we overtook the *Peron* and I led the boarding group." He shook his head. "Anyone who played poker with those odds would be an idiot."

"It was all we had, Jargy."

"I know. But it wasn't figurable; it was all wild cards. So that's how I'm naming my ship, Bran Tregare. It's *Deuces Wild*."

They drank to that while impatience rioted in Tregare, and he thought, *first Kickem, then Limmer, now Jargy. It begins to* move!

From the *Peron*—now *Deuces Wild*—came one other item of possible future gain. Eda Ghormley, *Inconnu*'s chief medic, told Tregare about it. "I talked with this woman on the other ship, one of their medical aides. She's a sleeper from the Underground, and she's going to do the cheek tattoos for Mr. Hoad and his new officers, so they can fake it at any UET colony."

Immediately interested, Bran said, "How about for us?"

"For us, she gave me a kit, and instructions. So if you want me to fix up Mr. Gonnelson and Ms. Prestor, and the new man—"

"If they're willing." Because about Leanne, he wondered. Would she go along with having her face marked?

Ghormley might as well have read his mind. "What I have here is new. For one thing, it's removable."

Tregare rubbed his own cheek. "Suppose you could fix this for me, where three promotions all look the same but don't match my first marking?"

She shook her head. "No, sir. That permanent stuff I can't do anything about. I'm sorry."

"Not your fault." *Comes to it, I'll have to think of something else, is all.*

The only other problem he could think of, along those lines, was that Frei Relliger wore a Second's tattoo but was Third on *Inconnu.* So Leanne Prestor, now Second Hat, would have to settle for being marked as Third. He hoped it wouldn't bother her much.

The Relliger part made no sweat because young Frei's promotion was recent and his tattoo was the erasable kind. Prestor, though, disliked the entire idea. "Why should I? Why do we have to? I don't *want* my face marked up."

At the moment, other worries on his mind, Tregare was close to having had it with Leanne. "In case we hit a UET colony, is why. Then he said, "If you'd stayed with Krieg Elman, you wouldn't have to worry about this small stuff, would you?"

In seconds she went pale, no doubt thinking of the debris and plasma that Elman's *Stump Farm* had become. "That's dirty, Tregare. That's really dirty. I—"

"You came on here and I took you in; you joined the team. Now it's one of two things. You take that damned tattoo—that *temporary* tattoo—or Relliger's my Second Hat and I find me a new Third who's not so picky."

"And what happens to me?"

He shrugged. "Chief rating, I guess."

"And do I stay here, or not?"

Oh, she was pushing! Narrow-eyed, he said, "That's up to you. For now."

He watched her absorb what he said. She made a sort of smile. "I guess I can put up with the tattoo."

"Good." He came to his feet. "I have to check some things."

He'd waited to go up to Control because he wanted to match with Junior Lee Beauregard's stint down in Drive. He was a little ahead of the Chief Engineer's sked, just long enough to take one more good look at the rather discouraging

Drive data. He called down for Junior Lee to call back when he came in, and not long after, that intercom channel sounded. "Beauregard here, cap'n."

"Right. Tregare here. Chief, I've been punching figures out of Tinhead, but I want you to tell me what they mean."

Junior Lee cleared his throat. "Well, 'em numbers, I know 'em good. Can't talk in 'em much, though. What y'all need?"

And that was the problem; Bran wasn't sure what he did need. All right, go in with what they both knew, and work from there. "Chief, I stretched the exciter and Nielson Cube both, chasing the *Peron*. Efficiencies are down, on both units, and once the drop starts it keeps dropping."

"Glad you know that, cap'n, same as I do."

"But I don't know how fast either unit loses efficiency. What the curve is. I tried a negative exponential but it wouldn't hold. So—"

The engineer cut in. "That ain't it. It's—lookyere, sir—what we do is, I punch you up 'em numbers to read. Better'n any try talkin' 'em things."

Hell, yes. If Junior Lee could "talk" with Tinhead's keyboard and readout, there was no need to put this stuff into words. Bran watched as the numbers began to emerge. On another input-output circuit he ran trial calculations, trying to find a curve that would match. And finally he had one, or almost. Starting with normal top Drive boost he found that once the effects of his abuse of those units began, the dropoff curve was a reciprocal log function. He told Beauregard as much. "Varies according to how close we push max, and there's a couple of constants I'm rough-guessing for now, but that's about it."

Silent for a time, Junior Lee said, "Put some numbers in that?" So Tregare did, and Beauregard's next answer was, "Then cap'n, either we coast us a whole bunch, or with the speed we got now, we don't turn course hardly at all."

"I agree," said Tregare. "When I work out which it is, I'll let you know." Already he was running star charts on his nearest aux screen. "And thanks, Chief."

He returned to quarters nearly an hour later than he'd said he would, and found Leanne, wearing a light robe, dozing curled up on her left side.

The clink of ice cubes, when he made a drink for himself,

woke her; she sat up, and he saw the small bandage on her left cheek.

He smiled. "Been busy, have you? I appreciate that."

"Yes. Temporary or not, though, the process still hurts and draws blood." She leaned forward. "So will the removal, if ever. Ghormley told me how the temporary part works. It's simply that the Underground developed dyes that can be neutralized by tattooing *again*, with a special fluid." She stood, and came to him. "Bran? What took you so long, up in Control?"

"Trying to figure where we go next." He told her of the Drive problems. "We need to get someplace where repairs can be made, and getting there we have to nurse what we got."

"Have you decided? Our destination, I mean."

"Not yet. It takes figuring, maybe even talking." He had his hands to either side of her waist. "Before I went upship you had a mad-on at me. You still do?"

"No. I thought it over. For UET an officer *does* have to look the part." She leaned up to him, and they kissed.

"Fine. I'll go sluice off a little sweat, and be right with you."

The trouble with the weakening Drive was that Tregare had to guess right the first time, what to do; a wrong guess meant drifting to eventual starvation. He'd already ruled out their original goal, Target Place. Chasing the *Peron* had put *Inconnu* far off course from that world; he could make the turn, or the decel and landing, but not both.

Terranova was a possibility, but he'd have to change course "immediately if not sooner" and even then it'd be close. They'd need to cut Drive and coast most of the way, until time for a slower, more extended period of decel than usual.

That's where the Long View came in, the time-dilation that came with high vee: Einstein was long dead, but his ideas still governed ships that chased light. The difference between running point-nine of c and point-nine-nine didn't make all that much difference by planets' time, but by ships' clocks it made a lot. With a healthy Drive, Terranova was maybe eight ship's months distant. With *his* Drive, Tregare was looking at more like two years. He wasn't sure his supplies would hold out that long.

* * *

Up in Control, when he thought he had it figured, he called council, presiding over his three Hats and with Junior Lee sitting in. He gave them the figures: Drive efficiency dropping on a reciprocal log curve ". . . active time, that is, and any time we run at less than max, helps stretch our reserve out." Requirements for a course change to point at Terranova. "Doesn't leave much leeway on the decel end, but maybe enough." He cleared his throat. "That's not the problem, though," and he gave them the time-stretch part. "We might make it, we might not."

"Choice?" That was Gonnelson, and Tregare caught his meaning.

"There is one, yes." He flashed the star chart on the aux screen. "I'm skipping one other UET colony and two Hidden Worlds we might reach, because none of them have Drive repair facilities the last I heard. Or likely to develop any such thing by the time we could reach those places."

"Some idee, though," said Junior Lee Beauregard, "you got up your sleeve. Ain't that so, skipper?"

Tregare nodded. "Sort of, Chief." With a light-wand's dot of brilliance he traced a path across the screen's chart. "The course we're on, we came to by chasing the *Peron*. It was going to Stronghold. Of all our possibilities, that's the most distant. But in ship's time, it's the place we could reach the quickest."

He watched their individual reactions to the idea. Stronghold: UET's fortress outpost, set up to guard against the alien Shrakken, lest those creatures come to avenge UET's murder of a Shrakken crew and taking of its ship. Well, that was the rationale Tregare had heard for Stronghold's existence.

Frei Relliger half stood, then sat again to speak. "I don't—sir, a Hidden World would be best, or even a UET colony. But Stronghold—it's a UET *military* outpost. What chance would we have there? How could we get away with it?"

It was about time, Tregare thought, that somebody made that point. Because it needed answering, and the answer seemed to be his own job. Carefully he kept a straight face as he said, "For one thing, we lie a lot. I grant you, Relliger, it'll take some study."

Gonnelson nodded. "Stronghold."

5. Stronghold

The long haul into Stronghold, with Junior Lee pampering the touchy Nielson Cube and Drive exciter, gave Tregare time to figure and rig the ship's cover story. Working from the data from Kickem Bernardez on UET's list of ships scheduled for Stronghold over the years, he picked a name. In council with his officers, Control and Engineering both, he said, "From here in, we're the *Alexander the Great.*"

So the ship's talker-beacon gained an *Alexander* program. Outside on the hull, the insignia was changed—not totally, but the name was overlaid and the symbols altered. Leanne Prestor designed the necessary decals, and Hain Deverel went outside in a standard suit to place the polarized-electret plastic overlays, which would withstand plowing air on landing. Floating out on a lifeline, Deverel relayed views of the new insigne to an aux screen in Control; Tregare said, "Yeah, good job, Hain. Come on in—I owe you a drink."

So the ship's outside would bear UET's scrutiny. The inside was more difficult. Hiding the ship's true log under a couple of levels of code-groups was no problem. Working up a fictitious log to fool UET's command at Stronghold—well, for a time there, Tregare missed a lot of sleep.

There was no use trying to begin the *Alexander*'s history at any real point of truth. But nothing wrong with working in a few truths concerning ships and persons; the trick would be to come up with items that UET's own records might confirm, while keeping the log free of entries subject to disproof. What made the job possible at all was that customarily ships gave only taped summaries at their ports of call. And personnel records in those summaries began with the date a person joined the ship plus citing the previous duty station. For ratings and unrated crew only the bare bones were required—UET was mostly interested in officers.

So Tregare began by having the *Alexander* detached, long before lift-off, from its Stronghold-bound fleet, which was due to arrive a year or two after Tregare would with luck be there and gone again. For its "original" officers he threw in names he knew UET couldn't check on—some real, some phony.

He checked the timing and decided that this hop should be the *Alexander's* third. All relatively short ones, and he had to run t/t_0 through several times to make it come out right. He put himself aboard for the second one, as First Officer off the *Hoover,* at Terranova. The next fictitious stop, at Johnson's Walk, logged Cleet Farnsworth off the ship to a new command, the *Pizarro,* with Tregare succeeding to the captaincy. Then he had to juggle his other officers' records, both to fit the dates and to seem credible.

When he thought he had it right, he called council again, ran the summary and called for criticisms. Except for a few details, most of his work drew approval. Hain Deverel chuckled once. "A nice touch, captain, having that Utie turncoat Farnsworth promoted. Wherever the bastard is, I hope his soul appreciates your charity."

Tregare grinned back as Leanne said, "The summary's fine, Bran—at least I think it is. But what if someone coming aboard wants to snoop the full log. And finds there isn't one?"

"That's right," said Bran. "I guess I haven't told anybody about that part yet. So now I will, because we'll need to get into practice first."

Approaching Stronghold, Tregare studied the data Bernardez had captured and passed on to him, and learned the rigamarole required before landing at the fortress outpost. Of course he had it in mind to ring a few changes.

A little less than three days out, the hail from groundside began to come clear. Frei Relliger had the watch, and per orders he called Tregare. "You'll want me to hold off answering, I expect?"

"Right. The way we're coming in, there's enough stellar wind that it's feasible we couldn't read them yet. Tape everything, though, and monitor while you're doing it. If there's anything you think I need to hear, tell me right away." The intercom went silent as Tregare reflected that the young man off the *Peron* was really a lucky acquisition.

Tregare got up from bed. He hadn't been asleep, just waking and dozing comfortably, almost ready to rise but lazily delaying the act. Now, though, he might as well start his ship's-time day.

The talk had wakened Leanne; she, too, sat up. "We're

close now, aren't we? Pretty soon the danger begins. How soon?"

Begins? He thought about it, and said: "The day you were born. And for me, the day I was."

Roughly thirty hours short of touchdown, Tregare decided he had all the info he could get from Stronghold's greeting-tape routine, and that he'd better start answering. As near as he could tell, Admiral Saldeen on Stronghold wasn't worried much about anything in the way of ships coming from human-controlled space, but he was getting a little impatient for an answer from this one. Not that the admiral came on the circuit himself, but whoever did the talking sounded more brusque and demanding as time passed.

At the comm-panel in Control, giving the comm-tech an extra break for snack or coffee or both, Tregare opened communication with groundside. First the standard chatter: "the armed ship *Alexander*, Bran Tregare commanding. . ."

In council they'd argued about using his own name. "But what if word's gotten there already, about you?"

Bran shook his head. "I've figured all that. The interval—"

"The what?" Frei Relliger's brows were raised.

"You didn't learn that? It's Pythagoras and right triangles, applied to the way ships chew time. Distance is one leg, time's the other, and interval's the hypotenuse."

Headshake. "If you say so, captain."

"Not me. Einstein said it first." The Third Hat nodded, and Tregare went on. "I checked the times UET learned anything about me after Escape, and figured time and distance from those places to when we get to Stronghold. And the odds have a lot of zeroes on them that the info won't be here yet."

Relliger still looked doubtful, but nobody argued.

Now, talking to Stronghold, Bran had covered all the standard stuff. The groundside spokesman said, after the wait for signals at lightspeed to reach Stronghold and return, "Then you'll be landing at about nineteen hundred hours. So let me give you the drill we have here. First you—"

Tregare quit listening, because that wasn't how it was going to be. When it was his turn, he said, "There'll have to be a few changes. Unless—is your garrison there, the entire personnel complement, inoculated against the Grey Plague from New Canada?"

The answer was a time coming. "Why, no. I don't think so."

Tregare wasn't much surprised. Because both the Grey Plague and New Canada were his very own inventions.

". . . quarantine procedures as worked out and applied by the medical departments . . . have proved effective and totally safe." Tregare read out the quarantine rules. They sounded most official. Both Leanne Prestor and Hain Deverel were good at helping paraphrase Tregare's ideas into officialese.

What it boiled down to was that only in spacesuits would ship's personnel leave the *Alexander* or groundsiders come aboard. And any time the airlock's outer hatch was opened, the lock would first be fumigated with a guaranteed disinfectant, Eda Ghormley had come up with an aerosol spray that smelled bad enough to be credible—it was normally used to kill moths, something like that. "Of course this means," said Tregare, "that except for fuel and water which can be piped directly, all supplies must be loaded onship by way of the main airlock, since we have no way of using the cargo hatch without fear of contamination. But then, nothing's ever perfect, is it?"

Then groundside's Chief Medic had a lot of questions, and Bran was glad he'd worked out some answers ahead of time. "No, sir; we were never given the planet's coordinates. Out somewhere past Far Corner, is the impression I got." And, "No, we had no deaths aboard ship. No cases, even. What happened, there'd been Grey Plague at Johnson's Walk and everybody had to be inoculated, including us. Because the problem is, the shots make *you* safe enough, but they also make you a carrier for a long time. So that's why the quarantine measures were imposed." He ventured a short laugh. "It's going to make for lousy liberty, here, but this crew knows how to obey orders, right enough."

"This Grey Plague. What are the symptoms?"

"Nobody seemed to want to talk about it, much. A grey color to the skin. Uncontrollable dehydration. Convulsions. Fever. Delirium. A lot of screaming, so probably it's very painful, but at that stage there's no ability to communicate. So—"

After transmission lag, groundside asked, "Can you provide us with samples of the inoculant?"

"The what?"

"Vaccine, serum, whatever it was in the shots *you* received."

This question, Tregare had been waiting for. He said, "No. We asked, but they wouldn't give us any. Said it was too dangerous to keep around, without someone special-trained to handle it. We thought our medic knew enough, but Johnson's Walk said no."

"I see. Well, I hope you won't mind if, any time your airlock opens, we douse it with our own antiseptic spray, also."

They were still too far out for the screen to show picture, but still Tregare repressed his grin. "Not at all. Sounds like a fine, sensible idea."

The conversation ended; Bran cut the circuit. Relliger said, "All well and good. But still—what happens when they board and somebody exercises authority to snoop in our computer files?"

Tregare didn't laugh at his Third Hat. All he said was, "You ever try to punch a terminal keyboard, wearing space gloves?"

So it was all working, but some misgiving nagged Tregare. He couldn't figure what it was, until he decided he needed a shave and saw himself looking back from a mirror.

The damn tattoo, was what! The parts that didn't look right. Sure, he'd got by with the discrepancy at Hardnose, but that was a piddling little colony with no firepower to speak of if someone *had* got suspicious. And they hadn't been there long, and half the time he'd fixed himself some grease smears on clothes and cheek and forehead, ostensibly from double-checking maintenance work. Here on Stronghold, though, once the ship set down he'd be up against people who outranked him and forces that hopelessly outnumbered him. And he couldn't get away with being grease-smeared *all* the time.

He couldn't think of a good idea so he asked for some. Leanne tried touching the circle up with surface paints; the job looked fine, but the stuff smeared too easily. "Thanks," said Tregare. "It'd work just fine on a viewscreen closeup, but—" And for that purpose, close now to Stronghold, it served admirably.

Frei Relliger suggested a faked injury, covered by a bandage. Bran shook his head. "Somebody'd want to look at it. A medic, maybe." Damn! There had to be some kind of answer. . . .

Gonnelson cleared his throat. "Shiner."

For a moment, Tregare didn't understand. Then Prestor said, "Oh! Like a black eye, you mean." And the First Hat nodded. "But that would smear, just like—"

"Real one."

With admiration, Tregare looked at his First Hat. "That'll *work*. If there's time for it to bloom—" He shook doubts loose from his head. "We just won't entertain guests on here 'til it does. And offship, through my helmet nobody can make a really picky inspection." He stood. "All right, Gonnelson. Get up and do the honors."

"Me?" The man looked horrified. *"No!"*

"Sure, you. It's your idea, you get the privilege. Why, just think—this is probably the only chance you'll ever have in your life to slug a captain and get away with it!" But the jollying didn't work at all, so Tregare went serious. With a hand to Gonnelson's shoulder, he said, "I've never seen you fight, but I heard about a thing that happened when somebody in a bar got to bullying you and wouldn't stop. You hit hard and you're accurate, is how I heard it. And I want this done right."

Slowly Gonnelson stood, his face paler than usual. Bran said, "Wrap something around your hand. We don't want any busted knuckles." When that was done, Tregare turned a little. "This about the correct angle?" Then, "I'd better shut my eyes. Otherwise I probably couldn't keep from ducking." He saw Frei Relliger move off to one side, out of his line of vision. He closed his eyes, and waited.

The impact dazed him; he stumbled backward and found himself held and supported from behind. At first the voice there made no sense, then he understood. ". . . way he wound up, I didn't want you slamming back against the bulkhead, skipper." Relliger . . .

The lights wore halos; so did everything and everybody else. He wanted to say something, but words wouldn't form. He waved a hand, meaning to signal that he was all right, but the people crowding around him and easing him into a chair didn't seem to pay much attention. Gonnelson—Gonnelson was *crying*.

Tregare couldn't have that. With great effort he put words together. "The hand—it's awright?" Massaging that one with the other, the man nodded. Now speech came better. "Good job, feels like," as he winced from the movements talking made. "If that doesn't do it, we'll need a sledgehammer. Thanks, Gonnelson."

First Tregare had himself a robust drink, then he ate. Chewing mostly on the right side—his jaw hadn't been struck, but the left side was sore, anyway. As much as possible, he ignored it; he was working on his cover story. "Small abortive mutiny, I think," he said to Leanne Prestor. "A little coup group—maybe three—been planning Escape and got desperate as we came closer to Stronghold." She started to interrupt but this was *his* story and he was still embroidering it. "—jumped me coming out of quarters, knocked me around some until I could get my gun out. Then, of course—"

Playing along with his scenario, she said, "What happened to them? And who were they? On the records, I mean."

Spreading his hands wide, Bran said, "Spaced 'em; what else? One dead, one hurt bad, one plain scared spitless. Names I'll pick from those dead in this ship's real mutinies and feed 'em into the log summary all the way, up to now. And next move, I go down and seal that corridor's bulkheads a little. Energy gun—that'll save me having to splotch blood around; they mostly cauterize."

Leaning forward across the table, Leanne clasped his hand. "But what if they—UET, I mean, on Stronghold—interrogate the crew about all this? How many people can you rehearse on it?"

He grinned. "No need. Nobody was there to see. All there are is rumors. And besides, UET never asks about anybody but officers. So *we'll* have the story straight, and that does it."

He went on viewscreen to Stronghold, next, with no bandage but a smear of colorful antiseptic over his swelling bruise. To the groundsider's question he said, "A little problem on here, yes. It's taken care of, and you get a full report when we're down."

Inconnu disguised as the *Alexander* was closing fast on Stronghold. Twice that world's rotation showed Tregare the main fortress and its spaceport. The first time he couldn't distinguish much, even on high-mag, but next exposure showed him that the Port held fourteen ships; nearly half of these would be armed. Well, this caper wasn't depending on muscle, anyway. Because if it did, Tregare was in deeper than he could handle.

It was about time to see how Frei Relliger could land a ship, so Tregare assigned him the job and rode sidebar for him. The new Third Hat seemed a little twitchy when the ship began plowing air, but he brought it down steadily and met the landing circle with only the slightest of jars. Seeing the man's apprehensive look, Tregare said, "Good sitdown, Frei. It buys you a drink." And as soon as he saw the log brought up to date, he took Relliger to captain's digs and paid off.

When he went groundside, Tregare took along Hain Deverel and two other ratings, all briefed on the "mutiny" story and all, of course, in suits. In the airlock they waited while nozzles installed by Junior Lee's people fogged the chamber with aerosol mist. Then the outer hatch opened, and using a hose running up the ramp from a tanker car, spacesuited UET personnel gave men and airlock another spraying. It was all going to be a big nuisance, Tregare thought—but the inconvenience and its supposed cause should distract UET's attention from other matters.

So the four of them left the ship. The suited groundside squad returned to their vehicle, leaving the hose in place. Tregare's group was beckoned to a large open groundcar. Its driver and its one passenger who wore captain's insignia were not spacesuited. Tregare thought they looked a little nervous. Well, that wasn't such a bad idea. . . .

Looking a little sheepish, too, the other captain reached to shake Tregare's gauntleted hand with his own bare one. "Welcome to Stronghold, captain. I'm Jase Hogarth, adjutant to Admiral Saldeen." He didn't introduce the driver, a youngish woman who wore Chief rating's stripes and a sandpaper haircut, but Bran did name his own people. Then they got into the car, moved off toward the nearest buildings, and Hogarth began pointing out the sights of the place.

To the left, "That big grey pillbox, it's the powerhouse. Most of the installation underground, of course, to save on shielding for the fusion cycle. Only fourteen years old, the plant is. Probably obsolete on Earth, though, by now." Bran mumbled something noncommittal; what he knew about power research on Earth he could stick in one ear.

They skirted the rest of the landing area, passing through shadows cast by the tall ships. Stronghold's sun, a fierce actinic dot so distant that Stronghold's year made fifteen of

Earth's, had risen less than halfway from horizon to zenith. To one side Hogarth noted the communications complex; its growth of antennae, in all shapes from spidery to disclike, made his identification redundant. Bran made approving comment anyway—it didn't cost him.

Up ahead, then, minimally sheltered by foothills beyond, stood the Headquarters complex, officer and civilian quarters, troop barracks—the one with the flagrant display of defense weaponry had to be the Committee Police contingent, but Tregare didn't state his deduction out loud. Instead he paid attention while Hogarth indicated the locations of other facilities: the warehouses and related supply functions, the fuel refinery sited well away from the main area, the storage tanks, main reservoir, crop lands off to the far side where Tregare couldn't really see them from here. All very interesting—because riding in this groundcar, not yet twenty minutes on this world, Tregare was getting himself one hell of an idea for future reference!

Peace take me, it can be done!

Admiral Saldeen was the far side of middle age, but his voice and movements showed vigor. Coming around from behind his desk, to shake hands, he grinned. "Glad to have you here, captain. Tregare, is it? Seems a shame, your having to wear that suit, but plague's nothing to fool with. Now—your report, sir?"

Deverel and the other two ratings were cooling heels in an outer room. They, and Tregare also, had been checked for weapons; no one entered the admiral's presence armed, except his personal bodyguard. Naturally Tregare and his group had brought no overt handweapons. Unarmed, though, they were not. Some of their suits' "air" tanks contained other substances, such as cough smoke and puke gas. Not that Tregare expected to need any of that stuff, but having it at hand made him feel a little more confident.

Now, handshake done with and both men seated, Bran answered, "My summary log is already sent into your computer files, sir. And that's about all the report I have. Actually, Admiral Saldeen, I'm here to get *your* report." Before the admiral could interrupt, Bran said, "Overall estimate of probabilities of Shrakken activity, for one thing. Morale situation: improving or deteriorating, here where we—" *We*. That's important to say. "—where we can only wait and watch. And that's another thing." He paused.

Saldeen frowned, then said, "*What* is? Explain, captain."

"As you'll see by our log, my mission has an option. In any case I receive your full report and return it to Earth as soon as possible." He tried to look apologetic. "*I'm* not being pushy, sir, but my orders came from the Presiding Committee itself." The admiral seemed to relax, so Bran continued, "The option is that if *you* think it's a good idea, then on leaving here I first take a loop out toward Shrakken space and scout for alien ships there. Now whether—"

The admiral shook his head. "We've done that. No sign."

Tregare leaned forward. "Of course, sir. But how far?" Saldeen told him. Bran pretended to consider the datum, then said, "It's the Long View, sir. When these orders were sent out, the Committee didn't know you had explored so extensively." He nodded. "Then I guess all we need to do, if, as I expect, you have my fuel and supplies replenished in short order, plus the Drive repairs I've listed, is for you to countersign the original orders and add your recommendation." Seeing the man's brows rise, he added, "Simply have it punched in by comm channel; no need to handle possibly contaminated readouts." He smiled. "And then we can get this damned Grey Plague worry well away from you."

"Yes. Hmm—not much of a rest stop for you, is it, captain?"

"No, it isn't. But already a few of our people are testing negative as carriers. By the time we reach Earth again, we should all be safe for normal folks to associate with."

"Umph. I certainly hope so. Now which level of report are you expected to receive and return? Total, redundant-reduced, edited by selective importance, or summary?"

Run that one past me again! How long since Stronghold had been established here? And on *Inconnu*, how much of Tinhead's memory space could be spared for this stuff, without cramping normal functions? Tregare made a guess: "Make it redundant-reduced for the first and latest decade of Stronghold's existence, summary for everything in between." What UET's Presiding Committee might want to see, Tregare had no idea. But the early days might have some clues for him personally, and the latest data he *had* to have.

A little more talk before leaving. "Sorry, captain, that those suits don't have facilities for me to feed you a drink. It's been a pleasure, though I must admit I'll be glad to see you take that damned Plague away safely." Then, after another mismatched handshake, Tregare collected his people and they got a ride back to the ship.

On the way, between reminding himself of the basics of Stronghold's layout, Tregare found himself thinking. Not everybody in UET was rotten. Admiral Saldeen, for instance. Too bad they were on different sides. Because Tregare *liked* that old rooster.

What made Tregare antsy was his Drive problem, but that work got underway immediately. The only tough part was not being able to use the cargo hatch, so that the exciter had to be broken down into components in order to get through the airlock.

The Nielson Cube made another problem. The thing itself was only about a meter each way, but its cryogenic crate measured twice that. Junior Lee Beauregard solved the difficulty—his crew pulled the old Cube and wrapped it in a blanket of thick, efficient insulation while at the same time at the foot of the ship's ramp a UET gang did the same for the new replacement unit, tapping it into flow from a portable tank of liquid helium to make sure it wouldn't warm enough to go sour between uncrating and installation. "Purely fast, we done gotta move, skipper," he said, and Tregare saw to it that extraneous personnel were kept the hell out of the way during those moves, until the new Cube was safely in place and the old one snugged into UET's crate groundside.

But the job did get done, and less than two hours later Junior Lee announced, "She balance real fine, cap'n. Rarin' to push, any ol' time."

Not all Stronghold's people were as helpful as Admiral Saldeen. For instance, Tregare wasn't exactly fond of Commodore Peldon when she came aboard with the announced intention of snooping into Tinhead for more details. What she looked like, Bran didn't know, because her suit's helmet was one-way opaque. Her voice and manner, though, held all the subtle charm of a backrub with a handful of poison ivy.

First off, the Commodore demanded full access to Tinhead's data banks. "All of them, captain. There'll be no secrets here."

Her advent had routed Tregare out of bed about three hours ahead of schedule, so he didn't feel especially conciliatory. "Course not," he said. "For starters, let's see your authorization."

"But I'm Commodore Peldon!"

"Anybody in that fishbowl mirror could say as much. What's on paper, to show me?" She handed over a flimsy, and ordinarily he'd have accepted it, but now he nitpicked three minor omissions on the authorization form. "Go get it done right; then come back." The Commodore used some surprising language then, but dutifully waddled her bulky-suited way off the ship.

"Are you sure," said Leanne Prestor, "that chasing her offship was really a bright move?"

Taking her arm, Tregare started them moving back toward the galley. "This time of morning I'm not sure which year it is. Come on." And when he'd had coffee and breakfast and more coffee, he said, "That's the hatchet lady, I chased off here. I don't know how or why, but she's trouble." He got on the intercom to Control, checking on progress of fueling and resupply. Four hours to completion, the answer came. "But I could cut upstairs earlier if we have to, right?" At Gonnelson's confirmation, Bran nodded, and turned back to Prestor. "See? We stall her, is all."

He couldn't stall the admiral, though. When Saldeen called to get Tregare's acknowledgment of receipt for Stronghold's report, Bran had to check with Frei Relliger to make sure the data was all logged into Tinhead. At the same time, with no audio going offship to the admiral, Tregare checked on fuel and supplies. The latter were complete, but a balky pump had fueling behind sked. "Another hour to top us off? Okay, thanks."

Then he got back to Admiral Saldeen, and the man's next request shocked him. "A passenger? But, sir—?" Because one goal of the Grey Plague story was to make sure no personnel could be transferred off or onto the ship. UET's custom, Bran knew, was to shuffle crews around a lot; in this case he couldn't let such a thing happen. His people didn't want to be tossed back into UET and he didn't want any Uties aboard, either.

He thought he'd beaten their system, but now Saldeen said, "That's right, captain. One passenger, to be delivered to Earth."

"Dead, that would have to be," Tregare said. "Nobody can

live in a suit that long, even if you fit it with input and output plumbing. Just the effects of isolation on sanity—"

"Captain, you are talking when you should be listening." So Tregare shut up; he was still in hostile country, and outnumbered. The admiral said, "Your cargo manifest shows that you have vacant area in your Hold, Portside Lower, which contains only sealed items that can't be opened without proper tools. That hold also is equipped with access to water and with one-way vented sanitary facilities, for the convenience of the loading crews. Do you follow me, so far?" Tregare nodded; the admiral grinned. "The passenger in question is a prisoner, a traitor. Drug interrogation proved that much, but Earth HQ has the new truth-field equipment; it is imperative that our people get *all* the information about this possibly dangerous conspiracy. Do you see?"

"Of course, sir. But the Plague—"

Saldeen frowned. "The prisoner boards your ship—suited, of course—along with those carrying the necessary supplies of food and so forth, all sealed. Once this person, baggage and all, is in the hold, you seal *that*, and spray it thoroughly with both your germicidal agents and our own. Leaving a plague-free environment in which the suit is no longer necessary."

Thinking fast, Tregare said, "And at the far end?"

"You've already told me, captain, that by the time you reach Earth, you and your people will no longer be carriers."

Tregare had run out of valid-sounding objections, so he said, "Then send the prisoner aboard, sir. We'll be ready."

And besides—*a prisoner, huh?* Or, just maybe, a sleeper.

Up in Control later, he knew when the prisoner was brought aboard and stuck into Hold, Portside Lower, after which the UET escort left the *Alexander*. He couldn't pay too much attention, though, because signals were coming in from offworld—signals that UET was also receiving. And the news wasn't good.

It was UET's biennial fleet from Earth approaching. Bran hadn't expected it to get here for another year, maybe two. Now he checked some figures (t/t_0, 1/x, Arc, Cos, Sine), shook his head and cursed a little. Gonnelson said, "Problem?"

"Yeah," said Bran Tregare. "I keep forgetting how just a little change in vee, up crowding light, affects time-dilation. Like the difference between twenty-to-one, and maybe twenty-two instead. In the fourth decimal place, is where it matters, and our instruments aren't that good. So what we have coming in is a bunch of ships we can't afford to hang around and meet."

Gonnelson's "Why?" was gesture, not word, and Tregare answered. "Because this is the fleet that includes the *Alexander*. The real one."

So to top it all off, here came Commodore Peldon, or somebody wearing a mirror helmet and using that name. The voice was the same, though. Tregare took the papers from her but didn't bother reading them; he used the time, pretending to look at the flimsies, to think fast. He sat the commodore down before a console and said, "I'll get somebody up here, so as not to disrupt my watch crew, on account of they're busy, to punch data for you. Here—let me plug you in an audio feed," and he did, because that feed preempted what she could hear from outside her suit and he didn't want her hearing what he needed to say to Junior Lee Beauregard.

"Ready as ever will be, cap'n," replied Junior Lee. So Tregare sat back while a comm tech arrived and began retrieving, for Commodore Peldon, computer data that in UET's hands would hang Tregare. Not that Stronghold likely used hanging as a method of execution, but the principle held.

"Junior Lee," said Tregare now, "get the final input valve closed."

"Right now?"

"Five minutes ago. We're topped off, near as makes no difference."

"You fixin' to lift? Best I advise groundside—"

"Advise, hell! We tear the feedpipe loose, it gives them something to do besides trying to intercept us. Especially when our Drive-node ionization ignites the fuel spill."

Junior Lee's cackling laugh wasn't his most lovable feature. "Sure 'nuff, cap'n. That there valve, she is now—close off!"

The offship intercom made its piping call; onscreen appeared the admiral. "Captain, I have a communication from the incoming fleet. It contains certain confusing items of information. Until the contradictions are resolved, I must ask you to consider yourself under arrest. You will not—repeat, will *not*—attempt to lift off and escape, or the fleet will blast you out of space. I—"

The hell with it. Push come to shove, Tregare answered,

"No, it won't. You'll order that fleet to swing well clear of my lift-off path, leaving me a safe corridor. Or else—" Or else *what*? He looked around and saw Commodore Peldon nodding as the comm tech began to feed her Tinhead's information. Okay—"—or else I will remove Commodore Peldon's helmet and expose her to the Grey Plague. And then I will set her down safely on Stronghold. But my airlock's tied up right now, so I guess I'll have to let her out the cargo hatch. So there goes your Plague security. Sir."

Silence, and then, "Tregare, you're a devil!"

"Yes, sir. I missed my calling."

"Eh? How's that?"

"I should have been on UET's Presiding Committee."

Escape wasn't all that easy, because nothing ever is; plan all you want, but something will screw up. On Tregare's topside screens he saw the hi-mag image of the incoming fleet sheering off from its direct approach; a few more minutes and those ships couldn't intercept him, if he timed it right. He had his fuel, his supplies, his Drive working. So why didn't he lift? Yet he didn't. And finally he realized what the problem was. It was Commodore Peldon, still busy accreting data. What to do with *her*?

The simple answer was take her upstairs and space her, so she couldn't deliver *Inconnu*'s history to UET. But although he thoroughly disliked the woman he'd never seen, Tregare wasn't quite prepared to kill her. So he gave Gonnelson certain instructions, and the two of them grabbed her. In the suit she wasn't easy to handle, but it didn't take long to strip away all the electronic hardware and leave her with nothing of Tinhead's data except what she might have heard and remembered. Then Tregare reached for the clamps that secured her helmet.

"What are you *doing*?" It was Prestor—and what *she* was doing here, peace only knew. "Bran—you can't!"

"Oh, for—!" Savagely, he shook his head. "I'm sending this Utie bitch off without a helmet. We need the diversion."

"They'll flame her dead! Anybody would, in this situation."

"And who cares? One Utie more or less, what's the difference?" But once she'd spelled it out like that, he couldn't do it.

So, helmet intact but suit's speakers smashed, the woman got marched downship to the main airlock. Leanne Prestor helped Tregare with that chore. At the top of the ramp, airlock opened to the ship's interior but sealed toward groundside with the spray routine ready to go, Tregare said to Commodore Peldon: "When you're cycled through, run down fast and get you some distance. When I lift, there won't be time to find cover." She didn't answer, so he said, "Do you understand?"

"Yes. I think so." Even leaning close to her helmet, he heard the voice only faintly.

"Then do it quick." Running upship to his own job, Tregare found Gonnelson ready to raise off. All right; the First Hat could do it—but Tregare sat in to make some changes once *Inconnu* got upstairs.

Then, as Bran watched screens and meters, the ship lifted. Some UET vessels tried to cut over for intercept, but the vectors gave them no chance. *Inconnu* got away from Stronghold, free and clean.

Entering his quarters, Tregare found Leanne sitting on the side of their bed and looking glum. "What's the matter?" He felt good, so when she didn't answer right away, he told her *why* he felt good. "This Drive—the new Cube, and Junior Lee's tuning every bit as good as Mallory's—we've got close to ten percent more oof than we ever had." He couldn't stop grinning. "Just the same, though, when we go behind the big gas-giant I'm going to swing course hard and then cut Drive."

"I don't understand." No wonder; she didn't look as though she were really listening.

So he explained. "They'll chase us anyway. And one of those ships might be a hotdog just like us. But they'll come scooting out, tailing our course the last they saw it; they'll do their scoot right on past us and diverging fast. With our Drive and beacon off they haven't a prayer of detecting us. And once we see they're gone by, building vee in the wrong direction, *then* we pour it on for Earth." At her frown, he said, "Oh sure, we'll still go there. Only thing is, I'll be fudging the orders some."

"I'm sure you will. Can I have a drink?"

"Coming up." And with one for himself, too, he sat and looked at her, wondering. And finally said, "You never did say what's wrong, Leanne. Something is, right?"

"That woman. What you did to her."

"The commodore? I didn't hurt her any. All we did—"

"You were going to kill her. If I hadn't—"

"I wasn't going to hurt a damned hair of her. I—"

"You'd have *sent* her to her death, and you know it!"

He knew she was right and he didn't like it, so he said, "Aw, she's high brass. And what she remembers from Tinhead's readouts is the only dope Stronghold has on us." He snorted. "She has any sense, she'd've used that info for leverage."

"As you would do, of course."

"Hell, yes." What the— "Leanne, what's going on here?"

She gulped the last of her drink. "It's—Tregare, you do things I can't live with. So I won't. Not any more."

She stood, and he with her. "You need any help, moving out? You have a room picked out yet?" Or a roommate? But that would be none of his business.

"I'll manage. You go upship and make sure of your sneaky course change. You wouldn't want to miss winning a trick."

He came close, then, to striking her. But he didn't. He said, "Maybe you think this is some kind of game, with UET. No such thing, and never has been." She started to turn away; he grabbed her arm. "No. You listen. You realize what I *did*, here? I took us into Stronghold with a bum Drive and brought us out with a good one. And with fuel, and supplies, and the Admiral's stamp on a set of orders I can use to get us in and out of *Earth*, if I work it right. I—"

"You, yes. You, you, *you*!"

He saw what she meant, there, and said, "Look, I give credit all around. You and everybody else did great, executing the plans." One deep breath he took. "But peace take you, they were *my* plans! And they will be at Earth, too, most likely." He made a snort. "Oh hell, it takes all of us to do it right; I know that. It's just—this is my ship and I have to be responsible for it. No matter what anybody says, it's my load."

She started to say something more, but he'd had plenty: "I'll get out and let you do your moving. Log your new quarters assignment in Control so the watch officer can reach you if necessary. And—no, I guess that's all."

As he turned away, she said, "Am I still Second Hat?"

"Long as you do your job. So far, you have; keep at it."

She tried to smile but it didn't quite work. "You're angry."

How else? The very banality broke his tensions; Tregare laughed. "Don't worry about it. I'll save it for UET." He left her then and went upship.

* * *

The plan worked. When *Inconnu* emerged from the gas-giant's shadow it ran dark. Hours later the UET pursuers, building vee rapidly, flashed past along Tregare's former course and soon were out of contact range. Then Bran swung ship and set course for Earth.

About that course, people had some questions. At the next Hats' counsel, Tregare tried to figure out his answers. "For starters, right here we have a perfectly good ship's ID all countersigned by Admiral Saldeen, along with his orders to *go* to Earth. Now what we do about all that, how we fudge it, is something else. But—"

"Why?" Gonnelson.

"Why Earth?" The First Hat nodded.

And that was the hard question. Tregare thought about it and then said, "I don't know, really. It's a hunch, is all. That getting a chance to get in and out of Earth at all is a peace-taking miracle, and I don't want to waste it."

Prostor spoke. "But what good will it do you, to go there?"

Shrugging, Tregare grinned. "Maybe I just need to find out what the place—the situation, I mean—smells like, these days."

Frei Relliger scowled. "To what purpose?"

Junior Lee Beauregard laughed. "Don't never ask a houn' dog that."

And Tregare decided that maybe Junior Lee had the answer.

6. Earth

Living alone made Tregare edgy. The split-up with Leanne frustrated the hell out of him. Getting cleanly away from Stronghold, bilking UET out of a new Drive and the rest of it, called for a celebration. What he really needed to do was get flatass drunk, but under the circumstances he couldn't afford to. He settled, the third day out of Stronghold, for hosting a moderately boisterous party, attended (off-and-on, so as not to disrupt the watches in Drive and Control) by all officers and senior ratings. Tregare took about half the booze he really wanted, reached a medium state of cheer, and was so nice to everybody that he could hardly believe it. To Leanne, even, but in her case he didn't exactly go overboard with cordiality.

So it was a relief to get away from her and talk with his Chief-rated Medic, Eda Ghormley. The thin, grey-haired woman was sipping on a surprisingly stiff-looking drink as he asked her, "You been keeping tabs on our prisoner?"

She nodded. "By the monitors, yes. I do look in occasionally. What do you plan to do about that one? And when?"

Bran checked his chronometer. "When? Let's say eighteen hundred, ship's tomorrow. Gives me time for some sleep and breakfast after this party winds down in a little while. Now as to *what*—"

He told her, and she said, "Why so complicated? And how do you keep it all straight in your head?"

"Fancy, because all we have is UET's word that this is any kind of rebel. When we're done, we'll know for sure. And how I keep it straight is, I plan my whole story on the basis that the Grey Plague is real."

Ghormley said, "Yes. You'd have to do it that way."

Tregare woke healthy, called for breakfast to be delivered from the galley, showered and ate and so forth, and dressed for the day. Then he called Eda Ghormley and had her listen while he spoke to the prisoner in Hold, Portside Lower. After three days, he figured that person could use some company. He said, "Get your suit on; you're being visited. We'll come in suited and then spray for safety so you can unsuit for discussion. You understand how it works?"

The answering voice was husky, almost a whisper. With no picture, Bran couldn't visualize the person speaking. "Discussion? You mean interrogation, don't you?"

"A few questions, sure. You'll be ready? Twenty minutes?"

"Yes, of course. Oh, yes."

Tregare cut that circuit and said to Ghormley, "You need any help with the gloves?"

"No, sir. And the drug kit's already packed."

"See you down there, then."

At the door to Hold, Portside Lower, Tregare and Ghormley met. Both were in space suits, but instead of gauntlets the medic wore surgical gloves, taped at the wrists to the suit's sleeves. Approving, Tregare nodded. "Let's go in."

Cradling the canister of foul-smelling antiseptic spray in one arm, he opened the door; they entered and he closed it again, to face another suited figure, and Tregare said, "All right, now we'll spray this place so you're safe, and then—"

But before he could finish, or do anything, the prisoner unlatched the suit's helmet and threw it to the deck. From a youngish haggard face the husky voice almost screamed. "You won't take *me* to Earth! You can torture me some more, but your damned Plague will make it stop, sooner or later. You don't have me forever. Not now, you don't!"

Eda Ghormley started to say something, but Tregare shushed her: dammit, this could *still* be a UET plant, if someone had gambled that the Plague was phony. So he grabbed the prisoner, and then Ghormley helped him wrestle the top half of the space suit off and get the person tied down, and somewhere along in there Bran realized that the stubble-headed, burn-marked prisoner was female. No matter; he gestured, and the medic gave the shot of the so-called "truth drug."

Then Tregare began asking questions.

She was a plant, all right, a "ringer"—but not from UET. She'd been planted *on* UET by Earth's Underground organization as a sleeper, and had performed well until betrayed and caught. Renni Lofall, age thirty-two—well, that was her official cover name and the age was probably close—thought the betrayal was a matter of ignorance rather than malevolence. Tregare had no way of knowing and no reason to give a damn; the woman had caught hell, but Stronghold was back *there*, and not apt to catch up.

The burns on scalp and cheek and breast and torso—first he'd thought they were from simple hot iron, but not so. UET used electric torture and some sadist had run the voltage up. Either way, Bran could understand why Renni Lofall had decided to take her chances with the nonexistent Grey Plague.

Lofall, now, was coming awake from the drug. She blinked and said, "Whatever you got from me, I hope it does your superiors no good at all. And *I* won't live to see them."

"Too right, you won't," said Bran Tregare. "Because I don't have any superiors." It took a while, before he got through to her that *Inconnu* was Escaped and Renni Lofall was, too. And that the Grey Plague did not exist. Then he and Ghormley took the woman upship to *Inconnu*'s small infirmary, and put her to bed.

"Earth, now," said Tregare, to the group assembled in his quarters. "To skim there, the story has to be perfect." Yes, he'd told Leanne he intended to fudge Admiral Saldeen's orders, and of course that's what he'd have to do—but all his thinking, to date, gave him no clear or complete idea *how* to do the fudging. So it was time to get his best people thinking loose, and kick some ideas around.

"The Grey Plague was fine for Stronghold," he said now, "because their medical facilities were limited. Earth's aren't. They'd be all over us, quarantining us aboard or even ordering us to evac for groundside isolation. We'll have enough problems without that kind of hassle."

Frei Relliger spoke. "Skipper, I don't see how we can chance it. Once we're groundside—"

"Don't land," said Gonnelson. Looking at his First Hat, Tregare nodded. Sure! He outlined the idea, fast: refuel and resupply from the pods in sync orbit, same as the near-Earth patrol ships would. To save on time and fuel, both. But to justify the option, and bar any exchange of personnel on or off the ship, what kind of mission orders could he fake?

"We're still the *Alexander*," he said, thinking it out. "And coming back immediately from Stronghold."

"Exceptin'," Junior Lee put in, "we got us a whole new crew. How you gone fix *that*?"

"Yeah," Tregare said. *How?* Yeah . . . "All right. Saldeen's recent files show several ships coming to Stronghold from colony worlds, not straight from Earth. The summary log we have to provide shows only a person's *latest* previous ship. Prestor, Relliger—check Saldeen's ship listings against our true log and try to frame capsule entries that could fit." Another thought. "Our people who joined us from groundside, just log them in off UET worlds, to whatever ship we say we got them from."

He grinned. "And I'll check you later, to be sure we don't need faster-than-light travel to explain any entry."

The "mission" parameters were still to be defined, but the session had run past some mealtimes and Bran was overdue to check the watch log, so he adjourned the meeting with thanks.

* * *

When Ghormley reported that Renni Lofall was out of shock and appeared reasonably healthy, Tregare invited Lofall up to his quarters for a private dinner. Even if this Underground agent's Earthside data was a decade or two obsolete, she'd still have information he needed. And her desperation, when she thought she was choosing a slow, painful form of suicide, had touched him more than he liked.

So now he welcomed her into captain's digs and fixed her a drink. Wearing a plain jumpsuit that almost fit her but not quite, she walked stiffly and sat with caution. Well, he'd seen what UET had done to her above the waist—he hadn't asked Ghormley about the rest. Not thinking, he said, "Comfortable?"

She half smiled. "No, but improving." His face must have shown embarrassment, for she said, "None of *your* fault, captain." Now she did smile. "It's still hard to believe I'm safe now."

He had to say it. "You're not, really. None of us are, until we figure a way to get in to and out of Earth." He leaned forward. "Maybe that's where you can help."

So while they sipped drinks and snacked on appetizers, he told her his very tentative plans, and asked for suggestions. "Let me think a little," she said, so when their dinner arrived and as they dined, he didn't push it. They made only light conversation, and not much of that.

Over coffee and liqueurs, though, she began to talk. The Shrakken, the possible alien menace—that was what Stronghold was there for. So perhaps . . . and by the third round of coffee, Tregare had the bare bones of his plan. "Warn Earth, yeah. And then the priority mission to alert wherever we decide the Shrakken are heading. The Twin Worlds, maybe, and Terranova."

"You have to high-code this warning," Lofall said, "and choose a code that fits the right year. They change them, you know."

"Sure. The Long View. Well, the Q-code still fits; all I need to figure is the progressive permutations." He laughed. "And to throw in a few glitches."

"I don't understand."

"Errors in the code paragraphs every so often. So the rest is gibberish until they computer-analyze. Slow 'em down a whole bundle. Time they figure it, with any luck we're gone."

"Then you think you have the problem solved, at Earth?"

"No. But we have us one good head start on it."

* * *

Lofall had other interesting facts to offer. Such as how to communicate with the Underground on Earth, how to do it from high orbit, how to decode the apparently random signals Tregare could elicit from groundside. Sitting by his keyboard terminal, Bran punched all these items into Tinhead. Finished, he said, "You must have a pretty good rank in the Underground. Or even in UET, for that matter. Communications is your specialty, right?" She nodded. "Mine too, until I got into the captain business."

"From our talk here, I'd gathered as much." Her brows lowered. "Rank, though. The Underground's so different, a comparison wouldn't mean anything. And on Stronghold, between spacers and groundsiders—well, I guess I outrank your Chief ratings but your officers outrank *me*." She looked at him. "Does it matter?"

"Not except for quarters assignment, now you're fit to move out of infirmary. Officers' digs are full up right now, and so are Chiefs' rooms. There's a couple of Firsts' cubbies open, so you could either take one of those or bump the least senior Chief. It's up to you."

She shook her head. "I'm not bumping anyone. I'm riding as supernumerary with no assigned duties. As yet. Certainly I don't want to throw my weight around. The cubby will be fine."

"All right. I'll walk you there. Stopping by the infirmary first, if that's where you have your gear stashed."

She stood. "Do I *have* to keep the space suit?" Noting how she said it with a straight face, Tregare decided he liked this Underground agent.

Over the next few days Tregare stayed busy. First he "adjusted" his orders from Admiral Saldeen, to allow for the phony Shrakken warning and the orbital refueling. Then he ran the permutation-updates an Q-code to the actual time he'd been at Stronghold, and coded the warning itself, not omitting the parts addressed to UET on the Twin Worlds and Terranova. He considered the computer image of the admiral's signature: his copy had to look nearly like the original but of course no two signatures are identical. Finally he ran the data-bits through a digital-to-analog converter and then put that signal through a distortion net until he came out with something just slightly different from his model. Then back to digital mode and into Tinhead. *If that doesn't fool the bastards . . .*

His plans were coming into focus now, but still a lot more risky than he liked. He'd put a lot of urgency and all the admiral's authority into that faked warning, and Stronghold itself gave evidence that the Shrakken scared UET spitless—but still, hanging around Earth very long invited meddling by UET groundside. He kept working on ideas. . . .

He needed a fake name and ID for himself, he'd decided, and certainly he couldn't simply invent one and hope to get away with it. So he asked Renni Lofall. "Is there anybody at Stronghold, looks somewhat like me, who'd be the right rank to command this ship by now?"

Thinking about it, she squinted at him, poised her hands to mask off first one part of his head and then another, and finally nodded. "Deet Armiger. Deet for Dietrich. He's been on Stronghold about six years, so he's perhaps sixteen out from Earth, groundside time. His record's good, and he's worked up to First Officer. A captaincy now would be plausible."

"And the resemblance? How close?"

"Around the eyes and nose, rather good. Not the same jawline at all. But if you had Deet's red hair and red beard, you'd pass."

Tregare thought, then laughed. "I have time to grow the whiskers. And if somebody on this bucket doesn't have some red dye that matches close enough, I miss my guess."

He located the dye, all right, and the bleach that would be needed first. He tried the stuff out on his sideburns, and Lofall okayed the results. Since the supply was limited, Tregare held off doing the full treatment until *Inconnu* would be nearing Earth. Lofall explained that to avoid an artificial, too-uniform appearance he should vary the bleach: "The beard's darker," she said, and, "I can't cut hair myself, but I can tell somebody else how Deet should look. For one thing, he has less forehead." She drew a rough sketch, and Bran saw what she meant. No problem.

Meanwhile, once she'd helped him pick the name, everyone aboard was instructed to use it at all times. "It's a nuisance, but we don't want any slips." By the time they reached Earth, he figured, the usage should be habit. Maybe even Junior Lee could get over snickering when he said it.

* * *

Renni Lofall's own hair was long enough, now, to hide the burned spots; except for one, burned too deeply, they showed only as shorter patches. On her cheek the scar was visible but fading. About any other marks, Tregare didn't ask.

She had, after calling first for permission, come to his quarters. She sat but declined a drink, and said, "There's an officer's cabin vacant, and—"

"You want it?"

"I wanted to ask whether anyone would be moving into it. And if so, whether it would be the senior Chief, or possibly me."

"You want it, it's yours. Need any help?" He knew she didn't, with the few things she'd brought aboard and hardly more she'd drawn from Ship's Stores, but it was polite to ask.

She shook her head, thanked him, and left, now moving smoothly and without stiffness. Bran looked at the closed door, thinking that Leanne could have told him herself. Because a vacant cabin meant somebody had moved in with somebody. It would hardly be Gonnelson, so Prestor had moved to join Frei Kelliger. Or more likely the other way around, her digs being the roomier.

Well, the hell with getting his feelings hurt. Maybe for morale and maybe for old times' sake, next chance he had, Tregare threw a small party for the new couple. Everybody seemed to enjoy it.

The plans for the Earth maneuver were as good as Tregare could figure them, but still he worried. Something was missing, and he couldn't guess what it might be. He knew what *kind* of thing he wanted and didn't have: some kind of edge, was what. But how to get it?

He was up in Control when *Inconnu*—or rather, the *Alexander*—met the UET patrol ship, some days short of Earth. Tregare had put his ship on decel early, taking longer at it than usual and staying well below redline; he needed all the options he could get, and coming in slow was one way to expand his choices.

The patrol ship obviously wasn't on station, and said so. "We've been back to the new refueling depot," its captain said. "Well, ten years is new enough, if you take the Long View. Anyway, the *Il Duce*, heading for Stronghold, had orders to take post at our station while we went for a refill. Did you meet the *Duce* on your way in, Captain Armiger?"

Tregare hadn't; he must have passed just outside detection ranges. For this meeting he hadn't bothered with the red dye; his new beard cloaked his jaw well enough, and any patrol ship skipper would have been well short of puberty when the real Deet Armiger left Earth. So Bran passed polite chat with this other captain, briefly since they weren't within talk range very long, and they parted with mutual well-wishings.

The one thing Tregare gained from the exchange was a handle on UET's refueling outpost. He had its coordinates, the characteristic signals of its beacon, and a couple of good ideas.

Maybe this was the edge he needed. Because damned few people understood how relativity's Long View really worked. And Bran did.

The orbiting depot wasn't hard to find; this far out, its natural Solar orbit took very little adjustment to keep the installation essentially at a sidereally constant position—that was to say, more or less on the line from Earth's sun to Stronghold's.

The thing had a haywire look to it, but why not? Out here it had no stresses to withstand. Approaching, on hi-mag Tregare saw an ungainly framework, a skeletal construction to which the major components were secured. He counted three large fuel pods, one full and two not quite. The one rigid-looking construct had to be the supplies warehouse, and probably quarters for station personnel. Off to one side floated an ice asteroid at the end of taut guying cables; it sprouted several plastic funnels ending in feedpipes. Inside those funnels would be the heating elements to melt the ice, and the pumps to supply ships with the resultant liquid. No ships were here now; the station's complement was two scoutships, moored to the base structure. Bran hadn't heard of this project before, but it looked like a workable design.

And for his purposes, it was perfect.

Still not bothering to recolor hair or beard, he hailed the station as Captain Dietrich Armiger of the *Alexander*, out from Stronghold and heading for Earth. "But we had a little chase back there, off our course and slowing enough to cut our t/t_0 some. Which is why we're here a little early."

The man at the other end of the circuit, not pictured too clearly yet at this distance, shook his head. "I've never understood that stuff too well, but I'll take your word for it."

Damn right! "And how can we help you, captain? And what was the chase about?"

"Sorry—that last question—it's what you might call Top Clam. But I can say this much: you know why you're out here, and our diversion was highly related. Now what we need—well, we have less fuel, because of the side-trip, than we should have at this point. Maybe it's safe to go on in as is, maybe not; the computer gives us marginal figures. So we'd like to top up some."

"Certainly, captain. And welcome to the *Arachne*." The man smiled. "The name's unofficial; comes from our structural makeup."

Well, the thing did look a little bit like part of a spider's web, with the solid components doubling for trapped insects, and folks in this kind of isolation needed all the in-jokes they could invent. Briefly, Tregare regretted having to hoodwink these people. But only briefly. What the hell—they were UET, weren't they?

If there was any hassle it would be [illegible] fuel, and he really had enough already. So he left that for last, maneuvering *Inconnu* to couple with a loading dock on the warehouse. He picked the side nearest the "iceteroid," so as to take on water at the same time. Agee Benbow, his contact on *Arachne*, seemed a little surprised. "Nobody's tried to double up those loadings before," he said. "It makes sense, though, if you're in a hurry."

"Which we are, and thanks for the cooperation." Tregare was watching the water feed. These orbiting ice cubes, he knew, were never plain ice; there had to be other components such as solid methane and ammonia. Finally he figured out how it worked. At the funnel's apex, just before it met the cylindrical feedpipe, valves gave streams of vapor to space. Well, the temperature differential wasn't touchy; he couldn't recall the boiling point of ammonia, but methane's was something like minus one-eight-four, Celsius. Neither compound was likely to get mixed up with liquid water, given enough heat to drive them out of solution at low pressure. So the water would be fit to drink; good. Tregare's chemistry wasn't all that accurate, but he thought he had it right.

If he didn't, that's what the filter system was for.

* * *

When water and other supplies—mostly food—were taken care of, Bran watched the disconnections and then shifted his ship over to the nearest fuel pod. When that feeding was begun, he accepted Benbow's invitation for a brief social visit to the depot's personnel areas. Along with him went Relliger, Prestor, and Deverel. Gonnelson was left to hold down Control. The visiting party was not unarmed, but you wouldn't know that fact by looking. It wasn't that Tregare expected any real trouble; he liked to take precautions, was all.

The depot's "scooters" were small chemical-reaction rocket craft, used to get the working crews from one part of *Arachne* to another. Max thrust might have lifted one off Earth's moon for a quick hop, but not much more than that. Here in no-grav space, range was limited by air supply; Tregare's casual questions determined that a work shift in a scooter shouldn't run into overtime too much. The thing seated up to ten, but not in comfort. Moving awkwardly in their controlled-magnet shoes, Tregare and his group met the two from *Arachne* at *Inconnu*'s small topside airlock, because coupling the scooter there was easier than at the larger main lock.

Waiting in the scooter were Agee Benbow and a woman who was somewhat older than her voice and movements indicated. "My Exec," said Benbow. "Lacey M'Guinness. Mac, for short." So Tregare, with handshakes all around, introduced his own people. Then everybody sat down and strapped in, and Mac did the uncoupling routines, pointed the scooter toward the warehouse, and applied thrust. Tregare felt the gentle push build.

By design he was sitting where he could watch every move she made at the controls. Probably he'd never have to fly one of these things, but just in case . . . well, it looked simple enough, as she took the spacesled a little wide and then slowed toward a docking point, touching with hardly any jar.

Then they all went inside. Into bare, unfinished-looking corridors for a time, but finally into a more cheerful room where another man and woman rose to greet them. Tregare heard the names but promptly forgot them.

So everybody sat down and had a few drinks, plus some snacks that accumulated to become a moderately-sized meal, and Tregare asked (with genuine interest) about the history of *Arachne*, which Benbow and Mac were quite willing to tell.

The depot group wanted to hear, in turn, about the *Alexander*'s travels. With a warning glance to his own people, Bran set off with a ship's history that made a few concessions to truth, but not many. Any time he caught himself talking his way into a hole, he had the easy out of invoking Security. And of course, in UET, that word slammed the door on any further inquiry. So, sneaking an occasional look at his wrist-chrono, Tregare strung out his story as long as he could stretch it.

Finally, though, Agee Benbow also checked the time and said, "Oh, I'm sorry, captain! It's been so pleasant, talking, that I hadn't noticed. But your partial refueling must have been completed hours ago, and I'm sure your crew is wondering what's happened to you. That is—you did say you were in a hurry?"

Nobody looked suspicious yet. Tregare said, "The hurry isn't just here, Benbow, it's on our overall assignment. So I thought, long as we're stopped here and hooked up, why not fill the tanks all the way? And save time at our Earth stopover, you see." He paused, and tried to remember how to look embarrassed. "Uh—I'd appreciate it if you all forget you heard that last part. I mean, I wasn't supposed—"

He paused, and Mac M'Guinness said, "Of course, captain. We didn't hear a thing. Did we?" She stared around the room, and the *Arachne* contingent shook their heads. "All right?"

For moments, watching Benbow's face take on a stubborn look, Tregare tried to rehearse the threats and arguments he'd have to improvise if things went wrong here. But that look passed, and Benbow said, "Yes. I should know better than to quibble about Security matters. But now then—" And whatever else, Tregare saw that the other man's previous cordiality had been rubbed dry. "—now, Captain Armiger, I don't wish to be inhospitable, but you know when your refueling will be done, and I don't. And I have duties to perform, which I've been happy to postpone in favor of this visit, but—"

"But now you'd like to know," said Tregare, "just how long we'd be hanging you up, here." *Say it right, now.* "My fault, I guess. Thinking back, I didn't make our fuel needs as clear as I thought I was doing." He knew the time, but for show he looked at his chrono anyway. "Okay." He raised his drink and without haste downed the last of it. "If we leave now, when we get to the *Alexander* it'll be time to start buttoning up and make ready to head in-system." He reached out a hand and Benbow accepted it. "And we do appreciate your welcome."

* * *

M'Guinness drove the scooter. This time Bran didn't watch the controls; he watched the woman. She wasn't young, but her lined face had vitality and her moves showed superb reflexes. When she docked at the topside airlock, Tregare waited while the rest of his party went into the ship. Then he stood, saying, "You're good with this scooter."

As they shook hands, she answered, "And you're a phony. I don't know what you're up to, but I don't believe a word."

"Then why—?"

The woman smiled. "Armiger—it takes one to know one." Then he went inside his ship and watched while she undocked and took the scooter back to *Arachne*.

Upship in Control, Tregare watched while *Inconnu* disengaged from the fuel pod and turned to initiate the curving course that would meet with Earth-orbit. The comm-tech expanded Gonnelson's usual monosyllables into precise instructions, and *Inconnu* began to move. Monitoring, Bran saw that the figures were right.

He nodded to Gonnelson. "Good job." Then he headed down to quarters. As he opened his door he turned to see Leanne Prestor coming toward him. "Hi. Something you wanted?"

"Yes. Do you have a minute?"

"Yeah, sure. What's on your mind?"

"What you did, there at the depot. I liked it."

"I didn't do anything. Faked 'em out, was all."

"That's what I *mean*. Our situation—I expected some kind of shoot-out, or violent bluff, at the least." Face flushed, she clenched a fist. "Things you'd done before—I expected—but this time you handled it without hurting anyone. If only you could have—"

So he knew what she meant. She liked things to work "nice." Well, so did he, but sometimes they wouldn't. Leanne didn't realize the difference; for peace' sake she thought it was *his* choice. And was she trying to come *back* to him, now? *Not that . . .*

He said first, "I always do what I have to." And then, "You and Frei, you getting along all right?" Then he waited.

Until she said, "What? Oh, yes. Just fine." Finally she left.

* * *

After Gonnelson's course had had time to put a few numbers into Tinhead, and Tregare had grabbed a few hours' sleep, he went up to Control and checked the situation. As he'd expected, the First Hat had set things up right. The trick was to start from *Arachne*'s "orbit," feed in the various gravitational influences—Sol's and Earth's being preeminent—and coast in on a compromise between least-time and least-fuel.

Near as Bran could tell, Gonnelson had it about perfect. So there wasn't much for a captain to do, up here just now. He hadn't had breakfast; now was a good time for it.

Entering the galley he met Renni Lofall coming out. "Captain—I'd like to talk with you."

"Sure. In here, though. I'm hungry." So while he ate she toyed with coffee she obviously didn't want, until he said, over his own second cup, "Okay, let's talk. What's the subject?"

"I want some work to do, on this ship."

Surprised, he said, "You're a comm-tech, aren't you? So—"

"You already have surplus in that specialty. Oh, I've filled in a few watches, learned things I didn't know about shipboard comm. But in that capacity I'm a fifth wheel."

He looked at her, seeing that a lot of strain had left her face. "What capacity you got in mind, then?"

"I'm an administrator, too. I can monitor the *systems* that keep an organization going, and make sure they're working correctly."

"Such as what?" Seeing her take his question as negation, he added, "Specifically, is all I mean."

Running fingers through her short, still uneven hair, she said, "What's your latest ship inventory? And how accurate?"

He thought about it. "I guess—well, I leave that up to Tinhead. We log supplies in when we load, and people are supposed to keep track of what's used. Like Groden, down in Stores. And—"

"And you know as well as I do that people sometimes forget. There's bound to be slippage. So, to be sure you don't someday find you're all out of some necessity you thought you had plenty of, it's imperative that regular inventories be conducted."

She was right, of course. So he told her she was, and thanked her, saying then, "Okay, you're in charge of inventory, just now. Ask Groden to line you up a work crew to help check. Take it easy on him, though; he tends to have a sore back, and I don't mean his muscles."

Lofall smiled. "Mr. Groden and I get along quite well in

these matters." At his raised eyebrows, she added, "Job-related, I mean. I'm making this proposal on his behalf as well as mine."

Tregare laughed. "All right, Lofall. You have yourself a job."

Passing through the Solar System's outer reaches, *Inconnu* passed two more patrol ships and—as the *Alexander*—exchanged greetings with them. Tregare tried to wangle some Earthside news but got nothing useful from either contact. Passing wide of Jupiter, though, *Inconnu* cleared that planet's interference-shadow and began picking up all sorts of miscellaneous signals from Earth and the inner System. So with Renni Lofall deciphering some of the fancier codes that were new since Tinhead's Earthside programming, Tregare got an earful of UET's local planning.

And some not so local. For instance, another fleet of ships was preparing to leave for Stronghold. Bran tried to count by Long View terms—how many would this be, at two years between fleets, since the one he'd dodged at the fortress world? He couldn't decide—five, probably—but one thing came to mind: UET was using a lot of its substance to guard against the Shrakken. Even though a lot of ships that went to Stronghold didn't necessarily stay there. *I can still take the place*.

But to plan for that move, he needed more info. He'd questioned Renni Lofall a little bit on that score, but not in detail. So when Renni brought the completed inventory summary to his quarters, he decided to get down to cases more.

First, though, the report. *Inconnu*'s supplies were mostly in good shape, but a surprising number of unglamorous necessities were running toward the low side: stuff nobody had the specific responsibility for keeping track of. But she'd logged the whole summary into Tinhead, so it would all be on the order readouts for the orbital resupply station at Earth.

"Good job," said Tregare. "Let me top up your drink."

"Haven't we finished our business, for the moment?"

"The inventory business, sure. But for a time now, I've been meaning to hear some more about Stronghold." So she agreed, and he started asking. And, of course, making notes.

He'd guessed that Stronghold's personnel complement was something less than ten thousand—and planned to grow slowly, as support facilities also grew. He was interested to learn how many were civilians, including nonworking "dependent" family members, how many troops—and the size of the Committee Police contingent. The latter was larger than he'd thought, but not enough to change his estimate of the forces *he'd* need. Because UET never allowed arms to any but Police and military.

"No problem," he muttered, and didn't realize he'd said it aloud until Lofall asked him *what* was no problem. "Oh, nothing. Not right now, anyway. Well, I guess that's all for this time, and thanks." He stood, ready to see her out.

She stood also, but came toward him instead, and put her hands to his shoulders. Puzzled, all he said was, "Yes?"

"Tregare—don't you get tired of living alone? I do. Unless you have a little something going on the side. I don't."

The trouble was, he hadn't been thinking of her in this way. And, maybe because first Erdis and then Leanne had rejected him, his first instinct was toward caution. So while he was still trying to find an answer, she pushed off from him. "Sorry. I forgot I'm all scarred and ugly."

On twin thoughts, that she'd been hurt a lot and that sure's hell he knew he could trust her, Bran's self-absorption broke. Moving fast, he caught her at the door. "You're not; no such thing. This was a little quick, is all. Grabbed me off guard. You want to talk some?"

"All right." So they sat. He expected her to say something; when she didn't, he asked two questions. Why him, and why now? Speaking carefully, she said, "You, because you accept me fully and were the first who did, aboard here. Now, because earlier I was too damned sore, but I think I'm healed well enough. And also because once we reach Earth you'll be too busy."

Oddly, her rather clinical manner aroused him; for the moment he tried to soft-pedal that reaction. "There's after, too."

She shook her head. "Maybe not. At Earth, I may go groundside." He wanted to know how and why, and she said, "Responsibilities, that I have to the Underground. Family I'd like to see, even knowing what the Long View's done to respective ages. Things like that. As to how—" She grinned. "You'll see. And I won't risk your security in any way."

"How about yours? UET Earthside has no handle on you now, but—"

"And won't. I have a solid cover identity." When he protested that living on phony ID could get tiresome, she said, "You don't understand. *This* is my cover ident. Once I get groundside, I'd take it off and blend back into the woodwork."

He didn't ask her real name because he had no need to know it. In fact he didn't ask much of anything, because now she was taking her clothes off, and it wasn't polite to let her get too far ahead of him in that activity.

To anyone who hadn't attended UET's Slaughterhouse, the woman's scars might have shocked arousal out of being. Bran had seen worse, though; in fact he *wore* worse. Not so cruelly and deliberately placed, however. At any rate he made no comments, and when she came to him, met her more than halfway.

About her state of recovery, it seemed she'd been a little optimistic. In the face of "too long since last time" Bran was *trying* to be easy with her, but saw her face contort with pain. So they switched to a position he found somewhat awkward, but it worked for both of them.

Anyway, sitting up after a while, Lofall looked as pleased as Tregare felt. She didn't talk about it; what she said was, "Your hair and beard. Earth's not far off now. Would you like me to do the coloring for you? I'm quite good at that, and can get rid of the excess curliness, too. Though as I said, someone else should give you the necessary haircut."

So after Tregare ordered them up a meal and they had that, she smeared him with one and another evil-smelling paste and eventually washed away each of them. Bran looked at the result and ran a finger across the lank red hair that fell over his forehead. "Why'nt you just chop this back so I can see better? That ought to do it." When she protested, he said, "After all, who says Deet Armiger always goes to the same barber?"

She tried it, and made several successive corrections. Finally Tregare said, "Let's quit while we're ahead." And at her startled look, added, "On my appearance, I mean."

With the urgency off, he was able to make love in the fashion he was most used to, and still keep it gentle enough for her.

A day or so later, *Inconnu* began to draw direct calls from Earth; the ship had been detected and groundside wanted some contact. Tregare didn't stall for long. He looked over his plans and went ahead with them, announcing the imminent arrival of the *Alexander the Great*, Dietrich Armiger commanding. He said, "I won't put the coded report and mission directive off to you until we're in better reception range, but part of it you need to know before we arrive. Which is, we refuel and resupply at whichever orbital station you assign us, and then move out ASAP on the next leg of our mission. Time's important and this crew is a briefed team, so Admiral Saldeen has ordered that no personnel transfers be made at this stop. The Admiral sends his apologies for any apparent highhandedness but says you'll realize the urgency when you see his coded report."

Tregare cut the circuit and wiped sweat from his forehead. He hoped his spiel, which Prestor and Deverel had helped phrase, carried the grade of conviction that would sell UET Earthside.

From the answers he got, after transmission timelag, it was going pretty well, so far.

Somebody groundside, though, seemed to need to put a spoke into the wheel of anyone citing any authority but his very own. This person was a Colonel Missouri (or something that sounded like Missouri, and the nasal twang surely fit). The colonel dictated that being an unscheduled arrival, the *Alexander* would take its turn at Station Five, and never mind that Station Five was preempted by the fleet for Stronghold.

Since there was no point at all in arguing, which would merely draw unwelcome attention, Tregare warped course so as to jump the line ahead of two ships making a more leisurely approach, and settled into a holding pattern immediately following the Stronghold ships.

He did ask Missouri's assistant, when the colonel left to exert his authority on some other caller, how come the ships for Stronghold needed refueling. "I mean," said Tregare, "they just now lifted off Earth." He was told that he was asking about a Security matter, so he apologized and cut the circuit.

"I can tell you that," said Renni Lofall, sitting in at comm. "Some years back, the first ship to lift in one of these fleets just swung off the wrong way and kept going. Never *was* caught."

Bran nodded. "So now they herd 'em a lot closer?"

"That's right. You'll notice, out there, two armed ships and four not. The armed ones came up first, almost fully fueled, and merely topped off. They're waiting while the other four, which lifted almost empty, refuel at Station Five. So—"

"Mother hens giving the chicks no chance to get lost." He shook his head. "With that grade of mistrust, how do they run their show at all?"

Lofall shrugged. "The only reason it works, Tregare, is that actual rebel activity is about a tenth of what UET's geared up to fight."

Tregare thought about it. "That situation needs correcting."

Not right now, though. Current drill was to minimize contact with UET but keep necessary dealings all smooth and nice. Coasting in Colonel Missouri's specified holding pattern, the *Alexander* accepted the airlock-docking of two courier craft, and in his digs Tregare entertained the midrange groundside brass commanding those little buckets, and sent them away happy. He didn't have to give them any coded reports because they lacked proper clearance, but he put the matter in a more face-saving way: "I expect you'll see all this stuff, groundside. It's just that *I* don't have authorization to release the info, except direct to HQ." Leanne Prestor, he could see, was truly impressed at his "tact." Her trouble, he decided, was that she'd never been at the Slaughterhouse.

And just as well. She'd never have lived through it.

When you have to wait, you might as well enjoy it. Tregare made a point of getting all the Earthside Tri-V channels monitored and taped. He had the major news circuit piped into the galley, because he wanted the whole crew to get a good look at what UET said was happening on Earth. And compare that with Underground data.

The latter, Renni was helping him with, readjusting one transceiver pair and its tape-handling accessories to handle the Underground's "wideband burst" method of secret communication, which traded bandwidth for time at an astonishing ratio. The principle was an old one; the Underground's trick was that each burst carried the coded key to shift the system's base frequency for the *next* burst. Without the codes, no one would be apt to intercept more than the occasional burst—

and wouldn't know what to do with it, anyway, since each burst carried parts of several different data blocks.

So retrieving the info was tricky, but with Lofall's help Tregare was getting the stuff into coherent order. He didn't much like the results, though: UET had North America in worse shape than ever, and still pushing. If the UG's observations were at all accurate, something like thirty percent of the continent's population now existed in Total Welfare Centers. And Bran knew what Total Welfare "clients" really were: government-owned slaves.

The rationale sounded reasonable. If you couldn't support yourself and your family, kindly ol' UET took over all your assets and liabilities, and placed you in a Welfare Center where you were fed, clothed, and housed. And sent out in work gangs hired by private industry or by UET itself. A small amount of your contracted wages went as "credit" into your personal account, and theoretically you could earn enough to buy out of Welfare. But damn few ever managed to reach that goal.

And of course it wasn't only bankrupts who went to Welfare. The Centers now probably contained more dissidents than any other category of client. Everybody knew it, but don't say so out loud!

Bran shut down the readout and turned to Lofall. "What say we grab some lunch?" So they went down to the galley. As they began eating, somebody turned up the Tri-V news monitor.

"Hey, let's see this," said Hain Deverel. "Some Welfare kid hit it big in the monthly lottery, and she's being interviewed."

"It's a replay," someone said. "Happened last month. The story now is that she's disappeared." Several people shushed the talker, and the newscaster could be heard.

Busy with his food, Tregare half listened. Several weeks ago, on her sixteenth birthday, which gave her adult status, a young Welfare "client" named Rissa Kerguelen had won the state-run lottery's grand prize, built to its largest-ever size by the drawing of a series of ineligible winners over previous months. Approximately a hundred million Weltmarks, the man said. Or maybe twenty-three million, Bran estimated, after taxes. A hell of a lot, anyway!

Now, it seemed, this record-high winner had disappeared. All possible means were being used to find her, and make sure of her safety. *Safety? Oh, sure, Mike!* Toward that end, then, her media interview on the day the prize was awarded was being shown again on Tri-V.

Tregare leaned forward and to one side, to see better. This could be interesting. The screen showed a drab auditorium; a surprisingly large press turnout half filled the place.

A fattish man with a lot of blond, slicked-down hair led in a young girl who wore a red dress. Somebody else's dress: it was several sizes too large and hung on her like a sack. Just guessing, Tregare bet she had nothing on except the dress.

Under Welfare-stubbled dark hair her face was so blank that Bran couldn't decide if she were pretty or ugly. Well, a Welfare kid—coping with something like this could freeze her.

The fat man took her up onto a small platform, with mikes. He smiled and smiled; Tregare tried to think where he'd seen that smile before. Certainly not on *this* butterball . . .

Then he remembered. "Plastic Smile" on the *MacArthur*, Butcher Korbeith's sadistic bodyguard. But Bran had killed that one. . . .

This one's name was Supervisor Gerard. When he got done talking about himself, he introduced his supervisee: Rissa Kerguelen, age sixteen just today, daughter of David Marchant and Selene Kerguelen, both unfortunately deceased, of a city Bran didn't recall hearing about before and promptly forgot.

As Gerard stepped down and left her standing there alone, the kid started to say something, but stopped when a question came from the floor. "What's your reaction to winning the big prize?"

Pause. Then, "Naturally, I'm delighted."

Another voice. "How does it feel to grow up in a Welfare Center?"

More quickly this time, Rissa Kerguelen said, "I can't answer that; I've never grown up anywhere else. How does it feel to grow up outside?" Laughter came, and Tregare thought, *good on you, kid!*

"The last big winner called it an utter miracle. Do you agree?"

Obviously gaining confidence now, the girl shrugged. "No. Why should I? Every month, as long as I can remember, it happens—with the winners announced on Tri-V. This time it's me, is all."

After a moment, "Who will you vote for in the next election?"

Kerguelen shook her head. "I don't understand."

"Which bidding conglomerate has your support?"

Slowly again, she answered, "I can't say—I don't know enough about any of them."

"Does that mean you don't favor the present Committee?" Some menace in that question? Maybe . . .

She was flustered; on the screen a close-up showed her biting her lip. "It doesn't mean *anything* yet. Give me time to learn."

A harsh voice. "You better learn fast, kid."

The implied threat stalled things, then the camera swung to a grey-haired woman: "What do you intend to do with the money you've won? And with your life, from now on?"

Not hesitating, Rissa Kerguelen said, "Buy my brother out of Welfare—my Uncle Voris, too, if he's still alive—and share with them. That's the money." Now, for the first time, she smiled, and Tregare decided she was better-looking than he'd thought. "My life? Well, I'm going off Earth and I'm going to grow my hair down to my butt—and the rest of it's my own business."

While Tregare chuckled at the kid's feisty answer, he heard gasps from the media reps, and one said, "You resent your present hairstyle?"

Again no hesitation. "What's to resent? A few sets of clippers are a lot cheaper than combs and brushes always getting lost and wearing out—anybody can see that. I don't have to like it, though, and I never did."

She'd slowed them down some, all right. Now someone asked, "What are you going to do, off Earth?"

"I don't know yet. What are *you* going to do, *on* Earth?"

Whether or not that reply ended the interview, now the screen cut back to the first newscaster. ". . . and that's all we have for you on the missing lottery winner Rissa Kerguelen. If anyone has any information leading to—uh, making sure of her safety and well-being, please contact us here at . . ."

Tregare quit listening; he knew bullshit when he heard it and that 'caster was full of it up to here. The kid, though—wherever she was, he hoped she was all right.

Renni came along to his quarters. Before anything else, she filled him in some about UET's lottery winners. "Those wins are UET's carrot, Bran. So they get lots of publicity. For a time, that is."

"And then?"

"Then it tapers off and disappears. And the winners, very quietly with no public mention at all, are taken in charge again."

"What—?"

"Arrested on any flimsy charges UET cares to make. The remaining prize money confiscated. And it's back into Welfare."

Until she yelped, he didn't realize how hard he was gripping her arm. "You mean, *that's* how the kid disappeared?"

Rubbing the arm, Renni said, "No. Not this time. Or they wouldn't be doing any of this on Tri-V. No, she got away. And I think I know how and where."

"But didn't you just now first hear of her, same as I did?"

"I'd seen earlier mentions, Bran—brief ones. But they didn't apply *here*, you see, so—well, anyway, some facts in that case clicked with some equally irrelevant material off the UG circuit. Irrelevant to this ship, I mean. And—"

"Are you going to *tell* it?"

She sat up straight. "Right. *Yes*, sir." Okay; he could put up with a little clowning, until she went on, "Young Kerguelen was taken from the Welfare Center by a reporter who is one of *ours*. The UG, I mean. Where she was taken is not important. *But*, from that place, a few weeks later, another of ours put a young woman on a low-level SST to Buenos Aires."

"And all that means what?"

"Put it together yourself. And add in Erika Hulzein's Establishment, which operates somewhere out of Buenos Aires and is most influential in keeping UET's fingers off that whole country."

Aunt Erika? Not thinking, Tregare said, "If the kid's with *that* old tiger, UET can go piss up a rope."

Lofall narrowed her eyes. "What do *you* know about the Hulzein Establishment?"

Now when Tregare took hold of her, it was gently. "More than I intend to tell you, Renni. Except that we're on the same side but never got along. All right?"

It must have been, because for quite a while there, everything else was.

For the rest of that day, in the back of Tregare's mind, the mystery of the Kerguelen youngster's fate nagged him. At one point he even toyed with the idea of trying to route some kind of illicit call through to the Hulzein Establishment in Argentina, and asking about the kid. But such a move would be just plain asking for trouble, and he was already surrounded with enough potential for that. So he didn't.

Instead he kept his ship waiting in line while the Stronghold fleet went, one ship at a time, through the supply feeds. He greeted and hosted two sets of couriers from groundside, who brought him flimsies of info that UET hadn't cared to trust to the airwaves, and in turn he gravely handed over printed (but still coded) readouts of the report that had Admiral Saldeen's slightly-edited signature on it. Groundside had had Tregare rerun that report to them, over tightbeam link, several times. But they couldn't seem to get the glitches out of it. Somehow Tregare wasn't too surprised.

When the second group was ready to leave, someone came running to join them. Panting a little, she said, "Catch a ride groundside with you? I was on the earlier shuttle and missed it going back. Met an old friend, we got to talking." She turned to Tregare. "Captain, I owe you an apology. May I speak with you a moment?"

Everybody was standing at the main airlock's inside hatch. Tregare motioned the others into the lock and drew Renni Lofall off to one side, out of earshot. "What the hell you think you're doing?"

With bright-colored lapels, epaulets, sleeve and leg stripes affixed to her jumpsuit, she looked the perfect courier: no denying that much. How had she done it? No time to ask. She said, "I told you I might be getting off. This is my move. You won't spoil it?"

He grinned. "Couldn't if I wanted to. Hope it works, is all." He looked around. "Nobody's watching. Kiss good-bye, Renni." They did that, and again; then he said, "Groundside, what'll you do? Do you have contacts to help you, once you land?"

"All set, yes. And—" She hugged him. "It's been good, Bran."

"Yeah. Same here." What else? "You—" But no more time. From the airlock someone was beckoning; she had to run. "Good luck, Lofall." Then the inner hatch closed, and she was gone.

Finally the *Alexander* was signaled ahead to a supply dock. Tregare sat monitoring Tinhead's record of the loading process. As he watched he felt grateful to Renni Lofall for insisting on taking inventory. It wasn't that *Inconnu* had been short of anything in a way that could endanger the ship—but he'd have felt stupid if, halfway between someplace and no place, he'd run out of soap or something. Now, thanks to Lofall, he wouldn't.

The input of solid supplies was nearing its end. So now was where push came to shove. Because having topped off fuel and water tanks at the *Arachne*, he couldn't accommodate much more of either item. And when that fact became evident, someone in UET HQ would want to know *why*. He had his story, of course: the Admiral's orders. But on a hunch he'd held it back, and he wondered if maybe the hunch had been wrong.

Now, as the ship undocked and instructions came for the *Alexander* to move ahead and take on water, on the forward screen Bran saw a triangle of three ships approaching. What he didn't like was that their path wasn't far from his own intended course for leaving here.

And then Bran *really* didn't like it. Because on hi mag, his main screen showed one of the nearing ships to be the *MacArthur*. And over a monitor came Arger Korbeith's gravel voice. "*Alexander*, hell! That ship is the *Tamurlaine*!"

And Korbeith's ships cut abruptly toward intercept.

There wasn't time to tell the supply station anything at all. Cutting his offship-send, Tregare told Gonnelson which way to point *Inconnu* and said, "Junior Lee. Fire the Drive, redline max. Now!" Slowly at first, *Inconnu* turned and moved.

It wasn't the comm-tech's fault; lacking other instructions the man obeyed Korbeith's transmitted order for two-way visual. The Butcher hadn't changed; that craggy yellowed face would probably look much the same in its coffin. Tregare could see Korbeith squint and blink at what he saw in *Inconnu*'s control area; then the man nodded and yelled, "Damn it, *all ships*! You've just resupplied an Escaped ship. And your Captain Dietrich Armiger is the pirate, Bran Tregare." Glaring, he yelled, "I see you, Tregare, you snot! Once, you got away from this ship alive. Not again, though." He cut voice-send, but Bran saw him barking orders. To his own crew and to his other ships, they'd be.

So Bran gave a few of his own. "Cut Drive to half-max,

Junior Lee—I need some time before this fight." And, "Gonnelson, head us straight for the center of their triangle." Tregare moved to another console, one that gave him more tools to work with. On intercom he called, "Anybody in Scout Bay Two, say so fast and get out faster." He activated the enabling circuits that would let him run that scoutship as a remote-control drone, then as no answer came to his order, opened the bay and fired up the scout's Drive. Only on idle, for the moment, and now he told Junior Lee Beauregard to run ship's Drive at redline again. Well, a little under, he wanted, but Junior Lee knew that.

There hadn't been time, what with all the rest of it, to get gunners up to the projector turrets, so Tregare slaved all his projectors to his own console. Hoping the turret controls were sitting on neutral, because from here he had no heterodyne control but only traverse and override capability, he fired three energy bursts straight ahead, just to get his heterodyne up toward peak range. Then, watching Korbeith's delta of killer ships approach, he waited.

Not for long. Korbeith's group opened fire early. This near to Earth, ionization of attenuated gases made coruscating tracer lines where the convergent lasers tracked—glowing streaks that dazzled vision. So under cover of that glare, Bran launched his scoutship from Bay Two. First hesitating, he decided its best use was to go directly between two of Korbeith's ships, the *MacArthur* and one of the others. When he had it pointed right, time came to use his own projectors—on the third ship.

Everything happened in a hurry. He got the third ship, all right. When the scout was between the other two, Tregare blew its Drive, and one ship blew along with it. Not the *MacArthur*, though; obviously damaged, it still held course, almost.

But Bran Tregare was past now—past the lot of them, and away clear.

7. South Forty

When it came to escape routes, what Tregare liked about making a sling turn and cutting Drive was that the pursuit could be expecting it and still couldn't do a damn thing about it. "Here we go," he said now, some days out from Earth. "We're out of sight behind Saturn—I'm swinging course. When the posse comes past the planet, we're dead-Drive coasting—about as easy to spot as a flea on a sheep dog." He laughed, then settled down to set course. "How many chased us, anyway? I've been too busy to check."

"Four," said Gonnelson. "Nothing fast." Tregare nodded.

He'd picked Saturn for his pivot because Jupiter was in the wrong direction, while Saturn lay within a radian of his chosen course and gave him leeway for the swing. Prestor thought the rings would be a problem because *Inconnu*'s closest approach obviously had to be well inside their spread. Tregare, though, simply went "under" them, below the planet's ecliptic. Which meant that the turn gave the ship a slight vector toward zenith. Well, that was all right—he'd be crossing a number of UET's regular shipping routes, and passing "above" them meant he'd be in a skew pattern with any Uties if he chanced to cross paths. Hard to intercept, that was the point of it.

Once they were back on Drive and well away, Bran held council; in captain's quarters he provided drinks and snacks while the group had a chance to look at a star-chart readout.

After a while, when everybody had settled down pretty well, he stood. "Okay, people: here's what I have in mind and I'd like to hear your thinking on it." He used a pointer at the chart. "Mostly I think we should stop in on Hidden Worlds—gather info, all that. Besides trading, of course. But it wouldn't hurt to raid a UET colony or two, if that option turns up handy by location."

He spelled it out, and some of the group had comments and some didn't, and the upshot was that *Inconnu*'s next stop should be a Hidden World called South Forty. It was off any major UET route, its settlements were well established, and it was fairly well in line for a considerable choice of second stops.

So, excusing himself with a gesture, Gonnelson went upship and set course.

Bran sat, after the others left, brooding over the tag-end of his drink. The knock startled him; he opened his door to a youngish woman whose jumpsuit bore no indications of rank. "Captain?"

"That's me." The odd thing was that he didn't recognize her. Well, maybe the short red hair, frizzed fluffy on top but tapered smooth at sides and back, was a new look for her. "I don't seem to recall your name," but he gestured her inside and to a seat. "How long have you been on this ship?"

"Since about twelve hours before we left Earth orbit. I came aboard as a courier." Pert-faced as she was, she had more age to her than showed at first—but the movements of her slim body showed an athlete's coordination.

Tregare frowned. To cover his surprise, he said, "Courier? Where's your fruit salad?" But then he saw, on the slightly faded suit, the darker places on sleeves and legs and shoulders where those decorations had been. *So that's where Lofall got all that stuff*. He moved a hand. "All right; I know where it went. I saw it go off the ship. But now then—who are you, and what the hell are you doing here?"

"My name is Tanit Eldon. I'm an Underground agent with roughly the same rank as the woman who left ship wearing my—" She grinned. "—my fruit salad. For about three months, since taking some brief training at the Hulzein Establishment in Argentina, I've been working undercover for UET at the main spaceport. And at the moment, since my report is long and dry, I'm waiting for you to offer me a drink, captain, sir."

Working undercover, was she? Maybe—*but who for?* Drinks made and served, because he could use a new one himself, Bran Tregare asked questions. A lot of them, and cutting back and forth from one subject to another, trying to trip her up.

Most of it fit—maybe all of it, but he didn't *know* all of it. She had code words, she had names—info that Renni Lofall had picked off the wide-burst channel for him. She described the layout and setup of Erika Hulzein's Argentine base, and maybe she'd been there and maybe not, but Bran hadn't so he could only go by what little he did know.

"How did you and Lofall get together?"

"She was loitering around where she could make eye contact with the couriers, or anyone else that came aboard, and now and then giving an Underground code sign." Again the grin, and Tregare felt he should be noticing something. Finally he did; occasionally her right thumb, the hand resting quietly in her lap, made an inconspicuous triple twitch: toward the back of the hand, forward, and again back. When he nodded, Tanit Eldon said, "When I responded, we did the usual drill—greeted each other like old friends and arranged to meet and talk in her room." She shrugged. "I wanted onship and she wanted off, so the details were easy. The only way it could have been easier would be if we wore the same size suit."

"That's nice." But one thing her story didn't explain. So he asked. "*Why* did you want to get on this ship?"

"Because word got back, from your wide-burst contacts with the UG, to Erika Hulzein. And she wants to make an alliance."

An alliance? *Erika?* Tregare said, "Just who is it, she wants to team up with?"

Eldon leaned forward. "Well, any Escaped ship would be better than none. But the way I was told, when Madame Hulzein put it together that here was a ship that was Escaped *and* armed, she said it had to be Tregare's *Inconnu*. And that's when I was pulled by the roots out of my previous assignment, and ordered to get on here at any cost." Pause. "Which I did."

He thought about it. Whether his aunt Erika knew who he really was, or whether Eldon did, made no difference. Because either way, no "alliance" could be made operative during Erika's probable lifetime (and how was his sickly cousin Frieda, Erika's daughter, doing these days?). Regardless, that stuff would have to wait.

What couldn't wait was finding out if Eldon told any truth.

Shrugging, she accepted being interrogated under truth drugs as a matter of course. "Now if you were UET I'd be trying to claw my way out of here. But at the port I didn't have that problem; the UG rather neatly got me into a job that didn't carry a high level of Security precautions."

So Eda Ghormley brought the kit upship and administered the injections, and Tregare ran his questions—or as many as he could keep in mind—through the mill all over again.

Tanit Eldon's story held up solidly. So Ghormley left, and Bran waited until the drugs wore off so that the woman came back to herself and knew where she was. Then he personally took her down to Stores, where Groden issued her the standard necessities, and finally Bran escorted her to the quarters lately vacated by Renni Lofall.

Still looking slightly whacked-out, Eldon said, "I can't simply *ride* this ship; I'll need a job. I don't know ships' needs, but I've worked as a junior administrator."

Tregare couldn't help saying, "Too bad we don't have any juniors to administrate," but then he smiled and said, "How are you at keeping track of inventory, monitoring actual count against the computer's version?" Because he didn't have time for that stuff, himself, and Renni Lofall had shown him the need.

She nodded. "I've done that kind of thing, yes."

"All right; tomorrow, show me a trial run. If you pass—" Suddenly he realized she couldn't know all the complicated stuff about rankings and owning shares in the ship; no time for all that, now. "If you pass I'll buy you a Chief's rating and you can pay me back out of work credits." She wanted to ask more but he shushed her. "I'll explain later; for now, don't worry about it."

Then he left, trying to figure what Erika's angle could be.

Danger seemed to unify the ship, and keep down the incidence of hassles. Since *Inconnu* first headed for Stronghold, Tregare had needed to hold court only twice, both for minor matters. So he'd nearly forgotten about that chore, until one day his Third Hat appeared at Tregare's door with a scowling Chief Rating named Sven Dahl, one of Junior Lee Beauregard's Drive techs. "We have a problem, skipper," said Frei Relliger.

Bran sighed; if he wanted problems he'd ask Tinhead for one. "Come on in." It didn't look like a social occasion, so except for seats he offered no hospitality. "What is it?"

"He gets his say first because he's brass; right?" said Dahl. Tregare looked at the man; the Chief was a "black Swede" or maybe Norwegian, swarthy with dark hair and high cheekbones. Big, and probably good-looking enough except for a nose that must have caught one fist too many.

And now the squarehead was spoiling for a fight. So Bran said, "If that's how you want it. All right, Relliger. What's the beef?"

Obviously embarrassed, the Third Hat tried to keep his story short but couldn't seem to manage. Since he and Leanne worked separate watches, they each had a lot of lonesome time. Dahl had started hanging around Leanne every chance he got, and making suggestions. And then—

"Just a minute," said Tregare. "Shouldn't she be here herself, to tell this part? You saying it, it's hearsay evidence."

"I asked her to. She wouldn't come, unless you make it a direct order." Tregare nodded; he'd hear these people first. Relliger continued. Finally Dahl had propositioned her outright, and she'd turned him down. "At which point he turned on her and was grossly insulting. He's not going to get away with that."

"You charging insubordination, or what?" Relliger shook his head, so Bran didn't wait for a verbal answer. "All right, Chief Rating Dahl. What's your side of it?"

"Sure I made a try, there. Where's the law against that? Or against striking out, either. But she set me back *snotty*. Like I wasn't good enough for her." Brows raised, Tregare waited. "So I told her she wasn't so much, shopping around like she does. First you, skipper, then him, so why too upnose for a Chief? I mean, it's not like she did the Slaughterhouse and brought her tattoo from UET." Arms folded, Dahl sat back.

"There's more than that," said Relliger. "He called her names."

"A couple, maybe," Dahl said. "But nothing real bad. I—"

"I do not *care*," said Bran. "I want to know one thing here, and one thing only. Exactly what is it that I am supposed to decide, about this?"

"It's not deciding," Relliger answered. "Just give us permission to fight; that's all."

Then it came to Bran, what they were after. After Escape he'd filed UET's Ships' Regs away and written a very brief paper entitled "NEW Ship's Regulations, by order of Bran Tregare." Looking back, he figured he'd put in some silly stuff, out of sheer smart-aleck bravado. But he remembered the first three; they came first because he meant them:

I. *Orders will be obeyed first and argued later.*
II. *No drinking or drugging on duty.*
III. *No fighting without captain's permission.*

All right. Now he said, "You want to fight?" Both nodded. "You'll each tell me why." He paused. "You first, Dahl."

"I want to show him I'm the better man. And her, too."

"It's debatable that winning a fight proves that, but I understand your point. And you, Frei?"

"He's not going to get away with insulting Leanne!"

Tregare thought about it, and weighed the odds. On the face of it, Dahl had the physique and quickness to make short work of Relliger. Dammit, Bran couldn't *afford* to lose another officer just now—and if he didn't specify otherwise, he knew this fight would be to the death. Yet if he shielded his Third Hat from danger, the man's usefulness would end as the crew lost respect for him. And the whole stupid mess over nothing more than a pair of bruised egos. . . .

There wasn't any good answer, so Tregare made one up. He made a show of thinking hard, but he was only figuring the details of how to say it. Let 'em wait a little . . .

He cleared his throat. "Scout Bay Two is mostly empty. First you stow the loose gear away; there'll be nothing used as weapons. Unarmed combat, and unclothed—no watches or rings, even."

"Wait a minute!" Dahl. "What are the rules?"

"Make up your own." Nobody answered; Tregare decided he was beginning to enjoy this. "What happens in there is your business. When somebody knocks to be let out, and not before, the door opens again." *Now the kicker.* "Don't take more than ten minutes at it, though. Because that's when I let the air out."

"But you said, no watches!" Both men protested.

Tregare shrugged. "*Your* problem." He saw the two of them looking at each other, and was pretty sure what they were thinking: no referee, no seconds, no cheering section for the winner . . .

Then Relliger said, "Dahl? Maybe if you'd apologize to Leanne—"

The Chief Rating shrugged. "I could do that. I guess I was a little rough. Got sore, you know, and—"

"Sure. But she'd appreciate your telling her so."

Talking almost like friends, the two men left. Bran Tregare poured himself the drink he'd been wanting, and grinned.

South Forty was a long haul from Earth and seemed longer. Twice *Inconnu* passed UET ships within shouting range, but Bran kept his beacon turned off and didn't bother to answer their hails. Since he couldn't spare time and fuel to try intercept, why give them any data about him? A further point was that even if intercept had been possible, he had no officer cadre to put onto a captured ship: Gonnelson didn't want command, and Tregare saw neither Prestor nor Relliger as command material. Not yet, anyway. And he wasn't exactly overstaffed with ratings, either.

He could have sidetracked to raid any one of three UET colonies not too far off *Inconnu*'s route. Bored, he figured the costs in fuel and time, and decided none of them were worth stretching the trip by months of ship's time. Heavenly Isles would have been the most economical side-jaunt, but as Tregare said in council, "It's a fairly new colony and the planet's mostly ocean. Likely all we'd get from a raid would be the fuel we'd waste stopping there." So they skipped Heavenly Isles; Tregare had t/t_0 still still riding above six by then, and would have hated to waste it.

Slowing toward the system where South Forty orbited, Tregare detected no other ship traffic. Not surprising; his data bank showed this Hidden World to have little commerce. But it was a place he wanted to check out, for future possibilities. A little isolation could be a good thing.

The sun was more orange and less bright than Earth's, but South Forty's orbit averaged only about point-eight of an A.U. so temperatures would be reasonably comfortable. Coming in past the usual gas giants, Tregare got a good hi-mag look at South Forty. His approach angle, by luck, showed the planet side-lit; checking the movement of planetary features on time-lapse tape, the degree of axial tilt was evident. About one-third radian, Bran guessed; slightly less than Earth's but not much. Looking, Bran Tregare nodded. The habitable zone on this world would cover a lot of latitude—and in that zone was plenty of land area.

But so far as he knew, there wasn't much habitation yet.

Closing so near that he'd spotted the major settlement and its spaceport, still Tregare got no hail from groundside. Finally he got on the horn and initiated the action. With straight talk, since this was a Hidden World: ". . . armed ship *Inconnu*, an Escaped Ship, Bran Tregare commanding, request landing instructions . . ."

Eventually an answer came. No screen picture, just a woman's voice, saying, "South Forty responding to *Inconnu*. Sorry to be such slow pay, but we get so little action these days that the port isn't manned full time. Please be welcome here. Pick any landing circle you want, but it'd be helpful if you'd burn the weeds off one that hasn't been used lately." She paused, then answered Bran's next question before he asked it. "We're well-fixed for fuel and supplies. In fact we had to shut the refinery down because we ran out of storage volume. So—"

"Right. Thanks for telling me." And in fact he *had* been wondering if this backwater could make it worth his while to expend the fuel needed for entering and leaving its gravity well. "See you down there pretty soon."

Two more orbiting spirals: then he plowed air and went in.

Number Six landing circle looked most overgrown. When *Inconnu* came to rest, the growth was gone. Leaving Gonnelson to hold down Control, Tregare's group waited in the main airlock until most of the smoke and dust had settled, then the hatch opened and the boarding ramp moved out and down.

Tregare led the way groundside. Following him were Frei Relliger, Hain Deverel, and a couple of other Chief Ratings. All wore their usual sidearms but no heavier weapons.

From the modest-sized Port Admin building, a party of three came to greet their visitors. The tall, lean woman in the lead looked to have about forty Earthyears, bio. When she gave a hail, Bran recognized her voice from the circuit contact. Then the groups met and everybody shook hands. "So you're Bran Tregare. We've heard about you, more than a little. And we have some messages for you, left by other ships."

"That's good; thanks." Distracted a little, Bran tried to keep the names straight. This blond woman, slightly greying, was Mayo Tolridge. The man was Theo-somebody, and the youngish brunette was somebody-Corelli; maybe he could fill the rest in later. "Who-all left messages? You happen to remember?"

The names rang few bells, so he decided the stuff would be mostly info from people he did know, relayed by some he didn't. And inside the building, that's how it turned out. Raoul Vanois had been here with *Carcharodon*, and left an uncoded voice tape for Tregare. "It's two as sends word for *Inconnu*." Contrasting with the odd grammar—and now Tregare recalled that Vanois was a Backwoodser and touchy about his planet's mode of speech—the voice itself came clear and sweet, like a child's. "I has first from Derek Limmer. He have your note is label Delta Five and say will or does mission at New Hope. I does not understand what year he says, but he meets you at Number One." There was more, but from it Tregare got little meaning.

Well, though—Limmer had agreed to visit the New Hope arsenal and pick up ships' weapons for delivery to Tregare's base. Long view or not, the network was beginning to function!

Two other tapes had been brought here and entered in the original versions. Kickem Bernardez, at time of recording, was still maintaining the *Hoover's* UET facade and visiting colonies with impunity. He didn't yet have Tregare's planning on hand, but "given any luck at all, Bran Tregare, I shall hear it from you in person, some landing, over a great untidy lot of drink."

And Jargy Hoad had raided a UET world and not only got away clean but came near to capturing a UET ship, groundside. "But I must have tipped our hand, Bran. With a quarter of his crew stranded groundside, and before he had his ramp up and his airlock closed, that skipper lifted off." A pause. "I just wish I could figure what I did wrong, there. So I wouldn't do it again."

None of the other material was anywhere near as interesting. Bran heard it through, recorded it in case some parts might be important later, and then spent another hour composing and taping messages *he* wanted to leave here. For the data net to work in the Long View, it needed all the input it could get.

On Hidden Worlds, Tregare's business rarely involved him with the ways their governments were organized. So he never did bother to find out Mayo Tolridge's position in the hierarchy at South Forty. She was, though, apparently in charge of all dealings with *Inconnu*, and that was fine with Bran Tregare. Because the woman stated her wishes clearly, made reasonable trade offers, and settled any given individual deal without undue bickering. Bran was used to more shuffling, but found it easy to get used to her style of commerce.

South Forty was at disadvantage because the Port's main computer had troubles. Nearly half its memory storage wouldn't access dependably; some days it worked, other times not.

Tregare offered to take a look, but found the problem was beyond his grade of skill. He wished Renni Lofall were still available, but wishing didn't help much.

When he mentioned the difficulty later, in *Inconnu*'s galley, Hain Deverel spoke up. "Mind if I have a try, skipper? If it's all right with groundside? I have a sort of knack with 'intermittents'—I get hunches, and sometimes they're right."

Well, Tregare had the same kind of ability in other fields, so he got Tolridge's okay for the attempt, and Deverel found and fixed the glitch in less than two hours. Notified, the woman said, "That's worth something in our trading. A bonus to your ship. I'll have to think what's suitable."

"Not the ship," said Tregare. "Pay Hain Deverel. He did the work." He wasn't quite sure why he put it that way; if he himself had found the trouble, he'd have assigned any bonus to *Inconnu*. Finally he decided it was because he held captain's shares and Deverel didn't.

A side effect of the incident was that the Port bought quite a lot of spare electronic hardware. "For backup and expansion both," Tolridge said. Then she and Bran looked over their respective inventories to see what else might be swapped to mutual advantage. Until she exclaimed, he'd forgotten the seed grains he'd picked up at one of *Inconnu*'s early landings. Some he'd traded at Number One as planned, but there was a lot left. Now Tolridge looked excited. "That's a problem here. Anything we plant, fertility's fine for some years, then starts dwindling. So we do need new stock."

Okay; the deal practically made itself, and this day's work seemed to be wrapped up. They'd been consulting in Tregare's quarters, so he invited Tolridge to share dinner with him there. She'd mentioned throwing a spread for him and his officers, but so far the event hadn't happened. Now, apologizing for that delay, she accepted his hospitality.

From the galley he ordered a moderately festive meal, featuring bushstomper steaks from Number One, and opened some wine from that planet. They ate leisurely and drank the same way, talking about widely varying subjects that had nothing to do with trade—or, indeed, with here-and-now. "Tell me about your life," she said, and he gave her a much-edited version: the overall flavor of UET's Slaughterhouse but none of the grimmer details, the same treatment of

Butcher Korbeith and of the triple mutinies leading to his Escape.

"Since then," he said, refilling her glass, "I've been here and there a lot. Ships don't give detailed itineraries, you know." She nodded. "Since UET already knows it by now, though, I don't mind admitting that I got in and out of Stronghold—and also Earth, though only in orbit; we didn't land."

Looking at him with an odd intensity, she said, "You take it right to them, don't you, Tregare? I suppose that's why you're becoming so notorious." She waved off any reply. "Oh, yes—nearly every ship leaves some kind of word about you and your doings. Some of it secondhand from UET worlds. Do you know what *they* call you? "Tregare the Pirate"—as though you were the only Escaped Ship that ever raided. I wonder why—"

"Simple enough, I'd think. Last I heard, *Inconnu*'s still the only Escaped Ship that can shoot at 'em. And has done it."

She blinked. Maybe a little on the drunk side, but not much, he thought, and restrained his hospitality, pouring her glass only halfway full, as she said, "How long, now, will you stay here?" Now that the trading and supplying were pretty well done, she meant.

"A few days. My crew's been working long hours; those people deserve some groundside leave, a chance to walk around and scan sky." He grinned. "Not to worry; they don't rampage a whole lot." Some, of course, but he expected she'd know that much.

"Another thing," he said. "I need some more computer time. Because in that blocked bank there could be some stuff for me that I couldn't access until Deverel got the jinx out."

"Of course. Any time. Tomorrow—or is it today, by now?"

He checked his chrono. "Close to it, but not quite. You like some more coffee?"

She laughed, then hiccuped. "No coffee. Who needs a wide-awake drunk?" Working at it, after a moment she stood. "I don't usually—" She shook her head. "Tregare? If you could walk me home I'd appreciate it. It's not all that far."

"Sure," so they went downship and out the ramp. The night held a bit of chill but not much. The sky showed bright stars, with a twinkling cluster low on the west horizon, but no sweep of galactic haze.

Not leaning on him greatly, of a sudden Mayo Tolridge

stopped and held him back. She was looking up as she said, "You've been a lot of places, Tregare. A *lot* of places."

"Well, a few more than most, I guess."

"And what do you think of the universe?"

He didn't know, so he said, "Mainly, it's *there*."

She laughed. "Right. And I've figured it out. Bran Tregare, the whole damn universe is one big Rorschach test!"

"If you say so. It's a new thought, anyway. Which way, now?"

"To our left, here," and soon they reached a fair-sized house, built all on one level. Tolridge couldn't find her keys, so she knocked, and after half a minute or so, a man opened the door.

"Mayo? Are you all right?" He squinted at her. "Carrying your cargo alist, eh?" To Tregare, "She doesn't do that often."

"I know. She told me. We were feasting a little, onship, after winding up trade arrangements; Ms. Tolridge has been a big help, so—"

"Oh, yes; you're Tregare." Bran accepted the offered handshake, heard the man's name, and promptly forgot it. "Well, thanks for escorting Mayo home. Care for a drink or anything?"

Politely, Bran declined, said his good nights, and headed back toward his ship.

His way took him through a grouping of small shops and other businesses. One place looked like a bar, and when he walked into it, that's what it was. Not crowded, this late, but several people sat in booths at either side of the aisle leading to the bar. Sometimes, Tregare decided, a man can use a drink just for the hell of it. So he walked the gauntlet of booths, bought his drink, and started back to find a booth of his own because the barstools didn't look all that comfortable. He paid no heed to the seated people; he wouldn't know any of them, anyway, and he wasn't in search of company.

But as a party of four came in, laughing and half-running, he stepped aside to let the group go by. And as he began to move again, someone took hold of his right sleeve. "What's the matter, captain? Are you stuck-up, or something?" The woman's voice restrained his first urge to pull away; he looked down to see, seated alone in the booth, redhaired Tanit Eldon. She said, "Twice you've walked past me. Don't you associate with Chief ratings, off duty?"

Come to think of it, he hadn't seen much of this woman *on*

duty, either, once her inventory readouts and Groden's reports assured him of her competence. Well, Erika Hulzein wouldn't waste training on stupid people. . . . Tregare said, "Wasn't expecting to see anyone I knew, so I wasn't looking. This seat taken?" She shook her head, so he sat, and took a sip of his drink. The taste wasn't what he'd expected.

Probably his face showed surprise, for Eldon said, "Is something wrong?"

"No, the drink's all right. But I ordered bourbon."

She laughed. "I had the same problem. On South Forty, that stuff *is* called bourbon."

"No place else would." Then they were both laughing.

After that drink, Tregare switched to beer, which even South Forty hadn't managed to turn into something else. Eldon was on a talking jag. ". . . the original Tanit was some kind of fertility goddess, back in Carthage or Babylon or someplace. I read about her, but somebody had cut all the sexy parts out of the tape." Sitting in the dim part of the booth, eyes shining in the shadow of her face, she looked at him. "My mother named me. Do you think she wanted me to be good at mating?"

Back onship in Tregare's quarters, he decided she probably thought she *was* good in bed. She had all the complex moves, and put considerable energy into them, but after a time he began to anticipate the routines, and it put him offstride. So he stopped moving, and waited until she did, too. "Tanit?"

"Yes?" Panting, she said, "Anything wrong?"

"Course not. Just, because you're such a good learner, I want to suggest something." She nodded. "Okay. This is a little tricky but I'm sure you can do it."

And she could. When asked, she could relax and do nothing except what her body's own reflexive responses dictated.

Then, for both of them, things worked a lot better.

Later, sitting up, she said, "I could learn a lot of things faster, Tregare, if I had more time to work with you directly."

"We could bend schedules that way, sure."

She blinked her eyes in the way he was learning to recognize. "I hear you're rooming alone now, captain. I could—"

"No." Too fast, that; he should explain more. "You're too

new aboard. No matter how you behaved, some people would say you were trading bed for status, And *being* new, shipside, you'd make mistakes and give the gripers something to chew on. So I'm afraid the word has to be no."

"Well, I didn't mean—"

"Sure not. Play it safe, is all."

She agreed, so he was off *that* hook. And not much after, late time or not, they tried bed again. She did remember what he'd told her before, so he found the occasion quite an improvement.

Next morning, waking alone, Tregare arose short of sleep, but all things considered he felt better than he probably had a right to. Well, being lovers with Tanit Eldon didn't hurt his morale any. He wondered—had he, maybe, got himself into this situation too quickly? No preliminaries, just jump to it? "Peace knows," he muttered to himself, "being hard up doesn't suit me a whole lot." Maybe it made him a little *too* vulnerable, too open.

But to make such decisions fast had always been his pattern. Well, almost always. And, for totally non-related reasons, he'd questioned Tanit under truth drugs; he *knew* her mind and liked it.

What else drew him? The red hair, short but still echoing the glorious mane of Phyls Dolan? Tregare shivered, hating to be reminded of that poor woman drifting all these years, space-frozen. If only he'd been able to move faster! . . .

He brought his mind to now, where it belonged. Dressed and ready to start his day, he headed upship, to the galley.

After breakfast he went groundside to dig further into possible ship data and messages. Mayo Tolridge had offered to set up a data link for *Inconnu*, but Tregare knew Tinhead's keyboard and control codes differed somewhat from those in Port Admin; he didn't want to chance throwing in errors without realizing it.

He found a certain amount of additional info which the malfunction had previously blocked away, but nothing crucial. Starting to leave, then, he passed the comm room and heard Tolridge's voice. Talking, apparently, to an incoming ship: ". . . helpful if you'd burn the weeds off one of the more overgrown ones." Tregare couldn't make out the answering words, but then Tolridge said, "*Inconnu*, yes. Leaving in a few days, I think." Turning back to the room's door, Bran caught something about hoping to talk with him, and then Tolridge said, "We'll see you down here soon then, *Graf Spee.*"

He walked into the room; the woman looked up. He said, "Who's upstairs, you were telling all about me?"

She looked startled. "*Graf Spee*. Ilse Krueger commanding."

The name rang a bell; after a moment he snapped his fingers. "Got it. I've heard of her, here and there. Smallest person ever to survive the Slaughterhouse. Hadn't heard she was Escaped, though." He scowled. "You sure it's not a UET trick? I mean, what name did the ship have, before?"

"Why, I don't know! But a woman, commanding—"

"Or claiming to command. Well, never mind. I'm going aboard ship now, and either way, I'll take care of it."

On *Inconnu*, up in Control, Tregare put his forward screen on hi-mag and monitored the incoming ship's descent. From this angle he couldn't see if it was armed or not, but coming down its weapons made no difference anyway. He had his own turrets slaved to the console in front of him; if that ship so much as twitched its Drive blast in his direction, the next second it would be a cloud of plasma. And to be certain, he warmed the projectors with a few harmless blasts into atmosphere, to bring his heterodyne into peak energy range.

Then he waited.

Circumspectly, with no way of knowing that Tregare's projectors tracked *Graf Spee*, that ship landed—a civil distance from *Inconnu* and never hinting any threat of Drive blast. When *Spee*'s ramp was down and the South Forty delegation came out to give greeting, so did Bran Tregare, accompanied by his First and Second Hats. Gonnelson didn't want to come along, but Bran told him he could merely shake hands and fake it.

Not far from either ship the three groups met. Tregare, waiting while Mayo Tolridge did the hellos and introductions, took an evaluating look at Ilse Krueger. Peace take it, she *was* small—a meter and a half, maybe, if that much. Slim but not fragile, and she moved well. Closer up he saw blue eyes with a barely discernible slant to match the Slavic cheekbones. Her blond hair, too short to hold a curl, lay smooth with only a slight hint of wave. Maybe that hair covered scars, but otherwise the Slaughterhouse experience showed only in a pale mark from above her right eyebrow back toward her ear. Of course, Bran reminded himself, limbs and torso no doubt carried worse souvenirs, because the woman *had* survived and graduated.

The introductions had got around to him and her. Her handshake didn't try to do anything much, but it wasn't limp, either. She smiled slightly, and said, "Tregare, eh? This is a fine occasion."

"Right." Then he said, "Congratulations on your Escape and command, Krueger. I don't think I know all the history."

Obviously she knew what he meant because she nodded. "I see. All right; under UET this ship was the *Bismarck*. Captain was Garrett Trumbull. Doul Falconer was First Officer and I was Second; Doul and I, we—" She shook her head. "I'll never get over missing him." Tregare watched her put her poise back together. "It was Doul who took charge of organizing Escape. I helped. The Third—hell, I don't *want* to remember the name of that little hyena. He's the one who got Doul killed." For a moment her face went pale and gaunt; then, quite matter-of-factly, she said, "Once I had the ship secured, I found time to cut his ratty little throat."

For once, Tregare had nothing to say. Krueger continued, "If it were up to me, I'd have named this ship *Falconer*, after Doul. But he'd picked *Graf Spee*, a joke he understood and I don't. So I've kept the name."

"Sure." Time to change the subject, so he asked where the ship had traveled since Escape, and what other ships she knew about. And mentioned the overall info net; she knew of it but had had only a few chances to feed it or draw on it. "Well, I put quite a lot of stuff in, here. You'll be getting it."

Then he accepted her invitation to dine aboard *Graf Spee*.

Gonnelson and Prestor didn't like the idea of his going aboard this stranger ship solo, but he went anyway, saying that an unarmed craft in need of refueling was in no position to pull anything tricky. "Not with *Inconnu* here, and two armed scouts."

"One," said Gonnelson.

"*They* don't know that." Anyway, Tregare's hunch said he faced no danger, so he went with it.

Krueger's Second Hat, an older man sporting no UET tattoo on his cheek, met Tregare at ramp-top and escorted him to captain's quarters. Wearing a light-blue outfit, something between a uniform and a jumpsuit, Krueger greeted him. She didn't have bourbon, but her Terranovan brandy was pretty good, and later Tregare enjoyed the dinner a lot. The main dish was a kind of stew or goulash; some of the blended flavors were new to him, but he decided they could be habit-forming in rather a hurry.

He was saying as much when the corridor door opened and in barged two large, sweaty young men. The sweaty part was easy to see because they were wearing only brief gym trunks. And they looked to be identical twins, obviously much involved with muscle-building routines. One pushed back his damp blond hair and said, "Done with our workout, captain."

The other mimicked the movement, but lefthanded. "A shower will feel good. Then, may we join you for dinner?"

"Yes—may we?"

Ilse Krueger shook her head. "Not this time, Helmuth—Gregor. Captain Tregare and I have business to discuss."

The two went into the bathroom, and Tregare said, "Couple of brawny lads there." Deliberately he refrained from asking any questions, or so much as raising an eyebrow. She'd tell him or she wouldn't; he didn't care which.

She did. "They live here. With me. Would you like something more? There's quite a bit left."

So Tregare ate again, slowly now for he was filling up. He wished the two youths would finish their stint in the bathroom—he had need of it himself. And finally he went in, anyway, to find Helmuth and Gregor fully dressed, just standing there.

He said hello and went to do his business, but Helmuth or maybe Gregor grasped his arm. "A word, captain."

"Yes?"

"Do not involve yourself with Captain Krueger."

"No?"

"No," said the other. "We belong to her. You do not." Then they left, and finally he could relieve himself.

When he came out, Ilse Krueger had poured coffee and some more brandy. She talked and he didn't, until she paused and said, "Is something on your mind?"

Tregare shrugged. "Not particularly." Then, "Well, yes, now that you mention it. Why did Ajax and Hercules think they had to tell me to keep hands off you?"

"They did that?" She laughed. "Because they know me, I

suppose." Her eyes narrowed. "Are you going to obey them? Are you afraid of them?"

"Yes, and no." She waited, so he said, "If you and I messed around, they'd sulk on you for a month. But they don't scare me."

"Why not?"

"Same reason they don't scare you. Those little trunks don't hide much. People with Slaughterhouse scars make me cautious. Those boys don't have any."

Again Krueger laughed. "I should have known. But we won't tell them, will we? It would hurt their pride."

The charade began to irritate Tregare. "Let's cut the games. I have something important to discuss." And he told her of his plan to gather a fleet of ships, the rendezvous at Number One and the approximate timing, and asked, "You want to be in on this?"

She paused, frowning. "I'll have to think about it. Offhand I like the idea—getting this ship armed, twisting UET's tail. But I have some commitments first. This network of yours—can I let you know by leaving word at message drops, and with any Escaped ships that pass within talking range?"

He shrugged. "That's how everybody else does it, who's not around to talk in person. Don't take too long, though, making up your mind. Rendezvous sounds like a long time from now, but don't forget how a trip or two *chews* time."

"I won't." Now Tregare stood. "Leaving so soon?"

"'fraid so. I need to run through my checklist and set the hour for lift-off. No point keeping the troops in suspense any longer than I have to."

She stood also, put her hands on his shoulders and leaned against him. "Some other time, Tregare."

"Could be, at that." He knew she wanted some sign that he found her desirable, so he leaned down and they kissed. She was really damned good at it; for a moment Bran was tempted, and the hell with the muscle twins. But then he disengaged. "Some other time, Krueger. Yeah."

Out in the corridor he was glad of the choice he'd made; both of the large young men were standing there, and he'd bet a stack that they'd been listening. They still didn't scare him, but not since boyhood had he taken pleasure in combat. Not since being introduced to the Slaughterhouse version.

Half-blocking his way, one of them said, "Leaving, captain?"

"That's right." Bran stepped and looked straight ahead. The man moved aside, and neither tried to stop him.

8. Fair Ball

A few hours later, picking his exact time to add the best resultant of planetary motion and rotation to his chosen course, Tregarc lifted *Inconnu* off South Forty. He did it himself because all the Hats had done it since his last turn and he didn't want to get rusty. In the direction he headed, he had several choices of destination. After a while he decided to look in on a small colony named UETopia. It was pretty well in line with several choices of a second stop, and the best part was that these shorter hauls wouldn't hurt him too much when it came to making rendezvous deadline on Number One. *I just hope to hell enough of us get there on time!*

The only trouble with UETopia was that it wasn't there. Either that or someone had entered the coordinates wrong, or the computer hiccuped on the readout. Whichever way, no UETopia. Well, the name irritated him, anyway.

Heading away from that empty space by Tinhead's guidance, *Inconnu* was up to point-two c when the comm-tech on Relliger's watch caught a beacon signal from about a radian off the ship's course. Advised, Tregare got out of bed, into shoes and pants, and grabbed a shirt which he put on while running upship.

When he got to Control, he shut up and listened. Long enough to learn that the beacon was from UET's colony Muspelheim. And that without consulting Tregare, Leanne Prestor (who wasn't even on watch, officially) had opened communications using the *Alexander the Great* ploy. Waiting until the long, transmission-delayed conversation ended and the circuit was cut, Tregare said, "Prestor. What do you think you're doing?"

She smiled at him. "Keeping our options open."

"You just closed down a bunch of mine. Why?" Mad as hell, he said, "Nobody but me decides for this ship. *Nobody*, and you know that. So tell me, fast and clear, why I don't unrate you where you stand, and pick me a new Hat."

"Pick two, then," said Frei Relliger. "We knew you were busy, and identifying us as the *Alexander* was the simplest alternative, whether you choose to land at Muspelheim or not."

It made sense, but Tregare didn't *like* it making sense, because he couldn't let these two get away with trying to run the ship on their own. Stalling, he said, "You back her on this, Relliger?"

"I do, yes."

"Then you can share the penalty." *I'm not armed. Are they?* Hell with it; either he was captain, or—"You're each fined a month's share-earnings." He paused. "Do you accept that?"

After a moment, both nodded. Hoping his relief didn't show, Tregare said, "All right. Past is past. Now let's see how we clean up this mess and turn it to *our* advantage."

Prestor wasn't done yet. "Captain, do you know what Muspelheim means?"

From childhood reading the answer clicked. "Sure. Norse myth; the land of the fire giants. Lots of vulcanism here, right?"

Prestor looked abashed. "Why—why, yes."

Abruptly, Tregare nodded. "Unless you got more questions, Leanne, what you say we get on with it?"

On points, landing didn't seem to be too bad an idea. The settlement wasn't big enough to support any large UET garrison, and the only ship currently groundside—the *Patton*—wasn't armed. Muspelheim's surface gravity was only about point-seven g, so even if refueling turned out to be a problem, *Inconnu* would have no trouble reaching any of several next-stop choices. Bran gave instructions—more detailed than were really necessary—on future contact with Muspelheim as the ship approached that world. Then he went back down to his quarters.

Eldon had been angry with him for leaving so abruptly, and when she saw him enter, she began again. He said, "Shut up, Tanit." He didn't say it loud but he didn't say it twice, either. "I had a problem upship and it couldn't wait. You could." He paused. "If you still want to. Do you?"

She looked more like wanting to sulk and argue, so he turned away and fixed himself a drink. When he sat facing her, she said, slowly, "Yes, Tregare. I do."

"Fine," said Tregare. Because, so did he.

Muspelheim's settlements, as they showed on *Inconnu*'s forward screens, lay on a narrow coastal plain. Behind that plain rose jagged-topped mountains, and Tregare saw that a number of them indeed bore smoke plumes. Evaluating the several towns and villages—plus areas obviously under cultivation—Bran guessed Muspelheim's population in the mid-five-figure range, with maybe a third living in or near the spaceport town. The port's Admin complex wasn't up to Number One's but looked about average for most colonies—UET or Hidden Worlds, either one.

He left the approach to Gonnelson, who had the watch, but reserved the landing for himself. Sitting beside the First Hat, ready to take over, Tregare watched the port move offscreen as the ship turned in preparation for sitdown. And for a moment, something caught his attention: the antenna setup on the main Admin building. Briefly he tensed, then relaxed—hell, a colony this size would naturally have missile defenses!

But now he was edgy, listening as groundside talked him in and the comm-tech on watch translated Gonnelson's monosyllables into English for the port's benefit. Absently, he noticed the squiggles on the visual monitor for that ship-ground frequency. And then, not so absently, saw squiggles that monitored frequencies he was *not* hearing.

So he remedied that lack, found the right scramble code on his second try, and caught himself an earful.

". . . to Port Control: of course I'm sure! The message just now . . ."

"Port Control to the *Patton*." Seeing the squiggle timed to be an answer, Tregare put that freq on audio, too. "You're saying that the incoming ship isn't the *Alexander*? Then what ship is it?"

"Dammit, I *told* you! It's *Inconnu* now, but it used to be the *Tamurlaine*, before the pirate Bran Tregare usurped command. And it's armed!"

"Armed?" Groundside sounded nervous. Gonnelson muttered something, and console lights showed Tregare that the First Hat had switched control over to him. The strained voice, distorted by less-than-perfect circuit tuning, continued. "Is he too close to blast with our missile defense, without endangering your own ship?"

"That's chancy." The *Patton*'s speaker hesitated, then said, "Let him land. As soon as he's near to touching down, I'll lift. *Across* him, you see? Lift, hover, and land again. Then your ground troops can attack, and clean up what's left."

Tregare cut the sound. Seeing startled looks, he said, "I heard all I need to." He hit another switch. "All-ship broadcast! Everybody strap in or hang on! Now!"

Then he attacked.

Inconnu had been coming down slow and easy. Taking his best guess, Tregare cut the force of his braking Drive and let the ship drop free; groundside's missiles would play hell tracking his angular velocity at this range. Then, closer to ground than he'd intended, he hit the preempt and fired Junior Lee's Drive close to redline max: *Inconnu* shuddered and stalled, as Tregare tipped nearly a radian to one side. He had the *Patton*'s audio signal on again, and by the yells and screaming he knew he'd made his point; that ship had caught Tregare's Drive blast at an angle and was toppling sidewise into crashing ruin.

Bran wasn't done yet. He hadn't spotted the port's missile sites, not for sure, but its guidance antennae sat atop the main Admin building. So with *Inconnu*'s Drive churning up the ground below it, but at much less than max now as the ship built altitude by mere meters, he kept the ship on a slant and walked it across the Port, across the Admin building, then with twitches that changed both the tilt and its direction, back around the area that probably held most of the missiles. And what that blast hit, it pulverized.

He looked at Gonnelson, and shrugged. "No point landing here, would you say?"

"No point."

So Tregare headed *Inconnu* straight up and lifted. Two missiles followed him, but not closely enough to worry about.

Before Muspelheim on the back screens had time to shrink from disc to point, Tregare told Gonnelson and Deverel to assemble all personnel with comm-tech training. "In the galley." When the two men looked puzzled, Bran said, "The *Patton* said something about a message. Which couldn't have come from anywhere except this ship. Which means somebody sent it. So wear your sidearms."

As they left, he began digging into the comm consoles' tape facilities. The aux positions held nothing that didn't belong there, but the main panel revealed an unlabeled tape container. With care, he withdrew it, and found it had been played to the end—and now would not rewind. The thing was warmer than it should be, so he knew the magnetic information-content no longer existed. In a hurry, he broke the box open; he wasn't surprised to find a small expended heat capsule, triggered by the tape's ending to disrupt the magnetic patterns and half-melt the plastic into a solid mass.

Hell with that, then; he went to the galley.

At least one of his people had used some initiative; besides the comm people, Eda Ghormley was there with her truth drug kit. Tregare explained the situation, then said, "I'm sorry, but to find one rotten Utie I have to inconvenience all of you. There's no other way." He heard some mumbling, but most of the group made a nod or gesture of assent. So Ghormley began her injections and Tregare asked questions.

One after another, the ratings checked out clean. Partway through, Bran was surprised to see Tanit Eldon receiving a shot. "Hey—you're not in Comm."

"I've had training, though; it's part of the UG routine, for people who might get onto ships."

"But you've already passed this stuff."

She smiled. "Under the circumstances, I prefer to ensure that there's no question. In *anybody's* mind."

Under the circumstances, yeah. The captain's lover, new on the ship, maybe needed more confirmation than most; he could see that. So in her turn he put her through the same questioning as everybody else.

The trouble was, she and everybody else passed. So over the next two days he ran *all* the crew—including Control and Engineering officers—through the interrogation. And, having heard a weird rumor that *he* was the culprit, had Ghormley run him through the procedure. Before witnesses.

He passed, too, though. So he had the ship searched for stowaways. But there weren't any.

Tregare stewed. Because of his experiences—desertion by his family, then surviving the Slaughterhouse, Butcher Korbeith and his guard Plastic Smile, the Utie Cleet Farnsworth's countermutiny—he found it hard to trust people, and he knew it. But here on his own ship, after all this time, to find a Utie traitor! Except that he *hadn't;* he knew there was one, though.

But *who*? He caught himself watching people, wondering. Then he'd shake his head; he had to trust his own people, or he'd go around the bend paranoid, like Krieg Elman.

In quarters with Tanit, both undressed but Tregare feeling no urge for sex, he talked about the problem. And ended up with no answers at all.

Frowning, she looked over to him and said, "Maybe there isn't the answer you're looking for." She cut into his protest. "No—I mean, maybe the person who fixed that tape isn't *on* the ship now. You've had people leave, haven't you, at one Port and another?" He nodded. "Then the tape could have been there for some time." Her brow wrinkled. "You had a closet Utie in your crew, let's say—someone who left ship at Earth or even before." Personnel did go groundside sometimes, though right now he couldn't put names to all of them, so he nodded.

Then shook his head. "No. Who arranged to *send* that tape?"

"Groundside did, is my bet." He knew he looked incredulous then, as she said, "The UG could have managed a similar hookup, a prearranged code group to trigger transmission *if* the proper circuits were set up in Comm."

He stood and reached for clothing. "I'm going up there and check that idea out."

"Forget it, Tregare. Those input circuits would be set to disconnect, totally, as soon as their job was done." So he flung the clothes across the room, and sat again.

His mind still gnawed the bone she'd thrown him. "Why didn't the tape do its trick at Earth?"

Her eyes widened, her brows rose. "How could I know that?"

He was thinking better now. "Two reasons I could go with. One: with all those UET ships milling around up there in orbit, nobody'd *expect* a lone Escaped maverick to show up. And two: we'd just come from Stronghold and had Saldeen's orders with us to prove it."

She smiled. "There's another possibility. Maybe your Utie didn't want any fireworks until he or she was safely offship."

Her eye-to-eye gaze moved lower. "You're feeling better now, aren't you?"

And he was.

In council, three days out from Muspelheim, Prestor was at it again. "Yes, I know it took some action to get us out safely—but all *that* killing? Tregare—what could be worth doing it?"

Exasperated, Bran found no words. Gonnelson said, "*Your* life?"

Then Tregare could laugh, as he said, "Leanne, when they're out to get you—and Muspelheim was—you don't just piss around. You give it your best shot, and hope to hell it's enough."

Tanit Eldon, first time he and she talked after Muspelheim, gave him no such crap. What she said was, "Tregare, when your neck's on the line, or your mission, you do what you have to do. The Underground taught me that." She made a one sided smile. "And I guess UET taught *you*. But not the way they intended." Relieved, Bran dropped the matter and got on to more pleasant business.

Now, though, when Frei Relliger cleared his throat, Tregare had no idea which way he was going to jump. And was relieved when the man said, "The captain's right. He couldn't afford to take chances."

So much for that. "Next order of business," said Tregare. "Where we go from here." As he pointed out, the impromptu lift-off hadn't given *Inconnu* a very good initial vector toward several of the possibilities for next choice of destination. "I punched up a holo-chart, and our best bet for fuel and time is Fair Ball." He told what he knew of the place, which wasn't much more than any member of the group could have dug out of Tinhead. Then he added, "The last I heard, Cade Moaker was heading there. And Moaker's a man I'd like to talk with again."

Since no one had any better ideas to propose, *Inconnu*'s course was swung toward the Hidden World known as Fair Ball.

Somewhat larger than Sol, the planet's primary shone whiter. Fair Ball itself, riding farther out than Earth did, had a longer year. Its orbit was tilted but its axis wasn't, much. Seasonal temperature changes were mostly due to the orbit's eccentricity. And, "Smallish radius, high average density," Tregare said. "Which puts surface gravity closer to one-gee than I'd expect." He shrugged. "Well, that's what the tape says."

Maybe because *Inconnu* was coming in on a slant from zenith, it was only about two days from landfall when Fair Ball hailed it. With a loop tape, repeatedly asking the ship to identify itself, and so forth. "If you haven't been here before, a few references might be in order."

Why bother with tape, replying? "The armed, Escaped ship *Inconnu*, Bran Tregare commanding. Did Cade Moaker make it here all right, with *Cut Loose Charlie*? If he did, he can confirm that it was on Number One he told me he was headed this way."

After the two-way transmission lag, groundside's loop tape stopped. Then a woman's voice came over the circuit. "I'm afraid Captain Moaker died a few years ago. He did mention you, though." She laughed. "Most ships' people do." A pause. "But as a double-check, to *prove* who you are, could you cite a few more names? For instance, do you know Sten Norden? Ilse Krueger? Malloy or Bernardez or Hoad or Quinlan? Rasmussen? And their ships?"

Now it was Tregare's turn to laugh. "Kickem Bernardez and Jargy Hoad I *roomed* with, back at the Slaughterhouse. Malloy and Quinlan, then, were running scoutships for summer training; I didn't know they'd Escaped." He thought back. "*Pig In The Parlor,* Malloy was going to name his ship. Krueger and Rasmussen I've met, and Derek Limmer—hell, I *got* his ship *Lefthand Thread* for him, on Freedom's Ring. Jargy has *Deuces Wild* and Kickem hasn't renamed the *Hoover* yet, far as I know."

Again the wait; then the woman, sounding impressed, said, "That's sufficient, I'd say. Now, captain, do you have any questions? And what is your estimated time of landing?"

He checked with Tinhead. "Roughly forty-eight hours from now, give or take a little, depending on where your port's longitude has rotated by the time I get there." Questions? Hmm. "What ships are in port now? And I could use some coordinates for that Port."

"You missed Quinlan's *Red Dog* by about a week, and *Strike Three* lifted yesterday, under Cyras Adopolous. So there's only *Charlie* here now. Grounded permanently, with the Nielson shut down and the nodes practically burned off in the landing here. Cade incorporated the ship as a business, and his people have done well."

Thinking about it, as the woman fed the coordinates along, then signed off, Tregare saw how a ship could operate as a going concern, groundside. Given fuel, which any spaceport had, the Drive's power systems could function as a generating plant for a fair-sized city. And few settlements had the kind of machine-shop, fabrication, and maintenance facilities a ship could muster. The skills of ships' personnel, hired out on groundside jobs, would bring in a fair grade of income. And for a ship that didn't need to fuel and resupply for space—liftoff and accel and decel and landing, and life-support systems now redundant—any reasonable cargo was good for years of profitable trading. Sure's hell, it would work!

Not that Tregare had any such ideas, but still it was interesting.

Now Bran checked the planetary data. Fair Ball had two major continents, antipodally located and both mostly in their respective temperate zones, semi-connected by strings of island chains. Baseline Port was on the northern land mass, about the middle of it in longitude and a few hundred kilos north of the southern shore. Most of that distance was desert, which was why no attempt had been made toward the more usual river-mouth settlement. The port was on the major north-south river, though, so it had waterborne access to the highlands farther north, where the rudimentary charts indicated such activities as mining, herd grazing, lumber harvesting, and (nearer to the port) agriculture.

Not a bad setup, Tregare thought. With a population of close to six figures, even spread out a lot, this place could prosper. Well, he'd seen all he needed, for now.

A little over twelve hours before *Inconnu* was due to plow air, Tregare was visited in quarters by Leanne Prestor and Frei Relliger. Maybe feeling in need of mutual support, most of the time they held hands. White-knuckled, Tregare noticed. Not the least bit at ease, obviously.

He offered drinks but got no takers. Well, the hell with it; it's their shoe so let *them* drop it. Relliger couldn't seem to decide what to say but eventually Prestor got it out. Yes, they both wanted off, groundside, and hoped Tregare wouldn't make any difficulty about whatever pay-off shares they might have coming. "No problem," said Tregare. "You figure 'em, I'll check 'em. If there's any real difference and a rerun doesn't straighten it out, there's always arbitration."

He thought Relliger would argue but the man didn't. Instead, Leanne began talking, high-pitched, about her feelings. "I know it's awful, us both deserting you like this. But we have to—well, I—" Bran gathered that the two planned to get on another ship someday. Not hardly right away, Tregare thought, because Leanne was pregnant by purpose, and most ships didn't favor officers who were pregnant or in charge of infants.

Bran said nothing of that side of things. "You're not deserting me. You're looking for where you fit better." Not allowing them a word in edgewise, "You're both competent, able ship's officers, but you don't belong on an armed ship and never did. Not one like this, that has to fight UET any way it can. Any way *I* can. So you can get off here with my blessings." They looked skeptical. "I mean that; you've both done good work."

Leanne Prestor shook her head. "I don't understand you. You can be such a mean, ruthless bastard—but now at the last minute we tell you we want off and you're *nice* to us. Why?"

He grinned. "Not nice. Fair, is all." Why was he always having to explain simple facts to people? But he did: "Outside of UET, captains who aren't fair don't last very long." He didn't want her getting soppy on him, so he said, "But against UET I can't afford fair. Just mean. Mean as I can think of, and the more the better." He looked at her. "You got it?"

"Maybe. I guess so." Changing the subject, she asked who might be replacing her and Relliger in the Hat berths.

"One I've decided, one I don't know about, yet. No idea, I mean. But that's my problem, not yours. Maybe there'll be a candidate waiting, groundside."

Then the two relaxed, and Relliger did have a drink. Leanne, being pregnant, settled for fruit juice.

When they left captain's digs, Tregare felt mostly relieved. Now he had his *options* open. Whatever they might turn out to be.

Coming in for the approach, Tregare checked the numbers and put on a little extra decel, to allow Baseline Port to pass the terminator and be well into daylight before *Inconnu* got there. Then he moved over to the aux pilot position and gave

Gonnelson the landing chore. It was either Relliger's or Prestor's turn, but they were getting off; Gonnelson could use the practice.

Inconnu's main forward screen showed Fair Ball's primary off to the left; thus, Tregare was nearing the planet from "behind" but landing against its rotational velocity. Tanit, sitting beside Tregare at an extra comm-panel position because she'd never viewed a landing, asked why he wanted to buck the rotation instead of going with it.

So he had to explain. Not that he minded; he could use a little distraction. "Far as need for decel goes," he said, "yes, sure, we have rotation working against us, but orbital velocity *with* us. So—"

"Why can't you have both?"

"On account of I want us to land in daylight." Using both hands, he gestured the layout of the vectors and hoped he was getting it straight—knowing something, and telling it, were sometimes different. But she seemed to understand. So he added, deciding it was too much work to get the exact [illegible] right now, "If that was Earth out there, the ratio of orbital velocity to rotational is about two hundred to three."

That part she got, just fine. And then pretty soon they were plowing air and setting down, Gonnelson's touch being as smooth as always.

Gonnelson didn't want to go visiting, and Prestor and Relliger were no longer connected with ship's business, so Tregare took Hain Deverel with him groundside to meet the "local admiral," Captain Gannes. Nobody said what he was captain of, but the stooped, elderly man greeted the two men in his office in Admin, and introduced his assistant, Marisa Hanen. The woman, round-faced and blue-eyed with a high forehead that looked to be going higher before too long, stood nearly Tregare's height and probably outweighed him. Her soft, clear voice belied the heavy-boned bulk of her, as she said, "I suppose you'll want, first thing, to make a search of all our computer entries from visiting ships. And I hope you'll have data to give us, in return."

With a smile, Tregare nodded. "Yes, I think so. Do you have a system of cross-checking all the entries, to give an overall picture of ships' movements in space-time?"

Gannes answered. "We're working on it. Cade Moaker

gave us the idea, when he brought *Charlie* here. It's a complex problem, though; I can't say we have the system running smoothly as yet."

Shrugging, Tregare said, "And what with the Long View, ships' times differing so much, maybe nobody ever will. But whatever you do have, I'm sure it'll be a help to both of us."

Then he asked about local customs regarding trade, refueling, and such. Gannes shook his head. "Out of my bailiwick. That's the Board of Trade, Suth Fairgrave's group. They meet down on the second floor, but they're not in session again until—let me see—three days from now. I hope the delay won't inconvenience you."

"Depends. Do I have to dicker *with* this Board for everything, or can I set up tentative deals for their okay, assuming they do?"

Gannes looked embarrassed. Hanen said, "A little of both. Officially you can deal freely. Unofficially, if Fairgrave doesn't like it, you may have a problem."

The situation felt entirely too damned familiar; Tregare felt himself tensing up, but said only, "Is his word final?"

Two headshakes. Gannes said, "Carries considerable weight, though."

Rising to leave, Tregare hoped his smile looked nicer on the outside than it felt on the inside. "So does mine."

Then he said polite good-byes, and he and Deverel left the building to walk under Fair Ball's pale sky that held a great amount of haze and only a touch of blue.

Back on *Inconnu*, after a quick lunch, Tregare arranged with groundside for a direct feed from the Admin computer to his ship. Needing nothing more than a word-readout display, he routed the feed down to his quarters and went there to browse at leisure.

Some of the entries were interesting but for a time he found nothing that seemed important. Quinlan on *Red Dog* had left the barest of info; obviously the man was a loner, so no point in trying to make contact with him. Ilse Krueger had been here, but some time ago, before he and she had met in person. Other people he knew—news of them was being relayed secondhand at the nearest. Well, that's how it *would* be. . . .

The ship *Strike Three*, that he'd missed by only a few days, interested Tregare. Its entered log was more detailed than most but still only hinted at the outlines of some obviously important events. At one entry he whistled—the *captain* of this ship had been bought out and got off here. Zelde M'tana: not a name he'd ever heard. So he thumbed the readout back a way; maybe this ship's history could use some looking into.

Strike Three was the ship's fourth name. It had started out, under UET, as the *Great Khan*, and its last UET commander had been Emilo Czerner. Hmm. All right—Tregare recognized another name or two. Escape had put command to Ragir Parnell, and the ship became *Chanticleer.* Tregare recalled, from Slaughterhouse days, the tall, serious cadet captain under whom Jargy Hoad had served after Jargy's transfer. A good man, yes. And then—the log got a little mixed up, there, as if entered by someone not used to the chore. Hmm . . .

Some more names he didn't know, and then this Zelde M'tana showed up as Third Hat. Tregare checked back. At first the woman wasn't on the roster at all; then, after Escape she was sharing captain's quarters. In between, she'd killed a Utie who wore a power suit! And then she came up with a Hat berth. He grinned.

Then he didn't. There had been a UET countermutiny, cat's-pawed by a UET hideout who had shipped as cargo. Cargo? Oh, yes—a hold full of women consigned to the cribs on UET's mining world, Iron Hat. *Cargo, huh*. Eyes narrowed, he read on.

Cyras Adopolous: after Escape, Parnell's First Hat. Disabled in a brawl in Parleyvoo on Terranova. UET country. What happened to the rest of the chain of command, Tregare couldn't figure, but all at once there was Zelde M'tana as Acting Captain, and a while later the adjective got lost. M'tana crushed the countermutiny but Ragir Parnell died; the log didn't say just how. And while she commanded, the ship was called *Kilimanjaro*.

Tregare punched for side-data on M'tana. It looked clear enough. She'd been bought off *Strike Three* and was looking to buy a Hat berth on some other ship. Well, he was short a Hat. It couldn't hurt to see and talk with her.

That evening, Bran and Tanit dined in his quarters and later took themselves to bed for a while. He was thinking, now that she'd had time to make a place for herself among the crew, to establish her bona fides, she might as well move in with him—assuming she still wanted to.

Their lovemaking varied a lot; on this occasion, when things were getting close to winding up, they switched to her being on top. To get some synchronizing feedback for their moves, Bran grasped her forearms as she braced herself on them. "Ow! That *hurts*, dammit!" It was a real yelp, she made then.

Startled and distracted, "What? *What* hurts?"

"My arm. I burned it today; the heat-marker slipped when I was marking some cargo crates."

"Sorry." In the dim light he couldn't see the burn but he took her word for it and shifted his grip toward the wrist. "Better?"

She nodded, but the momentum was broken. Eventually Tregare came to climax, but Tanit couldn't. "It's not your fault," she said afterward. "I can't take pain much; it spoils my concentration." Sipping the drink he'd fixed for her, she said, "Maybe it's just as well I'll be groundside the next few days."

"Groundside? What—"

"Yes. What's the point of leaving Earth if I don't get to see anything of the other worlds? Please, Bran?"

He didn't like the idea much, but in fairness he had to agree.

Over the next three days he took care of ship's business that didn't need Board of Trade approval, at least not in the preliminary stages. He set up dickers for cargo *versus* supplies, got *Inconnu*'s water tanks topped off, put in tentative offers for new cargo, and got the John Hancock of Captain Gannes on his schedule for liberty parties. Actually that was his first concern; the other matters were less urgent. And in all the dickering, the only item that seemed to trouble anyone was fuel for the Drive. Everything else, Tregare gathered, the Board would rubber-stamp. Fuel, though . . .

He couldn't figure it out, so he decided to wait and see. Meanwhile, Relliger and Prestor were packed to leave ship, so next morning Tregare requisitioned a groundcar and small open trailer, and drove them to a wood-built inn called River House, on the outskirts of the town of First Base. He left the trailer there, and Relliger to unload it, and took Leanne Prestor to City Hall where she could register herself and

Relliger with Immigration. Tregare hadn't been into First Base before but Hain Deverel had, and had given Tregare a good description of where the main points were. When Prestor came out again, Bran drove her back to the inn and rehitched the now empty trailer, as Relliger emerged from the building and said, "In case we don't see you again, join us inside for a farewell drink or two."

"Thanks, but I need to get back to the ship now." Tregare shook the man's hand. Prestor looked to be feeling kissy but also settled for a handshake. Smiling then, glad to be done with all this ritual that didn't *move* anything, Bran said, "Good luck to both of you." And got into the car and drove it back to the Port.

Back onship, he felt restless. He missed Tanit; of all his ship's people, she was the one he could *talk* with best, to keep from brooding his way back into paranoiac suspicion. And she'd gone off to see some mines and some herd-grazing camps; wasn't due back for several days yet.

He checked his chrono. Nearly an hour until he had to be at the trade meeting. Time for a drink. He made it a short one, though.

Although the Board of Trade began its meeting shortly after noon, *Inconnu*'s business didn't receive consideration until nearly four hours later. Working up a slow burn, Bran Tregare sat and watched the proceedings. Especially he watched and evaluated Chairman Suth Fairgrave, a heavy-set, red-faced man with thinning sandy hair and a loud, ponderous voice. At their initial handshake Tregare learned that Fairgrave was a knuckle crusher; Bran gave him no leverage and assumed a poker-faced grin to mask the effort needed to withstand the crushing grip. Equally deadpan, the chairman showed no disappointment at his failure to bully *Inconnu*'s captain.

Throughout the afternoon Fairgrave did most of the talking, at great and unnecessary length. Even the simplest, most routine items, it seemed to Bran, took hell-and-forever for Fairgrave to understand and approve. Yet clearly the man was not stupid; rather, he seemed to enjoy making everyone else hang by the thumbs.

Fairgrave's age, Tregare couldn't guess. He was a youngish-looking man who somehow gave the impression that the appearance of youth wouldn't last much longer; his physical movements had more speed than precision. All in all, Bran disliked him more than not.

After the first half-hour Tregare dismissed the other seven Board members from serious consideration; whatever Fairgrave said, most of them went along with him. Bran did catch and recall some of the names: Zinsmann was the gaunt one, the balding Farley smiled a lot and said very little, Horner was the dark-haired woman who might be interesting on a more personal basis. Chavez made a few comments that showed quickness of mind. The other three, including the spectacular redheaded woman teetering on the far edge of her prime, bore names Bran couldn't remember. And after a while Captain Gannes' assistant Marisa Hanen joined the group but didn't say much.

Boiling inside, trying not to show it, Tregare waited through the tedious session. Finally his bladder called recess on him—coffee was at hand and boredom had made him drink too much of it. When he returned to the meeting, Fairgrave said, "*Well*, captain. We've been waiting for you."

Tregare's patience, never one of his strong points, stretched almost to breaking. He took one deep breath and said, "Then I'll try to cover my part of the agenda as quickly as possible." He'd brought his own readout sheets and now, sitting, rattled off the first items.

Fairgrave interrupted. "One at a time, captain; one at a time. Now the matter of water: you took it upon yourself to top off without Board approval?"

I don't believe this! "Excuse me, Chairman. Are you saying that there was any question of my ship being *denied* water?"

Headshake. "No, of course not. But—"

"But nothing moves here until you say so. Is that it?"

"Well, there *is* the matter of protocol, and—"

"If you'd been available, I'd have asked. You weren't, not to me, until I got back from the john just now. Fairgrave, a ship's needs take some time, and they can't wait on one man's preset schedules. You understand that?"

Face redder than usual, the man half rose. "Do *you* understand, captain, that I—" He looked around the table and corrected himself, "—that *we* are responsible for trade at this port? And that we do not take our responsibility lightly?"

Frantically, Bran tried to think of an answer that would be logical without being totally insulting to this bureaucrat. *Oh, the hell with it!* "It's your *authority* you take so seriously you take it to bed with you." Overriding Fairgrave's protests, Tregare slammed a fist to the table. "Well, you've run into something, Fairgrave. What it is, is that you will approve this readout or you will give me a counter-offer on the whole list, and I'll consider it, and we'll dicker. But the whole thing, not one dinky piece after another." He handed the readout over. "Look at it, and fast. It's simple enough." *Even for you!*

Now the Chairman did his quibbling, item by item, in mumbles to himself alone; the process took nearly as long as before but Tregare could see no reasonable way to protest. Foot-draggers always have the edge. . . .

And eventually, nearly an hour later, Suth Fairgrave stated his reservations—one at a time, naturally, until Tregare barked out, "The overall figure, peace take you!"

"Well, for everything except fuel, which of course must be treated separately—" and while Tregare was digesting that one he followed the man's figures with the top of his head, decided the percentage of gouge was too small to argue about, and nodded.

"All right. Seal it approved and get your people moving stuff right now. Nightshift rates will be paid, but because *your* stalling makes it necessary, the Port pays half the differential."

He thought Fairgrave was going to buck that point, but the man didn't. So Tregare said, "Now let's get to fuel."

Some hours later he wished they'd done that part first, when he wasn't so tired.

They'd talked and yelled it and done a certain amount of cursing back and forth; now, several hours past normal time for eating dinner, stalemate held. Standard rates for the fuel Tregare needed were sixty thousand Weltmarks; Fairgrave was demanding twice that, *unless:* "Tregare, we have to begin hitting back at UET. With your ship you could take the Far Corner colony and hold it against them. If you'll agree, we can—"

It was stupid; it was all wrong; Bran tried to explain why. During the times when the Chairman recited his piece, over and over again, Tregare thought about his options. He didn't *have* to go along with this crap; if necessary, he had enough fuel to wipe this Port and take what he needed by sheer plunder. Or, using his remaining scout, he could accomplish the same thing with much less damage. Except that he didn't *want* to have to do any such thing to a Hidden World. To his own people, who were all he had to work for. Even *this* clabberhead . . .

So he gave it one more try. Standing, to give himself that much extra impact, again he whomped fist to desk. At vision's edge he sensed a tall figure entering the room, but had no time to glance aside and see who it might be. "You *will* refuel me, just as the Compact states. Or I'll orbit a beacon, blacklisting you with every ship that comes into signal range."

Fairgrave played his vocal record again. ". . . matter of price, same as with the food. Now if you'll undertake our mission . . ."

Tregare sat down. "Your *stupid* mission." By this time he hardly listened to his own words. ". . . hold Far Corner against UET?" A little cussing, and then, "You think I'll waste my life on that mudball?"

It went on and it went on, Fairgrave saying how the taking of Far Corner was *important*, and Bran answering, "You wouldn't know important if it bit you on the leg. I—" Seeing a shadow on the desk in front of him, he looked up to see who was casting it.

She was tall, big-boned, and very black. Her strong-featured face betrayed her age not at all, and her ships-issue jumpsuit outlined a trim figure, definitely female but still ripening. As she stood over him, saying nothing, he noticed that one earlobe carried a heavy-looking gold ring—and that the other ear had no lobe at all. Those features were obvious because her tightly-curling hair was clipped to the semblance of a tight cap of black felt. "You!" Tregare said. "Who are you? What's your business here?"

"Zelde M'tana." Deep-voiced for a woman, still she spoke softly. "My business, it's with the computer terminal over there. Go right on yelling—it won't bother me none." And without waiting for an answer she stepped past, toward the terminal.

Fairgrave began talking again, Bran cutting in now and then, trying to reach some kind of understanding. Possibly because of M'tana's gibe, they kept the noise level down now. But none of it helped matters, and when the tall woman came back past Tregare he welcomed the distraction. "You get done what you wanted—M'tana, is it?"

She looked down to him. "Some part of it, yeah."

Marisa Hanen began to protest that a very important meeting was being interrupted, but Tregare cut in. "What else you need, M'tana?"

"To talk with you. Stay all night here, you still get no place—and you know it. I bet nobody's had dinner, though it's late for that." True enough, and Tregare's stomach confirmed it. "Tregare—buy me a drink on your ship, and a meal with it. We need to talk."

Predictably, Suth Fairgrave began to shout. "—most arrogant, ridiculous thing—you walk in here and—"

That did it; Bran slapped the desk, and stood. "If *you* don't like it, it has to make sense." He declared the meeting recessed. "Come on, M'tana—you just bought yourself some drinks and dinner."

"*And* talk."

He touched her shoulder. "Yeah, that too." And they left.

Outside the building she detoured to a waiting aircar; near as Tregare could see, she handed something to the man inside it, then came out carrying a travel case. Rejoining Bran she said, "Ole, my pilot. Flew me down from upriver a ways. I was paying him, just now."

"Sure." He walked her over to *Inconnu*, up the ramp, and then straight to his quarters. On the intercom he ordered their dinners from the galley and offered drinks. She chose bourbon; they clinked glasses and sipped.

It was about time, Tregare thought, to get down to business. "First now—tell me who you are." What he wanted was *her* version of what he'd read from *Strike Three*'s computer-entered log. What she handed him was an envelope; inside was a letter of recommendation signed by Cyras Adopolous, Captain. Knowing part of the facts already but not prepared to admit it, Tregare scanned the sheet. ". . . joined ship at Earth . . . chosen for training . . ." Communications, navigation, weapons, the power suit: these things caught Bran's attention, and so did her test marks, scored by Adopolous and the late Ragir Parnell. ". . . appointed Third Hat, then Acting Second; assumed command in emergency and so functioned for the duration of the trip. Under trying circumstances, performed all duties effectively."

So far, so good—but now, maybe, a little pressure wouldn't hurt. Handing the papers back, he said, "Yes. I've skimmed the bulletin-board circuit. So you're the one who wants a Hat berth." She nodded, and he sank the hook. "Worked up from cargo, did you—all the way to captain, for a while—by way of the skipper's bed?"

She looked puzzled, not angry, as he explained that her ship's log didn't list her—and a number of others—at all, until after Escape, and then suddenly she was in captain's digs with Parnell.

Unsmiling, she shook her head. "It wasn't like you think. Tell you sometime, maybe. For now, I'll stand on what Dopples wrote."

Delivery of two food trays interrupted Bran's reply. He handed one to her. "Eat now, M'tana. Talk later."

Afterward, sipping tart wine with a tangy afterbite, they talked. Yes, she wanted to buy into a Hat berth; well, he had one open, and briefly he explained why. Then he went to questions: her background, knowledge, experience, ships she knew about. All of it.

The background surprised him. He'd heard of the Wild Kids on Earth, gangs of fugitive children who roamed semi-deserted towns and countryside, forming their own societies and dodging UET's Welfare roundups. Zelde M'tana had *been* one of them. "The worst was the Committee Police their own damned selves," she said. "I got one of those, with a spear gun, but the raid went wrong; that's how come I got caught." She was skipping a lot of it; he could see that. But anyway, she wound up as cargo on the *Great Khan*, headed for the cribs of Iron Hat to service miners and keep them happy for UET. And then, instead, Escape . . .

They were out of wine; he opened another bottle. "Yeah. I wondered what training you had. Now I know—from UET, nothing. Out on the loose, though, you learned command before you were fourteen. But if Parnell hadn't logged it, that you by yourself took out an armed man in a power suit—"

"It took me luck; he stood at the edge, when I jumped to kick." She told how the armored man had slammed back and forth, falling, how it seemed his shrieks would never stop. For a moment her young eyes looked haunted.

So he changed the subject. "The thing is, you won. Now tell me, what ships did you meet, or speak?" Well, after Escape they'd had a skew pass with Bernardez, but neither he nor Parnell admitted they were Escaped. At Parleyvoo on

Terranova they'd barely missed Malloy, and his message hinted that "soon there'll be a pig in the parlor." Tregare explained the reference; Malloy had then been preparing his own Escape. Zelde herself had spoken Ilse Krueger on *Graf Spee*, in space, and Ilse had confirmed that she would join Tregare's effort. "Well, I figured she would." Then he had to explain the loose information net a little more.

And, feeling that maybe he'd had a drink too many, Tregare spoke his own mind a little. "Fairgrave's idea—he has the wrong place, is all. Stronghold! That's the key." *I'm talking too much!* So he went back to asking questions.

Her answers came freely. "No, I never lifted off or landed for real, yet. Showed good on the sims, though." On weapons, "You know we wasn't armed, the ship. I know just portables."

So far, she sounded good. One more thing, though, Tregare needed to learn. "How did you get up to captain? Tell it all."

"Ragir's hurts brought him down," and in the saying, her own face showed pain. "Then Dopples, out flat so long. He took a knife in the gut at Parloyvoo. Went after the bandit that cut my ear—" She touched the lobeless one.

"He saved your life, did he?"

She frowned, he could see she was trying to figure how to say it. "Not that. The other two I killed, myself. What he did, Dopples he brought me back that part of my ear, and the ring in it. And killed him the one that tooken it. But that gutstab brought him real low, a long time." Her mouth twitched, almost to a smile but not quite. "And that there was when he didn't even *like* me. But still we was shipmates; you see that?"

"Yeah. I do. Then what happened?" It got complicated. M'tana told a story pretty well, except that Tregare got lost in sidelights that were obviously important to the woman but bogged him down in more unfamiliar names than he could keep track of. Especially since he was busy dealing with the fact that Zelde M'tana impressed him a lot more than anyone had in quite some time.

"Tzane was in line for Acting Captain but wouldn't take it, so that put me leapfrogging her. Some didn't like that; I had to kick ass a lot—like before, with Honcho, a time back." Tregare couldn't remember who Honcho was. Somebody from when Zelde was still with the Wild Kids, he thought.

"Carlo never got over me making Third when he was

bumped for screwing up. So when he had it again, that's how Franzel, the Utie hideout, stuck her hooks in him to try the takeover." Peace on a mountain—the *intensity* of her, now! Blinking back tears, she said, "If I hadn't of had to go fight, right then, maybe Ragir'd not've died." She shook her head. "Anyway, I got to the power suit we had left—it worked good enough, except no way to use the projector that went with it, and—and I took the ship back, is all."

Not meaning to, Tregare laughed. She looked at him; he reached to squeeze her hand, then refilled her glass. "Hell, M'tana—in a way we're *twins*, you and I!" And he told her of the *Tamurlaine*'s Escape and Cleet Farnsworth's countermutiny, and how Bran himself, in a power suit, pretty well cleaned the ship of Uties.

Looking more relaxed then, she continued. "Well, when we got to here, nobody except me to run the ship all that way, too many couldn't live with it. Cargo to captain, me. I had to sell off. You see it?"

"Sure. On *Inconnu*, though, you wouldn't have that problem. All I'd log for record is what Adopolous gave you to show around." He paused. "I could use you on here, M'tana. But the question is, can I afford you?"

"What's that mean?"

"Weltmarks—I need a lot, maybe you gathered, and I have only the Hat berths to peddle for them." He thought he knew what she'd say next so he didn't let her say it. "Don't offer to come aboard as a rating—I'd never ship an ex-officer in a pride-hurting job. Too risky; you people found that out with—what's his name?"

"Carlo. Carlo Mauragin. But I—"

"So if you can't afford to buy a berth, you're out. I'm sorry."

"Sorry, yeah. What kind of figure you got, on Second Hat?"

"Two hundred thousand. Do you have it?"

Her headshake wasn't a simple negative. "What I got, or what I don't—seems you're pricing kind of high, though."

With impatience, he gestured. "You heard what they're trying to do to me here! I *need*—"

No hesitation; she said, "One-forty, I'll go. Out of that, I'll see you fueled."

"No." It wasn't enough. He swallowed some wine. "That leaves me only twenty thousand fluid credit from the deal. I need more than that, a lot more."

Totally surprising him, the woman laughed. "You *got* more."

She handed him a printout sheet, and while he tried to figure it, she said, "See? I *own* that fuel—bought it at regular price and you get it the same way. Leaves you—"

"Eighty thousand clear, yeah!" Hmm, she'd bought a fair amount of food, too. He looked more closely. "You—the time code on this tape—"

"That's right." For the first time she smiled freely. "Heard the argument, you see, and—"

Not meaning to, he slammed his glass down so hard it broke, and leaned back, laughing. "*That's* what you were doing on the computer? Buying up fuel before Fairgrave changed prices officially?"

She nodded. "Seemed like a good move."

Twice Bran pumped his right fist up and out. On the intercom he called Control; Gonnelson had the watch. Tregare told him to advise Port Admin that *Inconnu's* business with the Board could wait until next day, midmorning. Then he signed out and sat back. "All right, Second Hat M'tana—and when I have the fuel and the eighty thousand that's who you are on this ship, long as you can hack it—let's have a drink."

They were back to bourbon; a deal like that, Bran thought, deserved more than wine. After the first sip he said, "You want to stay here tonight? Or do you have things to take care of, in town?"

She didn't—or nothing that couldn't wait. "No—Second Hat quarters on here sounds fine."

But that wasn't exactly what he'd meant. Tanit was gone off someplace and this woman *stirred* him. Without quite lying, he implied that the Hat quarters weren't available yet, and said, "What I had in mind, M'tana, was right here."

First she paused, but before he could say more: "You said you was shorthanded—means you got space. Somewhere I can be, for now." Her hand waved off any interruption. "One thing you should know, Tregare. My men—*I'm* the one does the picking." While he thought that one over, she said, "This change anything? I mean—you want some other Second Hat—and get your fuel someplace else, too?"

For a moment, anger came, but then he saw the tension in her face, and felt his own relax. *She's been through a helluva lot!* "No problem. You're right—there's space. There's time, too."

"Wasn't out to mad you up. Just had to say it."

And Tregare had to laugh. Both of them standing now, he gripped her arms, holding her face to face with him. "If you couldn't stand up to me, M'tana, how could you stand up *for* me?" Now he touched the lobeless ear. "Tell me about that sometime, will you? The whole thing, I mean."

"Sure. It wasn't so much."

"I'll bet." Hands on her shoulders now, he shook her, but only gently. "Stick with me, M'tana, you'll have your own ship again someday. And maybe more."

Talk time seemed to be over. He showed her to a clean, freshly-supplied Chief Rating's cabin and left her there. Back in quarters he had a small nightcap and thought about the entire evening, deciding that except for the one disappointment it could hardly have gone better. *That one's a tiger.* And tomorrow he'd promote Hain Deverel to Third, and have a full quota of watch officers again.

9. The Islands

The Board of Trade meeting took twenty minutes. Fairgrave didn't like it, but nothing said he *had* to like it. For the next two days matters moved fast and without interference, and on a sunny, characteristically hazy midmorning, the day after Tanit Eldon returned on sked, *Inconnu* prepared to lift.

At council, held in Control, Tregare had jockeyed coordinates out of Tinhead and maneuvered them on one of the aux screens. He wished he had a holographic projector working, but the ship's had been inoperative since someone's energy beam slagged its innards during Escape. So Bran made do with what he had, trusting Tinhead to follow directions and swing perspectives correctly.

Noting the distances and angles between various UET colonies and Hidden Worlds, translating these into time and costs and fuel and risks, the group reached a consensus. Most of it, Tregare liked. Their first destination, though, a UET world listed as The Islands, he wished he knew more about. All Tinhead had to offer was that the planet's surface was mostly water with nothing you could really call a continent, that its major resource seemed to be fuel ore, and that it was obviously the most time-efficient stop they could make. So, with some reluctance, Bran agreed to it. And out in this part of space he figured they could still get away with the *Alexander the Great* schtick.

The liftoff he assigned to Zelde M'tana. When she protested "But I never done this!" he said it was time she tried. He didn't mention that sitting alongside her he would have the takeover switch in case of need; she would know that much.

Before she could ask for instructions he said, "Just take it up the way you'd prefer to ride it," and tried not to show his delight when she boosted exactly the way he himself would have done if he were in a little hurry but no real emergency. Straight up, then bending half a radian toward rendezvous with the gas-giant Bran had pegged to give them a sling-turn boost. When she finished setting course, she turned to him, and he said, "Rock steady, M'tana. Not a wobble." And before she could answer, added, "On the sims, now, you might want to practice landings." First she looked puzzled, then nodded, and grinned at him.

With two new Hats to acclimate, Tregare wanted to bring Hain Deverel along fast, too. But the slingshot turn was trickier than Bran cared to load on someone with Deverel's limited experience. Instead, he took it himself but put the new Third alongside him, using controls that didn't affect the ship's moves but made a record of what the ship *would* have done. "That way," Bran said, "we can compare after, and see which of us made the least mistakes. Okay?"

Deverel nodded. "It's a good training system."

The turn ran on tracks. Then, comparing Tregare's tape with Deverel's on splitscreen, they saw that the Third had overcontrolled early-on but made quick recovery and came out as close to exact course as Bran had. "All right, Hain. Next time you do it yourself, while I take a nap."

Deverel had to know Tregare was joking, but his expression showed he appreciated the compliment.

Once course and timing were determined, Tregare went down to Stores to see what shape the ship's inventory was in. He got a pleasant surprise; after working first with Renni Lofall and then with Tanit Eldon, Storesmaster Groden had begun to learn the new inventory system and was doing well with it. The stooped, middle-aged man had shed the grumpy manner Bran had accepted for so long; now he was accommodating and even cheerful. So Tregare hinted, broadly, that another promotion was in store.

"Well, thanks, cap'n; I'd like that. Could you stretch that and boost my assistant, too? Mayly Dunbar—she's not here right now—she's still only a Second rating. And she may have to fill my job, not too long from now."

Tregare's brows raised. "You want off the ship, Groden?"

Headshake. "Not me. I'm happier on here than I ever was. It's my arthritis, wants off. The gee-changes, see? More and more, they give me pure hell. But I'm good for a while yet."

"I hope so. Have you seen Eda Ghormley about the problem?" Ghormley, *Inconnu's* closest answer to a full-fledged medic, might be able to help or might not.

"No, not yet. But maybe it's a good idea, at that."

Until *Inconnu* was set on a straight-accel heading, Tregare had had little time to be with Tanit Eldon: briefly, the night of her return, they'd been together, but not since then. Now, though, Bran could relax a bit; he and she arranged a dinner and evening in his quarters, and, as usual, she arrived on time.

After the hug-and-kiss greeting, after he'd changed two empty glasses into full ones, they sat. He said, "What did you learn about Fair Ball? That interested you, I mean?" But he didn't listen too closely, as she talked about commerce along Main River, and mining and agriculture and the herding of meat animals. He was looking at her, trying to see her as he first had done, to see if she had changed, and how.

Well, the hair was different; hair grows, and gets chopped back. The top frizz and short back-and-sides had changed to a full smooth cap, neat at the edges. And she wore less makeup now. But, as always, she looked good to him.

So he was puzzled to realize that somewhere along the line he'd decided *not* to ask her to move in with him. Not just yet, anyway. He liked her; he needed her to talk with; nowadays she made bed a delight. But still . . . he decided that maybe the problem was, it still bothered him that she'd insisted on being away from him for over a week when he really felt need for her.

So for now he said nothing about the roomies idea. After dinner, though, Bran enjoyed their activities very much.

Officers didn't usually work projector turrets, but Tregare wanted M'tana checked out on them anyway. "On account of when it hits the fan," he told her, "nobody ever knows who might have to do what." In her usual quiet way, she agreed. And by now he knew the woman well enough to realize she didn't bother to disagree about small stuff, but when she did balk, she truly meant it. He conducted himself accordingly.

On the firing-run simulations up in Turret Six, at first the tall woman couldn't seem to master the problems of coordination: when she kept her heterodyne indication to a circle the range lights got away from her, and vice-versa. Finally Tregare cut the sim in mid-run. M'tana turned to look at him as he said, "What's the matter? Do you have any problems seeing?"

"Not like you mean that, I don't think." She scowled. "But, I watch the circle, I lose the range lights. Or t'other way 'round."

Tregare's sigh was relief. "Oh, *that*. I should have told you. Don't look back and forth. Unfocus your eyes a little, so you see it all at once."

She nodded. "Makes sense. You want to start that thing again?" And after a run that showed flashes of accuracy and another that improved it a lot, she seemed to have the knack. Bran ran her through the rest of the series; her scores weren't great, as yet, but he saw that with practice she could be one hell of a gunner.

Shutting the sim down, he said, "That buys you a dinner. My place, in half an hour. Okay?"

Climbing down from the gunner's seat, she said, "Sure. I—" And just as one foot touched the deck, *Inconnu* gave a lurch. Not a big one, just the watch officer making an accel correction, but it caught her off balance and she fell against the console's rounded corner, hitting her head.

Before Tregare could get to her, she was standing, but her eyes didn't look focused. He saw the skin at the right side of her forehead coming back from an indentation, leaving a red mark but no cut, and the red fading slowly. He put an arm around her shoulders, in support. "Hey! You're all right. There's no—"

No blood, he was going to say, but surprisingly she shoved at him, separating them. "Don't never do that!"

"Do *what*? All I—M'tana, *are* you all right?"

"Trying to ease me, you was. Don't never. I can't—dunno why, but it puts me dizzy. Can't think straight. A long time I didn't know what done me that way. Learned a while back, though. So—" She touched the bruise, winced a little and shook her head.

Carefully, he said, "Is dinner still on, Zelde?"

"Sure." She grinned. "Can't hurt a Wild Kid, hitting her in the *head*."

During and after the dinner, Bran didn't feed his Second Hat too much booze. Possibility of concussion, and all. But she seemed to be tracking fully. Several days later, when she racked up an average score of 60 in the turret with a top run of 68, he repeated the invitation and this time didn't ration the bourbon. Well, by now he knew that Zelde M'tana was good at holding her liquor because she knew how to *monitor* herself. Tregare appreciated that skill, since it was one of his own, too.

Still curious about this woman with the unorthodox background, he asked questions. Some she answered, some she wouldn't, and some she simply didn't know. Such as her ages, either bio or chrono. "Back on Earth, what year it was, nobody never told me. The Utie woman, one as put me on the *Great Khan*, she guessed me fourteen or fifteen, maybe. Could of been wrong, and said so. And from there, bringing it up to now—" Her brow furrowed. "Eighteen, maybe twenty bio, best guess I got." Shrugging, "Ain't like it mattered."

She seemed so much older, so matured by experience. But that happens, Tregare thought, when you're up against the Long View.

Now she talked more freely. Tregare began to wish he'd known more of Ragir Parnell, the man she still obviously mourned. She'd saved his life at Escape, moved into captain's digs to care for him, overcome total ignorance of ships' ways to earn a rating and then abrupt, unexpected elevation to Third Hat. "And weren't Ragir, put me up for it. Dopples done it, Dopples not even liking me then, 'cause he hated women as dealt on their men's rank." Shaking her head, "That, I never done. And finally Dopples knew it."

Other events on the multi-named ship, Tregare couldn't get so clear. It wasn't that M'tana couldn't do brief, solid reports, but now she was ranging back through memories that held a lot of feeling. There was something about a Policebitch at Terranova who bluffed her way aboard ship just at liftoff time and turned out to be an Underground agent making her own individual Escape. Tregare couldn't figure that one out, but decided he didn't need to.

With *Inconnu* on decel toward The Islands, Bran keyed Tinhead to the fake *Alexander* log and did a little creative updating. Then he gathered his Control officers plus Junior Lee Beauregard, to look through it for discrepancies and suggest improvements. Junior Lee was a couple of centimeters shorter than M'tana or Tregare. On first meeting her he'd said, "New Second Hat, you are? My, my—y'all *are* a big one."

Eyes narrowed, Zelde said, "That all right with you?" But Junior Lee's wide grin and quick reach to shake hands made it clear that the Chief Engineer, in his own way, was being friendly.

Now, as the update reading ended, Beauregard sat back. "Looks spit-slick to me, cap'n." Hain Deverel suggested deletion of some questionable details of the "*Alexander's*" visit to a colony none of them knew except by report, and Tregare accordingly put that section into vaguer terms.

After a few other comments were discussed, the meeting broke up. M'tana had the watch. Tregare went to the ship's infirmary, to talk with Eda Ghormley.

He found the thin woman sorting through medical supplies, making an inventory sheet. As she greeted him, Tregare noticed that the chronic frown was almost gone; maybe working in an Escaped ship felt better than doing the same job under UET. And it probably hadn't hurt matters when he'd decided, a time back, that a Chief's rating wasn't prestigious enough for the Chief Medic. Back at Number One his council had okayed raising Ghormley to officer status, roughly equal with Second Hat.

Now he asked her: "How's the lame duck business? You got many in residence?" He knew from the log, but asked anyway.

"Just Schroeder from Drive, and she'll be up on crutches in a day or two. Maybe next time she won't try to skip a landing going downship, late for watch or not."

Tregare laughed. "Not while she has the cast on, she won't. But what I came for—are you having any luck yet, rigging something that looks like UET's cheek tattoos and won't smear? Because coming into The Islands, we'll need that pretty soon."

She nodded. "I think so. Let me show you." And a few minutes later, after she peeled the decal off the hairless underside of his forearm and the colored design dried in place, she showed him that no amount of scratching or soap-and-water would smear the pattern. But the special solvent took it off clean. "So any time you want, bring your Hats in and I'll do them up properly."

He fingered his own cheek, where the later-added segments didn't match well with the quadrant originally received from UET. "Could you cover *this*, you think, so's it'd pass better?"

"Well, let's try." It took a little doing, getting everything to match, but he found the result hard to fault.

Still well out from The Islands, Tregare began growing his Dietrich Armiger beard. Zelde M'tana found it funny; in fact, once it gave a case of the giggles to that extremely ungiggly woman. "Come on, M'tana," he said. "Chuckle at the whiskers some other time. After all, this is *your* fake history we're trying to fool Tinhead and make it look good." So she sobered down, and the resultant entry was a fictional masterpiece, if Tregare did say so himself!

He held off the bleaching, trimming and dyeing of hair and beard as long as possible ("For one thing, it itches"), but made and aired a loop tape to the planet they were nearing, well before *Inconnu* came into detection range.

"Deet Armiger calling The Islands. Captain Dietrich Armiger, for the armed ship *Alexander the Great*. Homing in with ETA approx ninety standard hours. Come in please, The Islands..." And every hour, the comm-tech on watch stopped the tape and changed the number.

With sixty-eight standard hours to go, The Islands responded.

Entering Control, Tregare motioned his comm-tech to stay seated at the main panel and sat at an aux position. The voice from groundside was live, not tape, and the male speaker sounded youthful. Tregare cut his own tape's transmission, idly watching the indicator show silence as he framed his own first reply. But before he'd spoken a word, the indicator came to life. His panel was *sending* something!

Only for about two seconds, though, before Tregare slapped the Off switch and cut transmission. It took him a little longer to find which tape drive had been operating; he rewound the short bit that had been sent, set the unit's output to local audio with no scramble or offship signal—and as an afterthought, put on a headset and plugged it in to preempt the speakers. Because this kind of thing had happened before, back at Muspelheim. And this time, Tregare wanted first listen.

He started the tape. And heard, "First, let me identify myself. I am—" All right—that's as far as the message could have played; he restarted it. "—an agent of the Committee Police. My cover name on this ship is Tanit Eldon."

Long enough to determine the betrayal would have been total, he listened. Damn *all;* how could it be? *But peace take me, it* is! Deverel was watch officer; Tregare turned to him. "You handle the palaver, Hain. Something I need to do."

"But, captain—"

"You're up to it; punch up the *Alexander*'s log and tell it like you believe it." He clapped a hand to the man's shoulder. "Sorry, but I'm in a hurry right now."

He checked his chrono, and nodded. Tanit should be asleep now, so he went to her room. But not taking anything for granted, Tregare went in fast, without knocking. And a good thing, too, because if a mat hadn't slipped under his foot, her clawing lunge would have taken his left eye.

He didn't have time to wonder how she'd known what the situation was, but something in the back of his mind told him she would naturally have monitors hooked up here, to check on how her treachery was going. Right now, though, he fended off the fierce, *expert* attack of the woman he'd made love with, only a few hours before. She knew moves he didn't, and his emotional shock took away any physical edge he had.

So she got in a few good ones on him, but the range was too close for any blow or chop to have much speed to it. As he realized he'd better do something fast or she would, by all the flavors of peace, *kill* him, he remembered Murphy, the scarred, one-eyed female combat instructor at the Slaughterhouse. *When in doubt, get closer; guard your eyes and balls; a woman's wrists are her greatest disadvantage.*

So, trying to ignore some jabs and gouges that would probably leave him hurting for a month, he *got* in close. His thigh blocked her knee; she had nothing to bite but his jacketed shoulder, and finally a hand came where he could grab the wrist. He took it, and twisted hard; it might be unfair that the female wrist had less width and leverage, but fair was for games, and this situation wasn't one. Ten seconds later he had that hand up behind her in a hammerlock and heard her shoulder creak near to dislocation.

And *then* she said, "Bran? What's this all about?"

He didn't figure the question deserved an answer. Right now, the questions would be going the other way. And since Tanit had obviously beaten the truth drugs, twice, he was going to have to use less sophisticated methods.

He didn't like it, but what choice did he have?

A chop to the neck half-stunned her; he kept it short of killing force. Off came her clothes; he used some of them in tying her to the room's armchair: forearms flat along the chair's arms, feet secured to its front legs, tied around waist and neck because she shouldn't be able to move much.

Then he thought about it; *now* what? He'd never tortured, and even now the idea nearly made him throw up. He knew the theories: not *just* pain or mutilation, but fear of it and of its results. Go too far with disfigurement and the victim simply abdicates; nothing you do will have any further effect. Yet you can't afford to bluff and have that bluff called, either. Why in the name of peace did this have to happen to *him*?

Or, for that matter, to her. Looking at her, even now he found her semblance dear. No, he couldn't destroy the beauty of that face or body. Stymied, suddenly he noticed he was rubbing his right thumb over the nail of that hand's middle finger. And remembering the agony of a childhood injury, he felt a grin forming. A very mean grin. Because he looked at that fingernail and saw no marks at all, from the earlier trauma.

"What are you going to do?" So Tanit Eldon, whatever her real name, was back to full consciousness. Ignoring her, he got on the intercom.

"Ghormley?" At her response, he said, "In about fifteen, twenty minutes, get here to Eldon's quarters with your medic kit. Make sure to bring some anti-shock stuff." He listened to her startled questions, and said, "You'll have a shock patient, all right. Take my word for it. Tregare out."

When a sharp piece of iron smashed nine-year-old Bran's fingernail and punched a vee-shaped segment under the rest of it, to put agonizing pressure on the bruised nerves, the boy had felt the worst pain of his entire life and nearly died of shock. So now he couldn't think of a simpler way to get the most impact with the least damage. Tanit Eldon was tougher than the boy Tregare had been; it took two fingers on each hand, and occasional harsh tapping on first one damaged nail and then another, before she gave up on pleading and began talking.

He had most of it from her before shock hit and he had to wait for Eda Ghormley to come up and counteract the effect. "Hypnosis, Tregare," she kept repeating. Automatically he ignored the screams and curses, listening only to the words that made sense. "The chemical *presence* of any truth drug in the bloodstream triggers the hypnotic implant; whatever my cover ID is, my cover story, under the drug it's *true* for me." Was she the only one like this? She didn't know, except that the technique was fairly new. And only one such agent would be slipped into any given ship.

Eldon hadn't been to the Hulzein Establishment in Argentina; she *had* been infiltrated into the Underground, though. Her story of Erika wanting an alliance was sheer improvisation; when she boarded *Inconnu* she didn't know its identity or status, she was one of an experimental group designed to go onto ships and be monitors. It wasn't her job to blow an Escaped Ship's cover immediately, but first to gather data, such as coordinates, on Hidden Worlds. "And I had two, now, so it was time. One's plenty, but Muspelheim went wrong." Then, for a time, shock took her.

Knowing the disabling effects of that reaction, before Ghormley arrived Tregare had Tanit Eldon untied and even clothed. Seeing the injuries, the medic gasped. "What *happened* to her?"

"I did." And then, "She's our traitor, and I had to know *how*." Further, "Twice she beat the drugs; I knew that. So—"

Shrugging, Ghormley punctured the blood-blistered nails to relieve the agonizing pressure, then administered the hypo to bring the woman back to consciousness. Tregare said, "Give her some pain-killing shots, too."

"Why—?"

"I've got most of what I need; the rest's not important. And just because she has to die in a few minutes, doesn't mean she has to hurt, up until I space her."

Bran didn't need any words then, from Ghormley, to know what kind of monster she thought he was.

Tanit didn't resist his further questions; she said, after answering them, "I wish we could have been on the same side."

Him supporting her, because drugs and trauma had her shaky, they were heading downship to the main airlock. "If you'd wanted to switch, you could have."

Headshake. "Couldn't. More hypnosis. I don't remember it, of course, but it's standard for field agents. Total loyalty to UET, total animosity toward its enemies. No choice." What her face did, then, was probably trying for a smile. "So you don't have to feel badly about spacing me; it's your only option."

"Thank you, Tanit." For what, he wasn't quite certain. But remembering Butcher Korbeith he forced himself to watch as vacuum drew her out the lock to death. She didn't scream or struggle or void her body wastes in panic; Tanit Eldon met death with dignity.

Heading back up to Control, Tregare wasn't sure whether her stoicism made him feel better or worse.

Almost, but maybe not quite, Tregare had himself back in gear. *I killed Tanit*. But he forced himself to listen to the playback of what Deverel had said to The Islands, and of what groundside had said back.

It smelled good. This place sounded less paranoid than most places Tregare had visited, UET *or* Hidden. Relying on M'tana's data, Deverel had cited Terranova as the ship's most recent stop, and near as Tregare could tell, The Islands believed everything Deverel had said.

When Tregare turned off the tape and said as much, Gonnelson cleared his throat. "Sure?"

"Sure as I *can* be, from up here. I've learned to judge these communications. Any time the other end hesitates, except to look up data, somebody's thinking something over—or up. On Deverel's tape, counting-in the decreasing range and transmission lag, the only real pause was when Hain asked for longitude of their port, with respect to the terminator, for our ETA. And that one, they had to look up."

"Hope so."

* * *

When Tregare entered his quarters, he found Zelde M'tana waiting, sipping a drink. There was one for him, too. As he sat, she said, "Heard what you had to do. Thought I might could help some." He felt his face go tight. "Bad, huh?" He nodded. "I done a Utie the same once. Carlo Mauragin. All the way downship, he yelled."

"This one didn't. And Zelde—I'd *loved* that woman. Or damned close to it, anyway." Honesty forced the qualification.

"Pretty one, too. Not a big skinny giraffe like me." Startled, not knowing what to think, he watched her pull her blouse off over her head. When her face came clear, she was smiling. "But I'm what's here. You want to see if it helps?"

One deep breath he took. "Yeah. I think I'd like that."

His prediction was quite correct.

Up again, both seated and clothed, they looked at each other. She said, "That settle anything? About today, or the want I seen, all along, you got for me?" Her eyes narrowed. "That how it is with you and any woman? Take us all to bed, you have to?"

Shocked out of any semblance of defense, Bran shook his head. "Sure I wanted you. You're not like anyone I've ever known, and I guess the difference made you a challenge. I can't help that, Zelde; it's just how things are." He shook his head. "But today—now—I wasn't after anything, and all I want to do is thank you. Because you didn't have to—"

"True's all hell I didn't. Tregare, it's not like you're Parnell. Him I needed, *had* to have. Same with Honcho, when I run a division for him, back on Earth. Biggest Wild Kid gang UET ever busted, and tooken 'em a nuke shell to do it." And Bran realized that while he'd survived risks and ordeals this tall black woman hadn't, the reverse was also true.

"All right," he said, "Just so we know how we stand."

"I ain't done yet. What I need you for is different. It's what you *are*, and what you gonna do. And except for this here, today, and sometimes we could both feel like it again, maybe that's what you need me for, too."

For seconds, the words silenced Tregare; then he said, "M'tana, you impress the total hell out of me. And I think you're right." Assessing himself, his state of being, he added, "How did you know what could put me back together? And why did you want to?"

He liked her grin, then. "Hell'sfire, Tregare; a little screwing helps damn near anything. And we're *friends*, ain't we?"

"Right. And peace knows, I'm glad of it."

But that night, the nightmares returned: the Slaughterhouse dorm was somehow in space, and part of the time Bran himself was Butcher Korbeith, and the redhaired woman who went out the airlock was Phyls Dolan and Tanit Eldon both at once, so he had to try to space her and rescue her at the same time.

Going in toward The Islands, it seemed that Bran's reassurances to his First Hat had been correct. At the planet's one spaceport, situated on its largest island, *Inconnu* landed just after sunrise and met a friendly welcome.

Only one other ship sat groundside: the unarmed *Erwin Rommel*, captained by Lane Tysdale, a heavy-set swarthy man close to twice Tregare's age. They met as Bran came out of Port Admin, having settled the necessary fuel-and-supplies transactions. Tysdale invited him aboard the *Rommel:* drinks and lunch, the usual. Normal drill would be to take a sideman along, and although Tregare could find nothing remotely suspicious about the situation, he felt edgy and could have used the confidence of some backup.

But inwardly he shrugged. If he let himself get scared of shadows, haunted by Tanit Eldon's betrayal, he could wind up like Krieg Elman. So he made do with informing *Inconnu*, from Tysdale's quarters, where he was and when he expected to be back on his own ship. "Anything needs asking, call me. Armiger out."

Having come directly from Earth, Tysdale was well stocked with bourbon. With ice tinkling as they sipped, the two men traded small talk. Tregare wasn't as relaxed as he hoped he looked to be, because he had to concentrate on keeping his story straight.

It didn't matter for long, though, because Lane Tysdale had something on his mind, and starting his second drink he told it. "Armiger, I've got one hell of a mess on this ship, and I don't know what to do about it." Politely, Bran gestured that he was willing to listen, and the man said, "They put me sixty women on here, Welfare clients, as cargo for Iron Hat. Sixty, in a space fit to hold half that many. And then, an hour before we lifted, changed the orders to come here *first*. I asked permission to unload the women—some of them, anyway—or to follow my original orders to Iron Hat and *then* come here." One side of his mouth quirked. "I guess you know, Armiger, how far I got, trying to argue with the Port Commander."

Tregare thought about it. "Couldn't you put some of them in freeze?" Or maybe the *Rommel*'s chambers, like *Inconnu*'s, were unreliable.

But that wasn't the answer. "Preempted. The reroute, here, was to deliver some VIPs. The new governor and his two secretaries, and their families, filled those chambers. And now the old governor's group has them." His voice went from bitter to more so. "We lost a crewman, Armiger—because we didn't have a spare chamber when there was a medical emergency too big for my medics." He shook his head. "And those poor damned women down there—what's left of them—"

Running figures through his head, Tregare felt shocked. Earth to Iron Hat was maybe eight months, ships' time. Earth to the Islands was a year or more, easily—and from here to Iron Hat nearly the length of the originally-planned trip. "Some of them have died? Why?"

"Jammed in, like I told you. Poor sanitary facilities, no exercise, short rations—no shorter than the rest of us had, but what with the other problems—well, you see it."

"No exercise? I'd think you could—"

"Let them out a few at a time, under guard? Worth the guards' lives, that would be. Armiger, we're the only people they have, close enough to be worth hating."

Tregare tried to think of suggestions, but they all fell flat. Tysdale couldn't unload the women here because UET orders said they went to Iron Hat where the Miners' Co-op would pay the *Rommel* for transportation costs. He couldn't give them more living space because he had none available. He couldn't improve sanitation because any work force going inside to do so would be attacked tooth and nail. "Hell, Armiger. Two of the deaths were women charging into energy guns protecting the food delivery crew."

Finally Tregare gave it up. "How soon you leave for Iron Hat?" Ten days, was the answer. "Well, if I think of something I'll let you know. Thanks for the drinks."

Walking back to *Inconnu*, Bran felt depressed. In quarters he sat, brooding, then had an idea. He called the Second Hat's cabin. "M'tana, you had enough sleep you could have dinner with me?" And before she could take the implication that his motive was sexual, he added, "Something I found out, I need to talk over."

When she arrived, after he poured drinks—a light one for him because they weren't starting even-up—he told her the story. "You rode cargo, yourself. Tell me about it."

"Wasn't like *that*, none. Crowded, sure, but not bad crowded." Brow wrinkling as she thought back to that time, she said, "Hold Portside Upper, we was in. About the same size as on here. And sixty of us didn't rattle much. Shared bunks, some of us. And—" She described the facilities. "Plumbing over where it tapped into Drive's, I expect. Three crappers, the squatover kind. Two shower closets. Four basins, two-way faucets, wash or drink, either one. Four-decker bunks along the side bulkheads. A sort of shelf with three slots over it; that's where the ration packets came out, twice a day. And a trash chute under it for the empty packets." She squinted a little. "The door out, it was two of 'em with a space between. Like an airlock, only not for vacuum. Security. And the rations—not great, but better'n I'd got in the UET lockup, earlier."

Bran paused to call the galley and order dinner, then he said, "Doesn't sound wonderful, but not any death trap, either. I—"

Leaning forward, Zelde grasped his wrist. "Tregare. Why don't *you* buy them women off him? One of the holds on here, we could fix it up good enough, and—"

He shook his head. "Zelde. You can't think, seriously, that *I'm* going to deliver a load of slaves, to whore for free in Iron Hat's cribs? Even if my schedules allowed time to go there?"

"Iron Hat, my ass! You—"

"And the ship simply can't *afford* to free those slaves and ferry them to some other world, a Hidden World, with no way to recoup the cost. I'm sorry, but—"

"Give a listen, damn you!" For moments, Bran almost expected physical attack. "Not Iron Hat. Find a ship going to Farmer's Dell, and make you a swap. The Dell—I heard on it, back in Hold Portside Upper on the *Great Khan*. Always been short of women, so they don't mind paying to get some. But then they're *free* women, treated right." She had a stubborn look, as she said, "Well, that's how *I* was told it."

He nodded. "I heard it that way, too. But—"

"You got to, Tregare. You *got* to!"

Caught between anger and frustration and peace knew *what*-all, Bran took refuge in an unconvincing laugh. It didn't get him off the point of M'tana's fierce stare, but gave him time to sort out what he felt. "Slavery, Zelde. I hate it, same as you do. UET—it's a slaveowner *system*. Total Welfare, women as cargo, the whole thing. I—"

"You gonna *do* it, then!"

His scowl went tight enough to pain him. "Damn all, quit *crowding*, just a minute."

Surprisingly, her expression softened. "Sure, Tregare. You need some time, you got it. But—"

Without volition he shook his head. "Human cargo on *my* ship? No better than U E rotten peace-fucking T?"

Almost like iron, her hand gripped his. "No such a thing, Tregare. Wouldn't be like that, on here. The hold, yeah, but not how they get treated. And come to money, I could—"

A knock interrupted her; their meal was delivered. Hardly paying attention to his food, Tregare said, "Let me think about it. The way I've traded, we're low on high-bulk cargo; I could clear most of Hold Portside Upper. What's left would be crates nobody could break into, bare-handed." What else? "Clothes. No way do we have enough extra, and what they may have now—"

Startling him, M'tana laughed. "Clothes? They got none. No more than we did on the *Khan*. So—"

"So that takes care of the laundry problem, which was the next thing bothering me." He nodded. "All right. I'll try to dicker with Tysdale. Is that good enough?"

"Being as I go with you, sure. And I'll set a gang up, move things, get at the plumbing and stuff, try to make it no more work for you than got to be. You—"

"Zelde. Get these matters *planned*, the materials located, all that. But don't move Crate Number One until we have a deal.

"If we can manage one."

A quick Hats' council agreed the ship could afford the venture, so that was that. So far . . .

Tysdale couldn't seem to believe it, and even if he did, foot-dragging was his specialty. First he wanted the full compensation he had expected to receive at Iron Hat, along with ironclad documentation to prove to UET that in essence he had made delivery as ordered. The papers didn't bother

Tregare any; Dietrich Armiger could swear to anything Tysdale wanted.

The money was something else. "You've got how many still alive, you say? Forty-eight? You guarantee they'll all live? And how about the fact that I'm transporting them a considerable time and distance, and deserve compensation for my expenses?" So Tregare haggled the *Rommel's* captain down to about half his original demands. And figured to lose money anyway—but that beat hell out of facing Zelde's reactions afterward, if he *didn't* make the deal.

Only after the papers were signed did Tysdale let *Inconnu's* captain and Second Hat see his human cargo. Part of the view camera's lens was smeared with something, and Tregare had a fair idea what it was. Even so, he could see the wretched creatures huddled in much too small a space. They lay listless, filthy, some with festering sores on limbs and torso. Forty-eight? He tried to count but gave up; for the moment he accepted Tysdale's estimate. He could count the bunks, though. Twenty, or originally one for every three confined persons.

And he saw one crapper and one drinking tap and no showers. Nothing that looked like feeding arrangements, so he asked. "They have bowls and spoons—at least those were issued to them. Once a day my galley people take down a kettle of stew. It's set down in the open doorway and they have half an hour to dig in. But as I said, I need armed guards at that doorway."

"Don't surprise me none." M'tana's usually quiet voice held an edge Bran hadn't heard before. "Tysdale, you got a way to talk in that place, a screen they can see who's talking?"

"Why, yes. Do you want me to announce the arrangements?"

Tregare was going to take the job on, but Zelde said, "Not so's you'd notice. I think that's for me to do."

It was loud and ugly and painful. When the prisoners saw the screen light up, they pelted it with excrement, which they had no trouble finding. Tregare said, "Peace take me, I've never seen such a pigsty."

"Be glad you can't smell it," Tysdale said, and Bran hoped he would never receive such a look as M'tana gave that man, then.

One deep breath, and she shouted, "Shut the hell up,

down there!" To Bran's wonder, they did. "All right, who runs things? Somebody got to, anyplace. Whoever, say your name and hear the news I got for you." Silence. "Speak up, goddammit!"

A woman, probably young and once vigorous, but now looking neither, moved to the forefront. "What can *you* tell us? Why don't you kill us and get it over with? Who are you, anyway?"

"I'm Zelde M'tana and one time I rode cargo, same as you." *Oh, hell! I hope she doesn't blow cover on us*. But it was her show so Tregare said nothing; he checked that his knife was handy, though. "Not all shitty like they done you here, it wasn't. And that's the news. You're coming out of there, to another ship. A clean place, like you'll be, too. Only you got to come peaceful, not try to fight, and all." As the shouting began again, Zelde cracked the volume control high and said, "Talk it over. I can wait."

Bran could see the woman below, shushing the others, before she said, "My name is Cherisse Frisco. Before the Presiding Committee confiscated everything I had and Welfared me, I could have bought and sold this ship twice over. Now all I have is my own will to live by. And what's the point of living if we end up on Iron Hat, anyway?"

Tricky question, that. Tregare held his breath, until Zelde said, "You ain't there yet. And while you ain't, you rather live clean, or dirty like now? Like I said, take your time, deciding. I got plenty, too, except mine smells better."

Below, the discussion was loud again, too many talking at once for anything coherent to come through the circuit. As Lane Tysdale said, "Armiger? I'll provide guards, to get them off this ship and onto yours. You can clean them up, there."

"Like bloody hell I will!" Bran found himself glaring at the man. "That's your job. I expect they came on here clean; you send them off the same way." Overriding the other's protest, Tregare waved a hand. "You let this mess happen; you clean it up and I care not apeshit if you have to dirty some of your facilities a little. Otherwise the deal's off." M'tana gave him a stricken look; then her face cleared, so she must have guessed he was bluffing from strength.

It all took a while. Some of the women couldn't walk without help, so two who could supported one who couldn't. Luckily the proportion of invalids left no one unaided. And two or three at a time, the women went into the three shower cubicles made available and scrubbed each other down. The first trio had no luck trying to cleanse hair so matted and filthy it simply couldn't be made clean in a reasonable time. Zelde took over, commandeering some hair clippers; stubble washed quickly.

Tregare began to see why his Second Hat, coming from cargo, had earned the steps of command so quickly. She *acted*.

So while she seemed to have the mechanics of the situation under control, Tysdale's armed guards standing by as safeguard but not needing to do much of anything, Tregare decided to lean on the other captain. Well, first he called *Inconnu* and told the leader of Zelde's work gang to start moving cargo and installing plumbing plus fixtures. Some of the stuff would need fabrication in the ship's machine shop, but the needs were simple enough.

Then Bran said, "Tysdale? While we're waiting, you might's well have some of your people go down and take out those bunks, fittings and all. Steamclean 'em and deliver them to my ship." Tysdale balked, until Bran said, "You wouldn't want me to walk out of here now, would you? With all those slaves on the loose?"

So he got that one. And then, "Sixty women came on here wearing clothes. What's left goes off the same way. Dig 'em out." And he realized that the reason Tysdale caved in, once again, was that he hadn't been paid yet. And wouldn't be until Bran Tregare was damned well ready to do so. On *Inconnu*, as agreed.

Once the women, bathed and clothed, were herded across the spaceport into *Inconnu* and then to Hold Portside Upper, Tregare made payment to Lane Tysdale and gladly saw the last of the man, going down the ramp to groundside. Bran went to the hold; Zelde was there, flanked by two armed guards. The prisoners, some wearing clothes and others only holding the folded garments here in warmed space, seemed bewildered.

Bran could see why. The hold's personnel-sized door was open and members of Zelde's work gang went in and out. One shower closet was in place and the other halfway erected. The crappers were in, and two of the washbasins with drinking-tap option. A small crew was installing bunks, and Tregare saw that the Shops had produced new ones using the pattern of one from the *Rommel*.

Bewildered these women might be, but still, Bran saw, wary and resentful and potentially very dangerous. The sickest of the lot lay on newly-installed bunks, but even they looked around the place like caged animals.

So he went over to Zelde, and said, "Time I talked, you think?" She nodded, so he made a shrill whistle to draw attention.

"Welcome aboard. I captain this ship and it's time you learned you're a lot better off than you've been thinking. For starters, you won't ever see the cribs on Iron Hat. There's a colony called Farmer's Dell—"

A shout interrupted him. In the press of women moving forward, he couldn't determine who was shouting. "That's what they told us on the *Rommel*, first. And before, when we signed up."

Zelde spoke. "Same on the *Great Khan*, when *I* rode cargo. But this here man, you can believe." She had them quiet now and went on to say, "How you think I went from cargo on there to Second Hat on here? Captain, even, on that other ship for a time. So you—"

The woman who pushed forward then, Tregare recognized as Cherisse Frisco. "Second *Hat*, you said? Not Second Officer." She turned to face the other women. "What she's saying, this Zelde M'tana, is that this is an Escaped Ship. So *we're* Escaped." She looked back, now, to Zelde. "Or are we?"

Tregare answered. "We are, and you are. So you'll understand why, until we lift from here, I take no chance of any word getting off this ship." Some didn't seem to like that, but Bran had more to say. "Frisco, I want you to organize, if you hadn't already, a peacekeeping squad to keep your whole outfit in line. Which means you stay in here because otherwise you'd get in the way. And nobody jumps the people who bring your food. I could use armed guards but that's a waste; I'd rather not. I could build a security 'airlock,' but if we won't need it, why bother? You have folks here that need medical attention, and I'd like it if our Medical Officer and her helpers could come in and work without needing protection." He paused. "Can you promise me those things?"

He saw Cherisse Frisco look to three or four women, one after another, and draw a nod from each. Then, to Tregare she said, "I can promise all of it. Anyone who breaks the rules, it's my responsibility to correct the matter."

Tregare grinned. "Frisco, we have a deal." He checked his chrono. "And you're all due a meal, too, about now. On here we'll feed twice a day, not once. For starters. Three would be a load on our galley staff, but if you need it, we'll do it. Then after chow, I think Ghormley and her medics will be geared to come down here and start work." He raised an eyebrow. "Any problems?"

Frisco said, "We guarantee your people perfect safety, here."

Before answering, Bran said to his two armed guards, "Why don't you folks go for a coffee break?" When they were gone, he told the sick, tired group of women, "No matter what happens, keep in mind—long as I can trust you, you can trust me."

Then he and Zelde went upship. He expected her to go to her own quarters but she accompanied him to his. Inside, she began to disrobe. "Tregare, you done great. Even Ragir—I don't see how he could of done better." She looked at him. "Get them clothes off, right now." So he followed suit, and they hugged. She pushed him back and said, "Why not in the shower?"

That much was fine and so was the talk later, while they ate. But when Zelde finally left and Bran was alone, suddenly he dreaded sleep. He was right, too: in his dreams, Hold Portside Upper, looking more like its counterpart on Tysdale's ship, was on Earth as a component of the Slaughterhouse. In fact, it was what he found when he opened the door to enter his squadroom—the women, naked and diseased, lying in filth, cried out to him, some with invitation and some threatening with jagged clawed nails. From one side, Jargy Hoad said to join the party. "Channery says he'll be along soon; he wouldn't want to miss you. . . ."

Sweating and shaking, Tregare found himself sitting bolt upright, half awake, but not totally. *Channery,* that goddamn raper of junior cadets! Bran hadn't thought of the rotten bastard since he couldn't remember when. *Things must be really getting to me*. Well, seeing those women, the way they'd been on the *Rommel*, could get to anybody. . . .

He got out of bed and poured himself a slug of whiskey, twice the size he'd normally take, let alone at this time of night.

And downed the whole thing; he might suffer for it tomorrow, but right now he needed to shut down the dreaming-function.

It worked. When he slept again, if he dreamed he woke with no memory of it. And got up feeling not half bad at all.

Probably there were rumors around the Port, but once the *Rommel* lifted off (for where, Tysdale didn't tell "Armiger"), Bran figured they would die of malnutrition. Most of his official transactions were done; mostly he was waiting for the work on Hold Portside Upper to be completed. But when it was, he got a call from Port Admin: a ship had come within detection range but not close enough to speak. Custom was that no ship deliberately missed groundside contact with another if only a few days' wait were involved; those contacts were too infrequent as it was. So Bran agreed to await the unknown ship's arrival.

Not unknown for long, though; it was the *Bonaparte*, commanded by Chalmers Haiglund. First Officer was Jimar Peralta.

The information came through Port Admin, not ship-to-ship direct contact. Tregare turned away from the comm-panel.

"Figured he'd have that ship by now," said Zelde.

"*You* know Peralta?"

"At Parleyvoo spaceport, on Terranova. The *Bonaparte* come in there, Tregare, while we was still working on the Nielson Cube, loading up supplies, mainly out fishing for some kind of Underground contact, so as to find us a Hidden World next."

Wondering, Bran shook his head. "Why haven't you mentioned this before?"

"Thought I did." A frown. "*Sure* I did. Well, the *Bonaparte*, anyway; Jimar Peralta, maybe not." She looked at Bran. "Why? You know that one too, maybe? Then I don't need to tell you, watch your ass all the way. Else he might could walk off with it."

Tregare chuckled. "Not likely. Though he has a claim, at that, having possibly saved it for me, a time or two."

So he told her about Butcher Korbeith and "airlock drill" where the Butcher might or might not put a naked cadet out into space, and how Peralta had twice intervened. And she told him how on Terranova the man had pressured Ragir Parnell toward trying to help him take the *Bonaparte*. "We drunked him up on trair, though, so he showed his hand. Then, 'till next day we knew he was safe to let go, we didn't do that."

Tregare didn't quite understand. "Zelde, back in UET's Space Academy, the Slaughterhouse, Peralta was one of the few decent people who had any authority. Ambitious, yes, but—"

"Ambitious, yeah; that's the worry. Wants command like a thirst-dried man wants water." She paused. "But how we knew he could be let loose, was what he said—why he couldn't take the rat way to command."

"Turn in an Escaped ship, and receive command of it from UET?"

She nodded. "He said like, all right, supposing he done that. Then when *he* Escaped, *where would he go*?" Zelde laughed. "He said, when *you* heard, you'd hunt him down if it tooken you all your life to do it. So might be you could still trust him."

"I'd hope so." He felt himself frowning. "That's not the problem." He stood. "Zelde, we haven't checked out this Port's missile defense and garrison facilities; there's been no need. But now—"

"You want I should send out some security snoops?" He nodded. "I will, that. But how come?"

"Because I want to know the odds on *our* helping Jimar Peralta take a good healthy ship for himself." Thinking: *if he'll agree to my terms, I couldn't ask for a better ally.*

Right on its announced ETA, the *Bonaparte* landed. On Zelde's advice ("this Haiglund, Ragir said, is all by the book, and sure seemed Ragir had him right") Tregare made a formal call to the other ship and, as the junior of the two captains, accepted his senior's invitation to bring his First Officer along for a drink or two on the *Bonaparte*. Bran thought to spare Gonnelson the ordeal but Zelde said, "Ragir took me last time, on account Lera Tzane knew Peralta from early and was scared of him. Anybody with you excepting First Hat, that Haiglund he gonna ask *why*. And *me*, on a new ship and all—"

So Tregare bulldozed Gonnelson into going along. "Now look! You've done this before and got by with it." So the First Hat, without any show of sulkiness, accepted the inevitable.

* * *

The ramp guard and the airlock guard who escorted Bran and Gonnelson upship were courteous and businesslike. Captain Haiglund, admitting the visitors to his quarters, smiled and shook hands with both. A tall, broad man, Haiglund was, looking younger than his grey hair would indicate. "Welcome aboard," and all that routine; then, inside captain's digs, Tregare found himself face to face with Jimar Peralta.

Only one way to play it. Tregare moved to shake hands. "Mister Peralta. I've heard of you. Favorably."

Peralta's eyes narrowed; Tregare couldn't be sure whether his disguise held, or not. "Captain Armiger. A pleasure indeed."

The ritual seemed to run on tracks: exchange of data on other ships met, drinks neither stingy nor prodigal, dinner that kept balance between stinting and opulence; the food was quite good. And through it all, Gonnelson made semblance of communication with one word for ten of everyone else's. It was strange, Tregare thought, how nobody else seemed to realize that Gonnelson didn't *talk*.

While Tregare, trying to analyze, watched Peralta. The man hadn't changed much, to look at—he was still lean and taut, and moved like a caged cat. His face showed few lines of aging, but Bran saw shadows forming at brow and mouth-corners. All in all, though, Tregare thought, the other man had stood up well against the pressures and frustrations of shipping with UET.

The one thing Tregare couldn't risk doing was to leave the *Bonaparte* without hanging a lifeline out to Jimar Peralta. Whether or not Peralta saw through the Armiger disguise, Bran had to assume he had done so. All right; when time came to accept Captain Haiglund's polite dismissals and leave the *Bonaparte*, midway through the handshakes and farewells Tregare said, "Mister Peralta? I think we know a lot of the same people in the Service, and might enjoy trading stories about them. Not suitable to do that here, we juniors—but if you'd like to drop over to the *Alexander* in a day or two, informally if Captain Haiglund can spare you for a few hours . . ." Bran looked to Haiglund and got a nod. ". . . then give me a call and come aboard, with my welcome."

Peralta signed assent; Tregare and Gonnelson went downship and left the *Bonaparte*. As they walked back toward *Inconnu*, Gonnelson said, "Why?"

"If it's at all possible," Tregare said, "we're going to take the *Bonaparte* for Peralta. Because we need that ship. Peralta's a fox. If I make sure I can trust him, I need that man."

First chance he had, Bran told Zelde about his visit in fullest detail, and also his own intentions. "What do you think?"

She finished the last spoonful of her dessert; then, with the spoon, she gestured. "You'll have him here, I expect?"

"Right. Captain's digs are proper courtesy. But you haven't answered."

"Well, say you do bust Peralta loose of UET. Dunno if he'll serve second to you nor any other—but sure's hell you set UET up for a good mess of trouble."

Tregare nodded. "Too right. But I think I have the bait that will hook Jimar to join me. Long enough to get the main job done."

"What bait?"

He grinned. "Sit in when he gets here. You'll see."

Next day, after a voice-call to set the appointment, Jimar Peralta was escorted to Tregare's quarters. Bran waited there alone. When the guard-escort left and the door was closed, Tregare did the obligatory handshake and said, "Welcome aboard. A drink should be in order. Bourbon all right?"

He busied himself preparing the drinks, aware that Peralta was watching him. They clinked glasses. "Cheers."

They sat, and after a moment Tregare said, "This room isn't bugged. And there's only one latrine in all of UET."

"Bran Tregare!" The two were up and hugging, pounding each other on the back. As they sat again, Peralta said, "I *thought* it was you—but it's been some years, and with your hair dyed, plastered down over your forehead this way—"

Tregare laughed. "It's a fair disguise, at that. Didn't fool the Butcher, though." And he told of his incursion at Stronghold, and of barely escaping the refueling orbit at Earth when Korbeith arrived and blew his cover. He told all these things because either he could trust Jimar Peralta or the man would never leave *Inconnu*. Then he said, "I think we have some business, you and I. You mind if my Second Hat sits in on that?" Peralta nodded, so Bran called Zelde's cabin. Without speaking her name, he said, "Mr. Peralta's here. I'd like you to meet him."

Then he waited, and when Zelde entered, Peralta's reaction was worth the wait. The man went from sitting to standing in one motion. "M'tana!"

"That's right." Shifting a bottle from right hand to left, she came forward to shake hands. "Brought you some trair, seeing as you liked it last time."

Peralta shook his head, not in negation but apparently to clear his thoughts. "I'm surprised. To see you here, I mean. I hadn't thought you'd ever leave Ragir Parnell."

"Wouldn't have, was he still alive. Tell you later, maybe."

"I'm sorry." From the look of him, and his voice, Peralta meant it. "He was a good man."

"The best," M'tana said. "Not meaning a thing against you two here, either one." Then, "You like a little trair?"

This headshake *was* negative. "Not until you explain how that delicious stuff put me out of orbit, *twice*, while you and Parnell stayed well on course."

Zelde, Tregare thought, sometimes had a really mean grin. "Guess you should know, yeah. Trair, it's got something in it, you drink and feel great but not drunk, so you keep going. But the stuff, keeps you sober, it wears off quicker'n the booze part does. So there you are, all've a sudden, ory-ass blasted. Whilst Ragir and me, we went slower, and waited you out."

First Peralta began a slow chuckle, then his laughter doubled him over. Finally, wiping tears away, he said, "So that's how you whipsawed me. Thanks for telling it."

"Sure. Well now—you want we have us some?" At his wary look, she said, "All starting even, this time, I mean, and we none of us take a whole lot." So he nodded, and she poured.

When they'd clinked glasses and were sitting, Tregare said, "Now, the business. Peralta, on Terranova the situation was that Parnell didn't dare try to help you take your ship. Bad odds. Let's talk, and figure out what the odds are here." He waved off any answer. "First, though, we need to set terms."

"What terms?" The other man looked puzzled.

Tregare leaned forward. "I have a job planned. The terms are that if I help you take the *Bonaparte*, you owe me service. On that mission only, and the key word is Stronghold. Before and after, the ship is yours free and clear."

"And *on* that job, it isn't?" Peralta's eyes were narrowed.

"It's still your ship, even then. But during that time, it and you are part of my command."

This was the touchy part and Tregare knew it. "Of the two of us, I'm well senior. Why should I serve under you?"

Tregare shrugged. "I could say, to pay me back for getting you a ship." Oh, the hell with it—*be honest*! "But I won't. Because we both know I owe you, for saving my life once and maybe twice, on the *MacArthur*. And we both know I want you free and loose, on our side, to bite UET's butt, almost as much as you want it."

Grinning, Peralta spread his hands. "So where's your leverage, Tregare?"

"You're getting a ship. How'd you like to have an *armed* ship?"

"Armed? But how—?"

It was Bran's turn to grin. "I'll take care of that part. You come join me on Number One, date to be determined, on *my* terms—and I'll arm your ship for you." He paused, then said, "Is it worth what I ask, Jimar?"

He could see the imperatives warring in the man. Then Peralta nodded. "To have an armed ship—Tregare, it's a deal!"

The planning got a little tricky. Obviously both ships should lift off as soon as Peralta had the *Bonaparte* safely in hand, but *Inconnu* had held only to wait and exchange information with the other ship—so Tregare had to ask Junior Lee Beauregard for some faked malfunctions, to justify delay.

More hellbent for command than ever, Peralta might be, but still he held the same scruples he'd shown at the Slaughterhouse. "Haiglund's a stuffed shirt and a Utie loyalist, but he's an honest man and a fair one; I don't want him dead. And when it comes down to cases, once we have the ship I want to put the surviving Uties groundside here, not space them. If we can."

"Yeah, Jimar. I remember; you always did hate waste."

The important parts. Things had to happen when Peralta himself had the watch in Control and one of his people held the Drive room. There was some talk about the power suits—since both Tregare and M'tana had used those decisively in takeovers—but Peralta said, "I'd rather the *Bonaparte*'s were disabled. Few of Haiglund's people are armed, and I can see that more of mine are; that should be enough force. A power suit—that way, it's too easy for killings to happen by accident."

So Tregare, with some misgivings, had to agree.

When they had it all figured, best they could, Bran again went over the parameters for the later rendezvous on Number One. "I'll have the ships' weapons there. You just be sure the *Bonaparte* arrives in plenty of time."

"It won't." Tregare blinked; then saw Peralta's grin. "What will arrive on time, Tregare, is my ship—*No Return*."

A few hours before *Inconnu*—or rather, the *Alexander*—was due to lift, a roistering band of its crew, led by a tall black woman, came back from town and insisted on boarding the *Bonaparte* to share a few drinks with their counterparts on that ship. From Control, Peralta gave orders to humor the intruders and avoid trouble. Bottles were passed around; Peralta's man in Drive told his watchmates to leave there and help maintain order, then locked the place from inside and reported "All secure." Captain Haiglund, alarmed by the commotion and getting no answers from Control, went charging upship and was taken into custody by strangers who didn't seem to be drunk, as had been reported.

Drumming knuckles on his own control console, Tregare had to make do with brief, fragmentary reports from Peralta, plus occasional items from Zelde whenever she was someplace where communications could get through. He knew she'd said a lot of things when she was in shielded areas, but now: ". . . gave up, so we locked 'em in a service cubby. Going downship now. M'tana out."

Well, so far, so good. But Tregare wished he could *be* there.

When his downview screen showed people coming down the other ship's ramp, Tregare began to relax. And on the scrambled channel, Peralta said, "Ship secured, Tregare. Superfluous personnel being herded groundside. We had some casualties, both sides, but less than I'd feared." Then, referring to an offer Bran had made earlier, "I'm accepting your contingent of volunteers, so we won't lift too shorthanded. Fourteen, I believe, and all to be upgraded one step for today's action." A pause, and then, "As soon as my discards and your people are clear of the safety perimeter, *No Return* lifts. Good landings, Tregare."

Below, not much later, Bran saw Peralta's "discards" milling off away from the danger area, and then *Inconnu*'s own people moving briskly aboard. He said, "Good landings; right. I'll look for you on Number One, Jimar."

"I'll be there."

He'd thought of putting the scout up to cover the liftoffs, but Peralta convinced him that if they timed it right they'd have both ships off before UET groundside could know there was any kind of problem. So why bother? He didn't.

Now Tregare watched *No Return*'s Drive nodes turn dirt to dust and steam as the ship began to rise—oh, so slowly, at first!—and then cant to one side and throw ionization into the missile-defense antennae. Not blasting them away, merely jarring them into temporary ineffectiveness.

For a moment, Tregare chuckled. But he didn't have time for it, because now it was *Inconnu*'s turn to lift; he gave Zelde M'tana the high-sign and felt his own Drive build and start to lift, moments behind Peralta.

And then on the downscreen a movement caught his eye. Someone, somebody groundsided from *No Return*, was running headlong *into* that ship's liftoff blast area. And ran, and ran, and hit the field's edge and turned into running flame, and fell.

As that view fell away, Zelde M'tana said, "Captain Haiglund, it was. We should of knowed he would. Tregare?"

"Yeah?" Bran tried to ignore his effort, not to throw up.

"Peralta, he don't need to know that."

"Right." So in the brief exchanges before the two ships went their different ways, Bran didn't tell him.

10. The Backslid

Figuring schedules the best he could, Long View and all, and realizing that no amount of urgency could hurry matters, Tregare decided how many junkets he could manage and still make it to Number One in time for the rendezvous he was arranging.

His next raid on a UET colony was the one that later made him Escaped Target Number One back at Earth. He got lucky that time; two armed UET ships were groundside, and coming down he wiped them both with his Drive before they could lift out of air. Then he plundered the place, and before leaving he blew its fuel refinery, so that any ship coming there would be grounded for a considerable time. His reason for being so punitive was that this colony ran to slavery; he wanted to turn the whole rotten mess upside down, and was fairly sure he'd done so. In fact, the remaining population seemed to think they were now Escaped, the equivalent of a Hidden World. He hoped they were right, but kept his next two raids a lot more modest. And then . . .

He went to Terranova using a totally improvised fake ID for the ship, and got away with it. But from that planet, he decided, he should start heading for Number One. And looking at his star charts, with the holographic projector still out of action, he decided that his best bet was to go by way of UET's small colony on the planet Far Corner.

So he lifted for there. The only trouble was that before *Inconnu* passed $t/t_0 = 2$, or maybe the other way round, in came incoherent signal from a beacon circling a world that was on no charts at all.

Not only incoherent, that signal, but intermittent as well. First it came on abruptly, rather than emerging gradually from the noise level. It stuttered, wavered, died, came on again—long enough for Hain Deverel to get a bearing on it—then died once more. "Old equipment," Tregare said. "Not maintained. On its last legs." Looking around at his Hats, gathered hurriedly in Control, he said, "Should we give a look?"

Consensus was in favor, so Deverel changed course—not more than a quarter of a radian, no great cost in fuel. Going with Gonnelson's distance estimate, Tregare had Junior Lee schedule Turnover.

Bran hadn't expected that he and Zelde would bed regularly or frequently, and indeed, now and then was the name of the game. With no coquetry or other emotional games, sometimes the occasion called for that kind of celebration. When it did, both seemed to know without asking. Tregare could have used a little more frequency, but after a while he got used to the way things were.

Now, though, they planned a tryst beforehand. Bran assigned Turnover to Hain Deverel with Gonnelson riding shotgun; he and Zelde took the opportunity for sex in free fall. As *Inconnu* swung 180 degrees while they, in midair, did not,

Zelde laughed. "Never done this way before. Fun, kind of." When they'd finished, just before Junior Lee—gently, as Bran had requested—brought the Drive up to thrust, she asked, "You done it lots of times, I expect?"

Drifting, they thumped softly to the deck. He shook his head. "Just once before. A long time ago." *With Salome Harkness.* "My first trip, as a cadet on the *MacArthur*." And where was Butcher Korbeith now? Would Tregare ever make good his vow to kill that man? But those thoughts he didn't tell M'tana.

With decel set at half-max, a few days later the planet's primary came into view, and then the world itself.

Hailings brought no answer; with the ship in low orbit, just short of plowing air, it took some time to spot where the spaceport had been. Around the flat-lying wreckage of a ship, a few huts clustered. But several kilos distant, Tregare saw a larger settlement. That terrain looked level enough to set down on, so he spread the "feet" on the ship's landing legs. After one more orbit, spiraling down, Deverel landed *Inconnu* safely.

The locals, gathering to meet the groundside party, didn't impress Tregare much. Unkempt, wearing makeshift clothing, they spoke a dialect that had drifted quite a way from standard speech; Bran found it hard to understand. Finally four of the younger men came carrying a sort of rickety palanquin, roofed but open-sided; inside sat a very old person of indeterminate sex, wearing a filthy robe that still bore traces of gold embroidery. When the conveyance was set down, supported by flimsy-looking legs unfolded from its lower frame, the person beckoned and said, "You've come at last. Who speaks for you?"

None of this crowd looked dangerous, so Tregare walked past them to the oldster's seat. "I do. Bran Tregare, captain of *Inconnu*. What's the name of this place? And your own?" And what the hell *happened* here? Well, that would take some asking.

"New Earth, we used to call it, at first when we still thought the ship could lift again. Fell down fifty years ago, it did. But the Nielson was bad, anyway. The Cast Out Ones still live alongside it, radiation and all. Worship it. Grabbed Chira, my great-granddaughter, the other day, for sacrifice."

A sniffle, and the person wiped it off with the back of a hand. "I'm Hugh Charlton, last one born aboard the *Conquistador* in space. Or am I? Last one alive, anyway." The old man coughed. "Lots more ships coming out, supposed to be; that's what my daddy said. But none of 'em came here. Not any. Not until you. You going to take us home, are you?"

Tregare looked around him. *Not hardly!* But he said, "We're supposed to conduct an inspection, is all. And make a report. Now could you tell me how the colony is progressing?"

Old Charlton's ramblings took a time, but Bran could put the picture together. After the bad landing, that left the *Conquistador* standing aslant and none too stable, at first the officers had used the colonists for forced labor, trying to get the ship repaired while also growing food crops. After a number of years—Charlton wasn't sure how many—there had been a bloody revolt. At its end, no technical personnel survived. Hugh emerged as the prophet of a new religion, devoted to simplified living and individual freedom. After half the survivors died of famine because nobody had to work if he or she chose not to, changes arose, but Hugh Charlton somehow managed to hang onto his—well, high priesthood seemed as good a word as any.

"What about the Cast Out Ones?" Well, living near the ship with its malfunctioning, radiating Nielson Cube, the colonists began having malformed offspring. Hugh vaguely remembered enough to realize that radiation caused the birth defects, so he moved the colony to its present location and cast out the defectives, who chose to stay near the *Conquistador*, even after it toppled over.

"We still get a bad birth here, sometimes. Soon as it's weaned, it goes to them. To raise or eat, whichever they choose."

Tregare had had just about enough of these degenerates, but before he could think how to end the interview, beside him Zelde M'tana spoke. He hadn't heard her approach. "Charlton! What's this sacrifice thing you said?"

"Chira?" The old man wiped his eyes. "They shouldn't have done that, taken her. Not supposed to. We paid them their dole."

"Wrong answer," M'tana said. "*What* is it, they do to her? And, they done it already, or not?"

The old head moved back and forth; Tregare felt he could

almost hear the neck creak. "Tomorrow; next day—when the moons cross. They tie 'em down to the Nielson, to purify. When their hair falls out, they're pure. That's when the cutting comes."

During the next few minutes, while Charlton placidly told what the ensuing rites were, Tregare wished it wouldn't be so undignified for a ship's captain to puke. Unlike the ancient Aztecs, the Cast Out Ones didn't cleanly cut the heart out. No, they opened the abdomen, carefully tied off all major blood vessels, and emptied the abdominal cavity, organ by organ. "Then," said Hugh Charlton, "they cast next year's auguries according to how far the sacrifice can walk or crawl. One I remember, made it more than a kilo." Sniff. "Doped up, likely."

Walking back to *Inconnu:* "Shut up, M'tana! I know we got to get that barbarian kid out of there. What I'm trying to figure, just now, is *how.*"

Walking would take too long and lifting *Inconnu* would waste too much fuel, so Tregare used the scoutship, fully crewed. He worried a little about M'tana being in charge of the combat squad, but he'd told her, "Nobody shoots until *I* say so," and no matter how gowed-up she was about this thing, he figured she'd obey orders.

He landed the scout back a way from the toppled *Conquistador* and left Deverel in charge with two guards to watch the ramp. The rest of them, Tregare leading, went to meet the ragged group that gathered around the wrecked ship.

He'd seen some bad things, Tregare had, but this bunch beat all of it. Radiation damage at its worst; after a first look he tried to ignore the scars, the burns, the other obvious mutilations. The one-eyed woman, leading that pack, was apparently in charge, so Tregare said, "We're here for the girl Chira. Where is she?"

The woman's mumblings were barely comprehensible. Tregare repeated himself and lit a drugstick and handed it over. The woman puffed, smiled, nodded, and passed it to the next in line.

M'tana nudged him. "Let me do this, huh?" She seemed to understand the group's gibberish, or else she faked it pretty well, because after a few minutes she said, "I thought they'd settle for a few packs of sticks, but it's more, they want. You got a knife you can spare?"

He was surprised, when he pulled the throwing knife from the sheath at the back of his neck, to find rust on the blade. But the Cast Out Ones didn't seem to mind; Zelde closed the deal.

Chira, led out with chains binding her and no other covering, shouted a constant stream of curses in a voice gone hoarse. Some of the words, Tregare had never heard before, so they must be new inventions. And with words he did know, most of the compoundings were unfamiliar. She tended to favor combinations of the scatalogical and the classically obscene. When she began to repeat herself, he realized she wasn't necessarily being original.

The noise was getting in the way, so Tregare yelled, "Chira! You want out of here alive, *shut up*!" When she did, on his second try, he said, "All right. Take those chains off her." Now that she was quiet, he looked at her more closely. Built strong, she was: not tall, but sturdy. No excess flesh at all; her muscles showed clearly.

She had to be some kind of Caucasian, but dark-complexioned, with a matted mass of curling, almost-black hair. Still mumbling, he saw, though not loud enough to hear, she made an occasional snarl as she jerked at the chains.

The one-eyed woman shook her head, and uncannily, Zelde seemed to understand her mouthings. "Says we take her as is, Tregare. Afraid if they let her loose she'll bust them up some."

Again Tregare spoke. "Chira." She looked at him. "If you won't follow orders I can't save your life. You hear me?" Chira nodded. "I'm going to take those chains off you. When I do, you come with us. And that's *all* you do. You don't attack any of these people, no matter how much you think they deserve it. Or else we leave you here, with them. You got that?"

She erupted again. ". . . shitkissers . . . plowed me every way . . . done every crap thing there is . . ." But finally she ran down, looked at Bran, and nodded. "You the boss. I don't kill none."

So the chains came off, and Tregare saw the effort it took Chira to keep her promise, as he and his people hustled her into the scout. Once inside, he wished there had been some way to bathe her first.

* * *

Never before had Bran docked the scout onto *Inconnu* with the ship groundside, but he'd practiced, both in free space and in orbit, so now he thought he'd give it a try. Making sure that the bay was cleared and inside-sealed first, he swung near to his ship, threw a drift toward the opened bay, and cut his Drive—to give it one impact-softening burst at the last moment. The landing jar was more than he liked, but it beat flaming his deck and bulkheads any more than need be.

Then he and Zelde took Chira back to her people.

"No!" Hugh Charlton shook his head. "If you leave her here—once the Cast Out Ones took her, she was dead. So we'd have to kill her." Tregare's angry protests got him nowhere as the old man said, "*I* never asked you to bring me back my dead."

And thinking back, Tregare had to agree. He turned to Zelde. "This was your idea. What do we do now?"

She shrugged. "There's spare bunks in Hold Portside Upper."

Except for a disgusted wrinkling of her nose, Chief Medic Eda Ghormley took Chira's advent in stride, as Tregare said, "Peace only knows what her health is like. Check on what you can, and fix what you can."

"After she has a bath," Ghormley said, "and a haircut. I can see the lice crawling in that mop, from here."

Chira didn't like it. "Nobody shitfuck Chira. I—"

Suddenly she made an indrawn gasp, and was silent. Bran saw that Zelde M'tana had two of Chira's fingers in her grasp and was exerting leverage: he knew the taming effect of that simple hold, so he waited, as Zelde said, "This lady, she's to help you. Anything she says, you do. Anything she does, you let her. Else you wish you had. You hear me?" From Chira's silent wince, Tregare guessed that Zelde had got her point across.

Washed and sheared, curling hair not much longer than Zelde's, then tested and prodded and inoculated, Chira still glowered. She didn't like all this, not one damned little bit; Bran could tell that much. But so far she was keeping her resentments more or less under wraps, as Ghormley reported, "She's healthier than I'd expect from such a flea-bitten rabble. In the bloodstream, a couple of bugs new to me, but no fever or other symptoms so probably nothing dangerous. I can't think of any other tests to try, so she's all yours, Tregare."

"Not exactly." Tregare didn't laugh, quite. "M'tana? You got time to help me escort our guest to Portside Upper?" He checked his wrist chrono. "It's coming up mealtime, there." He turned to Ghormley. "Would you advise the galley to add one more ration packet from now on?" Then, looking again at Chira, how the issue jumpsuit hung on her, "Maybe you better make that two extra. This one has some catching up to do."

As they went downship, Tregare noticed that the unfamiliar surroundings seemed to give Chira no unease. Either she was adaptable as all hell or had no imagination; he couldn't guess which. At the hold's door she said, "Locked in? I—"

"Just a place to stay, for now," he said. "You'll have a lot of new friends here, while we go to another world."

"Friends?" But she went in without arguing.

Then Tregare and Zelde climbed to the galley; breakfast was a long time ago. He thought of asking her to his quarters, for after, but didn't. Because he could sense that they were out of phase; he was in a mood for sex and she wasn't. He didn't know why, and wasn't sure he liked it, but couldn't put a finger on how to change anything. At least Zelde had turned out to be someone he could *talk* with, better than anyone since—*dammit, forget that!* So he guessed he'd settle for what he could get.

At the meal's end he did ask her up for a drink, after all, but in a way that made it clear he was asking nothing more. So they were sitting, talking over the day's events, when the intercom sounded. It was Gonnelson. "Captain! The hold. The new woman. Trouble."

Jeez—more words than the First Hat usually said all week. "I'll be right down there. I assume you have a squad on the way." Hearing the confirming syllable, Tregare signed out, and he and Zelde headed downship considerably faster than safety regs allowed. Passing the impromptu guard station at the open door of Hold Portside Upper, Tregare went in to see a real mess.

Cherisse Frisco had blood on her face but the wound was superficial. Three women lay on bunks while Eda Ghormley and two of her helpers worked over them. At Tregare's quick question, Ghormley said, "Nothing fatal. But you have to get that new one out of here." And then Bran saw Chira, a little bloody herself, and bruised about the face, handcuffed to a stanchion.

He shook his head. "What the hell happened here?"

"That peacepissing *savage* of yours, is what happened. She—" Apparently Chira didn't know the meaning of the word rations—that is, one to a customer, or in her own case, two. When the packets were brought in and the delivery crew left, Chira began grabbing as many as she could, and fighting the others for them. Shaking her head, Frisco continued, "Nobody could talk to her; she hit and kicked and bit. So finally the lot of us overpowered her and held her until the guards brought those handcuffs." She quieted while Eda Ghormley cleaned her face and covered the cut with a small bandage. Then, "Damnedest brawler I've seen in a long time. Not trained, though; that was *our* luck."

The group's leader wasn't done talking yet, but Bran's slight wave of hand put her into listening mode. He said, "You think you and she—all of you, I mean—can get along now?"

A frown, and violent headshake. "My people here, they took enough crap already; you know that. Not complaining, Tregare; I know you're treating us as well as conditions permit, and we all appreciate it. But you take that savage out of here or I can't guarantee she'll be alive tomorrow."

And before he could answer, she added, "Several have said, she has to sleep sometime. But she doesn't have to wake up."

No argument with that kind of thinking, and Tregare knew it. He looked to M'tana in time to see her shrug, but asked anyway. "Ideas, Zelde?"

"You can't turn her loose anyplace, and my room won't hold two, even was I willing. I guess you're stuck with her."

He guessed so, too. So he began. "Now look, Chira..."

He let her bring along two of the disputed ration packets, and on the way upship he tried to tell her how it would have to be. "You behave yourself, cause no trouble, keep your hands off anything you don't understand, you can stay with me, for now." She nodded, and he hoped the nod meant comprehension and acceptance. "You screw up, Chira—you screw up *any*—and you're down there again with the property. Where they don't like you very much."

Scowl. "I go home. Nobody kill Chira. Just they try, they turdwhackers; I show better."

For a moment he was tempted to turn her offship and forget her. But if he did, Zelde would never let him hear the last of it. So he said, "Too late for that. Ship's sealed; we lift soon." And only by a few minutes was he lying, his reason being that he figured the woman would have *no* chance groundside; she might think she was tough, and be partly right too—but the community Hugh Charlton headed reminded Tregare of a pack of jackals; in the longer haul, no single animal could withstand them.

Entering his quarters he touched her shoulder and she did not flinch. "You're safe here. You'll be fed all you want. We're going to a different world with different people and you can live better, there. All you need to do, now, is be peaceful, not fight, not mess with anything you don't know. You *want* to know, ask and I'll try to tell you." He stopped moving, because she had turned to face him.

She said, "Plow me, I got to let you?"

Carefully, Tregare did not laugh. He said, "No. No, Chira. On this ship, that's not how it is."

The girl wasn't malicious, nor, as it turned out, even stupid. What she was, though, was a damned nuisance. Part of it was her developing curiosity, once she emerged from the shock of her ordeal. It wasn't safe to leave her alone, because without some admonishing presence at hand she *couldn't* keep her hands off things. And somehow she'd decided that Tregare could tell her what to do, or Zelde or another officer, but no one else. Well, except Eda Ghormley. On promise of seeing a Nielson Cube that was safe to touch or stand next to, she admitted Junior Lee to the select company. Afterward the Chief Engineer told Tregare, "Given a li'l book learnin', that ol' gal might *be* somebody."

Ghormley had done some teaching, once, so Bran saddled the Chief Medic with a daily stint as schoolmarm. The assignment took some pressure off Tregare and his Hats, since they'd practically had to arrange duty shifts for watching Chira.

And Tregare couldn't bring himself to lock her up, even if Zelde would have stood still for that solution.

* * *

Right away, Tregare figured how to Chira-proof his quarters. His intercom panel and the adjacent console mounted a sizable number of control switches he couldn't afford to let her play with, and there were times when he couldn't keep an eye on her, such as when he slept and she didn't. So he checked the diagrams and found where to insert a key-operated switch in the common-battery lead. Incoming signals weren't interfered with, but without the key, Chira could flip switches until Hell froze, without harm.

In the interests of good sense, though, such flipping was still forbidden.

A week out of Backslid, as Tregare dubbed the ship's most recent stop, he woke feeling feverish and nauseated. He called and asked Gonnelson to take "Chira duty" for a while; oddly, the girl understood the First Hat's monosyllables better than many of his shipmates did. That matter arranged, Bran visited the infirmary.

Ghormley couldn't find any probable cause. She gave him some pills and the time-honored advice: "Stay in bed as much as possible and drink lots of fluids." She scowled. "I don't mean booze, skipper."

Hoping he wouldn't puke until safely back in quarters, Tregare tried to smile. "I figured that."

That day and the next were pretty bad: shakes and fever, and the alimentary canal purging itself both ways long after he felt it had to be empty. Chira wasn't around; he had no idea who had the care of her and was too drained to want to ask. The third day was better; by late afternoon he ate something and it stayed down. And near as he could tell, the fever was dropping, too. But still he was glad the infrequent mandatory reports from Control kept saying his presence wasn't needed there.

That night he woke drenched in sweat and felt the fever gone. He got up and showered and changed the bedding; he ate his first full meal since the bug had hit him. And every bite tasted delicious. But still he was weak, and more shaky than not, as he returned to bed.

He woke slowly and confused, not sure where he was or whether he still dreamed. There'd been a nightmare sequence, something about Butcher Korbeith spacing women out the airlock and bringing them, dead and frozen, back to the Slaughterhouse for the cadets to sleep with. But before Bran could see whether the one in his bed was Phyls Dolan or Tanit Eldon, everything changed—the bed was *real*, and so was someone else, with him. Was this a sex dream, or did he wake? He hadn't asked Zelde to stay over with him, had he? For a dream, this was more than he was used to—the rising urgency . . . He opened his eyes to see Chira moving above him, and it was too late to reconsider, because the Big Train was already rolling, and no brakes.

Judging from the sound she made as she collapsed onto him, she'd made it pretty big, herself.

Still joined, now she lay partly to his side. He said, "I thought you didn't want this." And realized, *hell, she doesn't even have an implant. Can't have. What—?*

With her strong, heavy jaw, Chira would never look delicate. But her tentative smile, the first he'd ever seen on her, had a sort of innocent quality to it. "Not for you, I be dead now." There had to be more, so he waited. "Me here allatime, you got nobody else. So—" She shrugged. "Good, too. Not like *them*."

"Well, I'm glad of that, Chira. And thank you. But now let's get up and go see Eda Ghormley. Maybe it's not too late for a contraceptive implant to take effect." She didn't understand, but she didn't argue, either.

Without explanations, feeling too drained to bother with them, Tregare made his request. Prim-mouthed, Ghormley swabbed Chira's thigh and disinfected the insertor before punching the little capsule into the muscle tissue. Then the Chief Medic couldn't hold back any longer. "Maybe it's not my place to say anything, captain, but I'm surprised and disappointed. Taking advantage of a girl this young! I wouldn't have expected it of you."

Tregare found no answer; the truth, even if Ghormley believed him, would sound like a whining excuse. So he stood, tongue-tied, while Chira looked back and forth between them. Frowning, she said, "Not him. Asleep, him." She jerked her thumb up to point at herself. "Me!"

Eda Ghormley's expression cleared, but only partway. "You mean you already have? Then you'll need a morning-after pill, too." She rummaged in a small, compartmented drawer,

"Here." When Chira had gulped the small tablet, the Medic said, "Is that right, Tregare? She caught you, not vice-versa?"

Maybe his grin didn't look sheepish but it sure felt that way. "The fever broke last night; afterward I was dead to the world. Don't remember hearing her come in, even."

Ghormley smiled. "Makes you feel silly, doesn't it? Well, *I* feel better about it, anyway. Not that it's any of my business. And don't you have someplace you should be, now?"

So Tregare thanked her, and he and Chira left.

Up in Control he found everything running on tracks, the way he liked it. The necessary course change had been made accurately by Gonnelson, and Turnover was still a time away. The only bad thing, aside from his own fatigue, was that when it came time for change of watch, Zelde M'tana called in sick.

Bran cut himself into the comm circuit. "You need any help, Zelde? You want to see Ghormley? I can send somebody down there right away, and we'll fudge the watches okay."

There was a pause—he could hear her retching—then, "Same thing you had, I think. I can get up to the infirmary, though, on my own. Better go while I still can. M'tana out."

Leaving Chira to Hain Deverel's care, in Control, Tregare went to the infirmary. Then, forcing his meager strength, he walked Zelde back to her own quarters before returning to question Ghormley. She didn't look happy as she said, "The girl brought it aboard, I'm afraid. Those bugs I noticed, that didn't seem to bother her. Some bacterium must have mutated, there on Backslid, and those people eventually developed immunity. But we haven't.

"I'd better take a culture, and see if I remember how to make a dead-bacterium vaccine. The live kind is beyond me."

Maybe the vaccine worked, partly, and maybe it didn't. No epidemic swept *Inconnu*, but cases of the new disease kept happening, a few at a time. And the bug seemed to grow in strength—Tregare had been flat-out ill for about three days, M'tana over a week, and later victims took longer and longer to recover.

The only good thing you could say about it, Tregare thought, was that nobody had died. Yet.

* * *

Turnover came and went; *Inconnu* was on point-seven decel for Far Corner. The worst three weeks were when the "Backslid Flu" hit Hold Portside Upper; nearly all the women caught the bug during that time and the place became a shambles. Even after the repeated moppings-up by crew members, the hold maintained a residual stench that would need draconian measures to clear away. And that grade of fumigation couldn't be done until the hold was empty of human occupation.

Tregare's own worst times came when Gonnelson and Deverel went sick two days apart, and *stayed* sick. Leaving Bran and Zelde, neither of them really fit to pull even a normal shift, to split the watches between them. And short-handed at that. The two had not been together sexually since Chira's advent, and now the whole idea became impossible. Well, he hadn't been doing all that much with Chira, either; he'd told her he needed his rest so she shouldn't wake him in the fashion she first had done. When she disobeyed him, he yelled through gritted teeth that if she had to behave like a spoiled brat, "Peace take you, you get treated like one!" Holding her sprawled across his lap by a wristlock, he took his doubled belt and whaled her butt red for her.

The effort nearly made him pass out. Panting, holding her down, he said, "Just one damned move, Chira, and you're down with the property!" And for a brief moment, he found himself wishing he was Butcher Korbeith.

Surprising him, she smiled. "Real man, you, Tregare. That good. Before, Chira not sure." As she went off to the shower—and thank peace she'd taken to cleanliness, once exposed to the chance for it—Tregare wondered about what had just happened.

He had a handle on her now and he knew it—but it wasn't the kind of handle he *wanted* on any woman; hitting had never been his style, and he didn't want to have to use it.

Finally he shrugged. Chira was Chira; he'd never known anyone like her before, and with luck he never would again, either.

Once more Chira tested the limits of his tolerance; then she settled down, mostly, and behaved herself. Sometimes she'd try a fit of the sulks or a little mild baiting, but nothing that bothered Bran too much. As to sex, she accepted the fact that if he had the energy he'd ask—or say yes if *she* asked. Nowadays, though, such occasions came very seldom.

For one thing, the nightmares. The bout of them following Tanit Eldon's treachery and execution had tapered off over the next month; now with the illness and its aftermath, the damned things were back, full force. Not since the Slaughterhouse, and on the *MacArthur* under Korbeith, had dreams so tormented Bran. Maybe that was why they seemed the worst ever. He could be in the Academy, or shipping with Korbeith, or anywhere else he'd ever been—but maddeningly, the people involved usually didn't fit the times or places.

Airlock drill! Alongside the Butcher stood Plastic Smile, suavely grinning above the handle of the icepick Tregare had thrust under the guard's chin and into his spine. Plastic Smile chuckled—the handle bobbed with his merriment—and pushed Bran's mother into the lock. Korbeith spaced her into vacuum. . . .

Tregare and Peralta were lifting off from The Islands. But wait—someone had been left behind! And running into Peralta's Drive blast, screaming and falling and curling up and frying, was Jargy Hoad.

And then the same thing, except now it was Megan Delange, already blotched and bloated from being spaced by the Butcher, who suffered further mutilation by flame.

Shaking his head, Tregare sat up. It was getting worse; he didn't know what to do. Sedative pills, when he tried them, didn't wear off in time when he needed alertness. One watch, he'd started to move the wrong control lever and caught himself just in time. Zelde, ready to leave but not gone yet, looked at him, until he said, "Sorry. Punchier'n a bird dog, these days. Guess I'll have to drop those peacewasting *pills*."

"How you figure to sleep, then, Tregare?"

He knew her concern, but stretched to breaking, all he could feel was anger. "Drop a rock on my head, why don't you?"

Her mouth registered a bad taste. "Tregare, was they any way I could do good to you—put Chira with Ghormley maybe, and *me* hold you, and wake you when I feel you going bad—that I'd do. But—"

"But there's only us to run the ship. Thanks, Zelde. Now flag your ass out of here and get some rest."

"Yeah, sure, Tregare. Wish *you* could, too, is all."

* * *

He hadn't thought his condition could worsen much more, but it did. Gonnelson and Hain Deverel stayed ill; for some time now they had been in Ghormley's infirmary, too weak to tend themselves. By the time Far Corner's beacon was heard, both Hats were able to be up and around part of the day, but nowhere near capable of standing a full watch.

Far Corner was a small colony; to Tregare's knowledge it mounted no missile defenses and had no organized UET garrison. He wasn't up to rigging a fake log, so he decided to go in as himself and dare anybody to do something about it.

"This is Bran Tregare speaking for the armed, Escaped ship *Inconnu*. Let me reassure you that if you deal fairly with me in matters of trade, refueling and the like, I will do this colony no harm. I can use some extra crew and am prepared to sign on any persons who satisfy me as to their intentions and loyalties." For a moment, he thought. "Passengers are something else. I can't divulge destinations. Tregare out."

He didn't expect much hassle but did figure on some, and was surprised when groundside made no protests at all. So on landing, he was wary. (M'tana did that landing; Bran wasn't fit for it.) But refueling and trade went entirely peacefully.

11. Tari Obrigo

Tregare's surprise ebbed when he tapped the computer logs at Second Site, Far Corner's spaceport town. By no means was his the first Escaped ship to visit this place; apparently the locals were pretty much laissez-faire in their politics.

Bran was pleased to find a coded note from Malloy, saying that *Pig in the Parlor* definitely hoped to make Tregare's rendezvous on Number One. The loose info network was working, all right.

When he began getting into more recent items, Tregare swore. He'd missed Kickem Bernardez, who still held cover by keeping his ship ensigned the *Hoover*, by less than a month. But Kickem's tape said, "Should an old squadmate of mine, from Cadre D of our beloved Academy, hear these words, I wish him to know that I shall make all endeavor to attend our planned reunion. Misfortunately I will likely have no chance to obtain a bottle of Irish poteen as would be most appropriate. But no doubt we can liberate something equally suitable." And then Bran had to chuckle. Kickem never changed much. . . .

Always tired, still Tregare dreaded sleep. After a time his mind had learned to give an alarm when nightmare began: if something truly didn't fit, somehow he made a mental twitch and woke up. So he was spared a lot of grueling horror—but he also lost a lot of sleep. Didn't help his disposition at all.

Daytimes, though his negotiations went peacefully enough, a lot of them carried a tedious amount of red tape. To keep his growing irritability within bounds, Tregare took to smoking a drugstick or two before each session; the things didn't help his fatigue, but did keep him short of blowing up in the face of unnecessary delays. Nothing he could do about feeling washed out all the time; as he explained to Eda Ghormley, he'd never been able to handle uppers and this was no time to try. One way and another, he lasted.

He had Ghormley sit in on all recruiting interviews; without questioning under truth drugs he was signing no one from a UET colony. Figuring time and distance, he was close to certain that no counterpart of Tanit Eldon could have reached this place yet. When he read off his list of questions, even one shaky answer scuttled the applicant; fair or not, securing *Inconnu*'s safety and integrity was the name of the game. Sometimes he wondered: was he letting Eldon's betrayal make him too jumpy? Way out here in the boonies, to suspect people of being planted agents rather than merely wanting to get free from UET? Well, maybe he was and maybe not. The hell with it; he was running enough risks already, without any unnecessary ones.

He'd relented enough to disclose to successful applicants that his next stop was Number One, but no one aboard except key navigating personnel knew that world's coordinates—and as far as Tregare was concerned, that was exactly how he wanted it.

At the end of his third day groundside, Bran had his ship full-up with new crew including trainable supernumeraries, plus as many passengers as could be crowded in. Since the passengers were going to Number One and nowhere else, thus were seeing the last of UET, in their cases he skipped the drugs.

When he checked his overall roster against quarters accommodations, Tregare realized he had literally filled the ship; if there were any vacant bunk except the spare in his own digs, he couldn't think of one. He was somewhat chagrined, then, to get a call from a trader named Bret Osallin, a one-armed man not much given to red tape, therefore easier to deal with than most here.

Now Osallin reminded him that he'd halfway promised to give consideration to a passenger represented by the trader, a woman who had been, while waiting for a ship to ride, taking a sort of tour of some of Far Corner's more interesting aspects. "She'd like to talk with you, Tregare. I told her you would."

Impatient, wanting to end the call, Bran considered. Damn it, he knew the background. Osallin had formerly captained a ship for UET, and was known as good to serve under. Then, one way or another, depending on which rumor you chose to believe, he'd lost the arm. And UET, with its usual generosity, had dumped him on this world with a meager and ironically-named "severance payment," to shift for himself.

So for several reasons, Tregare didn't want to turn this man down flat. Earlier, before the ship filled up, he'd hinted that maybe Osallin could use a lift out of UET country, but the man smiled and said, "No, thanks; I have a job to do, here." Well, certainly that was an attitude Bran understood.

But it didn't help him find an answer. Now he said, "I really have a full ship. Unless your client would like to ride in Hold Portside Upper where the bunks are four deep and some sleeping double. But—oh, hell, I owe you, I guess. For being good to deal with. So bring your client out, any time today. Maybe I can discourage the old bat and it won't be your fault."

Even without a screen, Osallin's grin was clear in his voice. "Maybe you can." Then the voice came serious. "But if you can possibly do so, Tregare, please consider taking this passenger. Her reasons are—well, rather urgent."

"We'll see. Bring her."

When Osallin—short, squat, his smile showing three gold teeth and missing one alongside that trio—brought his client into Tregare's quarters and introduced her, Bran saw what the grin he'd sensed was all about. No "old bat" was Tari Obrigo. Somewhere in her early twenties, Tregare guessed. Not tall, slim but somehow not at all fragile—quickly he assessed the identifying details. Clothes weren't anything he noticed much; her dress was a dark orange, fitted well, and wasn't showy. She had an oval face, dark brown eyes, black hair curling down around her shoulders. What else? Front teeth a little prominent, brows arched more than nature probably intended, and at the left nostril a small, fleshy mole. All right—now he'd recognize her. The only thing that bothered him was the way she moved—he remembered that from someplace, but couldn't figure quite where. . . .

Meeting Osallin's awkward lefthanded handshake, Tregare said to the woman, "Passage? I have room for one, only."

"I wish passage; my friend Osallin does not. How much?"

Damn, but she was arrogant. So he said, "What am I bid?" and when she seemed confused, added, "I'm not running a charity, Ms. Obrigo. Highest bidder rides."

"I see. And you have other bids?" Somehow irritated by the precision of her speech, he lied, saying that of course he did. *Why am I letting her get to me? Her self-assurance, maybe? Or—?* She asked to see those bids; sparring, he said everything had been verbal. She wanted to know the amounts; off the top of his head he quoted a sum that should certainly back her away. But all she said was, "And does that include the freeze-chamber?"

Serve her right if he said yes! But, "No freeze on here. The damned things aren't working right. Unreliable." Then, still sounding as if *she* ran this show, she asked how long the trip would be, ship's time. He shook his head, saying he didn't give out that kind of information, but that if she figured on a year she wouldn't miss it too far, either way.

From the look of her, she was ready to drop the matter and leave. But Osallin spoke. "Did I forget to mention, Captain Tregare, that Ms. Obrigo is a Hulzein protege? I believe you occasionally do business with Hulzein agents, other than myself?"

And then Bran knew where he'd seen it before, the way this woman moved. His aunt Erika Hulzein, the one who'd tried to have him killed: the time he'd seen her do combat display. Tregare's eyes narrowed. If *that's* it . . . All right—let's see how far they're willing to go. So he said, "Okay—the price is half of what I just told you. But no less. Not for anybody." *Now we'll see.*

Obrigo raised her arched brows. "What about the other bidders?"

"What you do on this ship is ride it. What you don't do is ask questions. You got it?" If he could drive her away, he would. But irrationally, he found himself hoping that he couldn't.

He saw her hesitate, then rally. "I always ask questions. Everywhere. But I agree—you have the right not to answer. And so do I."

Without intent, he found himself smiling. "We lift day after tomorrow, around sunset. Bring your gear aboard two hours early. No time for last-minute stuff; you see?"

"I understand." So Tregare nodded and led the two people to the door, where the guard waited to take them down off the ship.

Then Bran sat down and poured himself a drink. Thinking, this Obrigo was a wild card he hadn't asked to be dealt. *Was* she an agent of Erika's? In that case, what would she want? *Oh hell, Erika's long dead*. But her daughter would carry the same genes, the same aims. Yet how could anybody know he'd come *here*? In the Long View, a rendezvous planned by only one side simply couldn't happen. But still . . .

His suspicions made no sense; he knew that, but couldn't shake them loose. His parents, on Number One where he was going next: no, there was simply no way they could be involved. Could they . . . ?

His hand moved, as if to brush away cobwebs of fear. This was all garbage; it was the woman herself who bothered him. Something familiar there: not only movement but appearance—yet he couldn't place her. Chance resemblance, probably—but who? Damn, if he could be his real self again, not this stretched-out wreck, he'd put her in her place fast enough, and show her what uppity really meant. Or did he really want to do that . . . ?

Hell with it; he polished off his drink and went upship, back to work.

The next two days went hectic; when Obrigo showed up he was arguing some mistakes with groundside suppliers. He didn't have to argue; he could say "go to hell," and lift off. But he rather liked the idea of Far Corner as a buffer between UET and the Hidden Worlds, so he kept patience beyond his wont. Only at the edge of vision did he notice

Obrigo climb to the entrance deck, and Chira go to meet her. He'd told Chira to greet Tari Obrigo, feed her some coffee or whatever in the galley, and take her to captain's digs. Chira, he noticed, didn't offer to help carry the passenger's luggage. Well, maybe that could be a good start. After a while he disengaged the argument without too much prejudice, and went to see how Chira was doing.

The door to his quarters was open; he heard Obrigo say, "Why must I carry my gear from one place to another, where I will not be staying?"

Entering, standing behind her, he said, "You're staying here, Ms. Obrigo. The rest of the ship is full."

Chira yelled, "Yeah? Where *I* go?" When he laughed, saying she could stay right here and they'd all have lots of fun, she spat. "I don't do that stuff. I *don't*."

"Neither do I," said Obrigo. "Do not worry." And to Tregare, "I have bought passage—only that. Or else I leave this ship."

The whole ploy had got out of hand, but he was stuck with it. Well, sooner or later he had to test the limits; why not start now? He reached out, clenched a hand in her hair, shaking her head slowly from side to side. "Nobody's getting off—and you stay here. Don't crap me how you don't do this or that, either; I know the Hulzein training program. You got it?"

Her only reaction was to say, "Let go of my hair."

He did; she hand-brushed it back from her face, and said, "Erika has more than one training program."

"I know," he said, and left quarters for Control. It was time for lift, and time to see if he could do it.

Liftoff went well enough; bent out of shape Tregare might be, but still functioning. He set course for Number One, waited until Tinhead confirmed that aim and accel were correct within limits of acceptable error, then went downship to quarters.

Tari Obrigo and Chira must have been getting chummy; when he came in they moved farther apart. Chira had a guilty look to her, and Bran noticed a couple of nearly-empty shotsized glasses. So they'd been at his best booze, too. All right . . .

Where to push it? The passenger's luggage. "Inspection

time," he said, and saw Obrigo hestitate before she opened the bags to him. He searched quickly, determined that there were no hidden compartments of any size, and came up with a lockbox. "Open it."

She shook her head. "That is private—Hulzein business." And when he said that he was in a lot of Hulzein business himself, she claimed she had no authority in this matter and couldn't even open the thing, herself.

He didn't buy it. "You almost lie like a Hulzein—but not quite."

"Believe what you wish. I cannot oblige you."

He looked at the box and recognized its mechanism—a photolock, keyed to its bearer's retinal patterns. With one hand to her nape he brought the lock to her eyes. "Keep 'em open." But the lock didn't yield. He let her go. "Well, I've opened photolocks before."

"If you try this one, do it somewhere else. Or let me out of here—and Chira, also."

"Booby-trapped, is it? Fine—you can tell me how."

"You know Erika better than that, if you know her at all. Would she allow me to be a possible weak link?" And finally she convinced him she *didn't* know. So he might as well drop the matter.

He said as much, adding, "If you can't open it yourself, I don't have to worry you've got a weapon in there."

Eyes slitted, she laughed. "Is *that* what you were afraid of?"

"Afraid?" While her scorn tore at his gut. "Don't use that word to me, you bitch!"

In flat tones, she said, "Why not, you bastard?" Then he hit her—a slap, not a fist blow—somehow wondering how this woman could so provoke him. Showing no reaction, she said, "I see. You can call names but I cannot? This is hardly a good beginning for a friendly relationship."

"Friendly? All right—let's see you be friendly."

Unbelieving, then, he watched her remove and drop her clothing.

"You see? No weapons on my person, either." Without haste she lay on the larger of the two beds and spread her legs. "Very well, let us get on with it. What are you waiting for?"

I didn't intend this. But I have *to call her bluff*. "You know something? You're not a very *feminine* woman, are you?"

"I did not have a very feminine upbringing. I am as I am."

"Yeah—well, we'll see." As he got rid of his own clothes he saw her eyes widen briefly—maybe she hadn't seen Slaughterhouse scars before. For a moment he wondered if he could manage sex just now, but it had been a long time; the surge he felt told him that fatigue would not betray him.

Second thoughts might, though. So that they'd have no chance to do so, he simply plunged ahead without preparation, forcing himself into her and hammering away as he hadn't done since he was sixteen and someone taught him better.

At first he could tell she was withholding any reaction whatsoever; then he felt movements that had to be deliberately helpful, before his own overdue climax took away all thought.

Eventually he sat up, saying, "You didn't come?"

"I seldom do."

"Didn't even fake it—try to make me feel good."

"That, I *never* do."

"Chira does." And for the first time he realized he'd done this thing with the barbarian girl watching. Well, too late now, so, "She does it real good—don't you, Chira?"

"Better than her. Any time." Pouting, she said that.

"Well, not right now. Go get us all something to eat."

"You, sure, Tregare. She can get her own."

There was no thought at all, no volition. But his slap knocked her skidding. "You forgetting how to take orders?" Then Obrigo had hold of his arm and was saying to Chira that the two of them could share the chore. Tregare looked at her. "Ms. High-and-Mighty Paying Passenger wants to help with the scutwork?"

"To accommodate one another in small matters, yes."

His hand scythed air. "Oh, get the hell out. And hurry it up—I'm hungry."

Unblinking, she said, "It would serve you right if we ate in the galley and *then* brought your food. Cold."

Effort turned his snarl to a laugh. "Talk all you want, Obrigo. You know better than to do it."

Then she clothed herself and the two women left; Tregare, showering and then dressing, wondered what the hell was going *on*, here. One thing he knew: right now, he didn't really like himself too much.

Dinner, and wine afterward, relaxed him; conversation came easier. After a time, somehow the exchange of information led him to tell Tari Obrigo of the taking of *Inconnu*; she'd mentioned the garbled version that had him gaining command by mutiny against his own people, and he had to correct that.

So he told of the tensions and dangers, the treacheries that could happen with Escape: how after Leon Monteffial assumed command, Cleet Farnsworth's countermutiny had nearly given the ship back to UET. Except that Farnsworth hadn't realized Tregare was working outside the ship in a power suit, and would come back in and "—well, clean house, I guess you'd say. But I wrecked the suit, doing it."

Obrigo nodded. "That is most interesting, Tregare. It explains a great deal."

"Like what?"

"An experience of that sort must not be easy to live with. I will remember, and make allowances."

Draining the latest refill Chira had given him, he said, "Nobody has to make allowances for Tregare. On this ship *I* make the allowances. Don't forget that."

"Very well." But her smile mocked him.

He wouldn't let her bait him again; he said, "You're a smart one, aren't you, Obrigo? I'll keep it in mind."

"And I will keep in mind, Tregare, that you are another."

The talk wound down. Feeling a little mushminded but more alive than he had in some time, Bran said, "Tonight you two can argue who gets which side of the big bed. I'll use the other."

As ship's days passed, Bran felt easier on one level but still anxious at a deeper one. His first thought, that Tari Obrigo was a weapon of Erika's against him, no longer seemed reasonable. But then, what *was* she here for?

The harem thing wasn't an item he was proud of, but he'd begun it without meaning to; he could see no graceful way to ease out. Now that his strength was returning (thank peace for small blessings!) he took his occasional turns with Chira and with Obrigo—though now he tried to have one out of quarters when bedding the other. It struck him that as time passed he was less inclined, though still as attracted, toward Obrigo. Maybe it was the way he sensed that her muscular control, which sometimes heightened his pleasure, could just as easily shut him off. Once, maybe at her purpose or maybe not, that failure happened. Later he said to her, "If I thought you were playing games with me . . ."

She laughed. "We all play games—it is our nature."

"I don't."

"Of course you do. You are playing one now. The name of it is 'I don't play games.' "

Baffled, he told her he ought to space her "and the Hulzeins be hanged!" But later, in bed, she erased his displeasure.

As before, hailing and recognition at One Point One, the planet's spaceport, went easily. And this time there were people on duty, considerably older now, who remembered Bran from his previous visit. One of them patched him through to the appropriate official, and Tregare arranged for refueling to begin as soon as he landed.

He wanted that landing to come when ship's morning was also the port's, so Gonnelson figured the requisite number of hours *Inconnu* should spend in orbit first, and at what height—a little short of synchronous, it turned out. Then, for the last dinner in space, he ordered up a real spread. Chira looked impressed, and even Tari Obrigo expressed appreciation without her usual hint of mockery. At the meal's end he brought out a dusty, oversized bottle of wine. "This stuff I save for special landings, and there's only enough for three more." Going into Far Corner, he reflected, he'd been too frazzled even to think of any celebration.

Sipping, Obrigo nodded. "Delicious. I hope you can replenish your supply."

Chira laughed. "Not hardly, he can't. Comes from UET's main base, off Earth. Armed ships all over, he says."

Tregare found himself explaining how he'd gone into Stronghold with fake papers, for repairs. "That trick won't work a second time. But you never know—someday I may try the place again."

Obrigo nodded. "Yes—with a few more armed ships . . ."

Was she a mindreader? "What have you heard?"

Nothing specific, she said, except that he'd taken at least one other Escaped ship, maybe more. So he was building a fleet. "Will you take more armed UET ships, or arm your own?"

He glared, but kept his voice low. "Nothing's safe from you, is it? All right—either, or both. I have—"

"You have someone trying to duplicate this ship's weapons. I will not ask where. But the projector unit missing from its turret—not removed for repairs, I think, because the defective freeze-chambers are still in place. And *why*, may I ask?"

"You trying to tell me how to run my ship?"

Now she glared, too. "Somebody should!"

She was sometimes a hard person to agree with. When he said, yes, he'd offload those chambers, immediately she told him to maintain ownership in case they could be repaired. He yelled a little. ". . . next you'll tell me how to zip my own shoes!"

Chira giggled. "You sure let her get you mad a lot."

Looking then from one to the other, all he could say was, "You're giving her bad habits, Obrigo—you know that?"

"I do not consider honesty a bad habit."

Tregare managed to turn his explosive laugh into a cough. "Yeah. Like she said, you do get me mad. But—you know? I'll miss you."

Surprisingly, she reached for his hand. "Tregare? At the first of this trip, I hated your guts."

"I wasn't crazy about yours, either. So?"

"I am not certain, Tregare, if I *like* you or not—or whether anyone should—but you are important to me. I wish you survival and success."

"Same to you and many of 'em. Anything else?"

"Yes. Tregare, will you sleep with me tonight?"

For some time he hadn't touched her; what moved her now, he couldn't guess. But in the big bed—once, and then again later—she showed him skills she'd never before displayed. Nor, in his personal experience, had anyone else. He didn't know why and he couldn't ask, but he felt deeply grateful.

In the dim light he saw, at the corner of one eye, a tear forming. "What's wrong?"

"This time—this time, Tregare, I truly wanted you. But my body would not believe that want."

There was nothing he could say and not much he could do. But he went to sleep holding her.

* * *

When the landing woke him, though—M'tana had the con—he and Tari were disarranged, lying spraddled all over the bed. He worked one leg free from under hers, disengaged other minor entanglements, and pulled the spread up to cover her when he left.

First he stopped by the galley and assembled a snack, which he took with him to Control; if a captain couldn't break his own rules, who could? Deverel was relieving M'tana at the watch. Tregare said, "Good landing, Zelde. If I hadn't been half awake already I'd've slept right through it." On her way out, the tall woman grinned and threw him a sketchy salute.

The log and instruments were all shipshape. Bran told Hain Deverel, "Except for the usual airlock guards for screening, we don't need Alert procedures here. I think you know what kind of items to handle by the routines, and what to call me for or record for me." Deverel nodded; Tregare took his empty tray back to the galley and went down to the main airlock foyer, where he expected—and found—a group of traders and brokers, all ready to haggle and smiling about it. But it didn't take long for the smiles to vanish and the voices to raise; Bran remembered that Number One was a place for loud and profane dickering.

So, whole-heartedly he entered into the spirit of the occasion.

Some of the dealings went easily, some harder, and some not at all. Meanwhile Tregare heard the fueling pumps start, and made a sort of nod to himself that there was *one* worry covered. Then he put his mind back to arguing with a rather cadaverous elderly man, mostly bald but sporting a thin, grey goatee. The man's nasal whine was irritating, but Alsen Bleeker held the handle on some categories of foodstuffs Tregare didn't want to have to pick up in dribs and drabs from smaller suppliers, so it made sense to make the extra effort. Suddenly the name and appearance clicked; Bleeker was the man who had tried to get cute with his prices on Tregare's earlier visit here. *So watch him*. He'd been on the young side of middle age then, but that was the Long View for you. . . .

A voice broke his concentration; over by the exit ramp, Tari Obrigo was calling to him. His hand waved the argument to a halt. "A few moments, gentlemen. A farewell to say, here." He went to her, gave her a one-arm hug around the shoulders. "So you're getting off. All done with me now."

"Done? Will that not depend on our travels, yours and mine? If I settle here, I may be old before you next return."

The idea hurt him. He looked away, but said, "I might like that. We'd go to bed and *you'd* be the grateful one."

She laughed; a thumb and knuckle nipped his earlobe. "Do not bet on it. But stay in communication when you can, and I shall, too. Good luck, Tregare."

He watched her, luggage-laden, walk to the ramp and down it, out of sight. Then he returned to the dickering. But somehow found it hard to keep his mind to it.

When he'd settled as many of his dealings as could be managed at this point, Tregare hosted a few of the traders—those who accepted his invitation—to lunch in the galley. Then, he decided, it was time to go visiting. Because the ship that sat down the port a way, easy walking distance, was Fell Quinlan's *Red Dog*.

The ramp guard was officious but not unfriendly. Going by protocol, Bran gave his name and that of his ship, then said of the woman beside him, "This is Zelde M'tana, my Second Hat." Zelde had told him about meeting with Quinlan on Fair Ball and declining his offer of a supercargo passage; in this case, though, there was no reason for her dodging the man.

After a brief talk on his hushphone the guard passed them, and at the airlock another took over, ushering them to the captain's digs. There Quinlan—still lean and tall, wearing a pointed, tawny beard—gave welcome. Handshakes, offer of drinks, then while busy at the pouring, "A long time, Tregare. And you, M'tana—I see you found your way off Fair Ball without help from me."

So they talked, exchanged info and anecdotes, until Tregare decided it was time to make his pitch: the fleet to take Stronghold, then wait and collect successive fleets sent out from Earth, and then—

Quinlan was shaking his head. "It might work—I wish you luck. But I operate solo, always have—and can't imagine doing it any other way." He raised his glass. "I'm sorry, Tregare."

Bran shrugged. "I knew it already. Had to ask, was all. But now—" He leaned forward. "Where you headed next? And how much filled up, with cargo?" The answers suited Tregare quite well. So then he made his *real* pitch.

* * *

"I lucked out fine, Zelde." He'd dickered with Quinlan for nearly an hour but now he and M'tana were walking back to *Inconnu*. "Farmer's Dell isn't too far off the course he was planning, and he can free enough space for the women to be comfortable. Well, reasonably." He looked at her. "You handle the workgang that moves the bunks over to *Red Dog*, will you?" She nodded. "I'm glad Pell can take care of the plumbing in a hurry, using his own people to do it."

She cleared her throat. "The women, now. You out to tell 'em the news, or me?"

"Let's do it together. I know you're worried about how it'll work, at Farmer's Dell, but the colony administration has a fund set up; it pays passage rates for any women brought in on the cuff."

"And then? I know, you *said* they're free, but—"

"Everything I've heard documents it that way." He smiled. "Ol' Pell, though. That fake log and ship's ID he worked up. I wish I had time to talk him out of a readout on that. It sounds better than anything I've ever done, along those lines." He shrugged. "Well, I remember enough to give me some good ideas."

"Too bad he's so much a one-man show, Tregare."

"Yeah. I could sure use him on the project. He's just not a man to take orders. Never was. But he'll cut himself some notches."

Upship and in quarters, first Tregare showered and changed clothes. Then he had a drink and told Chira about his latest deal. "So that saves me some worries. And without gouging Quinlan I netted about ten percent over expenses, on the operation. He'll make three times what I did, but I don't have to sidetrack to Farmer's Dell!"

He knew the financial side meant nothing to her, so her frown puzzled him. She said, "I go there, too. With them."

"But—" He shook his head. "Maybe you forgot. Those women down there—last I heard, they didn't like you pretty much."

"Not now, that way. Food runs, I been helping. Talk some. First on here, I didn't *know*. Told 'em, sorry. Nobody mad, now." Her face had a pleading look. "You good to me. But on here—" She spread her hands. "No wind. No rain. No *sky*."

So he said, "All right. You come downship with us when

Zelde and I announce the latest development, and we'll see how it goes. Okay?"

So they went down to Hold Portside Upper, and first Zelde and then Tregare explained the situation. The woman Cherisse Frisco looked maybe a decade younger than when she'd been brought aboard *Inconnu*; there was something to be said for decent food and adequate sanitation. She asked questions, and so did others, but eventually they seemed reasonably satisfied. "I wish there were a way you could get us to a Hidden World, not a UET colony," Frisco said, "but I know economics. It *cost* you, to buy us out of that shitbox, and your ship's resources are finite. Besides, Farmer's Dell doesn't sound too bad."

"The place does have a good name," said Bran. "Now one more thing." He motioned toward Chira. "This young woman was yanked out of a backslid savage culture and came aboard here without much in the way of manners. First thing, she got a bunch of you killing-mad. She thinks she's cleared that up, since, and wants to ride with you to Farmer's Dell. Tell me honestly, Frisco—is that a good idea? For her?"

Cherisse Frisco smiled. "Sure it is. So she *did* act like a rotten little savage, then. Thinking back on it, the rest of us weren't too much better. Don't worry; there'll be no problems."

Zelde's work crew was beginning to disassemble bunks, with the women's help. Tregare took Chira back upship to pack the few belongings she'd accumulated. Briefly he wondered why he hadn't suggested simply turning her loose here on Number One, then he realized she couldn't handle herself, alone on a strange world. But as part of a group, she'd be all right.

She went in for a shower. He thought she'd come out dressed and ready to go downship and join the others, but she didn't. Unclothed, she tossed her garments onto a chair, and said, "I told you, you been fine, Tregare. Now I go, fuck you a good one first. For to remember."

This time he was pretty sure she didn't fake her climax.

And next day she and the others were off to Farmer's Dell.

With a few things off his mind, Bran got around to checking the Port's computer for messages; maybe his growing data net had some good news for him, or maybe not.

Only a little, was the answer. Jimar Peralta had been here

once; his comment was, "You picked the right world, Tregare, for your staging base. I didn't venture to inspect your own private spaceport in person, but on hi-mag it looks shipshape, and having it out away from the civilians is a good idea." And after a brief pause, "I'm off, now, on what you might call a raiding tour of UET colonies; the more they're shaken up, the better. My planned schedule will have *No Return* back here during your rendezvous period." Another pause. "I still feel we need to restructure the administrative side a bit, but I'm sure it can all be worked out." And Tregare thought, *he's still after part of command, Peralta is. . . .*

In the next few messages Tregare found nothing important. Then came a voice he barely remembered and at first couldn't place. But before she spoke it, he remembered the name of Erdis Blaine. ". . . a job in Port Admin, the greeting and querying of ships, before and since your son was born. He's Bran Leon Blaine, by the way." So she'd commemorated Leon Monteffial, her lover killed in Farnsworth's countermutiny. Tregare nodded; the man deserved as much. ". . . leaving now on Keath Farrell's *Spark Plug*, and I hope our destination is a place where Bran Leon can grow up peacefully. Blaine out." Well, he hoped she got her wish.

Alsen Bleeker didn't seem to be a quick learner. Some days later, when *Inconnu*'s loading neared completion, the man suddenly tried to change his terms. "Some of that electronics gear you brought," he said. "You have it priced higher than I can sell it." That, Tregare thought, was probably an outright lie, but when he tried to check with Port Admin's computer, the data came out garbled. Cute trick! So the hell with it; Tregare left the trader standing there groundside, went upship and sent an armed squad down to safeguard the rest of the loading.

Only when that was done did he lift the ramp and close ship. And that's when he learned that Junior Lee had found a bug in the Drive; *Inconnu* couldn't lift right away.

Well, all right. He put his downside screens to showing the area around the ship, and opened communications on groundside frequencies to Bleeker. When the man answered, Tregare said, "I'm checking the computations, but I'm having a little computer trouble. Would you have Admin feed me the manifest figures again?" Seemingly relieved, Bleeker agreed, and this time the data came through clearly. Bran wasn't surprised to find most of Bleeker's prices raised considerably from the terms previously set. Well, the best thing, for now, was just plain stalling. Tregare did a rather artful job of it.

Meanwhile he eavesdropped on Bleeker's shorthaul talkset. The man was rounding up an unofficial army, claiming that Tregare had cheated him and possibly several others. "After all, he *is* known as a pirate." Tregare made a face—if he was a pirate, what did that make Alsen Bleeker? But, not to give away his advantage in overhearing, he said nothing.

By the time Junior Lee announced readiness for liftoff, armed groundsliders ringed the safety perimeter around *Inconnu*. "Normal" safety perimeter, that was; if Tregare made a max lift he'd probably kill no one but he could sure bounce a few around. The group's weapons didn't bother him much; besides a couple of two-hands energy guns that might scar the hull at that range, all he saw was standard handguns. They'd make pretty sparks but nothing more.

What did worry him some was eavesdropping on Bleeker's pitch to interdict *Inconnu* with the Port's defense missiles. Only one side of that argument, Tregare got; whatever frequencies the Port was answering on, Bran's comm-tech couldn't find them. So when Bleeker said, "Thirty minutes? Can't you get faster authorization? Well, I guess it'll have to do. And thanks—" When Bran heard that much, he told Junior Lee to lift in fifteen unless delayed by Tregare's personal countermanding. And at max.

"Right y'all purely are, cap'n. Thisyere ship, she gonna show 'em sump'n, you bet my tired ol' tailend."

Before Bran could finish giving Beauregard the usual supportive thanks, Gonnelson pointed at the forward screen. "Aircar!"

The comm-tech hit a switch; Tregare yelled, "You up there! What you trying to pull? Clear off or get shot down." Then to groundside: "*You*, Bleeker—I thought you had better sense. Call off your pipsqueak Air Force—and damned fast!"

As the aircar turned away, still circling the ship but at a more civil distance now, Bleeker spoke high-pitched and fast. It wasn't his, he swore. He knew nothing about it; he'd been right here ever since Tregare closed ship. "All I want is my money, you pirate!"

"You got it—exactly as agreed, beforehand." Bleeker whined that it wasn't *his* fault if prices went up. Tregare snorted.

"Your prices always go up; that's an old groundhog trick. And like it or not, most ships pay. But not *Inconnu*!"

Incredibly, Bleeker didn't know the ship was refueled, and tried to use fuel as leverage. Bran laughed and corrected his ignorance. "That's an old *spacer* trick." Then he signed off, and called the aircar again. "Who are you? What's your business?"

The answering voice came low and sounded concerned, not excited. "Tregare! It is I—Tari Obrigo. I must talk with you."

He shook his head. What—? "Too late; no time. Bleeker'll be programming the defense missiles on me; I've got to lift." He paused. "Glad you came, though. See you someday."

"Wait! Your father is here. He brought me."

"Hawkman? Sorry, but for him it's *years* too late—ever since they left me in that UET hellhole."

"They could not help it; they had no choice! And they—they love you—they want to see you."

"The pirate, the mutineer, in Hulzein Lodge? I doubt it."

"Bran Tregare, the girl speaks truth." Hawkman! "And she cares enough that she would have come here against Liesel's command."

Obrigo would have defied Liesel Hulzein? Somehow Tregare wasn't too surprised. He said. "She's quite somebody, Hawkman. See that you treat her right."

He missed a word or two, then "... we miss you. Are we never to see you again?"

For a moment, his guts wrenching, Tregare couldn't speak. Then he said, slowly, "I'll think about it. Next time, maybe."

"And how long? Will your mother live to see that time?"

"I—I hope so." Then, hearing what Bleeker was saying on the other channel, he called down to Junior Lee. "Liftoff coming; sixty seconds and counting." Then to the aircar again, "Scoot hard and fast, Hawkman; this lift is going to make waves. Not like the time with you, Tari." The car sheered away as Tregare got confirmation from Junior Lee. He said a few more words to Tari and to his father, then *Inconnu* lifted.

Before dust hid groundside, Bran saw the armed posse rolled away like rag dolls by the mere blast-outskirt pressures. Then they began to get up and run away.

If Bleeker got any missiles aloft, he wasted them; the ship's backscreens showed no sign. Tregare set course, cutting back to less than half-max accel, and called council. "We've talked all this over, but I want a last-minute check, to see if anybody has improvements to offer." So, in no hurry, they kicked the plan around.

Basically, *Inconnu* was going to be on a combination of listening-post and patrol duty. Number One's sun had a very large planet—practically a grey dwarf—that rolled sullenly around its primary at roughly two week's ship-distance from Number One. And for a number of years that world, Big Icecube (though actually it had considerable internal heat), had been and would be in a position to monitor most ship traffic between Number One and other inhabited places. So for the period during which Tregare was hoping other ships would make the rendezvous he'd spent years trying to arrange, *Inconnu* would stay in energy-saving orbit around Big Icecube. Relaying data from incoming ships long before groundside gear could have detected the signals, for one thing. All right? So far, so good.

"Now then." Tregare waited while Gonnelson, the one-drink man, saw to fillups for the others, who weren't being too thirsty, themselves. When the First Hat was done, Bran said, "Soon as we pass the range a scout could be detected from groundside, I take our scoutship back to Number One, going in on a blindside spiral. The gear's loaded and the work crew's picked, for what we need to do at my bases, across the Big Hills from One Point One."

Zelde M'tana spoke. "Crew's picked, you said. Not all, though. Who's to strawboss for you? *That* ain't said yet."

"You want the job?"

She shook her head; at her left earlobe the heavy gold ring swung. "Makes me no mind. I'll do it or ride here, either one."

Tregare smiled. "It happens I think I need you on here—you and Gonnelson. Pick a couple of bright ratings to help out on the watches." She nodded as Bran looked to his Third Hat. "Hain, I'd like you to help handle things at the bases." And before Deverel's reaction could develop past looking startled, "You and Anse, that is." Then the officer relaxed, and a little later the council convened.

Carrying the dozen that the scout could hold comfortably, that small craft emerged from *Inconnu* and put on decel to head back to Number One. Maintaining a blindside course, so as not to be spotted on his way in, Tregare timed his moves closely. Number One's major, circular-orbiting moon helped a lot.

Gingerly, all senses at max alert, he brought the scout down at Base Two, the rudimentary spaceport he'd ramrodded when he first visited this world. The appearance of the place delighted him—with absentee management he'd tried not to be too optimistic, but he saw no clutter nor plant overgrowth, and the buildings looked shipshape, well-tended.

Since nothing ensured this was still *his* base, he went down the ramp armed and not alone. At groundside he paused until a man and woman, also armed, came out of a quarters building. Tregare raised his voice to carry. "Do you work for MacDougall and Aguinaldo? If you do, you work for me."

Approaching, the woman said, "You're Tregare?" He nodded. "Mac's retired; got a leg smashed, hunting bushstomper. He still does Pete's books, but no full-time work."

"Sorry to hear it." Time for business. "You two here alone?"

"No." The man whistled, and another weaponed couple emerged from behind an innocent-looking scrap pile. *Nice caution.* Everybody shook hands. The woman pointed out the Base office and comm building, then said, "Captain? Now that you're back, do we still have jobs here?"

"Sure. Things'll change, but likely we'll need more people, not less." Inside the office prefab, Tregare saw it was too small for his needs. But a larger one was empty, so he assigned space there for his administrative kipple and left the work crew to see to it while his own people got the scout unloaded. Emila Thorndeck, the stocky thirtyish woman who spoke for the mainenance gang, seemed to have things in hand—so, taking only Deverel and Kenekke with him, Bran lifted the scout for his Base One, the cabin on the higher, gently sloping plateau.

Setting down, he wondered what, after all this time, to expect. Buildings and ground seemed well maintained. Operating his key in the trick sequence that nullified alarms, he found the cabin's interior bare, stark, and dusty, but intact. All the fixtures were there, and so were the stored emergency rations. The attic tank gave only driblets of stale water, so Tregare started the pump and heard fluid surge through the pipe—his well still functioned. Leaving the other two to shake the place down, since they'd be staying there while Bran dossed in the scout, he went out to check the rest of the premises.

It looked good; Pete and Mac had done the job right. Back against the rising cliff his small warehouses were stocked as specified; he was surprised to find two empty crates that had held ships' turret projectors, and couldn't imagine what cooperative act of piracy had brought them here. But gift horses by definition have perfect teeth—so, grinning, Tregare headed for the gully-end of his escape tunnel, followed it to the upward side-exit, and found the projectors mounted in his pillbox. The power switch worked; the units traversed either separately or together, to cover the plateau or guard the cabin. Cutting power to a trickle, so as not to alarm the two men indoors, he fired—the faint hiss and ionization trails said the guns were operative.

Missile control tests showed Ready, too. Yeah, the place was in good shape. Just like he wanted it.

Back in the cabin, Kenekke was cooking dinner. Not "iron rations" but food from the scout. Joining the party, Tregare ate, and had a beer with Deverel. Then at the scout he rigged a relay circuit, so the cabin's intercom could talk with Base Two, below. When he went back to the cabin and tried it, the first thing he didn't like was that Emila Thorndeck had no aircars on hand; one was down for repairs and the other two were across the Big Hills in One Point One. He didn't like his base letting *all* its mobility go someplace else, but he didn't want to start off hassling these people, either. So he asked about the comm situation, Base Two to city or Port, and that was better: the scatter circuit had been down for a while but was okay now. So he could say, "Good," and ask for delivery of an aircar to him as soon as posible, and add, "First chance, I'd like to see Pete. Preferably this side of the Hills, and do the talking over a few drinks I owe him."

Thorndeck chuckled. "I think Pete would hold still for that."

Signing off the call, Bran went to the cabin's front window. Out past the plateau's edge the last of sunlight tinged the horizon, far out on that vast upland plain. *There's nothing like it*. Checking his wrist chrono, he turned to the two men. "Everything else I need to do tonight is from the scout. See you in the morning." So now Deverel and Kenekke would know that even though it was his cabin, he wouldn't be invading their privacy.

Aboard the scout he checked his charts and swiveled the little ship's antennae the best he could figure. Then he set up a loop tape, calling *Inconnu*. Round-trip comm lag had grown to boring length, but he waited. All he got, though, was a rating filling in as watch officer, and confirming that the ship was on course and on sked.

Hell with it. Making a polite acknowledgment, he ended the call. Early still, for sleep. But maybe a little extra would do him good. If his nerves would ease down and *let* him.

Pete Aguinaldo, bringing the aircar next day, didn't look as old as Tregare expected. He was still slim, fluid of movement, his hair black and face unlined. The main difference was that Pete's familiar smile wasn't there *all* the time.

Finally Tregare figured it out. For almost the only time since Bran had first met him, Pete wasn't stoned. There wasn't any way to ask about the change, so Tregare didn't. Well, he had no need to; he knew about "negative tolerance" and could think of no lesser force that would have weaned Pete Aguinaldo from cannabis.

So, with a little bourbon for lubrication, they got down to business. Looking around the scout, Pete said, "You still keep it shipshape, Tregare. And it's been a time."

"Longer for you than for me." *The Long View*, and somehow Bran didn't want to know how long it had been, here, groundside. So he reached for the Base Two inventory readouts Pete had brought, scanned them and made notes. Handing them back, he said, "Back at One Point One, see if you can order this stuff out for me and have it delivered to the Port. I could do it over the circuits, but in-person usually works better."

"Sure. I'll tell you when it's ready for pickup." Aguinaldo frowned a little "Tregare? I was surprised you didn't get in touch when *Inconnu* was here."

Bran waved a hand. "I wanted to. But too many deals to make in a hurry. And then get the ship out safe. Little problem with Alsen Bleeker, I guess you heard."

A nod. "He's still running around, claiming you cheated him."

Tregare felt his face go rigid; was this man doubting him? "He tried to gouge me on prices, after terms were set. I didn't let him, was all."

The familiar smile came. "I thought so. I've dealt with you and Bleeker both, and what you say fits what I know."

So *that* was all right. Pete accepted one refill on his drink, talking, catching Bran up on events he'd missed here. Tregare thought to order out two aircars for his own use, and Pete agreed. Not long after, while the pass would still hold daylight, Aguinaldo took his leave.

When one scoutsized load of supplies, including an aircar, was ready at the Port, Bran lifted across the Hills and accepted delivery. Part of the stuff was for Two and part for the cabin. And now, with his new aircar, he could shuttle between bases without wasting the scout's fuel.

Next day Aguinaldo called to say the other car was ready, and a pilot could bring it across by afternoon. Tregare said, "I'll be down at Two; send it there. I'll get the pilot back to town on tomorrow's shuttle run." Pete, less talkative than usual, agreed and signed off.

At Base Two, Tregare was rearranging his landing circles; the first setup was fine for safety but not handy for loading a *group* of ships. *And when the hell will they get here?* But he wanted his tractor, towing loaded flats, to have clear runs from warehouses to any ship. And then there was refueling. So he wound up with his circles in a zigzag line, the buildings on one side of it and the tanks on the other.

Done with that chore, he was having coffee in Emila Thorndeck's cramped office when he heard the first sounds of an approaching aircar. No hurry; he finished the coffee, not strolling outside until the car landed.

He got ten paces beyond the door. Then he stopped. Climbing out of that aircar was a very tall man.

Tregare's father, Hawkman Moray.

12. Rissa Kerguelen

Fighting shock, Tregare stood rooted. *He hasn't changed much*. As his father came forward, one hand out for greeting, Bran found words. "What the hell are *you* doing here?" His voice, high-pitched and strained, didn't sound right to him.

Hawkman's smile hadn't changed, either. As Bran submitted to the handshake but glared away any thought of embrace, the older man said, "Why, I brought your aircar. Obviously."

"Pete's letting just anybody come in here? I thought security was one of the things I was paying for. I—" Dammit, if only his head would stop pounding. . . !

"Not just anybody." The deep voice was mild. "And I've never been here before, to either of your bases; I've only seen them from the air, and at a distance. Interesting, though."

"Spying on me? Is that it?"

"Not at all. Bran, *everybody* knows you have something set up out here; Mac and Pete kept close wraps on their dealings with you, but things do leak out. Though your zigzag pass through the Hills—or rather, how to get through it safely—is still largely a secret." Again the smile came, but rueful now. "I know how because I was along on the hunt with Mac when he got bushstomped; he couldn't fly the car himself so he *had* to talk me through. That made me one of the gang, I suppose; Pete showed me the eastbound strategy, next time *we* went hunting."

With his gut sometimes a lump of ice and sometimes a blazing coal, Tregare nodded. "Okay, thanks for bringing the car. A drink goes with that, so come on in. I'll set you up for meals, and a bunk tonight, and the shuttle can run you back in the morning."

Following into Tregare's own, new office, Hawkman said, "Thank you, Bran. That's fair enough."

Without asking, Tregare poured bourbon. Not very big slugs, because his hands trembled and he didn't want to betray his weakness by spilling anything. The damned *tension*! He tried to analyze it: not fear. Not even anger, as he knew anger—yet he was stretched as tight as even Butcher Korbeith had been able to manage. Now he *knew* he'd been right, all these years, to stay the hell away from his family.

Sitting down, across from Hawkman who was also seated, helped some, but when Tregare raised his glass he needed both hands to hold it halfway steady. Trying to ignore his shame at the loss of control, he said, "Cheers, I suppose."

They sipped. Hawkman said, "Bran? Don't you realize? *We had no choice*."

"But you *left* me!" He tried to stop, to say no more, but his voice kept going anyway: the Slaughterhouse, the awful brutality. Butcher Korbeith, his filthy ways of piling fear. Megan Delange at Korbeith's airlock, her body spewing as though she were trying to get rid of it. Phyls Dolan—feeling his face contort into pain, Bran saw tears run down Hawkman's cheeks.

As if a maul hit his solar plexus, Tregare doubled over in cramp. He lost hold of his glass and heard it shatter on the hard floor. His belly wrenched and spasmed; grimly he made effort and did not vomit.

But it wouldn't *stop*. He felt arms around him and tried to shake free, but he had no strength. Vertigo struck; it felt like having drunk twice too much and fighting to keep from passing out. The beat of blood in his head brought pain and more pain. He tried not to hear the voice saying, "Bran, Bran—" It was too much; he couldn't stand it; something would break.

And then it did. He heard a dull groaning, half roar and half wail, and knew he made that sound himself but could not stop it.

Slowly the pressure drained; the great, choking sobs abated, and finally, clasped in his father's arms, Bran Tregare was only crying. And so was Hawkman.

When they could sit up and look at each other, mopping away the tears and—Bran, at least—feeling sheepish, Tregare fixed new drinks. His hands, now, were steady. Hawkman said, "Breaking out of armor can be a terrible experience, can't it?" At Tregare's nod, he said, "Why did you need it to be *so total*?"

So Bran explained: at the Slaughterhouse, the seductive dreams of home and family, always ending in dread and shock at waking, until his only defense was to turn against his past, his family, and *hate* them.

Hawkman heard him through, then said, "Do you still hate us?"

"Reflex, yes; reason, no."

The tall man nodded. "Then can we lean toward reason now? Because I have a favor to ask you before I go to my bunk here."

Tregare stood. "Bunk, hell. Come on; we'll fly up to the cabin and stay in the scoutship tonight. We're overdue for dinner, I expect, but Pete gave me some bushstomper steaks for the freezer."

Almost like Earth beef, bushstomper had a special tang to it. After both men had eaten heartily and were tapering down with wine and coffee, Tregare sat back, more relaxed than he felt he should be. Well, *acting* relaxed and businesslike was helping a lot. He cleared his throat. "A favor, I think you said?"

Half-shrugging, Hawkman spoke. "Local politics here. A protégé of ours, Liesel's and mine, you could say. She's in trouble and we'd like to help her, and *not* only because she owns sufficient wealth to become an oligarch and a good ally."

Tregare frowned. "What's the help problem?" He didn't understand, and said so.

"Are you married, Bran? At the moment?"

"Never have been. Why?"

"Then to give Rissa Kerguelen the protection of Hulzein Lodge, through a critical time that's coming, your mother and I would like you to marry her."

Memory took its time, clicking in. Rissa Kerguelen? Oh sure—back on Earth. The stubble-headed kid on the Tri-V, the one who lucked out in UET's lottery and was buying free of Total Welfare. And taking precisely no crap at all from the Tri-V interviewers. Tregare said only, "Yeah. I know who she is. But how the hell did she get *here*?"

"Why, on your ship, of course." Tregare waited, and finally Hawkman said, "I believe you knew her as Tari Obrigo."

That one, peace take it! Who had put up with indignities, on *Inconnu*, that would hardly leave her fond of one Bran Tregare. Thinking fast, he said, "She might not care for the idea. Anybody ask her?"

Headshake. "Not until the crisis point. Liesel wants her Hulzein-connected by marriage; it's a matter of mutual strength." He sighed. "It's also contingent. Because Rissa must first survive a death duel with Stagon dal Nardo. It seems he tried to bully her, but the end result was his own humiliation."

From so long ago, the name took a moment to register. "That overgrown calf? Yeah—last time I was here, he tried to give *me* trouble."

"A calf no longer, Bran. A bull now, and dangerous; he heads that clan of assassins and has murdered his way to high standing."

Tregare's eyes narrowed. "*I* could take him. So why not—?"

"The rules. You'd need to wait your turn, after he's met Rissa's challenge."

"*She* challenged?"

"She was more or less forced to it. But in any case, I doubt Rissa would allow you to preempt. I've seldom seen such inflexible pride in a young person."

Thinking back to his own dealings with Tari Obrigo, Tregare made a number of reevaluations, and said, “Sometimes it's not all that easy to see what somebody's really like.”

Briefly, Hawkman smiled. “I have the impression that Rissa has come to the same conclusion about you.”

Wary as always, Tregare asked more questions. *Why* this marriage thing? The answers sounded plausible, but plausible wasn't good enough. Who was going to set it up, and how? Was his own identity as a Hulzein heir going to be revealed? “In short, Hawkman, how phony does this thing have to stack up?”

Tregare's father looked placid enough. “You needn't be named at all, at the time. In fact it's better if you're not. Arrive in hooded garb, if you like.”

“Will *she* know?”

“That's up to Liesel, or to your sister Sparline.”

His sister—he hadn't thought of her in years. He said, for want of anything else to say, “How old is Sparline now, bio?”

“Perhaps a year older than yourself, whereas the opposite was once true. Does it matter?”

“I guess not.” A big difference *would* have mattered.

“Well, then,” Hawkman said. “Will you do it? If Rissa survives?”

Tregare thought about it, then nodded. “All right. But don't tell her I know who she really is. I want to do that myself. Assuming she lives to hear it.”

Suddenly, to Tregare the whole situation seemed unreal. Earlier this same day he had been engrossed in the problems of his own long-term goals. Now, without warning, his past had struck—and hard enough, apparently, to derail the train of his concentration and common sense. Now he shook his head, not in negation but to earn a pause. “Hold it—I have to think.”

Hawkman chuckled. “Surely. And from hearsay, not to mention heredity, I gather you're well equipped to do so.”

For moments his father's warm humor took Bran back to his childhood, the safe home he'd lost so long ago—memory bridging the years between and easing them. By effort, Tregare brought himself back to the now that was. “If I do this for you, what's in it for *me*?”

“What is it that you want?” In Hawkman, Bran saw no guile.

“For starters, you might sit on Bleeker a little. And a few

others who have the idea they can gouge me on supplies I need." A hand forestalled interruption. "This much I can tell you. I intend to gather some ships here; they'll all need supplying, and it'd save me a lot of trouble, not having to push weight all the time. Bleeker seems to be sparking the groundside traders, to make things difficult."

"Not for much longer," Hawkman said.

"Oh? You're after him already, on your own?"

"To absorb him, let's say, while leaving him nominally in oligarch status. Your mother is gathering power in true Hulzein fashion." Hawkman grinned. "Her sister Erika chased us off Earth because she feared competition for control of a relatively small country: Argentina. Liesel, if I'm not mistaken, has a good chance to dominate this entire planet."

"But not me." Flatly, Tregare said that. "Not my ships."

The older man shook his head. "Groundsiders can't control ships. Except for UET, and you're part of the living proof that even that tyranny scores poorly over the Long View. No, Liesel won't try to tie *you* down." He leaned forward. "What she might like, mind you, is some exchange of information, and other cooperation."

Tregare nodded. "I could manage that, I expect. But back to Bleeker and his group. What's in mind, there?"

"As a matter of fact, Rissa has more or less taken over that problem. She's inveigled Bleeker into making a bet he can't afford to pay off, without losing control of his own holdings, on the outcome of her death duel with Stagon dal Nardo."

A picture came to Tregare's mind: the slim young woman he'd known as Tari Obrigo, facing the powerful dal Nardo, now grown to full strength. "What kind of weapons will they use?"

"None," said Hawkman, "except themselves. By Rissa's choice, they'll fight nude and weaponless."

Halfway rising, Tregare sat back. "She's insane!"

Hawkman nodded. "That's been the general consensus, but Rissa disagrees. And after she did a few practice sessions with Ernol Lombuno, who's the best unarmed combat specialist we have at Hulzein Lodge, the consensus isn't so solid." He shook his head. "I wish I could stop fearing for her, though. And while Liesel doesn't let on much, she's worried, too."

Abruptly, Tregare made up his mind. "If Tari—Rissa—agrees, I'll do the marriage thing for you, all right. Make it clear that afterward she won't be bound by it if she doesn't want to be, in anything other than legal formalities. As long as *they* may be needed." He paused. "Now then—you say there's nothing I can do about this dal Nardo duel, to head it off, or get to the bastard *first*?"

"No, Bran. If you killed him while he had a challenge pending, you'd be outlawed here." Hand gesture; Tregare held his reply. "Yes, I know you're outlawed on more worlds than I know of, and don't give two small damns. But *here* you want to outfit a fleet. If you killed dal Nardo, unlawfully by our customs, you'd be totally cut off from supplies. And Hulzein Lodge couldn't do one thing about it."

No way past that edict; all right: "Then I promise you only this. If Stagon dal Nardo kills that woman, he won't outlive her. Not long enough to get hungry."

Near time to bunk down, Hawkman asked if Tregare could get him a talk circuit to Hulzein Lodge. "Sure." But Bran had to go through Base Two, then to Port, where a lazy-sounding operator patched through faster than her drawling voice might have suggested. When he heard "Hulzein Lodge" he handed the phone to Hawkman and left the scout's control room, to give his father reasonable privacy with his call. A time later, out of sheer boredom Tregare was preparing to light one of his rare cigars when Hawkman opened the door and beckoned to him. So he went in and picked up the handset. "Yes? Tregare here."

"And about time, too." Liesel's voice, his mother's. "All right, I know pretty well why you've avoided us. Are you done with that nonsense?"

"Nonsense?" He needed time—time to fight against being pushed back into his childhood. He said, "That's not what it felt like. Still doesn't, if you want to know." Inside him, leaping, came the spark of challenge from long distant in his past. "Your side of it, I'd like to hear."

More stalling, that was, because she could only say what he already knew, and that's what came over the circuit. When she was done with it, she said, "Hulzeins don't ask forgiveness; you know that much. What I'm asking is, are you ready to do business?" And that, of course, was exactly how it would be, with Liesel Hulzein. Looking over to Hawkman, Tregare felt his breath come shuddering out. "Business, yeah. Hawkman told me about it, the marriage and all." Oddly, he felt tremors within him that he didn't understand. So he said, "We've talked that out; he can fill the story for you. Me, I've had a long day. The duel, whenever—I'll see you there."

He handed the phoneset back to Hawkman, walked out and to bed.

Neither the next day nor the day after did Hawkman return to One Point One. He said he wasn't needed there until it came time for the duel, and meanwhile Tregare found himself enjoying the chance to show his father the facilities and planning at both bases: the cabin defenses, the escape tunnel and pillbox, the embryonic spaceport down at Two. At dinner in the cabin with Deverel and Kenekke, Hawkman shook his head. "You're prepared, here, for just about anything that could happen and much that can't."

Bran sipped wine. "You think I'm overdoing it?"

"Not at all. Or rather, if you didn't, I'd worry about the entire concept of heredity." He laughed. "But you restore my faith, if it had ever been shaken, in the Hulzein genes."

And Tregare said, "I don't think your side short-changed me, either." The look on Hawkman's face made him glad he'd said it.

The morning they were to leave, Tregare packed a travel bag. Seeing his father's raised eyebrows, he said, "I expect to be gone from here more than just the day."

"I was planning to invite you to the Lodge. Will you come?"

"If I'm alive, I will." *Yes, now it's time for that.*

They went to the aircar; Bran took the passenger's seat and gestured Hawkman to the controls. The older man said, "You want me to fly the pass?"

"Sure. Maybe you can show me some pointers." So Hawkman brought the propulsors up to speed and they lifted from the plateau, making a wide climbing sweep to head upslope toward the pass itself.

Hawkman's technique was, to begin with, neither flashy nor overly cautious; as the summit approached and the cut's walls began to narrow, he maintained a safety cushion of about a hundred meters' altitude. He needed at least half of that, because at the dogleg's first turn he dipped the car into a vertical bank and threw the nose ninety degrees left, broadsiding. His half-roll, then, gave him a few seconds to spare before broadsiding the rightward turn also. The dogleg was on the downslope side, so the lost height in the two maneuvers gave no real risk.

Then the strong westward current caught the aircar and spat it free of the pass, at a height that allowed Hawkman to make another lazy swing and head for One Point One. "Do I qualify?"

What impressed Tregare about his father's maneuvering in the pass was its sheer efficiency. "How many times, you've done that?"

"This was my third experience, piloting westward."

"You're a quick study; I'll say that."

"Possibly I take after my son, who did it first and with no guidance at all."

"I had a lot of luck." Bran laughed. "Maybe that's heredity, too. I hope so."

"Perhaps the heredity factor is the tendency to *make* luck."

Descending on a smooth slant, the aircar bore to the left of the spaceport. Ahead, Hawkman pointed out a small enclosure, alongside an open space where an aircar and two groundcars sat. "The arena's bare dirt. The fence keeps gawkers away."

Tregare said, "Who's all the company, then?"

Preoccupied with landing, Hawkman waited until he'd brought the car to a stop not far from the enclosure's gate. "The aircar's not one of ours, so the dal Nardo contingent must be here first. The groundcars would be the referee's and medic's teams."

"Referee, huh?" Bran began to realize he didn't know much about this situation. "You know who it is? You satisfied?" He was pulling on the hood mask, glad in the day's warmth that the thing was lightweight porous fabric.

"I have no idea. But the officials must be approved by both sides, and I can't imagine anyone slipping a ringer past Liesel." And as Bran started to leave the aircar, Hawkman said, "We must disarm ourselves now. Only the referees may have weapons."

Tregare didn't like it, but rules are rules.

The wooden fence stood about three meters; at the small gate a young grey-robed woman asked for bona-fides. "We're with the Obrigo group," said Hawkman. "I understand there'll be three more—plus our principal, of course."

She nodded. "That's the agreed number. Go on in, please, Mr. Moray." She looked a question at Tregare but didn't say it.

Inside, Bran was surprised at how small the place really was. Roughly fifteen meters across, total, and the dueling ring itself no more than seven. Without asking, he guessed that being forced outside that ring meant defeat, with the loser's life forfeit; that was the way such events usually worked. The dirt surface was dry and solid, with only a few piles of loose dust here and there.

Tregare looked at the others already present; besides himself and Hawkman there were ten. All right—the black robe and two grey were the officials; the man and woman in white coats had to be medics.

Then he put attention to the dal Nardo group. Hawkman was right—Stagon was grown to be a bull indeed. Bellowing like one, too—mostly at the referee and that person's aides. Tregare looked at the man, closely and with heed to detail. Obviously he outweighed Tari—*no, Rissa, damn it!*—by more than two to one, with strong thick limbs and a neck like that same bull. A black beard, trimmed short but not neatly; no doubt the man cut it so as to give his opponent no grabbing handle. The gross belly was probably misleading; the way the man moved, quickly for his great size, the fat hid hard muscle.

Hovering around dal Nardo were five others: two men and one woman (Tregare's instincts dismissed those three as inconsequential), a hulking shape that stood completely concealed by robe and hood, and a slim young man, gaudily clad, who moved like quicksilver. Bran nudged his father. "Who's the Fancy Dan there?"

Hawkman was frowning. "I don't like this. That's Blaise Tendal; he kills for hire and has collected for more than twenty assignments. He's impotent with women, one hears, and hates them for it. Of course he can't be armed here, but still—"

"Course he can't." Tregare grinned. "'tother hand, you and I, one at each foot, shake him upside down a little, we'd know for sure."

Hawkman smothered a chuckle. "I wish we could; I really do. But the referee's duty would be to stop us, at gunpoint if necessary." He clasped Bran's shoulder. "I like your thinking, though."

Before Tregare could answer, again the gate guard admitted a group. Four, this time: in front, Tregare's sister Sparline Moray walked beside a young black man; next was the woman Bran knew as Tari Obrigo and was trying to rethink as Rissa Kerguelen. In the rear walked a man built like a bear and moving like one.

Bran again nudged Hawkman. "Besides Sparline and Rissa, should I know about the others?"

"Ernol Lombuno, up front; he's the one Rissa's been training with. Behind is Splieg; he's here if we need muscle. Splieg once, not too long ago, stunned a charging bushstomper with his bare fist. He's not fast, but not easy to stop, either."

Tregare grinned. "Nice you have some talent on hand. Just in case." But he was looking at Rissa Kerguelen. She was the Tari Obrigo he knew, and yet she wasn't, quite. *What's the difference?*

She moved the same—or maybe better now, with the recent combat training. Not black, today, the tied-back hair, but dark brown—and the sun brought a few reddish glints to it. He squinted, sharpening his distance vision across ten meters or so, and noticed that there was no mole at the left nostril, and that when a brief smile showed teeth, the upper incisors no longer protruded. "Disguise, huh?" Hawkman nodded. "Good job, it was."

"Subtle, Bran. That's the trick of it."

"I—" But now, a distraction. Stagon dal Nardo's raucous voice had receded in importance to mere background noise, but the younger medic called something to "Tari" and the bullish, bullying man was crying foul. Whereupon Rissa shook her head, seemed to shout without raising her voice much, and said, "Claim and be damned to you!" She added a few choice remarks, then turned to confer with Sparline. Hawkman moved over toward them; Tregare followed, but stayed back when his father hugged the young woman and spoke to her in low tones that Bran couldn't hear.

The black-robed referee spoke. "It is time. Tari Obrigo challenges Stagon dal Nardo to the death. Weapons, none. Clothing, none. Seconds and other agreed parties are present. Now, if they wish, the opponents may speak. Challenged party speaks first."

At the Slaughterhouse and serving under Butcher Korbeith, Tregare thought he had learned about cruelty and sadism.

But hearing Stagon dal Nardo, Bran decided he'd been playing in a beginners' league. Point by point, dal Nardo detailed the breaking and crushing and gouging and biting-away that would constitute a vivisection, by teeth and nails, of his young opponent. Feeling shock dim his mind, Tregare shook his head to clear it, and was reminded of his promise to Hawkman: that dal Nardo would not outlive this woman. *Not long enough to get hungry.* It helped a little, but he could have used something more. *And what's all this doing to HER?*

Then the roaring man, with one jerk, disrobed the hulking figure beside him: a tall woman who was a shape of horror. Not just the battered, crudely-stitched face—could there possibly still be an eye in that bleeding socket?—but also the bruises and gaping cuts, one arm bending at the wrong places, the blackening breast half torn away, the few broken teeth that showed behind swollen bloody lips. Peace take it, was there *any* part of her not bloody? And dal Nardo laughing: "Here's what I do, only in *practice*!"

With no thought, Tregare began a lunge toward the man, but Hawkman pulled him back. "You can't. Not now."

Gasping for breath, Bran let himself be stopped. He saw his sister lean toward Rissa, and heard: "*It's a fake*, most of it." And then, coming to himself a little, looked and realized that most of the woman's mutilations *were* a clever job of makeup. Not the arm, or some of the cuts, but a lot of it. Still, though . . .

His mind leveled out on two imperatives: he would not throw up and he would stay conscious. The rest blurred on him. He heard dal Nardo gloat over the sexual indignities he intended to inflict between the time he rendered his victim helpless and the moment of death; accordingly Tregare decided that if it were his lot to end dal Nardo, the man would not die a functional male.

After dal Nardo's invective ran downhill, calling Rissa Kerguelen "fertilizer" and "mouse," it was her turn. She didn't say much. Bran caught, "If I squeak like a mouse . . . you shit like a bull, but from your mouth." Her face, pale under sun-color, showed no expression as she taunted dal Nardo into obvious rage. At the end she thanked him for the warning of his sexual intent. "I shall make certain you are unable to fulfill it."

Then the seconds began to prepare their principals. Tregare saw Sparline saturate Rissa's hair with grease and then, after discussion he didn't understand, spread the stuff over her entire nude body, leaving only hands and feet free of the stuff. Again dal Nardo cried foul and Bran realized the man had his own hands coated with adhesive and was demanding a share of his opponent's lubricant; the referee gave him short shrift. Finally the argument stopped; the huge man and slim woman stepped to face each other.

"I see the bull is constipated," said Rissa Kerguelen.

Afterward, Tregare could never sort out the action in sequence. The man charged. True to her word, Rissa in diving aside clawed for the crotch—drawing blood but doing no real damage. First grabbing himself, dal Nardo cursed and waved a bloodstained hand.

Wrong move. She caught his thumb in both hands, braced to slam both feet into his face, and somersaulted backward to face him again. That thumb, now, jutted at an odd angle. He charged; she dropped and tripped him to fall over her, but before she could get up and away he recovered, and hit her across the mouth and chopped at her ribs. He missed a kick as she rolled free; the black man's shout warned her she was too near the ring's edge. She scuttled and feinted, turned at someone's shout and caught a handful of dust, thrown directly into her face. From outside the ring.

The coxcomb! Tregare reached for a weapon he didn't have, then shrugged off Hawkman's restraining hand. "Yeah, I know. But just *wait*!"

Others were crying foul; the big man Splieg had one hand at dal Nardo's chest, the other fist raised like a maul. Rissa wiped knuckles at her eyes. She must have seen the gaudy man skulking back, for her hoarse croak said, "Dig your grave, Blaise Tendal! If I live, you are a dead man!" And Ernol Lombuno shouted that Tendal was dead, either way.

With order restored, again the duel began. Now it was all hitting and feinting and dodging, dal Nardo getting most of the better of it. Rissa backed away, and shouted, "It is time, dal Nardo!" But she was losing; what could she do? With the sweating Bran could see, and the panting he could hear . . .

Feints to eyes and groin, a wrench to the broken thumb. Then a full lunge, stiffened fingers to the larynx. But the thrust slipped off, and his arms closed in effort to crush her slim rib cage.

Hawkman's clutch hurt Tregare's arm; it wasn't needed; he couldn't have moved anyway. He saw her try to kill by concussion, both palms slammed to the ears; it didn't work. The man was bending her backward; the spine didn't have much more leeway before it would break. The heel of her hand punished dal Nardo's smashed nose, to no avail. She clawed for the carotid and drew blood, but nowhere enough.

She had to be close to death; for a moment her hands dropped. Then she thrust a thumb into his right eye and his arms refused to hold their killing grip. Released, she drove her other hand at the larynx again.

This time, Stagon dal Nardo fell and died.

If there was anything Tregare didn't need, it was more confusion. Staggering, Rissa challenged Blaise Tendal. That treacherous man said *he'd* do the challenging. Hawkman shut them both up as Sparline and the medics worked over Rissa and got her into a robe. And then somehow Hawkman was announcing a marriage, as of now, between "our victor, Tari Obrigo," and, gesturing toward Tregare, "one not to be named publicly at this time." Bran heard Rissa mumble, through swollen, bloody lips, something about having the wrong legal identification; apparently Hawkman reassured her.

As they all walked forward, Rissa supported by Hawkman, Tregare saw his battered bride gesture toward himself. "But how can *he* be here?" Whatever his father answered, Rissa nodded.

Bran's own questions gave Hawkman no pause, either. He'd asked if the marriage was to be oldstyle or freestyle. Headshake. "We don't make the distinction here. Now let's begin."

Not one word of that ceremony stuck in Tregare's memory. At the end of it Rissa turned to him; he tasted blood on her abused lips. Then she reached her head up and lightly touched her tongue to each of his eyelids. "If this is all you will show—" and he realized his face was still hooded.

Hawkman was trying to wind things down. While Bran was trying to find an answer for his new wife, Blaise Tendal began to shout, challenging her as "the murderer of Stagon dal Nardo!" Wrenching away from Bran, she shouted an acceptance, but Hawkman in a cold voice negated the entire proposition: as a Hulzein connection by marriage, "Tari" was out of Tendal's status range for dueling. Tendal claimed he was a dal Nardo the same way she was a Hulzein. A short man, one of Stagon dal Nardo's retinue, calling himself Talig dal Nardo and claiming to be Stagon's heir to power in the clan, told Tendal that his nominal marriage to Stagon's prepubescent daughter was annulled. Tendal, red-faced, threw his hat down and cursed the lot of them. "You all hide behind status, don't you? Well, dealing with Blaise Tendal, it won't help you! I'll get her anyway!"

Enough of this shit. I want that one. Tregare stepped forward. "Tendal! If I headed the dal Nardo clan, I'd kill you this minute. If the new head doesn't, he should. Because I'm sure he knows, if you don't, what happens to anyone connected with the fool who harms the wife of Bran Tregare!"

For seconds he thought it would work. Insane and raging, the man was, but Tregare was in position to stop him from getting near Rissa, and moving forward, too. Hawkman didn't hold him back. Bran stepped ahead, slowly. When he saw the man's mouth twisting and knew something was wrong, it was too late. The knife came from nowhere into Tendal's hand—*so much for their damned Security here*—and went far afield of Tregare's frantic grab. He heard a gasp, a shout; he couldn't turn fast enough to see where the knife had gone, but in front of him Blaise Tendal's chest exploded into red steam. The black-clad referee put away her energy gun and said, "I should have done that when he threw the dirt."

The shout had been from Ernol Lombuno; now Tregare saw that the hilt of a knife protruded from the palm of the black man's hand, and the blade out the back of it. But Lombuno was grinning. "Best catch I ever made!" There was blood but not a whole lot, and shortly the senior medic worked the blade loose and opened skin enough to make sure there was no tendon damage, then administered antibiotics and closed the wound.

Later they went out to the aircars. The others—the dal Nardos with the corpse to carry, the referees' group and the two medics (after the younger of those two had hugged Rissa for a time)—left earlier. Hawkman assigned passengers to his and Bran's car. A small man, thin-faced and with a crooked nose, was waiting outside the arena; Hawkman said, "Lebeter, I wish we'd had you inside, there. The dal Nardos had a knifester who got in, armed. Nearly killed our principal."

Lebeter shook his head. "Bad. Who was it?"

"Blaise Tendal. So damn' *fast*."

Lebeter spat on the ground. "I *should* of been there." And Hawkman laughed, clapping a hand to the little knifeman's shoulder. They both grinned, and Lebeter said, "Your car's crowded. I'll fly Splieg with me. Anybody else?" Hawkman shook his head; Lebeter said, "If you need no more now, I'll leave."

That car lifted; not long after, the remaining group boarded Tregare's car. He waved Hawkman to the pilot's seat; after all, the man knew the way to Hulzein Lodge and dark would be coming soon. Sparline was making Rissa, sedated close to sleep, comfortable on the car's wide rear seat. That done, she turned to face Tregare. "It's been a long time, Bran. Are you reconciled to us now, or—?" He stared at her, and found that all the long hurt was somehow gone. So he hugged her, this tall beautiful sister he didn't really know. "All of a sudden, seems so. We'll talk later; okay?"

"I'd like that. Rissa's said you're not so bad as people say."

He laughed. "I hope to hell not. Go sit down, so's Hawkman can lift us."

Strapping in, Tregare found himself sitting beside Ernol Lombuno, and said, "How's the hand? Hurting much?"

"Some. Not too badly." A pause, and then, "So you've married her. I hope you know what she's worth."

Tregare thought that remark over. "Maybe. Do you?"

Lombuno cleared his throat. "Her worth, I do know." Before Bran could answer, he said, "We had moments. I fought her in practice. Fought *with* her when that Tendal tried ambush, once. Made love together, after." Sidelong glance. "Does that bother you?"

Tregare shrugged. "Why should it? People don't own each other. Never have, never can, never will."

In peripheral vision he saw the other man shrug. "I'm glad you see it that way. Because if you held anything against her, you'd answer to me, for it."

In wonderment Tregare looked at the man beside him. "I think I need to tell you something, Lombuno. Which is, we're on the same side."

Seeing the wounded bandaged hand reach out for handshake, Bran Tregare made his clasp gentle.

As Hawkman, in early dusk, approached Hulzein Lodge, Bran found the place even more impressive at close range. The entire complex sat at the edge of a high valley, with a wooded sweep dropping away below. Landing near the Lodge itself, Hawkman taxied the aircar to the front entrance. Tregare unfastened his harness and went back to see how Rissa was doing.

She was awake, maybe still a bit drug-punchy but not much. He and Hawkman helped her out the aircar's door; then she said, "I can walk unaided now, I think. Let me?" And though she moved as awkwardly as stiffened bruises might justify, Tregare contented himself with staying close in case she stumbled.

As they entered, he spoke softly to her. "On the ship I took you when I had no right to. Now I've got the right—but I won't come to you until you say so."

She touched his arm, then his tattooed cheek. "Be with me now." He must have looked surprised, because she added, "No—only to talk, while I soak out some hurt, in a hot tub."

He nodded—and so, approaching now, did Liesel Hulzein. Bran waited for some unbidden emotional surge within him, but nothing came except curiosity: what would his mother say?

Her response was pure Liesel. She hugged him as though he'd been away for the weekend, and said, "Yes, go with her, Bran. We all need to talk, but that can wait." Quickly she gave Rissa some comforting words and an embrace to match, then asked Hawkman to go with her and give a full report. "I want to hear all of it." Looking after them, Bran shook his head. *Those Hulzein women!* And half his genes were theirs....

Guiding Tregare to her upstairs room, Rissa needed to lean on his arm. Inside, she shed her robe. The marks she bore would have fit well on a Slaughterhouse snotty.

Finding the bathroom, Tregare ran water into the tub, gauging and adjusting the temperature as hot as a person could stand without real pain, or injury. "I look like a gargoyle!" He turned to see her before a mirror, and had to agree: bloody, swollen lips, the purple-bulging right eye above the bandaged cheek. As she touched fingers to her upper front teeth, he saw her wince. "He has loosened a few; for some days I shall not chew well."

Then she entered the tub, sliding down until only her face appeared above the water, and asked him to bring her some brandy, in the flask's oversized cap. The first sip made her shudder; the second brought what she probably meant to be a smile. But not today, it wasn't. Pulling a chair over, to sit beside the tub, he said, "You ever marry before?" Her headshake was slow and lazy. "Neither have I. It feels . . . odd."

"Do not worry. Sparline said we need not be bound, after this crisis." She shrugged. "Whatever that might be."

He tried to explain: Bleeker, the oligarchy's reactions to learning Tregare's Hulzein status, the dal Nardo succession, and more—but she wasn't interested. Interrupting, "Say instead how you are here. *Inconnu* was not at the Port—did you land elsewhere and travel overland?"

She was kneading lather into her hair, and he could see her wince at working with sore arms. "Here—let me do that." While he did so, he explained how he had *Inconnu* out circling the big planet ("almost a grey dwarf") and serving as a relay station for incoming ships, and that he'd sneaked back to Number One in his scoutship. "Landed at a place I have, the other side of the Big Hills, and called Hawkman to come parley."

And heard what he said: *why did I lie?* Because he wasn't ready to tell her, or anybody else, how he'd fallen apart, was why. *Someday . . . ?*

"That is where he has been?"

"Right. Now hold your breath—" And for the next minute or so, Rissa's attention was distracted by being underwater longer than she truly enjoyed, while Bran scrubbed away at lather. When she came up spluttering he apologized; both offense and apology were horseplay—and meanwhile he could change the subject. . . . "That thumbnail you tore, there, in the duel—I'll have to fix it. Might's well cut back those other claws, too. We need any more fighting around here, it's my job."

"No! Married or not, I do my own fighting. And you forget—Sparline said the ceremony was for political reasons. We are not bound unless we both wish it."

He stopped filing the broken nail. Suddenly he knew what *he* wished. He couldn't stop his scowl. "Forget politics. You want free of me so soon, without even trying the marriage? Without seeing what it's like?"

She looked at him. He was pretty sure what she was

thinking, and that he wasn't going to like it. But he had to listen. "I cannot know, Tregare, what I will want later. But mask and all, I recognized you *before* the ceremony. And now—there will be time, for both of us, to decide our wishes.

"Will you help me out of here? My muscles have turned to wax." Like his scowl earlier, he had no control over the grin that came now. He aided her to stand and leave the tub, then handed her a large towel for herself and took a smaller one to begin the drying of her long hair. When he stood back, as much done as a towel would manage, she put her own towel aside and again he saw the swollen, distorted attempt to smile. "How can I have such hurt, from blows I do not remember?"

He helped her into her robe. "I don't know. How could anyone your size stand up against the likes of dal Nardo—and kill the bastard?"

"Dal Nardo was not trained by Erika Hulzein." Well, he couldn't argue with that answer. . . . With an arm around her, he walked Rissa into the bedroom and brought a chair so he could sit beside her bed. "Something I didn't know before. On *Inconnu*, any day you could have killed me. The way I treated you, how come you didn't?"

Lying down, it's hard to shrug, but she managed. "First, because no stranger kills a captain on his own ship and survives. Later—as I said before our landing here—I ceased to hate you."

"Ceased to hate? Is that all, Tari?" Tari? His mind had slipped back to the *Inconnu* time with her—and that was all right, because he wanted *her* to do the telling.

Her answer belied her headshake, then—what was she thinking? "More than that, Tregare—but probably not what you would like to hear. Toward the end I felt a kind of sympathy, a precarious comradeship—but also that you were a dangerous man who might still be useful to me."

Useful? She was certainly laying it on the line! "You still feel that way?"

"After what you said to Tendal before he threw the knife? Ah, no, Tregare—whatever happens between us or does not, I will never try to *use* you. Can you say the same to me?"

He found one fist pounding into his other palm. "Peace, yes! But I can't speak for the rest of the family. They—"

Then they came near to arguing, Rissa saying she begrudged no advantage Liesel gained by their dealings, Tregare telling her that to Hulzeins *everyone* was expendable if the stakes were high enough. "*I* sure as peace was." And found himself rehashing the old grievances, until by main will he stopped himself. "Oh, I believe it now, that they had to leave me in hell to save my life." Shaking his head, "*You* wouldn't believe what UET does to young kids, to weed out all but the very toughest. Either you turn into a kind of monster, or you die."

Staring, he didn't really see her. "I didn't die, Tari—*I didn't die*."

Her hand touched his; by reflex he jerked away, then came back to himself and clasped hands with her. "There—you see? Thinking back to that, any touch—even yours—is a threat."

"But only for a second—then you recovered quickly enough."

"I don't know. It's been years, and still—"

"To let go of old hurts, there are methods. I can show you, if you like—if you will let me."

"Maybe. If we ever have time for it, maybe I will." At first he couldn't identify the feeling that came to him then, because not since he lost his home had he known it, much. That feeling was, he finally decided, *trust*. He also decided it scared him a little.

She was trying to say something and he hadn't been listening. "And I—" in a small voice, then nothing more. His questions brought no response; she changed the subject to the matter of dinner. "Soft foods, please." The loosened teeth; sure. So over the intercom he ordered up a meal. He thought he'd done a good job of it, so that couldn't be why she was frowning. Then she said, "Tregare? As married persons, should we not know one another by our true names?"

All right, it was *her* surprise; he wouldn't spoil it. Pretending ignorance, he played straight man; yes, the disguise, and so *that* was why the lockbox wouldn't open, and so on. When he saw she was on the verge of exasperation, he said, "You want me to ask, don't you? All right, I'm not married to Tari Obrigo. Who, then?"

"I am sorry it makes little difference to you." She was wrong, there, but he didn't interrupt. "To me, it does. I am Rissa Kerguelen. Now, I suppose, we can talk about something else."

Faking surprise he said, "Sure! I remember now—" and told of seeing her Welfare press conference back at Earth—his glee at the spunk she'd shown and at learning of her later escape from UET. Then his smile faded; he could feel it go. Done with acting, he said, "On the ship—I wish I'd known. I wouldn't have—"

"Ease your mind, Tregare. If you are in dire need of something to regret, I am sure we can find a more worthy subject."

Their meal's arrival interrupted any further protest. As she looked at the tray he said, "Does my order suit you? Does it—Rissa?"

A nod. "Yes."

"Real names. If they're important to you, mine's Bran." She'd know already, of course, but this was the way he wanted to do it.

"Yes—Bran."

"That's better. Let's eat."

Later they talked more. On the matter of names, Rissa's view was that only in private were the usages important. "Because publicly we use automatic defenses. By ourselves we must discard these or remain strangers." He wasn't sure he followed her thinking, but it *felt* right.

In light of her physical state, at bedtime he offered to leave, but she said, "Not unless you wish to go. I am in invalid status, but if you would like merely to *stay* with me, this bed is large and your presence would comfort me."

"Maybe yours will comfort me, too." Her lips would pain her too much to accept a kiss, so he settled for her forehead. And in bed, knowing how stiff and sore she must be—bath or no bath—he attempted no cuddling.

But once, in the night, he woke to find her snuggling close. Yawning, he smiled, and let sleep come again. Without nightmares.

Next morning, Rissa had a bone to pick. Two, in fact. First, the woman Chira; well, sooner or later he'd have to explain so why not now? He told about it: "...bought her for a packet of drugsticks and a rusty knife, because she was next up for sacrifice to their tribal god, a nasty bastard as such things go," and how by no purpose of his own he'd wound up stuck with her. Next, the women in Hold Portside Upper. So he told that, too: the buying and transportation, and the lucky deal to send them off to Farmer's Dell with Pell Quinlan. And that Chira had gone with the rest. Ending, "That suit you, or do you still think I lie to you?"

Smiling, she shook her head. "Bran Tregare, you are too proud to lie—except, of course, in the line of business. You are what my father used to say—a brass-plated sonofabitch who takes no crap from *anyone*. There is much to be said for that kind of person. So I accept you . . . no, not *yet*, you ravisher of cripples!" But his hands were gentle on her, and she laughed, even leaning to touch her damaged lips to his.

"Rissa—how can you fit into the stretched-out life I must lead?"

"How could I know? But for now, while we are here, I think I can. Shall we try?"

Later when he'd run another hot bath to soothe her aches, she lay near-submerged, only eyes and nose and mouth above the steaming water. "Bran Tregare? Now I shall trust you."

"If you do, then except for my people on *Inconnu*, you'll be the first." *But I won't let you down.*

She couldn't have heard him; as he spoke, she had ducked her head under water. No point in saying it again, the said or unsaid, either one. He'd *show* her, was all.

As she sported, lazily, in the steaming tub, Bran did some thinking. It wouldn't be easy, putting together a fleet to go take Stronghold. Then the gamble he couldn't even estimate: lying in wait to take UET's incoming ships, and finally moving against UET on Earth itself. But he had to try—*it's what I'm built for.*

His odds were better now. Looking back, he saw that since the Slaughterhouse had begun to warp him, he hadn't been truly a whole person. *All that waste—walling off Hawkman and Liesel and Sparline. I had to do it, but—if it hadn't been for Krieg Elman's example, I could have turned just as bad. And a paranoid can't do this job of mine; who'd follow him?*

After Tanit Eldon he'd thought he could never trust another woman. How could he accept Rissa so easily? Well, Zelde M'tana had taken the edge off—impossible that *she* could be phony. And Rissa, instead of ingratiating herself as Tanit did, had faced up to him, brought him to a standstill sometimes. That made her *real*.

She'd had her own years of hell—*Total Welfare!* Maybe that was why he and she could respect, and accept, each other. Sipping Rissa's brandy, Tregare sighed, in release of tension.

Dripping, blowing water from her nose and swollen lips,

Rissa bounced up sitting. Bran looked at her, and thought: as long as new things were possible, they didn't have to be easy. Breaking the barriers against his family—damned near broke him in half, but sure worth it. And Rissa, growing up a slave in Total Welfare—what barriers might *she* still have?

He shook his head. It didn't matter. *Because* they knew each other's hellish pasts, they had a handle on something together. And his feeling was, what they had, would last.

Thumbing water from her eyes, she raised her arched brows in query. "Why so solemn, Bran Tregare?"

He couldn't tell her now; it might take years. All he said was, "Come on out of there, will you? Before you turn into a prune, or something."

13. Epilogue: Return to Stronghold

Coming off duty from her watch trick as Third Hat on *Inconnu*, Rissa joined Bran in captain's digs. He cut his terminal screen, where he'd been studying a star chart, and watched her pour coffee for herself, shaking his head as she offered to refill his own cup. "Thanks, though." She sat near him. He said, "What's our latest ETA for Stronghold?"

She sipped, then said, "Six weeks, I would say—give or take a day or so. Within expected limits, is it not?"

He thought about it: t/t_0. "Yes. We're just below twelve percent of c, then." She nodded, set her cup aside and came to kiss him. A time later he put his mind back to business.

He hadn't brought together all the ships he wanted or had expected, only the bare minimum that might do the job. He felt full trust in his captains—Gowdy, Vanois, Derek Limmer, Zelde M'tana and Ilse Krueger. He wished that Kickem Bernardez had made rendezvous on time and that Jimar Peralta's thirst for command hadn't cost—but this was no time for mourning.

Because now it was all, everything, up for grabs.

But for Bran Tregare, when had things been any other way?